THE
MAMMOTH BOOK OF
BEST NEW
HORROR 13

Edited and with an Introduction by
STEPHEN JONES

CARROLL & GRAF PUBLISHERS
New York

Carroll & Graf Publishers
An imprint of Avalon Publishing Group, Inc.
161 William Street
NY 10038-2607
www.carrollandgraf.com

First Carroll & Graf edition 2002

First published in the UK by Robinson,
an imprint of Constable & Robinson Ltd 2002

ISBN 0-7867-1063-2

Printed and bound in the EU

STEPHEN JONES lives in London, England. He is the winner of two World Fantasy Awards, three Horror Writers Association Bram Stoker Awards and two International Horror Guild Awards as well as being an thirteen-time recipient of the British Fantasy Award and a Hugo Award nominee. A former television producer/director and genre movie publicist and consultant (the first three *Hellraiser* movies, *Night Life*, *Nightbreed*, *Split Second*, *Mind Ripper*, *Last Gasp* etc.), he is the co-editor of *Horror: 100 Best Books*, *The Best Horror from Fantasy Tales*, *Gaslight & Ghosts*, *Now We Are Sick*, *H.P. Lovecraft's Book of Horror*, *The Anthology of Fantasy & the Supernatural*, *Secret City: Strange Tales of London* and *The Mammoth Book of Best New Horror*, *Dark Terrors*, *Dark Voices* and *Fantasy Tales* series. He has written *Creepshows: The Illustrated Stephen King Movie Guide*, *The Essential Monster Movie Guide*, *The Illustrated Vampire Movie Guide*, *The Illustrated Dinosaur Movie Guide*, *The Illustrated Frankenstein Movie Guide* and *The Illustrated Werewolf Movie Guide*, and compiled *The Mammoth Book of Terror*, *The Mammoth Book of Vampires*, *The Mammoth Book of Zombies*, *The Mammoth Book of Werewolves*, *The Mammoth Book of Frankenstein*, *The Mammoth Book of Dracula*, *The Mammoth Book of Vampire Stories By Women*, *Shadows Over Innsmouth*, *Dancing With the Dark*, *Dark of the Night*, *Dark Detectives*, *White of the Moon*, *Keep Out the Night*, *Exorcisms and Ecstasies* by Karl Edward Wagner, *The Vampire Stories of R. Chetwynd-Hayes*, *Phantoms and Fiends* and *Frights and Fancies* by R. Chetwynd-Hayes, *The Conan Chronicles* by Robert E. Howard (two volumes), *The Emperor of Dreams: The Lost Worlds of Clark Ashton Smith*, *James Herbert: By Horror Haunted*, *Clive Barker's A-Z of Horror*, *Clive Barker's Shadows in Eden*, *Clive Barker's The Nightbreed Chronicles* and the *Hellraiser Chronicles*. You can visit his web site at <www.herebedragons.co.uk/jones>.

CONTENTS

ACKNOWLEDGMENTS

I would like to thank Kim Newman, David Barraclough, Nick Austin, Andy Cox, Mandy Slater, Rodger Turner and Wayne MacLaurin (sfsite.com), Andrew I. Porter, Harris M. Lentz III, Richard Dalby, Bill Congreve, Gordon Van Gelder, Robert T. Garcia, Tina Rath, Jo Fletcher, Sara Broecker, Mick Sims, Alan M. Clark, Michel Parry, Brian Mooney, Stephen Gallagher, Robert Morgan, Barbara Roden, David Pringle, Jason Williams and John Pelan for all their help and support. Special thanks are also due to *Locus*, *Interzone*, *Science Fiction Chronicle*, *Variety* and all the other sources that were used for reference in the Introduction and the Necrology.

In memory of
Cherry Wilder
(1930–2002)
who was always a delight to work with,
and
Harry Nadler
(1940–2002)
who gave me my first break as a writer.

INTRODUCTION

Horror in 2001

IN 2001, BOOK SALES IN THE UK were boosted by the success of the *Harry Potter* series to more than £1 billion. Almost 130 million titles were sold by booksellers, although a higher proportion of books are now purchased over the Internet.

Horror titles were up in America for the first time since the mid-1990s. However, the number of horror books published in Britain dropped to its lowest since the late 1980s and, according to *The Bookseller*, accounted for just 2.4 per cent of the total books published.

In February, the Crown Books chain filed for Chapter 11 bankruptcy again, having only emerged from bankruptcy protection in November 1999. Books-A-Million bought the inventory and property leases on a number of stores, while the remainder closed down. Crown was once the third-largest book retailer in America.

With the failure of its online bookselling business, Borders Group, Inc. turned over its website Borders.com to rival Amazon in April.

Meanwhile, according to a Gallup poll, two-thirds of Americans read ten books or fewer a year, and 13 per cent read no books at all. Even more disturbing is that more than half of adult Americans spend less that thirty minutes every day reading printed matter of any kind – and that includes newspapers and food labels!

Britain's Bloomsbury Publishing announced a tenfold rise in profits in September, mostly due to the continuing success of the

Harry Potter books. Pre-tax profits rose from £273,000 to £2.85 million in the first six months of the year, and turnover was up 100 per cent at £22.7 million.

With worldwide sales passing 100 million in May, *Harry Potter* author J.K. Rowling became the highest-paid female author in the world, earning a reported £45 million and bringing her estimated worth to around £220 million. She was invested as an Officer of the Order of the British Empire by Prince Charles in March, for her contributions to children's literature.

However, young fans were disappointed to learn that there would be no new adventure of the boy wizard in 2001. Rowling broke a promise to produce a *Harry Potter* adventure every year for seven years because she was reportedly too busy with the movie version and supervising merchandising deals.

In Stephen King's alien-contact novel *Dreamcatcher*, the survivors of a bizarre encounter twenty-five years earlier were re-united as adults on an annual hunting trip, where they came upon a disoriented stranger who gave birth to something with very sharp teeth.

Black House, King and Peter Straub's much-anticipated sequel to their 1984 collaboration *The Talisman*, featured a grown-up Jack Sawyer on the trail of a child-eating serial killer known as 'The Fisherman'. He was aided in his quest by blind DJ Henry Leyden and The Thunder Five, a group of Harley bikers. The novel also included references to a number of other King books, including 'The Dark Tower' sequence. The two authors were reportedly paid a $20 million advance, and the book went to the top of the bestseller list in the US with a first printing of two million copies. A one million-copy mass-market paperback re-issue of *The Talisman* contained a teaser first chapter from *Black House*.

Clive Barker's *Coldheart Canyon* was a big Hollywood ghost story dating from the 1920s. The author himself appeared on the cover of the American edition, suitably attired in period costume and earring.

Somewhat aptly, HarperCollins designated October as 'Ray Bradbury Month' in America with the publication of the author's latest work, *From the Dust Returned: A Family Remembrance*. First conceived more than fifty-five years ago, this beautifully written novel about the weird family, the Elliotts, who live in October Country, was constructed around seven previously published stories, including the classic 'Homecoming'. Along with an afterword by the author, the US hardcover also featured a dust-jacket illustration by Charles Addams. An audio version was released simultaneously, read by actor John Glover.

In another honour, Mayor James K. Hahn of Los Angeles declared December 14th 'Ray Bradbury Day'.

James Herbert's *Once . . .* was an adult fairy tale about the dark side of magic. A clever promotion involving the placing of chained elves around London landmarks had to be scrapped on September 11th after the terrorist attacks on America. The beautifully illustrated and designed hardcover (which included four full colour plates) was published in two editions by Macmillan with complementary black and white dustjackets.

One Door Away from Heaven by Dean Koontz had 500,000 copies in print after three printings. It involved a woman on a quest to save a disabled child from the girl's strange stepfather, who believed that she would be taken by aliens before her tenth birthday. *The Paper Doorway: Funny Verse and Nothing Worse* was a young-adult poetry collection by Koontz, illustrated by Phil Parks. In Britain, Headline published a paperback omnibus of Koontz's *Watchers/Mr Murder*.

Anne Rice's *Blood and Gold: The Vampire Marius*, the tenth book in 'The Vampire Chronicles', featured one of the oldest members of the undead and his meeting in the present day with a creature of snow and ice.

The End of the Rainbow by V.C. Andrews® was the fourth in the Gothic 'Hudson' series, while *Cinnamon, Ice, Rose, Honey* and *Falling Stars* comprised the five-volume 'Shooting Stars' sequence. They were all still probably written by Andrew Niederman. A paperback omnibus of Andrews's four 1999 'Wildflower' novels was also published. Meanwhile, Niederman's own novel, *Amnesia*, was a twist on the Circe myth.

Ramsey Campbell's *The Pact of the Fathers* was about the daughter of a dead movie producer who discovered that her father had made a diabolical deal involving his first-born.

Neil Gaiman's *American Gods* was the author's most assured novel to date, about an impending war between the old and new gods and a quest to the dark heart of the United States. An audio version was read by George Guidall.

Despite reusing the title of a Roger Zelazny novel (itself a quote from Edgar Allan Poe), Richard Laymon's *Night in the Lonesome October* involved a young man's encounter with a mysterious girl while taking a scary stroll at night. Laymon's posthumously published novel *No Sanctuary* was about a couple's meeting with a serial killer during a vacation in the wilderness.

Graham Masterton's *Swimmer* was the fifth volume in the 'Jim Rook' series, while *When the Cold Wind Blows* was the fifth volume in Charles Grant's *Black Oak* series. This time Grant's paranormal investigators followed up rumours of a wolf man in the Georgia swamps.

Caitlín R. Kiernan's much-anticipated second novel, *Threshold: A Novel of Deep Time*, dealt with a woman who was recruited by a strange girl with alabaster skin to battle an ancient evil.

Authorized by the late author's estate, Simon Clark's *The Night of the Triffids* was a disappointing sequel to John Wyndham's classic 1951 novel, set twenty-five years after the events of the original. Much better was Tim Lebbon's apocalyptic chiller *The Nature of Balance*, in which most of mankind were destroyed by their own nightmares and the few remaining humans tried to survive in a world seeking vengeance. It was published as a deluxe limited hardcover by Prime Books and in paperback by Leisure Books.

Dorchester Publishing launched its Leisure hardcover line with Douglas Clegg's *The Infinte*, yet another haunted-house novel involving a ghost hunter and psychic investigators.

Broadcaster Muriel Gray's third horror novel, *The Ancient*, came with a recommendation from Stephen King. It involved the raising of a demon amongst the piles of garbage in Lima and a supertanker loaded with terrifying trash.

The Fury and the Terror was John Farris's long-awaited sequel to *The Fury*, involving a young psychic and a government mind-control conspiracy. It was 'The Most Dangerous Game' time again in John Saul's *The Manhattan Hunt Club*, as a secret society hunted human prey in the tunnels beneath New York.

Graham Joyce's impressive *Smoking Poppy* was set in a spirit-haunted Thailand and involved a father's search for his wayward daughter. *Whole Wide World* by Paul McAuley was a murder mystery and conspiracy thriller set in a future London monitored by a computer surveillance system.

In Simon R. Green's *Drinking Midnight Wine*, bookseller Toby Dexter followed a mysterious woman through a door in a wall that was not there into a world of magic and monsters. Green's 1994 novel *Shadows Fall*, about the eponymous supernatural haven threatened by a serial killer, received a welcome paperback reissue from Gollancz.

Robin Cook's *Shock* was another medical thriller from the author of *Coma*.

Alan Dean Foster's *Interlopers* involved archaeologist Cody Westcott investigating the cause of random acts of evil, while a man learned he was to be possessed by demons in Richard Calder's *Impakto*.

A Crown of Lights and *The Cure of Souls* were the third and fourth volumes, respectively, in Phil Rickman's series featuring female exorcist Merrily Watkins.

The prolific Christopher Golden's *Straight on 'Til Morning* was a reworking of the *Peter Pan* story, as a teenager's girlfriend was stolen away to a nightmare Neverland. An illustrated version was also available from CD Publishing, limited to 1,000 signed copies and a lettered edition.

Past the Size of Dreaming was Nina Kiriki Hoffman's sequel to *A Red Heart of Memories*, about a haunted house in a small Oregon town, and *Evil Whispers* by Owl Goingback was set in Florida's backwater lagoons.

The Hauntings of Hood Canal by Jack Cady took place along the eponymous waterway in Washington State and involved the disappearance of a number of vehicles into its murky depths.

The Leisure imprint continued to churn out attractive-looking paperbacks every month: *The Lost* by Jack Ketchum (aka Dallas Mayr) and *Wire Mesh Mothers* by Elizabeth Massie were both non-supernatural horror novels, as was Mary Ann Mitchell's *Ambrosial Flesh*, about a devout cannibal.

Gerald Houarner's *The Beast That Was Max* featured a demon-possessed assassin, while *The Evil Returns* by veteran Hugh B. Cave involved voodoo in Haiti. Tom Piccirilli's *A Lower*

Deep featured a satanic coven, and a man discovered that his memories were not his own in *Affinty* by J.N. Williamson.

A living edifice built over a murder site was the location for *House of Pain* by Sèphra Girón, and a writer found evil on his doorstep in Donald K. Beman's *Dead Love*, also from Leisure.

Jeffrey E. Barlough's *The House in High Wood*, which mixed Dickens, Lovecraft and Poe in its tale of a 19th century haunted manor, was the second volume in the 'Western Lights' series about an alternate England. In Gregory Maguire's ghost story *Lost*, a writer searching for her cousin in London invoked the spirits of Jack the Ripper and Dickens's Scrooge.

Sherlock Holmes and the Terror Out of Time was a Lovecraftian novella featuring Conan Doyle's consulting detective and H.G. Wells's Professor Challenger, from Gryphon Books. Randall Silvis's *On Night's Shore* was a 'Thomas Dunne' mystery featuring Edgar Allan Poe.

A couple moved into a bizarre community in Bentley Little's *The Association*, and a woman had a premonition about her own death in *Fear Itself* by Barrett Schumacher.

A contemporary murder was linked to ancient Egyptian magic in *The Alchemist* by Donna Byrd, while an archaeological team in the Amazon jungle discovered *The Altar Stone* by Robert Hackman.

Bone Walker was the third volume in Kathleen O'Neal Gear and W. Michael Gear's anthropological 'Anasazi Mysteries', and genetically engineered chimpanzees went wild in the same authors' *Dark Inheritance*. There were more biomedical experiments gone awry in Alan Nayes's *Gargoyles*.

A dark god was reborn in Los Angeles in D.A. Stern's *Black Dawn*, and the dead were reborn on an alternate Earth in Eugene Byrne's *Things Unborn*.

The restoration of a haunted house in Maine awakened past nightmares in *The White Room* by A.J. Matthews (aka Rick Hautala). Will Kingdom's second suspense novel, *Mean Spirit*, involved four people trapped in a Victorian neo-Gothic castle in the Malvern Hills, menaced by a psychopathic killer and voices from beyond the grave.

Tananarive Due's *The Living Blood* was a sequel to the author's *My Soul to Keep* and involved a race of African immortals, and an immortal killer menaced a small mountain community in Tamara Thorne's *Eternity*.

The Burning Times by Jeanne Kalogridis (aka J.M. Dillard) was an historical horror novel about witchcraft and the Inquisition. A man's girlfriend disappeared in front of his eyes in T.J. MacGregor's *Vanished*, and the owner of a successful construction business discovered that his past was about to come back and haunt him in Lucy Taylor's *Nailed*.

An executed serial killer returned to possess a married woman on the brink of death in the paperback original *Ghost Killer* by Scott Chandler (aka Chandler Scott McMillin).

Scottish writer Anne Perry's *Come Armageddon* was a sequel to *Tathea* and continued the battle between Good and Evil as the great and final war approached. Australian author Kim Wilkins's *Angel of Ruin* was based on Milton's *Paradise Lost*, and featured that writer's daughters and their collective relationships with a dark angel they had conjured up.

The Family: Special Effects Book 1 by Kevin McCarthy and David Silva was the first volume in a new series packaged by Tekno Books for DAW. *Full Moon Bloody Moon* was the second in the horror/mystery series by Lee Driver (aka Sandra D. Tooley) featuring hero Chase Dagger.

Fool Moon and *Grave Peril* were the second and third books, respectively, in Jim Butcher's series 'The Dresden Files' as Chicago's only professional wizard and paranormal investigator discovered that werewolves turned up in different guises and something was stirring up the city's ghosts.

Mark Ramsden's kinky characters Matt and Sasha became involved with animal-rights fanatics, a midwinter neo-Nazi festival and a satanic cult known as the Black Order in *The Sacred Blood*, the author's S&M sequel to *The Dungeonmaster's Apprentice*, also published by Serpent's Tail.

Vampires were as popular as ever in 2001. An Interpol agent was on the trail of the undead Miriam Blaylock in *The Last Vampire*, Whitley Strieber's long-awaited sequel to *The Hunger*.

Necroscope: Avengers was the third and final volume in Brian Lumley's *E-Branch* trilogy, in which Ben Trask's team of talented psychics, including necroscope Jake Cutter, pursued three powerful Wamphyri lords who had joined forces.

Narcissus in Chains was the tenth volume in Laurell K. Hamilton's popular 'Anita Blake, Vampire Hunter' series, once again given a classy-looking hardcover release in America. This time a changed Anita had to call on both her rival vampire and werewolf lovers to search for a kinky were-leopard who had disappeared from the eponymous S&M club. An excerpt from the novel appeared in the paperback anthology of 'paranormal romance', *Out of this World*, which also included original novellas by J.D. Robb, Susan Krinard and Maggie Shayne.

A Feast in Exile was Chelsea Quinn Yarbro's latest novel of Saint-Germain, this time set in 15th-century India. Karen Taylor's *The Vampire Vivienne* featured vampire Deidre Griffin and her ex-cop husband in the fifth in the 'Vampire Legacy' series, and P.D. Cacek's *Night Players* was the second book featuring new vampire Allison Garrett.

Laws of the Blood: Companions was the third volume in Susan Sizemore's paperback series. This time undead 'Enforcer of Enforcers' Istvan and his unwilling companion, Chicago homicide detective Selena Crawford, uncovered a more serious motive behind the murder of a vampire.

Mick Farren's *More Than Mortal* was a follow-up to his novels *The Time of Feasting* and *Darklost* in the series of 'Victor Renquist' Lovecraftian/vampire thrillers.

Set in 1899 London, a doctor investigated a series of apparent vampire murders in Sam Siciliano's *Darkness*. *The London Vampire Panic* was the sixth in the series by Michael Romkey, set in Victorian Europe, and P.N. Elrod's *Quincey Morris, Vampire* was yet another sequel to Stoker's *Dracula*.

Stephen Gresham's *In the Blood* was a Southern Gothic about a cursed family of vampires. Clairvoyant cocktail waitress Sookie Stackhouse discovered that her new boyfriend was a bloodsucker suspected of murder in Charlaine Harris's (aka Charlaine Harris Schulz) Southern Vampire Mystery *Dead Until Dark*.

Psychologist Meghann O'Neill encountered a vampire in *Crimson Kiss* by Trisha Baker, while James M. Thompson's *Night Blood* featured a vampire doctor infected with Creutzfeldt-Jakob disease (CJD).

A senior in high school who fell prey to the family curse of vampirism and a billionaire industrialist fighting his own battle with mortality confronted each other in Billie Sue Mosiman's *Red Moon Rising*, packaged by Tekno Books.

A woman working in a health resort discovered that her employers were vampires in Tamara Thorne's *Candle Bay*, and Australian author Stephen Dedman's *Shadows Bite* was a martial-arts mystery set in Los Angeles involving vampires, demons and the Yakuza.

Bound in Blood was a gay erotic novel by David Thomas Lord about a nineteenth-century vampire in modern New York. *Vampire Vow* by Michael Schiefelbein was another gay vampire novel.

A book critic in Venice investigated vampires and werewolves in Shannon Drake's *Deep Midnight*.

Alice Borchardt's *The Wolf King* was the third volume in the historical werewolf series by Anne Rice's sister, while a man in Saxon times became involved with a trio of shapechanging siblings in Susan Price's *The Wolf-Sisters*.

Gillian Bradshaw's medieval thriller *The Wolf Hunt* contained elements of lycanthropy and was based on 'Lai de Bisclavret' by Marie de France. *Bitten* was a debut novel by Kelly Armstrong, about the first female werewolf.

In Sarah A. Hoyt's debut novel, *Ill Met by Moonlight*, a young Will Shakespeare was drawn into a realm of elves and faeries in pursuit of his missing family. The book's prologue and first two chapters were self-published as a chapbook sampler.

A vengeful spirit haunted a modern housing development in *Wringland* by newcomer Sally Spedding. *The Music of Razors* marked the debut horror novel of Cameron Rogers (aka Penguin Australia children's editor Dmetri Kakmi). It was a coming-of-age story involving a fallen angel and the tools it fashioned from bones.

In Jonathan Carroll's *The Wooden Sea*, the seventeen-year-old self of middle-aged Chief of Police Frannie McCabe turned up and told him that he had lived his life all wrong, just before he got a glimpse of the day he was going to die.

Jeremy Dronfield's *The Alchemist's Apprentice* was about the eponymous bestselling novel written by Madagascar Rhodes, which nobody appears to remember having read.

Jay Russell's offbeat detective Marty Burns returned in *Greed & Stuff*, a novel set in the Los Angeles TV industry and involving a classic *noir* film, *The Devil on Sunday*.

Steve Aylett's comedic *Only an Alligator* was the first book set in the demonic city of Accomplice, situated one step to the left of reality.

A new trade paperback edition of Bram Stoker's *Dracula* from Random House included an introduction by Peter Straub, plus various review extracts and a reading guide.

The Library of Classic Horror was an instant-remainder hardcover featuring the complete novels *Dracula, Frankenstein, Dr Jekyll and Mr Hyde* and *The Island of Dr Moreau* along with two other stories by Robert Louis Stevenson and six by Edgar Allan Poe.

Published as a slightly updated trade paperback in Dover's Thrift Editions series, *A Bottomless Grave and Other Victorian Tales of Terror* was a welcome reprint of editor Hugh Lamb's superior 1977 anthology *Victorian Nightmares*, featuring twenty-one stories by Ambrose Bierce, Guy de Maupassant, Richard Marsh, Erckmann-Chatrian, Guy Boothby and others.

The Collected Ghost Stories of E.F. Benson was a new edition of the 1992 volume edited by Richard Dalby that contained fifty-four tales, an essay by the author, and an introduction by Joan Aiken.

From Dutch publisher Coppens & Frenks, *The House on the Borderland* was a limited edition of William Hope Hodgson's 1908 novel, with a new introduction by Brian Stableford.

Là Bas: A Journey Into the Self was a new translation of the 1891 literary black-magic novel by French 'décadent' writer Joris-Karl Huysmans, published by Dedalus with an introduction by Brendan King and an afterword and chronology by Robert Irwin. From the same imprint, Geoffrey Farrington's *The Revenants* was a revised edition of the author's 1983 vampire novel with a new introduction by Kim Newman.

Black Seas of Infinity: The Best of H.P. Lovecraft was a collection of nineteen stories and three non-fiction pieces from the Science Fiction Book Club, edited by SFBC editor Andrew Wheeler.

Edited by S.T. Joshi, *The Thing on the Doorstep and Other*

Weird Stories was the second collection of H.P. Lovecraft's fiction published as part of the prestigious Penguin Twentieth-Century Classics series. With David E. Schultz, Joshi also edited and annotated HPL's *The Shadow Out of Time*, a trade paperback from Hippocampus Press that contained the restored text of the original manuscript (discovered in 1995), along with an early draft and notes.

The ubiquitous Mr Joshi also edited and introduced *The Mark of the Beast and Other Horror Tales* by Rudyard Kipling, a collection of seventeen stories from Dover, and *The Three Impostors and Other Stories*, the first volume of *The Best Weird Tales of Arthur Machen* from Chaosium. Along with three other classic stories, this trade paperback also included the complete text of Machen's 1895 linked novel.

The Conan Chronicles Volume II: The Hour of the Dragon was the second omnibus volume in Gollancz's Fantasy Masterworks series collecting Robert E. Howard's eight remaining Conan stories (including the title novel), edited with an afterword by Stephen Jones.

Richard Matheson's *The Incredible Shrinking Man* was a reissue of the omnibus from Tor containing the eponymous short novel and nine classic short stories.

R.L. Stine's young-adult series *The Nightmare Room* continued with *They Call Me Creature*, *The Howler*, *Shadow Girl* and *Camp Nowhere*, some of which may have been written by George Sheanshang.

A famous YA horror writer apparently inspired a school-based mystery in *The Mysterious Matter of I.M. Fine* by Diane Stanley.

Murder victims were found mysteriously incinerated in *Burning Bones* by Christopher Golden and Rick Hautala, seventh in the 'Jenna Blake' young-adult mystery/horror series.

Golden's own *Prowlers*, *Prowlers: Laws of Nature* and *Prowlers: Predator and Prey* launched a new series about a group of teenagers investigating reports of werewolves.

Tartabull's Throw was a time-travel novel about werewolf detective Cyrus Nygerski and the third in the series by Henry Garfield after the adult books *Moondog* and *Room 13*.

Dr Franklin's Island by Ann Halam (aka Gwyneth Jones) involved a group of teenage plane-crash survivors who were genetically altered into shapeshifters. A giant bat attacked researchers in the Amazon in Paul Zindel's *Night of the Bat*.

In Pete Johnson's *The Frighteners* a new girl in school was befriended by a strange boy whose drawings had the power to call up the eponymous supernatural creatures. *Dark Things II: Journey Into Tomorrow* by Joseph F. Brown once again featured Jarrod, who had the ability to make what he imagined real.

Musician Chris Wooding's *The Haunting of Alaizabel Cray* was a gaslight romance set in Victorian London and inspired by *Gormenghast* and H.P. Lovecraft.

Margaret Mahy's *The Riddle of the Frozen Phantom* was 'A Vanessa Hamilton Book'. In Eva Ibbotson's comedic *Dial-a-Ghost*, the eponymous agency mixed up its hauntings, and a teenager believed that ghostly phenomena may have had something to do with the arrest of his father in Nick Manns's *Operating Codes*.

A girl who didn't realize she was dead looked after the children living in her house in *The Ghost Sitter* by Peni R. Griffin, while a young boy encountered a Civil War phantom in *Ghost Soldier* by Elaine Alphin. *My Brother's Ghost* was a novelette by Allan Ahlberg.

A girl's dreams seemed to hold the answer to her parents' disappearance in Joseph Bruchac's *Skeleton Man*, and a young girl attempted to help her missing friend in Jonathan Stroud's *The Leap*.

Vampire Mountain was the fourth volume in *The Saga of Darren Shan* and the first in a three-part sequence. The character returned in *Trials of Death*. Eponymous schoolboy author Shan is a pseudonym for Darren O'Shaughnessy.

A young witch discovered that one of her classmates was a vampire in Amelia Atwater-Rhodes's *Shattered Mirror*, while *Witch Hill* was a time-travel fantasy by Marcus Sedgwick. With the help of a strange sea captain, two children battled the Night Witches in Michael Molloy's *The Witch Trade*.

Cate Tiernan's *Sweep 1: Book of Shadows, 2: The Coven, 3: Blood Witch, 4: Dark Magick, 5: Awakening, 6: Spellbound* and *7: The Calling* were the initial volumes in a packaged series about a teenager who discovered she was a witch.

Silver RavenWolf's *Witches' Night of Fear* and *Witches' Key to*

HORROR IN 2001   13

Terror were the second and third volumes, respectively, in the *Witches' Chillers* series of occult murder mysteries, from Llewellyn Publications.

Isobel Bird's *Circle of Three* series about a trio of modern-day teenage witches included *1: So Mote it Be*, *2: Merry Meet*, *3: Second Sight*, *4: What the Cards Said*, *5: In the Dreaming*, *6: Ring of Light*, *7: Blue Moon*, *8: The Five Paths*, *9: Through the Veil*, *10: Making the Saint*, *11: The House of Winter* and *12: Written in the Stars*.

T*witches #1: The Power of Two by H.B. Gilmour and Randi Reisfeld was about twin sisters, separated at birth, who meet in a theme park and discover that they share strange powers. It was followed by *2: Building a Mystery* and *3: Seeing is Deceiving* from the same authors.

Australian Kim Wilkins's *Bloodlace* was the first volume in a new young-adult psychic detective series featuring Gina Champion, who investigated a mystery based on a past murder set in a seaside suburb of Sydney.

Ninth Key and *Darkest Hour* by Jenny Carroll (aka Meggin Cabot) were two new titles in the ongoing series *The Mediator*, about a girl who talked to the dead.

From Headline Australia, *Shades 1: Shadow Dance*, *2: Night Beast*, *3: Ancient Light* and *4: Black Sun Rising* was a young-adult horror adventure series by Robert Hood, about a group of teenagers trapped in a ghostlike existence who battled an invasion by creatures from the shadows.

Scholastic's 'Point Horror Unleashed' continued with Celia Rees's *The Cunning Man*, about the eponymous shipwrecker. Paul Stewart's *Fright Train* involved a ride through Hell, and a young girl paid a high price for consulting *The Bearwood Witch* in Susan Price's novel.

Hair Raiser by Graham Masterton and *Fly-Blown* by Philip Wooderson, the latter about intelligent mutated blowflies, both appeared as 'Mutant Point Horror' titles.

Decayed: 10 Years of Point Horror was an omnibus containing the novels *Trick or Treat* and *April Fools* by Richie Tankersley Cusick and *Blood Sinister* by Celia Rees.

Bruce Colville's *The Monsters of Morley Manor* was significantly revised and expanded from its 1996 serialization.

Shadows & Moonshine was a new collection of thirteen stories by Joan Aiken, while Vivian Vande Velde's *Being Dead* collected seven stories about ghosts and the undead.

R.L. Stine's *The Haunting Hour* featured ten stories, each illustrated by a different artist, including John Jude Palencar and Art Spiegelman. Spiegelman and Françoise Mouly edited *Little Lit: Strange Stories for Strange Kids*, a graphic anthology of sixteen stories by such authors as Jules Feiffer and Maurice Sendak.

Brian Lumley's *The Whisperer and Other Voices* collected eight reprint stories, plus the short Cthulhu Mythos novel '*The Return of the Deep Ones*' and a new introduction by the author.

Published in trade paperback by Serpent's Tail, *The Devil in Me* was the latest collection from Christopher Fowler, containing twelve stories and a new foreword by the author. From the same imprint came a welcome reissue of Fowler's 1998 collection *Personal Demons* in a matching edition.

M. John Harrison's *Travel Arrangements* collected fourteen stories, and Ed Gorman's *The Dark Fantastic* collected seventeen stories with notes by the author and an introduction by Bentley Little.

Faithless: Tales of Transgression collected twenty-one stories (one original) by Joyce Carol Oates. Meanwhile, the author's psychological Gothic novella *Beasts* was published as a trade paperback by Carroll & Graf.

HarperCollins produced a special sampler for the UK edition of Peter Straub's collection *Magic Terror* containing the story 'The Ghost Village'.

The second of Dorchester Publishing's hardcover Leisure titles, *The Museum of Horrors* was presented by The Horror Writers Association. Although perhaps not up to the quality of some of editor Dennis Etchison's previous compilations, it was still one of the best anthologies of the year. Even though most of the eighteen original stories did not appear to fit into the loose 'theme' of the book, and a few were surprisingly similar to each other, it still boasted some memorable contributions from Joyce Carol Oates, Ramsey Campbell, Peter Atkins, Tom Piccirilli, Joel Lane, Conrad Williams, Charles L. Grant, Lisa Morton, S.P. Somtow and a stunning but annoyingly incomplete tale by Peter Straub. It was all the more a shame that such a fine volume and its editor became embroiled in a totally unnecessary controversy publicized through the HWA itself.

Although subtitled *Extreme Visions of Speculative Fiction*, editor Al Sarrantonio's massive new anthology *Redshift* actually contained some excellent dark fantasy stories amongst its thirty all-new contributions by Dan Simmons, Ursula K. Le Guin, Michael Moorcock, Thomas M. Disch, Stephen Baxter, David Morrell, Elizabeth Hand, Michael Marshall Smith, Gene Wolfe and the editor himself (who was also responsible for yet another self-congratulatory introduction).

Edited by P.N. Elrod (and probably an uncredited Martin H. Greenberg), *Dracula in London* contained sixteen stories about the vampire count living in some very peculiar interpretations of the city by Tanya Huff, Fred Saberhagen, Chelsea Quinn Yarbro, Nancy Kilpatrick and others, including a collaboration between the editor and actor Nigel Bennett.

Vampires: Encounters with the Undead was a huge, 600-page hardcover from Black Dog & Leventhal Publishers, edited and with commentary by the erudite David J. Skal. Along with classic short stories by J. Sheridan Le Fanu, Bram Stoker, M.R. James, Sir Arthur Conan Doyle, Robert Bloch, Fritz Leiber, Richard Matheson, David J. Schow, Kim Newman, Caitlín R. Kiernan and others, this value-for-money volume also contained articles, essays and extracts, all profusely illustrated with film stills and artwork.

Lords of Night: Tales of Vampire Love contained three romance novellas by Janice Bennett, Sara Blayne and Monique Ellis.

Hammer horror star Ingrid Pitt graced the cover and contributed the introduction and an original story to *The Mammoth Book of Vampire Stories By Women*, an anthology of thirty-three stories (fourteen original) and one poem edited by Stephen Jones with illustrations by Randy Broecker. Other contributors included Anne Rice, Poppy Z. Brite, Tanith Lee, Lisa Tuttle, Connie Willis and Chelsea Quinn Yarbro.

Mike Ashley's excellent *The Mammoth Book of Fantasy* reprinted twenty-three classic tales by Robert E. Howard, Clark Ashton Smith, Fritz Leiber, Tanith Lee, Harlan Ellison, A. Merritt and many others.

Published in hardcover by The British Library, *Meddling with*

Ghosts: Stories in the Tradition of M.R. James was a handsome reprint anthology selected and introduced by Ramsey Campbell. Among the sixteen authors included were J. Sheridan Le Fanu, F. Marion Crawford, Sabine Baring-Gould, Fritz Leiber, L.T.C. Rolt, A.N.L. Munby, T.E.D. Klein, Sheila Hodgson, Terry Lamsley and Campbell himself. Rosemary Pardoe also contributed a useful guide to writers who followed in James's literary footsteps.

Edited by Don Hutchinson, *Wild Things Live There: The Best of Northern Frights* reprinted sixteen stories from the Canadian anthology series by Nancy Kilpatrick, Nalo Hopkins and others.

Into the Mummy's Tomb, edited with a long introduction by John Richard Stephens, contained fifteen reprint stories, two excerpts and an abridgement by such authors as Louisa May Alcott, Tennessee Williams, H.P. Lovecraft, Agatha Christie, Mark Twain, Sir H. Rider Haggard, Edgar Allan Poe, Ray Bradbury, Rudyard Kipling, Sir Arthur Conan Doyle, Elizabeth Peters, Sax Rohmer, Anne Rice and Bram Stoker.

Edited by Marvin Kaye, *The Ultimate Halloween* contained seventeen stories (five reprints) about the horror holiday by Esther Friesner, Ron Goulart and others. *Isaac Asimov's Halloween* was edited by Gardner Dozois and Sheila Williams and reprinted ten stories from *Asimov's Science Fiction*. Andy Duncan, Lawrence Watt-Evans, Howard Waldrop, Steven Utley and Ian R. MacLeod were amongst the authors included.

Winning Tales of the Supernatural edited by Joyce Booth O'Brien contained eleven 'prize-winning' stories, while *Nor of Human* edited by Geoffrey Maloney was an Australian anthology published by the Canberra SF Guild writers' group.

Published in trade paperback by Polygon, *Damage Land*, an anthology of *New Scottish Gothic Fiction* edited and introduced by Alan Bissett, contained twenty stories (six reprints) and a bibliography.

The busy Martin H. Greenberg teamed up with John Helfers to edit the all-original *Villains Victorious* and *The Mutant Files*. The former contained fourteen stories of evil triumphant, the latter sixteen tales about the next step in human evolution. The contributors (many of whom were featured in both books) included Charles de Lint, Tanya Huff, Alan Dean Foster, Janet Berliner, David Bischoff, Nina Kiriki Hoffman, Kristine Kathryn Rusch,

Ed Gorman, Peter Crowther and Peter Tremayne (with a new Sherlock Holmes story).

Greenberg was joined by Brittany A. Koren for *Single White Vampire Seeks Same*, an anthology of twelve stories based on paranormal personal ads from such familiar names as Rusch, Crowther, Hoffman, de Lint and Huff (a 'Henry Fitzroy' vampire tale). With Jean Rabe, Greenberg also edited *Historical Hauntings*, featuring eighteen original stories by Andre Norton, Bruce Holland Rogers and others.

The Mammoth Book of Best New Horror: 12 edited by Stephen Jones contained twenty-two stories and novellas, along with the usual comprehensive overview of the previous year in horror, a detailed necrology and a list of useful contact addresses for aspiring writers and horror fans. Ellen Datlow and Terri Windling's *The Year's Best Fantasy and Horror: Fourteenth Annual Collection* reprinted forty-four stories and nine poems, plus the annual summations by the two editors, Ed Bryant and Seth Johnson, obituaries by James Frenkel, and a list of so-called 'Honorable Mentions'. The Datlow/Windling and Jones books overlapped with just four stories from Ramsey Campbell, Kathe Koja, Terry Lamsley and Paul McAuley.

After much ballyhoo in the small-press world and to the anger of many of its contributors, *The Year's Best Dark Fantasy: 2000*, the first in a proposed new annual series announced by editor Steve Savile, was abruptly cancelled by print-on-demand publisher Cosmos Books.

HarperCollins globally launched its e-book imprint PerfectBound in February with titles by Raymond E. Feist, Joyce Carol Oates and an omnibus of *The Nightmare Room* by R.L. Stine, containing six novels.

Following the May launch of AOL Time Warner's digital imprint iPublish, The Authors' Guild warned its 8,000 members that the new company's publishing contract was 'among the worst the Authors' Guild has seen from a publisher of any size or reputation'. The Science Fiction Writers' Association agreed, describing the publisher's non-negotiable terms as 'rights stealing'.

Ignoring the criticism, iPublish announced a new popularity contest in conjunction with the monthly publication of three works discovered through its website. However, in an unexpected move in December, AOL Time Warner pulled the plug, citing a slowdown in the overall economy as its reason for the decision. The company concluded that a separate electronic publishing division was not currently viable at that time. While iPublish titles remained available for the time being, electronic book sales were moved to other groups within Time Warner Trade Publishing.

In a landmark decision in June, the US Supreme Court ruled 7 – 2 on *The New York Times* v. Tasini case that publishers must obtain consent for the electronic reproduction of work originally created by freelancers for print. This resulted in thousands of articles being deleted from electronic databases and on the Internet.

After buying 'exclusive electronic rights' to around 100 backlist titles by authors such as Kurt Vonnegut, new e-book publisher RosettaBooks was sued by Random House, who claimed that their existing contracts with the authors giving them the right to publish the works in 'book form' included digital rights. In July, a federal judge in US District Court in Manhattan ruled against Random House's request for a preliminary injunction, and the publisher subsequently appealed.

Barnes & Noble Digital debuted on September 11th with an original e-book by Dean Koontz, *The Book of Counted Sorrows*, but delayed the launch of its other titles until mid-October. Economic fallout from the 9/11 terrorist attacks may also have caused Random House to fold its AtRandom electronic imprint, launched in June 2000.

At the beginning of the year, editor Paula Guran announced that it had become obvious to her that the only way for her weekly electronic newsletter *DarkEcho* to evolve was 'for it to head directly into extinction', which it did. However, after publishing more than 300 issues since 1994, Guran did revive the title occasionally as a once-in-a-while informal newsletter.

Along with co-sponsoring a story contest, Leisure Books began sponsoring original fiction by new and established authors on Brett Savory's quarterly webzine *The Chiaroscuro*.

Delirium Books' website was removed by its host server in November after a complaint about the site's graphic content. As a result, certain features such as the 'Gross-Out Tournament' were moved to another server.

The Spook was a fully downloadable electronic horror magazine in Adobe Acrobat (PDF) format launched in June by publish-
er/editor Anthony Sapienza. Featuring short fiction, celebrity
profiles, reviews, cartoons and poetry, among the featured
authors were Ramsey Campbell, Poppy Z. Brite, Dennis Etchison,
Damon Knight, John Shirley, Chelsea Quinn Yarbro, Jonathan
Carroll and Joyce Carol Oates. Features included interviews with
Neil Gaiman, Jonathan Carroll, actress Linda Blair and artist
Alan M. Clark, plus articles on *Halloween*'s Michael Meyers, the
Zodiac Killer, the witchcraft of Shirley Jackson and the truth
behind Disneyland's Haunted Mansion. Ramsey Campbell's
opinion column (originally in *Necrofile*) began running from
the second issue onwards. Because it was sponsored by adver-
tisers, the full-colour monthly magazine was free to readers and
received more than 4,000 hits in the first forty-eight hours.

Gothic.net underwent its annual make-over and the $15 sub-
scription entitled readers to get the 'premium' short fiction,
change the colour scheme, post comments and receive regular
updates.

Among the authors whose stories were featured on Ellen
Datlow's *Sci.Fiction* on *SciFi.Com* in 2001 were Charles
Beaumont, Terry Dowling, Ian R. MacLeod, James P. Blay-
lock, Geoffrey A. Landis, Lucius Shepard, Gerald Kersh,
Glen Hirshberg, Richard Matheson, Pat Cadigan and many
others.

After six issues as a print publication, Paul Lockey's *Unhinged*,
subtitled *Disturbing Fiction for Discerning Adults*, became a
twice-yearly online magazine in May with articles, reviews and
fiction by Sean Russell Friend, Mark Howard Jones, Michael
Chant, T.M. Gray, Ray Clark and others.

Paul Fry's *Peep Show*, published by Short, Scary Tales Publications, featured erotic horror fiction by David J. Schow and
others, and more horror stories could be found on John Urban-
cik's webzine *Dark Fluidity*.

The Zone SF, a non-fiction site, went live in mid-September
with interviews with Dan Simmons and Simon Clark, and a list of
the Top 10 Heavy Metal Albums with SF Themes.

Edited by Sara Creasy, *aurealisXpress* was a monthly science
fiction and fantasy e-bulletin for subscribers to Australia's twice-
yearly *Aurealis* magazine. The electronic update was issued eleven

times a year (except January), and you could subscribe to both magazines by visiting the website and printing off an application form.

Pam Keesey's *Monsterzine.com* looked at monster movies and was linked to the related site, *BioHorror.com*, while *Ghoul Britannia* was a tribute site for Hammer Films and other Brit horror movies.

Douglas Glegg's 'The Infinite Road Diary' debuted on the Cemetery Dance website. While the author travelled across America promoting his new hardcover novel *The Infinite* with bookshop signings, he updated his electronic diary every few days. Neil Gaiman's electronic diary was also credited with boosting sales of his latest novel, *American Gods*.

Stealth Press marked Halloween on its website with a free downloadable PDF e-anthology, *All Hallows-e: Halloween Tales from Seven Masters of Terror*, compiled by Paula Guran. It featured reprints by such Stealth authors as Ray Bradbury, F. Paul Wilson, Chelsea Quinn Yarbro, John Shirley, William F. Nolan, Al Sarrantonio and Peter Straub.

Stealth's e-freebie page also featured a downloadable e-chapbook of Nolan's 1967 *Playboy* short story 'The Party', from his new collection *Dark Universe*, and a sample from Wilson's novel *An Enemy of the State*, featuring a new introduction by the author along with the prologue and five chapters.

A follow-up to the previous year's impressive electronic anthology, *Brainbox II: Son of Brainbox*, edited with an introduction by Steve Eller, featured contributions from eighteen writers, including Brett A. Savory, Charlee Jacob, Brian A. Hopkins and Mort Castle. Another CD-ROM anthology was Lone Wolf Publications' *Extremes 3: Terror on the High Seas*, edited by Brian A. Hopkins and illustrated by Thomas Arensberg.

The UK print-on-demand publisher House of Stratus, which reissued much of Brian Aldiss's backlist along with many other titles, ceased trading in June and apparently went into administration in September. Booksellers had apparently complained of late deliveries and poor billing.

After the cancellation of *Enigmatic Tales*, editors L.H. Maynard and M.P.N. Sims pretty much recreated their magazine as the first two volumes of the trade paperback anthology series

Darkness Rising Volume One: Night's Soft Pains and *Volume Two: Hideous Dreams*, from Cosmos Books, an on-demand imprint of Wildside Press. Along with obscure reprints by Howard Jones and Huan Mee introduced by Hugh Lamb, the books included original stories, with notable work from Lynda E. Rucker and Donald Murphy.

Also from Cosmos, *Similar Monsters* was a decade-spanning collection of fifteen stories (five original) and an afterword by Steve Savile, while *City of Saints and Madmen: The Book of Ambergris* collected four novellas by Jeff VanderMeer with an introduction by Michael Moorcock.

Dan Clore's *The Unspeakable and Others* was a collection of forty-seven Lovecraftian tales and non-fiction pieces, with an introduction by S.T. Joshi. Stephen Mark Rainey's *Balak* from Wildside Press was a Lovecraftian novel involving a woman searching for her missing child.

Fluid Mosaic collected thirteen horror stories (one original) by Michael Arnzen. *Gemini Rising*, *Downward to Darkness* and *Worse Things Waiting* were substantially revised versions of Brian McNaughton's novels *Satan's Love Child* (1977), *Satan's Mistress* (1978) and *Satan's Seductress* (1979), while McNaughton's *Nasty Stories* and *Even More Nasty Stories* collected twenty-five stories (eight original) and twenty-one stories (two original), respectively.

Strange Pleasures was an anthology of fourteen stories edited by Cosmos Books' Sean Wallace and featuring contributions by Keith Brooke, Adrian Cole, Barrington Bayley, Maynard and Sims, John Grant and others.

Wallace also announced a new imprint, Prime Books, which would include a number of titles originally announced by Imaginary Worlds. These included books by Tim Lebbon, Jeff VanderMeer, Brett Savory and Michael Laimo. Subsequently, Jeff VanderMeer's Ministry of Whimsy Press became a print-on-demand imprint of Prime.

Edo van Belkom's *Teeth* from Meisha Merlin was an erotic police procedural about *vagina dentata*, introduced by Richard Laymon. From the same publisher, Lee Killough's *Blood Games* was the third in the series featuring vampire detective Garreth Mikaelian.

David Nordhaus's online imprint DarkTales launched the

collections *Dial Your Dreams & Other Nightmares* by Robert Weinberg, *Cold Comfort* by Nancy Kilpatrick and the erotic *Six-Inch Spikes* by Edo van Belkom at the Seattle World Horror Convention. Later in the year, the publisher released the novels *Soul Temple* by Steven Lee Climer, *A Flock of Crows is Called a Murder* by James Viscosi, and the second volume in the *Asylum* anthology series, *The Violent Ward*, edited by Victor Heck and featuring stories by D.F. Lewis, James Dorr, Gerard Houarner and others.

Harlan was a new novel by David Whitman, while *The Charm* was the first book in the reissued 'Shaman Cycle' series of Southwestern supernatural thrillers by Adam Niswander. It was followed by *The Serpent Slayers* and *The Hound Hunters*, with more volumes in the projected thirteen-volume series due from DarkTales.

Harry Houdini and Sir Arthur Conan Doyle teamed up to battle dark magic in Harry R. Squires's print-on-demand novel *What Rough Beast*.

Published in a signed and numbered 500-copy hardcover by Oregon's IFD Publishing, *Escaping Purgatory: Fables in Words and Pictures* by Gary A. Braunbeck and Alan M. Clark contained seven thematically linked stories (five original) and a foreword by Peter Crowther, illustrated throughout by Clark. From the same imprint, *Flaming Arrows* was a collection of short-short stories by Bruce Holland Rogers, published in both trade paperback and hardcover, with an introduction by Kate Wilhelm. Set in a ridiculously huge typeface, the twenty-seven tales (many of them reprints) were illustrated by Jill Bauman and publisher Clark.

Edited by Elizabeth Engstrom, *Imagination Fully Dilated Volume 2* contained twenty-nine stories by such authors as Ramsey Campbell, Poppy Z. Brite and Charles de Lint, based around Alan M. Clark's artwork. With an introduction by Paula Guran, the hardcover was limited to 600 signed copies from IFD.

Independent Texas imprint Clockwork Storybook was founded in 2001 by a writers' collective and published nine titles in its first year. These included the trade paperback collection *Beneath the Skin and Other Stories*, containing six original stories and a somewhat pretentious introduction by Matthew Sturges, and Chris Roberson's *Cybermancy Incorporated*, a collection of two stories and two linked novellas introducing modern-day pulp hero Jon Bonaventure Carmody and his associates. The Clockwork Reader was a trade paperback sampler containing work by the above-mentioned authors, along with Mark Finn and Bill Willingham. Hundreds of short stories, novels and sample chapters were also available for free download on the publisher's website.

William E. Rand's *Painted Demons* was a collection of nine linked horror stories available from iUniverse/Writers Club Press. Rand's *That Way Madness Lies* and Rita Dimitra's *The Blood Waltz* were vampire novels from the same imprint.

Gus Smith's *Feather & Bone* was a debut novel from British print-on-demand publisher Big Engine and involved an ancient spirit loose in a Northumberland farming community beset by BSE.

Edited by Forrest J. Ackerman, *Rainbow Fantasia: 35 Spectrumatic Tales of Wonder* from Sense of Wonder Press featured stories with colours in their titles by Ray Cummings, Robert W. Chambers and others.

From Subterranean Press, Douglas Clegg's *Naomi* was originally published as an online serial novel. About a man pursuing a ghost into the underground world that exists beneath New York City, it was limited to 1,500 signed copies. Clegg's other novel from Subterranean, *Dark of the Eye*, involved a woman whose healing powers made her a target for evil forces.

Joe Lansdale's *Zeppelins West* was a wild parody of Westerns, alternate universes and pulp stories, involving a cast of historical characters, the Frankenstein Monster and Captain Nemo and his intellectual seal, Ned. Illustrated by Mark A. Nelson, it was available in a signed hardcover edition limited to 1,500 copies with full-colour endpapers.

Ray Garton's *Sex and Violence in Hollywood* lived up to its title, while John Shirley's novel *The View from Hell* was published in a signed edition of 1,000 copies and a twenty-six-copy lettered edition.

Published as an attractive hardcover limited to 750 signed and numbered copies, Thomas Tessier's novella *Father Panic's Opera Macabre* concerned a successful historical novelist who stumbled upon a remote Italian farmhouse filled with supernatural secrets.

The story was unfortunately marred by some extremely graphic depictions of Nazi tortures.

Delayed from the previous year, David J. Schow's collection *Eye* contained thirteen stories (two original) and a witty afterword by the author, limited to 1,000 signed copies. An extra new story was included in the lettered-state edition.

Edward Bryant's *The Baku: Tales of the Nuclear Age* contained a new introduction by the author, three short stories and a previously unpublished teleplay, bought by *The Twilight Zone* but never produced. It was limited to 500 signed copies and a twenty-six copy lettered edition.

Guilty But Insane was a collection of Poppy Z. Brite's non-fiction, limited to 2,000 signed hardcover copies with a full-colour dust jacket and autograph page art by J.K. Potter. Brite and Caitlín R. Kiernan each had a new story plus a collaboration in *Wrong Things*, an attractive hardcover illustrated by Richard Kirk and published in a signed edition of 1,500 copies and a lettered edition.

Subterranean also revived the old Dark Harvest *Night Visions* series with the tenth volume. Edited by Richard Chizmar and illustrated by Alan M. Clark, it contained new novellas by Jack Ketchum and John Shirley, along with five original short stories by David B. Silva. The volume was available as a trade hardcover and a 500-copy limited edition.

Simon Clark's new novel, *Darkness Demands*, appeared from Cemetery Dance in a signed edition limited to 1,000 copies. It involved a writer of true-crime stories faced with choosing between the survival of his daughter or the rest of his family. A reissue of Clark's 1995 end-of-civilization novel, *Blood Crazy*, was also available from the same publisher in a signed edition of 1,000 copies.

The signed, limited edition of Christopher Golden's *The Ferryman* came with a quote from Clive Barker and involved a woman who spurned the eponymous soul-taker during a near-fatal medical ordeal. The book's prologue was published as a chapbook with illustrations by Eric Powell.

Tim Lebbon's short novel *Until She Sleeps* was about a young boy's battle against a resurrected 300-year-old witch who released her suppressed nightmares on a quiet village. It was available in a deluxe limited edition of 1,000 signed copies.

Edward Lee's *City Infernal* was a Southern Gothic horror novel set in Hell and also limited to 1,000 copies.

The Cemetery Dance hardcover of Richard Laymon's *Night in Lonesome October* was the first US edition of the late author's Halloween novel. Also from CD, *Friday Night at Beast House* was a short novel that was nominally a sequel to the author's previous three books in the series. Laymon's fable *The Halloween Mouse* was a thin, oversized hardcover illustrated in full colour by Alan M. Clark and limited to only 300 signed and numbered copies inside a handmade cloth slipcase.

Richard Matheson's *Camp Pleasant* was possibly an early novel, about a murder at a children's summer camp, while a limited edition of 1,500 copies of Jack Ketchum's *The Lost* was published by Cemetery Dance simultaneously with the Leisure paperback.

Edited by Richard Chizmar, *Trick or Treat* was the first in a new hardcover anthology series celebrating Halloween. It collected five original novellas by Gary A. Braunbeck, Nancy A. Collins, Rick Hautala, Al Sarrantonio and Thomas Tessier. It was also available in a signed edition, limited to 400 slipcased copies.

F. Paul Wilson's *Sims Book Two: The Portero Method* was the second in a new series of hardcover novellas published exclusively by Cemetery Dance in a limited edition of 750 signed copies. Wilson's latest 'Repairman Jack' novel, *Hosts*, appeared from Gauntlet Press in a signed, limited edition of 475 copies, with cover art by Harry O. Morris. It introduced the enigmatic Jack's sister, Kate Iverson, and featured an insidious virus that threatened to deprive humanity of its individuality.

Originally published in 1991 as a paperback original, Nancy A. Collins's second novel, *Tempter*, appeared from Gauntlet Press in a completely rewritten version that the author considered the preferred text. It was available as both a signed and numbered hardcover and in a lettered, leather-bound and tray-cased edition priced at $150.

Edited by Donn Albright, Ray Bradbury's classic collection *Dark Carnival* was limited to only 700 numbered and slipcased copies signed by Bradbury and Clive Barker (who contributed the afterword). This edition added five stories not contained in the 1947 Arkham House edition, along with several black and white pulp-cover reproductions and an archival section featuring photos of manuscript pages, letters, and some other rare items. Bradbury produced the dust-jacket art and interior illustrations himself. A lettered, leather-bound, tray-cased edition of fifty-two copies, containing an extra twenty-five pages, sold for $1,000 apiece.

For those who purchased the book directly from the publisher, there was also a chapbook of Bradbury's story 'Time Intervening', limited to 752 copies.

The deluxe reissue of Richard Matheson's classic *The Shrinking Man* contained a new afterword by David Morrell, photos from the movie and several pages of facsimile script. It was limited to 500 numbered copies signed by Matheson and Morrell.

Gauntlet's new Edge imprint concentrated on publishing mass-market trade paperbacks and hardcovers. Released as an Edge title, Barry Hoffman's serial-killer novel *Judas Eyes* was the third in the series about bounty hunter Shara Farris, with an afterword by Jack Ketchum.

The *Gauntlet Press Sampler* was a chapbook featuring new stories by Richard Christian Matheson, Barry Hoffman, Rain Graves and Richard Matheson, along with a poem by Clive Barker, illustrated by Harry O. Morris and David Armstrong.

Launched in November 2000 by Craig Spector and a venture capital company to sell books directly through the Internet, Stealth Press consolidated its publishing schedule in 2001 with a raft of nicely produced hardcover volumes that were not initially available in bookstores.

Celebrating the fortieth anniversary of Dennis Etchison's first professional short-story sale, *Talking in the Dark: Selected Stories* was a handsome collection of twenty-four tales (one original), the earliest dating back to 1972. Unfortunately, despite being a commemorative volume, the book contained neither an introduction nor any story notes by the author.

Darkness Divided collected twenty-two stories (four original) by John Shirley, presented in two sections – one featuring stories set in the past and the present, and the other set in myriad futures. The book included collaborations with Walter Gibson and Bruce Sterling, plus a short introduction by Poppy Z. Brite.

Dark Universe contained forty-one stories that author William F. Nolan considered to be amongst his best work from the past fifty years, with an introduction by Christopher Conlon. Chelsea

Quinn Yarbro's *Tempting Fate*, her third Saint-Germain vampire book from Stealth Press, weighed in at more than 600 pages.

In December, Stealth published a 800-page-plus edition of *Clive Barker's Books of Blood*. The massive collection was available as a trade hardcover, a 500-copy signed edition and as a lettered edition of fifty-two copies that sold out pre-publication. Featuring a cover photograph by the author and a new preface by Peter Atkins, it was the first and only edition containing all six books in one volume (including the final story, 'On Jerusalem's Street', previously unavailable in any North American printing).

However, having gone through a reported $1.3 million in venture capital, Stealth suspended all publication at the end of the year and let its consulting staff go. Amongst those who found that they were out of a job were Craig Spector, Pat LoBrutto, Peter Schneider, Paula Guran, Douglas Clegg and Peter Atkins, while imminent editions of Ray Bradbury's poetry collection *They Have Not Seen the Stars* and Tabitha King's *Small World* were left in limbo.

Sporting a jokey dust jacket by Gahan Wilson, *Acolytes of Cthulhu* was the third Lovecraftian anthology edited and introduced by Robert M. Price and published in hardcover by Fedogan & Bremer. It contained twenty-eight stories (two original) by Joseph Payne Brennan, C.M. Eddy, Manly Wade Wellman, Henry Hasse, Edmond Hamilton, David H. Keller M.D., Jorge Luis Borges, Randall Garrett, S.T. Joshi, Dirk W. Mosig, Don Burleson, Peter Cannon, Gustav Meyrinck, Neil Gaiman and others.

Fedogan also reissued H.P. Lovecraft's *Fungi from Yuggoth* as an audio CD containing thirty-five sonnets and with an accompanying booklet.

Inspired by Lovecraft and the Cthulhu Mythos, *Strange Aeons* from Wiltshire's Rainfall Records was an atmospheric two-disk CD collection of words and music produced and directed by artist Steve Lines. Contributors to the audio anthology included Ramsey Campbell, Brian Lumley, Simon Clark, John B. Ford, Joel Lane, Robert M. Price and Tim Lebbon.

Robert T. Garcia's American Fantasy imprint published a 600-copy signed and slipcased edition of Michael Moorcock's *The Dreamthief's Daughter: A Tale of the Albino*, in which Elric of

Melniboné, Count Ulzic von Bek and other characters battled the evils of Hitler's Nazi Germany. The beautifully designed volume, illustrated by Randy Broecker, Donato Giancola, Gary Gianni, Robert Gould, Michael Kaluta, Todd Lockwood, Don Maitz and Michael Whelan, was also issued in a twenty-six-copy lettered and tray-cased edition.

Ranging from Lovecraftian horrors to hard SF, *Claremont Tales* was a collection of twelve recent stories (one original) by Richard A. Lupoff, illustrated by Nicholas Jainschigg and published by Golden Gryphon Press.

Peter Crowther's PS Publishing released Tracy Knight's impressive and offbeat debut novel *The Astonished Eye* (originally scheduled to appear from the now defunct Pumpkin Books) with an introduction by Philip José Farmer and dust-jacket illustration by Alan Clark. The hardcover was limited to 500 signed and numbered copies and twenty-six deluxe lettered editions.

Introduced by Paul Di Filippo, Eric Brown's novella *A Writer's Life* concerned an apparently immortal author whose previous incarnations included Ambrose Bierce. Conrad Williams's *Nearly People* included an introduction by Michael Marshall Smith and concerned a woman's quest through a decaying and dangerous landscape. Both were published by PS in limited signed and numbered editions of 500 paperback copies and 300 hardcovers.

Manchester's Savoy Books reprinted Anthony Skene's (aka George Norman Philips, 1886–1972) incredibly rare 1936 pulp detective novel *Monsieur Zenith the Albino* as an attractive hardcover with an introduction by Jack Adrian, a foreword by Michael Moorcock, and numerous black and white illustrations and cover reproductions throughout.

From the same publisher, David Britton's *Baptized in the Blood of Millions* was the third 'Lord Horror' novel with illustrations by the author, set in a bizarre alternate England spanning World War II and featuring the traitorous Lord Haw-Haw, British film star Jessie Matthews and poet Sylvia Plath as characters.

From editor David Sutton's Shadow Publishing imprint, *Phantoms of Venice* was a solid anthology of ten tales (two reprints) by Peter Tremayne, Cherry Wilder, Conrad Williams, Mike Chinn, Tim Lebbon, Brian Stableford and others, including one by the editor himself, set in the 'Serene Republic' of dark canals. The hardcover also included an informative foreword by Joel Lane and dust-jacket art by Harry O. Morris.

Produced in conjunction with The British Fantasy Society, Telos Publishing was launched with *Urban Gothic: Lacuna and Other Trips* edited by David J. Howe, a trade paperback and hardcover anthology based on the disappointing Channel 5 TV series. Along with a very brief introduction by actor Richard O'Brien and interviews with the creators of the show, it included three original tales about London (the first two of them reprints) by Christopher Fowler, Graham Masterton and Simon Clark and a trio of stories by Paul Finch, Steve Lockley and Paul Lewis, and Debbie Bennett based on previously produced scripts by Tom de Ville.

Telos also began publishing a series of original hardcover *Doctor Who* novellas. The first, *Time and Relative* by Kim Newman, appeared as a standard hardcover and in a deluxe signed edition featuring a colour frontispiece illustration by Bryan Talbot.

Published in trade paperback by Brooklyn's Small Beer Press, *Stranger Things Happen* was the first collection from the talented Kelly Link, containing eleven quirky, spooky and smart stories (two original). *Meet Me in the Moon Room* from the same imprint contained thirty-three often surreal tales (six original) by Ray Vukcevich.

California's Dark Regions Press issued the attractive trade paperback collections *Strange Mistresses: Tales of Wonder and Romance* containing fourteen stories (two original) and thirteen poems by James Dorr with an introduction by Marge Simon, *Winter Shadows and Other Tales* featuring twenty stories (four original) by Mary Soon Lee, and *Salt Water Tears*, a collection of ten stories (one original) by Brian Hopkins with an introduction by Gary A. Braunbeck. All three volumes featured cover art by A.B. Word.

Gary Braunbeck's *This Flesh Unknown* was an erotic ghost novel from Foggy Windows Books/Chimeras, while D.G.K. Goldberg's . . . *Doomed to Repeat It*, published by The Design Image Group, was about a woman with an abusive ghostly boyfriend.

From Overlook Connection Press, Gary Raisor's *Graven Images* appeared in various signed editions with an introduction by Edward Lee, who also somewhat predictably supplied the introduction for *Duet for the Devil*, a hard-core horror novel by T. Winter-Damon and Randy Chandler about serial slayer The Zodiac Killer. It was published by Florida's Necro Publications in a signed and numbered edition of 400 trade paperbacks and 100 hardcovers.

Necro's Bedlam Press imprint, dedicated to bizarre, weird and darkly humorous fiction, was launched with *Tangy Bonanza!*, a collection of two novellas by Doc Solammen published in a signed and numbered trade paperback edition of 300 copies and a fifty-two-copy signed and lettered hardcover.

Published by Delirium Books, Scott Thomas's *Cobwebs and Whispers* collected twenty-six stories (seventeen original) of quiet horror with a foreword by Jeff VanderMeer and an introduction by Michael Pendragon in a signed hardcover edition limited to 250 numbered copies.

Also from Delirium, Greg F. Gifune's *Heretics* contained eight short horror stories with an introduction by Brian Hopkins and was limited to just fifty signed and numbered hardcover copies. This also became the first title in Delirium's new trade paperback line.

From the same publisher and edited by Shane Ryan Staley, *The Dead Inn* was an anthology of hardcore horror subtitled *Gross Oddities, Erotic Perversities & Supernatural Entities*. It featured stories by Don D'Ammassa, Charlee Jacob, Steve Beai, Mark McLaughlin, John B. Rosenman, Trey R. Barker, Jeffrey Thomas and others, including the editor. *4x4* contained eight stories by Michael Oliveri, Geoff Cooper, Brian Keene and Michael T. Huyck, Jr., with an afterword in which the authors/collaborators discussed why they write horror.

From Shadowlands Press, Tom Piccirilli's *The Night Class* involved a college student who found his life unravelling around him, while Steven R. Cowan's *Gothica: Romance of the Immortals* was a time-travel tale from Southern Charm Press involving vampires.

New York's Soft Skull Press published Nick Mamatas's novel *Northern Gothic*, about two serial killers connected over more than a century by the city's bloody history.

Confessions of a Ghoul and Other Stories from Silver Lake Publishing contained seven stories by M.F. Korn and an introduction by D.F. Lewis. Boasting 'Six Honorable Mentions' in *The Year's Best Fantasy and Horror* on the cover, *Odd Lot: Stories to*

Chill the Heart was a collection of nine stories (one original) written and published by self-proclaimed 'Storyteller of the Heart' Steve Burt, illustrated by Jessica Hagerman.

The Bubba Chronicles was a collection of eleven stories (including several collaborations) by Selina Rosen from Yard Dog Press. *Bubbas of the Apocalypse* was a follow-up anthology edited by Rosen containing sixteen stories and three poems set in a zombie-filled post-holocaust future. From the same editor and imprint, *Stories That Won't Make Your Parents Hurl* contained fifteen young-adult stories and three poems inspired by the Brothers Grimm.

Edited by Nicola Griffith and Stephen Pagel, *Bending the Landscape: Horror* was an anthology of eighteen original gay and lesbian horror stories published by Overlook Press.

Published by Chicago's 11th Hour Productions and Twilight Tales, *Blood & Donuts* was a 250-copy trade paperback anthology edited by Tina L. Jens and containing eighteen crime/mystery stories (twelve original) by Jody Lynn Nye, Jay Bonansinga, Steve Lockley, Robert Weinberg, Brian Hodge, Yvonne Navarro, Edo van Belkom, Wayne Allen Salle and others.

John B. Ford's collection of ten stories and four poems, *Tales Of Deviltry & Doom*, was published by artist Steve Lines's Rainfall Books in a limited hardcover edition of 250 signed and numbered copies. *Dark Shadows on the Moon* contained a further thirty-six stories (seven original) by the same writer, published in trade paperback by Hive Press with an introduction by Simon Clark.

Meanwhile, Ford's own BJM Press issued David Price's *The Evil Eye*, Quentin S. Crisp's *The Nightmare Exhibition* and Paul Kane's *Alone (in the Dark)*, each as trade paperback collections with introductions by the publisher.

Dark Whispers by Peter Ebsworth was a collection of ten stories published in trade paperback by Storybook, an imprint of David Searle's Searle Publishing.

Edited and introduced by Nikolas Schreck for Creation Books, *Flowers from Hell: A Satanic Reader* featured stories, poetry and novel excerpts about the Devil by Edgar Allan Poe, John Milton, Charles Baudelaire and others.

The 1920s Investigator's Companion to Chaosium's *Call of Cthulhu* role-playing game included background material by

Keith Herber, John Crowe, Kenneth Faig, Jr. and others. Bruce Ballon's award-winning *Call of Cthulhu: Unseen Masters* was another guide to the game, including a scenario partly inspired by Philip K. Dick. The trade paperback was illustrated by Paul Carrick and Drashi Khendup.

Also from Chaosium, *Song of Cthulhu: Tales of the Spheres Beyond Sound* edited by Stephen Mark Rainey contained twenty Lovecraftian stories (nine original) by Thomas Ligotti, Caitlín R. Kiernan and others.

Nameless Cults: The Cthulhu Mythos Fiction of Robert E. Howard was the latest Chaosium anthology edited and introduced by Robert M. Price. It included thirteen vaguely Lovecraftian stories by Howard plus five collaborations (including the round-robin tale 'The Challenge from Beyond' by Howard, C.L. Moore, A. Merritt, H.P. Lovecraft and Frank Belknap Long), illustrated by H.E. Fassl and Dave Carson.

Robert Price also contributed an introduction to *The Gardens of Lucullus*, a Cthulhu Mythos/Roman gladiator novel by Richard L. Tierney and Glenn Rahman, published as an attractive trade paperback by the enigmatic Sidecar Preservation Society.

Introduced by David G. Rowlands, *A Ghostly Crew: Tales from The Endeavour* was a welcome collection of fifteen all-reprint stories by Roger Johnson, published by Robert Morgan's Sarob Press in a hardcover edition of 300 copies. *Spalatro: Two Italian Tales* was a slim 250-copy hardcover containing two stories from the *Dublin University Magazine* by J. Sheridan Le Fanu, edited and introduced by Miles Stribling and superbly illustrated by Douglas Walters.

The Sistrum and Other Ghost Stories by Alice Perrin (1867–1934) was the fifth volume in editor Richard Dalby's 'Mistresses of the Macabre' series, with illustrations by Paul Lowe. The publisher had to revise the binding specifications for *The Haunted River & Three Other Ghostly Novellas* by Mrs J.H. Riddell (1832–1906), which included an introduction by editor Dalby and twenty-four full-page original illustrations that accompanied the *Routledge's Christmas Annual* publication of the four stories. Both books appeared in 300-copy numbered hardcover editions.

Published the same month by Sarob was *Can Such Things Be? & By the Night Express* by the mysterious Keith Fleming, with an introduction by John Pelan, an afterword by Dalby, and dust-jacket and interior art by Randy Broecker. It contained the title novel from 1889 and three supernatural novellas ('By the Night Express', 'Dolores' and 'Love Stronger than Death') from the very rare 1889 paperback *By The Night Express*. The book was limited to just 250 hardcover copies.

From San Francisco's Night Shade Books came *The Devil is Not Mocked and Other Warnings* and *Fearful Rock and Other Precarious Locales*, the second and third volumes respectively in *The Selected Stories of Manly Wade Wellman* series edited by John Pelan. Ramsey Campbell contributed a reminiscent introduction to the former and Stephen Jones to the latter. These welcome collections were once again only marred by the poor interior artwork.

The Man With the Barbed-Wire Fists was a large collection of twenty-four stories (two original) by Norman Partridge, while *Face* was a new novel by Tim Lebbon about a supernatural hitch-hiker. Both books were also issued in 100-copy signed/slipcased editions that included extra chapbooks.

. . . *And the Angel with Television Eyes* was a new fantasy novel by John Shirley, loosely based on the short story of the same title, and *Lies & Ugliness* was a big new collection from Brian Hodge, containing two new stories. The signed/slipcased edition of the latter also included a CD by the author's musical side project, Axis Mundi.

Also from Night Shade, editor S.T. Joshi's *The Ancient Track: The Complete Poetical Works of H.P. Lovecraft* eventually appeared in hardcover and trade paperback after a few delays.

Edited with an introduction by Joshi, Robert Hichens's *The Return of the Soul and Other Stories* from Seattle's Midnight House contained eight reprint tales and was the first of a proposed two-book set presenting the definitive collection of the prolific author's supernatural tales.

The Scarecrow and Other Stories was an expanded edition of the 1918 collection containing seventeen tales by G. (Gwendolyn) Ranger Wormser (1893–1953), edited by Douglas A. Anderson. As a follow-up to the author's earlier collection *The House of the Nightmare and Other Stories*, the same publisher also issued Edward Lucas White's (1866–1934) *Sesta & Other Strange Stories*, which included fifteen stories (several previously unpublished), two poems, an introduction by Lee Weinstein and a bibliography.

Nineteen of Fritz Leiber's best horror tales were collected in *The Black Gondolier & Other Stories*, the first of two hardcover volumes edited by John Pelan and Steve Savile.

The Beasts of Brahm was a reprint of the rare 1937 novel by the possibly pseudonymous Mark Hansom, with a fascinating introduction by Pelan. The equally obscure H.B. Gregory's *Dark Sanctuary* was another rare British novel also rescued from obscurity, with an historical introduction by D.H. Olson. Both volumes appeared on the late Karl Edward Wagner's list of 'forgotten' works of fantasy and horror and, like all the titles from Midnight House, were published in hardcover editions of just 460 copies with cover artwork by Allen Koszowski.

From Tartarus Press, *Ghost Stories* by Oliver Onions collected twenty-two classic tales. First published in 1931, Forrest Reid's *Uncle Stephen* was a dream-story with a new introduction by Colin Cruise, while L.P. Hartley's *The Collected Macabre Stories*, also from Tartarus, contained thirty-seven ghost stories by the author of *The Go-Between*, with an introduction by Mark Valentine. All were limited to just 350 copies.

L.T.C. Rolt's *Sleep No More: Railway, Canal and Other Stories of the Supernatural* was a trade paperback collection of fourteen classic ghost stories from Sutton Publishing, with an introduction by Susan Hill.

From Ash-Tree Press, *Where Human Pathways End: Tales of the Dead and the Un-Dead* collected all ten of the supernatural short stories of 1930s author Shamus Frazer, whose story 'The Fifth Mask' is cited as an influence on Ramsey Campbell, with an introduction by editor Richard Dalby. Edited and introduced by John Pelan and Dalby, *The Shadow on the Blind and Other Ghost Stories* reprinted the 1895 collection of nine stories by Alfred Louisa Bladwin, along with a previously uncollected tale, and included seven illustrations by Symington from the first edition.

The Golden Gong and Other Night-Pieces by Thomas Burke reprinted twenty-one tales complete with an introductory essay by editor Jessica Amanada Salmonson.

Edited by David Rowlands and limited to 500 copies, *Mystic*

Voices by Roger Pater (aka Dom Gilbert Hudleston), a member of the Order of St. Benedict, collected fourteen stories about psychic squire-priest Father Philip Rivers Pater, along with a chapter from a companion work, *My Cousin Philip*, and a contemporary obituary of the author.

Mrs Amworth, the third volume of *The Collected Spook Stories of E.F. Benson*, was limited to 600 copies and contained sixteen short supernatural stories (dating from 1922–23), with an introduction by editor Jack Adrian. Adrian was also responsible for *Couching at the Door and Other Strange and Macabre Tales*, which collected the supernatural stories of popular novelist D. (Dorothy) K. (Kathleen) Broster (1877–1950), including one previously unpublished tale. It was also limited to 600 copies, with dust-jacket art by Jason Van Hollander.

As usual, Adrian edited *The Ash-Tree Annual Macabre 2001*, which was limited to 500 copies and contained thirteen stories, only one of which had appeared in book form before, by writers better known for working in other genres. These included such well-known names as Marjorie Bowen, Jessie Douglas Kerruish and Leigh Brackett.

After Shocks was a collection of eighteen 'classical' supernatural stories by prolific small-press contributor Paul Finch, and Steve Rasnic Tem's *The Far Side of the Lake* was a welcome collection of eight of the author's 'Charlie Goode' ghost stories and twenty-five other horror tales, limited to 500 copies.

The Five Quarters by Steve Duffy and Ian Rodwell collected five novellas about meetings of the eponymous society with a handful of members, at which the talk inevitably turned to the supernatural. It was limited to 500 copies, and the dust jacket was illustrated by Paul Lowe.

Probably Ash-Tree's finest achievement of the year was *A Pleasing Terror: The Complete Supernatural Writings of M.R. James*. With a preface by Christopher and Barbara Roden, and an introduction by Steve Duffy, the $75.00 hardcover reprinted thirty-four annotated stories plus prefaces, several rare fragments, articles, letters, translations, appendices, a bibliography, and information on James on film, radio and television. Paul Lowe also provided thirty-three illustrations along with a full-colour dust jacket.

The series of chapbooks published by the mysterious and elusive Sidecar Preservation Society (named after a classic Prohibition-era cocktail) continued with Richard L. Tierney's *The Blob That Gobbled Abdul and Other Poems and Songs*, a collection of thirteen Lovecraftian verses, illustrated by Dave Carson and with an introduction by Ramsey Campbell. Tierney in turn introduced Campbell's time-travel story *Point of View*, illustrated by Allen Koszowski.

Hugh B. Cave's *Loose Loot* was a detective yarn featuring Officer Coffey with an afterword by Milt Thomas, while *Swedish Lutheran Vampires of Brainerd* was a humorous story by Anne Waltz, with an afterword by Karen Taylor and cover art by Jon Arfstrom.

Edited by D.H. Olsen, *A Donald Wandrei Miscellany* contained a number of shorter pieces of fiction, non-fiction, verse and humour by the late author, and Lee Brown Coye's *Chips & Savings and Another Writing* (already in its second printing) was a collection of the artist's homespun newspaper column in the *Mid-York Weekly* during the 1960s. Each of the Sidecar booklets was limited to 100 numbered copies (except for the Cave, which totalled 175), some of which may have been bound in boards by the publisher.

From Subterranean Press, Graham Joyce's chapbook *Black Dust* contained the 1994 story 'The Apprentice' along with the previously unpublished title story, limited to 250 signed and numbered copies. From the same imprint, Graham Masterton's *The Scrawler*, about an urban monster, was limited to 500 numbered copies.

Also from Subterranean, *On Pirates* was a deluxe chapbook by William Ashbless (a pseudonym for Tim Powers and James P. Blaylock) with interior two-colour illustrations by Gahan Wilson. Limited to 1,000 signed and numbered copies, it included 'Slouching Toward Mauritius', a short pirate story written more than twenty-five years ago but never published, along with a lengthy pirate poem, 'Moon-Eye Agonistes'. Powers and Blaylock supplied the introduction and afterword respectively.

Cat Stories by Michael Marshall Smith was published by Paul Miller's Earthling Publications, collecting three tales (one original) featuring fantastique felines in an attractive 350-copy chapbook designed by the author. Fifteen lettered and signed hardcover copies were also issued in a slipcase, along with a facsimile of the original handwritten manuscript for Smith's short story 'The Man Who Drew Cats'.

Chico Kidd's self-published *Second Sight and Other Stories* contained four rousing supernatural adventures introducing readers to turn-of-the-century sea captain Luís Da Silva, who had the power to see ghosts after losing his left eye to a demon. It proved an impressive showcase for one of the genre's most interesting and genuinely original new characters.

From Sean A. Wallace's Prime Books, *The Hidden Language of Demons* was a 33,000-word modern novella by L.H. Maynard and M.P.N. Sims which was billed as 'Poe in his Sgt. Pepper period'.

Limited to 100 copies, W. (Wilum) H. (Hopfrog) Pugmire's *Songs of Sesqua Valley* was published by Imelod and contained thirty-three weird sonnets inspired by H.P. Lovecraft, The Cthulhu Mythos and various dark places, with an introduction and cover illustration by Peter Worthy. From the same author, *Tales of Love and Death* published by Delirium Books was a 300-copy signed chapbook containing sixteen horror and Lovecraftian short stories (two original).

Mark McLaughlin's *Shoggoth Cacciatore and Other Eldritch Entrees* was a chapbook collection of ten Lovecraftian stories (six original) also from Delirium, with an introduction by Simon Clark. *The Night the Lights Went Out in Arkham* was an anthology of Lovecraftian stories set in the 1970s from Undaunted Press. It contained five new tales by Shawn James, Megan Powell, Octavio Ramos, Jr., Lawrence Barker and the ever-popular McLaughlin.

Louis de Bernieres's *Gunter Weber's Confession: The Final Chapter to Captain Corelli's Mandolin* was a thin chapbook from Tartarus Press, published in a special limited edition of 350 numbered copies. Hand-set in Perpetua type and printed and bound by Alan Anderson at the Tragara Press, it was available in a 250-copy edition on Teton paper or as one of 100 special copies on Zerkall paper signed by the author for $120.00.

Eden was a novelette by Ken Wisman about a drug-fuelled spiritual journey, published by California's Dark Regions Press. *True Tales of the Scarlet Sponge* by Wayne Allen Sallee and

Weston Ochse's *Natural Selection* were both available from DarkTales.

Billed as 'A Double Shot of Repugnance', the first release in the new Necro Chapbooks line from Florida was *Partners in Chyme*, featuring Ryan Harding's 'Gross-Out Contest'-winning story 'Damaged Goods' paired with 'The Dritiphilist' by Edward Lee. It was published as a 300-copy signed and numbered chapbook and a twenty-six-copy signed and lettered hardcover.

Quantum Theology Publications was a new chapbook line from Canada that launched with *The Narrow World*, a collection of five stories by the talented Gemma Files, including a new vampire tale, plus an introduction by Michael Rowe.

Colorado's new online bookstore and specialty press Wormhole Books launched its limited-edition Contemporary Chapbook line in May with *Pioneer* by Melanie Tem, briefly introduced by Nancy Holder, and *A Sad Last Love at the Diner of the Damned* by Edward Bryant, with a new introduction by S.P. Somtow and an afterword by the author.

Also from Wormhole, *Pink Marble and Never Say Die* were two short stories by Dawn Dunn with an introduction by Nancy Kilpatrick, and Dunn also contributed an author biography to *While She Was Out* by Bryant. Steve Rasnic Tem's bizarre novella about a travelling salesman, *In These Final Days of Sales*, included an autobiographical afterword by the author and interior photography by Bryant.

Each Wormhole booklet was limited to 750 signed copies, a 200-copy hardcover edition and a fifty-two-copy lettered edition, featuring full-colour covers, illustrated interiors and archival materials.

Fallen Angel Blues was an apocalyptic round-robin novella from Succubus Press/horror.net which, despite owing a little too much to Stephen King's *The Stand*, succeeded because of the enthusiasm of its ten collaborators, who included Suzanne Donahue, James Newman, Steve Savile and Mark Tyree.

Lee Martindale's *The Folly of Assumption* was a chapbook collection of five stories (one original) from Yard Dog Press, while *A Game of Colors* by John Urbanick was a novella from the same publisher.

The Exchange by Nicholas Sporlender (aka Jeff VanderMeer) was a beautifully produced little enveloped chapbook illustrated by Louis Verden (aka Eric Schaller) and published by Hoeg-bottom & Sons to celebrate the city of Ambergris's 300th Festival of the Freshwater Squid. It was available in a 300-copy edition or as a 100-copy deluxe limited signed edition in a box containing several items traditionally used during the Festival.

The Haunted River produced Oliver Onions's *Tragic Casements: A Ghost Story* as a seventy-five-copy chapbook with an introduction by Jonathan Harker. Published by Athanor Press, *Because Horrors Linger* contained four classic tales by Terence Ekenan.

The second volume of Jeff Paris and Adam Golaski's *New Genre* included new SF and horror stories by M.J. Murphy, Jan Wildt, Barth Anderson, Jon-Michael Emory and Zohar A. Goodman.

Darrell Schweitzer's *They Never Found His Head: Poems of Sentiment and Reflection* collected twelve Lovecraftian poems, four of which were Cthulhuoid hymns, in a chapbook published by Zadok Allen.

Defacing the Moon and Other Poems by Mike Allen was a slim chapbook from DNA Publications with illustrations by the poet. From Dark Regions Press, *A Box Full of Alien Skies* collected thirty-one poems by G.O. Clark in a signed edition of 200 copies.

Published by New Jersey's Flesh & Blood Press, *What the Cacodaemon Whispered* by Chad Hensley and Jacie Ragan's *Deadly Nightshade* both collected thirteen poems each and were limited to 150 copies apiece. *The Temporary King* by P.K. Graves was a short story also available from the same imprint.

Travelers by Twilight was the first volume of a portfolio of selected illustrations by Allen Koszowski with an introduction by Brian Lumley and an appreciation by fellow artist Jason Van Hollander. It was published by Magic Pen Press in an edition of 350 numbered copies.

It was reported that *Famous Monsters of Filmland* was facing an uncertain future after US Bankruptcy Judge Arthur Greenwald declared that its publisher, Ray Ferry, fraudulently transferred the magazine's ownership to his housemate, Gene Reynolds. In 2000, a Van Nuys jury found Ferry liable for breach of contract, libel and trade-mark infringement and awarded the title's creator and former editor Forrest J. Ackerman $518,000 and rights to the pen name 'Dr Acula'.

Ferry then transferred his assets to Reynolds and filed for bankruptcy protection. However, the judge found the asset transfers fraudulent because Ferry was trying to keep them away from creditors (including Ackerman) and continued to function as the magazine's editor. As a result, a US Bankruptcy trustee filed suit for $750,000 plus punitive damages against the law firm that represented Ferry in the case.

Published in Canada, Rod Gudino's *Rue Morgue* is probably the most attractive and informative magazine currently covering horror in popular culture. The glossy bi-monthly featured interviews with Dario Argento, William Lustig, Alan Moore, Rob Zombie, Guillermo del Toro and many others, along with plenty of film, DVD and video, book, audio, toy and gaming news and reviews.

As usual, *Weird Tales* produced four issues from DNA Publications with fiction and verse by Keith Taylor, Ian Watson, editor Darrell Schweitzer, Tanith Lee, Stephen Dedman, Thomas Ligotti, Ashok Banker, David Langford, Phyllis and Alex Eisenstein and others, along with articles by Douglas Winter (on Clive Barker), Gary J. Weir (on how he rediscovered his father through the latter's correspondence with H.P. Lovecraft), S.T. Joshi (reviews of Cthulhu Mythos fiction), and John Betancourt (on vampires).

From the same publisher, but far less professional-looking, was the quarterly *Dreams of Decadence: Vampire Poetry and Fiction*. Edited by Angela Kessler, contributors included Brian Stableford, Sarah A. Hoyt, N. Lee Wood, Wendy Rathbone and others.

Meanwhile, DNA's *Aboriginal SF*, the semi-professional magazine first published in 1985, folded with the spring issue. Editor Charles C. Ryan cited the periodical's excessive time demands, rather than any failure of the magazine, for his decision. *Aboriginal*'s inventory was absorbed by *Absolute Magnitude*, which also agreed to fulfil all outstanding *Aboriginal* subscriptions with its own magazine.

Edited by Richard Chizmar, Robert Morrish and Kara L. Tipton, the long-running *Cemetery Dance* published four issues featuring fiction by John Shirley, Jack Ketchum, Richard Laymon, Christa Faust, Dennis Etchison, Richard Christian Matheson, Simon Clark, Al Sarrantonio, Darrell Schweitzer, David B. Silva, Tim Lebbon, Bentley Little, Nancy Holder, T.M. Wright, Conrad Williams, Michael Cadnum and others. The magazine also included interviews with Bentley Little, Douglas Clegg, Simon Clark, Peter Straub, Tim Lebbon, Kim Newman, T.M. Wright and Al Sarrantonio, the usual review and opinion columns by Poppy Z. Brite, Bev Vincent (Stephen King news), Thomas F. Monteleone, John Pelan, Michael Marano, Charles L. Grant and various tributes to Richard Laymon.

Paula Guran's *Horror Garage* published a further two issues featuring pin-up covers of a woman in a fur bikini and another wielding a bloody cleaver. That aside, there was fiction by the mandatory John Shirley, Kim Newman (a new 'Anno Dracula' story), Peter Crowther, Don Webb, Gerard Houarner, Bruce Holland Rogers and others, a reprint interview with China Miéville, Norman Partridge's Drive-In reviews and various other regular columns.

As usual, Gordon Van Gelder's *The Magazine of Fantasy & Science Fiction* featured an impressive selection of fiction by such authors as Lucius Shepard, Esther M. Friesner, Michael Bishop, Geoff Ryman, Lucy Sussex, Michael Cadnum, Robert Sheckley, Thomas M. Disch, Paul McAuley, Ron Goulart, Terry Bisson, Ian Watson, the late Poul Anderson, James Morrow, Ray Bradbury, Gene Wolfe, Neil Gaiman, Carol Emshwiller, Michael Blumlein, and even actor Alan Arkin! There were also all the usual book and film review columns by Charles de Lint, Elizabeth Hand, Robert K.J. Killheffer, Michelle West, James Sallis, Kathi Maio and the always excellent Lucius Shepard, plus other non-fiction from Mike Ashley, Paul Di Filippo, Jeff VanderMeer, Bradley Denton and Barry N. Malzberg, amongst others. Unfortunately, a number of copies of the April issue were printed without any punctuation, and the bumper October/November issue appeared without its cartoons, although all the gag-lines were included!

David Pringle's *Interzone* published stories by Stephen Baxter, John Whitbourn, Graham Joyce, Ian Watson, Ashok Banker, Eric Brown, Liz Williams, Ian R. MacLeod, Gwyneth Jones, Thomas M. Disch, Lisa Tuttle, Gregory Benford and Richard Calder's interminable 'Lord Soho' series based around famous operas and operettas. The monthly magazine also featured interviews with Calder, Stephen Baxter, John Clute, Frank Kelly Freas, Lucius

Shepard, Ian R. MacLeod, Ian McDonald, Connie Willis, David Zindell and John Christopher (the March issue was a special celebration of his career), an always lively letters column, David Langford's 'Ansible' column, Gary Westfahl's opinion column, Evelyn Lewes's controversial media commentary, plus various book and film reviews by Nick Lowe, Paul McAuley, Tom Arden, Liz Williams, Chris Gilmore, David Mathew, Paul Beardsley, Matt Colborn, Phil Stephensen-Payne, Paul Brazier, John Clute and others.

Having finally succumbed to illustrated covers, Paul Fraser's *Spectrum SF* produced two issues featuring fiction by John Christopher, Stephen Baxter, Michael Coney, Mary Soon Lee, Eric Brown and Charles Stross. The best thing about this paperback periodical was its extensive listing and often grumpy reviews of recent publications.

Realms of Fantasy included a feature on Stephen King's best and worst, and managed to spell the author's name incorrectly on the cover!

Christopher Fowler joined Andy Cox's *The Third Alternative* with a regular column about the cinema. The three issues published also featured fiction by James Lovegrove, Simon Ings, Mike O'Driscoll, Joel Lane, Muriel Gray, James Van Pelt, Douglas Smith and others; interviews with Lovegrove, Gray and Graham Joyce, and articles about film directors Michael Powell, Andrei Tarkovsky and Tim Burton. With Issue 28, there was a subtle title change to *The 3rd Alternative*.

Also edited by Andy Cox, *Crimewave 5: Dark Before Dawn* featured three novellas and seven short stories, the stand-out being Christopher Fowler's contribution.

The ever-busy Mr Cox also launched the first two issues of *The Fix: The Ultimate Review of Short Fiction* from TTA Press, featuring interviews with Gordon Van Gelder and Ellen Datlow, columns and features by Mat Coward, Peter Tennant, Tim Lebbon and others, and numerous reviews of magazines, anthologies and collections.

For vampire fans, Arlene Russo's *Bite Me: The Magazine for the Night People* from Scotland, included interviews with 'Gothic supermodel' Donna Ricci, film director Kevin J. Lindenmuth, authors Nancy Kilpatrick and Fred Saberhagen, articles about Hammer's *Blood from the Mummy's Tomb* and *Captain Kronos,*

Vampire Hunter, plus such useful hints as '10 Ways to Become a Werewolf!'

The fourteenth issue of the impressive French magazine *Ténèbres* featured modern ghost stories by L.H. Maynard and M.P.N. Sims, Stephen Laws, Rick Hautala and others, articles by Brian Stableford, Ramsey Campbell and Maynard and Sims, and interviews with Laws and Hautala.

The *Book and Magazine Collector* contained a useful article by David Whitehead looking at books about 'Horror Stars', while 'Relaunch of Clive Barker' was a special sixteen-page magazine 'outsert' by Jeff Zaleski which appeared in *Publishers Weekly* to tie-in with the publication of Barker's latest novel, *Coldheart Canyon*.

After publishing two bi-monthly issues in 2001, Sovereign Media officially terminated Dan Perez's editorship of *Sci Fi* at the end of May, following the breakdown of negotiations between the publisher and the Sci Fi Channel regarding the transfer of ownership and the future management of the magazine.

Despite the tragic death of founder Frederick S. Clarke, *Cinefantastique* still produced six issues under publisher Celeste C. Clarke and editor Dan Pearsons. These included a *Farscape* double issue and cover features on *Hannibal*, *The Mummy Returns*, *Planet of the Apes*, *Ghosts of Mars* and *The Lord of the Rings*.

Produced on a strict monthly schedule, Tim and Donna Lucas's *Video Watchdog* featured the usual fascinating articles on James Bond, AIP's Beach Party series, both versions of *The Haunting of Hill House*, *Godzilla 2000*, *Frank Herbert's Dune*, Hitchcock on DVD, the restorations of *The Lost World* and *Planet of the Vampires*, superheroes and an interview with Mel Welles. With a list of contributors that included Kim Newman, Douglas E. Winter, Stephen R. Bissette and Tom Weaver, the quality of the reviews was exemplary. However, readers were once again left wondering whether Lucas's long-promised book on Mario Bava would ever be published.

From Visual Imagination Limited, David Miller's *Shivers* included cover features on *Shadow of the Vampire*, the cinema's greatest bogeymen, the *Buffy* monster make-up, *Resident Evil*, *Jeepers Creepers* and a bumper edition on *The Mummy Returns*.

Cult Movies featured a fascinating piece about Bela Lugosi visiting England, while Dennis J. Druktenis's enthusiastic *Scary Monsters Magazine* reached its fortieth issue and celebrated ten years of publication with the usual articles on TV horror hosts, regional conventions and old movies.

Alternative Cinema, the magazine of independent and underground film-making edited by Michael J. Raso, included interviews with Donald F. Glut, Julie Strain and Sam Sherman, plus an article about the making of *Erotic Witch Project 2*.

The revived *Castle of Frankenstein* magazine began reprinting Don Glut's series of novels *The New Adventures of Frankenstein* in an appallingly illustrated magazine format from Druktenis Publishing. At least they also included a black and white reprint of Dick Briefer's *Frankenstein* comic book from the 1950s.

For serious fans of model kits, the fortieth issue of *Kitbuilders* was a special Halloween edition featuring some impressive monster models.

After twenty-one years, Rosemary Pardoe's acclaimed M.R. Jamesian publication *Ghosts & Scholars* rounded out the year and its print incarnation with issues 32 and 33 featuring fiction by David Longhorn, C.E. Ward, Anthony Wilkins, Don Tumasonis, James Doig, David G. Rowlands, Katherine Haynes and Michael Chislett, plus articles by Pardoe, Christopher and Barbara Roden, and Andy Sawyer.

With Pardoe's fine fanzine transformed into a web-based, non-fiction magazine and the recent demise of Maynard and Sims's *Enigmatic Tales*, David Longhorn launched *Supernatural Tales* to fill the gap in the British small-press market. The first two issues contained some fine new supernatural stories by Chico Kidd, Michael Chislett, David G. Rowlands, Tina Rath and Steve Duffy. However, the dull presentation and lack of artwork did not do the new title any favours.

As usual, Gordon Linzner's *Space and Time* published two issues, featuring fiction and poetry by Mary Soon Lee, Darrell Schweitzer, Bruce Boston and others, plus interviews with Ursula K. Le Guin and James Morrow. Joe Morey and Bobbi Sinha-Morey's *Dark Regions: A Journal of Fantasy, Horror & Science Fiction* also managed two issues that included stories and poems by Charlee Jacob, Bruce Boston, P.D. Cacek and James S. Dorr.

James Van Pelt, Denise Dumars and Bruce Boston were amongst those contributing fiction and poetry to Patrick and Honna Swenson's *Talebones*, which also featured interviews with Dan Simmons and Charles de Lint and a review column by Edward Bryant.

The twelfth issue of Mark McLaughlin's *The Urbanite* was a special 'Zodiac' issue featuring stories by Christopher Fowler, Shane Ryan Staley, John Pelan, Hugh B. Cave and others, plus an impressive poetry suite by Jo Fletcher.

Subtitled 'a journal of parthenogenetic fiction and late labelling', the first edition of *Nemonymous* was an attractively designed collection of sixteen stories, whose author bylines would not be revealed until the second issue.

Graeme Hurry's *Kimota* published its regular two issues, with stories by Peter Tennant, Joel Lane, Hugh Cook, Paul Finch and others, along with articles on old radio drama and artist Sidney H. Sime, the usual reviews and letters columns, and more outstanding artwork from 'T23'.

Indigenous Fiction, edited by Sherry Decker, featured the usual mix of fiction, poetry and reviews, while Jack Fisher's *Flesh & Blood: Tales of Dark Fantasy & Horror* included an interview with Tom Piccirilli.

Paul Bradshaw's *The Dream Zone* reached its tenth number with two issues packed with fiction and poetry by Ian Watson, Mark McLaughlin, Allen Ashley, Peter Tennant, Rhys Hughes and many less familiar names, plus reviews and letters columns, and a useful article aimed at writers explaining how to avoid rejection.

Robert M. Price's *Crypt of Cthulhu* No.104 featured fiction and poetry by Joseph S. Pulver, Sr., Darrell Schweitzer, Richard L. Tierney, Frank Searight and David E. Schultz, articles by Ross F. Bagby, Rawlik and T.G. Cockcroft, plus the usual 'Mail-Call of Cthulhu' and 'R'lyeh Reviews'.

The Lovecraftian *Dark Legacy* from 'H'chtelegoth Press included Cthulhu Mythos fan fiction and poetry from James Ambuehl, Phillip A. Ellis, Ron Shiflet and Peter Worthy, plus artwork by Sinestro. There was more of the same in *Cthulhu Cultus*, including work by James and Tracy Ambuehl, and Chris Loveless.

The fourth issue of Pentagram Publications' *Lovecraft's Weird*

Mysteries featured four stories and a poem, plus an old interview with *Weird Tales* cover artist Margaret Brundage.

Brian Lingard's *Mythos Collector* was a new magazine devoted to Lovecraft with fiction by Christopher O'Brian and James P. Roberts, an interview with artist John Coulthart, and articles on collecting Mythos-related material.

Paul Fry's *Peep Show* was launched by Birmingham's Short, Scary Tales Publishing with a colour cover by Mike Bohatch and fiction from Sheri White, Daniel Harr, Michael O'Connor, Alex Severin, Glen Hamilton, Kobe Nihilis and Jim Lee.

The latest double issue of *Aurealis*, Australia's longest-running science fiction and fantasy magazine, was mailed to subscribers just before Christmas. It included fifteen stories by Dirk Strasser, Robert Hood, Robert Browne and others, plus a warts-and-all interview with outgoing editors Strasser and Stephen Higgins, an interview with author Ian Irvine, Bill Congreve's book reviews, and new editor Keith Stevenson's plans for the future of the title.

Also from Australia came the second issue of small-press magazine *Orb*, edited by Sarah Endacott, and former Allen & Unwin publicist Darran Jordan launched two issues of a new magazine called *Eschaton* from his Eclectica imprint.

The July issue of the monthly *The New York Review of Science Fiction* had an article about Clark Ashton Smith and the 1999 tribute anthology *The Last Continent*, while the November issue included a special forty-four-page supplement with reactions to the terrorist attacks of September 11th.

Charles N. Brown's monthly *Locus* boasted new cover designs by Arnie Fenner and included interviews with Frank Kelly Freas, Ellen Datlow, John Crowley, Thomas M. Disch, Harlan Ellison, Bob Eggleton, Andy Duncan, Lucius Shepard and several others, along with all the usual news and reviews.

Now available through Warren Lapine's DNA Publications, *Science Fiction Chronicle* was almost back on schedule, producing eleven issues with founder Andrew I. Porter staying on as news editor. Along with introducing interior colour, the magazine also revived Marvin Kaye's opinion column, premiered Brian Keene's new horror column, and featured interviews with various SF writers.

As always, *The Bulletin of The Science Fiction and Fantasy Writers of America*, edited by David A. Truesdale, contained plenty of useful articles and business advice for writers. Contributors included Harry Harrison, Michael Cassutt, Mike Resnick and Barry Malzberg, Barry B. Longyear, Kevin J. Anderson and others. The four quarterly issues also featured tributes to Gordon R. Dickson and Poul Anderson, a history of the Nebula Award, an interview with Patrick Nielsen Hayden, and market reports by Derryl Murphy and Randy Dannenfelser.

Despite a couple of confusing format changes and an editorial switch, The British Fantasy Society's newsletter *Prism* still managed to produce six bimonthly issues for members. These featured the usual news and reviews along with articles on young-adult fantasies, regular columns by Tom Arden and Chaz Brenchley, plus interviews with Lisa Tuttle and Canadian director John Fawcett.

The society also published two square-bound volumes of *Dark Horizons*, both of which were all-fiction issues edited by Debbie Bennett and featuring D.F. Lewis, Paul Lewis, Tina Rath, Peter Tennant, Mark McLaughlin and Allen Ashley, amongst others. The second volume of *F20*, published by Enigmatic Press and the BFS, and co-edited by David J. Howe with Maynard and Sims, was an all-fantasy issue themed around the seven deadly sins. Contributors included Freda Warrington, Juliet McKenna, Storm Constantine and Louise Cooper.

Voices from the Vault, the newsletter of Britain's Dracula Society, included obituaries for actor Francis Lederer (by Basil Copper) and author R. Chetwynd-Hayes, along with various reviews.

The Official Newsletter of the Horror Writers Association, edited on a monthly schedule by Kathryn Ptacek, featured all the usual columns and the editor's extensive market reports, plus a fascinating article on reverting rights by Richard Laymon, an interview with Laymon by Vincent Fahey, an extensive tribute to R. Chetwynd-Hayes, and self-congratulatory reports on the 2001 World Horror Convention/Bram Stoker Weekend.

Most of the March issue was devoted to remembrances and tributes to HWA President Laymon, who died suddenly in February. Former vice-president David Niall Wilson succeeded the author as the group's president, with Tim Lebbon stepping into the role of VP until the next regular election, when both were officially returned to office.

Barbara and Christopher Roden's excellent *All Hallows: The Journal of the Ghost Story Society* included numerous book reviews, Roger Dobson's film news and Richard Dalby's obituary column, Ramsey Campbell's take on *The Blair Witch Project*, articles on Vernon Lee, *Blood of the Vampire* (1958), *The Ghost Breakers* (1940) and *The Skull* (1965), and an interview with Douglas Clegg by Michael Rowe. There was also fiction by Stephen Volk, Paul Finch, Geoffrey Warburton, Peter J. Wilson and others, plus artwork by Paul Lowe, Douglas Walters, Dallas Goffin, Iain Maynard and veteran Alan Hunter.

The Stephen King Universe: A Guide to the Worlds of the King of Horror by Stanley Wiater, Christopher Golden and Hank Wagner was a chunky trade paperback from Renaissance Books which looked at the influences on King's work by grouping the author's novels and stories by setting and theme. A deluxe, signed, limited edition containing extra text and illustrative material not included in the paperback version was available in hardcover from Cemetery Dance Publications at $75.00.

The Essential Stephen King was yet another reference guide by Stephen J. Spignesi ranking 101 books, stories and movies by King.

Douglas E. Winter's long-awaited authorized biography, *Clive Barker: The Dark Fantastic*, stretched to more than 650 pages and contained useful primary and secondary bibliographies, two eight-page photo inserts, headings by Barker and a story written when the author was fourteen years old.

A follow-up to his 1990 volume *The Weird Tale*, *The Modern Weird Tale* was S.T. Joshi's critical study of such authors as Stephen King, Clive Barker, Anne Rice, Ramsey Campbell, Peter Straub, Robert Aickman, Shirley Jackson, William Peter Blatty, T.E.D. Klein, Thomas Ligotti and Thomas Tryon.

Published by Liverpool University Press, *Ramsey Campbell and Modern Horror Fiction* was an in-depth study of the Liverpool-based horror writer by the prolific Joshi, including a detailed bibliography plus a look back at his early life by Campbell himself. From the same publisher and author, *A Dreamer and a Visionary: H.P. Lovecraft in His Time* proved that there were still more minutiae to be squeezed out of poor HPL's short life.

From 1923 until 1937, C.M. Eddy, Jr. and Muriel E. Eddy

enjoyed a close relationship with H.P. Lovecraft. Fenham Publishing's trade paperback *The Gentleman from Angell Street: Memories of H.P. Lovecraft* contained four essays/memoirs of HPL, three poems about Lovecraft by Muriel Eddy, and several pages of photographs. A collection of five of Eddy's weird tales, *Exit Into Eternity: Tales of the Bizarre and Supernatural*, was reprinted by the same publisher, with an introduction by the author's wife.

After researching his subject for more than twenty years, Mike Ashley's *Starlight Man: The Extraordinary Life of Algernon Blackwood* (aka *Algernon Blackwood: An Extraordinary Life*) was a long-anticipated and fascinating illustrated biography published on the fiftieth anniversary of the death of the acclaimed writer of the supernatural.

In Search of Dr Jekyll and Mr Hyde by Raymond T. McNally and Radu R. Florescu looked at Robert Louis Stevenson's novel and its cultural impact.

Edited by James Van Hise, *The Fantastic Worlds of Robert E. Howard* was an illustrated guide to the work of the *Weird Tales* writer, with contributions from Rusty Burke, Rick Lai, Roy Krenkel and others, mostly taken from The Robert E. Howard United Press Association (REHUPA).

Subtitled *Friends of Yesteryear: Fictioneers & Others* and limited to 4,000 copies, *Book of the Dead* was written in the 1970s and contained wonderful personal reminiscences by the late E. Hoffman Price about friends and colleagues such as H.P. Lovecraft, Robert E. Howard, Clark Ashton Smith, Seabury Quinn, Henry Kuttner, August Derleth and others. Unfortunately, like other recent Arkham House volumes, the book was poorly edited and filled with unnecessary typos.

Greenwood's *The Supernatural in Short Fiction of the Americas* by Dana Del George was a somewhat skewered look at short horror fiction by such authors as Poe, Hawthorne, Bradbury and others. However, most modern writers were notable by their absence. Bob Madison's *American Horror Writers* was a young-adult study of ten authors, including King, Lovecraft and Poe.

French fan Alain Sprauel added to his series of attractive self-published bibliographies with a chronological listing of Peter Straub's published work in France.

One of the best art books of the year was *Fantasy of the 20th Century: An Illustrated History* written by artist Randy Broecker. Beautifully designed and printed by Collectors Press, the stunning oversized hardcover not only contained around 450 exemplarily chosen full-colour illustrations (including many rare pulp and paperback covers), but also a detailed history of the genre and its practitioners that was immaculately researched and presented with an infectious enthusiasm for its subject matter.

From the same publisher, Richard A. Lupoff's *The Great American Paperback: An Illustrated Tribute to Legends of the Book* contained more than 600 lavishly produced cover reproductions from all genres.

After issuing a profits warning in January, Collins & Brown Publishing, owner of Pavilion and the Paper Tiger art-book imprint, was taken over by the Chrysalis Group in a reported £2.1 million deal.

The Art of Richard Powers by Jane Frank was a beautiful and in-depth tribute from Paper Tiger to the American artist (1921–1996) whose often surreal covers graced many horror collections and anthologies in the 1950s and early 1960s. It additionally included a foreword by Vincent Di Fate; a memoir by the artist's son, Richard Gid Powers; a previously unpublished interview and a checklist of book covers. Also from the Paper Tiger imprint, *Offerings* was the latest full-colour collection of Brom's dark depictions of demonic heroes and villains.

Testament: The Life and Art of Frank Frazetta was the third and final volume in the Frazetta series from Underwood Books, edited by Cathy and Arnie Fenner. It included a wealth of previously unpublished material and appreciations by Bernie Wrightson, Dave Stevens, Michael Kaluta and others.

Introduced by Dave Stevens, *Wings of Twilight: The Art of Michael Kaluta* included much of the artist's comics work plus illustrations for *The Lord of the Rings*, *Prince Valiant*, *Vampirella* and *Metropolis*.

The Wally Wood Sketchbook was a large-sized paperback from Vanguard Productions which featured fascinating commentary on the comics artist by Steranko, Al Williamson and Joe Orlando.

Visionary, edited by Mark Wheatley and Allan Gross, collected

the art of Gray Morrow from the late 1950s onwards, with an
introduction by Al Williamson.

From Cemetery Dance Publications, *Dark Dreamers: Facing
the Masters of Fear* was a book of monochrome photographs by
Beth Gwinn, with commentary by Stanley Wiater and an introduction by Clive Barker. Just over 100 horror authors, artists,
editors and film-makers were featured, along with a short commentary by the subject or from Wiater, who also supplied brief
recommended reading lists. Some of the most poignant shots were
those of people who are no longer with us – Robert Bloch, R.
Chetwynd-Hayes, Richard Laymon, and Karl Edward Wagner
(with an uncredited Lynne Gauger). There were also signed,
limited and leather-bound lettered editions. Despite the dull dust
jacket, the book was billed as the official companion volume to
Dark Dreamers, a weekly Canadian television series hosted by
Wiater.

Dynamic Forces released two full-colour lithographs of 'Universal's Mightiest Monsters'. Alex Horley's *Dracula: Crimson
Kiss* and Greg and Tim Hildebrandt's *Bride of Frankenstein* were
available both as regular prints and in limited editions signed by
the artists.

Co-authored in German and English by film director Jörg
Buttgereit (*Nekromantik*), *Nightmares in Plastic* looked at hor-
ror-inspired model kits through nearly 150 photos of completed
kits and box art.

Despite his death the year before, Edward Gorey continued to
have wicked fun with the month-by-month misfortune that
mysteriously plagued *The Deranged Cousins*. Edited by Karen
Wilkin, *Ascending Peculiarity: Edward Gorey on Edward Gorey*
collected interviews, photographs and unpublished artwork by
the late artist.

Probably the most superfluous book of the year was *The
Quotable Sandman: Memorable Lines from the Acclaimed Series*
by Neil Gaiman. Unless such pithy *pensées* as 'That which is
dreamed can never be lost, can never be undreamed' had some
kind of resonance for the reader, the attractive pocket hardcover
was only worth acquiring for the full-colour illustrations by 'a
remarkable ensemble of artists', including Dave McKean, Kent
Williams, Glenn Fabry, Charles Vess, Rick Berry, Brian Bolland
and others.

It was also hard to know who would want *Edison's Franken-stein 2002 Calendar*, featuring twelve rare stills from the 1910 film, with anecdotes, trivia and interesting facts written by Frederick C. Wiebel, Jr. At least Midnight Marquee's *Attack of the Movie Monsters 2002 Calendar* included stills from 1950s and 1960s sci-fi films featuring 'Damsels in Distress and the Monsters Who Terrorize Them'.

The Classic Movie Tin Sign set contained poster reproductions of *The Day the Earth Stood Still*, *The Invisible Man* and *Creature from the Black Lagoon*.

An original poster advertising Boris Karloff's 1932 *The Mummy* sold to a telephone bidder at Christie's in London for £80,750 in March. Designed by artist Karoly Grosz, it was one of only three copies known to have survived and was discovered amongst a collection found in a garage in Arizona.

From Pentagram Publications, *Dracula: The Graphic Novel* reprinted the 1966 Ballantine Books comic strip with introductions by Bela Lugosi and Christopher Lee.

Dark Horse Comics' *Buffy the Vampire Slayer* featured a four-part mini-series, *False Memories*, scripted by Tom Fassbender and Jim Pascoe, which explored the effect that Buffy's younger sister Dawn had on the history of the Scooby gang.

Also from Dark Horse came a 168-page *Buffy the Vampire Slayer* graphic novel, which included such reprint stories as TV scriptwriter Doug Petrie's 'Food Chain' and 'Double Cross', plus Christopher Golden and Tom Sniegoski's first *Buffy* collaboration.

Meanwhile, *Buffy* creator Joss Whedon made his comic writing debut with Dark Horse Comics' eight-issue miniseries *Fray*, which was set in a future where vampires, demons, and other supernatural creatures existed. The books were illustrated by newcomer Karl Moline.

Neil Gaiman's *Books of Magic* character Tim Hunter returned, somewhat older and wiser, in DC/Vertigo Comics' *Hunter: The Age of Magic*, a new series written by Dylan Horrocks and illustrated by Richard Case, which picked up three years after the recent mini-series *Names of Magic*.

DC/Vertigo's *House of Secrets: Façade* was a two-issue mini-series scripted by Steven T. Seagle and illustrated by Teddy

Kristiansen in which human witness Rain Harper fled the Spirit Court.

Despite a promise by publisher Brian Pulido that the character would never return after being killed off, Chaos! Comics launched a new series of *Evil Ernie* on Halloween while, from the same publisher, Phil Nutman continued the original story of Tommy Doyle from the lacklustre movie *Halloween IV* in the somewhat confusingly titled comics *Halloween II* and *Halloween III: The Devil's Eyes* (which featured a variant cover design).

As usual there were novelizations of the summer blockbusters, such as *The Mummy Returns* by Max Allan Collins and Dave Wolverton's young-adult *The Mummy Chronicles: Revenge of the Scorpion King*, *Lara Croft Tomb Raider* by Dave Stern, *Final Fantasy The Spirits Within* by Dean Wesley Smith and *Planet of the Apes* by William T. Quick.

Frankenstein: The Legacy and *Night of Dracula* were a pair of pot-boilers updating the classic monsters by Christopher Schildt, featuring introductions by Sara Jane Karloff and Bela G. Lugosi, respectively.

Larry Mike Garmon's *Return of Evil: Dracula*, *Blood Moon Rising: The Wolf Man* and *Anatomy of Terror: Frankenstein* were the first three volumes in Scholastic's young-adult series *Universal Studios Monsters*, about a trio of children battling the classic movie monsters when the latter were released during a special film transfer.

David Jacobs's *The Devil's Night* was the second volume in another series featuring all the classic Universal Monsters.

A.A. Attanasio's *The Crow: Hellbound* was the latest novelization of the movie and comic-book series created by James O'Barr.

Based on the Hallmark Entertainment TV miniseries, *The Monkey King* by Kathryn Wesley (aka Dean Wesley Smith and Kristine Kathryn Rusch) contained sixteen pages of colour photos.

There was no sign of the series of *Buffy the Vampire Slayer* novelizations slowing down. Yvonne Navarro contributed *The Willow Files Vol. 2* and Nancy Holder's latest was *The Book of Fours*. *The Faith Trials* by James Laurence contained eight pages of colour stills, and the prolific Christopher Golden published his four-volume serial novel *The Lost Slayer*, comprising *Prophecies*, *Dark Times*, *King of the Dead* and *Original Sins*. *Tales of the Slayer Vol. 1* was an anthology of seven stories about different Slayers by Nancy Holder, Yvonne Navarro and others.

As if that was not enough, Holder and Jeff Mariotte published the *Buffy/Angel* crossover trilogy *Unseen: The Burning*, *Door to Alternity* and *Long Way Home*, while *Angel* continued in his own series of novelizations with *Avatar* by John Passarella, *Soul Trade* by Thomas E. Sniegoski, *The Summoned* by Cameron Dokey and *Bruja* by Mel Odom.

TV's witchy Halliwell Sisters appeared in the young-adult *Charmed* novelizations *The Legacy of Merlin* by Eloise Flood, *Soul of the Bride* by Constance M. Burge and *Beware What You Wish* by Diana G. Gallagher. *Blair Witch Files: The Death Card* by Cade Merrill was the fifth in the unlikely young-adult series.

She may be growing up on TV, but *Sabrina the Teenage Witch* still proved popular with younger readers in *Pirate Pandemonium* and *Dream Boat* by Mel Odom, *Wake-Up Call* and *From the Horse's Mouth* by Diana G. Gallagher, *Witch Way Did She Go?* by Paul Ruditis and *Milady's Dragon* by Cathy East Dubowski.

Hidden Passions: Secrets from the Diaries of Tabitha Lenox was purported to be written by Juliet Mills's evil witch from the daytime soap opera, but was more likely authored by series creator James E. Reilly.

Lawrence Miles's *The Adventures of Henrietta Street* was set in 18th-century England and featured the eighth *Doctor Who* encountering a coven of comely witches. *The Ghost Hunter's House of Horror* by Ivan Jones was a young-adult novelization of the BBC-TV series.

Resident Evil 6: Code Veronica by S.D. Perry was based on the popular zombie video games.

Featuring his mismatched heroes Gotrek Gurnisson and Felix Jaeger, William King's *Beastslayer* and *Vampireslayer* were the author's fifth and sixth *Warhammer* novels in the new series from Black Library, based on the fantasy role-playing game.

White Wolf's ever-popular *World of Darkness* series, based on the role-playing games, continued with *Predator & Prey: Judge* and *Jury*, both by Gherbod Fleming. *Heralds of the Storm* was Book One in the 'Year of the Scarab' trilogy by Andrew Bates, and *Tremere: Widow's Walk* and *Widow's Weeds* were the first two books in a new trilogy by Eric Griffin based on the *Clan* series.

Inherit the Earth edited by Stewart Wieck, collected nine stories based on *Hunter: The Reckoning*. *Silent Striders and Black Furies*, *Red Talons and Fianna* and *Shadow Lords and Get of Fenris* were all omnibus volumes in the 'Tribe' series based on White Wolf's *Werewolf: The Apocalypse* game.

Diablo #1: Legacy of Blood by Richard Knaak was based on the Blizzard Entertainment computer game.

Inspired by Eden Studios' zombie survival role-playing game *All Flesh Must be Eaten*, editor James Lowder's trade paperback anthology *The Book of All Flesh* contained twenty-five original stories about the walking dead by Scott Nicholson, L.H. Maynard and M.P.N. Sims, Michael Laimo, Mark McLaughlin, Scott Edelman and others.

Edited by the busy Stanley Wiater, *Richard Matheson's The Twilight Zone Scripts* was the first volume of a projected two-volume trade paperback set from Gauntlet Press/Edge Books that would publish for the first time all fourteen of Matheson's scripts for the legendary TV series. The collection also included extensive commentary by Wiater on each episode, new interviews with Matheson, plus supplementary material.

Published as a large-sized softcover by Reynolds & Hearn, *Christopher Lee: The Authorized Screen History* was an excellent biography of the Hammer horror star by Jonathan Rigby, with a foreword by George Lucas and profusely illustrated with numerous black and white stills and a useful film and television filmography. Lee (who was busier than ever in 2001) became a Commander of the British Empire (CBE) in the Queen's Birthday Honours List in June.

Daniel O'Brien's *The Hannibal Files* from the same imprint was an unauthorized guide to the Hannibal Lecter trilogy, illustrated with two colour spreads.

Boasting a foreword by actor Ian Richardson, David Stuart Davies's information-packed *Starring Sherlock Holmes* from Titan Books detailed every Holmes movie, TV show and stage production, illustrated with numerous rare stills and posters. This beautifully designed hardcover also had a reversible cover for those readers who preferred either Basil Rathbone or Jeremy Brett as their ideal Holmes.

From the same publisher, Stephen Jones's *Creepshows: The Illustrated Stephen King Movie Guide* looked at the movies, sequels, spin-offs and TV adaptations of books and stories by King, illustrated with posters, stills and book covers. It also included an introduction by director Mick Garris and an exclusive career interview with King.

The Greatest Sci-Fi Movies Never Made was a fascinating volume in which David Hughes looked at movies that never went into production or eventually emerged from development hell. These included Ridley Scott's *I Am Legend*, the confusion over *The Watchmen*, the truth behind *Supernova* and the disasters that befell Richard Stanley's *The Island of Dr Moreau*. It was published in hardcover by Titan Books, with a foreword by H.R. Giger and an eight-page colour section of pre-production artwork.

Hollywood Vampire: A Revised and Updated Unofficial and Unauthorized Guide to Angel was a new version of the 2000 book by Keith Topping. Edited by Roz Kaveney, *Reading the Vampire Slayer* was subtitled *An Unofficial Critical Companion to Buffy and Angel* and included some heavy academic essays along with an episode guide to the plots.

Andy Lane's *Randall & Hopkirk {Deceased}: The Files* was an illustrated guide to the revived TV series, with an introduction by producer Charlie Higson.

Scarecrow Press reprinted the late Curt Siodmak's 1997 autobiography, revised under the new title *Wolf Man's Maker: Memoir of a Hollywood Scriptwriter*.

From McFarland & Company, Lisa Morton's *The Cinema of Tsui Hark* was an illustrated hardcover that looked at the career of one of China's most famous film-makers.

David Kalat's *The Strange Case of Dr Mabuse: A Study of the Twelve Films and Five Novels* was an illustrated look at the career of the super-villain created by German author Norbert Jacques and most famously filmed by Fritz Lang.

The Zombie Movie Encyclopedia by Peter Dendle was an A-Z guide of the walking dead, while *White Zombie: Anatomy of a Horror Film* was Gary D. Rhodes's in-depth illustrated study of the 1932 poverty-row film starring Bela Lugosi, with a foreword by the late George E. Turner.

The Gorehound's Guide to Splatter Films of the 1960s and 1970s by Scott Aaron Stine was an A-Z guide of gore films.

John Kenneth Muir's *Terror Television: American Series, 1970–1999* was another hefty reference work, while the same author's *An Analytical Guide to Television's 'One Step Beyond', 1959–1961* looked at the now-obscure 'reality' anthology show.

In *I Was a Monster Movie Maker: Conversations with 22 SF and Horror Film-makers*, the talented Tom Weaver talked with such nearly-forgotten actors as Faith Domergue, Ray Walston and Maureen O'Sullivan.

Also from McFarland, Harris M. Lentz III's monumental *Science Fiction, Horror & Fantasy Film and Television Credits: Second Edition* combined four earlier books and updated and revised more than 2,000 pages into one of the most important and impressive reference volumes of the year.

From Midnight Marquee came *Memories of Hammer Films*, editors Gary J. Svehla and Susan Svehla's collection of interview transcripts from the annual FANEX convention in Baltimore, Maryland. Amongst those profiled were Christopher Lee, Barbara Shelley, Ingrid Pitt and Jimmy Sangster. In *Monsters Mutants and Heavenly Creatures*, Tom Weaver interviewed the people behind the drive-in classics.

From the same publisher, *The Spawn of Skull Island* was Michael H. Price and Douglas Turner's revised and expanded edition of the 1975 volume *The Making of King Kong* by the late George E. Turner and Orville Goldner. *Forgotten Horrors 2: Beyond the Horror Ban* was Price and Turner's follow-up to their previous volume about poverty-row horrors.

Published by The John Hopkins University Press as an oversized softcover, Chris Fujiwara's *Jacques Tourneur: The Cinema of Nightfall* was a welcome reissue of the 1998 illustrated study of the director of *Cat People*, *I Walked with a Zombie* and *Night of the Demon*, with a foreword by Martin Scorsese.

In *Italian Cannibal and Zombie Movies*, Jay Slater looked at the gory sub-genre from the 1970s through to the early 1990s, and *The Horror Movie Survival Guide* by Matteo Molinari and Jim Kamm was a pointless A-Z list of movie monsters and their various attributes.

From Maryland's Sense of Wonder Press, *Famous Forry Fotos: Over 70 Years of AckerMemories* was a softcover collection of black and white stills from the archives of legendary fan and editor Forrest J. Ackerman, who turned eighty-five in November and celebrated with a party at The Friar's Club in Beverly Hills, California. To commemorate the event, guests received *It's Alive @ 85*, a special publication limited to 250 copies with an introduction by Ray Bradbury.

Among the attendees at Ackerman's birthday celebrations was director John Landis, who guest-edited *The Best American Movie Writing 2001*, which included essays by Jack Kerouac, Tom Weaver, Lawrence Kasdan, John Irving, Stanley Kubrick and others.

Although *Gladiator* walked off with Best Picture at the 2001 Academy Awards, the martial-arts fantasy *Crouching Tiger Hidden Dragon* picked up Best Foreign Language Film, Best Art Direction, Best Cinematography and Best Original Score Oscars, while *The Grinch* won Best Make-up for Rick Baker.

Arthur C. Clarke presented the Oscar for Best Screenplay Based on Material Already Published or Produced via a pre-recorded clip from his home in Sri Lanka. He did not know in advance that *Traffic* was the winner.

Meanwhile, the terrorist attacks of September 11th had an immediate effect on Hollywood, with studios shelving, postponing or abandoning any films that might have appeared insensitive. These included Tim Allen's new Disney comedy *Big Trouble* and Arnold Schwarzenegger's *Collateral Damage*.

Somewhat more bizarrely, even just the inclusion of the World Trade Center's Twin Towers resulted in scenes being changed and promotional campaigns being pulled. The trailer for Sam Raimi's *Spider-Man* film was withdrawn from theatres and the Internet because it contained a scene (produced exclusively for the trailer) in which a helicopter was trapped in a giant spider's web strung between the two buildings. Meanwhile, the producers of Columbia Pictures' sequel *Men in Black 2* announced that the ending of the movie would be re-shot because the World Trade Center was used as a backdrop. Any other scenes featuring the structures would also be changed.

Warner Bros. even postponed by one week its planned 500 sneak previews of the Stephen King adaptation, *Hearts in Atlantis* starring Anthony Hopkins. It didn't help, and after an opening of

$9.8 million the film took less than $21 million at the US box office.

Costing £90 million to make and £30 million for Warner Bros. to market, Christopher Columbus's *Harry Potter and The Philosopher's Stone* (retitled *Harry Potter and The Sorcerer's Stone* in America) was released the first weekend in November and smashed box-office records on both sides of the Atlantic. In the US, where it was released on a quarter of all the screens in the country, it easily beat the previous record set by *The Lost World – Jurassic Park* ($71 million) and the *Potter* movie became the first film to make $100 million in its first four days. In the UK it beat the previous weekend record set by *Star Wars I: The Phantom Menace* (£14.7 million), and the film went on to take more than $300 million worldwide.

At almost three hours, Peter Jackson's version of J.R.R. Tolkien's *The Lord of the Rings: The Fellowship of the Ring* (filmed for $270 million back-to-back with the two sequels, to be released a year apart) was truly an epic. Although it had a lower box-office opening than *Harry Potter*, the film went on to gross more than $290 million in the US. Ian McKellen was perfectly cast as Gandalf, and there was some nice villainy from Christopher Lee.

Directed by The Hughes Brothers (Albert and Allen), *From Hell* was based on the grim graphic novel by Alan Moore and Eddie Campbell and grossed an impressive $70 million in the US: Johnny Depp gave a powerful performance as the opium-smoking psychic Inspector Abberline, investigating the Jack the Ripper killings in 1888 London.

Ridley Scott's *Hannibal* was the much-anticipated sequel to *The Silence of the Lambs* (1991), based on the novel by Thomas Harris (which had a different ending). Anthony Hopkins reprised his role as cannibal killer Dr Hannibal Lecter, Gary Oldman hammed it up as one of his mutilated victims, and Julianne Moore ably stepped into the role of FBI agent Clarice Starling.

Thir13en Ghosts, Steve Beck's loose remake of the disappointing 1960 William Castle film, involved a strange house that was actually an occult machine powered by the trapped souls of twelve ghosts designed to open a gateway to Hell. Co-scripted by Adam Simon, Ernest Dickerson's *Bones* brought rapper Snoop Dogg back from the dead as the eponymous 1970s ghetto pimp for a very brief Halloween run at the box office.

Although boasting a rave quote from Clive Barker and having Francis Ford Coppola amongst its executive producers, much of the criticism surrounding *Jeepers Creepers* centred on its controversial director, convicted paedophile Victor Salva. It opened in the US at No.1 with $15.8 million, and went on to gross $33.6 million.

In *Soul Survivors*, a woman slipping in and out of a coma attempted to recall the events that led to her predicament. Writer/director Stephen Carpenter's teen horror film suffered from being cut by its distributor from an 'R' rating to a 'PG-13' in America.

When it came to the summer blockbusters, Stephen Sommers's *The Mummy Returns* was a fun action sequel to his 1999 original which enjoyed a record-breaking opening weekend before finally taking a worldwide total of more than $400 million.

Despite cameos from original stars Charlton Heston and Linda Harrison, Tim Burton's disappointing and impersonal $100 million 're-imagining' of *Planet of the Apes* took $69.5 million during its first week in late July at the US box office. Only the first *Jurassic Park* had enjoyed a better opening weekend at the time. However, audiences quickly dropped off and the film ended up grossing just under $170 million. Meanwhile, extras from the film announced that they were suing the producers, claiming they were exposed to a cancer-causing substance during a dust storm scene.

Executive producer Steven Spielberg handed *Jurassic Park III* over to director Joe Johnston, and the result was a short but impressive 'B' movie. Filming reportedly began without a finished script, and it showed, despite the film earning $168 million.

Based on the successful interactive game, *Lara Croft-Tomb Raider* starred Angelina Jolie as the eponymous upper-crust adventurer attempting to prevent the Illuminati from tracking down the secret of an ancient device that could alter space and time.

Although Marlon Brando pulled out, reportedly suffering from pneumonia, after agreeing to appear in a cameo for $2 million, the dire *Scary Movie 2* still went on to take nearly $70 million in the US.

Ice Cube, Natasha Henstridge and Pam Grier found themselves battling centuries-old spooks in John Carpenter's incompetent *Ghosts of Mars*, which opened and closed with a miserable $3.8

million. Woody Allen's 1940s spoof *The Curse of the Jade Scorpion* did even worse, grossing just $2.5 million.

Denise Richards and David Boreanaz were among the suspects as a cupid-masked killer cut up the teen cast in the derivative slasher *Valentine*, and three teens travelling across the desert found themselves battling the undead in J.S. Cardone's low-budget vampire thriller *The Forsaken*.

David Caruso was part of a crew sent into an abandoned mental hospital to clear asbestos who were soon affected by the building's brooding atmosphere in Brad Anderson's *Session 9*. Daniel Minahan's low-budget *Series 7: The Contenders* involved a lethal TV game show where the last surviving contestant was the winner.

A good Jet Li battled an evil Jet Li from a different dimension in *The One*, Jake Gyllenhaal played a schizophrenic teenager who listened to a man-sized rabbit with a twisted face in *Donnie Darko*, and Steve Railsback portrayed the Wisconsin cannibal killer who inspired *Psycho* and *The Texas Chainsaw Massacre* in Chuck Parello's *Ed Gein*.

Jeremy Irons and Bruce Payne hammed it up as villains in the juvenile sword-and-sorcery adventure *Dungeons & Dragons*, which also starred Thora Birch. The young American actress also turned up in *The Hole*, a low-budget British chiller about a group of boarding-school teens trapped in an old war bunker.

In Rob Green's *The Bunker*, a group of German soldiers took refuge in an underground storage tunnel and wished they hadn't. *Urban Ghost Story* starred Jason Connery as a journalist involved with a Glasgow family bothered by moving furniture and other spooky occurrences after the daughter's near-death experience.

Chris Rock discovered he was dead before his time in *Down to Earth*, an unnecessary remake of *Heaven Can Wait*, while Martin Lawrence travelled back in time to visit Camelot in the equally pointless *Black Knight*.

Despite the acrimonious divorce of star Nicole Kidman and co-producer Tom Cruise, *The Others*, from young Spanish writer/director/composer Alejandro Amenábar, was a classic haunted house story set in 1945 that grossed an impressive $90.6 million. Meanwhile, Guillermo de Toro's ghost story *The Devil's Back-*

bone was set in a boy's orphanage during the last days of the
Spanish Civil War.

Sophie Marceau played the eponymous ghost in *Belphegor:
Phantom of the Louvre*, based on the popular 1965 French TV
mini-series. Julie Christie and Juliette Greco had cameos. Chris-
tophe Gans's *Brotherhood of the Wolf* saw an 18th-century
gardener and his Iroquois Indian blood brother sent to Gevaudan
to track down a legendary beast. A box-office hit in its native
France, it was apparently that country's highest-grossing genre
film ever.

Veteran Kinji Fukasaku's *Battle Royale* was a combination of
gruesome game show and *Lord of the Flies*, while Alex de la
Iglesias's gory homage to Hitchcock, *La Comunidad*, was
banned worldwide by George Lucas because one of the characters dressed like Darth Vader. Lucas also sued the producers
of the porno movie *Star Ballz*, claiming consumers could be
confused into thinking that Lucasfilm sponsored the hardcore
Star Wars spoof.

Billy Crystal, John Goodman and Steve Buscemi were among
those who voiced the nightmare inhabitants of Monstropolis in
the Disney and Pixar computer-animated *Monsters Inc.*, which
opened in November and took more than $244.8 million. How-
ever, it was overshadowed by rival DreamWorks' revisionist fairy
tale *Shrek*, featuring the vocal talents of Mike Myers, Eddie
Murphy, Cameron Diaz and John Lithgow. The computer-
created cartoon grossed $255.5 million, consequently blowing
Disney's traditionally animated adventure *Atlantis – The Lost
Empire* out of the water!

Inspired by the video game, *Final Fantasy: The Spirits Within*
went one step further and created its realistic human characters
and alien invaders totally through CGI animation.

In May, director William Friedkin and screenwriter William
Peter Blatty sued Warner Bros. and others for unspecified da-
mages in the federal court, claiming they were denied residuals
from both the 1973 and 2000 versions of *The Exorcist*. They also
maintained that the latter version violated federal copyright law
by identifying the studio as the movie's author and by failing to
register the film as a derivative of the original.

Despite having already been shown on UK satellite television,
in August the British Board of Film Classification finally passed

Tobe Hooper's long-banned 1986 sequel *The Texas Chainsaw Massacre 2* uncut with an '18' certificate.

In America, films such as *Harry Potter* and *Lord of the Rings* helped boost cinema attendances to their highest levels since the 1950s. Ticket sales rose to 1.5 billion in 2001, a 5 per cent increase on the previous year and the highest since 1958. Despite the September 11th attacks, US box-office takings were a record $5.9 billion. The same upward trend was also to be seen in Britain, where the number of admissions rose by four million to 141 million, the highest figure since 1972.

Unjustly banished to video, Ellory Elkayem's *They Nest* was an enjoyable chiller set on a remote island invaded by mutated African cockroaches that nested inside the bodies of their victims. A likeable cast (including Thomas Calabro, Dean Stockwell and John Savage), fine special effects and a knowing script raised this often gory chiller into a whole different class.

Despite featuring music from Kid Rock, Rob Zombie and others, the third film in *The Crow* series, *Salvation*, starring Kirsten Dunst and Eric Mabius, went straight to video and DVD in most markets.

Tom Arnold and Tiffani-Amber Thiessen investigated a series of murders at the Bulemia Fall High School in the slasher spoof *Shriek If You Know What I Did Last Friday the 13th*.

Venomous starring Treat Williams and some genetically engineered snakes was just what you would expect from director Fred Olen Ray and co-producer Jim Wynorski working under pseudonyms.

Brian Yuzna's Spanish-made *Faust: Love of the Damned* featured Andrew Divoff and Jeffrey Combs and was based on yet another comic book series.

Donald F. Glut's low-budget softcore comedy *The Erotic Rites of Countess Dracula* was simply embarrassing. The unlikely-named Brick Randall played a singer bitten by Count Dracula (a sick-looking William Smith), who lived in Hollywood with her faithful servant Renfield (Del Howison). From the same producers, Glut's half-hour short *The Vampire Hunters Club* resembled a home movie. John Agar, William Smith, Bob Burns, Dave Donham and Forrest J. Ackerman played members of the eponymous group, still searching for a young girl kidnapped in 1958 by Dracula (Daniel Roebuck). This included special guest appearances by Belinda Balaski, Conrad Brooks, Del Howison, Irwin Keyes, Carla Laemmle, Brinke Stevens, Mink Stole, Carel Struycken, Mary Woronov and others.

Erotic Witch Project 2: Book of Seduction was another of Seduction Cinema's softcore lesbian romps from the production team of producer Michael Beckerman and director John Bacchus, who were also responsible for *The Erotic Ghost*. Terry M. West's *The Sexy Sixth Sense* was more of the same, also from Seduction.

From Video Outlaw, *Cremains* was a shot-on-video anthology movie from writer/director Steve Sessions that featured Lilith Stabs and Debbie Rochon. In David A. Goldberg's *Demon Lust*, Brinke Stevens was a sexy demon confronted by Tom Savini's hit man for the mob, while Jeff Burton's *The Night Divides the Day* was about a psychopathic killer stalking a group of students camping in the woods.

Blood: The Last Vampire was an *animé* about a sword-wielding girl battling shapeshifters on an American military base during the Vietnam war.

All Day Entertainment's *The Horror of Hammer* and *Tales of Frankenstein* contained numerous trailers of varying quality, while the latter also included the 1958 Hammer TV pilot *Tales of Frankenstein* as a bonus.

Some of the scariest bogeymen to appear on film, including Jason, Freddy, Michael Myers, Chucky, Leatherface and Pinhead, were profiled in *Bogeymen: The Killer Compilation*, a three-hour documentary featuring an audio commentary by Robert Englund.

Jay Holben's *Paranoid* was an eight-minute short adapted from the 100-line poem 'Paranoid: A Chant' by Stephen King.

Hallmark Entertainment's *The Infinite Worlds of H.G. Wells* was an enjoyable three-part mini-series, based upon the author's short stories. Tom Ward portrayed Wells, interviewed by a secret government agency about the mysterious adventures he and his future wife (Katy Carmichael) were involved with.

Co-produced with The Jim Henson Company, *Jack and the Beanstalk: The Real Story* was an inventive two-part TV movie in which a millionaire industrialist (Matthew Modine) discovered that the fairy tale lied. Daryl Hannah and Richard Attenborough turned up as giant gods.

Allan Arkush's *Prince Charming* was just as good, as two humans (Sean Maguire and Martin Short), transformed into frogs 500 years earlier, found themselves in contemporary New York. Hallmark's *Snow White* was yet another version of the fairy tale by the Brothers Grimm, with the princess (Kristin Kreuk) menaced by Miranda Richardson's wicked queen. Clancy Brown played a creepy Granter of Wishes, and Warwick Davis and Vincent Schiavelli were amongst the dwarves named after the days of the week.

The Disney cable TV movie *Halloweentown II: Kalabar's Revenge* reunited the cast of the 1998 original, including veteran Debbie Reynolds, for an inferior sequel where everyone living in Halloweentown was placed under a warlock's spell.

Christopher Lloyd played the zombie who helped a town overcome its Halloween curse in the Fox Family movie *When Good Ghouls Go Bad*, based on a story by R.L. Stine.

In *The Evil Beneath Loch Ness*, Patrick Bergin and Lysette Anthony discovered that a giant prehistoric creature had been released from an underwater abyss. Infinitely better was the two-part BBC-TV movie of Sir Arthur Conan Doyle's *The Lost World*, in which Bob Hoskins's gruff Professor Challenger led an expedition to discover superb-looking CGI dinosaurs.

Murder Rooms: The Dark Beginnings of Sherlock Holmes was a series of four superior BBC films created by David Pirie. Charles Edwards portrayed Arthur Conan Doyle, who teamed up with his old friend Dr Joseph Bell (the superb Ian Richardson) to investigate various murders. *The Kingdom of Bones* (scripted by Stephen Gallagher) included a number of allusions to Doyle's *The Lost World* while, in *The White Knight Stratagem*, comedian Rik Mayall gave a stand-out performance as the likely inspiration for Professor Moriarty.

A totally miscast Matt Frewer played Doyle's great detective in Hallmark's Canadian version of *The Sign of Four*, the second in a series of 'public domain' adaptations of the Sherlock Holmes stories.

John Fawcett's impressive Canadian cable TV movie *Ginger Snaps* linked lycanthropy and menstruation when the weird Brigitte (Emily Perkins) realized that her rebellious older sister (Katharine Isabelle) was turning into a sexy werewolf.

Wolf Girl was a USA Cable Entertainment movie for Halloween in which the eponymous hirsute heroine was trapped in a freak show run by an over-the-top Tim Curry.

The Cinemax/HBO series *Creature Features* comprised loose 'remakes' of five old AIP movies – *She Creature*, *The Day the World Ended*, *How to Make a Monster*, *Earth vs. The Spider* and *Teenage Caveman* – executive-produced by the late Samuel Z. Arkoff and with special effects credited to Stan Winston on all but the last title. Despite the presence of such stars as Rufus Sewell, Nastassja Kinski, Randy Quaid, Colleen Camp, Julie Strain, Dan Aykroyd and Theresa Russell, the results were definitely mixed.

Lost Voyage, starring Judd Nelson and Lance Henriksen, was a fun, low-budget horror thriller set on a cruise ship that disappeared in the Bermuda Triangle and returned from Hell possessed by evil. Almost exactly the same story was told in Lewis Teague's inferior *The Triangle*, a TBS movie starring Luke Perry and Dan Cortese amongst a group of vacationers killed off by evil spirits on a lost liner.

Judd Nelson also reprised his role as psychotic screenwriter Stanley Caldwell in the USA Cable Entertainment sequel *Return to Cabin by the Lake*.

Bo Derek was the professor with a killer curriculum in the Sci Fi original movie *Horror 101*, while Fox's *The Rats* apparently had nothing to do with James Herbert as the verminous creatures ran riot through a Manhattan department store where Mädchen Amick was trying to shop.

UPN's *Curse of the Talisman* featured killer gargoyles, and in *Robin Cook's Acceptable Risk*, from TBS, Chad Lowe discovered that a drug made out of a strange fungus had horrifying side effects.

Showtime's *On the Edge* anthology featured a trio of actresses making their directorial debuts with three half-hour shorts: Helen Mirren's 'Happy Birthday' was based on a Keith Laumer story and featured John Goodman, Beverly D'Angelo and Christopher Lloyd; Anthony LaPaglia starred as a terminally ill scientist in Mary Stuart Masterson's 'The Other Side', based on a story by Bruce Holland Rogers, and the multi-talented Anne Heche both scripted and directed 'Reaching Normal' from Walter M. Miller's short story, starring Andie MacDowell and Joel Grey.

In 2001, *Buffy the Vampire Slayer* lost its sense of humour, while spin-off series *Angel* finally found one, at least for a while.

Vampire Spike (James Masters) fell in love with Buffy (Sarah Michelle Gellar), Buffy's mother (Kristine Sutherland) died, and the evil god Glory (Clare Kramer) discovered that the hidden 'Key' she was searching for was actually Buffy's younger sister Dawn (Michelle Trachtenberg). The fifth season of *Buffy* ended with the 100th episode as the eponymous Slayer sacrificed her own life to save Dawn.

After very public arguments over the price paid per episode, the sixth season of *Buffy* moved from The WB to UPN in October with a two-hour premiere featuring Gellar as the android Buffy-bot. Once resurrected by Willow's (Alyson Hannigan) dark magic, Buffy had hot sex with Spike, battled a trio of super-nerd villains and went to work in a fast-food outlet. Meanwhile, Willow allowed her use of magic to get out of control. The best episode was done entirely as a musical.

There were also rumours that *Buffy* creator Joss Whedon was developing a spin off series for British character Giles (Anthony Stewart Head, who left the series after the first few episodes of the new season) which would be made in collaboration with the BBC. *Buffy* also finally went into syndication five nights a week on FX.

Meanwhile, over on *Angel*, the eponymous vampire's (David Boreanaz) obsession with Wolfram & Hart broke up the team, which eventually reunited only to travel to The Host's (Andy Hallett) alternate demon dimension. For the new season, Angel and his companions were joined by Amy Acker's physicist Winifred 'Fred' Burke. Darla (Julie Benz) announced she was pregnant with Angel's child, and Angel was pursued by an old enemy, vampire hunter Holtz (Keith Szarabajka), seeking revenge for the deaths of his family.

With David Duchovny's Agent Mulder apparently gone for good, and Gillian Anderson's Scully now a mother, the ninth season of Fox's *The X Files* added Annabeth Gish's FBI agent Monica Reyes as a full-time lead alongside Robert Patrick's John Doggett. Cary Elwes joined the cast as an FBI assistant director, and former *Xena* actress Lucy Lawless also turned up for a couple of episodes.

Unfortunately, the quirky spin-off series *The Lone Gunmen* failed because it ignored the core genre audience that had made *The X Files* so successful.

The reworked pilot for CBS-TV's *Wolf Lake* was delayed after the terrorist attacks in September. *Twin Peaks* met *The Howling* as a Seattle detective (Lou Diamond Phillips) traced his missing girlfriend to the eponymous Pacific Northwest town where most of the humans turned into wolves. The hour-long series, created by John Leekley, lasted just eight episodes in America.

Yancy Butler starred as Sara Pezzini, a New York cop who used a mystical gauntlet to battle evil in the TNT series *Witchblade*, based on the Top Cow comic book.

After the series was renewed by The WB for three more seasons, actress Shannen Doherty quit *Charmed* as one of the witchy Halliwell sisters. In her final episode (which she also directed), Doherty's character Prue was killed by a demon assassin. At the start of the new series, the remaining two sisters discovered that they had a long-lost half-sister who had magic of her own. After such actresses as Tiffani Thiessen and Jennifer Love Hewitt were reportedly considered, Rose McGowan joined the cast as Paige in a two-hour season premiere.

Dawson's Creek met *The X Files* in the hit WB series *Smallville*, about the contemporary adventures of Clark Kent/Superboy (Tom Welling) and his friends Lana Lang (Kristin Kreuk) and Lex Luthor (Michael Rosenbaum). Each episode usually involved green meteor fragments giving other people strange powers. John Glover had a recurring role as Lex's industrialist father, Lionel Luthor.

In UPN's *All Souls*, a young doctor (Grayson McCouch) began inquiring into a series of mysterious deaths in a hospital, while Rae Dawn Chong and Adrian Pasdar were back investigating mysteries and miracles in a second series of *Mysterious Ways* on PAX and NBC-TV.

The Sci Fi Channel's *The Chronicle* was about a tabloid newspaper that researched bizarre but true stories, and The WB's *Dead Last* was about the members of a rock band who obtained the power to see ghosts from a mysterious amulet.

In UPN's *Special Unit 2*, a covert branch of the Chicago Police Department investigated 'the monsters of every child's nightmare'. These apparently included gargoyles, virgin-craving mermen, werewolf stockbrokers and a ninja mummy, all created by Patrick Tatopoulos.

Following the movie pilot featuring Eric Roberts and Judd Nelson, *Strange Frequency* was an anthology series on VH1 hosted by Roger Daltrey, who appeared as a satanic talent agent in the first episode. Meanwhile, Aidan Quinn, Lou Diamond Phillips and Samantha Mathis were among the stars of the Fox anthology series *Night Visions*, which also failed to identify its audience.

The second series of *Shockers* comprised three offbeat hour-long dramas written by Stephen Volk, Joe Ahearne and Chris Bucknall.

In the Halloween episode of *Relic Hunter*, Sydney (Tia Carrere) teamed up with charismatic vampire novelist Lucas Blackmer (Adrian Paul) to find Vlad Tepes's mystical chalice.

Season four of the Sci Fi series *Lexx* included a two-part episode, co-written by Tom De Ville, in which Stanley (Brian Downey), Xev (Xenia Seeberg) and Kai (Michael McManus) travelled to the Transylvanian castle of Count Dracul (John Standing) and encountered the power of the revived Vlad (Minna Aaltonen). Veteran Lionel Jeffries turned up briefly as a priest.

Vampire High was a Canadian teen series in which five young vampires were entrusted to the Mansbridge Academy, where they would learn to tame their instincts and live among mortals.

More *Land of the Lost* than Conan Doyle, the Australian syndicated series *Sir Arthur Conan Doyle's The Lost World* featured episodes in which members of the stranded expedition discovered a mysterious valley full of werewolves and received psychic visions from the knife belonging to Jack the Ripper. Judith Reeves-Stevens and Garfield Reeves-Stevens were creative consultants, and a slightly more risqué version apparently aired on DirecTV in America.

Filmed in New Zealand, the *Dungeons and Dragons*-inspired fantasy series *Dark Knight*, created by co-producer Terry Marcel, included episodes in which Ivanhoe (Ben Pullen) and his companions came to the aid of a village menaced by an ancient werewolf cult and battled an Egyptian mummy raised from the dead by a band of Templar Knights.

In the second season of the syndicated *BeastMaster*, Dar (Daniel Goddard) and Tao (Jackson Raine) encountered the shapechanging demon Lara (Sam Healy and Danielle Spencer) and the original film series' star, Marc Singer, joined the cast as spirit guide Dartanus.

TV's Tarzan, Ron Ely, turned up as a villain in *Sheena*, starring Gena Lee Nolin as the shapechanging heroine, while TV Batman Adam West was among those battling *Black Scorpion*.

During the fifth season of Melissa Joan Hart's *Sabrina, The Teenage Witch* (how long can they keep using that title?), Sabrina finally moved out and lived with roommates on campus.

Creator R.L. Stine described his anthology series *The Nightmare Room* on Kids' WB as 'a *Twilight Zone* for kids'. Tippi Hedren (Hitchcock's *The Birds*) was one of the guest stars.

Dr Terrible's House of Horrible was a not very funny BBC series created by and starring comedian Steve Coogan. Spoofing everything from Hammer Films to Sax Rohmer's Fu Manchu and the Amicus anthology movies of the 1970s, the shows did feature such interesting guest stars as Oliver Tobias, Sheila Keith, Warwick Davis, Angela Pleasence, Tom Bell and Graham Crowden.

In the crazy world of American daytime soap operas, NBC-TV's *Passions* featured homages to five classic horror films before 300-year-old witch Tabitha (Juliet Mills!) lost her head and had it sewn back on by little Timmy (Josh Ryan Evans). Meanwhile, Timmy's magic left Charity with some odd side effects.

Over at ABC-TV's even wackier *Port Charles*, after a twelve-week 'telenovella' involving time-travel, the town's inhabitants found themselves succumbing to schizophrenic vampire Caleb (Michael Easton). The characters also saw the year out with an apocalyptic plot involving angels and devils.

Not to be outdone, on ABC-TV's *All My Children* Gillian (Esta TerBlanche) was shot in the head by an assassin and then visited by the ghostly spirits of previous characters from the show, who helped her find her way towards the bright light.

Reworking themes and characters from *The Mummy Returns*, the Universal cartoon series *The Mummy* featured the ancient Egyptian sorcerer Imhotep searching for the ancient Scrolls of Thebes. In one episode, Rick O'Connell (voiced by John Schneider) was bitten by a wolf in Ireland and transformed into a werewolf.

Shown on the digital TV channel BBC Choice, *The Fear* was a series of fifteen-minute readings (with dramatized inserts) by such actors as Marianne Jean Baptiste, Jason Flemyng, Anna Friel, Sadie Frost, Kelly Macdonald, Neve McIntosh, Nick Moran,

Sean Pertwee and Ray Winstone. Authors whose work was adapted included Honore de Balzac, M.E. Braddon, F. Marion Crawford, Arthur Conan Doyle, John Berwick Harwood and Edgar Allan Poe.

American Movie Classics' hour-long Halloween tribute to American International Pictures, *It Conquered Hollywood*, featured interviews with Beverly Garland, Roger Corman, Bruce Dern, Samuel Z. Arkoff, Dick Miller, Susan Hart and others.

Produced for Channel Four Television by Pete Tombs and Andy Starke, *Mondo Macabro* was a wonderful half-hour documentary series looking at exploitation and genre film-making in Argentina, Brazil, Indonesia, Mexico, the Philippines, South Asia and Turkey. Among those interviewed were Eddie Romero and José Mojica Marins (aka Coffin Joe/Zé do Caixâo).

SF:UK was a jingoistic documentary series written and hosted by the irritating Mathew De Abaitua for Channel Four and The Sci-Fi Channel. Topics included *Frankenstein* and *War of the Worlds*, and Mark Gatiss and Kim Newman were among the regular contributors.

Gatiss and Newman also turned up in *Inventing Monsters*, an impressive half-hour documentary for digital channel BBC Knowledge hosted by Professor Christopher Frayling, who looked at the attraction of monsters in popular culture. Other contributors included David J. Skal, Marina Warner, Anne Billson and Ingrid Pitt, plus archive interviews with Jimmy Sangster and Yutte Stensgaard.

Mario Bava, Maestro of the Macabre was an hour-long documentary about the cult Italian director with commentary from film-makers Tim Burton, Joe Dante, John Carpenter, John Saxon, Samuel Z. Arkoff, Lamberto Bava, John Philip Law, Alfred Leone and Daria Nicoldi and from critics Allan Bryce, Tim Lucas and the ubiquitous Kim Newman.

Michelle Trachtenberg from *Buffy the Vampire Slayer* hosted the half-hour Discovery Kids series *Truth or Scare*, in which she looked at such subjects as Dracula, The Curse of Tutankhamun, werewolves and Irish ghosts with the help of Dr Leonard Wolf, David J. Skal, James V. Hart and Professor Nina Auerbach.

In September, Canada's Corus Entertainment launched the country's first twenty-four-hour digital-access horror channel, entitled *Scream*. Horror author Edo van Belkom hosted the midnight-movie programme *Post Mortem*, supplying commentary during breaks in the films.

Peggy Sue Got Married, the stage musical starring Ruthie Henshall and based on the 1986 movie, became the first theatrical casualty of the September 11th terrorist attacks when it closed after just six weeks in London's West End, blaming plummeting audience figures. It was soon followed by *Notre-Dame de Paris*, in which Hazel Fernandez had replaced Dannii Minogue after the Australian actress/singer walked out in June, and *The Witches of Eastwick*, in which Clarke Peters had taken over from Ian McShane as the Devil.

The Secret Garden at London's Aldwych Theatre in March was the Royal Shakespeare Company's musical version of Frances Hodgson Burnett's classic children's fantasy. From October, the RSC mounted a new dramatization of Lewis Carroll's *Alice in Wonderland and Through the Looking Glass* in London and Stratford-Upon-Avon.

The Northern Ballet Theatre's production of *Jekyll and Hyde* at Sadler's Wells the same month had received poor reviews when it originally opened in Leeds. Daniel de Andrade played Henry Jekyll while the leather-clad Edward Hyde was portrayed by Jonathan Olliver.

The Russian Ice Stars mounted a chilling version of *The Phantom of the Opera on Ice* at London's Wimbledon Theatre in April.

Writer Jeremy Dyson and actors Mark Gattis, Steve Pemberton and Reece Shearsmith took *The League of Gentlemen*, based on the cult radio and TV show, to the Theatre Royal in Drury Lane in March.

The Perrier Award-winning stage spoof *Garth Marenghi's Netherhead* featured the eponymous 'Sculptor of Nightmares' and 'Duke of Darkness' talking about his bestselling literary career and giving advice to would-be horror writers. Unfortunately, the show was neither as funny nor as clever as it thought it was.

Supposedly inspired by the works of H.P. Lovecraft, *Alone in the Dark – The New Nightmare* was the fourth interactive computer game in the supernatural series featuring occult detective Edward

Carnby, armed with just a flashlight to keep the evil creatures at bay on Shadow Island.

Clive Barker's Undying from EA Games was promoted with the tag-line, 'What does not kill you will make you wish it had'. Set in Ireland in the 1920s, it involved an undead family attempting to destroy its last surviving member.

Silent Hill 2 was set in a fogbound town where strange creatures inhabited a blood-splattered mental asylum and an abandoned apartment block, while *Soul Reaver 2* was based in a world filled with vampires.

The *From Dusk Till Dawn* game picked up from the end of the 1995 movie, with Seth Gecko imprisoned on a prison ship infested with vampires, and *Blade* featured the eponymous Marvel Comics character hunting down his undead brethren.

Alien Versus Predator 2 pitched the two movie monsters against a gun-toting marine, while *The Mummy* recreated the 1999 Universal movie, including video sequences, as Rick O'Connell confronted Imhotep and other marauding mummies.

Return to Castle Wolfenstein was set during World War II, when the Nazis of Wolfenstein had cellars full of genetically-created, fire-breathing zombies.

A sword- and pistol-wielding demon hunter/investigator battled more supernatural foes in *Devil May Care*. Created by the team who came up with *Resident Evil*, it was one of the most eagerly anticipated games of the year. Meanwhile, *Resident Evil Code: Veronica X* picked up the plot from *Resident Evil III: Nemesis* as heroine Claire Redfield searched for her lost brother in a world filled with zombies, worms, freaks and mutants.

In 2001 it seemed that almost any film character could be turned into an action figure or a collectable. Sideshow Toys' series of eight-inch Universal figures finally included Bela Lugosi as a fully articulated Count from *Dracula*, Lugosi again as the broken-necked Ygor from *Son of Frankenstein* and Lon Chaney, Sr. as the Red Death from *The Phantom of the Opera* with a variant unmasked head. There was also a translucent green plastic *Creature from the Black Lagoon* special-edition figure with fourteen points of articulation.

The same company also released twelve-inch figures of Lugosi's

Dracula, Chaney Jr.'s Wolf Man and Chaney Sr.'s Phantom, plus vampire figures from *London After Midnight*, *Nosferatu* and *Son of Dracula*, The Invisible Man (with a clear plastic head!), and a trio of figures from Mel Brooks's *Young Frankenstein*.

A set of three six-inch articulated figures from Full Moon's *Demonic Toys* series was also released, along with a twelve-inch figure of Pimp from *Blood Dolls*.

Another twelve-inch figure released during the year was The Fly from the sequel *Return of the Fly*.

Mezco's 'Reel Masters', the second series of *Silent Screamers* six-inch figures, included Graf Orlock from *Nosferatu*, Edison's Frankenstein, the 1920 Dr Jekyll and Mr Hyde and the *Metropolis* robot Maria, all with their own diorama bases.

The *Shadow of the Vampire* deluxe figure set featured F.W. Murnau with movie camera filming Max Schreck in a detailed display case.

Produced by McFarlane Toys, *Clive Barker's Tortured Souls* featured six Cenobite-like action figures – I: Agonistes, II: The Scythe-Meister, III: Lucidique, IV: Talisac, V: Venal Anatomica and VI: Mongroid – each accompanied by a connected short story written by Barker. The concept was subsequently sold by Barker and Todd McFarlane for a mid-six-figure option to Universal Pictures.

McFarlane continued its *Movie Maniacs* series with figures of Tony Todd as Candyman and Todd McFarlane's version of The Blair Witch.

The Mummy Returns spawned a series of articulated figures from Jakks Pacific, including The Rock's Scorpion King, Rick O'Connell with a pygmy mummy, Anubis and Alex O'Connell, and Imhotep.

Special-effects expert Stan Winston teamed up with X-Toys to produce *Stan Winston's Creature Features*, a new line of toys that was launched in October. The initial releases included five new characters developed for a series of films based on old AIP movies of the 1950s, accompanied by a CD-ROM detailing the design, sculpting and development of each figure. At least five additional lines were also being developed – Monster Mythology, Nightmare Demons, Extreme Gargoyles, Stan Winston's Alien Universe and Animal Kingdom, the latter featuring half-man, half-beast creations.

Ray Harryhausen fans could choose between the X-Plus USA series of limited-edition four-inch chess pieces (which included harpies, hydra, Selenites and sword-fighting skeletons), and the twelve-inch cold-cast statues of Kali, the Ymir and various mythological creatures.

From Japan there were twelve-inch poseable vinyl figures of Harryhausen's Cyclops and Dragon from *The 7th Voyage of Sinbad*, and Talos from *Jason and the Argonauts*.

The Japanese also seemed to go crazy for Tim Burton's *The Nightmare Before Christmas* with a fourteen-inch Jack Skellington coffin doll, a gold 'Millennium' edition and a twelve-inch version dressed in pyjamas; a ten-inch Sandy Claws doll; a reversible pillow featuring Jack; a hand-painted set with Lock, Shock and Barrel, or a similar set of four vampires; a set of pull-back racers featuring Jack's faithful dog Zero and Jack's snow-mobile; a Zero choker necklace, and various die-cast Jack key-chains, amongst numerous other items.

A Halloween treat for little girls with a twisted sense of humour was the Barbie-and-Ken-as-*The Munsters* gift set. The dolls were surprisingly faithful recreations of Lily and Herman from the cult 1960s TV show. And if that wasn't enough, there was always Mezco Toyz's series of nine-inch *Living Dead Dolls* complete with their own death certificate!

The *Scooby-Doo* five-piece bendable gift set included five-inch figures of Scooby, Shaggy, Velma, Daphne and Fred.

A series of limited-edition retro tin lunch boxes from NECA included designs for *Evil Dead* and *Halloween*, each with a free metal thermos and holographically numbered. Stephen King's 1958 Plymouth Fury *Christine* turned up as a 1/8th scale die-cast model.

For Christmas trees, Clayburn Moore designed and sculpted a *Vampirella Ornament* complete with crescent moon and vampire bat.

William Marshall's *Blacula*, David Hedison's *The Fly* and a Morlock from George Pal's 1960 movie of *The Time Machine* were recreated as quarter-scale resin bust kits sculpted by Joe Simon.

Sculpted by Richard Force, the *Nosferatu* mini resin model kit featured Max Schrek playing with a yo-yo and was limited to just 200 figures. A ten-inch caricature of Boris Karloff from *Mad*

Monster Party? was sculpted by Tony Cipriano and limited to 500 pieces at $100 each.

Lovecraft fans could choose between a 'Collect Call of Cthulhu' T-Shirt or a 'Pokéthulu' T-shirt, while a company called Java's Crypt offered in sterling silver an Elder Sign Brooch/Pin, an Elder Sign Pendant and Elder Sign earrings. Bad Boy Designs introduced Cthulhu Beer Glasses with four designs – Innsmouth Golden Lager, Ithaqua Ice, Wizard Whateley's Dunwich Ale and Witch House Dark ('It's the beer you've been dreaming of').

Meanwhile, Mythos Books launched its second revised edition of *The Lovecraft Tarot*, containing twenty new cards and an expanded book by Eric Friedman.

In celebration of the 70th Anniversary of three of Universal's most famous Classic Monsters, in October Universal Studios Home Video and Madame Tussaud's–New York unveiled lifelike wax figures of Count Dracula, Frankenstein's Monster and The Mummy to pay tribute to legendary horror icons Boris Karloff and Bela Lugosi.

From Giant Manufacturing came a Classic Horror T-shirt depicting Universal's The Mummy.

The Mummy Returns trading cards featured scenes from the movie or early designs of CGI characters, while the *Ghosts of Mars* trading cards included plenty of background information and even a limited-edition card signed by director John Carpenter himself.

The 2000 Bram Stoker Awards for Superior Achievement were presented on May 26th at the Horror Writers' Association Banquet, held in conjunction with the World Horror Convention in Seattle, Washington. *The Traveling Vampire Show* by late HWA president Richard Laymon predictably won in the Novel category, while Brian A. Hopkins's *The Licking Valley Coon Hunters Club* was chosen in the First Novel section. Steve Rasnic Tem and Melanie Tem's chapbook *The Man on the Ceiling* won for Long Fiction, and Jack Ketchum's 'Gone' (from *October Dreams*) picked up the award for Short Fiction. *Magic Terror: Seven Tales* by Peter Straub was the winner in the Fiction Collection category, and *The Year's Best Fantasy and Horror: Thirteenth Annual Collection* edited by Ellen Datlow and Terri Windling won the Anthology award. Stephen King's autobiographical *On Writing* was the Non-Fiction winner, Alan Moore's *The League of Extraordinary Gentlemen* was voted best Illustrated Narrative, while Steven Katz's *Shadow of the Vampire* collected the Screenplay award. Nancy Etchemendy's *The Power of Un* won in the Work for Younger Readers category, Tom Piccirilli's *A Student of Hell* won in the Poetry Collection section, and Patricia Lee Macomber, Steve Eller, Sandra Kasturi and Brett A. Savory's web site *The Chiaroscuro* won the Other Media award. The Specialty Press Award went to William K. Schafer for Subterranean Press, and Nigel Kneale was honoured with the Lifetime Achievement Award.

Held over July 19th-22nd on the Roger Williams University campus in Bristol, Rhode Island, the guests at the informal Necon XXI were Tim Powers and Elizabeth Massie.

The International Horror Guild's awards recognizing outstanding achievements in the field of horror and dark fantasy were presented on September 1st during Dragon*Con in Atlanta, Georgia. Best Novel was *Declare* by Tim Powers, *Adams Fall* by Sean Desmond was voted best First Novel, *The Man on the Ceiling* by Melanie and Steve Rasnic Tem won in the Long Story category, while Steve Duffy's 'The Rag-and-Bone Men' (from *Shadows and Silence*) won in the Short Story section. *I Feel Sick* #1 – 2 by Jhonen Vasquez won the Illustrative Narrative award, and there was a tie for Collection between *City Fishing* by Steve Rasnic Tem and *Ghost Music and Other Tales* by Thomas Tessier. Best Anthology went to *October Dreams: A Celebration of Halloween* edited by Richard Chizmar and Robert Morrish, *At the Foot of the Tree* by William Sheehan won in the Nonfiction category, and Paula Guran's *Horror Garage* was voted Best Publication. Joel-Peter Witkin won Best Artist, *American Psycho* was voted Best Film, and *Angel* picked up the Television award.

The International Horror Guild also presented shock-rock performer Alice Cooper with its Living Legend Award. Cooper also received Dragon*Con's 'Julie' Award – named for science fiction/comic legend Julius Schwartz – which recognizes universal achievement spanning multiple genres.

The 2001 British Fantasy Awards were presented on September 23rd at the British Fantasy Society's one-day 30th Birthday Bash in London's West End. The winners of this year's awards were announced by Guests of Honour Hugh Lamb and Simon Clark: The August Derleth Award for Best Novel went to *Perdido Street Station* by China Miéville, *Hideous Progeny* edited by Brian Willis was judged Best Anthology and Kim Newman's *Where the Bodies Are Buried* won Best Collection. Tim Lebbon's zombie novella 'Naming of Parts' was voted Best Short Fiction, Best Artist was Jim Burns, and Peter Crowther's PS Publishing was named Best Small Press. The special Karl Edward Wagner Award was presented to legendary anthologist Peter Haining.

The 2001 World Fantasy Awards were presented on November 4th at the World Fantasy Convention in Montreal, Canada. Guests of Honour were Fred Saberhagen, Joël Champetier, artist Donato Giancola and toastmaster Charles de Lint. The Best Novel result was a tie between *Declare* by Tim Powers and *Galveston* by Sean Stewart. Steve Rasnic Tem and Melanie Tem's *The Man on the Ceiling* picked up yet another award with Best Novella, while 'The Pottawatomie Giant' by Andy Duncan was voted Best Short Fiction. *Dark Matter: A Century of Speculative Fiction from the African Diaspora* edited by Sheree R. Thomas was considered the Best Anthology, Andy Duncan made it a double when his *Beluthahatchie and Other Stories* won Best Collection, and the artist award went to Australian Shaun Tan. Tom Shippey received the Special Award: Professional for *J.R.R. Tolkien: Author of the Century*, and the Special Award: Non-Professional went to Bill Sheehan for *At the Foot of the Story Tree: An Inquiry into the Fiction of Peter Straub*. Life Achievement Awards were announced for Philip José Farmer and Frank Frazetta.

Unsurprisingly, the staff and clientele of California book-dealer Barry R. Levin voted J.K. Rowling the Most Collectable Author of the Year. Charnel House won the Collector's Award for Most Collectable Book of the Year for the lettered-state edition of *From the Corner of His Eye* by Dean Koontz, and the Lifetime Collectors Award went to Henry Hardy Heins for his outstanding bibliographic contributions to the study of the works of Edgar Rice Burroughs.

I guess it was inevitable that, in view of the terrorist attacks of September 11th on New York's World Trade Center and Washington's Pentagon building, and their continuing consequences for the entire world, any other topic I might attempt to address in this introduction would just seem trivial, even in context.

Like millions of others, I watched dumbfounded as events unfolded live on television. As a babyboomer, born after World War II, the images I saw that afternoon were amongst the most horrific I have ever witnessed. Yet there was also a sense of awe. A sense of unreality. I was genuinely astonished that anybody could create such wholesale destruction and massive loss of life in what I, probably naively, considered to be a 'civilized' world. I was appalled that something I had only ever encountered in the movies or science fiction was actually happening in real life while the world tuned in.

Perhaps more than anything else, I was aware that the events taking place in front of us all would shape the still-fledgling twenty-first century for years, perhaps decades, to come.

So what has all this to do with horror – the fictional kind?

Well, in the aftermath of '9/11' (as American media pundits quickly dubbed the attacks) fiction sales dropped dramatically around the world. Almost immediately, and especially in America, reading tastes shifted towards non-fiction titles and self-help books. With media coverage focused on terrorism and war news, new books were unable to get the publicity they needed. This, coupled with a looming global economic recession, meant that the already struggling horror field was even further marginalized.

In general publishing, the *New York Times* claimed that book sales had slumped by at least 15 per cent, while bestselling novels by top authors were off by as much as 25 per cent to 40 per cent. Although the *Harry Potter* books and *The Lord of the Rings* reissues continued to sell well, supported by blockbuster movies, new books from such authors as Stephen King, Anne Rice and James Herbert were said to be selling well below expectations. And if those authors were not doing well, you can imagine how much worse it was for mid-list horror writers.

Meanwhile, the series of anthrax attacks through the mail in America resulted in some publishing houses refusing any longer to accept unsolicited manuscripts.

Although fiction sales began to pick up again in mid-December, publishers were already having to tighten their belts by laying off staff (including editors), cancelling sales conferences, cutting the number of books published, reducing authors' advances and marketing budgets, and cutting print runs.

The consequences of these actions will affect the publishing industry for a long time to come.

Perhaps even more bizarrely, given the movie industry's knee-jerk reaction to the attacks, the US Army held a meeting with Hollywood writers and directors (including Danny Bilson and Spike Jonze) to brainstorm ways to prevent further terrorist assaults on America. Life really was beginning to imitate art.

Soon after the attacks I expressed publicly my concern that once again the horror genre, which was still desperately trying to crawl out of a decade-long recession, would be caught in some kind of moral and media backlash. We had seen it happen before, and there was no reason to assume that this time – given the immensity of the tragedy – events would be any different.

Thankfully, my fears ultimately proved to be unfounded. A few days after the attacks, Stephen King's radio station WKIT raised money for the American Red Cross Disaster Relief Fund with listeners pledging a minimum of $10.00 to hear a song. Stephen and Tabitha King matched all pledges dollar-for-dollar, and the estimated total raised reached $140,000.

The New York City Chapter of the Horror Writers Association published *Scars*, a charity anthology whose proceeds also went to the Red Cross on behalf of victims of the World Trade Center attack. Authors involved in the project included Gerard Houarner, Jack Ketchum, Michael Laimo, Gordon Linzner and Monica O'Rourke.

As Halloween approached, there was a real possibility that parents more concerned with anthrax spores or hijacked airplanes would prevent their children from celebrating ghoulies, ghosties, and things that go bump in the night.

However, according to one Internet source, Uncle Sam, Lady Liberty, Rudolph Giuliani and firefighter and rescue-worker masks were big sellers at Halloween. We were already beginning to adapt.

Horror writers have always argued that their stories can be cathartic – by embracing our fictional fears we can sometimes overcome our real-life demons – and this was never more evident than in 2001.

As critic Douglas E. Winter has said: 'Great horror fiction has never really been about monsters, but about mankind. It shows us something about ourselves, something dark, occasionally monstrous . . . Its writers literally drag our terrors from the shadows and force us to look upon them with despair – or relief . . .'

Proof that horror could perhaps be therapeutic was evidenced when Stephen King and Peter Straub's collaborative novel *Black House*, initially released the week of the terrorist attack, finally reached the top of the American bestseller lists, despite an initial postponing of print advertising.

'The current context makes these things more relevant, more important,' Straub was quoted as saying. 'You say, yes, the world is really like this. The writing my colleagues and I do is to awaken people to the fragility of existence and the possibility of extremity.'

For the foreseeable future the world has new monsters to fear, new bogeymen to keep us awake at night. It may not mean much in the greater scheme of things, but horror fiction also has a role to play in our recovery.

The world as we knew it before that fateful day will never be the same again. Yet horror fiction, as it has always done, can help us move towards confronting our fears and, by allowing us to recognize them for what they really are, we can use it to hopefully lessen the hold they have over us.

The Editor
May, 2002

CHICO KIDD

Mark of the Beast

CHICO KIDD HAS BEEN WRITING GHOST STORIES since 1979 under the name of A.F. Kidd. They have been published (mostly illustrated by the author) in such small-press magazines as *Ghosts & Scholars*, *Dark Dreams*, *Peeping Tom*, *Enigmatic Tales*, *All Hallows* and the author's own series of chapbooks.

Others have appeared in anthologies such as *Vampire Stories*, *The Mammoth Book of Ghost Stories 2*, *The Year's Best Horror Stories X*, *XVI* and *XVIII*, and the hardcover *Ghosts & Scholars*. She remains, apparently, the only non-Antipodean author to appear in the Australian magazine of SF and fantasy, *Aurealis*.

'In September 2000,' recalls Kidd, 'a Portuguese sea-captain called Luís Da Silva barged into a tale called "Cats and Architecture" and demanded to have his story told. Since then he has appeared in nine more short stories and two-and-three-quarter novels – *Demon Weather*, *The Werewolf of Lisbon* and *Resurrection* – which are currently under consideration by a publisher.'

'Cats and Architecture' (which is also reprinted in this volume) first appeared in *Supernatural Tales* 2, and the next four Da Silva stories in a chapbook entitled *Second Sight*. More recently, 'Handwriting of the God' was published in *Dark Terrors 6* and another of the tales, 'Zé and the Amulet' (featuring two characters who also appear in 'Mark of the Beast'), is scheduled for *Supernatural Tales* 4.

' "Mark of the Beast" has more than a nod in Kipling's direction,' continues the author, 'both in its setting and its title. It came from trying to find a new angle on the werewolf story, and it introduces Harris the Werewolf, who seems to have taken on a life of his own. I had no idea, when he first appeared, that he was going to be an important character in the series. Other characters reappear, some quite frequently, but haven't yet graduated to "Scooby Gang" status. For anyone interested, this story takes place about two and a half years after the "Death in Venice" section of "Cats and Architecture".'

B LOOD IN THE NIGHT.
In the warm moist darkness, the town was a cacophony of smells – vivid, exciting, thrilling, delicious. Each one told a story, each held a promise. Hunger writhed in his belly, but the odoriferous stew was so seductive that he could almost ignore the gnawing compulsion, almost push it to one side in order to explore the exhilarating possibilities opening up to him in every direction. Secrets. Secrets.

He sniffed the air with delight, drinking in the rich brew, and let his scent-sense wander over the profusion of smells, much as a shopper might scan the goods on view in a bazaar. Here a pi-dog bitch in heat had urinated, and she would already be mated; there an ailing beggar had lain for a while, and he would die soon of his sickness.

Yet in the end hunger became the imperative, and he filtered out, not without a little regret, the odours that did not promise food and focused on one particular, juicy, blood-rich odour. It led him along a maze of streets and finally down an alleyway that, to human eyes, would have been impenetrably dark. But to him, to whom scent both marked his way and told him the history of every place he passed, it was as bright as a gaslit street. To a man's nose, too, it would have smelled foul, at least to one that was unused to its stink.

Human debris lived in this place along with the rats and other scavengers – families crowded in makeshift shacks of cardboard and corrugated iron, picking over the rubbish of those just a little more fortunate. Here lived beggars, cripples, lepers, the weak and the poverty-stricken: here were rich pickings for a creature hungry for an easy meal.

Small children were the easiest to take, and, he had found, the sweetest meat, especially the little males, whose mothers pampered them as best they could despite poverty: their flesh soft and buttery, their bones crunchy and filled with the most delicious fatty marrow. He salivated at the thought, if he could be said strictly to have thoughts. They were more like olfactory pictures, impressions, memories.

Now that one particular scent was very strong, so tempting, so mouth-watering. Licking his lips, he peered carefully round the corner, yellow eyes glinting, and sensed the prey, a sleeping toddler of no more than two years. It slumbered just a few feet away, just on the other side of a makeshift wall of splintered plywood, and he padded up to this barrier that was no barrier and nosed under it. Inside, a little fire of dried cow-dung sent up a pungent smoke that almost made him sneeze, and something cooked on it in a rusty iron pot – it was an unappetizing concoction of rice, he registered, thinly flavoured with a chicken bone. His meal, that slept plumply just by the fire, was far more appetizing, with plenty of meat on its bones.

As if sensing danger, the child opened its eyes. But it was too late to cry out.

The shipping agent was a diminutive babu with slicked-down hair and an oleaginous manner. He spoke rather rancid Portuguese and insisted on calling Luís Da Silva *chefe*. After an hour in his office, the captain felt as if he had been deep-fried.

It was also damnably hot and humid. The stickiness of the atmosphere was not at all alleviated by a sail-like fan that a boy in the corner was desultorily operating with a string tied to his toe. It barely stirred the air, except perhaps for a foot or so in front of it.

His shirt was wringing wet as if he had been swimming in the ocean – admittedly a rather unlikely occurrence, since the water around the port differed from an open sewer in name only: at low tide, the harbour smelled like a midden. But even that was a minor discomfort compared with wearing an eye-patch in this hellish climate.

Captain Da Silva lit what was probably his sixth cheroot – after that many, his mouth felt like old carpets – and regarded the other man with irritation. He was almost at the end of his patience, and badly in need of a drink. The agent, whose name was Gomes, had offered him tea. The captain was of the opinion that only the

English could possibly enjoy tea, despite the fact that it had come to them via Portugal in the first place, but he thought he would probably have melted away into a little puddle on the floor without it and had accepted a cup of the sweet, revolting stuff.

But whether under the jurisdiction of the Portuguese or the English, as he knew from experience, the subcontinent moved at its own pace. You just had to let events roll along. Until in the end they would gather so much momentum they were in danger of becoming a juggernaut. The trick was to catch them just before they reached that stage – to catch the tide, as it were, at precisely the right time. Which was easy enough to do with a ship, but damnably difficult when it was a tide in the affairs of men.

Outside, palm leaves rattled with a noise like rain. Beneath them, a pair of crows were brawling raucously. Da Silva eyed them sourly through the open window, thinking, come to the tropics and you expect exotic birds, jewel colours, sweet trilling songs. And what do you get? Crows.

Money changed hands and the next level of wheels was lubricated. That done, the agent leaned back and smiled, displaying an alarming set of false teeth that appeared to have been rifled from a corpse, and saying with patent insincerity, 'We are being sorry for all the delays,' in a way that made Da Silva want to hit him. 'It is the fault of the damn superstitious peasants in this town,' he explained.

At the word *superstitious* the captain became attentive, although he made no outward show of the fact. 'Indeed?' he said in a disinterested tone, blowing smoke in Gomes's direction.

'Oh yes,' replied the agent, leaning over the desk to impart information and treating Da Silva to a gust of truly horrific breath, perhaps in retaliation. 'All bloody ignorant peasants. They are saying there is a wolf stealing children from their homes, you know? As if damn wolf would come into the town! And not normal wolf, oh no, that is not good enough, they must have it that it is some kind of supernatural. Well, *chefe*, what do you expect, they are all low-caste heathens and untouchables, not even Christians like you and me.'

A number of comments rushed through Da Silva's mind at that remark. But all he did was shrug his shoulders. 'And this affects our business how?' he asked, fighting the urge to stick a finger under his eyepatch and somehow dispose of the sweat accumulating there.

'Oh, you are knowing what the people are like here, *chefe*, no?' said the agent, apparently unaware of any irony. 'Too damn ignorant to know any better. Werewolves and *nagas* and ghosts, pah,' he added – thus neatly encompassing East and West in one contemptuous phrase – and appeared to be preparing to spit until he caught sight of Da Silva's expression and thought better of it, turning the aborted expectoration into a cough.

Da Silva, who had no objection at all to spitting as an expression of contempt, wondered with some amusement what Gomes would say if the agent knew that *he* saw ghosts all the time. Including the faint shade of a long-forgotten bureaucrat – who had presumably, therefore, died in harness – in this very office. Not only that, but the captain had encountered far more dangerous creatures. More dangerous than wolves in many ways.

It was curious, though, the way the subject had come up. Or maybe not so curious. *I ought to be getting used to it by now*, he thought resignedly, feeling a little like spitting himself. *You'd think I was some kind of lodestone. So wouldn't that just be a surprise if it does turn out to be a werewolf or something of the sort, just waiting for Da Silva to put into port.*

Gomes, unaware of the captain's thoughts, prattled on. 'But I have good news! I can do you a favour! I am hearing of a sailor who is looking for a ship, a man with the mate's chitty, right here in town.'

Da Silva grunted non-committally. Though he had not met Gomes before, he recognized the type. There were Gomeses in every port in every country in the world, and somehow they made the wheels of commerce go round and kept him in business. But, like all the others, this man was more likely to tailor his reportage to what a listener wanted to hear rather than anything that resembled the truth. *Probably some decrepit old pirate who spends his days so drunk on palm whisky he can't find his arse without a map*, he thought. 'Really.'

'Oh, yes, *chefe*,' the other said unctuously. 'An American man,' as if this negated anything the captain had been thinking. 'I shall be arranging a meeting, yes?'

It couldn't do any harm to meet the man, Da Silva said to

himself with a sigh, on the off chance that Gomes was actually correct. 'Yes, go ahead, Senhor Gomes,' he said.

Which was why Captain Da Silva was currently awaiting the arrival of one Edward Harris, lately of Boston, Massachusetts, while sweating and soundly cursing each and every equatorial land for its vile climate. Formality be damned, he had decided, and had shed his coat. Now he was mopping moisture from the humid zone under his eyepatch in a vain attempt to make wearing the thing more comfortable. *You could probably grow mushrooms under there*, he thought irritably.

However the captain was not thinking about the imminent Harris but was contemplating the ghosts that mingled with the breathing crowds at the quayside under the sullen monsoon sky. They were of little help, but that was no more than he expected. The damned things were only shades, after all, memories of the people they had been, haunting the place where they had died. Very few of them seemed to retain any kind of awareness for very long, yet today they seemed – restive, somehow. Disturbed. Sometimes he thought they were able to communicate with each other in a kind of dim, distant way, and now it was almost as if they were all infected with nervousness, odd though that sounded. What would make a ghost nervous?

He knew a way to ask, but that involved summoning a real spirit, something he was reluctant to do. Even now he found the thought of necromancy repellent, and always would. It was a kind of slavery, and that purely disgusted him. Having been, for many years, as good as owned himself, he was reluctant to force another soul to his own will. Even if the body it had once inhabited was no longer living.

The char-wallah who had supplied Gomes with tea, and whom he had collared on leaving the agent's office, had not only confirmed the man's story but had added a considerable amount of grisly detail of his own, presumably in the interests of artistic verisimilitude, in exchange for appropriate remuneration – not to mention offering to bring the hysterical mother of the latest victim for a small additional sum. Da Silva had turned this last down.

I can't just let it rest, he thought. *Damn it*. And was wondering what to do about it when the man he was waiting for arrived.

Harris was unmistakable, especially in a crowd whose main racial mix, ghostly and living alike, consisted of Indian and

Portuguese in various combinations. He was nearly six feet tall, heavily built, and as red-haired as Judas Iscariot.

The captain hastily replaced his eyepatch. Informality was one thing, but he knew the scar that ran from eyebrow to cheekbone was not a sight to let loose on anyone at a first encounter. On the quayside, Harris caught his gaze and gave an odd little wave, one that might one day grow up to be a salute.

'Captain Da Silva?' he called.

'Senhor Harris, I presume?'

'That's me, skipper. Permission to come aboard?'

'Come along, Senhor Harris.'

Twenty minutes later, the *Isabella* had a new third mate, and Da Silva was silently apologizing to the absent Gomes: Harris seemed both sober and competent. Which probably meant there *was* something wrong with him. But for the time being the captain was willing to give him the benefit of the doubt, being a firm believer in letting people have enough rope to hang themselves rather than trying to do it for them.

This captain seems like a regular sort, even if he does look like a pirate with that black eyepatch. I guess he's been at sea since Pontius was a pilot, but I'd bet fifty dollars that he's never come across a sailor with my particular problem before. I've gotten used enough to signing on for one trip and being given my papers when we tie up at the other end that it don't bother me no more, but I don't reckon I'll ever get used to the change that comes over me every full moon, and neither will any skipper. Still, after kicking my heels in this godforsaken hole all this time I reckon I would have shipped out with the Flying Dutchman if he'd happened to put into port.

I recall feeling pretty goddam down, watching the Nimrod *shrink into the distance. It wasn't so much being without a berth again, like I said, I'm used to that – it was where I was stuck ashore. Places like these, they ain't healthy. If the malaria don't get you the yellow fever will, and if the typhoid don't, the dysentery will, what ignorant fellows call the dire rear. Though I can't say I'm prone to catching regular human-type diseases any more it don't mean I couldn't go down with distemper or rabies, and I wasn't fixing to put it to the test.*

Last month I'd gotten away with it by locking my door – my granma could have picked the lock but I pushed the bed against it – and tethering myself to the bedframe with my collar and chain. It's what I aim to do every month, but on a ship there ain't no privacy. I tell my messmates I'm going down sick, but when they see what sort of sick they can't wait to leave me be. Since this thing happened to me, Mrs Harris's little boy's been worse than a pariah, but working the sea's all I know how to do.

Da Silva shook hands with Harris. The American's hand was the size of a bear's paw but his grip was merely firm, not bone-crushing. With hands that big, he had no need to prove anything. The captain lit a cheroot and offered one to Harris, who refused politely.

'You needn't be in any hurry to quit your lodgings, if you don't want to,' Da Silva said. 'We're mired down in seventeen levels of bureaucracy, as usual. If it weren't for that we could be out of here tomorrow. Oh, and the fact that there seems to be a werewolf on the loose.'

Watching Harris closely for any reaction, but not really expecting one, he was surprised to see the American's eyes widen for a bare instant. *Now I wonder what that was about?* he thought curiously, drawing in smoke.

'Werewolf, huh?' drawled the mate. 'How do they work that one out?' And he took a cigarette out and lit it. Da Silva smiled faintly, being quite used to reading body language. He raised an eyebrow.

'The Indian penchant for melodrama, perhaps,' he suggested, somewhat disingenuously, and shrugged his shoulders.

Harris looked doubtful. 'They must have a reason, don't you think, skipper?'

'Justification, then,' said the captain, feeling the scar on his cheekbone absently. It still felt strange, a strip of smooth slippery skin. 'So they wouldn't have to admit that they weren't watching a child, they say the wolf that took it had supernatural powers.'

'A wolf in the town, though?' Harris said, unconsciously echoing Gomes, and turned away, ostensibly eyeing the crowd at the waterfront.

'Whatever it is,' said Da Silva, 'it's a convenient excuse for more delays. Anyway, Senhor Harris, I'll send word when I need you.'

'Right, skipper,' said the *Isabella*'s newest crew-member, and took his leave.

The man was shocked when he heard about the werewolf, Da Silva thought. *But not surprised to hear me say the word.* A drop of sweat ran down his nose, and he wiped at it irritably. *Damned stupid climate.* The captain took off his eyepatch, his hand encountering damp hair as it cleared his head. His shirt was glued to him, and all the folds of his clothes were sodden. *I wish to God I was back in Lisbon. Where it gets hot in summer, but you don't liquefy in it.* He rubbed at the patch ineffectually, grimacing.

'Who was that?' asked a curious voice by his elbow.

'New third mate,' he said, ruffling his son's hair automatically and finding it as clammy as his own.

'Oh *mãe*,' said Zé disgustedly. 'Someone else to boss us around.'

'That's what 'prentices are for,' Da Silva informed him.

'What's his name?'

'Harris,' said the captain. 'He's an American, so I expect you'll be learning a few new swear words.'

Zé grinned at the prospect, and did a little dance round his father. When he had been nine years old, a sailor from Providence, Rhode Island, had taught him to say *goddamn* – much to Da Silva's private amusement – and given him a silver dollar, which Zé would not be parted from. 'When are we sailing? It's too hot here.'

'Too hot, too wet, too stuffy, too dirty. I don't know, Zé. As soon as we can. As soon as all those bloody bureaucrats decide I've paid them enough in bribes. Heaven only knows.' A yawn caught him by surprise. *My God, I'm tired*, he thought, *how did that happen?* He wiped his hand over his face, the sweat feeling greasy on his palm and his fingers, then dragged it through his hair, mopping his forehead with his shirtsleeve as it followed through. Zé looked at him and giggled.

'Your hair looks like a bottle-brush,' he said.

'Haven't you got any studying you should be doing?' asked the captain, ominously, and his son took the hint and scuttled off. Da Silva watched him go, a small smile on his face. He hadn't really wanted the boy to follow in his footsteps at all, but it had soon become obvious to both him and his wife that Zé would get himself to sea by fair means or foul. So they had concluded that the safest thing had been to take him on the *Isabella* where he could at least be watched some of the time. And Da Silva had to admit that he was doing well.

He lit another cheroot, put the thoughts of Emilia – whom he missed every day – that Zé had awakened firmly out of his mind, and wondered what he should do about the werewolf.

Hell and damnation, why is the skipper interested? What does he know? How can he know?

Get yourself under control, Harris. He don't know about you. There's something else going on in this burg. Someone else, that don't care about killing people. Well, good God Almighty, life is cheap here. Ain't that the truth.

But that ain't the point, is it? The point is, I can't tie myself up no more, case someone finds me and kills me before I can do anything about it. Kills me for something I ain't done. But Jesus, what happens then, when the beast comes to me? Can I control it?

I remember. I remember. It was the George Washington *from Liverpool to Riga. Freezing Baltic waters. Rime on the sheets. Danny O'Leary got pneumonia and nearly died. We put into port a day before it iced over, and there we were, stuck fast till she thawed. And wolves in the streets, leaving paw prints in the snow and yellow stains of piss on the frozen buildings. Marking out their territory. Hell, folks said they was even out on the sea, running on the ice.*

So what the devil was a sailor supposed to do, take up woodcarving?

It was poker was my undoing, like my Ma always said it would be. Except I don't reckon she meant it like it happened. I didn't go with no hookers, didn't want to catch the pox. Didn't go drinking, at least not too much, rots your brain. Took care of my brain and my prick but lost my goddam humanity when I stepped outside for a smoke to clear my head.

Yellow eyes in the night, hot and yellow as molten gold poured into a mould, the same deep fierce glow. Lips, black, stretching back from a mouth full of fangs. Smell of decaying blood, new blood.

And I'm dead.

Only I'm not.

Then, a month later, pain. Excruciating pain. My spine is broken, my legs and arms dislocated, even my skull feels like it's exploding. I fall to the floor screaming. Some bones stretch, some shrink, everything re-forms. It feels like there's hot lead running in my veins. It hurts so much I have no more breath to cry out, and it goes on and on and on and a furnace heat builds until I think I'm really on fire, with actual flames shooting from my skin. But I can't see them burning because when I open my eyes their perception has changed, the entire concept of seeing has altered.

I don't see with my eyes any more, but with my nose. Sight is no more than shadows. The sense of smell is totally overwhelming, the scent of blood irresistible.

I'm a wolf.

So I go hunting.

José Da Silva, known to everyone – except to his mother when he was in for a hiding – as Zé, sat in the 'prentices' cabin and pretended to study. But however convincing this outward appearance of diligence, he was actually rerunning the last part of his father's conversation with Senhor Harris in his head, over and over.

The two men had been talking in English, of course, but Zé had inherited the captain's gift for languages and already spoke it pretty well himself. Added to which an addiction to penny dreadfuls, a form of literature to which O'Rourke, the ship's doctor, had introduced him, had made him familiar with words like *werewolf*.

Zé had long suspected that his father knew rather more about uncanny things than he ever let on, and this seemed to confirm it. Except that he hadn't said it was actually a werewolf, had he? But that was uninteresting. The possibility of real werewolves was, on the other hand, decidedly intriguing, not to say exciting.

Zé chewed the end of his pencil and rubbed his left cheekbone in unconscious imitation of the captain. *I could ask Vik*, he thought, *except that I can't figure out how*. This was a native boy a year or so older than Zé who appeared to be indigenous to the dockside, and with whom he had struck up a sort of friendship despite the lack of a common language. Vik had a smattering of Portuguese and English, and had taught Zé a few words of

Hindi, but it was hardly a sufficient linguistic basis for explaining such a sophisticated concept as that of a man who turned into a wolf. The greater part of most of their conversations was conducted in sign language, with odd words thrown in here and there – usually very loudly, since Vik seemed convinced that Zé would understand him if only he shouted loudly enough.

Another drop of sweat fell on his book, and he wiped it off absently, noticing in passing that the page was quite pocked with damp patches. It had been uncomfortably hot and humid ever since they had put into port, even when the skies opened – as they did fairly often – and released a torrent of rain as solid as the sea. Zé found this quite remarkable, being used to the air feeling fresher after rain had fallen.

If it is a werewolf, he thought, *I wonder if Father has silver bullets for his revolver?* And that led to another idea, just as exciting: did his *mother* make them for him? Emilia Da Silva was a jeweller, and he had watched her casting small metal trinkets often enough; though since the captain had acquired the *Isabella* she also ran the business from an office in Lisbon, and that took up much of her time. Zé visualized his father stalking something in deep shadows, gun in hand, but his picture of the werewolf itself was somewhat hazier. The illustrations in O'Rourke's books showed hairy beasts that bore very little resemblance to actual wolves – not that Zé had ever seen a real wolf, except a stuffed one once – but he wanted the werewolf to be more formidable, somehow, than those often ill-drawn pictures. To be a better adversary.

Unaware of his son's train of thought, Da Silva headed away from the stinks of the waterfront into the only slightly different stinks of the town, making for a small grey church that sat on a bare sward that perhaps once had been green with grass, incongruous amongst tall palm trees and leathery-leaved frangipani.

The Portuguese who had colonized this shore had been as much evangelists as explorers and, like most zealots, had been enthusiastic in suppressing local religions and, often forcibly, substituting their own. That missionary zeal meant that there was no shortage of priests in the area, which should have been good news, since in most places a priest was a reliable, not to say indefatigable source of information.

Father Miguel Domingues did not look, at first sight, like the kind of ascetic who wore a hair shirt, being decidedly on the plump side. But on closer inspection, his chin and his round skull alike had both been shaved to within an inch of their life, and his lips were bracketed with deep furrows and were too thin for his full face. It gave him a forbidding air, and Da Silva's heart sank. *He looks like a damned Jesuit*, he thought.

The priest arched his nostrils at Da Silva and eyed the captain haughtily, taking in eyepatch and scar and incongruously blue eye, and damp untidy hair and four o'clock beard, somehow combining an expressionless stare with the appearance of being singularly unimpressed. Da Silva returned the stare and decided the feeling was mutual, though how Domingues managed to cope with wearing full clerical fig without apparently raising a sweat was, admittedly, quite a trick.

'What can I do for you, my son?' he enquired, in the peculiarly gentle tone that some priests affected, and that never failed to set the captain's teeth on edge. They probably took a special course on it at the seminary, he decided. Unctuous condescension certificate.

Da Silva had already made up his mind not to beat about the bush by skirting around the topic. He lit up a cheroot, partly because the priest looked the type to be irritated by smoke, with his flaring patrician nose – though God knew his sinuses must have had to put up with much worse things than cigars, living here – and said bluntly, 'Have you heard about this wolf that's supposed to be eating children?'

The priest gave him a raking stare that said plainly, *What business is it of yours*? but answered in an indulgent tone. 'Of course. Tragic. But these things happen, my son. I fear that despite all our efforts, many of these poor souls remain unenlightened.'

And that makes it all right if they're eaten, does it? Da Silva thought. He blew smoke out, and wiped sweat from his upper lip. 'It doesn't worry you?'

'It saddens me deeply,' replied the priest. 'If those poor children had been baptized they would now be with God, however unfortunate their lives on earth.'

There's my problem, thought the captain. *I don't believe that any more, if I ever did. Why should God be so petty as to turn them away?* Aloud, he said, 'What do you think about the rumour that it's some kind of supernatural beast?'

At that, Father Domingues chuckled indulgently, his prejudices about seafarers obviously confirmed. 'My son, my son,' he said, overt condescension creeping into his voice that implied not only *superstitious sailor* but also, and not very far behind at that, *ignorant peasant* as well. 'I do hope that we have put that sort of superstition behind us. We are, after all, living in the twentieth century now.'

The captain, who was rather more than half inclined to dismiss the better part of religion's trappings as superstition invented by priests to subjugate ignorant populaces – especially those parts which led the ordained to believe in their own superiority, if not omnipotence – bared his teeth in something that was almost a smile. 'But a lot of people do still believe in that sort of thing. Don't you believe in the Devil, Father?' he added. A little to his surprise the priest reddened, but the captain was careful not show his amusement.

'Evil can come in many forms,' the priest said sharply, looking at Da Silva with narrowed eyes. 'But prayer is always effective.'

Da Silva stared back, suddenly furious at the sheer stupidity of the man's arrogant ignorance, and bit back an angry retort. *Prayer is always effective! Yes, and I'm the grand panjandrum of all India.* He had to take care not to show his anger, though, so merely raised an eyebrow fractionally. 'I'm sure I can count on your prayers, then,' he said, and turned to go.

To hell with the whole pack of them, he thought viciously. *If they're too bloody narrow-minded to see what's in front of their noses, then I'll get the information I want from someone who knows.* Still imagining he could feel Father Domingues's gaze on him, he took a few deep breaths to steady himself. An unwise reaction, given the truly heroic level of putridity in the street.

Carefully he picked his way along, skirting deep, opaque, chalky-yellow puddles that you would never even consider putting a foot into. Not if you wanted to keep your boot intact, that was. And then he frowned, feeling another presence watching him, though when he looked round there was nothing suspicious to be seen. Not even the priest.

He was roused from his thoughts by a voice cutting through the cacophony of the street and speaking cultured Portuguese. 'Excuse me, senhor *capitão*, but perhaps I can be of help.' He turned round abruptly, his accoster having come up on his blind side, to see an elderly man clad only in a dhoti and a coat of dust. This ancient recoiled slightly at Da Silva's grim expression, but persisted. 'If you were wanting to know about the . . . wolf, that is.'

'That was the general idea,' replied the captain, rubbing at his scar and feeling sweat run down his face.

'Allow me to introduce myself,' the old man said, oddly formal. He looked a good deal older than Methuselah, but his brown eyes were bright and alert in his seamed face. 'My name is Mohan Das. And I am at your service.'

Intrigued, Da Silva asked, 'What can you tell me?'

'Will you walk a little?' Mohan Das moved off, and Da Silva fell in beside him. Not a tall man, he topped the diminutive Indian by several inches, and had to moderate his normal pace. In fact, in most eastern countries he could feel tall, and was vain enough to enjoy the sensation – a reaction that amused him.

They had hardly begun to walk when he was obliged to stop almost immediately as an inordinately large and solid-looking ghost surged up in front of him. The captain swore silently, irritated that any shade could still have the capability of startling him. He walked through it determinedly. His companion, however, either did not notice or affected not to do so.

The knife he wore concealed down his back chafed, and sweat pooled and ran inside his clothes. Da Silva wished he could emulate Mohan Das and strip off, and grinned to himself – more at the picture it presented than at the possible reaction it could cause. Which would probably be none at all, here. 'May I ask why you are hunting this thing?' the old man asked, curiously. 'Are you on some kind of crusade?'

Well, yes, the captain thought, startled, although he would not have put it quite that way. But, on reflection, he *did* feel he had an obligation. A duty to get rid of such things whenever they crossed his path. As they did now, since he began seeing ghosts. A little taken aback, as much by his own response as by the question, he said, resignedly, 'It looks like it.' And felt as though he had taken an irrevocable step.

The other nodded, as though it were the most natural thing in the world. 'And you can see ghosts, too.' That was not a question. Da Silva wondered how he knew. 'How long have you had this ability?'

Da Silva indicated his eyepatch. 'Ever since this happened.' He sometimes wondered whether it was the precise nature of the entity that had destroyed his left eye that had enabled his second sight, rather than the loss itself. Since it had been a demon. This information he did not intend to share with the old man.

'May I ask *how* it happened?'

'You may ask,' said Da Silva, in a tone that brooked no argument, 'but I won't tell you.'

Mohan Das seemed unperturbed by his refusal. 'In some cultures, shamans' eyes were ritually put out before they could come into their full powers,' he remarked, conversationally. 'And seers and sibyls were often blinded, too.'

The captain raised his eyebrows. *Shamans*, he thought. *What next, witchdoctors?* 'I'm not a seer.'

'What is a name?' asked the other. 'You see ghosts. You fight evil. What does that make you?'

'Captain of the *Isabella*,' retorted Da Silva. Mohan Das laughed, and executed a neat manœuvre to avoid a particularly persistent beggar. He moved through the crowd the way a fish does through water, quite at home in his own element. Da Silva, who had to dodge ghosts as well as people, fared less well, although he was gradually learning to walk *through*, rather than round, the shades that thronged the streets wherever he went. Even after nearly two years, though, it was still not quite automatic.

'You will find,' observed his companion, without looking up at him, 'that you are not unique. But neither are you alone.'

He had half-suspected it. But hearing it said, especially by someone who, however educated he sounded, came from a culture profoundly different from his own, was more disconcerting than comforting.

'Can you help me?'

'Only with information, senhor *capitão*.' The old man smiled, all the wrinkles in his face gnarling, like the bark of a tree, and Da Silva wondered just how old he was. 'Oh, yes, I have done things in my time – been a hero. How old are you?' he asked abruptly, and the captain, taken by surprise, answered automatically.

'Forty-two.'

'You are a young man still. I am more than twice your age now. Much more.' His expression sobered. 'And I must warn you, if you have not already realized it, that your task will become more dangerous as time goes by.'

'More dangerous,' repeated Da Silva. *Oh good. That's just the sort of thing I wanted to hear.* 'Why?' he asked, bluntly.

The old man looked up at him, his eyes hooded. 'Because they know you now. Your sight, and your actions, mark you, and they will recognize you.'

And the proof of that is that I know exactly what he means by they, he thought mordantly, and expelled a deep lungful of smoke. 'You said,' he reminded Mohan Das, 'that you could tell me something about the wolf.'

'Ah yes,' the other agreed. 'The wolf.' But he said no more. Da Silva wiped sweat from his face again and wondered once more how people managed to live, even thrive, in such a climate. He looked up to see clouds building in the lead-coloured sky.

'It's going to rain,' he observed.

'Yes. We should take cover.'

Da Silva thought he wouldn't have minded getting wet if it would cool him down at all. But the last time he had been caught in a monsoon downpour all it had done was soak his clothes still further without noticeably decreasing his discomfort.

He followed the old man under a low doorway, ducking instinctively although he had only ever met one low enough to smack his head on, and sat down where indicated in a stuffy, sweat-smoke-and-spice-scented dimness.

Mohan Das spoke to someone unseen in such a quiet voice that the captain could catch not a single word, which annoyed him. 'The wolf?' he prompted after a silent moment, and heard rain begin to drum on the roof.

'This is, as people have surmised, not a natural wolf,' the old man said. 'At least, not natural in the sense that it was not born a wolf but has, as we might say, acquired wolfhood – had wolfhood thrust upon it, as it were.'

'You're saying it *is* a werewolf, then?' said Da Silva. 'Can it be killed? What I mean is—'

'You are asking about silver bullets, I imagine. Yes?'

'Yes, I suppose so,' the captain admitted, a little irritably, since despite Zé's fancies he had no such ammunition for the revolver in his pocket.

The old man looked at him shrewdly, dark eyes glittering. By now the noise of the rain was so profound it sounded as if they were inside a drum, and Da Silva had to strain to hear him when he spoke.

'I expect you know that certain metals are, by their nature, more potent against . . . unnatural things. Just as some substances are apt to evil. Although the effectiveness of both is affected by the nature of the wielder.'

A steaming glass was placed in front of Da Silva, and he sniffed it suspiciously. *Oh God, more tea*, he thought. *What I'd give for a decent brandy*. There probably wasn't one this side of Constantinople – even the stuff in the decanter in his cabin had come from Greece and was, frankly, gut-rot. 'And that means?' he asked.

'I am sorry,' said Mohan Das. 'What I mean to say is, you would find it easier to kill such a thing with a bullet made of silver than with one made of lead, but depending on how much . . . virtue you have of your own it might add effectiveness to the lead. I think, though, that unless you were very fortunate, you would need to decapitate the creature extremely quickly after shooting it with an ordinary bullet. Otherwise you would have a wounded and angry werewolf on your hands, which would not be a pleasant prospect.' He took a sip of the scalding tea. 'May I see your knife, senhor *capitão*?'

Long past the stage of asking how the old man knew things, Da Silva unsheathed it carefully in the limited space and offered the hilt to him. Mohan Das took it, which made the captain feel decidedly uncomfortable, and scrutinized it for some minutes. The only sound was the rhythmic thunder of the rain, like a huge engine very close by. After a while, the captain could stay silent no longer. 'Well?' he demanded.

'A formidable weapon,' said the old man, handing it back. 'Silver and steel. I would think it should suffice.'

'You would *think*?' Da Silva repeated, holding the knife loosely in his sweating hand. 'You aren't sure?'

'Senhor *capitão*, nothing is sure. But I believe you are well enough armed, should you wish to pursue this thing.'

The captain's mouth and throat were so dry by now that he took a mouthful of tea in desperation. It shocked his taste buds, being black, bitter and astringent. But being also devoid of either condensed milk or sugar, it was more palatable than the sweet glop he had drunk in Gomes's office. He drained the glass, and suddenly realized that the great piston sound of the rain had ceased. *I wonder when that happened?* he thought, and put away his knife.

'Do you know where I might find it?' he asked. Mohan Das closed his eyes and slowly opened them again.

'I think it will find you, senhor *capitão*,' the old man said quietly, and Da Silva felt a shiver along his spine despite the heat of the day.

The idea of silver bullets having once occurred to Zé, he found himself quite unable to shake it off. After a while he gave up even the pretence of studying and just stared into space. The gentle, almost imperceptible motion of the ship was soothing, but a strange sense of urgency was building in him, fuelled by his own imagination. He was supposed to be meeting his new friend Vik soon, who had promised (he was *almost* sure) to take him to see a man who could perform the famous Indian rope trick. But that could wait. Zé had already seen enough of India and its denizens to realize that their sense of time was a flexible notion, even in those who possessed timepieces, which Vik certainly didn't.

He wondered later whether if Felipe, his fellow 'prentice, had been around to talk to, he would even have been thinking about it. But it was Felipe's watch, it being the captain's policy to keep the two boys on separate duties in order to keep them out of mischief. Which precaution was patently not working right now.

At length Zé got up and, after checking that the coast was clear, padded aft in his bare feet to the captain's cabin. His heart was pounding as he turned the door-handle and slipped inside.

Empty, the cabin smelled of his father in some indefinable way that was more than the odour of smoke. It was also close and airless, and Zé felt himself start to sweat again. This brought on the sudden dread that the captain might be able to detect that *he* had been in here by *his* smell, and he had to sit firmly on the irrational fear.

Zé looked at the tantalus with its anchored decanters of brandy, port and madeira without feeling tempted – an episode of sampling all three in unwise quantities at the age of eleven had rather put him off the idea of alcohol – and his gaze passed on to a framed photograph of his mother. He approached the desk still staring at this, and a drop of perspiration ran down his nose and fell on the blotter. A section of his father's spiky handwriting, reversed, ran immediately into a blob, the black ink fringing to a strange bronze colour. Zé flinched back, muttering an oath that his mother would have boxed his ears for.

Nervously, he slid open the desk drawer, but feared to hunt through the chaos within lest he leave a sign of his presence. He fingered a silver hip flask – which he could not recall ever having seen his father use – but immediately rejected it as being too big, and then guiltily had to wipe his smeared fingermarks off it with his shirt-tail. The gun that he had expected to see was not there, but a box of ammunition for it was. Zé poked at it, finding ordinary bullets, and took one out carefully. He took another overview of the drawer's contents, and sighed. As he closed it, his gaze lit on a key-fob.

And then the answer struck him, and he castigated himself for an idiot. He could use his lucky silver dollar.

When he slipped ashore, a silver bullet sat in his trouser pocket where previously there had been a coin.

Zé wormed through the crowds in search of Vik, and spotted him fairly quickly. He was tall for his age, which Zé estimated to be about a year older than him, and that made him easier to see in a throng of people.

'Namaste,' he said, and Vik replied with 'Boa tarde.' Which made Zé smile. Languages were such fun. He had been brought up in Venice, where Portuguese had been his family's private tongue. And now they were based in Lisbon, the Venetian dialect of Italian served the same purpose. Any new language delighted him, though – the way everything fitted together so neatly – and had the added bonus that people genuinely seemed to appreciate his attempts to learn it. Even if his accent occasionally caused amusement.

Vik grinned at Zé, white teeth flashing (except for one gap), and Zé passed the other boy one of the captain's cheroots. Along with alcohol, this was another vice he did not share with his father, also due to having sampled rather too much of it at an earlier age.

'Come,' Vik said, tucking the smoke somewhere in his grubby clothing, and set off at a pace that left Zé panting in his wake. The crowd flowed round them, gulped them down, digested them, and he was overwhelmed by its assault on all his senses. Smells, intriguing and inviting and revolting by turns. Some foods and spices were identifiable, and some made his mouth water while others seemed utterly disgusting. Sewage, too, was a familiar stink, as was the powerful odour of unwashed humanity. But there were a thousand others that were totally unrecognizable.

The noise, too, was indescribable, people shouting in a dozen or more different dialects, singing, chanting, perhaps praying, but what was the strange brazen instrument he could hear? Dogs he heard, too, and donkeys, goats and cows, but also something that – exciting thought – could be an elephant, perhaps. Of motorized traffic there was very little, the internal combustion engine not only being a relative newcomer but there being, also, a conspic-uous lack of roads that vehicles thus powered could run upon. But he heard motor horns, nonethelesss: what else could that mechanical braying be?

Beggars thrust deformed limbs at him, hawkers everything from jewellery and little carved statues to fruits and flowers and sweetmeats and cups of glutinous tea. At times Zé nearly lost Vik in the tumult. There was so much to see that he almost wished he could, and drown in the sensory overload. Sweat was pouring down his face and body, but he hardly noticed it, except when it stung his eyes. A three-legged yellow dog, so agile it hardly seemed to miss its lost limb, darted by with a bone, black with flies, in its mouth, trailing a faint carrion stink of tainted meat; and a fat child stumbled by in half-hearted pursuit, squeal-ing like a stuck pig.

Rushing to keep up with Vik, Zé nearly ran smack into a white cow with a flaccid hump on its back. Someone had painted its horns red and garlanded the beast with glass beads and flower chains, but it still smelled of shit and its legs were mired to the knees, if cows had knees. He skidded in the beast's wake, and almost fell, putting his hand on its warm flank to steady himself. Where was Vik? The taller boy had vanished in the throng, as he had been threatening to do.

Zé cursed, but half-heartedly. Either he would find Vik, and they could go to see the conjurer; or he would not, and he could then find something different to do in this fascinating crowd. He stuck his sweaty hands in his pockets, but immediately took them out again, and slowed his pace, following – on nothing more than a whim – the scent of woodsmoke. It quickly blended with a delicious frying smell, and his stomach growled. Vik more or less forgotten, Zé headed towards the prospect of food.

I wish I knew what the skipper was up to. Does he think he can go blundering after a werewolf, just like strolling down the main street? And why would he be interested, anyhow? Hell, it ain't none of my concern. No, I guess it is. I've signed on the Isabella *now, so he's my captain. Jesus, as if life wasn't complicated enough.*

Harris paused in the act of stuffing his belongings into his sea-chest for long enough to light a cigarette, and then went back to his packing.

This is going to be tricky. I can't follow him no more, I swear he knew I was there. But I can't see myself changing in some back alley. Too risky. So I have to make sure it happens in here, then go after him. Least I reckon I can find his scent. Hell, ain't many folks have themselves a . . . wolf bodyguard. Then tomorrow I get out of this dive.

Goddam it, it's getting dark already. No – I'm wrong. Just thought for a moment there I felt the change coming on. I'm thinking about it too much, is what it is. Pull yourself together, Harris. There's too much riding on this for you to lose focus now. If you don't ship out on the Isabella *you're going to be stuck here. And I don't know how long I can cope with that. I ain't killed anyone yet since this happened but I sure as hell can't guarantee that's going to stay the case if I have to stop here much longer.*

He looked out of the window at the lowering sky, yellow-grey clouds still bulging with unshed rain. They hid the sun; would hide the moon, when it sailed into the air above them. But nothing could stop its pull. He was a creature of tides now, as subject to the moon as was the sea, and when it was full and in the sky, he became a wolf. That was not to be changed now, he knew, and it was pointless to regret it. And now he had to use it.

And as my ma used to say, What can't be cured must be endured. Though I don't reckon she had this kind of thing in mind when she came out with that particular gem.

The small squalid room which he had inhabited for the past two months was on the ground floor of the building, and ease of access – and egress – more than made up for the multitude of spiders, roaches, lizards, rats and other assorted urban wildlife that shared it with him. The rats, indeed, found themselves preyed upon rather than predators when the moon was plump and high, and that had the added advantage of assuaging the Harris-wolf's hunger for a time. He smiled without humour, both at the thought and the memory of the taste. Not when he had actually consumed them, but at the foulness in his mouth when he came back to himself.

Pain lanced through him, and he doubled over in agony, falling to the floor and trying to curl round the hurt. Which was impossible, because it was his entire body.

Oh no, not yet. Please.

Leaving Mohan Das, Da Silva was surprised to find most of the day gone. The sense of being watched, however, was now absent, and he stepped out into the steaming street, skirting new and deeper puddles that had appeared. Above, some of the clouds had thinned slightly, and were turning the colour of steel as the sun they hid tumbled unseen towards the horizon. A faint feeble breeze stirred the awnings of the stalls that lined the street.

His conversation with the old man had disturbed him, as if something had taken away part of his free will. *I will be damned if I'll exchange one sort of slavery for another,* he thought savagely, *however noble or heroic its aim. If I hunt werewolves, or vampires, or whatever the hell else is loose in the night, I'll bloody well do it because it needs to be done. Not because I've been chosen to do it. I didn't fight any of those other things because someone ordered me to do it. If I do this, it's on my terms.*

He pushed the anger down, and lit a cheroot. The tip glowed redly in the fading daylight, and steadied his thoughts a little. *So,* he said to himself, *I have a talent. That's all. It's no different from being able to sing, or add up. That's why Emilia does the books, and I don't. That's why Caruso sings Verdi and not music-hall ditties, and the snake-charmers in the marketplace pipe their thin music at cobras. They do it because they're good at it.*

And I – I see ghosts.

Somewhat calmer now, the captain wiped the sweat from his face and began to walk along the street, past shops that sold spices in sacks and fireworks and bolts of multicoloured silk, cooking pots and trinkets and woodcarvings, tobacco and cashew nuts and palm whisky. Now he was more annoyed with himself for getting angry. *Never mind all that now*, he thought firmly. *Think about the matter at hand.*

By this time dusk had fallen with the usual tropic suddenness, though it was not noticeably cooler. He lifted his eyepatch away from his face in the hope that the tiny breeze would ease the discomfort, but without success, and he sighed.

The lighted shops and doorways took on the distance that lamplight imbues them with to an outside observer, that warm and welcoming glow that at the same time excludes the life within from those without.

Not a part of the crowd, but now further distanced from it, he attempted to filter out the living and concentrate on the dead. Of whom there were, in fact, more. As Harris had noted, and Da Silva knew well, life was cheap here. The pattern of the ghosts that drifted amongst the press of humanity bore that out, for mostly they were the shades of victims. Women and children, the weak and the sick, beggars and prostitutes, the robbed and the beaten and the raped. A crowd of miserable souls. Literally.

But nothing lupine ran among the shades, and there was no threat hanging in the air save the echo of Mohan Das's voice.

I think it will find you, senhor capitão.

Yet his hackles had risen, and it was not, this time, with the sense that he was being watched. It was the unshakeable feeling that, between one heartbeat and the next, something was loose in the night.

The grey wolf lay on the dirt floor, panting in the aftermath of almost unendurable pain. But now he lived in the moment, and the memory of agony did not remain in his mind. He heaved himself to his feet, feeling renewed strength flowing through his body. Power far greater than his feeble human form, and a fierce joy at the prospect of the hunt.

This time there was in his nostrils the smell of one particular human being. Not a tiny child this time, and therefore a little less tempting. He shook his head, puzzled. Why should he scent this one, when he knew that there were far richer pickings in the shacks and hovels where he had preyed before?

Keeping to the shadows – not a difficult task – he crept swiftly on the trail, an imperative that tugged at him with strange urgency. He could taste his quarry, and it knew nothing of his

pursuit, which was the first thrill of the hunt. When it sensed him
and knew the first small stirrings of fear, that was the second joy
of the hunt. And the third was the kill, the taste of its terror that
sweetened the meat. Yet there was that about this prey which
seemed to promise more than soft small children. Some spice,
some savour. Something he did not understand.

Impelled by this odd compulsion as much as by the need to
feed, he padded along a path he discerned as easily as a man
would a broad road; and if anyone sensed his passage it caused
them no more than a momentary unease.

Zé, his senses completely overloaded, was immersed in a micro-
cosm of India's vastness, drinking in sights and sounds and smells
the like of which he had never imagined. He had just eaten some
pastries, stuffed with mind-blowingly-hot spiced vegetables, that
he'd bought from a hawker, and was now sucking in breaths of
air in an attempt to cool his mouth. He paused to watch a snake-
charmer, a lithe brown boy of about his own age who was playing
his pipe to the swaying hooded head of an enormous cobra. The
spectacle markings stood out clearly on the reptile's back, and Zé
watched its motion, as fascinated by the snake as the cobra itself
was by the music.

Close by, another boy was trying to interest passers-by in a
somnolent python that was looped hugely round his shoulders.
He had hold of it just behind the head, and was lunging at people
with it, a manic grin on his face, laughing uproariously if they
flinched back and capering ponderously under the snake's
weight.

This scene was lit by a sputtering fire that cast shadows at
strange angles when the flames spurted and sparked, and Zé
abruptly realized, with a start of guilt and alarm, how dark it had
grown. Oh! he was going to be in hot water. He stared round the
crowd in sudden apprehension at the inevitability of punishment.
Seeing a gap in the direction in which he thought the waterfront
lay, he headed for it purposefully, nimbly dodging the boy with
the python.

Ten minutes later he halted, panting heavily, a stitch stinging
his side, thoroughly and comprehensively lost.

And then, behind him, in the darkness, something growled.

Da Silva's scalp prickled. *What is this, another new sense?* he wondered sourly. He considered unsheathing his long knife, but decided against it. It would be too conspicuous. Instead he fingered the revolver in his pocket, and wondered briefly about silver bullets. *Well, I'll just have to rely on virtue, won't I?* he thought, with a mirthless grin that made him look more than a little wolfish himself.

It was not just a tingle of unease. All his nerve endings felt raw and exposed. And his whole back was as taut as rigging in a high wind. Sweat trickled into his eye and he flicked it away automatically with a finger, scanning the crowd of living and dead with every sense he could muster. Sight was less important in the gathering dusk than his awareness of ghosts and this new sensitivity to . . . something evil in the night.

Rounding a corner, he found himself abruptly in another world altogether, and cursed at the realization. He had stepped out of the populous town into its noisome underbelly, stinking mud underfoot, noxious drifts of garbage to either side, uncertainly lit by fires here and there. The stench made him gag.

Da Silva took out his revolver and cocked it, holding it in his right hand. He was left-handed, but finding a target was easier this way round since he had lost his left eye. Besides, it kept his other hand free should he want to draw his knife. And that, he thought, turning his head to look at his surroundings, was a distinct possibility. At times like these it was a distinct disadvantage to have no sight at all on one side. Sweat crawled in his hair and ran down his sides. He felt his heart pounding. In fact, he could *hear* his heart pounding, and damned loud it sounded, too. Raising the gun, he stepped cautiously forward.

The scent of the quarry was very strong now, so powerful that it quite overwhelmed everything else. Saliva surged into his mouth in anticipation, and he loped along, tasting the prey's fear, feeling no need to hide in shadows any more.

Close now, so close – and then, just as he was on the point of springing, something else intruded. An alien sense, like a knife-blade in his brain, and his senses splintered: *sight*, or the memory of it, spilled into his mind, putting him off. And he remembered.

He knew this prey – this *boy*. It – *he* – was his friend. He could not kill it. But it was not, he suddenly became aware, what he had really been seeking: it was merely an echo of it. His real quarry was – *there*.

Disbelief almost stopped Da Silva in his tracks, disbelief and dismay. What in the name of Christ and all the saints was Zé doing here? But he saw his son standing in the dingy, fire-lit alley, and he saw the wolf at the same time. And it saw him.

He sensed, rather than saw, its muscles bunched to pounce, and raised the gun. As he did so a voice he almost recognised shouted indistinctly, 'Leaf'im, ski'-er!'

'I can't,' he said. 'That's my son.' And he fired.

His shot caught the wolf in mid-spring, right in the centre of the chest, but the beast's momentum propelled it forward almost unchecked by the force of the bullet to smash into him. They crashed to the ground together with an impact that drove the breath from his lungs and the gun from his hand – he swore as he heard it skitter off in the darkness – and then the wolf's wide, fanged, stinking, snarling jaws were an inch from his face.

Da Silva stuffed his right arm in the beast's maw while he fought to unsheathe his knife from underneath his body. Fangs slid into his forearm like hot knives into butter and he hissed through his teeth at the pain, and then something knocked the creature off him. He felt his flesh tear as the beast relinquished its grip, and heard Zé shout something.

Gasping for breath, Da Silva whipped out his knife as he lurched to his feet, to see another wolf battling with the first one. This beast was much larger, and had reddish fur. Its teeth were in the grey wolf's throat.

Zé grabbed his hand and pressed the revolver back into it. 'It's got a silver bullet in it,' he whispered, wide-eyed with fright.

The captain shot him a glance that was both astonished and relieved as well as threatening retribution to come, and took hold of the weapon, pushing Zé behind him. Blood running down his arm made the grip slippery, but he brought the gun up, only to shrug helplessly at the growling, snapping mass of fur that was the two battling wolves.

A moment later, the bigger animal's strength and size told, and the grey wolf was pinned to the ground beneath it.

'Shoo' i', ca'-n,' the red wolf panted, barely intelligible. Its mouth had not been designed to frame human words.

'Harris,' said Da Silva, and put the gun to the grey wolf's head. 'I'll need to talk to you later,' he added as he pulled the trigger.

The recoil jarred his bitten arm painfully, but the smaller beast spasmed in death, blood and bone and brain matter spurting from the exit wound. Zé made a small sound of disgust, and the red wolf stepped back, its eyes on Da Silva, who nodded once, with a slight smile. Then it turned and padded away into the shadows.

'Look!' said Zé. The dead wolf that lay on the ground seemed to shiver, and its outline blurred. Its body jerked and twitched, as if things were moving under the skin. Which was exactly the case, Da Silva realized, sheathing his knife. The grey fur seemed to fade into the flesh, the muzzle of the face shrank, the shape of the skull changed as if an unseen hand were remoulding it like clay, and a naked boy lay there with a gunshot wound in his head.

'Mother of God,' said Da Silva, slipping the gun back into his pocket. He squatted down to look for the bullet, gritting his teeth at the pain eating his arm.

'It's Vik,' Zé breathed in a mixture of wonder and horror. Then he turned away and abruptly lost the pastries he'd eaten earlier. Da Silva found the bullet and straightened, pressing his bleeding arm against his ribs.

'Come on,' he said, putting his other arm round his son's shoulders and giving him a rough hug. 'Let's get out of here.'

When they got back to the *Isabella* Zé, somewhat to his surprise, did not get the anticipated hiding, and he thanked the sailor from Providence for that.

CHRISTOPHER FOWLER

Crocodile Lady

CHRISTOPHER FOWLER'S SHORT FICTION is collected in *City Jitters, The Bureau of Lost Souls, Flesh Wounds, Sharper Knives, Personal Demons, Uncut, The Devil in Me* and *Night Nerves*. His short story 'Wageslaves' won the 1998 British Fantasy Award, 'The Master Builder' became a CBS-TV movie starring Tippi Hedren, while an adaptation of 'Left-Hand Drive' won Best British Short Film.

Fowler's novels include *Roofworld, Rune, Red Bride, Darkest Day, Spanky, Psychoville, Disturbia, Soho Black, Calabash, Full Dark House*, and the recently completed *Plastic*, about a shopaholic housewife trapped in a blacked-out building. He also scripted the 1997 graphic novel *Menz Insana*, illustrated by John Bolton, and has written a book about the cinema, *Electric Darkness*.

'I first had the idea for this story in 1979,' explains Fowler. 'Back then it was called "Red Rovers", referring to the all-day tickets you could buy to ride the buses. I always wanted to write a story about a schoolteacher losing a pupil, which must be the ultimate nightmare – or dream – of many a teacher. Then I remembered that the author Joanne Harris used to be a French teacher, so I talked to her about the problems of controlling classes, and she gave me plenty of observational tips. I'm also getting into training for when I eventually do my Underworld London book.'

I: Finchley Road to Swiss Cottage

L ondon has the oldest underground railway system in the
  world. Construction began in 1863 and was completed in
1884. Much later it was electrified, and since then has been
periodically modified. A great many of the original stations have
been abandoned, renamed or resited. A partial list of these would
include Aldwych, British Museum, Brompton Road, York Road,
St Mary's, Down Street, Marlborough Road, South Kentish
Town, King William Street, North End and City Road. In many
cases the maroon-tiled ticket halls remain, and so do the railway
platforms. Even now, some of these tunnels are adorned with
faded wartime signs and posters. Crusted with dry melanic silt
produced by decades of still air, the walls boom softly as trains
pass in nearby tunnels, but the stations themselves no longer have
access from the streets above, and are only visited by scuttling
brown mice. If you look hard, though, you can glimpse the past.
For example, the eerie green and cream platform of the old Mark
Lane station can be spotted from passing trains to the immediate
west of the present Tower Hill Station.

'You know what gets me through the day? Hatred. I hate the little
bastards. Each and every one of them. Most of the time I wish
they would all just disappear.' Deborah fixed me with a cool
stare. 'Yeah, I know it's not the best attitude for a teacher to have,
but when you know them as well as I do . . .'

'I think I do,' I replied.

'Oh? I thought this work was new to you. Being your first day
and all.'

'Not new, no.'

'My boyfriend just decided he wants us to have kids. He never
liked them before. When he was made redundant he started
picking me up from school in the afternoons, and saw them
running around my legs in their boots and rain-macs asking
endless questions, and suddenly he thought they were cute and
wanted to have a baby, just when I was thinking of having my
tubes tied. I don't want to bring my work home with me. We
still haven't sorted it out. It's going to ruin our relationship. Hey,
hey.' Deborah broke off to shout at a boy who was trying to
climb over the barrier. 'Get back down there and wait for the

man to open the gate.' She turned back to me. 'Christ, I could use a cigarette. Cover for me when we get there. I'll sneak a couple in while they're baiting the monkeys, that's what all the other teachers do.'

Good teachers are like good nurses. They notice things ordinary people miss. Ask a nurse how much wine she has left in her glass and she'll be able to tell you the exact amount, because for her the measurement of liquids is a matter of occupational observation. The same with teachers. I can tell the age of any child to within six months because I've been around them so much. Then I got married, and I wasn't around them any more.

But old habits die hard. You watch children constantly, even when you think you're not, and the reflex continues to operate even in civilian life. You bump into pupils in the supermarket. 'Hello, Miss, we didn't know you ate food.' They don't quite say that, but you know it's what they're thinking.

If there's one thing I know it's how children think. That was why I noticed there was something wrong at Baker Street. My senses had been caught off guard because of the tunnels. Actually, I sensed something even before then, as early as our arrival at Finchley Road Tube station. I should have acted on my instincts then.

God knows, I was nervous enough to begin with. It was the first day of my first week back at work after twelve long years, and I hadn't expected to have responsibility thrust at me like this, but the school was understaffed, teachers were off sick and the headmaster needed all the help he could get. The last time I had worked in the education system, the other teachers around me were of roughly the same age. Now I was old enough to be a mother to most of them, and a grand-mother to their charges. I wouldn't have returned to Invicta Primary at all if my husband hadn't died. I wasn't surprised when the bank warned me that there would be no money. Peter wasn't exactly a rainy-day hoarder. I needed to earn, and have something to keep my mind occupied. Teaching was the only skill I was sure I still possessed.

Which was how I ended up shepherding twenty-seven eight-year-old boys and girls on a trip to the London Zoological Gardens, together with another teacher, Deborah, a girl with a tired young face and a hacking smoker's cough.

I hadn't been happy about handling the excursion on my first day back, especially when I heard that it involved going on the Tube. I forced myself not to think about it. There were supposed to be three of us but the other teacher was off with flu, and delaying the trip meant dropping it from the term schedule altogether, so the headmaster had decreed that we should go ahead with the original plan. There was nothing unusual in this; the teaching shortage had reached its zenith and I'd been eagerly accepted back into the school where I'd worked before I was married. They put me on a refresher course, mostly to do with computer literacy, but the basic curriculum hadn't changed much. But things were very different from when I was a pupil myself. For a start, nobody walked to the school any more. Parents didn't think it was safe. I find parents exasperating – all teachers do. They're very protective about some things, and yet utterly blind to other, far more obvious problems. If they found out about the short staffed outings, everybody would get it in the neck. The parents had been encouraged to vote against having their children driven around in a coach; it wasn't environmentally friendly. It didn't stop them from turning up at the school gates in people-carriers, though.

Outside the station the sky had lowered into muddy swirls of cloud, and it was starting to rain. Pupils are affected by the weather. They're always disruptive and excitable when it's windy. Rain makes them sluggish and inattentive. (In snow they go mad and you might as well close the school down.) You get an eye for the disruptives and outsiders, and I quickly spotted the ones in this group, straggling along at the rear of the Tube station hall. In classrooms they sit at the back in the corners, especially on the left-hand side, the sneaky, quiet troublemakers. They feel safe because you tend to look to the centre of the class, so they think they're less visible. Kids who sit in the front row are either going to work very hard or fall in love with you. But the ones at the rear are the ones to watch, especially when you're turning back towards the blackboard.

There were four of them, a pair of hunched, whispering girls as close as Siamese twins, a cheeky ginger-haired noisebox with his hands in everything, and a skinny, melancholy little boy wearing his older brother's jacket. This last one had a shaved head, and the painful-looking nicks in it told me that his hair was cut at home to save money. He kept his shoulders hunched and his gaze on the ground at his feet, braced as though he was half-expecting something to fall on him. A pupil who hasn't done his homework will automatically look down at the desk when you ask the class a question about it, so that only the top of his head is visible (this being based on the 'If I can't see her, she can't see me' theory). If he is sitting in the back row, however, he will stare into your eyes with an earnest expression. This boy never looked up. Downcast eyes can hide a more personal guilt. Some children are born to be bullied. They seem marked for bad luck. Usually they have good reason to adopt such defensive body language. Contrary to what parents think, there's not a whole lot you can do about it.

'What's his name?' I asked.

'Oh, that's Connor, he'll give you no trouble. Never says a word. I forget he's here sometimes.' *I bet you do*, I thought. *You never notice him because he doesn't want you to.*

'Everybody hold up their right hand,' I called. It's easier to count hands than heads when they're standing up, but still they'll try to trick you. Some kids will hold up both hands, others won't raise any. I had lowered my voice to speak to them; you have to speak an octave lower than your normal register if you want to impose discipline. Squeaky high voices, however loud, don't get results. They're a sign of weakness, indicating potential teacher hysteria. Children can scent deficiencies in teachers like sharks smell blood.

'Miss, I'm left-handed.' The ginger boy mimed limb-failure; I mentally transferred him from 'disruptive' to 'class clown'. They're exuberant but harmless, and usually sit in the middle of the back row.

'I want to see everybody's hand, now.' *Sixteen*, and the four at the rear of the ticket hall. 'Keep right under cover, out of the rain. You at the back, tuck in, let those people get past.' *Seventeen*, the clown, *eighteen*, *nineteen*, the Siamese twins, *twenty*, the sad boy. 'We're going to go through the barrier together in a group, so everybody stay very, very close.' I noticed Deborah studying me as I marshalled the children. There was disapproval in her look. She appeared about to speak, then held herself in check. *I'm doing something wrong*, I thought, alarmed. But the entry gate was being opened by the station guard, and I had to push the sensation aside.

Getting our charges onto the escalator and making them stand on the right was an art in itself. Timson, the class clown, was determined to prove he could remount the stairs and keep pace with passengers travelling in the opposite direction. An astonishingly pretty black girl had decided to slide down on the rubber handrail.

'We step off at the end,' I warned. 'Don't jump, that's how accidents happen.' My voice had rediscovered its sharp old timbre, but now there was less confidence behind it. London had changed while I had been away, and was barely recognizable to me now. There were so many tourists. Even at half-past ten on a wintry Monday morning, Finchley Road Tube station was crowded with teenagers in wet nylon coats, hoods and backpacks, some old ladies on a shopping trip, some puzzled Japanese businessmen, a lost-looking man in an old-fashioned navy-blue raincoat. Deborah exuded an air of weary lassitude that suggested she wouldn't be too bothered if the kids got carried down to the platform and were swept onto the rails like lemmings going over a cliff.

'Stay away from the edge,' I called, flapping my arms at them. 'Move back against the wall to let people past.' I saw the irritation in commuters' faces as they eyed the bubbling, chattering queue. Londoners don't like children. 'We're going to be getting on the next train, but we must wait until it has stopped and its doors are open before we move forward. I want you to form a crocodile.'

The children looked up at me blankly. 'A crocodile shape, two, two, two, two, all the way along,' I explained, chopping in their direction with the edges of my palms.

Deborah gave me a wry smile. 'I don't think anyone's ever told them to do that before,' she explained.

'Then how do you get them to stay in lines?' I asked.

'Oh, we don't, they just surge around. They never do what they're told. You can't do anything with them. The trouble with children is they're not, are they? Not children. Just grabby little adults.'

No, I thought, *you're so wrong*. But I elected not to speak. I looked back at the children gamely organizing themselves into two wobbly columns. 'They're not doing so badly.'

Deborah wasn't interested. She turned away to watch the train arriving. 'Crocodile, crocodile,' the kids were chanting, making snappy-jawed movements to each other. The carriages of the train appeared to be already half-full. I had expected them to be almost empty. As the doors opened, we herded the children forward. I kept my eyes on the pairs at the back, feeding them in between my outstretched arms as though I was guiding unruly sheep into a pen. I tried not to think about the entrance to the tunnel, and the stifling, crushing darkness beyond it.

'Miss, Raj has fallen over.' I looked down to find a minuscule Indian child bouncing up from his knees with a grin on his face. I noted that no damage had been done, then lifted his hands, scuffed them clean and wrapped them around the nearest carriage pole. 'Hang on,' I instructed as the doors closed.

'Miss, how many stops is it?' asked a little girl at my side.

'We go to Swiss Cottage, then St John's Wood, then Baker Street, then we change from the Jubilee Line to the Bakerloo Line and go one stop to Regent's Park.'

'Miss, is there a real cottage in Swiss Cottage?'

'Miss, are we going to Switzerland?'

'Miss, can you ski in Swiss Cottage?'

'Miss, are we going skiing?'

'We're going skiing! We're going skiing!'

The train pulled away and everyone screamed. For a moment I sympathized with Deborah. I looked out of the window as the platform vanished. When I married Peter we moved out to Amersham, at the end of the Metropolitan line, and stopped coming into central London. Peter was a lecturer. I was due for promotion at the school. In time I could have become the headmistress, but Peter didn't want me to work and that was that, so I had to give up my job and keep house for him. A year later, I discovered that I couldn't have children. Suddenly I began to miss my classroom very badly.

'Miss, make him get off me.' Timson was sitting on top of a girl who had grabbed a seat. Without thinking, I lifted him off by his jacket collar.

'I wouldn't do that if I were you,' said Deborah. 'They'll have you up before the Court of Human Rights for maltreatment. Best not to touch them at all.' She swung to the other side of the central pole and leaned closer. 'How long has it been since you last taught?'

'Twelve years.'

'You've been away a long time.' It sounded suspiciously like a criticism. 'Well, we don't manhandle them any more. EEC ruling.' Deborah peered out of the window. 'Swiss Cottage coming up, watch out.'

II: Swiss Cottage to St John's Wood

Many projects to build new Tube lines were abandoned due to spiralling costs and sheer impracticability. An unfinished station tunnel at South Kensington served as a signalling school in the 1930s, and was later equipped to record delayed-action bombs falling into the Thames that might damage the underwater Tube tunnels. The Northern Heights project to extend the Northern Line to Alexandra Palace was halted by the Blitz. After this, the government built a number of deep-level air-raid shelters connected to existing Tube stations, several of which were so far underground that they were leased after the war as secure archives. As late as the 1970s, many pedestrian Tube subways still looked like passageways between bank vaults. Vast riveted doors could be used to seal off tunnels in the event of fire or flood. There was a subterranean acridity in the air. You saw the light rounding the dark bend ahead, heard the pinging of the albescent lines, perhaps glimpsed something long sealed away. Not all of the system has changed. Even now there are tunnels that lead nowhere, and platforms where only ghosts of the past wait for trains placed permanently out of service.

Trying to make sure that nobody got off when the doors opened would have been easier if the children had been wearing school uniforms. But their casual clothes blended into a morass of bright colours, and I had to rely on Deborah keeping the head-count from her side of the carriage. In my earlier days at Invicta the pupils wore regulation navy blue with a single yellow stripe, and the only symbol of non-conformity you saw – apart from the standard array of faddish haircuts – was the arrangement of their socks, pulled down or the wrong colour, small victories for little rebels.

I avoided thinking about the brick and soil pressing down on us, but was perspiring freely by now. I concentrated on the children, and had counted to fifteen when half a dozen jolly American matrons piled into the car, making it hard to finish the tally. I moved as many of the children as I could to one side, indicating that they should stay in crocodile formation. I instinctively knew that most of them were present, but I couldn't see the sad little boy. 'Connor,' I called, 'make yourself known please.' An elliptical head popped out between two huge tourists. So unsmiling. I wondered if he had a nemesis, someone in the class who was making his life hell. Bullies are often small and aggressive because of their height. They go for the bigger, softer boys to enhance their reputation, and they're often popular with games teachers because of their bravado. There's not much I don't know about bullies. I was married to one for twelve years.

'I've got these new assignment books in my bag,' said Deborah, relooping her hair through her scrunchie and checking her reflection in the glass. 'Some government psychology group wants to test out a theory about how kids look at animals. More bloody paperwork. It's not rocket science, is it, the little sods just see it as a day off and a chance to piss about.'

'You may be right,' I admitted. 'But children are shaped far more by their external environment than anyone cares to admit.'

'How's that, then?'

'They recently carried out an experiment in a New York public school,' I explained, 'placing well-behaved kids and those with a history of disruption in two different teaching areas, one clean and bright, the other poorly lit and untidy. They found that children automatically misbehaved in surroundings of chaos – not just the troubled children but all of them, equally.'

Deborah looked at me oddly, swaying with the movement of the train. Grey cables looped past the windows like stone garlands, or immense spider webs. 'You don't miss much, do you? Is that how you knew Connor was hiding behind those women?'

'No, that's just instinct. But I've been reading a bit about behavioural science. It's very interesting.' I didn't tell her that before I was married I had been a teacher for nearly fourteen years. The only thing I didn't know about children was what it was like to have one.

'Well, I'm sorry, I know it's a vocation with some people, but not me. It's just a job. God, I'm dying for a fag.' She hiked her bag further up her shoulder. 'Didn't your old man want you to work, then?'

'Not really. But I would have come back earlier. Only . . .' I felt uncomfortable talking to this young woman in such a crowded place, knowing that I could be overheard.

'Only what?'

'After I'd been at home for a while, I found I had trouble going out.'

'Agoraphobia?'

'Not really. More like a loss of balance. A density of people. Disorienting architecture, shopping malls, exhibition halls, things like that.'

'I thought you didn't look very comfortable back there on the platform. The Tube gets so crowded now.'

'With the Tube it's different. It's not the crowds, it's the tunnels. The shapes they make. Circles. Spirals. The converging lines. Perhaps I've become allergic to buildings.' Deborah wasn't listening, she was looking out of the window and unwrapping a piece of gum. Just as well, I thought. I didn't want her to get the impression that I wasn't up to the job. But I could feel the pressure in the air, the scented heat of the passengers, the proximity of the curving walls. An over-sensitivity to public surroundings, that was what the doctor called it. I could tell what he was thinking: *Oh God, another stir-crazy housewife.* He had started writing out a prescription while I was still telling him how I felt.

'We're coming into Baker Street. Christ, not again. There must have been delays earlier.' Through the windows I could see a solid wall of tourists waiting to board. We slowed to a halt and the doors opened.

III: Baker Street to Regent's Park

The world's first tube railway, the Tower Subway, was opened in 1870, and ran between the banks of the Thames. The car was only ten feet long and five feet wide, and had no windows. This claustrophobic steel cylinder was an early materialization of a peculiar modern phenomenon: the idea that great discomfort could be endured for the purpose of efficiency, the desire to reach

another place with greater speed. An appropriately satanic con-
traption for a nation of iron, steam and smoke.

'This is where we change,' called Deborah. 'Right, off, the lot of
you.'

'Can you see them all?' I asked.

'Are you kidding? I bet you there's something going on somewhere as well, all these people, some kind of festival.' The adults
on the platform were pushing their way into the carriage before
we could alight. Suddenly we were being surrounded by red,
white and green-striped nylon backpacks. Everyone was speaking
Italian. Some girls began shrieking with laughter and shoving
against each other. Ignoring the building dizziness behind my
eyes, I pushed back against the door, ushering children out,
checking the interior of the carriage, trying to count heads.

'Deborah, keep them together on the platform, I'll see if there
are any more.' I could see that she resented being told what to do,
but she sullenly herded the class together. The guard looked out
and closed the train doors, but I held mine back.

'How many?' I called.

'It's fine, they're all here. Come on, you'll get left behind.'

I pushed my way through the children as Deborah started off
toward the Bakerloo line. 'You worry too much,' she called over
her shoulder. 'I've done this trip loads of times, it's easy once
you're used to it.'

'Wait, I think we should do another head check—' But she had
forged ahead with the children scudding around her, chattering,
shouting, alert and alive to everything. I glanced back anxiously,
trying to recall all of their faces.

I saw him then, but of course I didn't realize.

Four minutes before the next train calling at Regent's Park. I
moved swiftly around them, corralling and counting. Deborah
was bent over, listening to one of the girls. The twins were against
the wall, searching for something in their bags. Timson, the class
clown, was noisily jumping back and forth, violently swinging his
arms. I couldn't find him. Couldn't find Connor. Perhaps he
didn't want me to, like he didn't want Deborah to notice.

'Let's see you form a crocodile again,' I said, keeping my voice
low and calm.

'Miss, will we see crocodiles at the zoo?'

'Miss, are you the crocodile lady?'

Some of the children at the back moved forward, so I had to start the count over. I knew right then. *Nineteen*. One short. No Connor. 'He's gone,' I said. 'He's gone.'

'He can't have gone,' said Deborah, shoving her hair out of her eyes. She was clearly exasperated with me now. 'He tends to lag behind.'

'I saw him on the train.'

'You mean he didn't get off? You saw everyone off.'

'I thought I did.' It was getting difficult to keep the panic out of my voice. 'There was – something odd.'

'What are you talking about?' She turned around sharply. '*Who* is pulling my bag?' I saw that the children were listening to us. They miss very little, it's just that they often decide not to act on what they see or hear. I thought back, and recalled the old-fashioned navy-blue raincoat. *An oversensitivity to everyday surroundings*. He had been following the children since Finchley Road. I had seen him in the crowd, standing slightly too close to them, listening to their laughter, watching out for the lonely ones, the quiet ones. Something had registered in me even then, but I had not acted upon my instincts. I tried to recall the interior of the carriage. Had he been on the train? I couldn't—

'He's probably not lost, just lagging behind.'

'Then where is he?'

'We'll get him back, they don't go missing for long. I promise you, he'll turn up any second. It's quite impossible to lose a small child down here, unfortunately. Imagine if we did. We'd have a bugger of a job covering it up.' Deborah's throaty laugh turned into a cough. 'Have to get all the kids to lie themselves blue in the face, pretend that none of us saw him come to school today.'

'I'm going to look.'

'Oh, for Christ's sake.'

'Suppose something really has happened?'

'Well, what am I supposed to do?'

'Get the children onto the next train. I'll find Connor and bring him back. I'll meet you at the zoo. By the statue of Guy the gorilla.'

'You can't just go off! You said yourself—'

'I have to, I know what to look for.'

'We should go and tell the station guards, get someone in authority.'

'There isn't time.'

'This isn't your decision to make, you know.'

'It's my responsibility.'

'Why did you come back?'

Deborah's question threw me for a second. 'The children.'

'This isn't your world now,' she said furiously. 'You had your turn. Couldn't you let someone else have theirs?'

'I was a damned good teacher.' I studied her eyes, trying to see if she understood. 'I didn't have my turn.'

There was no more time to argue with her. I turned and pushed back through the passengers surging up from the platform. I caught the look of angry confusion on Deborah's face, as though this was something I had concocted deliberately to wreck her schedule. Then I made my way back to the platform.

I was carrying a mobile phone, but down here, of course, it was useless. Connor was bright and suspicious; he wouldn't go quietly without a reason. I tried to imagine what I would do if I wanted to get a child that wasn't mine out of the station with the minimum of fuss. I'd keep him occupied, find a way to stop him from asking questions. Heavier crowds meant more policing, more station staff, but it would be safer to stay lost among so many warm bodies. He'd either try to leave the station at once, and run the risk of me persuading the guards to keep watch at the escalator exits, or he'd travel to another line and leave by a different station. Suddenly I knew what he intended to do – but not where he intended to do it.

IV: King's Cross to Euston

There exists a strange photograph of Hammersmith Grove Road station taken four years after the service there ceased operation. It shows a curving platform of transverse wooden boards, and, facing each other, a pair of ornate deserted waiting rooms. The platform beyond this point fades away into the mist of a winter dusk. There is nothing human in the picture, no sign of life at all. It is as though the station existed at the edge of the world, or at the end of time.

I tried to remember what I had noticed about Connor. There are things you automatically know just by looking at your pupils. You can tell a lot from the bags they carry. Big sports holdalls mean messy work and disorganization; the kid is probably carrying his books around all the time instead of keeping them in his locker, either because he doesn't remember his timetable or because he is using the locker to store cigarettes and contraband. A smart briefcase usually indicates an anal pupil with fussy parents. Graffiti and stickers on a knapsack mean that someone is trying to be a rebel. Connor had a cheap plastic bag, the kind they sell at high-street stores running sales all year round.

I pushed on through the platforms, checking arrival times on the indicator boards, searching the blank faces of passengers, trying not to think about the penumbral tunnels beyond. For a moment I caught sight of the silver rails curving away to the platform's tiled maw, and a fresh wave of nausea overcame me. I forced myself to think about the children.

You can usually trace the person who has graffitied their desk because you have a ready-made sample of their handwriting, and most kids are lousy at disguising their identities. Wooden pencil boxes get used by quiet creative types. Metal tins with cartoon characters are for extroverts. Children who use psychedelic holders covered in graffiti usually think they're streetwise, but they're not.

You always used to be able to tell the ones who smoked because blazers were made of a peculiar wool-blend that trapped the smell of cigarettes. Now everyone's different. Spots around a child's nose and mouth often indicate a glue-sniffer, but now so many have spots from bad diets, from stress, from neglect. Some children never—

He was standing just a few yards away.

The navy-blue raincoat was gabardine, like a fifties school-child's regulation school coat, but in an adult size. Below this were black trousers with creases and turn-ups, freshly polished Oxford toecap shoes. His hair was slicked smartly back, trimmed in classic short-back-and-sides fashion by a traditional barber who had tapered the hair at the nape and used an open razor on the neck. You always notice the haircuts.

He was holding the boy's hand. He turned his head and looked through me, scanning the platform. The air caught in my lungs as he brought his focus back to me, and matched my features in his memory. His deep-set eyes were framed by rimless spectacles that removed any readable emotion from his face. He held my gaze defiantly. We stood frozen on the concourse, staring at each other as the other passengers surged around us, and as Connor's head slowly turned to follow his new friend's sight line, I saw that this man was exhilarated by the capture of his quarry, just as I knew that his initial elation would turn by degrees to sadness and then to anger, as deep and dark as the tunnels themselves.

The tension between their hands grew tighter. He began to move away, pulling the boy. I looked for someone to call to, searching faces to find anyone who might help, but found indifference as powerful as any enemy. Dull eyes reflected the platform lights, slack flesh settled on heavy bodies, exuding sour breath, and suddenly man and boy were moving fast, and I was pushing my way through an army of statues as I tried to keep the pair of them in my sight.

I heard the train before I saw it arriving at the end of the pedestrian causeway between us, the billow of heavy air resonating in the tunnel like a depth charge. I felt the pressure change in my ears and saw them move more quickly now. For a moment I thought he was going to push the boy beneath the wheels, but I knew he had barely begun with Connor yet.

I caught the doors just as they closed. Connor and the man had made it to the next carriage, and were standing between teenaged tourists, only becoming visible as the tunnel curved and the carriage swung into view, briefly aligning the windows. We remained in stasis, quarry, hunter and pursuer, as the train thundered on. My heart tightened as the driver applied the brakes and we began to slow down. Ahead, the silver lines twisted sinuously toward King's Cross, and another wall of bodies flashed into view.

As the doors opened, fresh swells of passengers surged from carriage to platform and platform to carriage, shifting and churning so much that I was almost lifted from my feet. I kept my eyes focused on the man and the boy even though it meant stumbling against the human tide. Still he did not run, but moved firmly forward in a brisk walk, never slowing or stopping to look back. The carriage speakers were still barking inanely about delays and escalators. I could find no voice of my own that

would rise above them, no power that would impede their escape.
Wherever they went, I could only follow.

V: Euston to Camden Town

*Once, on the other side of that century of devastating change,
Oscar Wilde could have taken the Tube to West End. The
Underground was built before the invention of the telephone,
before the invention of the fountain pen. Once, the platform walls
were lined with advertisements for Bovril, Emu, Wrights Coal
Tar Soap, for the Quantock Sanitary Laundry, Peckham, and the
Blue Hall Cinema, Edgware Road, for Virol, Camp Coffee and
Lifebuoy, for Foster Clark's Soups and Cream Custards, and
Eastman's Dyeing & Cleaning. These were replaced by pleas to
Make Do And Mend, to remember that Loose Lips Sink Ships,
that Walls Have Ears, that Coughs And Sneezes Spread Diseases.
Urgent directional markers guided the way to bomb shelters,
where huddled families and terrified eyes watched and flinched
with each thunderous impact that shook and split the tiles above
their heads.*

On through the tunnels and passages, miles of stained cream tiles,
over the bridges that linked the lines. I watched the navy-blue
raincoat shifting from side to side until I could see nothing else,
my own fears forgotten, my fury less latent than his, building with
the passing crush of lives. Onto another section of the Northern
Line, the so-called Misery Line, but now the battered decadence
of its maroon rolling stock had been replaced with livery of dull
graffiti-scrubbed silver, falsely modern, just ordinary. The maroon trains had matched the outside tiles of the stations, just as the
traffic signs of London were once striped black and white. No
such style left now, of course, just ugly-ordinary and invisible-
ordinary. But he was not ordinary, he wanted something he could
not have, something nobody was allowed to take. On through the
gradually thinning populace to another standing train, this one
waiting with its doors open. But they began to close as we reached
them, and we barely made the jump, the three of us, before we
were sealed inside.

What had he told the boy to make him believe? It did not
matter what had been said, only that he had seen the child's

weakness and known which role he had to play: anxious relative, urgent family friend, trusted guide, helpful teacher. To a child like Connor he could be anything as long as he reassured. Boys like Connor longed to reach up toward a strong clasping hand. They needed to believe.

Out onto the platform, weaving through the climbing passengers, across the concourse at Euston and back down where we had come from, toward another northbound train. We had been travelling on the Edgware branch, but it wasn't where he wanted to go. Could he be anxious to catch a High Barnet train for some reason? By now I had deliberately passed several guards without calling out for help, because I felt sure they would only argue and question and hinder, and in the confusion to explain I would lose the boy for ever. My decision was vindicated, because the seconds closed up on us as the High Barnet train slid into the station. By now I had gained pace enough to reach the same carriage, and I stood facing his back, no more than a dozen passengers away. And this time I was foolish enough to call out.

My breathless voice did not carry far. A few people turned to look at me with anxious curiosity. One girl appeared to be on the edge of offering her help, but the man I was pointing to had suddenly vanished from sight, and so had the boy, and suddenly I was just another crazy woman on the Tube, screaming paranoia, accusing innocents.

At Camden Town the doors mercifully opened, releasing the nauseous crush that was closing in on me. I stuck out my head and checked along the platform, but they did not alight. I could not see them. What had happened? Could they have pushed through the connecting door and – God help the child – dropped down onto the track below? They had to be on board, and so I had to stay on. The doors closed once more and we pulled away again into the suffocating darkness.

VI: Kentish Town to South Kentish Town

The tunnels withstood the firestorms above. The tunnels protected. At the heart of the system was the Inner Circle, far from a circle in the Euclidean sense, instead an engineering marvel that navigated the damp earth and ferried its people through the sulphurous tunnels between iron cages, impervious to the world above, immune to harm. Appropriately, the great metal circles that protected workers as they hacked at the clay walls were known as shields. They protected then, and the strength of the system still protects. The tunnels still endure.

He had dropped down to his knees beside the boy, whispering his poisons. I had missed him between the bodies of standing, rocking travellers, but I was ready as the train slowed to a halt at Kentish Town. I was surprised to see that the platform there was completely deserted. Suddenly the landscape had cleared. As he led the boy out I could tell that Connor was now in distress, pulling against the hand that held him, but it was no good; his captor had strength and leverage. No more than five or six other passengers alighted. I called out, but my voice was lost beneath the rumble and squeal of rolling steel. There were no guards. Someone must see us on the closed-circuit cameras, I thought, but how would eyes trained for rowdy teenaged gangs see danger here? There was just a child, a man, and a frightened middle-aged woman.

I glanced back at the platform exit as the train pulled out, wondering how I could stop him if he tried to push past. When I looked back, he and Connor had vanished. He was below on the line, helping the child down, and then they were running, stumbling into the entrance of the tunnel.

We were about to move beyond the boundaries of the city, into a territory of shadows and dreams. As I approached the entrance I saw the silver lines slithering away into amber gloom, then darkness, and a wave of apprehension flushed through me. By dangling my legs over the platform and carefully lowering myself, I managed to slide down into the dust-caked gully. I knew that the raised rail with the ceramic studs was live, and that I would have to stay at the outer edge. I was also sure that the tunnel would reveal alcoves for workers to stand in when trains passed by. In the depth of my fear I was colder and more logical than I had been for years. Perhaps by not calling to the guards, by revealing myself in pursuit, I had in some way brought us here, so that now I was the child's only hope.

The boy was pulling hard against his stiff-legged warden, shouting something upwards, but his voice was distorted by the curving tunnel walls. They slowed to a walk, and I followed.

The man was carrying some kind of torch; he had been to this place before, and had prepared himself accordingly. My eyes followed the dipping beam until we reached a division in the tunnel wall. He veered off sharply and began to pick a path through what appeared to be a disused section of the line. Somewhere in the distance a train rattled and reverberated in its concrete causeway. My feet were hurting, and I had scraped the back of my leg on the edge of the platform. I could feel a thin hot trickle of blood behind my knee. The thick brown air smelled of dust and desiccation, like the old newspapers you find under floorboards. It pressed against my lungs, so that my breath could only be reached in shallow catches. Ahead, the torch beam shifted and hopped. He had climbed a platform and pulled the boy up after him.

As I came closer, his beam illuminated a damaged soot-grey sign: SOUTH KENTISH TOWN. The station had been closed for almost eighty years. What remained had been preserved by the dry warm air. The platform walls were still lined to a height of four feet with dark green tiles arranged in column patterns. Every movement Connor made could be heard clearly here. His shoes scuffed on the litter-strewn stone as he tried to yank his hand free. He made small mewling noises, like a hungry cat.

Suddenly the torch beam illuminated a section of stairway tiled in cream and dark red. They turned into it. I stopped sharply and listened. He had stopped, too. I moved as quickly and quietly as I could to the stairway entrance.

He was waiting for me at the foot of the stairs, his fingers glowing pink over the lens of the upright torch. Connor was by his side, pressed against the wall. It was then I realized that Connor usually wore glasses – you can usually tell the children who do. I imagined they would be like the ones worn by his captor. Because I was suddenly struck by how very alike they looked, as though the man was the boy seen some years later. I knew then that something terrible had happened here before and could so easily happen again, that this damaged creature meant harm because he had been harmed himself, because he was fighting to recapture something pure, and that he knew it could never again be. He wanted his schooldays back but the past was denied to him, and he thought he could recapture the sensations of childhood by taking someone else's.

I would not let the boy have it stolen from him. Innocence is not lost; it is taken.

'You can't have him,' I said, keeping my voice as clear and rational as I could. I had always known how to keep my fear from showing. It is one of the first things you learn as a teacher. He did not move. One hand remained over the torch, the other over the boy's right hand.

'I know you were happy then. But you're not in class any more.' I raised my tone to a punitive level. 'He's not in your year. You belong somewhere different.'

'Whose teacher are you?' He cocked his head on one side to study me, uncurling his fingers from the torch. Light flooded the stairway.

'I might have been yours,' I admitted.

He dropped the boy's hand, and Connor fell to the floor in surprise.

'The past is gone,' I said quietly. 'Lessons are over. I really think you should go now.' For a moment the air was only disturbed by my uneven breath and the sound of water dripping somewhere far above.

He made a small sound, like the one Connor had made earlier, but deeper, more painful. As he approached me I forced myself to stand my ground. It was essential to maintain a sense of authority. I felt sure he was going to hit me, but instead he stopped and studied my face in the beam of the torch, trying to place my features. I have one of those faces; I could be anyone's teacher. Then he lurched out of the stairwell and stumbled away along the platform. With my heart hammering, I held Connor to me until the sound of the man was lost in the labyrinth behind us.

'You're the Crocodile Lady,' said Connor, looking up at me.

'I think I am,' I agreed, wiping a smudge from his forehead.

Unable to face the tunnels again, I climbed the stairs with Connor until we reached a door, and I hammered on it until someone unlocked the damned thing. It was opened by a surprised Asian girl dressed only in a towel. We left the building via the basement of the Omega Sauna, Kentish Town Road, which still uses the station's old spiral staircase as part of its design. London has so many secrets.

The police think they know who he is now, but I'm not sure that they'll ever catch him. He's as lost to them as he is to everyone else. Despite his crimes – and they have uncovered quite a few – something inside me felt sorry for him, and sorry for the part he'd lost so violently that it had driven him to take the same from others. The hardest thing to learn is how to be strong.

Everyone calls me the Crocodile Lady.

RAMSEY CAMPBELL

All for Sale

RAMSEY CAMPBELL HAS BEEN NAMED Grand Master by the World Horror Convention and received a Lifetime Achievement Award from the Horror Writers Association. A film of his novel *Pact of the Fathers* is in development in Spain from director Jaime Balagueró, *The Darkest Part of the Woods* is his latest supernatural novel, and he is currently working on another, *The Overnight*.

Campbell's M.R. Jamesian anthology *Meddling With Ghosts* is published by The British Library, and he has co-edited *Gathering the Bones* with Jack Dann and Dennis Etchison. S.T. Joshi's study *Ramsey Campbell and Modern Horror Fiction* is available from Liverpool University Press, while *Ramsey Campbell, Probably* is a large non-fiction collection from PS Publishing.

'The germ of this tale came from our first stay in Turkey,' remembers the author, 'where one morning our hotel in Kusadasi proved to have been surrounded overnight by a market.

'Another detail dates from the 1980s, when the swarthy proprietor of a large television and video shop on London's Tottenham Court Road where I was browsing did indeed take hold of my tits and declare "You are nice" (much to the outrage of my old editor Nick Austin when I told him over a Greek lunch at the Lord Byron, now defunct, alas). The first draft of the story was written in the mornings of two weeks in August 2001, on the terrace of an apartment in Petra on Lesvos.'

ONCE THEY WERE OUTSIDE THE Mediterranean Nights Barry could hear the girl's every word, starting with 'What were you trying to tell me about a plane?'

'Just I, you know, noticed you on it.'

'As I said if you heard, I saw you.'

'I know. I mean, I did hear, just about.' While he gazed at rather than into her dark moonlit eyes that might be glinting with eagerness for him to risk more, he made himself blurt 'I hoped I'd see you again.'

'Well, now you have.' She raised her small face an inch closer to his and formed her pink lips into a prominent smile he couldn't quite take as an invitation to a kiss. Not long after his silence grew intolerable, unrelieved by the hushing of the waves that failed to distract him from the way the huge blurred scarcely muffled rhythm of the disco seemed determined to keep his heartbeat up to speed, she said 'So you're called Baz.'

'That's only what my friends call me, the guys I was with, I mean. I don't know if you saw them on the plane as well.'

'I told you, I saw you.'

Her gentle emphasis on the last word encouraged him to admit 'I'm Barry really.'

'Hello, Barry really,' she said and held out a hand. 'I'm Janet.'

He wiped his hand on his trousers, but they were as clammy from dancing. Her grasp proved to be cool and firm. 'So are you staying as long as us?' she said, having let go of him.

'Two weeks. It's our first time abroad.'

'There must be worse places to get experience,' she said and caught most of a yawn behind her hand as she stretched, pointing her breasts at him through her short thin black dress. 'Well, I'm danced out. This girl's for bed.'

He could think of plenty of responses, but none he dared utter. He was turning his attention to the jittering of neon on the water when Janet said 'You could walk me back if you liked.'

As her escort, should he take her hand or at least her arm or even slip his around her slim waist? He didn't feel confident enough along the seafront, where the signs of the clubs turned the faces of the noisy crowds outside into lurid unstable carnival masks. 'We're up here,' Janet eventually said.

The narrow crooked street also led uphill to his and Paul's and Derek's apartment. Once the pulsating neon and the throbbing competitive rhythms of the discos fell behind, Janet began resting her fingers on his bare arm at each erratically canted bend. He thought of laying a hand over hers, but suspected that would only make her aware of his feverish heat fuelled by alcohol. He became conscious of tasting of it, and was wondering what he could possibly offer her when she clutched at his wrist. 'What's that?' she whispered.

He'd thought the trestle table propped against the rough white wall of one of the rudimentary houses that constricted the dim street was heaped with refuse until the heap lifted itself on one arm. Apparently the table served as a bed for an undernourished man wearing not even very many rags. He clawed his long hair aside to display a face rather too close to the skull beneath and thrust out the other hand. 'He just wants money,' Barry guessed aloud, and in case Janet assumed that was intended as a cue to her, declared 'I've got some.'

He didn't think he had much. Bony fingers snatched the notes and coins spider-like. At once, too fast for Barry to distinguish how, the man huddled back into resembling waste. 'You didn't have to give him all that,' Janet murmured as they hurried to the next bend. 'You'll be seeing more like him.'

Barry feared she thought he'd been trying to impress her with his generosity, which he supposed he might have been. 'We like to share what we've got, don't we, us Yorkshire folk.'

Before he'd finished speaking he saw that she could think he was making a crude play for her along with emphasizing her trace of an accent more than she might like. Her silence gave his thoughts time to grow hot and arid as the night while he trudged beside her up a steep few hundred yards – indeed, overtook her before she said 'This is as far as I go.'

She was opening her small black spangled handbag outside a door lit by a plastic rectangle that might as well have been a sliver of the moon. 'I'm just up the road,' he told her.

Did that sound like yet another unintentional suggestion? All she said was 'Maybe I'll see you in the market.'

'Which one's that?'

She gazed so long into the depths of her bag that he was starting to feel she thought his ignorance unworthy of an answer when she said 'What are you going to think of me now.'

He had to treat it as a question. 'Well, I know we've only—'

'Denise and San have got the keys. I didn't realize I'd drunk that much. Back we go.'

She was at the first corner before he'd finished saying 'Shall I come with you?'

'No need.'

'I will, though.'

'Suit yourself,' she said and quickened her pace.

He felt virtuous for not abandoning her to pass the man on the table by herself. In fact that stretch was as deserted as the rest of the slippery uneven variously sloping route. The seafront was still crowded, and she had to struggle past a haphazard queue outside the Mediterranean Nights. 'I won't be long,' she told him.

She was. Once he felt he'd waited longer than enough he tried to follow her, but the swarthy doorman who'd been happy to readmit her showed no such enthusiasm on Barry's behalf. Even if he'd had the money, Barry told himself, he wouldn't have paid to get back in. He supposed he could have said that Paul and Derek would vouch for him – that was assuming they weren't in an especially humorous mood – but he couldn't be bothered arguing with the doorman. If Janet's friends had persuaded her to have another drink or two, or she'd met someone else, that had to be fine with him.

He did his best to look content as he tramped back along the seafront, and was trudging uphill before he indulged in muttering to himself. He fell silent as he passed Janet's lodgings, the Summer Breeze Apartments, on the way to swaying around several jagged unlit bends that hindered his arrival at his own quarters. Some amusement was to be derived from coaxing the key to find the lock of the street door and from reeling up the concrete stairs, two steps up, one back down. Further drunken fumbling was involved in admitting himself to the apartment, where most of the contents of his and Paul's and Derek's cases had yet to fight for space in the wardrobe and the bathroom. At the end of an interlude in the latter, more protracted than conclusive, he lurched through the room containing his friends' beds to the couch in the kitchen area. Without too many curses he succeeded in unfolding the couch and, having fallen over and onto it, dragging a sheet across himself.

Perhaps all he could hear in the street below the window were clubbers returning to their apartments, but they sounded more like a stealthy crowd that wasn't about to go away. He was thinking, if no more than that, of making for the balcony to look when the slam of the street door sent Paul's and Derek's voices up from the muted hubbub. Soon his friends fell into their room, switching on lights at random. 'He's here. He's in bed,' Paul announced.

'Thought you'd pulled some babe,' Derek protested.

'She didn't have her key,' Barry roused himself to attempt to pronounce. 'You didn't see her coming back, then.'

'You could have brought her up here as long as you let us know,' Paul said.

'Put a notice on the door or something,' said Derek.

'Next time,' Barry told them, not that he thought there was much of a chance. Still, he could dream, or perhaps he could only sleep. He hadn't the energy to ask what was happening outside. The murmur from the street and the blundering of his friends about the apartment receded, bearing his awareness, which he was happy to relinquish.

Snoring wakened him – at first, only his own. The refrain was taken up by Derek, who was lying on his back, while Paul gave tongue into a pillow. The chorus was by no means equal to the noise from the street. Unable to make sense of it, Barry dragged the floor-length windows apart and groped between them into unwelcome sunlight. Leaning over the rudimentary concrete balustrade, he blinked his vision into focus. The street had disappeared.

Or rather, its surface had. From bend to bend it was hidden by the awnings of market stalls and by the crowd the stalls had drawn. Barry supported himself on his elbows, though the heat of the concrete was only just bearable, until he succeeded in dredging up some thoughts. His mouth was dry and yet oily with reminiscences of alcohol, his skull felt baked too thin, but shouldn't he wander down in case Janet was hoping to encounter him? Mightn't she have waited, not realizing he'd given away the contents of his pocket, for him to rejoin her in the Mediterranean Nights? He picked his way to the bathroom and, having made space for it, drank as much water as he could stomach, then showered and dressed. 'I'll be in the market,' he said, receiving a mumble from one of his friends and an emphatic snore from the other.

In the lobby the owner of the apartments was crammed into a shabby armchair overlooked by a warren of compartments, some lodging keys, behind the reception counter. He wore a flower-bed of a shirt too large even for him, which framed enough chest hair to cover his bald head. He opened his eyes half an inch and used a forearm to wipe his heavily ruled brow as Barry took out his traveller's cheques. 'You want pay?' the owner said.

'Please.'

'How much you pay?'

'No, we paid in England. My friend Derek had to show you the voucher when we checked in, remember.' When the man only scowled at the beads of sweat his tufted forearm had collected, Barry tried to simplify the point. 'The paper said we paid.'

'Now you pay for things go smash. Nothing smash, money back.'

'Derek's in charge of booking and stuff like that. You'll need to speak to him,' Barry said, knowing that with a hangover Derek would be even more combative than usual. 'He's the man in charge.'

'So why I talk to you?'

Barry pointed at the sign beside the pigeonholes:

TRAVVLER'S' CHEKS CACHED.

'It says you give money.'

For a breath that threatened to pop his shirt buttons the man seemed inclined to misunderstand, and then he thrust a ballpoint bandaged with several thicknesses of inky plaster across the counter. 'You put name.'

Barry signed a cheque for a hundred pounds as quickly as possible – the pen felt unpleasantly clammy – and handed over both, together with his passport. After the merest blink at Barry's signature, the owner ran his gaze up and down him between several glances at the photograph. At last he leaned back, heaving his stomach high with his thighs, to unlock a drawer and count out a handful of large grubby notes. 'You pay me nothing,' he complained.

Presumably he meant there was no commission. Barry shoved the notes into his shirt pocket – they felt clammier than the pen had – and was holding out his hand when the man dropped the passport in the drawer. 'What you want give me?' the owner said, leering at the hand.

'I need my passport.'

'I keep now,' the owner said and locked the drawer. 'You want more pay, you come me.'

'I don't think so,' Barry told him, but made for the street. Further argument could wait until Paul and Derek were there to join in – all right, and why not, to support him.

As he opened the door he was overwhelmed by heat that competed with the light for fierceness, by the sullen roar of the fire that was the crowd, by the smell of hot wallets, which were all the table nearest the apartments sold. Its immediate neighbour was devoted to leather goods too. The stalls were packed so close together that once he sidled between them he couldn't see the sign above the door – the Summit Apartments, though they were well short of the top of the hill.

Most of the crowd was making its sluggish way upwards, unlike him. Whenever he glanced about for possible souvenirs or presents, and often when he didn't, stall-holders launched themselves and whatever English they had at him. 'Good price,' they persisted. 'Special for you.' Beyond the corner was a clump of stalls blue with denim, and past that a stretch of trademarks, each of them almost as wide as the T-shirts and other clothes that bore them. Which stalls were likely to appeal to Janet? That was assuming she was even out of bed. He wasn't sure how either of them would have reacted to the other in sight of the next expanse of tables, which were bristling with phallic statues and orgiastic with couples, not to mention more than couples, carved from stone. He dodged the sellers as the hot crowd pressed around him, and struggled to the lower bend.

Had it brought him back to Janet's lodgings? He was trying to see past stalls heaped with electrical goods when a stall-holder, or surely an assistant, younger than himself stepped in front of him. 'What you look?'

'Summer Breeze.'

The boy made circles with his hands above the stall as if to conjure Barry's needs into view. 'Say other.'

Barry's head was so full of heat and light and clamour that he could think of nothing else. 'Summer Breeze,' he heard himself reiterate.

The boy's thin intense face gave up its frown. 'Briefs,' he said with a gesture of lowering his own and presumably his shorts as well.

'Breeze.' Barry jabbed a finger at the building the stall hid, then waved one limp-wristed hand. 'Wind,' he said in case that could possibly help.

'Here.'

As Barry grew aware that the exchange of gestures had made the nearest members of the crowd openly suspicious, he saw the boy pick up a pocket fan and switch it on. 'No, that's not it,' he said.

'You try,' the boy insisted, thrusting it at him.

'No, it's all ow.' Barry meant to wave away the offer, but the whirling blades caught his forefinger. 'Watch out, you clumsy bugger,' he cried.

The boy turned off the fan, which had developed an angry rattling buzz, and peered at it. 'You break. You pay.'

'Don't be daft,' Barry mumbled, sucking his finger, which tasted like a coin. 'Your fault, so forget it.'

He'd hardly presented his back to the stall when the boy raised his voice. 'Pay now. Pay,' he called, and other words that Barry didn't comprehend.

Barry saw a scowl spread like an infection through the crowd, who seemed united in obstructing him. He was willing the commotion to attract Janet and her friends – anyone who would understand him – when the crowd parted downhill. Two policemen were heading for him.

They wore khaki shirts and shorts, and pistols in holsters on their right hips. Their dark moist faces bore identical black moustaches. 'What is trouble?' the larger and if possible even less jovial officer said.

'He cut me,' Barry blurted, displaying his injured finger, and at once felt guilty. 'I'm sure it was an accident, but now he wants me to pay.'

'You listen.'

It was only when the policeman confined himself to glowering that Barry grasped he was required to observe the interview with the youth, which involved much gesturing besides contributions from nearby vendors and members of the crowd. The conference appeared to be reaching agreement, by no means in his favour, when Barry tried to head it off. 'I'll pay something if that'll quiet things down. It oughtn't to be much.'

The policeman who'd addressed him brushed a thumb and

forefinger over his moustache, and Barry had a nervous urge to giggle at the notion that the man was checking the hair hadn't come unglued. He stared at Barry as if suspicious of his thoughts before growling 'You go other place. No trouble.'

'Thanks,' Barry said, though his unpopularity was as clear from the policeman's face as from every other he risked observing. To retreat uphill to take refuge with his friends he would have had to struggle through hostility that looked capable of growing yet more solid. He swung around faster than his parched unstable skull appreciated to dodge and sidle and excuse himself down to the next bend, where he saw light through a shop. Once he was out of the back entrance he should be able to find his way to the rear of the Summit Apartments.

He launched himself between two stalls piled with footwear and into the building, only to waver to a halt as darkness pressed itself like coins onto his eyes. Outlines had only started to grow visible as he headed for the daylight, so that he was halfway through the interior before he realized where he was: not in a shop but in somebody's home. Nevertheless the contents of the trestle tables were unquestionably for sale, a jumble of bed-clothes, icons, cutlery, a religious tome with dislocated pages, dresses, spanners and other tools, toys including a life-size baby that the dimness rendered indistinguishable from a real one . . . He couldn't judge how many people were crouched in gloomy corners of the single room; of the one face he managed to discern, he saw only eyes and teeth. Their dull hungry gleam prompted him to fumble the topmost note off his wad and plant it between the baby's restless feet as he made for the open at a stumbling run. He barely glimpsed all the denizens of the room flinging themselves at the cash.

He'd emerged into more of the market. Only the space just outside the door was clear. Stall-holders and their few potential customers swivelled their heads on scrawny necks to watch him. They looked as uninviting as the tables, which were strewn with goods like a rummage sale. Here were clothes he and his friends might have packed to slouch in, here were the contents of several bathrooms – shaving kits, deodorants, even unwrapped bars of soap. The stares he was receiving didn't encourage him to dawdle. He set off as fast up the narrow tortuous dusty street as his hung-over legs would bear.

He hoped any rear entrance to the Summit Apartments would be both accessible and open. Though there were alleys between the streets, all were blocked by stalls or vans or refuse. He kept catching sight of the crowd, not including anyone who'd witnessed his difference with the youth. He might have considered dodging through a house to reach his street, but the old people dressed like shadows who were sitting in every open doorway looked worse than inhospitable. At least there weren't many more stalls ahead.

The next offered an assortment of electrical goods: cameras, camcorders and battery chargers, a couple of personal stereos, whose rhythmic whispers reminded him that before he'd gone to university and after he'd left it as well, his parents had often complained the stereos weren't personal enough. Suddenly he yearned to be home and starting work at the computer warehouse, the best job he'd been able to sell himself to, or even not having come away on holiday with his old friends from school. He glanced past the stall into an alley and saw them.

'Paul,' he shouted, 'Derek,' as their heads bobbed downhill, borne by the sluggish crowd. They'd looked preoccupied, perhaps with finding him. He would have used the alley if the bulk of a van hadn't been parked mere inches short of both walls. 'I'm here,' he yelled, digging the heels of his hands into his chin and his fingertips into the bridge of his nose. 'Over here,' he pleaded at the top of his voice, and Paul turned towards him.

He would have seen Barry if he'd raised his eyes. Having surveyed the crowd between himself and the alley, he said something to Derek that caused him to glance about before vanishing downhill. The next moment, as Barry sucked in a breath that almost blinded him with the whiteness of the houses, Paul had gone too.

Barry bellowed their names and waved until his finger sprinkled the wall with a Morse phrase in blood. None of this was any use. Members of the crowd scowled along the alley at him while the vendors around him glared at him as if he was somehow giving them away. As he fell silent, the personal stereos renewed their bid for audibility. Wasn't the one at the front of the stall playing his favourite album? He could have taken it for the stereo he'd left in the apartment. He reached for the headphones, but the stall-holder, whose leathery face seemed to have been shrivelled in the course of producing an unkempt greyish beard, tapped his arm with a jagged fingernail. 'Buy, you listen,' he said.

Barry had no idea what he was being told, and suddenly no wish to linger. He might have enough of a problem at the apartments, since he hadn't brought a key with him. Best to save his energy in case he needed to persuade the owner to admit him to his room, he thought as he toiled past the final stall. It was heaped with suitcases, three of which reminded him of his and Paul's and Derek's. Of course there must be many like them, which was why he'd wrapped the handle of his case in bright green tape. Indeed, a greenish fragment adhered to the handle of the case that resembled his so much.

As he leaned forward to confirm what he could hardly believe, the stall-holder stepped in front of him. He wore a sack-like garment that hid none of the muscles and veins of his arms. His small dark thoroughly hairy face appeared to have been sun-dried almost to the bone, revealing a few haphazard blackened teeth. His eyes weren't much less pale and cracked and blank than the wall behind him. 'You want?' he said.

'Where'd you get these?'

'Very cheap. Not much use.'

The man was staring so hard at him he could have intended to deny Barry had spoken. Barry was about to repeat himself louder when he heard a faint sound above the awning, and raised his unsteady head to see the owner of the Summit Apartments watching him with a loose lopsided smile from an upper window. 'What do you know about it?' Barry shouted.

If the man responded, it wasn't to him. He addressed at least a sentence to the stall-holder, whose gaze remained fixed on Barry while growing even blanker. Barry was about to retreat downhill in search of his friends when he noticed that the vendors he'd encountered in the lesser market had been drawn by the argument or, to judge by their purposeful lack of expression, by whatever the man at the window had said. 'All right. Forget it. I will,' Barry lied and moved away from them.

At first he only walked. He'd reached the first alley that led to the topmost section of the main market when the owner of the Summit Apartments blocked the far end. Sandalled footsteps clattered after Barry, who almost lost the remains of his balance as he twisted to see the vendors filling the width of the street. An understated trail of blood led through the dust to him. He sprinted then, but so did his pursuers with a clacking of their sandals, and the owner of the apartments managed to arrive at the next alley as he did. Above it there were only houses that scarcely looked entitled to the name, with rubbish piled against their closed doors, their windows either shuttered or boarded up. A few dizzy panting hundred yards took him beyond them to the top of the hill.

Two policemen were smoking on it. Though he saw nothing to hold their attention, they had their backs to him. Beyond the hill there was very little to the landscape, as if it had put all its effort into the tourist area. It was the colour of sun-bleached bone, and scattered with rubble and the occasional building, more like a chunk of rock with holes in. A few trees seemed hardly to have found the energy to raise themselves, let alone grow green. Closer to the hill, several goats waited to be fed or slaughtered. Barry was vaguely aware of all this as he hurried to the policemen. 'Can you help?' he gasped.

They turned to bristle their moustaches at him. It didn't matter that they were the policemen he'd encountered earlier, he told himself, nor did their sharing a fat amateur cigarette. 'All my stuff is in the market,' he said. 'I know who took it, and not just mine either.'

The officer who'd previously spoken to him held up one large weathered palm. Barry kept going, since the gesture was directed at his pursuers. 'You come,' the man urged him.

Barry had almost reached him when the policemen moved apart, revealing a stout post, a larger version of those to which the goats were tethered. He saw the other officer nod at the small crowd – more than Barry had noticed were behind him. As the realization swung him around, his hands were captured, handcuffed against his spine and hauled up so that the chain could be attached to a rusty hook on the post. 'What are you doing?' Barry felt incredulous enough to waste time asking before he began to shout, partly in the hope that there were tourists close enough to hear him. 'Not me. I haven't done anything. It was him from the Summit. It was them. Don't let them get away.'

The stall-holders from the cheapest region of the market were wandering downhill, leaving the owner of the apartments together with three other people as huge and glistening. The only woman looked pained by Barry's protests or at least the noise of them. The policemen deftly emptied his pockets, and while the man who'd spoken to him in the market pocketed his cash, the other folded the traveller's cheques in half and stuffed them in Barry's mouth. Barry could emit no more than a choked gurgle past the taste of cardboard as the Summit man waddled up to squeeze his chest in both hands and tweak his nipples. 'You nice,' he told Barry as he made way for the others to palpate Barry's shrinking genitals and in the woman's case to emit a motherly sound at his injured finger before sucking it so hard he felt the nail pull away from the quick. All this done, the four began to wave obese wads of money at the policemen and at one another. Barry was struggling both to spit out the gag and to disbelieve what was taking place when he saw three girls appear where the houses gave way to rubble.

The girl in the middle was Janet. Presumably she hadn't been to bed, since she was wearing the same clothes and supporting or being supported by her friends, or both. They looked as if they couldn't quite make out the events on top of the hill. Barry threw himself from side to side and did his utmost to produce a noise that would sound like an appeal for help, but succeeded only in further gagging himself. He saw Janet blink and let go of one of her friends in order to shade her eyes. For an instant she seemed to recognize him. Then she stumbled backwards and grabbed at her companions. The three of them staggered around as one and swayed giggling downhill.

If he could believe anything now, he wanted to think she hadn't really seen him or had failed to understand. He watched the bidding come to an end, and felt as though it concerned someone other than himself or who had ceased to be. The woman plodded to scrutinize him afresh, pinching his face between a fat clammy finger and thumb that drove the gag deeper into his mouth. 'Will do,' she said, separating her wad into halves that the policemen stuffed into their pockets.

While she lumbered downhill the owner of the apartments handed Barry's passport to the policeman who had never spoken to him, and who clanked open a hulk of a lighter to melt it. The last flaming scrap curled up in the dust as the woman reappeared in a dilapidated truck. The policemen lifted Barry off the post and slung him into the back of the vehicle and slammed the tailgate.

The last he saw of them was their ironic dual salute as the truck jolted away. Sweat and insects swarmed over him while the animal smell of his predecessor occupied his nostrils and the traveller's cheques turned to pulp in his mouth as he was driven into the pitiless voracious land.

PAUL McAULEY

The Two Dicks

PAUL MCAULEY HAS WORKED AS a researcher and lecturer in biology in various universities before becoming a full-time writer. His novels and short stories have won the Philip K. Dick, Arthur C. Clarke, John W. Campbell and British Fantasy awards. His latest novel, *Whole Wide World*, is a near-future thriller set in London and Cuba.

McAuley's other books include *Four Hundred Billion Stars*, *Fairyland*, *The Secret of Life* and his acclaimed 'The Book of Confluence' trilogy, *Child of the River*, *Ancients of Days* and *Shrine of Stars*.

'I meet up with a bunch of North London writers every other Friday for lunch and catharsis,' the author reveals. 'I owe the title of the story to one of them, the great American ex-pat Jay Russell.'

P HIL IS FLYING. He is in the air, and he is flying. His head full of paranoia blues, the Fear beating around him like black wings as he is borne above America.

The revelation came to him that morning. He can time it exactly: 0948, March 20, 1974. He was doing his programme of exercises as recommended by his personal trainer, Mahler blasting out of the top-of-the-line stereo in the little gym he'd had made from the fifth bedroom. And in the middle of his second set of sit-ups something goes off in his head. A terrifically bright soundless explosion of clear white light.

He's been having flashes – phosphene after-images, blank moments of calm in his day – for about a month now, but this is the spiritual equivalent of a hydrogen bomb. His first thought is that it is a stroke. That his high blood pressure has finally killed him. But apart from a mild headache he feels perfectly fine. More than fine, in fact. Alert and fully awake and filled with a great calm.

It's as if something took control of me a long time ago, he thinks. *As if something put the real me to sleep and allowed a constructed personality to carry on my life, and now, suddenly, I'm fully awake again. The orthomolecular vitamin diet, perhaps that did it, perhaps it really did heighten synchronous firing of the two hemispheres of my brain. I'm awake, and I'm ready to put everything in order. And without any help*, he thinks. *Without Emmet or Mike. That's important.*

By this time he is standing at the tall window, looking down at the manicured lawn that runs out from the terrace to the shaggy hedge of flowering bougainvillea, the twisty shapes of the cypresses. The Los Angeles sky pure and blue, washed clean by that night's rain, slashed by three white contrails to make a leaning *A*.

A for affirmation, perhaps. Or *A* for act.

The first thing, he thinks, because he thinks about it every two or three hours, because it has enraged him ever since Emmet told him about it, *the very first thing I have to do is deal with the people who stole my book.*

A week ago, perhaps inspired by a precursor of the clear white flash, Phil tried to get hold of a narcotics-agent badge, and after a long chain of phone calls managed to get through to John Finlator, the deputy narcotics director, who advised Phil to go straight to the top. And he'd been right, Phil thinks now. *If I want a Fed badge, I have to get it from the Man. Get sworn in or whatever. Initiated. Then deal with the book pirates and those thought criminals in the SFWA, show them what happens when you steal a real writer's book.*

It all seemed so simple in the afterglow of revelation, but Phil begins to have his first misgivings less than an hour later, in the taxi to LAX. Not about the feeling of clarity and the sudden energy it has given him, but about whether he is making the best use of it. There are things he's forgotten, like unformed words on the tip of his tongue. Things he needs to deal with, but he can't remember what they are.

He is still worrying at this, waiting in line at the check-in desk, when this bum appears right in front of him, and thrusts what seems like an unravelling baseball under Phil's nose.

It is a copy of the pirated novel: Phil's simmering anger reignites, and burns away every doubt.

It is a cheap paperback printed by some backstreet outfit in South Korea, the thin absorbent paper grainy with wood specks, a smudged picture of a castle silhouetted against the Japanese flag on the cover, his name far bigger than the title. Someone stole a copy of Phil's manuscript, the one he agreed to shelve, the one his publishers paid handsomely *not* to publish in one of those tricky deals Emmet is so good at. And some crook, it still isn't completely clear who, published this cheap completely illegal edition. Emmet told Phil about it a month ago, and Phil's publishers moved swiftly to get an injunction against its sale anywhere in the USA. But thousands of copies are in circulation anyway, smuggled into the country and sold clandestinely.

And the SFWA, Phil thinks, the Science Fiction Writers of America, *Emmet is so right about them, the Swine Fucking Whores of Amerika, they may deny that they have anything to do with the pirate edition, but their bleatings about censorship and their insidious promotion of this blatant violation of my copyright proves they want to drag me down to their level.*

Me: the greatest living American novelist. Erich Segal called me that only last month in a piece in The New York Review of Books; *Updike joshed me about it during the round of golf we played the day after I gave that speech at Harvard. The greatest living American novelist: of course the SFWA want to claim me for their own propaganda purposes, to pump my life's blood into their dying little genre.*

And now this creature has materialized in front of Phil, like some early version or failed species of human being, with blond hair tangled over his shoulders, a handlebar moustache, dressed in a buckskin jacket and faded blue jeans like Hollywood's idea of an Indian scout, a guitar slung over his shoulder, fraying black sneakers, or no, those were his *feet*, bare feet so filthy they looked like busted shoes. And smelling of pot smoke and powerful sweat. This aborigine, this indigent, his hand thrust towards Phil, and a copy of the stolen novel in that hand, as he says, 'I love this book, man. It tells it like it is. The little men, man, that's who count, right? Little men, man, like you and me. So could you like *sign* this for me if it's no hassle . . .'

And Phil is seized by righteous anger and great wrath, and he smites his enemy right there, by the American Airlines First Class check-in desk. Or at least he grabs the book and tears it in half – the broken spine yielding easily, almost gratefully – and tells the bum to fuck off. Oh, just imagine the scene, the bum whining about his book, his property, and Phil telling the creature he doesn't deserve to read any of his books, he is *banned for life* from reading his books, and two security guards coming and hustling the bum away amid apologies to the Great American Novelist. The bum doesn't go quietly. He screams and struggles, yells that he, Phil, is a fake, a sell-out, man, the guitar clanging and chirping like a mocking grasshopper as he is wrestled away between the two burly, beetling guards.

Phil has to take a couple of Ritalin pills to calm down. To calm his blood down. Then a couple of uppers so he can face the journey.

He still has the book. Torn in half, pages frazzled by reading and rereading slipping out of it every time he opens it, so that he has to spend some considerable time sorting them into some kind of order, like a conjuror gripped by stage-flop sweat in the middle of a card trick, before he can even contemplate looking at it.

Emmet said it all. What kind of commie fag organization would try to blast Phil's reputation with this cheap shot fired under radar? Circulating it on the campuses of America, poisoning the young minds who should be drinking deep clear draughts of his prose. Not this . . . this piece of dreck.

The Man in the High Castle. A story about an author locked in the castle of his reputation, a thinly disguised parable about his own situation, set in a parallel or alternate history where the USA lost the war and was split into two, the East governed by the Nazis, the West by the Japanese. A trifle, a silly fantasy. What had he been thinking when he wrote it? Emmet was furious when Phil sent him the manuscript. He wasted no words in telling Phil how badly he had fucked up, asking him bluntly, what the hell did he think he was doing, wasting his time with this lame sci-fi crap?

Phil had been stuck, that was what. And he's still stuck. Ten, fifteen years of writing and rewriting, two marriages made and broken while Phil works on and on at the same book, moving farther and farther away from his original idea, so far out now that he thinks he might never get back. The monster doesn't even have a title. *The Long-Awaited. The Brilliant New. The Great Unfinished.* Whatever. And in the midst of this mire, Phil set aside the Next Great Novel and pulled a dusty idea from his files – dating back to 1961, for Chrissake – and something clicked. He wrote it straight out, a return to the old days of churning out sci-fi stories for tiny amounts of money while righteously high on speed: cranked up, cranking out the pages. For a little while he was so happy: just the idea of finishing something made him happy. But Emmet made him see the error of his ways. Made him see that you can't go back and start over. Made him see the depth of his error, the terrible waste of his energy and his talent.

That was when Phil, prompted by a research paper he discovered, started on a high-protein, low-carbohydrate diet, started dosing himself with high levels of water-soluble vitamins.

And then the pirated edition of *The Man in the High Castle* appeared, and Emmet started over with his needling recriminations and insinuations, whipping up in Phil a fine hot sweat of shame and fury.

Phil puts the thing back in his coat pocket. Leans back in his leather-upholstered First Class seat. Sips his silvery martini. The anger is still burning inside him. For the moment he has forgotten his doubts. Straight to the top, that's the only answer. Straight to the President.

After a while, he buzzes the stewardess and gets some writing paper. Takes out his gold-nibbed, platinum-cased Cross fountain pen, the pen his publishers gave him to mark the publication of the ten millionth copy of the ground-breaking, genre-busting *The Grasshopper Lies Heavy*. Starts to write:

Dear Mr President: I would like to introduce myself. I am Philip K. Dick and admire and have great respect for your office. I talked to Deputy Narcotics Director Finlator last week and expressed my concern for our country . . .

Things go smoothly, as if the light has opened some kind of path, as if it has tuned Phil's brain, eliminated all the dross and kipple clagging it. Phil flies to Washington, D.C. and immediately hires a car, a clean light-blue Chrysler with less than a thousand miles on the clock, and drives straight to the White House.

Because there is no point in posting the letter. That would take days, and it might never reach the President. All Phil would get back would be a photograph signed by one of the autograph machines that whir ceaselessly in some White House basement...

No, the thing to do is subvert the chain of command, the established order. So Phil drives to the White House: to the White House gate. Where he gives the letter to one of the immaculately turned out Marine guards.

> *Because of an act of wanton piracy, Sir, the young people, the Black Panthers etc etc do not consider me their enemy or as they call it The Establishment. Which I call America. Which I love. Sir, I can and will be of any service that I can to help the country out. I have done an in-depth study of Drug Abuse and Communist Brainwashing Techniques . . .*

Phil walking up to the White House gates in the damp March chill, handing the letter, written on American Airlines notepaper and sealed in an American Airlines envelope, to the Marine. While still buzzing from the uppers he dropped in the LAX washroom.

And driving away to find the hotel he's booked himself into.

Everything going down smoothly. Checking in. Washing up in his room. Wondering if he should use the room menu or find a restaurant, when the phone rings. It's his agent. Emmet is downstairs in the lobby. Emmet wants to know what the hell he's up to.

And suddenly Phil is struck by another flash of light, igniting at the centre of his panic, and by the terrible thought that he is on the wrong path.

Phil's agent, Anthony Emmet, is smart and ferocious and tremendously ambitious. A plausible and worldly guy who, as he likes to put it, found Phil under a stone one day in the early 1950s, when Phil was banging out little sci-fi stories for a living and trying to write straight novels no one wanted to publish. Emmet befriended Phil, guided him, mentored him, argued with him endlessly. Because (he said) he knew Phil had it in him to be huge if he would only quit puttering around with the sci-fi shit. He persuaded Phil to terminate his relationship with the Scott Meredith Agency, immediately sold Phil's long mainstream novel *Voices from the Street* to a new publishing outfit, Dynmart, guided Phil through endless rewrites. And *Voices*, the odyssey of a young man who tries to escape an unfulfilling job and a failing marriage, who is seduced by socialists, fascists and hucksters, but at last finds redemption by returning to the life he once scorned, made it big: it sold over two hundred thousand copies in hardback, won the Pulitzer Prize and the National Book Critics Circle Award, was made into a movie starring Leslie Caron and George Peppard.

But the long struggle with *Voices* blocked or jammed something in Phil. After the deluge, a trickle: a novel about interned Japanese in the Second World War, *The Grasshopper Lies Heavy*, which received respectful but baffled reviews; a slim novella, *Earthshaker*, cannibalized from an old unpublished novel. And then stalled silence, Phil paralysed by the weight of his reputation while his slim oeuvre continued to multiply out there in the world, yielding unexpected translations in Basque and Turkish, the proceedings of a symposium on the work of Philip K. Dick and Upton Sinclair, an Australian miniseries that blithely transposed the interned Japanese of *The Grasshopper Lies Heavy* into plucky colonial prisoners of war.

Phil hasn't seen his agent for ten years. It seems to him that Emmet still looks as implausibly young as he did the day they first met, his skin smooth and taut and flawless, as if made of some material superior to ordinary human skin, his keen black eyes glittering with intelligence, his black hair swept back, his black silk suit and white silk shirt sharp, immaculate, his skinny black silk tie knotted just so. He looks like a 1950s crooner, a Mob hit man; he looks right at home in the plush, candlelit red-leather booth of the hotel bar, nursing a tall glass of seltzer and trying to understand why Phil wants to see the President.

'I'm on the case about the piracy,' Emmet tells Phil. 'There's absolutely nothing to worry about. I'm going to make this –' he touches the frazzled book on the table with a minatory forefinger '– go away. Just like I made that short-story collection Berkley wanted to put out go away. I have people on this day and night,' Emmet says, with a glint of dark menace. 'The morons responsible for this outrage are going to be very sorry. Believe me.'

'I thought it was about the book,' Phil says. He's sweating heavily; the red-leather booth is as snug and hot as a glove, or a cocoon. 'But now I'm not sure—'

'You're agitated, and I completely understand. A horrible act of theft like this would unbalance anyone. And you've been self-medicating again. Ritalin, those huge doses of vitamins . . .'

'There's nothing wrong with the vitamins,' Phil says. 'I got the dosages from *Psychology Today*.'

'In a paper about treating a kid with schizophrenic visions,' Emmet says. 'I know all about it. No wonder you're agitated. Last week, I understand, you called the police and asked to be arrested because you were – what was it? – a machine with bad thoughts.'

Phil is dismayed about the completeness of Emmet's information. He says, 'I suppose Mike told you about that.'

Mike is Phil's driver and handyman, installed in a spartan little apartment over Phil's three-door garage.

Emmet says, 'Of course Mike told me that. He and I, we have your interests at heart. You have to trust us, Phil. You left without even telling Mike where you were going. It would have taken a lot of work to find you, except I just happen to be in Washington on business.'

'I don't need any help,' Phil tells Emmet. 'I know exactly what I'm doing.'

But he's not so sure now that he does. When the light hit him he knew with absolute certainty that something was wrong with his life. That he had to do something about it. He fixed on the first thing that had come into his head, but now he wonders again if it is the right thing. *Maybe*, he thinks unhappily, *I'm going deeper into what's wrong. Maybe I'm moving in the wrong direction, chasing the wrong enemy.*

Emmet, his psychic antennae uncannily sensitive, picks up on this. He says, 'You know *exactly* what to do? My God, I'm glad one of us does, because we need every bit of help to get you out of this mess. Now what's this about a letter?'

Phil explains with great reluctance. Emmet listens gravely and says, 'Well, I think it's containable.'

'I thought that if I got a badge, I could get things done,' Phil says. The martini he's drinking now is mixing strangely with the martinis he drank in the air, with the speed and Ritalin he took in LAX, the speed he took just now in his hotel bedroom. He feels a reckless momentum, feels as if he's flying right there in the snug, hot booth.

'You've got to calm down, Phil,' Emmet says. Candlelight glitters in his dark eyes as he leans forward. *They look like exquisite gems*, Phil thinks, *cut with a million microscopic facets*. Emmet says, 'You're coming up to fifty, and you aren't out of your mid-life crisis yet. You're thrashing around, trying this, trying that, when you just have to put your trust in me. And you really shouldn't be mixing Ritalin and Methedrin, you know that's contraindicated.'

Phil doesn't try and deny it; Emmet always knows the truth. He says, 'It's as if I've woken up. As if I've been dreaming my life, and now I've woken up and discovered that none of it was real. As if a veil, what the Greeks call *dokos*, the veil between me and reality has been swept away. Everything connects, Emmet,' Phil says, picking up the book and waving it in his agent's face. Loose pages slip out, flutter to the table or to the floor. 'You know why I have this book? I took it from some bum who came up to me in the airport. Call that coincidence?'

'I'd say it was odd that he gave you the copy I gave you,' Emmet says. 'The agency stamp is right there on the inside of the cover.' As Phil stares at the purple mark, he adds, 'You're stressed out, Phil, and that weird diet of yours has made things worse, not better. The truth is, you don't need to do anything except leave it all to me. If you're honest, isn't this all a complicated ploy to distract yourself from your real work? You should go back to LA tonight, there's a Red Eye that leaves in two and a half hours. Go back to LA and go back to work. Leave everything else to me.'

While he talks, Emmet's darkly glittering gaze transfixes Phil like an entomologist's pin, and Phil feels that he is shrivelling in the warm darkness, while around him the noise of conversation and the chink of glasses and the tinkle of the piano increases, merging into a horrid chittering buzz.

'I hate this kind of jazz,' Phil says feebly. 'It's so goddam fake, all those ornate trills and runs that don't actually add up to anything. It's like, at LAX, the soupy strings they play there.'

'It's just background music, Phil. It calms people.' Emmet fishes the slice of lemon from his mineral water and pops it in his mouth and chews, his jaw moving from side to side.

'Calms people. Yeah, that's absolutely right. It deadens them,

Emmet. Turns them into fakes, into unauthentic people. It's all over the airwaves now, there's nothing left but elevator music. And as for TV . . . It's the corporations, Emmet, they have it down to a science. See, if you pacify people, take away all the jagged edges, all the individualism, the stuff that makes us human – what have you got? You have androids, docile machines. All the kids want to do now is get a good college degree, get a good job, earn money. There's no spark in them, no adventure, no curiosity, no rebellion, and that's just how the corporations like it. Everything predictable because it's good for business, everyone hypnotized. A nation of perfect, passive consumers.'

Emmet says, 'Is that part of your dream? Christ, Phil. We really do need to get you on that Red Eye. Away from this nonsense, before any real damage is done. Back to your routine. Back to your work.'

'This is more important, Emmet. I really do feel as if I'm awake for the first time in years.'

A man approaches their booth, a tall overweight man in a shiny grey suit and cowboy boots, black hair swept back and huge sideburns framing his jowly face. He looks oddly bashful for a big man and he's clutching something – the paperback of *The Grasshopper Lies Heavy*. He says to Phil, 'I hope you don't mind, sir, but I would be honoured if you would sign this for me.'

'We're busy,' Emmet says, barely glancing at the man, but the man persists.

'I realize that, sir, so I only ask for a moment of your time.'

'We're having a business meeting,' Emmet says, with such concentrated vehemence that the man actually takes a step backward.

'Hey, it's okay,' Phil says, and reaches out for the book – the man must have bought it in the hotel shop, the price sticker is still on the cover – uncaps his pen, asks the man's name.

The man blinks slowly. 'Just your signature, sir, would be fine.'

He has a husky baritone voice, a deep-grained Southern accent.

Phil signs, hands back the book, a transaction so familiar he hardly has to think about it.

The man is looking at Emmet, not the signed book. He says, 'Do I know you, sir?'

'Not at all,' Emmet says sharply.

'I think it's just that you look like my old probation officer,' the man says. 'I was in trouble as a kid, hanging about downtown with the wrong crowd. I had it in my head to be a musician, and well, I got into a little trouble. I was no more than sixteen, and my probation officer, Mr McFly, he straightened me right out. I own a creme doughnut business now, that's why I'm here in Washington. We're opening up a dozen new franchises. People surely do love our deep-fried creme doughnuts. Well, good day to you, sir,' he tells Phil, 'I'm glad to have met you. If you'll forgive the presumption, I always thought you and me had something in common. We both of us have a dead twin, you see.'

'Jesus,' Phil says, when the man has gone. The last remark has shaken him.

'You're famous,' Emmet tells him. 'People know stuff about you, you shouldn't be surprised by now. He knows about your dead sister, so what? He read it in a magazine somewhere, that's all.'

'He thought he knew you, too.'

'Everyone looks like someone else,' Emmet says, 'especially to dumb-ass shit-kickers. Christ, now what?'

Because a waiter is standing there, holding a white telephone on a tray. He says, 'There's a phone call for Mr Dick,' and plugs the phone in and holds the receiver out to Phil.

Even before Emmet peremptorily takes the phone, smoothly slipping the waiter a buck, Phil knows that it's the White House.

Emmet listens, says, 'I don't think it's a good idea,' listens some more, says, 'He's not calm at all. Who is this Chapin? Not one of – no, I didn't think he was. Haldeman says that, huh? It went all the way up? Okay. Yes, if Haldeman says so, but you better be sure of it,' he says, and sets down the receiver with an angry click and tells Phil, 'That was Egil Krogh, at the White House. It seems you have a meeting with the President, at 12.30 tomorrow afternoon. I'll only ask you this once, Phil. Don't mess this up.'

So now Phil is in the White House – in the ante-room to the Oval Office, a presentation copy of *Voices from the Street* under his arm, heavy as a brick. He's speeding, too, and knows Emmet knows it, and doesn't care.

He didn't sleep well last night. Frankly, he didn't sleep at all. Taking a couple more tabs of speed didn't help. His mind racing. Full of weird thoughts, connections. Thinking especially about androids and people. *The androids are taking over*, he thinks, *no doubt about it. The suits, the haircuts, the four permitted topics of conversation: sports, weather, TV, work. Christ, how could I not have seen it before?*

He scribbles notes to himself, uses up the folder of complementary hotel stationery. Trying to get it down. To get it straight. Waves of anger and regret and anxiety surge through him.

Maybe, he thinks in dismay, *I myself have become an android, dreaming for a few days that I'm really human, seeing things that aren't there, like the bum at the airport. Until they come for me, and take me to the repair shop. Or junk me, the way you'd junk a broken toaster.*

Except the bum seemed so real, even if he was a dream, like a vision from a reality more vibrant than this. Suppose there is another reality: another history, the real history. And suppose that history has been erased by the government or the corporations or whatever, by entities that can reach back and smooth out the actions of individuals that might reveal or upset their plan to transform everyone and everything into bland androids in a dull grey completely controlled world . . .

It's like one of the weird ideas he used to write up when he was churning out sci-fi stories, but that doesn't mean it isn't true. Maybe back then he was unconsciously tapping into some flow of greater truth: the truth that he should deliver to the President. Maybe this is his mission. Phil suddenly has a great desire to read in his pirated novel, but it isn't in his jacket pocket, and it isn't in his room.

'I got rid of it,' Emmet tells him over breakfast.

'You got rid of it?'

'Of course I did. Should you be eating that, Phil?'

'I like Canadian bacon. I like maple syrup. I like pancakes.'

'I'm only thinking of your blood pressure,' Emmet says. He is calmly and methodically demolishing a grapefruit.

'What about all the citrus fruit you eat? All that acid can't be good for you.'

'It's cleansing,' Emmet says calmly. 'You should at least drink the orange juice I ordered for you, Phil. It has vitamins.'

'Coffee is all I need,' Phil says. The tumbler of juice, which was sitting at the table when he arrived, seems to give off a poisonous glow, as of radioactivity.

Emmet shrugs. 'Then I think we're finished with breakfast aren't we? Let's get you straightened out. You can hardly meet the President dressed like that.'

But for once Phil stands his ground. He picked out these clothes because they felt right, and that's what he's going to wear. They argue for ten minutes, compromise by adding a tie Emmet buys in the hotel shop.

They are outside, waiting for the car to be brought around, when Phil hears the music. He starts walking, prompted by some unconscious impulse he doesn't want to analyse. *Go with the flow*, he thinks. *Don't impose anything on top of it just because you're afraid. Because you've been made afraid. Trust in the moment.*

Emmet follows angrily, asking Phil what the *hell* he thinks he's doing all the way to the corner, where a bum is standing with a broken old guitar, singing one of that folk singer's songs, the guy who died of an overdose on the same night Lenny Bruce died, the song about changing times.

There's a paper cup at the bum's feet, and Phil impulsively stuffs half a dozen bills into it, bills that Emmet snatches up angrily.

'Get lost,' he tells the bum, and starts pulling at Phil, dragging him away as if Phil is a kid entranced beyond patience at the window of a candy store. Saying, 'What are you thinking?'

'That it's cold,' Phil says, 'and someone like that – a street person – could use some hot food.'

'He isn't a person,' Emmet says. 'He's a bum – a piece of trash. And of course it's cold. It's March. Look at you, dressed like that. You're shivering.'

He is. But it isn't because of the cold.

March, Phil thinks now, in the antechamber to the Oval Office. *The Vernal Equinox. When the world awakes*. Shivering all over again even though the brightly lit ante-room, with its two desks covered, it seems, in telephones, is stiflingly hot. Emmet is schmoozing with two suits – H.R. Haldeman and Egil Krogh. Emmet is holding Haldeman's arm as he talks, speaking into the man's ear, something or other about management. They all know each other well, Phil thinks, and wonders what kind of business Emmet has, here in Washington, DC.

At last a phone rings, a secretary nods, and they go into the

Oval Office, which really is oval. The President, smaller and more compact than he seems on TV, strides out from behind his desk and cracks a jowly smile, but his pouchy eyes slither sideways when he limply shakes hands with Phil.

'That's quite a letter you sent us,' the President says.

'I'm not sure,' Phil starts to say, but the President doesn't seem to hear him.

'Quite a letter, yes. And of course we need people like you, Mr Dick. We're proud to have people like you, in fact. Someone who can speak to young people – well, that's important isn't it?' Smiling at the other men in the room as if seeking affirmation. 'It's quite a talent. You have one of your books there, I think?'

Phil holds out the copy of *Voices from the Street*. It's the Franklin Library edition, bound in green leather, his signature reproduced in gold on the cover, under the title. An aide gave it to him when he arrived, and now he hands it to the President, who takes it in a study of reverence.

'You must sign it,' the President says, and lays it open like a sacrificial victim on the gleaming desk, by the red and white phones. 'I mean, that's the thing isn't it? The thing that you do?'

Phil says, 'What I came to do—'

And Emmet steps forward and says, 'Of course he'll sign, sir. It's an honour.'

Emmet gives Phil a pen, and Phil signs, his hand sweating on the page. He says, 'I came here, sir, to say that I want to do what I can for America. I was given an experience a day ago, and I'm beginning to understand what it meant.'

But the President doesn't seem to have heard him. He's staring at Phil as if seeing him for the first time. At last, he blinks and says, 'Boy, you do dress kind of wild.'

Phil is wearing his lucky Nehru jacket over a gold shirt, purple velvet pants with flares that mostly hide his sand-coloured suede desert boots. And the tie that Emmet bought him in the hotel shop, a paisley affair like the President's, tight as a noose around his neck.

He starts to say, 'I came here, sir,' but the President says again, 'You do dress kind of wild. But that I guess is the style of all writers, isn't it? I mean, an individual style.'

For a moment, the President's eyes, pinched between fleshy pouches, start to search Phil's face anxiously. It seems that there's something trapped far down at the bottom of his mild gaze, like a prisoner looking up through the grille of an oubliette at the sky.

'Individual style, that's exactly it,' Phil says, seeing an opening, a way into his theme. The thing he knows now he needs to say, distilled from the scattered notes and thoughts last night. 'Individualism, sir, that's what it's all about, isn't it? Even men in suits wear ties to signify that they still have this one little outlet for their individuality.' It occurs to him that his tie is exactly like the President's, but he plunges on. 'I'm beginning to understand that things are changing in America, and that's what I want to talk about—'

'You wanted a badge,' Haldeman says brusquely. 'A federal agent's badge, isn't that right? A badge to help your moral crusade?'

Emmet and Haldeman and Krogh are grinning as if sharing a private joke.

'The badge isn't important,' Phil says. 'In fact, as I see it now, it's just what's wrong.'

Haldeman says, 'I certainly think we can oblige, can't we, Mr President? We can get him his badge. You know, as a gift.'

The President blinks. 'A badge? I don't know if I have one, but I can look, certainly—'

'You don't have one,' Haldeman says firmly.

'I don't?' The President has bent to pull open a drawer in the desk, and now he looks up, still blinking.

'But we'll order one up,' Haldeman says, and tells Emmet, 'Yes, a special order.'

Something passes between them. Phil is sure of it. The air is so hot and heavy that he feels he's wrapped in mattress stuffing, and there's a sharp taste to it that stings the back of his throat.

Haldeman tells the President, 'You remember the idea? The idea about the book.'

'Yes,' the President says, 'the idea about the book.'

His eyes seem to be blinking independently, like a mechanism that's slightly out of adjustment.

'The neat idea,' Haldeman prompts, as if to a recalcitrant or shy child, and Phil knows then, knows with utter deep black conviction, that the President is not the President. Or he is, but he's long ago been turned into a fake of himself, a shell thing, a mechanical puppet. *That was what I was becoming*, Phil thinks, *until the clear white light. And it might still happen to me, unless I make things change.*

'The neat idea,' the President says, and his mouth twitches. It's meant to be a smile, but looks like a spasm. 'Yes, here's the thing, that you could write a book for the kids, for the, you know, for the young people. On the theme of, of—'

' "Get High on Life",' Haldeman says.

' "Get High on Life",' the President says. 'Yes, that's right,' and begins a spiel about affirming the conviction that true and lasting talent is the result of self-motivation and discipline; he might be one of those mechanical puppets in Disneyland, running through its patter regardless of whether or not it has an audience.

'Well,' Haldeman says, when the President finishes or perhaps runs down, 'I think we're done here.'

'The gifts,' the President says, and bends down and pulls open a drawer and starts rummaging in it. 'No one can accuse Dick Nixon of not treating his guests well,' he says, and lays on the desk, one after the other, a glossy pre-signed photograph, cuff links, an ashtray, highball glasses etched with a picture of the White House.

Emmet steps forward and says, 'Thank you, Mr President. Mr Dick and I are truly honoured to have met you.'

But the President doesn't seem to hear. He's still rummaging in his desk drawer, muttering, 'There are some neat pins in here. Lapel pins, very smart.'

Haldeman and Emmet exchange glances, and Haldeman says, 'We're about out of time here, Mr President.'

'Pins, that's the thing. Like this one,' the President says, touching the lapel of his suit, 'with the American flag. I did have some . . .'

'We'll find them,' Haldeman says, that sharpness back in his voice, and he steers the President away from the desk, towards Phil.

There's an awkward minute while Egil Krogh takes photographs of the President and Phil shaking hands there on the blue carpet bordered with white stars, in front of furled flags on poles. Flashes of light that are only light from the camera flash. Phil blinks them away as Emmet leads him out, through ordinary offices and blank corridors to chill air under a grey sky where their car is waiting.

'It went well,' Emmet says, after a while. He's driving the car – the car Phil hired – back to the hotel.

Phil says, 'Who are you, exactly? What do you want?'

'I'm your agent, Phil. I take care of you. That's my job.'

'And that other creature, your friend Haldeman, he takes care of the President.'

'The President – he's a work of art, isn't he? He'll win his third term, and the next one too. A man like that, he's too useful to let go. Unlike you, Phil, he can still help us.'

'He was beaten,' Phil says, 'in 1960. By Kennedy. And in 1962 he lost the election for governor of California. Right after the results were announced, he said he would give up politics. And then something happened. He came back. Or was he brought back, is that what it was? A wooden horse,' Phil says, feeling hollow himself, as empty as a husk. 'Brought by the Greeks as a gift.'

'He won't get beaten again,' Emmet says, 'you can count on that. Not in 1976, not in 1980, not in 1984. It worked out, didn't it – you and him?' He smiles, baring his perfect white teeth. 'We should get you invited to one of the parties there. Maybe when you finish your book – it'll be great publicity.'

'You don't want me to finish the book,' Phil says. He feels as if he's choking, and wrenches at the knot of his tie. 'That's the point. Whatever I was supposed to do – you made sure I didn't do it.'

'Phil, Phil, Phil,' Emmet says. 'Is this another of your wild conspiracy theories? What is it this time, a conspiracy of boring, staid suits, acting in concert to stifle creative guys like you? Well, listen up, buddy. There is no conspiracy. There's nothing but a bunch of ordinary guys doing an honest day's work, making the world a better place, the best way they know how. You think we're dangerous? Well, take a look at yourself, Phil. You've got everything you ever dreamed about, and you got it all thanks to me. If it wasn't for me, you'd be no better than a bum on the street. You'd be living in a cold-water walk-up, banging out porno novels or sci-fi trash as fast as you could, just to keep the power company from switching off your lights. And moaning all the while that you could have been a contender. Get real, Phil. I gave you a good deal. The best.'

'Like the deal that guy, the guy at the hotel, the doughnut guy, got? He was supposed to be a singer, and someone just like you did something to him.'

'He could have changed popular music,' Emmet says. 'Even as a doughnut shop operator he still has something. But would he have been any happier? I don't think so. And that's all I'm going to say, Phil. Don't ever ask again. Go back to your nice house, work on your book, and don't make trouble. Or, if you're not careful, you might be found dead one day from vitamin poisoning, or maybe a drug overdose.'

'Yeah, like the folk singer,' Phil says.

'Or a car crash,' Emmet says, 'like the one that killed Kerouac and Burroughs and Ginsberg in Mexico. It's a cruel world out there, Phil, and even though you're washed-up as a writer, be thankful that you have me to look after your interests.'

'Because you want to make sure I don't count for anything,' Phil says, and finally opens the loop of the tie wide enough to be able to drag it over his head. He winds down the window and drops the tie into the cold gritty wind.

'You stupid bastard,' Emmet says, quite without anger. 'That cost six bucks fifty. Pure silk, a work of art.'

'I feel sick,' Phil says, and he does feel sick, but that's not why he says it.

'Not in the car,' Emmet says sharply, and pulls over to the kerb. Phil opens the door, and then he's running and Emmet is shouting after him. But Phil runs on, head down in the cold wind, and doesn't once look back.

He has to slow to a walk after a couple of blocks, out of breath, his heart pounding, his legs aching. The cold, steely air scrapes the bottoms of his lungs. But he's given Emmet the slip. Or perhaps Emmet doesn't really care. After all, Phil's been ruined as a writer, his gift dribbled away on dead books until nothing is left.

Phil thinks, *Except for that one book*, The Man in the High Castle. *The book Emmet conspired to suppress, the book he made me hate so much because it was the kind of thing I was meant to write all along. Because I would have counted for something, in the end. I would have made a difference.*

He walks on, with no clear plan except to keep moving. It's a poor neighbourhood, even though it's only a few blocks from the White House. Despite the cold, people are sitting on the steps of the shabby apartment houses, talking to each other, sharing bottles in brown paper bags. An old man with a terrific head of white hair and a tremendously bushy white moustache sits straight-backed on a kitchen chair, smoking a cheap cigar with all the relish of the king of the world. Kids in knitted caps and plaid jackets bounce a basketball against a wall, calling to each other in clear, high voices. There are Christmas decorations at most windows, and the odours of cooking in the air. *A good odour*, Phil thinks, *a homely, human odour*. A radio tuned to a country station is playing one of the old-time ballads, a slow, achingly sad song about a rose and a brier twining together above a grave.

It's getting dark, and flakes of snow begin to flutter down, seeming to condense out of the darkening air, falling in a slanting rush. Phil feels the pinpoint kiss of every flake that touches his face.

I'm still a writer, he thinks, as he walks through the falling snow. *I still have a name. I still have a voice. I can still tell the truth. Maybe that journalist who interviewed me last month, the one who works for the Washington* Post, *maybe he'll listen to me if I tell him about the conspiracy in the White House*.

A bum is standing on the corner outside the steamed up window of a diner. An old, fat woman with a mottled, flushed face, grey hair cut as short as a soldier's. Wearing a stained and torn man's raincoat that's too small for her, so that the newspapers she's wrapped around her body to keep out the cold peep from between the straining buttons. Her blue eyes are bright, watching each passer-by with undiminished hope as she rattles a few pennies in a paper cup.

Phil pushes into the diner's steamy warmth and uses the payphone, and then orders coffee to go. And returns to the street, and presses the warm container into his sister's hand.

DOUGLAS SMITH

By Her Hand,
She Draws You Down

DOUGLAS SMITH IS A TECHNOLOGY EXECUTIVE for an international consulting firm. He lives just north of Toronto, Canada, with his wife and two sons. His stories have appeared in more than thirty professional magazines and anthologies in eleven countries and nine languages, including *Amazing Stories*, *Cicada*, *Interzone*, *The Third Alternative* and *On Spec*.

In 2001, he was a John W. Campbell Award finalist for best new writer, and won an Aurora Award for best SF&F short fiction by a Canadian. Like the rest of humanity, he is working on a novel.

'This is the first horror story I ever wrote,' admits the author, 'and given that you're reading it here, I just may try another sometime. The inspiration for the tale resulted from the hard work in which you can often find writers engaged: staring out a window. Actually, it was the window of a bus. I wanted to write a story about some form of creativity other than writing. Perhaps the constant flow of visual images flashing by the window led to the idea of a visual artist. From there, I thought of the portrait artists that I'd often see during visits to Ontario Place, a lake-front tourist attraction in Toronto, and Cath and her situation was born.'

By her hand, she draws you down.
With her mouth, she breathes you in.
Hope and dreams and soul devoured.
Lost to you, what might have been.

B Y *HER HAND, SHE draws you down . . .*
  Joe swore when he saw Cath doing a kid. He had left her
for just a minute, to get a beer from the booth on the pier before it
closed for the night. Walking back now, he could see Cath on her
stool, sketch pad on a knee, ocean breeze blowing her pale hair. A
small girl sat on another stool facing her, a man and a woman,
parents he guessed, beside the child.

Kid's not more than seven, he thought. *Cath promised me no*
kids. She promised.

The sun was long set and the air had turned cool, but people
still filled the boardwalk. Joe wove through the crowd as fast as
he could without attracting attention. Cath had set up farther
from the beach tonight, at the bottom of a grassy slope that ran up
to the highway where their old grey Ford waited.

'Last night tonight,' Cath had said when they had parked the
car earlier. '*It* wants to move on. I can feel the change.'

Joe had swallowed and turned off the ignition. He was never
comfortable talking about it. 'Where's it headed?'

Cath had just shaken her head, grinning. 'Dunno. That's part
of the fun, isn't it? Not knowing where we're going next? That's
fun, isn't it Joe?'

Yeah, loads of fun, he thought now as he approached Cath and
her customers. It *had* been fun once, when they'd met, before he
learned what Cath did, what she had to do. When his love for her
wasn't all mixed up with fear of what she would do to someone.

Or to him.

The child's parents looked up as Joe came to stand beside Cath.
The father frowned. Joe smiled, trying to hide the dread digging
like cold fingers into his gut. Turning his back to them, he bent to
whisper in Cath's ear. That flowery scent she had switched to
recently rose warm and sweet in his face. *Funeral parlors,* he
thought. *She smells like a goddamned funeral parlor.*

'Cath, she's just a kid,' he rasped in her ear.

Cath shook her head. Her eyes flitted from the girl to her pad.
'Bad night. I'm hungry,' she muttered, ignoring Joe.

Joe looked at the drawing. It was good. But they were always good. Cath had real talent, more than Joe ever had. She would set up each night where people strolled, her sketches beside her like trophies from a hunt. People would stop to look, sometimes moving on, sometimes sitting for a portrait.

Eventually Joe and Cath would move on too. When the town was empty, Cath said. When the thing inside her wanted to move on. They had spent this week at a little New England vacation spot. At least they were heading south lately, he thought. Summer was dying and Joe longed to winter in the sun. Sleep for Joe was rare enough since he'd met Cath. Winters up north meant long nights in bars. Things closed in then, closed in around him. On those nights, he would lie awake in their motel bed, feeling Cath's stare on him, feeling her hunger.

He looked at the sketch, at the child captured there, perfect except for the emptiness that spoke from the eyes, from any eyes that Cath drew. And the mouth.

Where the mouth should have been, empty paper gaped. Cath left the mouth until the end. The portraits always bothered Joe when they looked like that. To him, the pictures weren't waiting to be completed, waiting for a last piece to be added. To Joe, something vital had been ripped from what had once been whole, leaving behind a void that threatened to suck in the world around it. An empty thing but insatiable. Waiting to suck him in too.

'Cath,' he whispered. 'You promised.'

She ignored him again. Joe wrapped his fingers around the thin wrist of her hand that held the sketch pad. 'You promised.'

Cath snapped her head around to glare up at him. Joe caught his breath as anger met hunger in her grey eyes, becoming something alive, something that leapt for him.

The father cleared his throat and the thing in Cath's eyes retreated. Cath turned to the parents. 'Sorry, can't get her right. You can have this.' Tearing the sketch from her pad, she shoved it at the mother. 'We gotta go.' Cath stood and folded her stool as the child ran to peek from behind the father's legs. Joe grabbed the other stool and the canvas bag that held Cath's supplies. He put an arm around Cath's waist, leading her away.

The father started to protest. 'But you're almost done. You just need to draw in the mouth.'

Cath stopped and Joe swore. He just wanted to get her out of there. She walked back to the man who exchanged glances with his wife. Cath touched a finger to her lips. 'Mouths are the hardest part. The most important part,' she said. 'Everyone – they say "the eyes are the windows of the soul." They say "Oh, you got the eyes just right." They don't know. They don't know it's the mouth you gotta get just right. That's what makes a picture come alive. Like it's gonna just start . . . breathing.'

The father cleared his throat, but the mother tugged at his shirt. Joe grabbed Cath's arm and pulled her away. The man muttered something, but Joe didn't care.

He led Cath to a gravel path that switched back and forth up the steep hill to the highway above. Halfway up, an observation area looked down on the pier and the beach and the boardwalk. Cath twisted away from him there. A low stone wall ran around the area's edge and two lampposts stood at either end. Putting her stool down under the nearest light, she began setting out her sketches against the wall.

Joe dropped the other stool and sat down. The fatigue that lived with him always now rose to engulf him. He felt dead inside, all used up, like the way Cath's pictures made him feel, waiting to be sucked into the void. 'We had a deal,' he said.

Cath sat, looking up and down the path. 'I'm hungry.'

'No kids, remember?' Joe said. 'And nobody with a family depending on them.' He tried to make his voice sound strong, but his hands were shaking.

She opened her pad. 'Kind of cuts down the field, Joe.'

'Use one of the sketches you've got put away.'

Cath laughed. A bitter, empty sound. Joe imagined the mouths she drew making that kind of sound. Cath looked at him finally. 'All gone. Used 'em all.'

Joe felt the emptiness again, a void gaping below, drawing him down. He leaned forward, head between his hands, fingers pressing hard on his temples, trying to make his fear go away. 'Jeez, Cath. All of them?' He searched her face for some hope.

Cath shrugged. 'Girl's gotta eat.' She stared past him and he heard gravel crunching underfoot. Joe turned, his hand slipping by reflex to touch the switchblade inside his boot top.

A fat man in black pants, white shirt, and paisley tie loosened at the neck was struggling down the steep path from the highway, a beach chair in each arm. He walked over to the stone wall and put down the chairs to rest. Nodding at Joe and Cath, he glanced at her sketches. He began to turn away but then looked back. His gaze ran over the portraits lined against the low wall like prisoners before a firing squad. The man whistled.

Joe sighed, from regret and relief. Cath would eat tonight.

With her mouth, she breathes you in . . .

The man's name was Harry. He haggled with Cath over the price, then he sat down, and Cath started sketching. Joe glanced at the two chairs that Harry had carried but he couldn't see a wedding ring so he kept silent.

Cath worked quickly, her hand slashing at the page, pausing only to switch the color of her pencil. When only the mouth remained unfinished, she put the pad down on her lap.

Harry looked down at the sketch. 'There's no mouth.'

'Mouths are special, Har,' Cath said. She puckered at him and Harry laughed, a nervous squeaky sound. Cath touched a finger of her drawing hand to Harry's lips. He gave that little laugh again but didn't pull away. Cath ran her fingertips slowly over his lips, tracing each curve and contour. Sitting on the stone wall, Joe thought of her fingers on his own skin at night in bed, tracing the lines of his body. Love and fear and lust – with Cath, they all mixed together, colors in a picture flowing into each other, until you couldn't separate one from another.

She lowered her hand to the paper, her eyes still on Harry's mouth. Picking up a red pencil and dropping her gaze, her hand began to stab at the paper in short urgent strokes. The mouth grew under her fingers as Joe watched. She finished in seconds. Removing the sketch sheet, Cath handed it to Harry. He regarded it for a moment, grunted his approval and paid her. Portrait under his arm, he picked up his chairs and nodded a goodbye.

After watching Harry labor down the path toward the board-walk below, Joe walked to where Cath sat cross-legged on the ground, her sketch pad on her lap. She carefully lifted a sheet of carbon paper from the top of the pad. A copy of the sketch of Harry she had just rendered stared up at Joe in black and white. *No color*, thought Joe. *As if all the life's been sucked out of it. No*, he thought. *Not all of it. Not yet.*

From her canvas bag, Cath removed a small rosewood box, its hinged cover carved with letters in a script that Joe thought was

Arabic. He'd never checked, wanting to know as little as possible about the thing. Cath opened the lid and withdrew what looked like a child's crayon but without any paper covering.

The crayon was as long as Joe's middle finger but thicker, and a red so dark it was almost black. Joe remembered drawing as a kid, the crayons, the names of the colors. Midnight blue, leaf green, sunshine yellow. He knew the name that this one would have carried – blood red. It glinted in the overhead light as if it would be sticky to the touch, but Joe had never touched it so he didn't know for sure. He didn't want to know.

Hunched over the portrait copy, Cath began to retrace the lines of the mouth with the red crayon, adding color and shading. She worked with almost painful slowness. Joe remembered how once, when she had made a mistake at this stage, the fury had burst from her like a wild thing caged too long.

At last, Cath straightened. She gave the mouth one last appraising look, then returned the crayon to the rosewood box. Joe walked back to the low stone wall. He knew he would turn back to watch her. He always did.

Below, Harry had reached the boardwalk. The big man put down one chair to wave to someone on the beach. Joe's stomach tightened. A woman waved back at Harry, and a small boy and girl ran to hug him. *Jesus, no*, thought Joe.

He turned back. Cath sat hunched over the portrait of Harry on her lap. Joe rushed to her, praying that it wasn't too late, a prayer that died when he saw the picture. It had started.

The portrait's mouth was moving, far lips squirming like slick red worms on the paper. A pale vapor rose thin and wispy from those lips. Cath bent her head over the mouth and sucked in that misty thing that Joe never wanted to name.

A scream rose from the beach. A woman's cry, a thing of pain and fear. Between her sobs, Joe could hear children crying.

He walked back to the low stone wall and looked down at the crowd gathered where Harry had fallen. Joe stood there, stare locked on Harry's still form, feeling the void opening below him again. 'Cath, we have to get out of here.'

Cath didn't answer him. Joe tore his gaze from the scene below and turned back to her. She was standing now, looking south, down the coastline. 'It wants to move on,' she said.

Hope and dreams and soul devoured . . .

Joe drove, staring at the white lane markers slicing the dark two-lane one after another, like brush strokes by God on a long black canvas. *White on black*, he thought. *The negative image of Cath's secret portraits. Black on white, white on black. Just the red missing. Just that blood red.*

How long before some cop put it together? A string of deaths, all the victims drawn by a young woman with a male companion. Christ, Harry had died with a sketch in his hand.

Cath stirred beside him and then he felt her stare on him. He could always feel her gaze, like a physical touch, like a brush dipping into him, drawing something from him. *Is that how you do it, Cath? How you take the thing you take? Capture it in your eyes, then cage it through your fingers onto the page? Have you been feeding on me too?*

'I'm still hungry,' Cath said. Her voice was small, almost childlike in the dark.

He knew what she meant. 'We'll hit town soon,' he said. But it would be three in the morning when they arrived. No one around. No one to draw. And she had no pictures left. Cath said nothing but looked away. After a while, he figured she was asleep. Then he felt her stare again.

'I don't *want* to hurt people, Joe.'

He swallowed. This was new. She never talked about it, even when Joe did. He should say something now, something smart, something that would lead them out of this. He should but he had nothing left to say. He could only nod. 'I know, babe.'

'It just gets so hungry. I get so hungry.'

'I know.'

'I can't stop it. It keeps pulling me, making me . . .'

Joe could feel her pain in those words. And his fear.

'I'm tired,' she said. 'So tired I wish I could just go to sleep and never wake up. Ever been that tired, Joe?'

Joe swallowed again. *All the time*, he thought, but he just nodded. Cath looked away and he took a breath as if he was coming up for air.

'I'm hungry,' she said again.

'I know.'

Her stare settled on him again like a beast on his chest.

'I could draw *you*, Joe.'

Joe's hands tightened on the wheel. Cath had said it the way a kid told you she could ride a bike or tie her shoe. The lines flashed by in the headlights. White on black, no red.

'Don't even need to see you,' she said. 'Know you so well.'

Joe stared at the road. *Don't look*, he thought.

'Know your face like I know my own,' she said.

The burden of her gaze lifted. He looked at her.

Her eyes were shut and her hand moved in her lap, mimicking drawing motions. 'Don't even need light. Could draw you with my eyes closed.' Her hand stopped and she leaned her head back. A few minutes later, Joe could hear her breathing slow and deepen.

So there it is, he thought. He always knew it would come to this. This was why he had stayed, even after he learned what Cath did, what she was. Afraid that when he left, when Cath no longer needed him, she would draw him down. Draw him down onto the page from memory, then drink him in like all the others.

The road lines flew at him like white knives out of the night. White knives and blackness. Just the blood red missing. Taking a hand from the wheel, he felt inside the top of his boot, running his fingers over the bone handle of his switchblade.

A few miles down the road, he found a wide shoulder and pulled over, turning off the engine and the lights.

Cath still slept. Hands shaking, Joe pulled the knife from his boot. *It's self-defense*, he thought. But he just sat holding the knife. It was for the best. How many more would she kill? But he still loved her. Could he do it? He was tired, so tired. He leaned back. He only slept now when Cath did, when he didn't feel her stare. He closed his eyes. Her breathing brushed his ears, soft and deep, soft and deep, soft . . .

Joe awoke to the sound of scratching on paper. He looked over. Framed against the moonlight, Cath sat hunched over her sketch pad, her hand moving in short, sure strokes.

'Kind of late for drawing, isn't it, Cath?' Joe asked. His throat was dry. He fumbled in his lap for the knife.

'Hungry,' she said, her voice barely audible.

'Dark, too,' he said, blood pounding in his ears.

'Don't need light. Drawin' from memory,' she whispered.

Drawing from memory. Drawing him. He knew she was drawing him. 'Don't, Cath.' His thumb found the blade's button.

'Tired of being hungry.' She sat back, her gaze on the sketch. Joe couldn't see the picture, but he saw the red crayon in her hand. She'd finished the mouth. 'Please, don't do it,' Joe said. His cheeks felt cool and wet. Joe realized he was crying.

Cath lifted the paper to her face. She was crying too.

'Don't!' Joe screamed. The knife blade clicked open.

'Bye, Joe. Sorry.' Cath breathed in through her lips.

Joe saw a pale wisp rise from the paper and move toward her mouth. Saw his hand gripping the knife flash forward. Saw the blade slice her white T-shirt and slide between her ribs.

Saw the red, the blood red, flow over the white of her shirt to blend with the black of the night and the shadows.

Cath spasmed and fell sideways onto him. Surprise mixed with peace in her face. 'Thanks . . . Joe,' she whispered. Her eyes closed and her head slumped back. A wisp of mist escaped her lips. That's *me*, Joe thought. Sobbing, he pressed his lips to hers, sucking in the breath and the grey mist from her mouth.

Bitter and sour, the thing burned his throat as he breathed it in. Something was wrong. Joe felt a presence of something dark, something . . . *hungry*.

His head spinning, Joe flicked on the dome light. Blood soaked into his shirt where Cath slumped against him, the picture still clenched in her hand. Joe stared at the sketch, a scream forming in his mind.

A familiar face stared back at him from the page, a face that Cath knew from memory. The face she knew best of all.

Not Joe's face.

It was Cath.

She hadn't been drawing him. She'd been feeding herself to the thing that had lived in her. Cath had been killing herself.

The emptiness that was the mouth in Cath's pictures gaped beneath him and Joe felt himself being drawn down.

Lost to you, what might have been . . .

A February evening, St. Pete's Beach. Joe sat on his stool, his back to the beauty of a Gulf sunset. His portraits lay strewn on the sand around him like the dead on a battlefield. A woman and man looked them over while Joe waited. The woman held the hands of a little girl and a boy. Twins, Joe guessed. Kids couldn't be much more than seven, he thought. He remembered when that would have meant something to him, before Cath died, before . . .

The little girl tugged on the mother's hand. 'They all look so sad, Mommy.' The mother hushed the child while the father haggled with Joe over the price. The day had been slow, so Joe agreed to do both kids for the price of one.

Joe started sketching. His hand leapt over the paper, and the images of the children grew around the emptiness where their mouths should have been. A tear ran down his cheek, but he kept drawing.

He had to. He was hungry.

POPPY Z. BRITE

O Death, Where
Is Thy Spatula?

POPPY Z. BRITE HAS PUBLISHED FOUR NOVELS: *Lost Souls*, *Drawing Blood*, *Exquisite Corpse* and *The Lazarus Heart*. She has had two short-story collections published, *Wormwood* (aka *Swamp Foetus*) and *Are You Loathsome Tonight?* and a collection of non-fiction, *Guilty But Insane*. She also edited two volumes of the erotic vampire anthology *Love in Vein*.

Wrong Things was a recent collection with Caitlín R. Kiernan, and she has two novels forthcoming, *The Value of X* and *Liquor*. Brite lives in New Orleans with her husband Christopher, a chef.

' "O Death, Where Is Thy Spatula?" is the second in my series of stories about my alternate life as Dr Brite, the coroner of New Orleans,' explains the author. 'This was my earliest career ambition, but unlike Dr Brite, I doubt I could have made it through the organic chemistry courses in medical school.

'The exquisite cuisine of Devlin Lemon was inspired by many New Orleans restaurants, including Marisol, Lilette, Gerard's Downtown, Dante's Kitchen, and Commander's Palace under the late chef Jamie Shannon, for whom the story was written.'

T HE MAIN THING YOU NEED to know about me is that I love eating more than anything else in the world. More than sex, more than tropical vacations, more than reading, more than any drug I've ever tried. I'm not fat – I'm actually quite slender – but I can't take credit for any kind of willpower or exercise regimen. The truth is, I'm not fat because I only finish eating things that are really, really good, and there just aren't that many of them in my opinion. I love eating, as I say, but I'm picky as hell. A French pastry, ethereal manifestation of butter, custard, and chocolate, designed like a little piece of modern architecture? I'm there. A slice of cold pizza? I might nibble at it until my hunger headache goes away, but no more.

So, for the tale I'm about to relate, this food-love is the central fact of my being. I have a job (coroner of New Orleans), five purebred Oriental Shorthair cats, a mixed-breed husband (Irish and Jewish; wire-haired; his name is Reginald, but I never thought that suited him, so I call him Seymour), a house, and a hell of a lot of books, but none of that is terribly important here. What's important is that you understand how much I love to eat.

All right – the fact that I am the coroner of New Orleans is somewhat important too, but I don't want to put you off right away. Just store that information for future reference.

People think New Orleans is a world-class food city. Possibly it is, but only in a very narrow sense. There's a saying that we have a lot of great food but only about five recipes. Gumbo – etouffee – jambalaya – oysters Rockefeller – and I don't even know what the fifth one is supposed to be. Maybe breaded, deep-fried seafood, because we certainly have plenty of that. I see arteries full of it on my tables every day.

Perhaps I'm being unfair. There are, in fact, a lot of good restaurants here. But most of them . . . well, did you ever see that episode of *Frasier* where Frasier asks Niles, 'What's the one thing better than a flawless meal?' and Niles answers, 'A great meal with *one tiny flaw* we can pick at all night'? Most of the places here are like that, except the flaws aren't tiny. I can easily think of twenty places with excellent appetizers, terrific entrees, and dessert lists dull enough to plunge me into despair (apple tart, bread pudding, the eternal Death By Chocolate). There's a good French restaurant on Magazine Street where, even though I always pay with my credit card, the waiters refuse to acknowledge my existence – 'May I clear that for you, sir?' they say, gazing lovingly at Seymour as they whisk away my salad plate. There's a simple neighborhood place where they used to have perfect fried chicken livers, but they hired a new fry cook, and now (no matter how I beg) the lovely little livers resemble nothing so much as deep-fried pencil erasers. I don't even want to talk about who and what you have to know to get a decent meal at the old-line venues like Antoine's.

There are problems everywhere. I eat at these restaurants anyway, and most of the time I enjoy them, but there is only one place where I know I can count on a flawless meal, without peer: Devlin Lemon's little restaurant in the Garden District. It's called the Lemon Tree and decorated with wrought-iron baskets full of bright yellow lemons with their leaves still attached. In lesser hands it could have some serious cuteness issues. In Devlin's hands, you just want to prostrate yourself on the cerulean carpet and cry, 'Feed me, you eponymous, lemon-stacking, brilliant fool.' Or at least I do.

Devlin came from the frozen North with a Culinary Institute of America degree and a love for local ingredients. Anything that passes through his hands – a steak, a lobe of Hudson Valley foie gras, an unpasteurized French cheese – is likely to come out tasting good, but he has always reached the apex of his talent with Louisiana ingredients: Gulf fish, artichokes, Creole tomatoes, andouille and tasso, cane syrup, even mirlitons. I've never met another cook who could make a mirliton taste like anything but a sweaty sock. Devlin bakes them with shrimp, garlic, and a shocking amount of butter until they release a hitherto untold sweetness.

(All right, you nitpicking foodies. Yes, I am talking to you. I know you've been squirming since you read the words 'unpasteurized French cheese', and I am quite aware that these ambrosial creations are legally forbidden to enter the country, let alone appear on a restaurant menu. The only thing I can say is all that's on the menu is not always all you can eat, and a good chef takes care of his regulars.)

Devlin knows everything I like and hate to eat. He knows that I am genetically disposed to think cilantro tastes like soap and that I can't stand cauliflower because it reminds me of certain cancers I see. He knows I will not eat amberjack under any circumstances; it was he who told me of the giant worms that lurk in its digestive tract. He knows how dearly I love sorrel, caviar, and clotted cream. At the Lemon Tree, I glance at the menu, but I usually end up telling my waitperson, 'Ask Devlin what Dr Brite should have today.'

Lest you get the wrong idea, nothing has ever 'happened', as they say, between us. We are both happily married. Any intimacy between me and Devlin is purely about his feeding and my eating.

It was May, close enough to my birthday that I had begun to wonder whether Devlin might find me something special – some Iranian caviar, perhaps, or some really fresh white truffles. I've never considered having my birthday dinner anywhere but the Lemon Tree, and some celebratory tidbit almost always finds its way onto the table.

I was at work in the basement of the big stone building at the corner of Tulane and Broad, where I spend a large part of my life. I'd spent the morning posting a young man killed in an automobile accident near the Calliope housing project (gross cranial trauma) and a fat old lady who died in her sleep (coronary event). I was beginning to think about lunch as my assistant wheeled out the last body that had come in the night before, a robbery victim who'd been shot in the head. I saw that the victim was wearing check-patterned chef's pants and work boots, but did not find this surprising. Kitchen workers keep strange hours and are often (wrongly) thought to be carrying large amounts of cash. His shirt had already been removed.

At first, I could only see that he was a young white man. The gun had been small and his cranium was intact, but even a low-caliber bullet to the head can distort facial features beyond recognition. This is mainly because the hemorrhaging of the brain produces gases that force blood into the tissues, particularly those around the eyes. This man's eyes were swollen shut and looked as if they had been smeared with heavy purple-black makeup. His lips were drawn rigidly across his teeth, and the teeth had dried blood on them. His hair was thickly crusted with blood; only a few clean strands told me that it had been strawberry-blond. This may have been when the first breath of suspicion touched me, but if so, I did not notice it.

I parted the hair with my latex-gloved fingers. 'Slightly stellate entry wound behind and below the right ear,' I said to my assistant, Jeffrey, who wrote it down. 'Stippling of the tissue around the entry wound. No exit wound. The bullet's still in there. What's his name?'

'That's a funny thing,' said Jeffrey. 'I can't find his report. I'm gonna have to call upstairs for the dupe.'

'Well, go do it, please. I'll get him undressed.' I picked up a pair of scissors and began to cut his pants off. As I did, his left hand slipped off the table and hung over the edge; rigor had not completely stiffened him yet.

Something about that hand caught my eye: a black-ink wedding band tattooed around the third finger. Many cooks don't like to wear wedding rings because they can so easily get snagged or lost, so this kind of tattoo is common. Devlin had one. His was done in a distinctive crosshatched pattern, just like the one on this man's hand.

I had opened one pants leg up to the crotch. Then I put the scissors down, moved to the head of the table, and looked carefully into the man's face. A warm rush of adrenaline spread through the muscles of my back as I saw what I had not seen before. The eyeball protrusion, tissue infiltration, and rigor had disguised him, but they could not hide his identity completely.

I was supporting my entire weight on the edge of the table when Jeffrey came back. 'I don't have to call upstairs,' he said. 'I found his paperwork on the floor in the cooler – Dr Brite? What's wrong?'

'I know him.'

'Oh, hell.'

'Let me see that paperwork.' I scanned the police report, but it told me nothing I didn't already know: he had been shot in a robbery leaving the restaurant; he had been dead about eight hours; he was Devlin Lemon.

'I'm not posting him,' I said.

'Well, of course not. We'll get Dr Garrison to post him.'

'*Nobody*'s posting him,' I said.

'What?'

'He can't – I mean, we can't – oh, God.' I bowed my head to hide the tears that stood in my eyes. Jeffrey had never seen me cry. No one at the morgue had ever seen me cry. I don't socialize a great deal, but inevitably I had seen acquaintances on my tables before. I see everyone who dies in New Orleans. But none had affected me like this. I took a deep breath. 'I have reason to suspect the presence of a communicable disease in this case,' I said. It was the only half-plausible reason I could think of to delay the autopsy. 'I'm keeping the body here until further notice.'

'His family won't like that. Getty said they were already talking about holding a wake.'

'I'll talk to them. I have no choice, Jeffrey. If there's a communicable disease involved, I can't release the body yet.'

'Well, then, shouldn't we take fluids?'

'Later,' I told him. 'I need to . . . I need to read up on this. We may have to take special precautions.'

Jeffrey's odd mint-green eyes met mine. He knew I was lying, and I knew that he knew. He trusted me, though; we worked well together. And he could see that I was rattled. He would drop the matter for now. 'Okay,' he said. 'Are you sure you don't want me to ask Dr Garrison to speak with the family when he comes in?'

'No. I'll do it. I'll call them after lunch. I'm going to have lunch now.'

I shut myself in my office just before the tears finally came. I curled up in my chair and hugged myself and cried. More than anything I wanted to call Seymour, but he and his brother were camping in Bogue Falaya for three days, unreachable.

Even if I could speak to Seymour, what would I say? I wasn't sure I could own up to what was in my head right now. I wasn't thinking of Devlin's family, or his youth, or the fear he must have felt when his murderer pressed the gun's muzzle against his skull. I wasn't thinking of Devlin at all, not exactly. I was thinking of the last appetizer I'd eaten at the Lemon Tree, a disk of beef marrow melting into a fricassee of chanterelles, its flavor brightened by a persillade so finely chopped you could barely see it. I was remembering the scent and savor of this dish. I could only remember it; I could not taste it, for the taste of loss was too bitter in my mouth.

When I finally washed my face and went back into the autopsy room, Devlin was gone. Jeffrey had zipped him into a body bag and rolled him back into the cooler. Maybe he'd feel comfortable there, I thought. Except for the presence of corpses, it was a lot like the walk-in refrigerator in a restaurant.

Was I losing my mind? It had been years since I thought that way about a dead person – as if he could feel comfortable, or feel pain, or have an opinion about his surroundings. Cutting open one body, sawing off the top of its skull, folding its face down and lifting the brain from its moorings had gone a long way toward convincing me that the dead do not care what is done to them. Doing these things thousands of times left me no doubt. I treat them with respect because they still matter to the living, but I no longer imagine them 'feeling comfortable'.

Now, though, I was.

I got through the rest of the day somehow. I even called Devlin's wife, whom I'd met once or twice at the restaurant. From the sound of her voice, I could tell she had been heavily tranquilized. She didn't argue when I told her I would have to keep Devlin's body for a few days. I expected to get a call from the wake-planning parents or siblings, but it didn't come. I left the morgue in the early evening, as twilight was falling over the city, and drove home. There I tried to eat some dry crackers, gagged on them, and crawled into bed with the cats.

A thin, sobbing, unearthly voice was trying to get me to hear it. 'I'm hungry,' it kept telling the darkness. 'I'm hungry.' It was trapped there, not knowing where it was or why. I tried to reply, but I could not form the words.

I wrenched myself awake, showered, and drove to the morgue hours before my next shift was scheduled to start. No one questioned my presence: they left me alone, assuming I had work to catch up on – which I did, in a way. I wheeled Devlin out of the cooler and slid him onto one of the tables, my back muscles knotting in protest. I ignored the pain. After measuring and photographing the bullet wound in his skull, I washed away the blood, used a disposable plastic razor to shave the hair around the area, and inserted a pair of long forceps into the hole. I was afraid that the bullet had ricocheted inside his skull, hiding itself among scrambled pieces of brain, but my forceps traveled a straight track to the region of his cerebellum and found metal. I pulled out a bloody bit of lead with a slightly flattened tip. I caught myself thanking God, or somebody, for my findings – his brain was not destroyed; the bullet had not shattered into fragments I would have to search out. What was I thinking? It didn't matter how little damage had been done. Devlin was still dead.

I wondered what was happening to me as I triple-bagged the bullet, put it in a padded envelope, and left the building with it tucked under my arm. I might not lose my job if anyone found out about this, but only because I am a good liar and could probably come up with a plausible reason for my actions. In truth, I didn't know what I was doing or why.

Usually Seymour brings me my coffee in bed, and I drink it with plenty of milk and sugar. This morning I drank it black in a Styrofoam cup from a gas station. Then I drove to the French Quarter, parked on Royal Street, and walked to St Louis Cathedral. I was not raised Catholic and had never been to a Mass, but I'd lit candles here to ask for various small favors, and they had all been granted. I lit a candle now, stuffing a ten-dollar bill into the collection box, looking into the porcelain faces of Mary and her small son. Then I slid into a pew and sat there for a long time.

I did not pray, exactly. I didn't know how. Instead I thought of marrow melting into chanterelles, of whole roasted snapper with wild-rice-stuffed figs, of fresh sweet Gulf shrimp on a bed of crispy fried spinach. I tried to remember everything Devlin had ever cooked for me, and as I did so, I slid my hand into the padded envelope and clutched the bullet in its triple layer of plastic.

I felt a little better when I came out of the cathedral. By noon, Jackson Square would be full of tacky fortune-tellers, bad musicians, and ugly tourists, but right now it was peaceful. My good mood lasted until I went back to work, looked in the cooler, and saw Devlin there. His face had begun to look haggard from dehydration, and the bullet that had been in his head was now in its padded envelope under the front seat of my car. Nothing else had changed. I don't know what I expected. If prayers could cause the dead to get up and walk away, I would have been out of work long ago.

'You look sick,' said Jeffrey. 'I swear you've lost weight since yesterday.'

'Thanks.'

'Why don't you go home? Dix and I can handle things here.'

'I'm fine,' I said. But after lunch – which I could not eat – I felt worse than ever. 'Do you really think you and Dix would be all right if I went home?' I asked Jeffrey.

'Absolutely. Get out of here and get some rest. And some food,' he called after me. 'Get yourself a hot meal.'

'I'm trying,' I muttered as I got into my car. Though it was only April, temperatures were already in the eighties, and I wondered if I was really picking up the dark rich smell of the blood on the bullet under my seat.

I did not go straight to my destination. Instead I stopped at a nice restaurant on St Charles Avenue and attempted to have lunch. There was nothing wrong with any of the food I ordered, but it all seemed to taste of ashes and decay. The waiter wanted to know if there was a problem. I said I'd had the flu and would take the leftovers with me, and he encased them in a foil swan, which I threw away as soon as I left the place. In two days I had managed to eat perhaps two grams of food. It was time to seek serious help.

I knew enough to stay out of the Quarter this time. The places that billed themselves as voodoo shops there were tourist traps, pure and simple. But I didn't know where to go. I had noticed a building on Broad Street, near my workplace, with words like CANDLES and HERBS and BOTANICA painted on its side. The woman behind the counter had skin the shade and texture of a Brazil nut. Her eyes were gorgeous: large and tilted, fringed with dark lashes, the irises a color somewhere between green and gold.

'Can I help you?' she asked, and I stood there stupidly. I had finally admitted to myself what I wanted to do, and in the same breath I had realized that there was no sane way to ask for it. I didn't particularly care whether I sounded sane, but if I asked how to raise the dead, the woman would probably throw me out of her shop.

I didn't know what I was going to say until I heard myself saying it. 'I'm a writer,' I said, and almost laughed. I *had* kidded myself that my ramblings had literary merit, once upon a time, but those days were long gone. 'I'm writing a story in which someone wants to bring a corpse back to life. Like they're supposed to do in Haiti. Do you have any information on that?'

Those devastating eyes regarded me levelly. 'Of course,' she said. 'There are books. Of course, the dead can't actually return to life – you understand that?' Perhaps my voice was a little too ragged, the skin around my eyes a little too red – but couldn't these be side effects of late writing hours?

'It's only a story,' I told her.

'Good.' She took a book from a shelf near the counter. Its black cover was embossed with a single word, VODOUN. 'The recipe is on page fifty-three. You'll recognize most of the ingredients – in fact, you'll find most of them in your kitchen. But you may not have heard of datura, also known as the zombi cucumber.'

'What's that?'

'A powerful hallucinogen, among other things.' She took down another book, this one titled *Plants of the Gods*. 'You can learn more about it in here.'

'Where can I, uh, where can my characters get it?'

'You can't. Not unless you grow it yourself, or find it growing wild – it's illegal.' Her eyes shone, and I wondered if she thought she was saving me from something.

'Then it won't work,' I said. I have killed every plant I ever tried to grow, and the idea of tramping around some wilderness trying to identify a hallucinogenic plant was just silly – I can't even stand to go camping with Seymour and his brother.

Nonetheless, I paid for both books, took them home, and spread them out on my desk. As the woman had promised, most of the ingredients in the voodoo (or vodoun) spell were familiar, but it was obvious that datura was central to the thing. This seemed like an insurmountable obstacle at first. Then I turned to the entry for datura in *Plants of the Gods*, and I began to wonder.

The book told me that datura grows in tropical and temperate zones in both hemispheres, and that all species have tropane alkaloids as their active principles. Organic chemistry was the only part of medical school that I found nearly impossible to get through, and I had studied it so hard that I still remembered most of it. Even if I hadn't, the names of three tropane alkaloids were listed in the book: atropine, hyoscyamine, and scopolamine. I handled at least two of these compounds on a weekly basis.

When a person dies at home, any medications he or she is taking are supposed to be brought into the morgue with the body. We note these medications on the autopsy report, count the pills, and (at least in theory) wash them down the sink. Atropine is the active ingredient in Lomotil, which is used to control severe diarrhea. Hyoscyamine is used in Cystospaz and Uriced, which are used for glaucoma, urinary obstructions, and bowel problems. These three drugs come in with bodies all the time; I was certain that there were some waiting to be counted in the morgue right now. Scopolamine is used in transdermal motion-sickness patches, which I don't see as often, but it would be easy to get one.

I wrote myself a prescription for a scopolamine patch and drove to a Walgreen's to fill it. I could write myself scripts for the others, too, but Lomotil is a controlled substance. I didn't want somebody recognizing my name and spreading rumors. I'd see if the drugs were available at the morgue. If not, the Walgreen's was open all night.

I could hardly make myself wait until midnight, but there was no way I could do anything at the morgue before then; too many people would be there. I gathered the other ingredients I needed and tried to make myself take a nap, but hunger pangs kept me awake. I fed the cats. I read more of the VODOUN book and learned that I was taking an enormous risk, not with Devlin, but with my own soul. I was tampering with the fabric of reality and would eventually have to pay a price. I didn't care. With Devlin dead, I thought I might never be able to eat again, so I would soon be dead too.

When midnight came, I forced myself to wait another half-hour. Then I packed up the things I needed and drove to work.

I had been afraid that a traffic accident or a house fire would have caused a spate of activity, but everything was quiet; only the night assistant and the janitor were there. Even so, I wheeled Devlin into the decomp room. He hadn't begun to decompose, but that room could be locked and there was no window in the door.

First I sewed up the skin over his head wound. I realized I should have done this earlier, as the skin had begun to curl and shrink away from the edges of the wound, but I did as well as I could. I had already cleaned the area around the wound, but now I washed all the blood from his hair, head, and neck. I didn't know what had happened to his shirt, so I had brought in the top of a green scrub suit. Rigor mortis had passed and his limbs moved easily, but I was not strong enough to wrestle him into the top. I put it on an instrument tray nearby.

Finding the Lomotil, Cystospaz, and Uriced had been no problem. I crushed the pills, cut the scopolamine patch into tiny pieces, and mixed them with most of the other ingredients in an organ-specimen jar. The copy of VODOUN was open to page fifty-three on the counter, and I checked the recipe to make sure I had done everything right. I had only the last two steps to go.

'The final ingredient,' the text read, 'is a finger bone taken from a living person.'

I sterilized my hands, my bone saw, and a heavy kitchen cleaver I'd brought from home. I had been tempted to grab a couple of painkillers along with the other pills, but I was afraid they would make me groggy. I had to be absolutely aware of what I was doing. I splayed my left hand on the steel table, expelled a long breath, and brought the cleaver down on the first joint of my forefinger.

This may seem senseless. The spell did not specify which finger to use, and I rely on my hands for my livelihood; why didn't I choose my relatively useless pinky finger? I'm not sure. I was doing what I felt I had to do – had been from the moment I first saw Devlin on my table, really – and all I can say is that my pinky didn't feel important enough. I didn't know how the spell would work, if it did work, but I understood that the finger bone had to be taken from a living person because it was a sacrifice.

I didn't need the bone saw at all. The cleaver went through the flesh, through the bone, and the joint skittered across the table's slick surface. It would have fallen to the floor if the table hadn't had a raised lip for catching blood and other fluids. I only looked at my left hand long enough to sink a few clumsy stitches into the raw flesh and slap on a butterfly bandage. The stitches were the most painful part of the whole procedure. When I had stopped the bleeding, I turned my attention to the severed joint. The book didn't say anything about meat, blood, or nerves: it said a finger *bone*, so I used a scalpel to dissect away as much of the other material as I could before dropping the slick little bone into the jar of ingredients.

As I mixed everything together, I felt ravenous. Hunger, exhaustion, and shock were preying on me now; I think I believed Devlin was going to get off that table and immediately fix me a nice meal.

It was ready. I had done everything else; there was only the last step to go. I tilted Devlin's head back, pulled his lower jaw down, and poured the mixture into his mouth.

Nothing happened.

Maybe the mixture had to dissolve, I thought. It wouldn't do so on its own because his mouth was so dried out. I ran some water into the jar and let it trickle between his lips.

Still nothing.

'Goddamn it,' I said. 'Devlin, you fucking asshole, *come back here*!'

I guess that was why the title of the recipe was 'Calling Back the Dead'. You had to actually call them. Because as soon as I spoke, Devlin opened his eyes.

I had the scalpel in my hand, not so much because I was afraid *of* him as because I was afraid *for* him. The book didn't say anything about what the person would be like when they came back. I didn't want a zombi, didn't want him in some mindless state of animated limbo. That would be worse than staying dead – and I doubted very much whether a zombie knew enough to hold a haunch of meat over a fire, let alone make a foie gras *crème brûlée*. If he was merely animated - if *Devlin himself* wasn't there - I was prepared to drive the scalpel into the base of his skull, doing essentially what the bullet had done before. I don't know what I thought I would do if that didn't work.

But I never had to worry about it, because as soon as he opened his eyes, I saw the man I knew in them. And as soon as his gaze met mine, he said, 'Dr Brite?'

Then the mixture hit the back of his throat and he began to cough. Wouldn't that have been cute, if I'd brought him back to life only to have him choke on my severed finger bone? 'Devlin,' I said, '*swallow*.' He did, and the obstruction went down.

'I feel terrible,' he said.

'We need to get you to a hospital.'

'Where are we? What happened?'

'You've been hurt. There was a terrible mistake, but it's going to be all right.'

And it was. There were questions, of course, but I stuck to my story that I'd found Devlin exhibiting vital signs after two days of refrigeration. It was highly unlikely but impossible to disprove, especially with the man sitting there, breathing and talking. Nobody ever connected my missing finger joint with Devlin's resurrection. I just said I'd had an accident while cutting meat, which was essentially true. Seymour may have been a little suspicious of this story, since he would have expected me to save the severed joint in formalin as a souvenir, but he must have seen that I was in an odd mood when he returned from his camping trip; he asked very few questions.

Devlin didn't remember anything after leaving the Lemon Tree the night of the robbery. The version of reality that most people came to accept – because any other version simply stretched the mind beyond its capacity – was that the bullet had not penetrated Devlin's skull at all, but had worked like a hard blow to the head, rendering him unconscious for a protracted period.

Only Jeffrey knew otherwise. He saw Devlin's body up close. He knows very well what a dead person looks like, and he knows me. But he has never said a word. That's one reason he is my favorite assistant.

For my birthday dinner, I had a Creole tomato aspic with lump crabmeat and sorrel, a dozen Kumamoto oysters topped with sevruga caviar, a plate of braised veal cheeks so tender they dissolved in my mouth, and a miniature heart-shaped chocolate cake with a chocolate sphere full of raspberry puree somehow concealed in the middle. The last item in particular made me think Devlin knew I had done something more than find him warm on the autopsy table. Like Jeffrey, though, he never said anything. He didn't have to. He continues to feed me all the thanks I need.

DENNIS ETCHISON

Got to Kill Them All

DENNIS ETCHISON HAS WON two World Fantasy Awards and three British Fantasy Awards. His short fiction has been collected in *The Dark Country*, *Red Dreams*, *The Blood Kiss*, *The Death Artist* and the e-collection *Fine Cuts*, a volume of stories about Hollywood available from Scorpius Digital Publishing. *Talking in the Dark* was a massive retrospective volume from Stealth Press marking the fortieth anniversary of his first professional sale, and his latest collection is *Got to Kill Them All & Other Stories* from CD Publications.

As an acclaimed anthologist, Etchison has edited *Cutting Edge*, *Masters of Darkness I-III*, *MetaHorror*, *The Museum of Horrors* and *Gathering the Bones*, the latter an international anthology of new stories, co-edited with Jack Dann and Ramsey Campbell. He has also recently adapted 150 episodes of the original *Twilight Zone* television series as radio dramas, released on audio cassette and CD in 2002.

'When I wrote "Got to Kill Them All",' recalls the author, 'the latest American success story was the triumphant return of big-money quiz shows to prime-time network television. Such shows had been enormously successful in the 1950s, until a Congressional investigation revealed that some of them were fixed. It turned out that certain contestants, including the scholar Charles Van Doren, were provided with answers in advance to manipulate the outcome and guarantee ratings; when the scandal broke careers were ruined and such programmes quickly disappeared from the broadcast schedule. Eventually smaller, less serious game shows reappeared on daytime and syndicated TV, emphasizing humour and celebrity guests, but allegedly serious, intellectually challenging quiz shows remained lost to history for more than forty years.

'The first of the new wave of retro quiz shows was *Who Wants to Be a Millionaire?* An American version of the British original, it debuted without fanfare as a low-budget, limited-run replacement series on ABC-TV. It became an unexpected hit, scoring such phenomenal ratings that it soon began airing several nights a week, opposite copycat shows on other networks, including a revived version of the infamous *Twenty-One*, another UK transplant called *The Weakest Link*, and even one simply and shamelessly entitled *Greed*.

'At around the same time (February, 2000), one could not help but notice that millions of American children had caught Pokémon fever. The word is the name of a wildly popular Nintendo Gameboy game that also inspired a Japanese *animé* series and a range of trading cards that picture hundreds of cartoon "pocket monsters". One of the characters is a boy whose job it is to protect the world by tracking down the "bad" monsters and defeating them in pitched battles with the "good" ones he's trained for the purpose. His motto, the signature phrase of the Pokémon universe, is "Got to catch them all!"

'It did not require much imagination to speculate that some shrewd, enterprising producer might attempt to combine these two hot trends and reach an even larger audience. Replacing the word "catch" with "kill" seemed obvious for the story's title, even reflexive to a horror writer. And what would the show be called? Well, green is the color of American money, which is after all what commercial television is really about . . .'

T HE SKY WAS GETTING DARKER all the time.
    I set the red can under the glove box and drove away from the pumps, steering with one hand so I could gulp down some of the coffee. Then I hit the brakes before I got to the street.
    The can worried me.
    It was still upright but I heard the gas sloshing. There were a lot

of turns between here and the house. What if it tipped over? I'd be sucking fumes before I got home.

I reached into the back seat, grabbed the plastic bag from B&B Hardware and wedged it next to the can. But it wasn't heavy enough. So I had to shut off the engine, climb out and make room in the trunk, between the spare tire and the suitcase. That way the can wouldn't move around, no matter how fast I took the corners. I turned the key again and headed east on Washington, picking up speed, with only one question in my mind:

Which of the following is a Burt Reynolds film? (a) Cannonball Run (b) Stroker Ace (c) Smokey and the Bandit or (d) The Night of the Following Day.

I couldn't remember the winning answer but it didn't matter now. The gas station was history.

The sky was so dark by now that I had a hard time believing it was still early afternoon. The clock on the dash said the same as my watch, a few minutes past three. Rush hour wouldn't be for a while yet. I changed lanes, weaving in and out, flexing my fingers till the joints popped, the sound like little arcs of electricity below the windshield. I thought I saw a barricade of squad cars at the next corner, colored lights spinning, but it was only a road crew setting out detour signs. Their red vests glowed in the underpass. I shook my head to clear it and noticed that the coffee was almost empty.

I worked my way over between the trucks and sport utility vehicles, heading for Venice Boulevard. It would have been a lot easier to take Sepulveda to Lincoln straight out of LAX. I'd be home now. But this way I had everything I needed. I could do the rest in my sleep. As I turned onto Venice another question flashed before me:

In what film does William Shatner appear? (a) The Intruder (b) The Brothers Karamazov (c) Big Bad Mama or (d) Anatomy of a Murder.

That one was easy. It was from Day Two, Show Five, the one we had just wrapped. How many hours ago? I could still see the answer on the card in front of me. I pretended to play the game, jabbing the steering wheel as if it were a buzzer. The horn went off and he glanced up.

The first thing I noticed was that he might have been anyone.

A beach boy, nothing special, the type you see around here all the time. Sun-bleached hair, sweat collecting in his squinty eyes, and a walk that said he was not going to slow down for anybody. He stepped into the street and one of us had to stop. I could tell by those eyes it had to be me. He glared back like a hot spot on the glass and didn't move.

Then he did something strange.

He folded his legs and sat down right there in the crosswalk, daring me to hit him. I didn't, of course. The light was red.

I opened the window.

'Hey, you want to move it?'

He shrugged. Not defiantly. He just didn't care.

Cars were stacked up behind me now and they didn't like this game. The light changed. I heard a horn tapping. *For God's sake*, I thought.

'What's your problem?'

When I leaned out his eyes got big.

'God, you're him!'

I shook my head. 'Move your ass.'

'Yeah! The guy on *Green*!'

Busted. I didn't even have my makeup on. Did I? No, that was hours ago, in Honolulu. I would have taken it off. I checked the rearview mirror. My eyes were like two cigarette burns. I had a hard time recognizing myself. The kid's legs unfolded as he got up. But not to move out of the way. He started walking toward me.

He was going to ask for my autograph.

The rest of the drivers leaned on their horns.

I had to make a decision fast so I unlocked the passenger door. I'd drive around the corner and dump him off once we were out of the intersection.

When he got in I took a close look at him. New Nikes, clean T-shirt and jeans, no dirt anywhere that showed. He was not a beach bum and he didn't really have an attitude. He had just plain given up. He probably didn't know he was going to until that moment and then something – the traffic, the sun, all the people on the street who couldn't care less – made him lose it. Now I could see that it wasn't sweat under his eyes. He had been crying.

He closed the door and wiped his face. 'Shit, I'm sorry. If I'd 'a known it was you . . .'

'What happened?' I said.

'Oh, nothin'.' He tried a laugh to make light of it. 'My old lady. We had a, you know, fight. She kicked me out.'

'Where?'

'Right here, in the middle of the street. Told me to fucking split. So I did.'

'I understand,' I said.

'You do?'

'She's a bitch.'

'Well . . .'

'Sure, she is. Acts like you're always bothering her. No time to talk. When you call, she's never home.'

'How did you know that?'

Which is proof that your wife is cheating? (a) Staying out all night (b) mysterious stains on her clothing (c) phone calls from someone who hangs up when you answer or (d) frequent trips to see her 'mother' in the hospital.

'They're all the same,' I said. 'Think about it.'

'Yeah,' he said, as if it had never occurred to him, 'I guess they are . . .'

Now we were close to Admiralty Way and the grid of side streets by the marina. It was hard to tell them apart in this light. *Got to bear down*, I thought.

'Where do you want me to drop you?'

'Wait,' he said. 'What do I do?'

What should you do once you know she is unfaithful? (a) Make her account for every hour of her day (b) hire a private detective (c) hide a Global Positioning Device in her car or (d) kill her.

'Only one thing to do,' I told him, 'isn't there? How about the corner?'

'It doesn't matter.'

'Where's your house?'

'I can't go back there.'

'Maybe you should.'

'Why?'

'To make it right.'

'I don't know how.'

'Yes, you do. Think about it.'

'Okay. I will.'

He squinted at the shadowy rows of condos as we neared the

end of the boulevard. We both saw sparks of light like tiny fires starting between the buildings. It could have been the sun on the ocean except that the sky had closed over.

'I have to let you out,' I said.

'Huh?'

'I can't take you with me. Not where I'm going.'

'That's cool. The market, okay?' There was a Stop 'N Start ahead, at the corner. 'I need some stuff.'

That was cool with me. I could get a refill on my coffee, as long as it didn't take too long.

I pulled in between a brand-new Land Rover and an exterminator's truck. The mannequin on the roof had a tux and top hat and a big rubber mallet behind his back and he was standing over an innocent-looking mouse. On the way to the glass doors I saw the little rat out of the corner of my eye, twitching his whiskers and scooting away over the hood. *Go on*, I thought. *You can run but you can't hide.*

Inside the convenience mart I poured a big 22-ouncer, black. The kid was in the aisle where they keep the dog food and soap and aspirin and Tampax, for when you're running late and she gave you a list and you promised. I popped a lid on the coffee and left a dollar bill on the counter, thinking: *Which method is best for a crime of passion? (a) Gun (b) rope (c) knife or (d) gasoline.*

'Good luck,' I said over my shoulder.

The kid had a couple of household items in his hands. He must have wanted to do the pots and pans or something as soon as he got home. So he was going to try and make up after all. He could hardly wait. The poor bastard. I went out while he was paying for his stuff.

The mousemobile was gone. Now a pool-cleaning truck was parked next to me, the kind I'd seen in the marina, sometimes in front of my own house even though our pool wasn't finished yet. I wondered if it was the same one. If it was maybe I could do something right here before I drove off and took care of the rest.

Let's see, I thought.

I hadn't figured on this part and didn't have the right tools for the job. It wouldn't take much to give him the message, say a screwdriver stuck in a sidewall or the radiator, like a note on his windshield only better. He'd know what it was for and look

194   **DENNIS ETCHISON**

around and I'd be gone. Or I could wait for him to come out and see what his sorry ass looked like. Was he inside? I hadn't noticed. *What should you do to her lover? (a) Make his life a living hell (b) tie him up and torture him (c) castrate him or (d) kill him*. But this was his lucky day. I wasn't sure.

Time to go.

The kid walked around and opened the passenger door like he wanted to get in.

'One question,' he said.

'What?' I swallowed hot coffee, put the cap back on and took out my keys.

'Can I get on the show?'

'I don't have anything to do with that,' I said, revving up.

'But if you put in a good word . . .'

'I'm out of here,' I said. The sky went black like a shadow had passed over the earth. Night was ready to fall. I could feel it in my head. 'Close the door.'

'Okay,' he said and got in.

Now he thought we were friends. He was really innocent. Like the Fool in a deck of cards, too busy smelling the flowers to notice that he's walking off a cliff. I didn't want to tell him the whole truth. He wouldn't be able to handle it.

'I guess you have to be pretty smart, anyway.'

'Do you watch the show?'

'Every week!'

'Then you know the rules,' I snapped. We were driving again and traffic was heating up. I couldn't waste any more time. 'It's not what you know. It's what—'

'"You don't know!" he finished for me. 'That's so cool. All those other shows, you have to get the right answer. But on *Green*, one right answer and you're—'

'History,' I said. 'Look, I have to be somewhere.'

'Sony Studios, Culver City, seven o'clock. Right?'

'Not tonight.'

'But this is Friday . . .'

'We tape the shows in advance.'

'You do?'

'Five a day. I just flew in from Hawaii. Yesterday San Francisco, Atlanta the day before, New York on Monday. A month in a week.'

'Jesus, when do you sleep?'

'It's been a while.'

He held out his hand. 'Ray Lands, right?'

'Lowndes.'

'I thought you were live.' He tried to give me some kind of brotherhood handshake but I got out of it.

'I used to be. Now they want it every night. We had to get some shows in the can.'

''Cause it's so popular?'

'Right.'

He put his bag of household crap in the back seat, cheered up already, sure everything was going to work out. It didn't take much. Even if she threw him out again he could sleep under a blanket of stars and eat dates off the palm trees while he figured another way to get her back. That would be cool. Somebody needed to burst his bubble but I didn't want to be the one. I had things on my mind.

What is the best way to obtain satisfaction? (a) Catch her in the act and take pictures (b) expose her betrayal on national television (c) beat her within an inch of her life or (d) tie her up and burn the house down.

'All ri-i-ght!' he said.

'What?'

He was still leaning over the seat and now he had his hand on the plastic bag from the hardware store. 'You go to B&B, too! Over on Washington, right? They have everything. It's great, huh?'

'Great.'

He reached into my bag and took out the long butane lighter. It balanced across his palm like a combat knife. He fingered the switch, ready to test it.

'I like these babies. For when you have to start a barbecue.'

'Leave it,' I told him.

'Duct tape, nails, rope . . .' He put the bag back down next to his. 'Need to fix something?'

'Yeah.'

'At your place?'

I stopped the car at the last corner.

'You better get out now.'

'Oh, yeah.' He took his bag from the back seat, then hesitated. 'Need any help?'

'No.'

A private security patrol car nosed out of the alley by the gate and sat there idling, the guard watching me from behind tinted glass. I hovered for a minute while I downed the rest of the coffee and let it absorb into my bloodstream.

I could see the stars already through my eyelids and then the streaked sky over Waikiki Beach, the way it was outside the window of the hotel room when the storm started moving in, and my hand as I picked up the phone to call her for the hundredth time. I felt the rumbling of the surf. It sounded like a car engine. I opened my eyes and checked the mirror.

So far there were no other patrol cars rolling up to block the way, only the one in the alley and while my eyes were closed he had camouflaged the front end so it looked like a trash can in the shadows. I saw waves churning in the marina. The water was blood red.

'You sure?' the kid said. 'I'm good with my hands.'

I would have bet that he was. I considered. If she was alone I could handle it and if she was out that would give me time to get set up while I waited for her to come home. But if she was not alone there might be complications.

'Still want to be on the show?' I said.

'Sure. Ten million greenbacks!'

'It's easy. All you have to do is give the wrong answer. Prove that you're an asshole, in other words, like everybody else.'

'I know.'

'If I gave you something to hold, could you do that, and not ask any questions?'

'Like what?'

'What would you do if you saw a rat?'

'Um, kill it, I guess.'

'That's right. You've got to kill them, don't you?'

'Hell, yeah.'

'Then come on.'

'Where are we going?'

'I want you to meet my wife.'

He swung his legs back in and closed the door. 'You'll put in the word?'

'Sure.'

'When?'

'Next week.'

'Cool!'

We drove around to the multi-level ranch houses at the end of Circle Vista.

'Uh, one thing,' he said, 'just so's you'll know. I'm not into anything weird.'

'That's cool,' I told him. 'Neither am I.'

Her lemon-coloured car was in the driveway. I took the hardware store bag from the back and as I climbed out a curtain flapped shut in an upstairs window. The bedroom.

'Wait here,' I said.

'You got it.'

I started along the flagstone walk to the side of the house. *Better check it out*, I thought, *before you bring the red can from the trunk, just to be sure.* Before I got very far the front door squeaked open and I heard a voice.

'Ray . . . ?'

I backtracked, holding the bag casually at my side.

'Hi, honey.'

I waited for her to ad lib an excuse to keep me outside. Her eyes were puffy, almost swollen shut. She hadn't been getting much sleep, either.

'Ray, I'm so glad you're here!'

'Are you?'

'You don't know . . .'

'What's wrong?'

'It's Mother.'

I nodded knowingly. 'Your mother? I see. Is she still "sick"?'

'She's . . . gone.'

'Oh, really? Where did she go?'

'She passed away last night. This morning. I tried calling you from Kaiser but you'd already checked out. I don't know what to do. I have to make the arrangements . . .'

I dropped the plastic bag and held her off, feeling her wrists trembling, so thin I could snap them like chicken bones. She came at me again and struggled as I pushed her away. Then her face twisted up and she started sobbing. I grabbed her around the waist and lifted her off her feet, carrying her out of the yard before the neighbors could see our hysterical little scene. The only one who saw was the kid. He watched from the car, taking it in.

'*What's wrong with you?*' she screamed as the sirens started closing in.

Why is a mouse when it screams I thought. *(a) Still shitting me (b) scared shitless (c) full of shit or (d) shit out of luck . . .?*

The next thing I remember is this:

She got her arms around my neck and then I wasn't fighting her anymore. I stood there feeling her lips against my neck and her breath was hot like a child's from the crying and my eyes finally closed all the way. And when they opened again it was like I was waking up.

I smelled her hair and tasted her skin and knew where I was. Everything else had been a dream. The sirens receded and there was only the quiet lapping of blue water behind our house. The weight lifted and the sky opened and there was light again and the pounding in my ears was her heart beating in my chest. Then her legs went out from under her and I had to hold very tightly to keep her feet from dragging as I pulled her inside.

I was sorry the kid had to witness any of this. He would have to walk home from here. I had a vague recollection of the bitter, twisted things I had said to him and felt ashamed. Someday he would understand how burned-out a man can get when he's really exhausted and wired and how bent out of shape things seem when you're like that, and maybe he'd forget this day. I had been out of my head. *It can happen to anybody*, I told myself.

Her clothes were so wrinkled she must have slept in them for days on a cold bench somewhere and her hair had come loose and there was no makeup on her pale face. I set her on the couch.

'I'm so sorry,' I said and kissed her forehead.

'I have to call the funeral home . . .'

'Let me.'

'And my brother—'

'I'll take care of it. Rest.'

'Where are you going?'

'The phone. I'll be right there, in the kitchen. Okay?'

She nodded.

I found her brother's number by the phone. No answer. He was probably on his way. I'd try again in a few minutes if he didn't show up. The next thing would be to call the funeral home. I didn't know which one it was. I started back to the living room and heard her cry out suddenly, louder and more desperate. The sound stopped before I got there.

The kid moved in front of the couch to block my way.

'Everything's cool,' he said.

'What is?'

Across the room the front door was still open. There were spatters on his clean white T-shirt. His bag from the convenience mart lay on the carpet with the contents spilling out: a blister pack of cheap steak knives, a roll of twine and a dispenser of wide package-sealing tape. In his hand was a pizza cutter.

She was where I had left her, only now her ankles were bound together with the twine, a piece of the tape covered her mouth and one of her arms dangled to the floor. Blood dripped from the wrist.

'I was gonna save my stuff,' the kid said, 'for when I get home. But I could tell you needed a hand.'

I tried to get past him before the room became any blacker.

He stepped aside and grinned.

'You really got it down, man, about the bitches. I guess I always knew. There just ain't no other way . . .'

'*What have you done?*'

'What you said,' and he winked at me, his eyes dancing wildly in his skull. 'I mean, like, you got to kill them all. Right?'

LYNDA E. RUCKER

No More A-Roving

LYNDA E. RUCKER WAS BORN IN BIRMINGHAM, ALABAMA, grew up in north-east Georgia, and made her way to Portland, Oregon, by way of Ireland, Nepal and the Czech Republic. (She has since found a better map.) She has held (and continues to hold, much to her dismay) the usual motley assortment of writers' jobs, among them waitress, ESL teacher, research assistant, burrito maker, receptionist, proof-reader and monitor for the postal exam.

Her two other published stories have both appeared in Britain's *The Third Alternative* magazine.

'With "No More A-Roving" I was thinking of the kind of people you meet sometimes when you're travelling,' explains the author, 'people who have been on the road for too many months or years and seem to have lost any sense of where they're going or why. Their lives have become little more than a random, disconnected series of occurrences, and they seem so jaded and dulled by their experiences, yet it's as though they don't know what else to do with themselves any longer.

'I wondered what would happen if some of these people were mysteriously drawn to the same place – and what sort of place that would be. Parts of the western Irish coast feel like the end of the world to me.

'Also, I wanted to write something in the spirit of Robert Aickman, whom I admire greatly. I hope I succeeded.'

THE SEAGULL HOSTEL WASN'T MENTIONED in Paul's battered copy of *Let's Go*, but the Australians he'd drunk with back in Cork had recommended it to him, as had his last lift across the Dingle Peninsula. Now dusk had come and gone and a good Irish mile or two out from town he'd begun to wonder if he hadn't been misled. The wind and the chill rain had redoubled their efforts against him, and the couple of cars out on the roads had flown past him in a spray of water. The backpack had seemed so light the first time he'd packed and hefted it. Now it sat like a ton of bricks across his shoulders and lower back. Perhaps he should hike back into town, before it got too late, and blow his budget on some cramped, overpriced bed-and-breakfast; but there it was, after all, a signpost pointing him down a muddy lane to a rambling wooden structure. In the dark of the night it was merely an outline. It looked deserted.

Paul swore under his breath as he approached it, but just as he was stepping up onto the porch the door swung open before him. 'Come in, love, you'll catch your death,' and the dumpy middle-aged woman was pulling him in out of the elements. Paul's eyes took a few minutes to adjust to the room before him: hostel-sparse and dingy, a few old chairs and a black and white television in one corner playing the theme to a soap opera, sunny Australian voices ringing incongruously across the gloom.

'Awful night for it,' the woman commented needlessly. 'Lucky you weren't knocked down by a car with no moon out there. Will you be wanting your own room or a bed in the dormitory, then?'

'Dorm,' he said. He'd get a night's sleep and head out in the morning. The Seagull, he realized now that he'd finally found it, was too far from town to suit him. Even a trip to the pub would require him to slog back through that endless wet rainy night. Hadn't the Australians described it as being closer in? Perhaps the name hadn't been the Seagull at all, perhaps it had been the Seabreeze or the Seaview. He might have missed his intended destination entirely in the storm. All the same, he might find someone interesting to talk to here, even a travelling companion.

'Right, dear. Six pound fifty. I'm Mrs Ryan and my girl Laura works from time to time too. Kitchen's through that door there.' She pointed. 'We don't lock you out during the day, but we ask that if you'll be staying you'll let us know by noon.'

Wandering past her, down a short passageway and into the

kitchen, he saw why he'd thought the place deserted. All the lit rooms were here at the back. Two girls sat giggling at a rough wooden table in the bare narrow room, spooning yogurt from tiny Yoplait containers. Paul lowered his backpack gratefully to the floor. He nodded at them and they giggled in return.

'I'm Paul,' he said. 'What's your names?'

They were from Cork, they told him, come here for work. Day in, day out, they gutted fish at one of the warehouses. Seventeen years old and their faces were hard and flat, their accents so thick he had trouble understanding them. Their complacency depressed him. When he wasn't directly addressing them, they whispered to one another and giggled more. At what, he wondered; his relentless American desire to strike up a friendly conversation? In the last year he had learned that things about himself that he had long imagined to be the very essence of Paul-ness were in fact culturally concocted mannerisms. The discovery was troubling, as though something vital had been stolen from him.

At last he got to his feet and retrieved his backpack, meaning to retreat to the dormitory. If no one there proved worth talking to either, at least he could read for a while before he went to sleep. Reading would distract him from thoughts of Alyssa; she'd stood him up in Scotland where they'd planned to catch the ferry to Ireland together. He'd even stayed two extra days in Stranraer, dull port town, waiting for her to arrive. Somehow, her behavior, though unexpected, hadn't surprised him. Presumably she'd gone on ahead of him, was most likely somewhere in Ireland still. Had he been Alyssa, he wasn't entirely certain he'd have waited for himself either; the real surprise was that she'd not ditched him earlier. And now he'd been travelling so long he found himself running out of reasons not to go home.

The dormitory was at the end of the hallway, past some doors he assumed were private rooms. Stocked with eight bunk beds, it was deserted save for a large young man snoring atop one. The bare walls and windows threw the harsh overhead light back at him. A door at the other end, open slightly to the outside, concealed the couple on the other side of it, a male and female speaking something that sounded like German, or maybe it was Dutch. The scent of hashish drifted languorously across the room.

Paul chose the bed farthest from the snorer to dump his pack. Something he'd seen earlier, in the reception room, worried at the back of his mind. Something he'd noticed, and he couldn't put a name to it.

He was too tired, and exhaustion was playing tricks on him.

He backtracked to the bathroom, a cavernous cold place, to change into dry clothes for sleeping, and brushed his teeth under a bulb that made his face look sickly and orange. So complete was the quiet and sense of isolation that he jumped when the door swung inward and a yellow-haired boy strode past to the urinal.

Paul heard voices in the passageway as he gathered up his shaving kit. They were still hanging around outside the dormitory room when he stepped into the hallway. Four of them, two girls and two younger-looking guys, their voices loud and edgy and frayed by alcohol and cigarettes. Paul found that all at once he didn't feel sociable any longer. Another moment and they were joined by the yellow-haired boy. Paul pushed past them and they gave him the indifferent glances of a well-established travellers' clique.

Another body had occupied the lower bunk opposite Paul's, a small form entirely hidden under the comforter save for some ginger curls strewn across the pillows. Paul rummaged in his backpack for one of the paperbacks he'd picked up in Dublin.

But the book bored him. He let it slide to the floor and rolled over, shutting his eyes against the glaring light overhead. He thought of home; it was like swallowing bile. Things would look better in the morning. As sleep overtook him, the something unremembered worried at the edges of his mind. Something he'd seen when he first came in, and only now had begun to realize the significance of. Sleep claimed him before he could sort it out.

He was awakened by the sound of a child crying. He opened his eyes to a room gone dark, and lifted his head before he realized the sound was that of the wind. He got up quietly, taking care not to irritate the vocal springs of the sagging bunk bed as the slow breath of sleepers rose and fell around him. There seemed too many of them, from the sound of it; only eight bunk beds and not all of them filled, but so many different breaths. A recollection of waking earlier, too, stirred in him, a memory of someone clambering onto the top bunk above him, but the bunk was empty, its bedding smooth. Stealing over to the window Paul saw that the rain had stopped and the sky had partially cleared; the wind blew heavy, fast-moving clouds across a moonlit sky. Under the sound of the wind the sea crashed, closer to the hostel than he'd realized. His own breathing fell into a rhythm with it. His eyes adjusted – indeed, the sea lay just beyond, moonlight glinting off the water. Paul leaned closer, pressed his face against the glass as if that might aid his vision. Surely he imagined the tiny boat on the water, manned by several figures, mere silhouettes in the moonlight. A rowboat. And somewhere out to sea, a distant glow, as if a lighthouse on some long-deserted island kept its covenant to beam would-be sailors to safety. Yet no one would dare that cold wild sea, even in daylight, in such a craft. A second possibility occurred to him: perhaps they were in trouble, perhaps there'd been some accident at sea and their vessel had sunk, and Paul was the only person in the world who could rescue them now. His gaze roamed wildly round the room as though he might find help there, wishing he'd never awakened, wishing someone else had spied the boat. He must have mistaken some trick of the moonlight. He would have to go outside, get closer, to be certain.

He felt his way along the wall till he found the door that had sat ajar earlier in the evening. He pulled hard on it, but it did not budge. Paul ran a hand over the knob, looking for some lock to be twisted, and above it in search of a deadbolt. Nothing. The surface of the knob and door were utterly smooth, yet as he tugged on the handle he felt not the slightest *give*.

Panic settled over him like a dream. Back to the window. He must alert someone. But who? Would he wake someone in the room, race to the reception telephone and phone the local police?

But he no longer spied the boat. A trick of the light, indeed. He scanned the surface of the water, uncertain of what he was looking for. Sometimes, when he was very tired, dreams lingered like afterimages. Surely that had happened tonight.

The stillness closed round him again. Something in the hostel was not waiting, not waiting for anything at all. He returned to his bed where sleep came much later, and troubled.

The next sound that awoke him was that of the heavy boy gasping his way through a round of calisthenics. In the harsher morning light – for the day dawned like slate – he saw that the boy was more of a man, at least in his late twenties or early thirties. The boy-man wore the clothes of someone even older, clothes

Paul associated with the middle-aged or elderly – white under-shirt, boxers, black socks pulled up to his knees. The man was trying to touch his toes. He bent at the waist and bobbed up and down. Paul closed his eyes again. His watching might be intrusive. When he opened them again, the man stood over him, sweating.

'Name's David,' he said, sticking out a fat, sweaty palm for Paul to handle. 'Welcome to the Seagull. Did you just come from Dublin?' He was English.

'Paul,' Paul said, though he didn't offer his own hand in return.

David remained undaunted. 'On holiday, are you? From America?'

Paul looked past him for the group from the previous night, or the German couple. But he and David were alone. It must be later than he realized. He was very tired. He'd been travelling so much lately. It might be good to stay another day or two and rest.

'Never really had any interest in going to America,' David said. 'Like it here.' He depressed Paul in some unaccountable way. 'You at university?'

'Yes,' Paul said. He started to offer more, but offering more led to conversation. Paul did not want to converse with David.

When he was able to escape, he located Mrs Ryan and told her he'd be staying another night. He was shocked to see by the clock behind her that it was almost noon. Mrs Ryan looked irritated, as if in waiting she'd had to turn away a bevy of travellers clamouring for his bed.

He showered and took a walk out the back of the hostel and down near the water. He found the coastline here forbidding. The green treeless landscape led right up to the edge of the sea, a sheer drop; to the south climbed a rocky cliff. Cold sea spray stung his face. He thought he saw two figures through the fog, clambering up the cliff. Perhaps the German girl and her boyfriend. He shouted after them. After all, they were staying there together, and it was perfectly permissible, expected even, to strike up a conversation under such circumstances. But they either ignored him or didn't hear, though the girl did turn once and stare at him, hair whipping about her face, before turning back to follow her boyfriend farther up and out of sight.

The beacon he recalled from the night before managed to penetrate the mist with a soft yellow glow. A lighthouse, perhaps,

on some rocky, craggy island off the coast here? He would ask
Mrs Ryan about it later. If the light he'd seen was real, had the
boat been as well? The dinghy caught his eye then, drawn up to
the shore below though he could see no way of getting down to it.
Seeing it there surprised him; he'd have imagined that at some
point high tide would obliterate the narrow stretch of beach,
making it a gamble to leave anything there. And the choppy sea
seemed hardly an ideal waterway for the poor craft. Paul shivered
against the chill, and in the next moment recalled his dream of the
night before. And certainly it had been a dream. Otherwise, the
people he'd seen in the boat had been lost at sea, their tiny boat
washed ashore. And it would have been his fault. He tried to
imagine it, adrift on that icy ocean, perhaps for days; perhaps
worried that to come too close to the rocky cliffs dotting the
shorelines there would break the boat up entirely, smash it
against the rocks.

His imagination was getting away from him again.

Later today he'd trek into town and pick up a few things to
eat and see about bus connections to Tralee and Limerick,
anyplace east of here. He'd had enough of the countryside,
enough of the coast, and this was seeming less like a restful
way station and more like a place where weary travellers went to
die. Something crawled down his spine at the thought, surprising
him. *Something just walked over my grave.* Paul stuffed his
hands in his pockets and turned his back to the sea, but the chill
still stung at the tips of his ears, the back of his neck, needling his
skin.

'That's Alyssa's scarf!'

Paul didn't think he'd meant to speak out loud. He'd been
watching television in the lobby, wrapped in his jacket against the
chill he hadn't noticed when he'd arrived the night before. But the
thing that had bothered him the previous night dawned on him
now; it was the soft grey woolen muffler snug against Mrs Ryan's
throat. How many times had he seen Alyssa wrap it round her
own beautiful neck?

'What, love?' Mrs Ryan, propped with a magazine, before a
tiny space heater looked over at him.

Paul recognized it as though it were a beloved article of clothing
belonging to him, the black threads woven throughout the grey in

a checkered pattern, the edges frayed because the scarf was old and Alyssa had loved it too much to throw it out.

'Did someone leave that here?' he asked. 'The scarf, I mean?' Mrs Ryan looked confused. 'My scarf?'

'Yes, I think it belongs to a friend of mine.' Impatient. Alyssa might be somewhere close by. She might have left only just before he arrived. She might have said where she was going. What he would say to her if he caught up to her, he would not think about.

'Why, no, that's impossible. My husband, God rest his soul, gave me this one Christmas – oh, six, seven years gone now it is. Keeps me warm as can be.'

'Did a girl named Alyssa stay here in the last week or so?' Paul demanded. Angry now, he tried to control his tone. She was lying. 'It's— I need to get in touch with her. It's very important to me to know if she's been here.'

'You're the first new guest I've had in a while,' Mrs Ryan told him placidly. He could hardly accuse her of anything, could he? He could hardly tell her outright that he knew she was a liar. Paul's hands curled into fists and he shoved them deep in his jacket pockets. Cheap old bitch. Wouldn't heat the place properly and stole from the guests. And he hadn't made it into town to check on bus connections after all. Well, tomorrow he'd just leave. He'd get up early and go and sometime during the day he was bound to catch either a bus or a lift out of town.

Paul pushed himself up from the chair and without another word to Mrs Ryan stalked down the hallway to the dormitory. The group he'd encountered the night before were apparently out again, as was the German couple. The form on the bed opposite his was still there, but this time the covers were thrown back to reveal a small face beneath the ringlets. Paul noticed a bottle of vodka peeking out from the girl's backpack.

Perhaps he'd try walking into town now. The night had cleared, and it wouldn't be such a bad walk as long as it stayed that way. He might even talk to someone about bus schedules. He asked David about a good pub.

'Try O'Flaherty's,' David suggested, and Paul realized with a sort of horror that David was preparing to accompany him. The thought of the pub immediately lost its appeal, and he began fumbling over excuses as to why he wasn't really interested in going *tonight*, especially. David, undaunted, took off for town, wearing a heavy overcoat and good boots. Soon Paul began to wish that he'd accompanied him after all. He had no wish to return to the reception room to watch television with Mrs Ryan, and the German couple returned but spoke in low voices with one another. Paul didn't remember falling asleep atop his covers with all his clothes on, and he didn't wake again before morning.

The rain started again soon after he got up, and he couldn't see heading out to hitchhike or wait for a bus in that weather. Anyway, he'd overslept again.

He boiled instant coffee in a deserted kitchen and later made his way out back once more to the sea. He looked for his fellow travellers again, perhaps on the cliffs, but saw no one. He smoked the cigarettes he'd bummed from David and threw the butts into the ocean. A bitter wind blew across the water, and somewhere through the mist the beacon shined for someone. He thought of the fishermen who made their living from this sea, of the thousands upon thousands dead because of blighted potatoes, years of famine scarring this green harsh land, and he thought of America. The more he thought of it the more it seemed to him to exist someplace very far away. He wondered if it would be there any longer if he crossed this sea. He wondered if he cared.

He strode to the edge, where he'd seen the dinghy below. The strip of shoreline remained, but the dinghy was gone.

It crossed his mind that perhaps it had broken free from its moorings somewhere, drifted up on the tide here and then back out again, but that hardly seemed likely. There had been a deliberateness about its placing on the shore below, as though someone had pulled it in from the water and carefully placed the oars crossways inside of it.

He asked Mrs Ryan about it that night in the reception room, but she shook her head. 'Oh, love, it might be anybody's. Still some fishermen in these parts, you know. We're not all in the business of providing warm beds for tourists.' But who would row a dinghy on that wild sea? And there were no lighthouses offshore around here, she assured him, she was certain of that. As she spoke Paul couldn't keep his eyes off that muffler round her neck. He was wild to get hold of it. He'd remembered how to be sure: something he'd teased Alyssa about. She'd written her name on the tags of all her clothes like a child going away to summer

camp: Alyssa Meiers. It was an oddly homey and endearing move
from the usually elusive, too-beautiful-to-be-true girl. Not the
kind of girl who usually fell for Paul. Not the kind of girl he could
expect to wait for him to catch up now. And the two of them,
together, would have always been that way: Alyssa, far ahead,
and Paul, lagging behind, trying to reach her.

In the kitchen he cooked up some packaged noodles and ate
them in front of the television. The ginger-haired girl made an
appearance outside of her bed at last. She said her name was
Rosie and she was from Melbourne. He wondered why she kept
getting up and leaving the room until he realized she was refilling
her Pepsi can with alcohol. Her speech became slurred and she
stumbled once across the rug at the threshold, and she tried to
laugh it off but she looked like she was crying. Then she left the
room again and didn't come back. Paul was glad. He waited until
he was pretty sure she'd gone to sleep, or passed out, and made
his way in there as well.

In the morning another girl kneeling beside Rosie, trying to
wake her, roused him from sleep instead. 'Ah, Rosie, did you have
too much to drink again?' the girl was saying, her voice a pleasing
Irish cadence, and Paul caught sight of Rosie's face, screwed up
tight against the morning like a little girl's, fists rubbing shut eyes.
He rolled over and tried to sleep again.

But, 'I don't want to go,' Rosie whined, 'the others have gone
and I don't want to go after them.'

'There, shhh,' the Irish girl whispered as though she were
soothing a small child. 'No need to fret about it.' Later, Paul
found the girl in the reception area. This was Mrs Ryan's Laura,
then. She was checking in the first new guest Paul had seen since
he arrived, a tall, heavy-set blonde girl.

'Did a girl named Alyssa Meiers stay here before I came?' Paul
asked Laura, hoping she'd be more receptive than her mother.

'Oh, I'm sure she didn't. I've a good memory for names,' Laura
assured him. He watched her as she spoke, looking for deception
beneath her cheerful ease.

The blonde girl said, 'You looking for somebody? She'll turn
up sooner or later. That's what happens, you know, you think
you've said goodbye to somebody forever and you run into them
three or four more times over the next couple months.' She had
the accentless voice Paul had come to associate with Americans

from the West Coast, and sure enough, she hailed from California.

'I've been traveling eighteen months,' she told him as they shared a cigarette in the kitchen. 'My friend was with me for a while, but she was raped in Spain. Hitchhiking. She went home after that. Before that we went all over Thailand, Malaysia, Nepal . . . you been to Southeast Asia?'

Paul said he hadn't.

'Man, that is a trip. Like, you wouldn't believe the drugs you can get there. And cheap! We stayed there a really long time, cause everything was cheap. Ireland costs too damn much.'

Paul was taking a dislike to the girl, her coarse and abrasive manner, her bulky body. 'When are you going home?' he asked, because somehow he felt the question might hurt her and he wanted to do just that.

She stopped, drew in a long drag of smoke and shrugged. 'Dunno. Why would I want to do that?'

And so it went. 'How long have you been staying here?' Paul asked Rosie once, and she just shook her head again and wouldn't talk to him anymore, just stared at the television as though mesmerized by the opening credits of a variety show. He dug through his address book but couldn't find the slip of paper where he'd written down the name of the place the night it had first been suggested. Perhaps it had been the Seashell, or the Albatross, in which case he was here *under false pretenses*. He said it to himself as a joke and didn't feel like laughing afterwards. If he wanted to stay in the area, it wasn't as though he had to remain *here*. He could ask around in town, perhaps get to the bottom of it, find the other, more pleasant hostel that he must have mistaken this one for. Surely no one would recommend this place to anybody.

For a long time no one arrived or left; and he eventually decided that the five travellers he'd encountered the first night were long gone, for he never saw them again. The German girl and boy spoke only to one another, even avoiding eye contact so it was impossible to strike up a conversation naturally. Late one morning he caught sight of them climbing the cliffs again. He could catch up to them; perhaps they'd been here long enough to remember Alyssa. They could hardly avoid him when it was only the three of them in that deserted landscape. And he was lonely. The other visitors depressed him.

The cliffs were slick and dangerous, sprayed with sea water. The couple were far more sure-footed than he. He clambered across the rocks, ignoring caution, curiosity rendering him careless, and still kept them barely in sight. At last they seemed to slow a bit, so he was able to pick his way more carefully. A glorious view awaited him. Even in the gloom, or perhaps because of it, the seascape spread before him bespoke a beautiful desolation. It was in one of those moments, gazing about him, that he nearly lost them again.

They had turned down a track, though, a path down the cliff. The way looked even more treacherous than the one he'd taken here. Paul might be able to follow them down, but he couldn't imagine making his way back up again. For a long moment he stood watching them, helplessly. He realized that if they continued as they were going they might reach the stretch of shoreline, if indeed it were possible to reach it at all.

Surely that wasn't safe. The tides came in swiftly. They might be trapped, cut off; but his concern was not great enough to send him after them. Cowardice, he supposed. He winced as he thought the word, however accurate it might be. It was a trait he'd been able to conceal from Alyssa in the short time they'd known each other. It was just as well he'd lost her; she'd have found him out anyway.

Paul waited until the couple re-emerged on a narrow rocky spit of shoreline farther to his left. Until now, he had not noticed the dinghy drawn up on the dry land there. The two of them shoved it off into the water, and the boy clambered in first, then helped the girl in. They both began to row, out to sea. Away toward the light that beamed feebly but steadily somewhere in the mist.

Eventually he lost track altogether of how many days he'd been at the hostel, and he approached Mrs Ryan with some bills again. She took some of them, and pushed back some change, which he pocketed. A thick haze had settled over everything, and Paul sensed October closing in on November: dank winter would soon overcome the Emerald Isle. Now he woke shivering in the night. The comforter provided by the Seagull was insufficient against the chill of the unheated room. David began to have nightmares. Sometimes he would cry out in his sleep and thrash about. He still went out some evenings, always asking Paul to go along, but Paul had the feeling David wasn't going to the pub at all. He saw him in town on a trip he made in himself, to purchase some supplies. David walked across the square with his overcoat flapping down around his ankles, and Paul called out to him, but David either didn't hear or ignored him.

There were only the four of them left there: he and David Rosie and the American girl. He'd not noticed when the girls from Cork went away but he had not seen them in a very long time. It no longer seemed curious to him that they rarely interacted, moving through the days as though each had erected an invisible but impenetrable barrier against the others.

One day Paul found himself sitting on his bunk composing a letter to his sister. He broke down crying. He wanted to go home. He paced up and down the room, cursing this grey inhospitable place, these people who flitted like ghosts here. He felt frantic to phone the airlines, to go screaming across the Atlantic and home again. He became panicked. Some nights before he'd dreamed of a mushroom cloud, and he wept, imagining this the last place left in all the world, and them the only people. He finished his letter to Robin, assuring her he'd be home soon, he just needed to make arrangements. 'As a matter of fact,' he concluded optimistically, 'you'll probably already have heard from me by phone by the time you get this!'

The words would be a talisman. He gave the letter to Mrs Ryan for posting. Afterwards he thought better of it, but when he asked her about it she stared at him with stolid incomprehension and said, 'Postman took it.' She still wore that scarf twisted defiantly about her neck, and Paul realized he no longer needed to look at any sort of label on it to confirm that it belonged to Alyssa. And he'd lost so much time here there was no hope of ever catching up to her.

'I'm heading back soon,' he told David, who did his exercises faithfully this morning as every morning. David lifted his head to look at him, red-faced.

'You'll be leaving, then?'

'Looks that way,' Paul said. 'Gotta get back to school. See my family again. My sister was pregnant, last I heard. Probably I'm an uncle now.' It felt funny to say it.

He walked into town and checked the bus schedules, arranged to take one into Tralee and from there to Limerick. The lazy appeal of hitchhiking had vanished. He thanked Mrs Ryan for her hospitality and informed her he'd be leaving early the next morning.

The wind and the sea woke him in the night, just as they had the first night he'd spent here.

This night, however, was moonless; no figures on the water to frighten him, no restless breathing in the room about him. But the sea was louder than ever before, the crashing of its waves palpably close, as though he could reach out through the window and dip his hand in those cold waters.

Paul woke again at dawn, before the others, and slipped outside.

He'd smoked his last cigarette the night before, and so he stood staring out at the water, nothing to do but gaze at the beam of light.

He climbed up the cliffs, as the German girl and her boyfriend had done, and scrambled down the slick path to the shore.

He found the dinghy waiting there for him. A solid, wooden vessel, splintery planks for seats. At one time he wouldn't have trusted it to take him across a pond.

But this was different.

Paul zipped his coat tighter against the winds that blew in across the water, and pulled on gloves. Rowing was difficult when the cold numbed your hands, though he wasn't really sure how much rowing he would have to do.

He pushed the boat most of the way into the water. He tried to climb in, still standing on dry land, but the boat tipped sideways and threatened to spill him into the sea as soon as he transferred all his weight. He would have to wade in, up to his shins. He gasped as the icy waters lapped at his jeans and seeped through to his skin.

Paul couldn't remember having handled a boat at all before. After a couple of false starts, in which he merely bobbed on the water and went in circles, he got the hang of it. Strong, slow, steady strokes sent him gliding against the current, against the constant breaking of the waves in toward land.

In the distance, he could see it, the beam of light, guiding his way. A chilling gust blew across him. Inside the jacket he was sweating, but his face, his lips and nose and ears, had gone numb in the cold.

Travelling, he'd always tried to remain on the move.

Paul kept rowing. The wind stung his eyes and extracted tears. Soon, his destination would become clear. The mist closed behind him and the land slipped away, and the glow beckoned him onward in the grey winter morn.

GRAHAM JOYCE

First, Catch Your Demon

GRAHAM JOYCE IS A FOUR-TIMES WINNER of the British Fantasy Society's August Derleth Award for Best Novel (for *Dark Sister*, *Requiem*, *The Tooth Fairy* and *Indigo*). His other books include *Dreamside*, *House of Lost Dreams*, *The Stormwatcher*, the young-adult science fiction novel *Spiderbite*, and the novella *Leningrad Nights*.

In 2001, Subterranean Press published Joyce's chapbook *Black Dust*, while his novel *Smoking Poppy* appeared from Gollancz in the UK and Pocket Books in America. His latest novel, *The Facts of Life*, is from the same publishers.

'This story is set in the scorpion-infested house I lived in on the Greek island of Lesbos in 1988,' the author remembers. 'Before I knew about the scorpions in the house, I was awakened one night by a bad dream and the word "scorpion" on my lips. I lit the oil lamp and saw three of the creatures on the wall – just as described in this tale.'

I MUST HAVE KNOWN THEY WERE there because some dark instinct jolted me awake. I sat upright in bed. The shutters were closed against the sirocco heat and there wasn't even the light from a single star. Fumbling for the matches I kept at the side of the bed, I lit an oil lamp. Not until then did I feel confident enough to swing my legs out of the bed without stepping on one of the disgusting things.

I lit two other oil lamps and the flame dancing behind each glass dispatched skittering shadows across the floor. Not helping at all. It was stifling. I opened the wooden shutters and the heat rolled over me. It was 4.00 a.m.

I looked under the bed. I looked behind the cupboard. I lifted the mat at the door. I knew they were there somewhere because a voice in my dreams had warned me, and I tend to take these things seriously. I didn't know whether to walk down to the water to throw myself in or to try to go back to sleep. Then I saw them.

Three of them.

My grandmother used to have three ceramic flying ducks on her living room wall. In the eighties, it was ironic-kitsch to display three Volkswagen Beetles, or three Supermen flying in strict formation. Such is our cleverness. But here in my beach house on the Greek island of Karpathos I'd managed to trump all that with three live scorpions. In ascending order: big, bigger, biggest. The largest not more than six inches away from where my dreaming head had slumbered moments earlier.

We should trust our dreams. They are trying to help us.

Well, I didn't like them, the scorpions. I'd heard they like to get into shoes and other warm, moist places. Perhaps if I'd been less of a lout I would have behaved like a proper naturalist, making sketches of these beautiful creatures, taking scholarly notes about their habitat and behaviour. But I'm not and I didn't. Plus I was thinking defensively about my own warm, moist places.

I marched outside to my patio kitchen and reached for a heavy iron skillet. Aspro, a feral white cat living on scraps from my table, looked puzzled. I weighed the frying pan in my right hand, returned to the scorpions and hit Number One so hard that what didn't stick to the underside of the skillet left a scorpion-shaped applique on the wall. Bang went Number Two, and fuck you all the way to hell thou slimy carapace, thou whoreson zed, thou mere cipher. I was saying all this and lining up for the hat-trick when Number Three, coming to its senses, dropped from the wall and scuttled toward my bare feet, sting cocked.

I leapt on my bedside chair, tipping over the oil lamp. The glass smashed and the burning oil spilled on the stone floor, raising a small curtain of flame between me and the surviving scorpion. I have heard that a scorpion encircled by fire will sting itself to death. Nonsense. Undeterred by the conflagration in its path, the scorpion – almost casually – stepped through the fire and came to a swaggering halt at the foot of the chair. Its sting remained cocked. My six-foot height advantage notwithstanding, it raised its pincers at me like a species of dense English football hooligan, drunkenly beckoning me on.

Then Aspro the cat appeared, and, properly challenged, the scorpion retreated to a crevice at the foot of the wall and was gone. I climbed down from my ridiculous perch and extinguished the small fire with a bedside glass of water. I examined the bottom of the skillet, where the crushed scorpions comprised no more than flimsy crisps of brown carapace and mucus. I let the cat have what it wanted, and anyway it saved me from having to clean the underside of the skillet. Aspro chewed thankfully and licked his paws.

'Sometimes, Aspro, you disgust me.'

The heat blanket made me sigh. Sweat ran in my eyes, down my back, trickled in my groin. There was no possibility of my going back to sleep. I decided to go and climb in the rowing boat, where at least I could sit with my feet in the water. I pulled on some shorts and Aspro followed me along the garden path to the boat.

I pulled up short. Someone was sitting in my boat. I didn't know who it could be. I had no friends and I discouraged all neighbours and strangers.

The sea was still, like oil, bearing a dermis of moonlight, but suffocating under the sirocco heat. The small, silhouetted figure hunched over the prow of the small rowing boat, gazing into the water. I stood under the fig tree at the gate to my garden, contemplating what to do. Aspro looked up at me as if to say, *what next?*

'You're in my boat,' I said rather fiercely.

I don't like visitors, invited or otherwise. I don't like people bothering me. I expected the intruder to be startled, or to spin round, or to take fright in some way. But the figure continued to gaze into the water. 'Yes.'

It was a woman's voice. I took a few steps closer, and I pulled up for a second time. There was a *naked* woman in my boat.

'You're in my boat,' I repeated, stupidly.

This time she turned languidly to face me. She sat with her knees drawn up together under her chin. 'You don't mind.'

It wasn't a question. It was a statement. Actually I did mind. I didn't want anyone around my place. Least of all a woman. Least of all a *naked* woman. I had to make an effort to avert my eyes from her breasts and the plump curve of her legs. Her lustrous black hair was cut in a fashionable bob. Her dark eyes trawled me with sensual laziness. She made no effort to cover herself. Indeed, I couldn't see any clothes with which she might.

'Look, if it really upsets you I'll get out of your boat,' she said. She stood up. Her skin was slightly wet. The weak moonlight slithered along her flanks like phosphorescence and her pubic bush glimmered with droplets of sea water.

I felt petty. 'No, you don't have to get out. I was just startled to see you there.'

She sat down again. 'I've been swimming. To get out of the heat.'

'Alone? You shouldn't swim at night alone. There are currents.'

'You're concerned for me? That's nice. But I wasn't alone. I went swimming with my two sisters. But when I turned around I couldn't find them.'

'Where? Where did you swim from?'

She gestured vaguely in the direction of Mesahori, where the illumined, whitewashed church squatted on a freakish outcrop of rock. I doubted she'd swum that far, but I didn't say anything. 'Go get some wine from your house. Let's drink together.'

I was taken aback by her commanding tone. So much so that I found myself returning to my kitchen for a bottle and two beakers. I also found her a towel. 'I don't have a cooler,' I said grumpily on returning to the boat. I tossed her the towel.

'Does it bother you?'

'Please just cover up.'

'I meant does it bother you, living without electricity.'

'Not at all. If you live without electricity you let other things into your life. Cheers.'

'Cheers to you.'

Her name was Sasha. When she told me she was a writer I felt my teeth grinding. The writers I have known have all been drunks, dreamers, deceivers and frauds. That was just the successful ones. I should know. I was an editor. I was the one who had to deal with these whining, self-centred, immature psychopaths for a living. Anyway, after divulging this piece of information she looked at me in anticipation of the usual questions. Perhaps she expected me to be interested, but I let it go.

We smoked cigarettes and drank the wine. The moon's image floated unbroken on the water. After a while Sasha produced a battered-looking reefer, and asked me for a light. She took a deep toke before passing it to me.

There was something disturbing about Sasha, something sexually ambiguous. She was simultaneously attractive and repulsive. As I squinted at her through the smoke from the joint, she ran her tongue along her upper lip, chasing the diamond-like beads of sweat there. Meanwhile I inhaled the smoke deeply and held it back for a long time, trying to impress myself. The smoke itself had a peculiar taste and odour. That is, another odour beyond the obvious scent of the beneficial herb. I couldn't put my finger on it.

'If you swam here,' it suddenly occurred to me to ask, 'how did you keep the reefer dry?'

She took the joint and inhaled passionately, holding my gaze until she blew out a plume of smoke. Then she winked.

I was appalled. I got out of the boat and walked back up to the vine-covered patio of my house. I had a hammock slung there, and I slumped into it. When I opened my eyes she was sitting nearby in a wicker chair, with her knees drawn up under her chin. I don't know why I'd bothered to give her the towel.

I had an unpleasant thought. 'You should be careful,' I said. 'This place is infested with scorpions.'

'Excellent! Where? Show me.'

I was a little taken aback by this response, though I lazily indicated that they were crawling all over the shop.

'Got a jar?' she said, springing to her feet. Without waiting for an answer she picked up a glass jam jar I used for burning candles outside. 'If there's one around, I'll find it.' She got down on her hands and knees, and, taking a draw on the joint, began blowing smoke into the cracks between the concrete floor and the external walls, moving methodically along the patio. I watched her do this for a few minutes and was about to speak when a medium-sized scorpion scuttled out of the crevices. She deftly trapped it under the jar. 'Hand me a knife. A big one.'

I swung out of the hammock and passed her a long-bladed kitchen knife. Lifting the jar half an inch, she manoeuvred the knife into place and expertly amputated the segmented abdominal tail from the creature. Satisfied, she lifted the jar, keeping her knife on the still-twitching tail. She picked up the disarmed scorpion, which was thrashing its lobster-like claws. 'You can go now,' she said, planting a kiss on its back. She set it down on the concrete. It would have scuttled away but Aspro the cat, having watched all these proceedings, pounced and ate it.

This seemed to displease Sasha. Still on her knees, she hissed at the cat. Aspro, chewing heartily, jumped back into the shadows. Murmuring something about hating cats, Sasha went on to give me a lesson in scorpion anatomy. 'The glands are at this end of the tail. You don't want the venom sac.'

'Don't I?'

'No. It would blow you apart. You want the glands, which are in a pair, here. You cut across here – see? – and here. Though I don't know why I'm telling you as you really shouldn't try this at home, as it were.'

'As it were.'

'You need a tiny drop of olive oil.'

'I do?'

'Just the tiniest drop to activate the neurotoxin.'

'The what?'

'Have you got any? Any oil?'

She crushed the segment she'd extracted from the scorpion and mixed it with a smear of olive oil. Then she asked me for a cigarette. She pinched a little of the tobacco from the end without breaking the paper, popped in her minute mix of God-knows-what and packed that in with the spare tobacco. Then she offered it to me to smoke.

'You must be fucking jesting.'

'No.'

'You first.'

'There's only one pop in it. The thing won't share.'

'Then you have it.'

'If you insist. I was trying to give you a treat.'

'A treat? What a pretty idea.'

She shrugged, and made to light up the concoction for herself. She struck a match and some cast to her eye, perhaps a glance of contempt as she looked across the naked flame at me, made me ask, 'What does it do?'

'Oh for God's sake. Do you want it or not?'

I stepped up to her, snatched the cigarette from between her lips, and put it to my own mouth. I could taste her lips on the filter. I grabbed her hand to steady the flame and put it to the tip of the cigarette. Catchlight from the watery moon flared briefly in her eye. I puffed on the cigarette and wiped sweat from my brow.

'Hold it deep in your lungs.'

I took another draw but nothing happened. Again, and this time something sizzled in the ciggie's red cone. I got a lungful, held it back; still nothing. Then my head cracked against the moon.

When I say my head cracked against the moon, I mean that literally. There was a sound like a ten-thousand-decibel mosquito and my brain inflated at unconscionable velocity, rushing outward at the speed of light. My chin banged on the concrete and my skull smacked up against the moon. (Later I was to realize I'd fallen over, but I didn't know that at the time.) The moon punctured and a shower of milky, resinous light drenched me, forming a brilliant membrane of ectoplasmic light around me, plugging my nostrils, my ears, my mouth. I could barely see through it. I had to hole the membrane to breathe and when I managed to drag the latex shroud off me my ears started popping to the cacophony of night sounds from my garden.

I heard a million insects and other wildlife excavating the ground under the house. A wave of heat rolled over me and I knew that I was lying on my back on the ground and that Sasha was fellating me. Every time I tried to open my eyes, all I could see was gold and silver flora exploding. After a moment the flora resolved into the shape of Sasha working away at my cock.

At last she hoisted herself onto my chest, her breasts quivering and I could see that from below her navel she was all scorpion and not woman at all. Half woman, half arachnid. She had human arms in place of the scorpion's lobster-like claws, but her body trailed eight legs. I shuddered, and gagged. She wiped her mouth with the back of her hand and smiled at me. Then her venomous sting appeared over her head, quivering slightly, waving from side to side. I made to scream, but no sound would come. The sting dipped, lightly touched my forehead, and I passed out.

When I came round it was morning and the bright sunlight lancing through the open shutters hurt my eyes. Someone clattered a pot in my patio kitchen. I swung my legs out of bed, and my vision suffered from a slight strobe effect. My dick was rather sore but apart from these things I felt quite well. I started to pull on some jeans that were lying on the floor; then, not wanting to find a scorpion in my tackle I remembered to shake them out. Sasha was outside making coffee. She must have been back to her own place because now she was wearing a simple black dress. She looked a little too much at home amongst my things.

'Come here,' she said, beckoning me off the patio. 'Want to show you something.'

I followed her down the path to the whitewashed breeze-block lavatory. She'd dislodged a stone near the base of the white wall. Two scorpions were locked in apparent combat in the small depression thus exposed. 'Mating is a dangerous business when you're a scorpion,' Sasha said. I looked closer. The creatures had engaged claws and were twitching their tails together. At last they hooked on, each having effectively neutralized the other. Then they proceeded to tug each other back and forth across the stony earth. 'The rocking makes him leave his seed on the ground and she picks it up on her belly.'

'Know a lot about scorpions, don't you?' I said, scratching the back of my neck.

'Sure do.'

We went back up to the patio. She poured coffee and offered me a cigarette. I looked at it doubtfully.

'There's nothing in it. You don't trust me an inch, do you?'

An inch? I didn't trust her the width of a brain synapse. Speaking of which, parts of my own brain were still tingling in aftershock. I found myself studying her surreptitiously, trying to see evidence of her nocturnal carapace. Though I will say she made decent coffee.

Sasha was content to hang around all day, sunbathing topless on the apron of grass between my house and the sea, sipping my ouzo and flicking through my magazines. She swam, later trying to wash off the salt water under the ramshackle shower, but the water drum on the roof was empty and I wasn't going to fill it up for her. No need – she did it herself, filling the bucket from the pump and climbing the ladder to empty the bucket into the drum. After showering she went around the place with a woman's fixing-up eye. She tidied my kitchen and rearranged my hanging system for my pots and pans. She swept out the room. I didn't like it one bit, but all I could do was growl into the encyclopaedia I was reading and feel the unwanted erection fattening inside my shorts.

'Encyclopaedia? You read encyclopaedias?'

'No. I read *one* encyclopaedia. This one.'

She leaned over me, her nipple an inch from my mouth, like the swollen pip of a pomegranate. 'You're only on C!' I don't know why she was surprised. It was a large encyclopaedia. 'What will you do when you get to the end?'

'I'll start again. Now leave me alone.'

'What's the last entry? Let's go straight to the end.'

'No.'

But Sasha wouldn't leave it. She teased and nudged me and tried to grab the book. At last I banged the encyclopaedia shut and grabbed her by the wrist, dragging her squealing from the patio into the room. Once inside I bent her over the bed and lifted her black dress over her head. Underneath she was nude. Though she pretended to resist, as I loosened my shorts she spread her legs. Released, my cock bobbed angrily and, with the startling quickness of a ferret into a rabbit hole, buried itself deep inside her. She gasped. And laughed.

I tend to fall asleep after the act. I understand this is supposed to make me a lousy lay. But when I came to moments later, she had massaged me to erection all over again. I couldn't seem to get enough of her, and this pattern was repeated over and over throughout the rest of the afternoon and evening. Just the smell of her inflamed me, and she in turn was determined to suck me dry.

At some point in the evening I got up to grab us something to eat. She followed me outside. We stood nude on the patio as the twilight settled on the water. She stood behind me with her arms around my waist as we watched a night fisherman glide silently by in silhouette, a lantern on the prow of his rowing boat. 'Know what I like about you?' she said. 'Your anger. I like it. Why are you so angry?'

I shook my head and struck a match to light the gas stove.

'It doesn't matter. You don't have to say. In fact it's better not to. I understand perfectly. Because I'm angry, too.'

Stars were winking awake. Orion, huge in the sky and hanging low. We stood looking out on the darkening ocean and with the ghostly fisherman gliding through the water, and with her hand stroking my belly, for a moment I felt truly happy. After we'd eaten she gave me something to smoke. I remember stumbling into bed in a daze, and her climbing in after me.

When I awoke it was in the hour just before dawn. She was gone from my side. The shutters were open and a buttery moonlight spilled into the room. Something on the wall moved, but at the periphery of my vision.

I turned my head very slowly. It was Sasha, clinging to the wall. Her eyes were half-closed in self-communion. Hanging on the whitewashed wall, she defied gravity. I was paralysed with fright. I pissed the bed. Huge boils of sweat erupted from my skin.

Sasha was nude and as I strained, trembling, to see how she clung to the wall I saw, faintly pulsating, like a brown shadow, the scorpion abdomen superimposed over her lower body. My teeth chattered, giving me away. Sasha slowly turned her gaze on me. Then she dropped from the wall and onto my bed with the lightness of a bug. As she crept towards me, her sting appeared from behind her head, wavering before it touched me lightly just below my left temple, and I passed out again.

Examining myself in my cracked shaving mirror the following morning, I found a sizeable lesion on the side of my head. Sasha was already up, frying eggs and bacon in the large skillet. She had tied a tiny apron round her waist as a precaution against the sizzling fat.

'Shouldn't you put some clothes on? Someone might come by.' As I spoke I noticed three scorpion carapaces scattered on the concrete patio. Either Aspro the cat had had a good night's hunting or Sasha had a gland-extraction factory going.

'Good morning, Ryan. And no one comes by here. Sleep well?'

'Actually I didn't.'

'Kind of grouchy today, aren't you?' She looked up from the chuckling, spitting frying pan. 'What's that on your head?' When I fingered the sore spot, she set the pan aside from the flame and came to look. 'Mosquito bite?' She went back to the eggs.

I sat down at the table. 'That stuff you gave me to smoke the other day. Do you think it could have after-effects?'

'Sure.' She served up the bacon and eggs. 'You can get flashbacks for days. Come and eat.'

'Not hungry.'

Whipping off her apron she straddled me, settling herself on my lap. 'If you're going to keep fucking me seven times a day, you're going to have to keep your strength up.' Then she kissed me, but I resisted. 'What's wrong? Tired of me already?'

'I don't feel good.'

She put a hand on my forehead, squinting at me doubtfully. 'You seem a little hot. Why don't you take a swim? You'll feel better.'

I picked up a towel and padded through the scorched grass down to the beach. I didn't want a swim, but I wanted to get away from her. Why couldn't I just kick her out? Just send her packing? I waded in the water up to my calf muscles, steadying myself against the boat to avoid stepping on the sea urchins. Looking back I saw Sasha hunkered over the table, not eating but engrossed in some new activity.

I returned to the house very quietly, coming up behind her while she thought I was still swimming. Over her shoulder I could see she was rolling another long joint. The papers were pasted together and the mixture of tobacco and resin was laid out on the paper. In her right hand was a syringe. Her left hand reached behind her head, lifting her hair as her fumbling fingers located a spot behind her ear at the base of her skull. In a shocking movement she jabbed the needle of the syringe into her neck and sharply upwards towards the region of the cerebellum. She jolted. I gagged, but she didn't seem to notice me behind her. Slowly she drained off some dark fluid into the syringe.

When she was done she made as if to squirt the fluid from the syringe onto the contents of the joint.

'What are you doing?' I gasped.

Turning to me slowly, she smiled. The brilliant Aegean sunlight fizzed in her eyes. She dropped the syringe and picked up the reefer, lasciviously rolling her tongue along the sticky paper edge as she proceeded to turn a neat, crafted joint. 'I'm gonna look after you,' she chuckled.

My feverish gaze swept the table. 'Where's that needle? The syringe, where is it?'

'What?'

The syringe was gone. I looked on the floor. Nothing. There was some cutlery on the table but that was all. 'I saw a syringe. In your hand.'

She picked up a stainless steel knife. 'I was just hot-knifing the resin. Give it a crumble. Say, you really are burning up, aren't you?'

I was perspiring insanely, and my temperature was rocketing, it was true. Sasha coaxed me back inside the house, her voice gentle, wheedling. 'I know what you want,' she said. 'I told you I'm going to take care of you.' Pushing me back onto the bed she whipped off my shorts and closed her mouth around my cock, sucking me to the point of orgasm. I lay back with my eyes closed, unable to resist. At the instant I ejaculated into her mouth she produced the syringe from somewhere and, bringing it down hard from above her head before swinging it round in a curving thrust, jammed it into my buttock.

I was still screaming when the hit came.

The first thing that happened was that I felt a scorching heat and my body crackled like cellophane in a fire. I was flung up in the air and out of the house. The roof blew outwards in a million tiny fragments. A golden wind shrieked in my ears as I went up and up, and my skin rippled and rolled with the g-force.

I remember corrosive sunlight stinging my eyes as I was sucked high above the clouds, up, up, up. I went ripping up through the stratosphere, through night-shining clouds and then on up into a sable darkness, passing through rises and falls of temperature until finally I passed through an exit zone of the atmosphere itself and into space, and although I knew it to be freezing, the raging inner heat of my body was keeping me alive. I was flung in a vertiginous trajectory, yoked by speed and feeling my bones cracking and resetting until I was reconfigured in a sequence of gleaming stars, major novae pulsating in a pattern almost cruciform, spine and forelimbs, while minor stellar bodies glittered superbly to complete a geometric form, pincers, legs, over-hanging tail loaded with brilliant venom, set among the heavens in a place outside the curve of time.

All that of course was hallucination. None of it happened.

It was some time before I came to my senses, to find myself back in my beach house. Sasha was still there, patiently awaiting my return. And I was glad she was there. My distaste for her presence had been resolved, and some of the rage inside me had been drained, or at least transformed.

We spend our days together quietly. Often we don't even feel the need to speak, enjoying the companionable silence of old couples. I feel my eyes glaze over and almost in a slumber I am prepared to let the days pass without event. We keep late hours.

Sasha is generous. Should a juicy black spider pop its head from between the cracks in the brickwork, she will let me have first strike as I hone my skills. Sometimes I glance up from my place on the wall to Sasha's place on the wall, and I have almost forgotten to marvel at how easy it is, with the extra limbs, to maintain my grip on the perpendicular. Aspro the cat had to go, of course. Sasha doesn't like cats and we had to chase Aspro away.

We wait for someone else to take over the house. It has been a long time and no one has come, though patience is a virtue that Sasha has been able to teach me.

Though for some reason I do miss the cat.

DONALD R. BURLESON

Pump Jack

DONALD R. BURLESON IS THE AUTHOR of the novels *Flute Song* (reprinted as *The Roswell Crewman* and a finalist for the Bram Stoker Award in 1996), *Arroyo* and *A Roswell Christmas Carol*. He has also had more than 100 short stories published in such magazines as *Twilight Zone*, *The Magazine of Fantasy & Science Fiction*, *Deathrealm*, *Wicked Mystic*, *Terminal Fright*, as well as in dozens of anthologies, including *The Mammoth Book of Best New Horror*, *Dark Terrors 4*, *Post Mortem*, *MetaHorror*, *100 Creepy Little Creature Stories*, *100 Wicked Little Witch Stories*, *100 Vicious Little Vampire Stories*, *The Cthulhu Cycle*, *The Azathoth Cycle*, *Return to Lovecraft Country*, *Made in Goatswood* and others.

He is the author of the short-story collections *Lemon Drops and Other Horrors*, *Four Shadowings* and *Beyond the Lamplight*, as well as the non-fiction study *The Golden Age of UFOs*. Burleson is the director of a college computer laboratory in Roswell, New Mexico, and is a field investigator and research consultant to MUFON – the Mutual UFO Network – of which he is State Director for New Mexico.

About the following story, the author explains: 'In the American Southwest oil wells are of course a common sight to travellers, standing against the desert sunset and nodding at the earth. While my wife Mollie and I have always found that there is something serene about these pump jacks, there is something creepy about them too, in an odd insectoid kind of way. And I guess that's all it takes for a diseased fancy . . .'

I T WAS STRANGE, BEING BACK in the desert.

That's what this land was, all right, however stubbornly a half-dozen generations of sheep ranchers had struggled to carve a living out of this sandy, mesquite-dotted soil.

Cal Withers pulled his rental car over to the side of the lonely road and got out and sniffed the air. After the clamorous squalor of city life, he wasn't used to all this space, all this quiet, and it tended almost to make him nervous. But the limitless deep blue sky was delectable, no denying that, especially when one was used to cramped city skies stained an ugly grey by skyscrapers.

All these years, back East, he had thought of the desert lands of southeastern New Mexico as a kind of childhood dream. This yellow prairie land had been his home for the first seven years of his life, till his dad, weary of farming, had found a new job and moved them all to the frozen northlands, leaving the old farmhouse in the dubious hands of Uncle Bill and Aunt Clara. Growing up in Boston on the banks of the Charles River, Cal had found it easy just to stay there, settle into life there, grow older there. But now he wondered whether he had made a mistake, never coming back here till now.

Well. He surveyed vastnesses of gently rolling ground, furred over with wheatgrass and spiked with yucca. What would he have done here, anyway, if he had stayed? Would he have had the patience to coax a living out of this ground, tend ragtag herds of sheep, run a ranch, like nearly all his family before him? He wondered. Probably not, the truth to tell; it took a different kind of mentality to live like that.

But damn, this clean, clear sky looked nice, with its regal flotillas of billowy white clouds driven onward by a tempest of sunlight. High above him, a hawk fell across the sky like a meteor, spread its wings, wheeled, and was gone, fluttering into the sun. Somewhere nearby, grasshoppers ratcheted lustily. Even in late October the air was warm and the land bristled with desert life. The place really brought back all the fond old memories.

And yet its pleasantness didn't quite banish the not-so-fond old memories.

The sky seemed to darken almost imperceptibly for a moment, until he realized that it was not the air but his own mood that was slipping into shadow. Funny – he hadn't thought about that other business for years.

And wasn't sure he wanted to think about it now.

He got back in the car and headed farther down the road, toward what the locals called the old Withers place. If he had his bearings straight, the venerable woodframe house wouldn't creep into view for several miles yet, and even then would only barely be visible from the road, a gabled gnome nestled back in a wilderness of chaparral. He would be there in a few minutes, and felt rather curious to see the old place again. But another sight greeted him first.

Here and there, now, at great intervals on both sides of the road, stood the eternal profiles of little oil wells.

There had never been any wells drilled on the Withers property, so far as he had ever heard, but you saw them all over the county, pretty much – here, there, one bundle of hope or another, pumping, pumping, imploring the ground for oil. These were the first wells he had seen in all the years since he was a child here. He stopped the car again, got out, leaned against a jagged post, and watched a nearby pump jack, perhaps only a hundred feet from the road. Somehow he had always found these things lulling, comforting, almost meditative to watch.

Except when he remembered—

But why dwell on that? Inane old stories, the wide-eyed foolishness of infancy. For now, he was content to watch the grasshopper-like head of the pump jack on the end of its long beam, nodding, nodding, nodding to the earth, piercing the desert soil again and again with its drilling rod like the proboscis of some strange hungry insect. Off in the distance, humming among waving seas of chamisa, other insect-heads slowly nodded and nodded, probing the dry earth to their own tune, and the tune of the sighing wind. There was no other sound, no other motion. It was like a scene in a dream, a bit of theater on a stage at the end of the earth.

Rousing himself, he drove on down the road, finally spotting the old two-storey house off at the end of a bumpy drive to the right. Arriving in a cloud of yellow dust, he parked beside a rocky ridge near the house and clumped up onto the creaky wooden porch. He had stopped in town for the key, but he needn't have bothered; the door was open. Out here where one measured the distance to one's nearest neighbor in miles, what did it matter? At his push, the door swung inward with an osseous creak, intruding upon shadow. In the window beside the door, the truculent fat face of Uncle Bill hung, scowling. But no, this was only a crumpled place in the brittle paper shade, an imagined face staring but not seeing, then not even staring. Uncle Bill and Aunt Clara were dead. If there was any certainty in the world, it was that their faces would not be present at dinner. Cal took a breath and stepped inside.

He switched on a light and looked around. It wasn't quite as bad as he'd expected, but bad enough, though there was no way of knowing how much of the general neglect here was due to an aging Bill and Clara's laxness at housekeeping, and how much was due to the fact that the house had sat empty for several months. Good thing he had arranged for the power to be on, because the place was morbid enough even in the light. Sea-bottom mantles of dust swam everywhere, undulating, blanketing the furniture, obscuring corners and angles. Old papers, clothes, rags, and nondescript debris cluttered the corners, the floors. The house smelled sour, and Cal pulled up a shade and pried open a window. No question, he had some cleaning up to do if he was ever going to sell this place. But who would buy it, out here? He cleared a path through the clutter and went down the hall toward the back of the house, to the kitchen.

Amazing, how clearly he remembered where everything was. Nothing much seemed to have changed all these years. The refrigerator was an addition, but the old stove was the same, only more battered-looking now. He hoped the butane tanks weren't empty, as he would have to bring his bag of groceries in from the car and do some cooking tonight.

For now, he had a lot to do, and figured he might as well be about it. Retrieving plastic trash bags from the car, he started making his way through the house, filling the bags, some with trash and some with things to take into Hobbs sometime later to give to charity: clothing, extra sets of dishes, a few books, countless odds and ends. What he was supposed to do with the furniture was a mystery. He didn't want any of this stuff himself; his own life had collected enough barnacle-clinging detritus, without taking on anyone else's. By the time he had made an initial pass through all the downstairs rooms, he had filled several bags, and they stood bulging in a row along the porch now like a strange gaggle of plump children. There were only two bedrooms and a bathroom upstairs, and Cal could see to those tomorrow. It was nearly sundown, and he was getting hungry.

Cooking a meal here wasn't quite the unpleasant chore he had somehow expected it to be. After washing his dishes he tamped some tobacco into his pipe and strolled outside and down the drive toward the road, and sat on a rock and smoked. He wanted to see the desert sunset.

Its explosion of color didn't disappoint him. In the west, long filaments of lithe cloud glowed red and gold and orange. Behind him, when he looked around, the distant windows of the old house gave the light back like pairs of feral eyes. For a few fleeting moments the effect of the sunset extended to the entire sky, painting wisps of cloud even on the opposite horizon in salmon-pink hues against the deepening blue, like pastel watercolors. Everywhere but in the west, the colors faded quickly to purplish black, but in the west it was another half-hour before the crimson oven-glow of the sky paled to a faint memory, then went out like embers.

And then it was night.

Real night. Night in the desert.

It came back to him, now, what that was like. The sky became a great vaulted dome frosted with stars. How *open* it was, how fathomless, an infinite black sea which, one felt, might come crashing down in titanic waves. One felt like an exhibit on black velvet here; the over-arching window of heaven was open, and all the universe looked on by starlight.

Not that the stars provided much in the way of light, he thought, getting up and making his way back to the path. Though he was facing the house now, he couldn't make out the faintest outline of it; even the desert terrain immediately around him was the vaguest of ghost-impressions, dark against dark. He rather wished the moon was out. As he started walking, the path somehow seemed rockier than before; in the inky dark his feet from time to time stumbled against large stones. This in itself was disorienting, and besides, the path must have branched, because by the time he had trudged through stony sand long enough easily to take himself back to the porch steps, he wasn't back there, but was staring out only at more blackness, more night.

Surely this was at least approximately the way back to the

house, though he might have been a little confused in the dark. He eased forward, feeling his slow way with his feet on what he hoped was still the path. Even now, when his eyes had had time to adjust to the dark, the chaparral around him loomed only as dim shadows without detail, and it made him uncomfortable to move on without quite being able to tell where he was going. He walked in this fashion for what seemed like a good while, and at length he felt his feet fetch up against a vertical object. This had to be the bottom porch step; he had to be back at the house. He had been mistaken about the moon; it was out, but had been obscured by low-scudding black clouds backlit now in wan yellow light, and as the clouds lifted the gibbous moon shone through, a half-eaten face of chalk. When he looked up he reflected that that angular object beginning to take form in the moonlight could only be a corner of the overhang to the porch.

But it wasn't.

Poised motionless above him, it was a pump jack, its oblong head raised as if contemplating the moon. Had it been pumping at the time, he would no doubt have heard it long before blundering into the edge of the platform on which the structure rested. The odd thing was that in the dark he must have wandered off the Withers property altogether.

But no – now that the light was better, he could see, traced along behind the oil well, a half-collapsed old fence stretching off into the night, rusty wire strands dividing the Withers property from the adjacent land to the west. And the pump jack was on this side of the fence. Did the fence, some yards back, look trampled down? How could it be? He must have been mistaken about the location of the pump jack.

Suddenly the sight of it, that sardonic metal head atop its walking-beam, filled him with nameless panic, and it wasn't until he had backed away from it and sprinted across the chaparral to the house and bounded up the steps, past the procession of trash bags and through the door, and had slammed and latched the door behind him – it wasn't until then that he thought consciously about what it was that was bothering him. Pulling the brittle shades down to shut out the night, he realized now that it must have been bothering him all along, ever since he saw the area again, maybe even before.

It was the old story of Pump Jack, with a capital P and a capital J.

It had never been clear to him, either when he was a child or later, whether this bizarre story was merely a family foible or a folktale of wider currency. In any case, Uncle Bill and Grandpa Willis used to terrify him with endless accounts of Pump Jack, the wayward oil well that wouldn't keep to its proper place,but tore out of its moorings and moved around at night – seeking, Uncle Bill warned him with great solemnity, seeking someone to punish. Bad little children were its favorite feast. And if it caught you, Grandpa intoned ominously as Aunt Clara fluttered her hands – well, sir, if it caught you, it would pounce upon you with its uprooted metal feet and drive its pumping rod straight into your heart like a giant mosquito and suck your body dry of blood, leaving you lying desiccated upon the sand, dry and dead as a lizard.

Cal snorted, going around and pulling more shades down, though he was not sure why he did so, since no one would be likely to be peering in at him, out here in the middle of nowhere in the dark of night. Pump Jack and his nocturnal feastings – perfectly delightful tales to tell an impressionable child! What in the world was wrong with Grandpa and Uncle Bill and the others? At least his own father had disapproved of such frightful storytelling. His father just might have been one of the few sane people in the family, when you got right down to it.

Not relishing any further reflections on the matter just now, Cal turned in early, choosing the front bedroom upstairs and making the bed over with fresh sheets. When the light was off and he was lying in bed listening to the night in the desert, where the wind made a forlorn moaning sound around the eaves of the old house, he half fancied he heard some furtive creature rooting and nuzzling about outside, somewhere near the house. But he fell asleep before he could worry about it, and apparently dreamed of things strange and vaguely disturbing, though he couldn't quite remember them in the morning.

He rose tired and moody. Breakfast did little to dispel the feeling, and he went about his work more out of duty than desire. By noon he had bagged up more than would even fit in the car. He packed as many bags as he could into the back seat and front passenger seat, and drove the fifty miles into town. The real-estate agent was typical of the profession, eager to help in any way possible, blithely confident that the property would sell quickly,

don't you worry about a thing, Mr Withers. Afterward Cal
disposed of his trash and his charity items, had lunch at a diner,
and spent a good portion of the afternoon just idling about town
before he realized that he was making excuses to himself to delay
going back out to the ranch.

Preposterous, of course. There was no reason to avoid driving
back out, and indeed he should have done so earlier, as there was
a good bit of work left to do today, and little of the afternoon left
to do it in. He pointed the car back out into the desert and was
bumping back up the rocky drive before sunset.

Desert sunsets were incomparable, but he wouldn't go out and
watch that spectacular event this evening. *Why not?* some corner
of his mind niggled. *Because,* his answer was, *there is simply no
point in it; I saw the sunset last night, and tonight I have more
pressing things to do.*

But he found himself not doing them. There was indeed a great
deal more in the house to bag up, including two closets full of
clothes that he hadn't even approached yet, but at dinnertime he
hadn't tended to any of it, and after his cheerless meal he felt even
less like bothering. There was no particular hurry, he thought,
pulling the shades down again and shutting out the encroachment
of night that yawned limitless beyond the windows. Why not just
grab a good book from his suitcase and settle into the easy chair
in the front parlor? He'd been working hard enough, and travel
itself had been tiring; he deserved a night off. He eased himself
into the chair with the copy of *Bleak House* he'd been promising
himself for weeks to start on, and he switched on a lamp and
began to read.

. . . *mud in the streets* (he read) *as if the waters had but newly
retired from the face of the earth, and it would not be wonderful
to meet a Megalosaurus, forty feet long or so, waddling like an
elephantine lizard up Holborn Hill.*

With no intended slight to Dickens, Cal's attention had already
begun to wander, because although he found himself looking
away from the page and thinking back over this Dickensian
image, or what should have been this image, the passage had
changed in some insane way of its own accord. *And it would not
be wonderful to meet Pump Jack, twenty feet long, waddling like
a bug up the hill from Hobbs,* he reflected, and chided himself the
next moment. Balderdash and nonsense. Cretinous drivel. It was

a sad comment on something or other, if a man couldn't keep his
mind from—
    What was that sound?
    He sat still, holding his breath, listening.
    Nothing. More nonsensical—
    No. No, there it was again. Like something bumping and
scraping around outside, near the porch. Probably some animal
looking for food, he thought, though this evening there were no
bags on the porch to tempt any four-legged scavengers. Sighing,
Cal got up to find out what was going on.
    When he stepped out onto the porch and switched on the light
out there, he could have sworn that something large and of
indeterminate shape scuttered away just beyond the reach of
the light. Now come on, this was getting to be absurd. If somebody was trying to— he had to go out and have a look around.
    Getting his jacket, he went down the steps and paced about the
area near the house, but saw nothing. At first. Then, off on the
horizon – something, he thought. Something moved in the moonlight. He walked in that direction, puzzling it over in his head.
What was he so distraught about? Some lunatic folktale designed
to scare children into submission? It had nothing to do with him
now. Maybe he *had* deserved a bit of censure from time to time
when he was a kid—
    You don't listen too good, do you, boy? Hey? Late for supper
again. Think you'd know better by now. And after dark too.
Why, old Pump Jack just loves to hunt 'em down, kids like you.
    Yeah, well, put a lid on it, Uncle Bill. Somebody already did put
a lid on you, as I recall, and about time too.
    Thinking this rather uncharitable thought Cal made his way,
through the mesquite and yucca and cactus, to the spot where he
thought he had seen something. But nothing moved here now
except crescents of mesquite-beans waving in the wind. Nothing.
    Wait – out there, farther off. Something *was* moving, by God.
Maybe it was a coyote. But it had given the impression of being
bigger than that. He loped across the sandy ground toward it, but
when he arrived, again there was nothing to see but the austere
moonlit trappings of the desert terrain. Then again, farther out –
another glimpse, or imagined glimpse, of movement.
    He ran on, determined to find out. Sable clouds drew them-
selves over the moon like ragged eyelids, and he began to have

trouble seeing where he was going. Slowing to a walk, he felt his way tentatively forward, having no desire to blunder into a cluster of prickly-pear cactus or sharp-spiked yucca, and no desire to put his foot in a rattlesnake hole. Now and again a bony bit of moon would slip out from behind the cover of cloud, but it was only enough to confuse him more, as things looked different when he caught sight of them in momentary moonlight to how he had expected them to look; where the land, he imagined, sloped down, it really sloped up, or where he thought there was an unobstructed way, a ridge of rock jutted in mute defiance.

Cal kept moving, increasingly wondering why he was out here, what he was doing. Even in the context of that ridiculous childhood legend, what should he have to fear?

He'd done nothing to be punished for.

Had he?

Nothing, except perhaps moving away?

Did the gods of the desert resent one for doing that?

He really *must* be getting daffy, even to entertain such a thought.

He hadn't been paying attention to where he was going, and now, as the moon came back out, he found himself standing in the very shadow of a great pump jack, its motionless head angled above him.

Was this the same one? In the same place? He couldn't tell. There didn't seem to be any fence nearby, and he had only a very uncertain idea as to where he was.

But in any event, the chase was over. Idiotic! Imagine, some animal scavenger makes some noise up near the house, and good old Cal goes running about the desert chasing phantoms, like a madman or a fool. He sat down on a rock near the pumping platform, and heaved a sigh of relief. He looked up at the profile of the pump jack, bizarre and cold-looking in the wan light, but harmless.

'Well, Jack, here's one old boy you're not going to terrorize. The desert may be a strange place sometimes, but it's not *that* damned strange.'

He waited. 'How's about it, Jack? Aren't you going to say anything?'

The pump jack sat silent, an absurd insectoid shape against a starry sky.

'That's what I thought.' Cal slapped his knees and got up off the rock and laughed outright.

The laugh, however, caught in his throat.

Whether it was the sight or the sound, he couldn't have said. But nothing that came afterward, right down to the end, would disturb him any more than that first impression, that first moment.

The moment when the great oblong head, perched atop its neck of steel, bestirred itself with an unthinkable metallic groan and turned, coldly predatory in the pallid moonlight – turned to look at him.

GALA BLAU

Outfangthief

GALA BLAU WAS BORN IN GERMANY, and divides her time between London and Berlin, where she designs jewellery and is a sometime singer with the band Scheintod.

The following story was her first published fiction, and she has a new tale, 'The Routine', in *The Third Alternative*. She is also currently planning her first novel.

' "Outfangthief" was inspired by a *Guardian* newspaper article concerning a "freelance" doctor who botched an operation,' explains Blau, 'killing a seventy-nine-year-old devotee of apo-temnophilia, a sexual fetish involving the voluntary removal of limbs for sexual gratification. I kept the idea of a mercenary doctor, but changed the fetish to acrotomophilia, which is a fetish enjoyed by those who prefer to have sex with amputees. The story is zero per cent autobiographical.'

AT THE MOMENT THE CAR SLID out of control, Sarah Running had been trying to find a radio station that might carry some news of her crime. She had been driving for hours, risking the M6 all the way from Preston. Though she had seen a number of police vehicles, the traffic had been sufficiently busy to allow her to blend in and anyway, Manser would hardly have guessed she would take her ex-husband's car. Michael was away on business in Stockholm and would not know of the theft for at least another week.

But Manser was not stupid. It would not be long before he latched on to her deceit.

As the traffic thinned and night closed in on the motorway, Sarah's panic grew. She was convinced that her disappearance had been reported and she would be brought to book. When a police Range Rover tailed her from Walsall to the M42 turn-off, she almost sent her own car into the crash barriers at the centre of the road.

Desperate for cover, she followed the signs for the A14. Perhaps she could make the 130 miles to Felixstowe tonight and sell the car, try to find passage on a boat, lose herself and her daughter on the Continent. In a day they could be in Dresden, where her grandmother had lived; a battered city that would recognise some of its own and allow them some anonymity.

'Are you all right back there, Laura?'

In the rear-view mirror, her daughter might well have been a mannequin. Her features were glacial; her sunglasses formed tiny screens of animation as the sodium lights fizzed off them. A slight flattening of the lips was the only indication that all was well. Sarah bore down on her frustration. Did she understand what she had been rescued from? Sarah tried to remember what things had been like for herself as a child, but reasoned that her own relationship with her mother had not been fraught with the same problems.

'It's all okay, Laura. We'll not have any more worries in this family. I promise you.'

All that before she spotted the flashing blue and red lights of three police vehicles blocking her progress east. She turned left on to another A road bound for Leicester. There must have been an accident; they wouldn't go to the lengths of forming a roadblock for her, would they? The road sucked her deep into darkness; on either side wild hedgerows and vast oily swells of countryside muscled into them. Headlamps on full beam, she could pick nothing out beyond the winding road apart from the ghostly dusting of insects attracted by the light. Sarah, though, felt anything but alone. She could see, in the corner of her eye, something blurred by speed, keeping pace with the car as it fled the police cordon. She took occasional glances to her right, but could not define their fellow traveller for the dense tangle of vegetation that bordered the road.

'Can you see that, Laura?' she asked. 'What is it?'

It could have been a trick of the light, or something silver reflecting the shape of their car. Maybe it was the police. The needle on the speedometer edged up to eighty. They would have to dump the car somewhere soon, if the police were closing in on them.

'Keep a look out for a B&B, okay?' She checked in the mirror; Laura's hand was splayed against the window, spreading mist from the star her fingers made. She was watching the obliteration of her view intently.

Sarah fumbled with the radio button. Static filled the car at an excruciating volume. Peering into the dashboard of the unfamiliar car, trying to locate the volume control, she perceived a darkening in the cone of light ahead. When she looked up, the car was drifting off the road, aiming for a tree. Righting the swerve only took the car more violently in the other direction. They were still on the road, but only just, as the wheels began to rise on the passenger side.

but i wasn't drifting off the road, was i?

Sarah caught sight of Laura, expressionless, as she was jerked from one side of the car to the other and hoped the crack she heard was not caused by her daughter's head slamming against the window.

i thought it was a tree big and black
it looked just like a tree but but but

And then she couldn't see much because the car went into a roll and everything became part of a violent, circular blur and at the centre of it were the misted, friendly eyes of a woman dipping into her field of view.

but but but how can a tree have a face?

She was conscious of the cold and the darkness. There was the hiss of traffic from the motorway, soughing over the fields. Her face was sticky and at first she thought it was blood, but now she smelled a lime tree and knew it was its sap being sweated on to her. Forty metres away, the road she had just left glistened with dew. She tried to move and blacked out.

Fingers sought her face. She tried to bat them away but there were many fingers, many hands. She feared they might try to pluck her

eyes out and opened her mouth to scream and that was when a rat
was pushed deep into her throat.

Sarah came out of the dream, smothering on the sodden jumper
of her daughter, who had tipped over the driver's seat and was
pressed against her mother. The flavour of blood filled her mouth.
The dead weight of the child carried an inflexibility about it that
shocked her. She tried to move away from the crushing bulk and
the pain drew grey veils across her eyes. She gritted her teeth,
knowing that to succumb now was to die, and worked at
unbuckling the seat belt that had saved her life. Once free, she
slumped to her left and her daughter filled the space she had
occupied.

Able to breathe again, she was pondering the position in which
the car had come to rest, and trying to reach Laura's hand, when
she heard footsteps.

When she saw Manser lean over, his big, toothy grin seeming to
fill the shattered window frame, she wished she had not dodged
the police; they were preferable to this monster. But then she saw
how this wasn't Manser after all. She couldn't understand how
she had made the mistake. Manser was a stunted, dark man with
a face like chewed tobacco. This face was smooth as soapstone
and framed by thick, red tresses; a woman's face.

Other faces, less defined, swept across her vision. Everyone
seemed to be moving very fast.

She said, falteringly: 'Ambulance?' But they ignored her.

They lifted Laura out of the window to a cacophony of whistles
and cheers. There must have been a hundred people. At least they
had been rescued. Sarah would take her chances with the police.
Anything was better than going home.

The faces retreated. Only the night stared in on her now,
through the various rents in the car. It was cold, lonely and
painful. Her face in the rear-view mirror: all smiles.

He closed the door and locked it. Cocked his head against the
jamb, listened for a few seconds. Still breathing.

Downstairs, he read the newspaper, ringing a few horses for the
afternoon races. He placed thousand-pound bets with his
bookies. In the ground-floor washroom, he took a scalding
shower followed by an ice-cold one, just like James Bond. Rolex
Oyster, Turnbull & Asser shirt, Armani. He made four more

phone calls: Jez Knowlden, his driver, to drop by in the Jag in twenty minutes; Pamela, his wife, to say that he would be away for the weekend; Jade, his mistress, to ask her if she'd meet him in London. And then Chandos, his police mole, to see if that bitch Sarah Running had been found yet.

Sarah dragged herself out of the car just as dawn was turning the skyline milky. She had drifted in and out of consciousness all night, but the sleet that had arrived within the last half-hour was the spur she needed to try to escape. She sat a few feet away from the car, taking care not to make any extreme movements, and began to assess the damage to herself. A deep wound in her shoulder had caused most of the bleeding. Other than that, which would need stitches, she had got away with pretty superficial injuries. Her head was pounding, and dried blood formed a crust above her left eyebrow, but nothing seemed to be broken.

After quelling a moment of nausea when she tried to stand, Sarah breathed deeply of the chill morning air and looked around her. A farmhouse nestled within a crowd of trees seemed the best bet; it was too early for road users. Cautiously at first, but with gathering confidence, she trudged across the muddy, furrowed field towards the house, staring all the while at its black, arched windows, for all the world like a series of open mouths, shocked by the coming of the sun.

She had met Andrew in 1985, in the Preston library they both shared. A relationship had started, more or less, when their hands bumped against each other while reaching for the same book. They had married a year later and Sarah gave birth to Laura then, too. Both of them had steady if unspectacular work. Andrew was a security guard and she cleaned at the local school and for a few favoured neighbours. They eventually took out a mortgage on their council house on the right-to-buy scheme and bought a car, a washing machine and a television on the never-never. Then they both lost their jobs within weeks of each other. They owed £17,000. When the law centre they depended on heavily for advice lost its funding and closed down, Sarah had to go to hospital when she began laughing so hysterically that she could not catch her breath. It was as Andrew drove her back from the hospital that they met Malcolm Manser for the first time.

His back to them, he stepped out in front of their car at a set of
traffic lights and did not move when they changed in Andrew's
favour. When Andrew sounded the horn, Manser turned around.
He was wearing a long newbuck trench coat, black Levis, black
boots and a black T-shirt without an inch of give in it. His hair
was black save for wild slashes of grey above his temples. His
sunglasses appeared to be sculpted from his face, so seamlessly
did they sit on his nose. From the trench coat he pulled a car jack
and proceeded to smash every piece of glass and dent every panel
on the car. It took about twenty seconds.

'Mind if I talk to you for a sec?' he asked, genially, leaning
against the crumbled remains of the driver's-side window. Andrew was too shocked to say anything. His mouth was very wet.
Tiny cubes of glass glittered in his hair. Sarah was whimpering,
trying to open her door, which was sealed shut by the warp of
metal.

Manser went on: 'You have 206 pieces of bone in your body,
fine sir. If my client, Mr Anders, does not receive seventeen grand,
plus interest at ten per cent a day – which is pretty bloody
generous, if you ask me – by the end of the week, I will guarantee
that after half an hour with me, your bone tally will be double
that. And that yummy piece of bitch you've got ripening back
home. Laura? I'll have her. You test me. I dare you.'

He walked away, magicking the car jack into the coat and
giving them an insouciant wave.

A week later, Andrew set himself on fire in the car, which he
had locked inside the garage. By the time the fire services got to
him, he was a black shape, thrashing in the back seat. *Set himself
on fire*. Sarah refused to believe that. She was sure that Manser
had murdered him. Despite their onerous circumstances, Andrew
was not the suicidal type. Laura was everything to him; he'd not
leave this world without securing a little piece of it for her.

What then? A nightmare time. A series of safe houses that were
anything but. Early-morning flits from dingy addresses in Brad-
ford, Cardiff, Bristol and Walsall. Manser was stickier than
anything Bostik might produce. 'Bug out,' they'd tell her, these
kind old men and women, having settled on a code once used by
soldiers in some war or other. 'Bug out.' Manser had contacts
everywhere. Arriving in a town that seemed too sleepy to even
acknowledge her presence, she'd notice someone out of whack

with the place, someone who patently did not fit in but had been planted to watch out for her. Was she so transparent? Her migrations had been random; there was no pattern to unpick. And yet she had stayed no longer than two days in any of these towns. Sarah had hoped that returning to Preston might work for her in a number of ways. Manser wouldn't be expecting it, for one thing; for another, Michael, her ex-husband, might be of some help. When she went to visit him though, he paid her short shrift.

'You still owe me fifteen hundred quid,' he barked at her. 'Pay that off before you come grovelling at my door.' She asked if she could use his toilet and passed any number of photographs of Gabrielle, his new squeeze. On the way, she stole from a hook on the wall the spare set of keys to his Alfa Romeo.

It took twenty minutes to negotiate the treacherous field. A light frost had hardened some of the furrows while other grooves were boggy. Sarah scuffed and skidded as best she could, clambering over the token fence that bordered an overgrown garden someone had used as an unauthorized tipping area. She picked her way through sofa skeletons, shattered TV sets, collapsed flat-pack wardrobes and decaying, pungent black bin bags.

It was obvious that nobody was living here.

Nevertheless, she stabbed the doorbell with a bloody finger. Nothing appeared to ring from within the building. She rapped on the door with her knuckles, but half-heartedly. Already she was scrutinizing the windows, looking for another way in. A narrow path strangled by brambles led around the edge of the house to a woefully neglected rear garden. Scorched colours bled into each other, thorns and convolvulus savaged her ankles as she pushed her way through the tangle. All of the windows at the back of the house had been broken, probably by thrown stones. A yellow spray of paint on a set of storm doors that presumably led directly into the cellar picked out a word she didn't understand: *scheintod*. What was that? German? She cursed herself for not knowing the language of her elders, not that it mattered. Someone had tried to obscure the word, scratching it out of the wood with a knife, but the paint was reluctant. She tried the door but it was locked.

Sarah finally gained access via a tiny window that she had to squeeze through. The bruises and gashes on her body cried out as she toppled into a gloomy larder. Mingled into the dust was an acrid, spicy smell; racks of ancient jars and pots were labelled in an extravagant hand: *cumin, coriander, harissa, chilli powder*. There were packs of flour and malt that had been ravaged by vermin. Dried herbs dusted her with a strange, slow rain as she brushed past them. Pickling jars held back their pale secrets within dull, lustreless glass.

She moved through the larder, arms outstretched, her eyes becoming accustomed to the gloom. Something stopped the door as she swung it outwards. A dead dog, its fur shaved from its body, lay stiffly in the hallway. At first she thought it was covered in insects, but the black beads were unmoving. They were nicks and slashes in the flesh. The poor thing had been drained. Sarah recoiled from the corpse and staggered farther along the corridor. Evidence of squatters lay around her in the shape of fast-food packets, cigarette ends, beer cans and names signed in the ceiling by the sooty flames of candles. A rising stairwell vanished into darkness. Her shoes crunched and squealed on plaster fallen from the bare walls.

'Hello?' she said, querulously. Her voice made as much impact as a candyfloss mallet. It died on the walls, absorbed so swiftly it was as if the house was sucking her in, having been starved of human company for so long. She ascended to the first floor. The carpet that hugged the risers near the bottom gave way to bare wood. Her shoes' heels sent dull echoes ringing through the house. If anyone lived here, they would know they were not alone now. The doors opened on to silent bedrooms shrouded by dust. There was nothing up here.

'Laura?' And then more stridently, as if volume alone could lend her more spine: '*Laura!*'

Downstairs she found a cosy living room with a hearth filled with ashes. She peeled back a dust cover from one of the sofas and lay down. Her head pounded with delayed shock from the crash and the mustiness of her surroundings. She thought of her baby.

It didn't help that Laura seemed to be going off the rails at the time of their crisis. Also, her inability or reluctance to talk of her father's death worried Sarah almost as much as the evidence of booze and drug use. At each of the safe houses, it seemed that there was a Laura trap in the shape of a young misfit, eager to drag someone down with him or her. Laura gave herself to them all, as if glad of a mate to hasten her downward spiral. There had been one boy in particular, Edgar – a difficult name to forget – whose influence had been particularly invidious. They had been holed up in a Toxteth bedsit. Sarah had been listening to City FM. A talk show full of languid, catarrhal Liverpool accents that was making her drowsy. The sound of a window smashing had dragged her from slumber. She caught the boy trying to drag her daughter through the glass. She had shrieked at him and hauled him into the room. He could have been no older than ten or eleven. His eyes were rifle green and would not stay still. They darted around like steel bearings in a bagatelle game. Sarah had grilled him, asking him if he had been sent from Manser. Panicked, she had also been firing off instructions to Laura, that they must pack immediately and be ready to go within the hour. It was no longer safe.

And then: Laura, crawling across the floor, holding on to Edgar's leg, pulling herself up, her eyes fogged with what could only be ecstasy. Burying her face in Edgar's crotch. Sarah had shrunk back from her daughter, horrified. She watched as Laura's free hand travelled beneath her skirt and began to massage at the gusset of her knickers while animal sounds came from her throat. Edgar had grinned at her, showing off a range of tiny, brilliant white teeth. Then he had bent low, whispering something in Laura's ear before charging out of the window with a speed that Sarah thought could only end in tragedy. But when she rushed to the opening, she couldn't see him anywhere.

It had been the Devil's own job trying to get her daughter ready to flee Liverpool. Laura had grown wan and weak and couldn't keep her eyes off the window. Sarah dragged her on to a dawn coach from Mount Pleasant. Laura had been unable to stop crying and as the day wore on, complained of terrible thirst and unbearable pain behind her eyes. She vomited twice and the driver threatened to throw them off the coach unless Laura calmed down. Somehow, Sarah was able to pacify her. She found that shading her from the sunlight helped. A little later, slumped under the seat, Laura fell asleep.

Sarah had begun to question ever leaving Preston in the first place. At least there she had had the strength that comes with knowing your environment. Manser had been a problem in

Preston but the trouble was that he remained a problem. At least back there, it was just him that she needed to be wary of. Now it seemed that Laura's adolescence was going to cause Sarah more of a problem than she believed could be possible. But at the back of her mind, Sarah knew that she could never have stayed in her home town. What Manser had proposed, sidling up to her at Andrew's funeral, was that she should allow Laura to work for him, whoring. He guaranteed an excellent price for such a perfectly toned, *tight* bit of girl.

'Men go for that,' he'd whispered, as Sarah tossed a fistful of soil on to her husband's coffin. 'She's got cracking tits for a thirteen-year-old. High. Firm. Nipples up top. Quids in, I promise you. You could have your debt sorted out in a couple of years. And I'll break her in for you. Just so's you know it won't be some stranger nicking her cherry.'

That night, they were out of their house, a suitcase full of clothes between them.

'You fucking *beauty*.'

Manser depressed the call-end button on his Motorola and slipped the phone into his jacket. Leaning forward, he tapped his driver on the shoulder. 'Jez. Get this. Cops found the bitch's car in a fucking field outside Leicester. She'd totalled it.'

He slumped back in his seat. The radio masts at Rugby swung by on his left, lights glinting through a thin fog. 'Fuck London. You want the A5199. Warp Factor two. And when we catch the minging little tart, we'll show her how to have a road accident. Do the job properly for her. Laura, though, Laura comes with us. Nothing happens to Laura. Got it?'

At Knowlden's assent, Manser closed his eyes. This year's number three had died just before he left home. It had been a pity. He'd liked that one. The sutures on her legs had healed in such a way as to chafe his thigh as he thrust into her. But there had been an infection that he couldn't treat. Pouring antibiotics down her hadn't done an awful lot of good. Gangrene had set in. Maybe Laura could be his number four. Once Dr Losh had done his bit, he would ask him the best way to prevent infection. He knew what Losh's response would be: *let it heal*. But he liked his meat so very rare when he was fucking it. He liked to see a little blood.

Sarah woke up to find that her right eye had puffed closed. She caught sight of herself in a shard of broken mirror on the wall. Blood caked half her face and the other half was black with bruises. Her hair was matted. Not for the first time, she wondered if her conviction that Laura had died was misplaced. Yet in the same breath, she couldn't bear to think that she might now be suffering with similar, or worse, injuries. Her thoughts turned to her saviours – if that was what they were. And if so, then why hadn't she been rescued?

She relived the warmth and protection that had enveloped her when those willowy figures had reached inside the car and plucked out her child. Her panic at the thought of Laura either dead or as good as had been ironed flat. She felt safe and, inexplicably, had not raged at this outrageous kidnap; indeed, she had virtually sanctioned it. Perhaps it had been the craziness inspired by the accident or endorphins stifling her pain that had brought about her indifference. Still, what should have been anger and guilt was neutralized by the conviction that Laura was in safe hands. What she didn't want to examine too minutely was the feeling that she missed the rescue party more than she did her own daughter.

Refreshed a little by her sleep, but appalled at the catalogue of new aches and pains that jarred each movement, Sarah made her way back to the larder where she found some crackers in an airtight tin. Chewing on these, she revisited the hallway and dragged open the heavy curtains, allowing some of the late-afternoon light to invade. Almost immediately she saw the door under the stairs. She saw how she had missed it earlier; it was hewn from the same dark wood and there was no door handle as such, just a little recess to hook your fingers into. She tried it but it wouldn't budge. Which meant that it was locked from the inside. Which meant that somebody must be down there.

'Laura?' she called, tapping on the wood with her fingernails. 'Laura, it's mum. Are you in there?'

She listened hard, her ear flush against the crack of the jamb. All she could hear was the gust of subterranean breezes moving through what ought to be the cellar. She must check it out; Laura could be down there, bleeding her last.

Sarah hunted through the kitchen. A large pine table sat at one end of the room, a dried orange with a heart of mould at its

centre. She found a stack of old newspapers from the early 1970s
bound up with twine by a back door that was forbiddingly black
and excessively padlocked. Ransacking the drawers and cupboards brought scant reward. She was about to give in when the
suck of air from the last yanked cupboard door brought a small
screwdriver rolling into view. She grabbed the tool and scurried
back to the cellar door.

Manser kept Knowlden still with a finger curled around his lapel.
'Are you carrying?'
     Knowlden had parked the car off the road on the side opposite
to the crash site. Now the two men were standing by the wreck of
the Alfa. Knowlden had spotted the house and suggested they
check it out. If Sarah and her daughter had survived the crash –
and the empty car suggested that they had – then they might have
found some neighbourly help.
     'I hope you fucking are,' Manser warned.
     'I'm carrying – okay? Don't sweat it.'
     Manser's eyebrows went north. 'Don't tell me not to sweat it,
pup. Or you'll find yourself doing seventy back up the motorway
without a fucking car underneath you.'
     The sun sinking fast, they hurried across the field, constantly
checking the road behind them as they did so. Happy that nobody
had seen them, Manser nodded his head in the direction of the
front door. 'Kick the mud off your boots on that bastard,' he said.
     It was 5:14 p.m.

Sarah was halfway down the cellar stairs and wishing she had a
torch with her when she heard the first blows hammering at the
door. She was about to return to the hallway when she heard
movement from below. A *lot* of movement. Creaks and whispers
and hisses. There was a sound as of soot trickling down a flue. A
chatter: teeth in the cold? A sigh.
     'Laura?'
     A chuckle.

The door gave in just before Knowlden was about to. His face
was greasy with sweat and hoops of dampness spoiled his
otherwise pristine shirt.
     'Gun,' Manser said, holding out his hand. Knowlden passed

him the weapon, barely disguising his disdain for his boss. 'You want to get some muesli down you, mate,' Manser said. 'Get yourself fit.' He checked that the piece was loaded and entered the house, muzzle pointing ahead of him, the grip held horizontally. Something he'd done ever since seeing Brad Pitt do the same thing in *Se7en*.

'Knock, knock,' he called out. 'Daddy's home.'

Just before all hell broke loose, Sarah heard Laura's voice, firm and even, say: 'Do not touch her.' Then she was knocked back on the stairs by a flurry of black leather and she was aware only of bloody-eyed, pale-skinned figures flocking past her. And teeth. She saw each leering mouth as if in slow motion, dark lips peeled back to reveal teeth so white that they might have been sculpted from ice.

She thought she saw Laura among them and tried to grab hold of her jumper. But she was left clutching air as the scrum piled into the hallway, whooping and screaming like a gang of kids let out early from school. When the shooting started she couldn't tell if the screaming had changed in pitch at all, whether it had become more panicked. But at the top of the stairs she realized she was responsible for most of it. There appeared to be some kind of stand-off. Manser, the fetid little sniffer dog of a man, was waving a gun around while his henchman clenched and unclenched his hands, eyeing up the opposition, which was substantial. Sarah studied them properly for the first time, these women who had rescued her baby and left her to die in the car. And yet proper examination was beyond her. There were four of them, she thought. Maybe five. They moved around and against each other so swiftly, so lissomely that she couldn't be sure. They were like a flesh knot. Eyes fast on their enemy, they guarded each other with this mesmerizing display. It was so seamless that it could have been choreographed.

But now she saw that they were not just protecting each other. There was someone at the heart of the knot, appearing and disappearing in little ribbons and teasers of colour. Sarah needed to see only a portion of face to know that they were wrapped around her daughter.

'Laura,' she said again.

Manser said, 'Who the fuck are these clowns? Have we just walked into Goth night down the local student bar, or what?'

'Laura,' Sarah said again, ignoring her pursuer. 'Come here.'

'Everyone just stand back. I'm having the girl. And to show you I'm not just pissing in my paddling pool . . .' Manser took aim and shot one of the women through the forehead.

Sarah covered her mouth as the woman dropped. The three others seemed to fade somewhat, as if their strength had been affected.

'Jez,' said Manser. 'Get the girl.'

Sarah leapt at Knowlden as he strode into the pack but a stiff arm across her chest knocked her back against the wall, winding her. He extricated Laura from her guardians and dragged her, kicking, back to his boss.

Manser was nodding his head. 'Nice work, Jez. You can have jelly for afters tonight. Get her outside.'

To Sarah he said: 'Give her up.' And then he was gone.

Slumped on the floor, Sarah tried to blink a fresh trickle of blood from her eyes. Through the fluid, she thought she could see the women crowding around their companion. She thought she could see them lifting her head as they positioned themselves around her. But no. No. She couldn't accept that she was seeing what they began to do to her then.

Knowlden slowed down as they ran towards the car. Manser was half-dragging, half-carrying Laura who was thrashing around in his arms.

'I'm nearly ready,' she said. 'I'll bite you! I'll bite you, I swear to God.'

'And I'll scratch your eyes out,' Manser retorted. 'Now shut the fuck up. Jesus, can't you do what girls your age do in the movies? Faint, or something?'

At the car, he bundled her into the boot and locked it shut. Then he fell against the side of the car and tried to control his breathing. He could just see Knowlden plodding towards him in the dark. Manser could hear his gasping lungs even though the man had another forty metres or so to cover.

'Come on, Jez, for fuck's sake! I've seen mascara run faster than that.'

At thirty metres, Manser had a clearer view of his driver as he died.

One of the women they had left behind in the house was

moving across the field at a speed that defied logic. Her hands were outstretched and her nails glinted like polished arrowheads. Manser moved quickly himself when he saw how she slammed into his chauffeur. He was in third gear before he realized he hadn't taken the handbrake off and he was laughing harder than he had ever laughed in his life. Knowlden's heart had been skewered on the end of the woman's claws like a piece of meat on a kebab. Manser didn't stop laughing until he hit the M1, southbound.

Knowlden was forgotten. All Manser had on his mind now was Laura, naked on the slab, her body marked out like the charts on a butcher's wall.

Dazed, Sarah was helped to her feet. Their hands held her everywhere and nowhere, moving along her body as softly as silk. She tried to talk but whenever she opened her mouth someone's hand, cold and rank, slipped over it. She saw the pattern in the curtains travel by in a blur though she could not feel her feet on the floor. Then the night was upon them, and the frost in the air sang around her ears as she was swept into the sky, embedded at the centre of their slippery mesh of bodies, smelling their clothes and the scent of something ageless and black, lifting off the skin like forbidden perfume. *Is she all right now?* she wanted to ask, but her words wouldn't form in the ceaseless blast of cold air. Sarah couldn't count the women who cavorted around her. She drifted into unconsciousness thinking of how they had opened the veins in their chests for her, how the gush of fluid had flooded over her face, bubbling on her tongue and in her nostrils like dark wine. How her eyes had flicked open and rolled back into their sockets with the unspeakable rapture of it all.

Having phoned ahead, Manser parked the car at midnight on South Wharf Road, just by the junction with Praed Street. He was early, so instead of going directly to the dilapidated pub on the corner he sauntered to the bridge over Paddington Basin and stared up at the Westway, hoping for calm. The sounds coming from that elevated sweep were anything but soothing. The mechanical sigh of speeding vehicles reminded him only of the way those witches' mouths had breathed, snakelike jaws unhinged as though in readiness to swallow him whole. The hiss of tyres on rain-soaked tarmac put him in mind of nothing but the wet air that had sped from Knowlden's chest when he was torn open.

When Manser returned, he saw a low-wattage bulb in the pub turning the glass of an upstairs window milky. He went to the door and tapped on it with a coin in a pre-arranged code. Then he went back to the car and opened the boot. He wrestled with Laura and managed to clamp a hand over her mouth. She bit down, hard. Swearing, he dragged a handkerchief from his pocket and stuffed it in her mouth, punching her twice to make her keep still. The pain in his hand was almost unbearable. She had teeth like razors. Flaps of skin hung off his palm; he was bleeding badly. Woozy at the sight of the wound, he staggered with Laura to the door, which was now open. He went through it and kicked it shut, checking the street to make sure he hadn't been seen. Upstairs, Losh was sitting in a chair containing more holes than stuffing.

'This was a good boozer before it was closed down,' Manser said, his excitement unfolding deep within him.

'Was,' Losh said, keeping his eyes on him. He wore a butcher's apron that was slathered with blood. He smoked a cigarette, the end of which was patterned with bloody prints from his fingers. A comma of blood could be mistaken for a kiss-curl on his forehead. 'Everything changes.'

'You don't,' Manser said. 'Christ. Don't you ever wash?'

'What's the point? I'm a busy man.'

'How many years you been struck off?'

Losh smiled. 'Didn't anybody ever warn you not to piss off the people you need help from?'

Manser swallowed his distaste for the smaller man. 'Nobody warns me nothing,' he spat. 'Can't we get on?'

Losh stood up and stretched. 'Cash,' he said, luxuriously.

Manser pulled a wad from his jacket. 'There's six grand there. As always.'

'I believe you. I'd count it but the bank get a bit miffed if they get blood on their bills.'

'Why don't you wear gloves?'

'The magic. It's all in the fingers.' Losh gestured towards Laura. 'This the one?'

'Of course.'

'Pretty thing. Nice legs.' Losh laughed. Manser closed his eyes. Losh said, 'What you after?'

Manser said, 'The works.'

Wide eyes from Losh. 'Then let's call it *eight* thou.'

A pause. Manser said, 'I don't have it with me. I can get it tomorrow. Keep the car tonight. As collateral.'

Losh said, 'Done.'

The first incision. Blood squirted up the apron, much brighter than the stains already painted upon it. A coppery smell filled the room. The pockets of the pool table upon which Laura was spread were filled with beer towels.

'Soft tissue?'

Manser's voice was dry. He needed a drink. His cock was as hard as a house brick. 'As much off as possible.'

'She won't last long,' Losh said.

Manser stared at him. 'She'll last long enough.'

Losh said: 'Got a number five in mind already?'

Manser didn't say a word. Losh reached behind him and picked up a Samsonite suitcase. He opened it and pulled out a hacksaw. Its teeth played with the light and flung it in every direction. At least Losh kept his tools clean.

The operation took four hours. Manser fell asleep at one point and dreamed of his hand overpowering the rest of his body, dragging him around the city while the mouth that slavered and snarled at the centre of his palm cupped itself around the stomachs of passers-by and devoured them.

He wakened, rimed with perspiration, to see Losh chewing an errant hangnail and tossing his instruments back into the suitcase. Laura was wrapped in bath towels that had once been white. They were crimson now.

'Is she okay?' Manser asked. Losh's laughter in reply was infectious and soon he was at it too.

'Do you want the off-cuts?' Losh asked, wiping his eyes and jerking a thumb at a bucket tastefully covered with a dishcloth.

'You keep them,' Manser said. 'I've got to be off.'

Losh said, 'Who opened the window?'

Nobody had opened the window; the lace curtains fluttering

inward were being pushed by a bulge of glass. Losh tore them
back just as the glass shattered in his face. He screamed and fell
backwards, tripping on the bucket and sprawling on the floor.

To Manser it seemed that strips of the night were pouring in
through the broken window. They fastened themselves to Losh's
face and neck and munched through the flesh like a caterpillar at
a leaf. His screams were low and already being stifled by blood as
his throat filled. He began to choke but managed one last, hearty
shriek as a major blood vessel parted, spraying colour all around
the room with the abandon of an unmanned hosepipe.

How can they breathe with their heads so deep inside him?
Manser thought, hypnotized by the violence. He felt something
dripping on his brow. Touching his face with his fingers, he
brought them away to find them awash with blood. He had time
to register, as he looked up at the ceiling, the mouth as it yawned,
dribbling with lymph, the head as it vibrated with unfettered
anticipation. And then the woman dropped on him, ploughing
her jaws through the meat of his throat and ripping clear. He saw
his flesh disappear down her gullet with a spasm that was almost
beautiful. But then his sight filled with red and he could understand no more.

Sarah had been back home for a day. She couldn't understand
how she had got here. She remembered being borne from the
warmth of her companions and standing up to find both men
little more than pink froth filling their suits. One of the men
had blood on his hands and a cigarette still smouldered
between his fingers. The hand was on the other side of the
room, though.

She saw the bloody, tiny mound of towels on the pool table.
She saw the bucket; the dishcloth had shifted, revealing enough to
tell her the game. Two toes were enough. She didn't need to be
drawn a picture.

And then somehow she found herself outside. And then on
Edgware Road where a pretty young woman with dark hair and a
woven shoulder bag gave her a couple of pounds so that she could
get the Tube to Euston. And then a man smelling of milk and boot
polish whom she fucked in a shop doorway for her fare north.
And then Preston, freezing around her in the early morning as if it
were formed from winter itself. She had half expected Andrew to

poke his head around the door of their living room to say hello, the tea's on, go and sit by the fire and I'll bring some to you.

But the living room was cold and bare. She found sleep at the time she needed it most, just as her thoughts were about to coalesce around the broken image of her baby. She was crying because she couldn't remember what her face looked like.

When she awoke, it was dark again. It was as if daylight had forsaken her. She heard movement towards the back of the house. Outside, in the tiny, scruffy garden, a cardboard box, no bigger than the type used to store shoes, made a stark shape amid the surrounding frost. The women were hunched on the back fence, regarding her with owlish eyes. They didn't speak. Maybe they couldn't.

One of them swooped down and landed by the box. She nudged it forward with her hand, as a deer might coax a newborn to its feet. Sarah felt another burst of unconditional love and security fill the gap between them all. Then they were gone, whipping and twisting far into the sky, the consistency, the trickiness of smoke.

Sarah took the box into the living room with her and waited. Hours passed; she felt herself grow more and more peaceful. She loved her daughter and she hoped Laura knew that. As dawn began to brush away the soot from the sky, Sarah leaned over and touched the lid. She wanted so much to open it and say a few words, but she couldn't bring herself to do it.

In the end, she didn't need to. Whatever remained inside the box managed to do it for her.

JOEL LANE

The Lost District

JOEL LANE LIVES IN BIRMINGHAM. His tales of horror and the supernatural have appeared in various anthologies and magazines, including *Darklands*, *Little Deaths*, *The Third Alternative*, *The Ex Files*, *White of the Moon*, *Dark Terrors 4*, *5* and *6*, *Swords Against the Millennium*, *The Museum of Horrors*, *The Darker Side* and *Gathering the Bones*.

He is the author of a collection of short stories, *The Earth Wire* (Egerton Press, 1994); a collection of poems, *The Edge of the Screen* (Arc, 1999), and two novels, *From Blue to Black* (Serpent's Tail, 2000) and *The Blue Mask* (Serpent's Tail, 2002). Lane has also edited *Beneath the Ground* (Alchemy Press, 2002), an anthology of subterranean horror stories and, with Steve Bishop, *Birmingham Noir* (Tindal Street Press, 2002), an anthology of tales of crime and psychological suspense.

'Influences on "The Lost District" include Fritz Leiber, Ramsey Campbell and *The X Files*,' explains the author. 'It was written for a Leiber tribute booklet that never got published. Then it was accepted for a horror anthology whose publisher went out of business. I began to suspect that it was fated to kill every project it was accepted into, like a paper version of the Red Death. Happily, it appeared in Andy Cox's excellent *The Third Alternative* with no fatal outcome for the magazine.'

These lost streets are decaying only very slowly. The impacted
lives of their inhabitants, the meaninglessness of news, the
dead black of the chimney breasts, the conviction that the wind
itself comes only from the next street, all wedge together to
keep destruction out; to deflect the eye of the developer.

Roy Fisher

Q uite recently, I heard some kid on the TV saying 'Nothing
ever changes'. It made me think about Nicola. Are we
really blind to what happened before our own lives? This
was just after the 1997 General Election, the first change of
government in eighteen years. There'd been this joke going round
that all the parties had trouble canvassing in the Black Country,
because none of the local people would go outside the street they
lived in. Which again reminded me of Nicola, and made me want
to go back to Clayheath and see what, if anything, had changed.

Back in 1979, I was in the fifth year at secondary school. It was
an odd time for me. People think 'teenage culture' is just one thing
that everybody gets into. But it wasn't that simple. In our school
there were punks, second-generation Mods, long-haired heavy-
metal kids and fledgling Rastas. Each crowd had its own language, politics and drugs. The rebels had gone by then, disappearing into casual work or street-life or youth custody. Those
who remained were only playing with fire, not living in it. Like the
girl who was sent home for wearing a slashed blazer. We were too
obsessed with our needs and resentments to communicate. None
of us knew what to say, what to feel, what to believe in. It didn't
matter: nothing was going to change.

After school, at a loose end, I often walked or ran through the
long strip of parkland along the Hagley Road. The first half was
neatly laid out, with flower beds and bowling greens. The second
half was more like woodland, an overgrown and sometimes
marshy surface flowing around the boles of huge trees. Now
that I no longer had to do Games, I missed the exhausting cross-
country runs that had made me feel connected to places like this.
It had been my only chance to look good in front of the heavy lads
who could fillet me on the rugby pitch. Out here, I could leave
them panting and clumping while I raced against the heartbeat of
an invisible partner, on into a mist of adrenalin and sweat. But at
sixteen, I was too lazy and self-conscious to race against anyone.

One chilly, bright day in April, I was strolling along the boundary between the halves of the park: a ragged line of birches, their silvery trunks slashed with rust. Phrases from my German homework were flickering through my head, alongside The Jam's 'Going Underground'. A pale-faced girl was sitting on a bench in front of a cedar tree, not far away. I walked past her, noting her short dark hair, white blouse and black skirt. In the thin afternoon light it was like a scene from an old film. Her gaze followed me impassively.

Driven by a sudden impulse to try and impress her, I ran up to the cedar tree. It was as wide as it was tall. I clasped my hands around the lowest branch and pulled myself up, kicking to gain height. A momentary shiver of sexual excitement passed through me. Using the rough trunk for support, I climbed upwards for another three or four branches. I felt a cold breeze shake the leaves around me, and didn't dare climb any higher. The girl was standing below me. I could see her upturned face, almost featureless at this height. A sudden vertigo snapped my eyes out of focus and I could see two of her, no less alone for it.

When I'd succeeded in climbing down, we stood awkwardly for a while. 'Which way are you going?' I said.

'Don't mind.' She smiled; her teeth were strong and very white. 'You just come from school?' I nodded. 'I'm from Clayheath. Y'know, out past Quinton. Came here on the bus.' Her accent was Black Country with a touch of something else, perhaps Irish. It was an old person's voice.

We walked along toward the road, where the traffic was beginning to thicken. 'Why are you here?' I asked.

'I have to get out sometimes. Just anywhere. It's bad at home.' I knew what she meant. I was in no hurry to get back to our narrow house in Smethwick: my tired parents bickering and shouting, my brother turning up the sport on TV to drown out everything, chores undone, dinner a communal stare. 'You don't know where Clayheath is, do you?'

I'd never heard of it. 'Never been there. Is it far?'

'Not really. It's just nobody goes there. Or leaves.' Along the Hagley Road, the lamp-posts were hung with election placards: mostly blue, a few red. Traffic punctuated our conversation. Her name was Nicola; she worked part-time in a garage. I guessed she was the same age as me. She looked unhappy even when she smiled; it was something in her gaze, always trying to run away. Her skin, stretched tight over her cheekbones, was as pale as a Chinese paper lantern. I wanted to make her blush.

When we reached her bus stop, Nicola said 'What are you doing on Sunday?' I shrugged. 'D'you want to come to Clayheath?' She gave me directions that involved catching a local train to Netherton, then taking the number 147 bus as far as the swimming baths. She'd wait for me there. 'Promise you won't let me down.' I promised. We stared at each other nervously until the Quinton bus arrived. Then Nicola leaned forward and kissed me, her eyes shut. Her lips were so soft I could hardly feel them, just her teeth and a whisper of breath. When the bus drove away, I turned round and walked back into Bearwood. After a while, I realized I'd passed my stop and was in a street I didn't recognize. All the shops had closed.

The train to Netherton stopped at Sandwell, Blackheath, Cradley Heath, and some other towns or districts I'd never heard of. The gaps between towns were a mixture of rural and industrial features: forests, waste ground, factories, scrapyards, canals. Parts of the line ran close to the backyards of terraced houses, where clothes jittered on washing lines and blurred figures moved behind windows. I pictured Nicola in such a room, brushing her hair. The only other people in the train carriage were three teenagers, not much older than me, who'd got on at Blackheath. The two girls sat behind me, whispering to each other. The boy sat in front of me, on the other side. He was wearing a brown jacket that he'd pulled up so it covered his head. After a few minutes of sitting like this, leaning sharply forward, he twisted his face around and snarled, 'A wooden vote for th'Layba.' The girls didn't respond. His pale, staring face rose above the seat like a mask. 'Ah said, a wooden vote for th'Layba *barstad*.' Then he relapsed into his leaning posture, forehead pressed against the back of his seat, jacket pulled over his ears.

The bus stop was in a narrow, old-fashioned high street with half-timbered buildings and wooden pub signs. The approaching streets were the usual Black Country mixture of small factories, houses and less easily identified buildings. Nothing was derelict, but everything had been patched up and reallocated many times over. Most of the buildings had the soft, grimy look of long-

ingrained pollution. A faint sunlight filtered through the streets
without catching any surface. Opposite a grey churchyard was a
tall Victorian building with stone steps: the swimming baths. As I
got off the bus, I saw Nicola step out from the shadow of the wall.
She was wearing a pale grey jacket and black jeans. I walked
towards her, wondering if I should kiss her or wait for a better
opportunity. Her pale hand gripped my arm; her lips brushed my
cheek. 'Glad you made it here,' she said.

We walked together through the centre of Clayheath, if a place
so marginal could be said to have a centre. All around us were
raw traces of industry a hundred years old: canals just below road
level, a brickworks wearing a loose scarf of smoke, black cast-
iron railings ornamented with crudely worked flowers, walls
studded with blue-green pieces of clinker from glass manufacture.
By contrast, the houses themselves were coldly uniform: narrow
grey terraces arranged in regular grids like the lines on a chess-
board. The district seemed overcast, though the sky was dead
white.

Nobody much was around. I remember a white dog pissing on
a lamp-post; a young woman pushing a pram; a few nondescript
grocery and hardware shops with figures moving behind the
window displays. 'It's dead here,' Nicola said quietly. 'Nobody
comes here, nobody goes away. It's always the same. Nothing
ever changes.' She was shivering; cautiously, I put my arm round
her shoulders. A faint smile ghosted her mouth, nervousness
mixed with resignation. She took my hand and curled it into a fist.

'Where do you live?' I asked.

'We've just passed it,' she said. I remembered a street of narrow
terraces, unlit basement windows behind iron railings like display
cases in a museum. 'Don't matter. We can't go there.' The houses
at the end of the street were derelict: windows smashed, doors
clumsily boarded over. Ahead, a new expressway crossed a
stretch of canal where rotting barges clung to the towpath.
Drivers raced over Clayheath without seeing it. I wanted to be
with them. I wanted Nicola, but not this featureless place where
she seemed little more at home than I was. Light flickered between
strips of pale cloud. The road dipped under a railway bridge, part
of a viaduct made from tiny bricks and blackened by industry.
Frozen worms of lime poked through the brickwork overhead. In
the shadow of the bridge, Nicola stopped and kissed me. For the

first time, I was really aware of her vitality: a fierce, bitter energy, like the charge you felt if you put a battery to your tongue. My hand moved from her shoulder to her breast, from the shape of bone to the shape of flesh. 'Come on,' she said. 'I know somewhere to go.'

Beyond the railway, a footpath led behind a row of allotments. They didn't seem to have yielded any crop except leaf mould and scabs of black ash. A few small lumps of greenish clinker studded the earth, like jewellery on a drowned body. As we walked, I told Nicola about my school, my parents, my hopes of being a journalist if the O levels worked out. 'I never took any exams,' she said. 'I was ill, and then it was too late. Makes no difference around here.' Her voice seemed more accented than it had been in Bearwood: the vowels flattened, worn out. In front of us, the outlines of buildings repeated themselves as if the sun were a cheap Xerox machine. 'I like it here. Away from the houses. It's here too, but you have room to be yourself.' I didn't know what she meant.

Ahead of us now, I could see the sun setting through trees: warm petals of orange and pink that belied the growing chill. A park. We stumbled through some undergrowth, skirting a pond that was crusted with grey flakes. The trees around it were short and wide, their branches tangled together. There was a smell of decaying wood and fungus. Nicola tripped and fell; I knelt to help her up. 'Are you okay?' She stared into my eyes. I put my arms around her. After a while, we spread our coats beneath us on the mossy ground.

It was too cold to undress, but we arranged our clothes to allow our bodies as much contact as possible. I remember the slow warmth of her, the sudden incredible heat. Then it was over. As I wiped her thighs with a tissue, I thought of all the times I'd wiped my residues from the centrefold of a magazine. She showed me how to give her pleasure with my fingers, and I felt less guilty. As we covered ourselves, Nicola laughing softly, I had an unmistakable sense of being watched.

Going from the waste ground to the park was like stepping back into the town. The edge was marked by a straight line of poplar trees, their shadows like the bars of a giant cage. We held hands as we shuffled through the grass; Nicola was still laughing, and I realized that something like love was keeping pace with us.

Then she stopped, the smile dissolving from her face like smoke. 'All laughing,' she said. 'All laughing, all dust, all nothing.' I kissed her. As if sex were a bandage for all kinds of unease and despair. You can be a lot older than sixteen and still do that.

Dusk was beginning to isolate the town, reducing it to a cluster of lights surrounded by industrial wasteland. Perhaps it wasn't a town after all. I was still wondering what was the matter with Nicola as we returned from the uncomfortably tidy park to the grey streets. A cat waddled past us like a drunk. 'Can't you feel it?' she said. 'They're used to it round here. But you'm not.' I frowned at her, then shook my head. Nicola shrugged with a quiet irony that I already recognized as characteristic of her. 'I've got to go to work now.'

The garage was a small plastic-roofed box, between the expressway and a low block of flats with iron railings in floral patterns. It had a long car park that smelled of petrol and old newspaper. There were two or three cars that looked abandoned, well away from the pumps. As we stood in the light of the garage window, the red above the houses fading to the blue of night, two figures emerged from the shadows. Boys, a year or two older than me. I registered the similarity of their denim jackets and blow-waved hairstyles before I realized they were twins. Nicola smiled at them. 'Hello.'

'Who's this one?' Nicola introduced me. I don't remember their names. They both seemed to have the same crooked half-smile; their eyes were hollows of darkness. 'What are you doing here?'

'He's doing her,' the other said. Like an echo. The first one looked at Nicola and said, 'Why do you bother?' She pulled at my sleeve nervously. 'This isn't your place,' one of them said to me. Maybe it was the failing light, but I couldn't see their teeth when they spoke. They were both shivering, but making no effort to get warmer.

'Whose place is it?' I said, inwardly preparing myself for trouble. I'd been through some fights in school and knew where to hit. But I had no illusions about violence being romantic.

'You'll learn.' Another blank stare, a half-choked snigger. 'Time's running out.' A car drove past, white eyes turning a dull red. Nicola tugged at my sleeve again, holding it. 'Let's go inside,' she said.

The twins watched us through the window, as faint as reflections in water, before moving on. Nicola lifted a wooden flap and stepped behind the counter, then fiddled with a display of cigarette cartons. A middle-aged man with greying stubble on his pink cheeks nodded at her sardonically and went back to writing figures in his accounts book. I fidgeted, bought a chocolate bar, touched Nicola's fingers when I gave her the coins. 'You'd better go home,' she whispered; not coldly. I nodded and turned away, then felt in my coat pocket for my diary and stub of pencil. I wrote down my name and my parents' phone number, tore out the page and gave it to her. She brushed it across her lips before folding it and slipping it into the pocket of her white blouse.

Outside, the cold went through me like a voice. I ran toward the lights at the higher end of the road, blinking, seeing double. I found the high street by chance and worked back to the swimming baths. The train rattled through a landscape of night shifts and distant fires. I stared out of the window and thought of home: my father asking 'Where the hell have you been?', my mother somehow knowing.

Ten days passed before Nicola rang. In that time, spring hardened into early summer. Light poured through trees, slipped on wet pavements. The rain tasted of smoke. Every morning, I got up half an hour early to deliver papers. They were full of the election, every tabloid but the *Mirror* hailing Thatcher as the saviour of England. I remember the election itself. Her clotted, suburban voice quoting St Francis of Assisi: *Where there is conflict, let us bring peace.* The newsagent whose papers I delivered was quietly jubilant. 'Now we'll get things back the way they were. The way they should have stayed.' Years later, I heard he'd been jailed for seducing a fourteen-year-old girl who was helping in his shop. He took her to bed, then gave her ten quid, a packet of cigarettes and a hot meal. The local paper said he'd been a pilot in the Second World War.

My paper round covered a strip of roads in between our house and the local primary school: the territory of my childhood. There was the fire station that sometimes jerked awake in the night, sending out wailing engines. The railway bridge where local bullies waited in shadow for younger boys to spit on or throw eggs at. The little car park with its row of disused garages where, when I was eleven, the twin girls who lived up the road led me through a broken wall into a sealed-off alley where they showed me their vaginas. There wasn't much to see, of course: just two scraggy folds of pale skin that reminded me of bacon left too long in the fridge. I had to expose myself too; it was probably the first time I had an erection, which I took to be somehow an effect of the cold.

Nicola phoned me late one evening; my father frowned at me as he passed me the receiver. She didn't say much. When I asked her what she'd been doing, she said 'Nothing.' Then she asked if I wanted to see her on Sunday. Same place, slightly earlier time. I agreed. It suited me to be away from home when I saw her. There was some interference on the line, making us echo each other's goodbyes – a verbal entanglement that felt somehow intimate. I put the phone down and slowly opened my eyes to see my father staring at me from his armchair. I said nothing.

Sunday was lukewarm and overcast. The train crawled through unconvincing stage sets of old factories and new housing, or vice versa. Rain chipped at the windows. I chewed a bag of aniseed sweets I'd bought in the chemist's shop that morning, having gone in to buy a packet of Durex and been inhibited by the young female assistant. In retrospect, I'm amazed at how little Nicola and I knew about each other's lives. I don't think that ever changes, but it's more obvious at a distance.

When I got to the swimming baths at Clayheath, Nicola wasn't there. I waited while a succession of ageing swimmers emerged slick-haired and red-eyed from the baths. Clayheath appeared to be dissolving into the rain. Blinking away ghosts of narrow buildings and metallic trees, I didn't see Nicola until she was close enough to touch. Her black umbrella covered us both as we embraced. 'Come with me,' she said. 'There's a place I want you to see. And we'll need somewhere to shelter from this.' As we walked along the high street, the umbrella a patch of darkness just above our line of sight, I slipped an arm around her pale jacket. She was tense, braced against the cold. Around us, the wind tore up scraps of light.

Nowhere seemed to be open. The narrow streets looked more compact than ever, as if the spaces between buildings had closed up, the district shrinking into itself. We walked past the edge of the park, the line of poplar trees like huge railings. There were no leaves on their symmetrical branches. I hadn't noticed that before.

Outside a scrapyard where rusting car parts were stacked up in mounds, two men were arguing. Something about a failed engine, where to find a replacement. I couldn't understand most of what they were saying, though it wasn't really dialect. It was like ordinary words in mouths that weren't quite alive. A dog started barking from behind the wire fence as Nicola and I passed. The sound echoed along the street. The sky felt as close as an iron lid.

'They've shut down the junior school,' Nicola said quietly. 'Not enough children to go there. It's been closed for years.' She pronounced *closed* with a break in the first vowel, almost making two syllables. 'But some of us who were there, y'know . . . we miss it. So we go back.' She laughed silently. I didn't see the joke. I somehow never did with her. We kept walking as the trees disappeared and more of the buildings began to seem derelict, their windows smashed or boarded. The canal network was visible every few blocks, crossed by narrow bridges, underlying the street plan like a mapmaker's grid.

The premature darkness of the rain clouds had begun to clear when we reached the school. It was like a smaller version of the swimming baths: a thin Victorian red-brick structure with an elaborate carved lintel above the door. The green chain-link fence on either side of the rusty gates was twisted and torn in several places, as if small animals had broken in. A thin strip of concrete playground ran across the front of the school and down the left-hand side. The windows were unbroken, but furred with white-wash on the inside. Some of them were covered by rusty wire grids.

'This way,' Nicola tugged my hand and led me along the side of the building, which was protected by spiked railings. At the back, two large dustbins were lying side by side. One railing was missing; Nicola squeezed through and I followed. To one side of the boarded-up door, an iron grille covered the basement window. The bars had been forced apart, the glass removed. Nicola smiled at me. Cautiously, but with a skill that suggested experience, she lowered herself feet first into the gap. It swallowed her eagerly. Her knuckles were white above the bars as her feet kicked in empty air. Then she fell, landing with a soft thud that I hoped was cushioned by more than dust. She climbed to her feet, breathless, and took something off a shelf. An electric torch, the batteries weak but not dead.

As I worked my way through the bars to join her, I had a sudden conviction that we were being watched. Not by human eyes, perhaps: a hidden camera, an electronic security system, or a guard dog that had been trained not to bark before it attacked. Then I was falling, too abruptly for vertigo, flailing in a sheet of damp air before landing on several thicknesses of rough sacking stitched with dust.

Nicola's torch cast a circle of pale light, wide but fading quickly from the centre. I could see a boiler and a series of pipes, lagged with dusty whitewashed bandages. Some used condoms littered the floor. It was very quiet. Nicola shone the torch in my face, dazzling me. When my vision cleared, the torch was off. By the grey light of the basement window, I could see Nicola removing her blouse. We stripped naked, then wrapped ourselves in our coats. The near-darkness helped me to relax, slow down. It was just the way a wet dream is. I mean all the different things superimposed, as if an hour were folded over or spliced into each minute, or as if we both had many bodies to make love with. Time and again.

A pigeon moaned outside as we finally separated and fumbled for our clothes. Dressed, Nicola was different: at once more confident and less self-possessed. 'I want to show you something,' she said. Holding the torch in front of her, she led me up the stone steps and through the open door to the hallway. The green-painted walls were livid with damp and mould. Strips of paint curled from the ceiling. Behind one of the side doors, something ran across the room to scratch the wall. Nicola glanced back, but didn't flinch. 'That was my classroom,' she said. The failing torch beam jittered in a huge cobweb, making it seem alive with darkness. Nicola tore it in half and stepped through. 'This is the hall where we sat for assembly. We did the Nativity play here. I was Mary. The baby was a doll from Woolworths.' She stopped, her torch beam lost in the cowebbed vaults above the dead mercury strip lights. I kissed her and realized, with a shock, that she was crying. 'Come on,' I said.

The first door in the next corridor had been locked, but the lock was smashed. 'The staff room,' she said. It was empty like all the others, smelling faintly of disinfectant. A side door, with no glass in it, was open by a crack. Nicola pushed it with her shoulder. The hinges snarled. Inside, shelves and crates were blurred with dust.

'This is the storeroom.' I stood beside her, my eyes following the weak torch beam as she moved it from side to side. First trying to make out what was there, then trying to make sense of it.

One set of metal shelves was filled with oblong wooden boxes, a foot or so long. They might have been games equipment, or costume items for a school play. Their lids had been crudely nailed in place. Another set of shelves, on the other side of the narrow room, was filled with murky-looking glass jars about a foot high. We stood there for minutes, Nicola banging the torch with her palm to make the battery keep working. The jars stank of formaldehyde.

It was a collection of preserved babies – or rather foetuses. I'm not sure they were entirely human. Were they deformed, or somehow a kind of hybrid? They floated, blind and colourless, shivering in the unstable light. Whatever their source, they'd been born without life. Perhaps others had survived, and these were the failures. Some had umbilical cords, I noticed; others were too distorted for anyone to tell where a cord might begin. A few looked like pairs of Siamese twins, so poorly separated that, in a photograph, you'd take them for a double exposure.

I stepped away from Nicola, walking until the darkness wrapped itself around me and I had to stop. For a moment, when she touched me, I wanted to push her away. Then I let her guide me back towards the steps and the basement, where the red sun glowed through the opening. We helped each other to climb out, then walked to the road in silence. Nicola glanced at her watch. 'I'd better go home,' she said. 'My shift's in half an hour.'

'Leave here,' I said. 'Come to Birmingham. Stay with me.'

We embraced briefly. 'There's no point,' she said. 'It's always the same. Nothing ever changes.' We might as well have been talking to ourselves. I remember thinking that everything changed, but that somehow you never noticed.

From the train, I watched the last residue of daylight spill like oil onto wet rooftops and roads. I got home late in the evening and showered, then went straight to bed. More than Nicola's body, I remembered kissing her. How soft her lips were, like shreds of tissue paper over her perfect teeth.

It was nearly a month before she rang again, late at night. My parents were out. I was listening to The Specials' 'Do Nothing' and trying to revise *Hamlet*. Her voice sounded faint and echoey; I could hear traffic going past. She must have been in a call box. 'Simon? Simon?'

'Nicola? Is that you?' The darkness of the living-room tensed around me. 'Are you okay, love?'

She was crying. 'Simon, I'm frightened. Please listen.' Her breath caught in her throat, and I thought she was going to choke. Then, suddenly, she was calm. 'I'm pregnant.'

'Oh, no.' I felt cold with guilt. As if I'd thrown up on the table and the whole family was watching me. 'I'm sorry, Nicola. It's all my fault.' She made an odd, throaty sound. 'What do you want to do?'

The same sound again. I realized she was laughing. 'Oh, Simon. You're such a div sometimes.' There was a pause. 'It's not you. I mean, it wasn't you. It's not yours.' In the silence that followed, I heard a car drive past; then another. I couldn't do anything but put the phone down. She didn't call back.

That weekend, I went to Clayheath. After a day spent with my revision notes, endlessly rereading the same text, I caught the train in mid-evening. I thought I'd try the garage, maybe leave a message for her there. By the time I reached the swimming baths, it was already dark. Sodium light painted the roadway. The garage was on the far side of the park. Or was it the near side? I tried to superimpose a memory of the district on the blank grid ahead of me, but all I could imagine was Nicola's face. And her body. Abruptly, I turned a corner and saw a featureless office building I didn't recognize. Two roads diverged from a traffic island with a tilted bollard. They were both lined with unvarying grey terraces, no lights visible behind the drawn curtains.

As I struggled to hold on to a sense of direction, a van swung around the corner from behind me. At the same time, a small dark shape loped awkwardly across the road towards me. The two collided with a scream of brakes and pain. The van slowed, then sped away. Its tyres left a thin red wound in the tarmac.

A cat. Probably the same cat I'd seen here a few weeks earlier. From where I stood, I could see that it was beyond help. I could also see what had made it so clumsy. Spilling from its torn gut was a litter of bald, helpless kittens. They must have been kittens. But in the flickering light of the street lamp, they reminded me of what I'd seen in the glass jars. Their enlarged heads, blind swollen eyes,

tiny clutching hands with pale fingers. There were seven or eight
of them, all exactly the same. Unable to live or die. Unable to
change.

Swallowing a mouthful of acid saliva, I turned and walked
slowly back to the swimming baths. Caught the bus. My head
was a whorl of milky light, a fingerprint on an icy road. On the
train going back to Birmingham, I began to feel steadier. What
made me vomit, weeping tears of pain and relief, was going to the
urinals in New Street Station and seeing a coin-operated Durex
machine.

There isn't much more to tell. I stayed in Birmingham, took my O
levels and passed most of them, applied myself to the task of
growing up in Thatcher's new Britain. Instead of becoming a
journalist, I became an accountant. Somehow, my curiosity about
the world had gone. In 1990, I moved to Guildford and became a
financial consultant. I put on some weight, bought a maisonette,
had a succession of girlfriends. Somehow I could never resist a
new face, or experience affection without desire.

One weekend in the spring of 1997, I was up in the Midlands
on business. Election fever was at its height, reminding me of
1979. I drove through South Birmingham, playing The Jam on
my car stereo: 'The Butterfly Collector', 'Going Underground',
'Dreams of Children'. That night, I decided to go back to
Clayheath.

But it wasn't there. When I looked for it in my new A–Z, the
district no longer existed. I wasn't even sure which districts it had
been absorbed into. I decided to let the train and bus route take
me to it; but the branch line had been discontinued. Finally I
checked the Yellow Pages for swimming baths within a few miles
of Netherton. There was only one.

It took me a long time to find it, driving through the narrow
Black Country streets on a quiet Sunday morning. The sky was
tinged with pink, like marble.

Perhaps I was distracted by images of streets that no longer
existed; or perhaps I didn't want to find real evidence of a place
I'd long ago bulldozed and redeveloped in my mind. But at last I
drove up a long straight road, behind a bus that stopped outside a
tall Victorian building with a carved lintel and several deep steps.

My neck stiffened, as if I had a chill. I parked the Audi and got out.

Apart from that building, nothing was the way I remembered it. In place of the crowded terraces, a jumble of housing blocks and prefabricated industrial units sprawled between the pitted roads. I couldn't see the park, nor any trees at all. A new expressway cut across the end of the high street before circling around a giant plastic-fronted garden centre, like a rubber ring around a baby floating in a pool of whitish concrete. I turned back towards the swimming baths. It wasn't only the image of Nicola that made me start to cry at that moment. It was the knowledge of how I'd been, then and ever since. Eighteen years of selfishness and waste. I blinked, rubbed my eyes and stared at my hands. Then I started running towards the car.

Ten minutes later I was speeding along the Halesowen Road into an acid sunlight, telling myself that what I'd seen had meant nothing. For those few moments, as I'd walked past the steps outside the old baths, I'd seen my hands somehow turn into hands that weren't left and right, that weren't mirror images of each other. They were the same hand twice: both palms up, both thumbs pointing to the right.

Nothing ever changes. We just tell ourselves it does.

RICHARD A. LUPOFF

Simeon Dimsby's Workshop

RICHARD A. LUPOFF CELEBRATED THE PUBLICATION of his fiftieth book, *The Great American Paperback*, in 2001. This was a work of cultural history that won glowing praise from periodicals as varied as *Playboy* magazine and the scholarly *Wilson Quarterly*. Most of his work, however, has been fiction, including several dozen novels and more than 100 short stories.

Much of his fiction has been collected in such volumes as *Before 12:01 and After*, *Claremont Tales* and *Claremont Tales II*. His latest publication is *Marblehead: A Novel of H. P. Lovecraft*, the manuscript of which was recently rediscovered, having been lost more than twenty-five years ago.

'In "Simeon Dimsby's Workshop" I return to the wondrous, long ago days when I was an avid reader and fan,' explains Lupoff, 'admiring the glamorous figures who filled the pages of lurid pulp magazines and dreaming of the time when I would join their ranks.'

IT TOOK REGIS HARDY SIX years to sell his first short story.

He would rise early each morning and put in an hour of mental effort, bending over a notebook, striving for the right combination of words that would elicit a letter of acceptance instead of the rejection slips to which he was accustomed. When he kissed his spouse, Helena, good-bye after a light breakfast of toast and half a grapefruit, he would ride the municipal bus to his job in downtown Elmwood, California.

The men and women around him occupied themselves in a variety of ways: perusing copies of the Elmwood *Daily Express-Bulletin*, listening to their favorite music on portable CD players, reading paperback novels. Often regular riders on the Number Eighteen line would greet one another and discuss the events of the world, or of their personal lives, as they traveled to work. High-school students engaged in horseplay. College students would take part in serious and arcane discussions of Kierkegaard, Aeschylus, or the millions of dollars they expected to make in the high-tech world as soon as they received their degrees.

Not Mr Hardy. He lived near the end of the Number Eighteen line and always got a seat on his way to work. He would ride with his eyes closed, imagining the doings of the men and women in his stories, striving to capture just the right event, image, or turn of phrase to make his current opus the one that would carry him across the threshold of literary status from that of ambitious amateur to that of acclaimed professional.

Mr Hardy worked at the Department of Social Services. He took his lunch each day in the department's cafeteria, notebook laid flat beside his plastic tray and yellow wooden pencil in hand, working, always working on his stories. And every night, after dinner with Helena, he would retreat to his private corner and work for another hour on his stories before joining his wife to watch the evening news.

Six years.

And then the miracle happened.

Mr Hardy received a letter from the editor of *Mayhem Monthly*. The editor had read Mr Hardy's submission, 'Vampire Town', and was pleased to tender the enclosed purchase agreement for the story.

The payment was minuscule and the magazine, which had rejected numerous of Mr Hardy's efforts in the past, was a minor one, but Mr Hardy was ecstatic. He could see a doorway opening before him. He imagined a room filled with the literary figures he had admired, almost worshiped, all his life, eagerly welcoming him to their world and to their own glamorous company.

Filled with pride, Mr Hardy showed the letter to his wife, who threw her arms around his shoulders and planted a congratulatory kiss on his cheek.

That night, inspired by the delicious taste of success, Regis

Hardy worked on his current story-in-progress for two hours rather than one. Later, lying in bed, Helena's soft breathing and warm presence filling him with marital contentment, he projected an imaginary motion picture on the ceiling, peopling each frame with characters of his own invention and creating a sound track filled with mood-inspiring music, crackling dialog and exciting sound effects.

It would be pleasant to report that Mr Hardy, having at last achieved the mystical transformation from amateur to professional writer, was immediately greeted with nothing but editorial accolades, but such was not the case. Following the solitary sale to *Mayhem Monthly* there came a series of rejection slips from a broad spectrum of periodicals.

But Regis Hardy was not one to surrender his treasured dream, especially after having sold 'Vampire Town'.

Some months later came a double red-letter day. There was another letter of acceptance, this one from *Interstellar Stories*. The work in question was a novelette titled 'Narcotics from Neptune'. The same day's postal delivery included a brown manila envelope. The envelope contained two copies of the issue of *Mayhem Monthly* featuring 'Vampire Town'.

The Hardys sat happily side-by-side admiring Regis's story and the black-and-white illustration that accompanied it. To be candid, the illustration was decidedly on the crude and slapdash side, nor had the artist captured quite the flavor of Mr Hardy's story, or the detail of his description. But Mrs Hardy patted Mr Hardy affectionately on the cheek, and he did feel that another milestone had been passed on the roadway to success.

As the months and years rolled by Mr Hardy found that he was receiving fewer rejection notices and making more sales. He was able to move to higher-paying and more prestigious markets. He cracked *Image of the Imagination* and *Exciting Adventure Annual* and finally *New Modern Gangster Quarterly*.

He built a proud 'brag shelf' of magazines containing his works. He admired the many black-and-white illustrations that accompanied them, and invited Mrs Hardy out for a celebratory cocktail and dinner when *Wilderness* magazine honored him with a full-color cover painting of a scene from his story 'Cannibal's Canoe'.

His hair was thinning and his temples were grey now, and he

suspected that Mrs Hardy's flaming titian locks retained their
brilliance only with the assistance of expensive chemicals, but he
chose not to raise the subject in conversation. He had never made
a living from his writing. He had kept his day job at the
Department of Social Services, but' he knew in his heart that
the job was merely a means to the end of supporting his writing
endeavors.

Only two goals had eluded him.

Despite numerous attempts he had never been able to sell a
story to *Grave Yarns*. In each case the story in question had been
successfully placed in another market, nor was *Grave Yarns* the
highest-paying or most prestigious of periodicals. But it was a
venerable publication, almost legendary in the community, and
Mr Hardy had long dreamed of winning a place in its pages. That
was the first of Mr Hardy's remaining unfulfilled ambitions.

The second was to see his stories collected into a book. He had
approached a number of publishers and been turned away with
the advice that he procure the services of a literary agent. He had
then approached a number of agents only to be turned away by
them with the advice that he write a novel if he wished book
publication. Collections of short stories were virtually impossible
to place, he was told.

By this time Mr Hardy was nearing retirement age and looked
forward eagerly to leaving the Department of Social Services. He
would then be able to devote all of his energies to his literary
endeavors. Mrs Hardy had already taken early retirement from
her own job, and offered her husband encouragement with his
plan.

By the time a letter arrived at the Hardys' modest home bearing
the return indicia of *Grave Yarns* Mr Hardy was forced to don his
trifocal spectacles in order to read it. But the game was most
assuredly worth the candle as Mr Hardy found that he had at last
captured the proverbial brass ring on the ever-turning carousel of
literature. The editor of *Grave Yarns* was pleased to accept Mr
Hardy's submission to the magazine, 'Even the Dead Have
Rights'.

Only one goal remained now on Mr Hardy's agenda, and that
was book publication. He had not been wholly frustrated in even
this enterprise, for several times his stories had been included in
anthologies. These books, some colorful and some drab, some of

them beautifully bound and jacketed volumes and others cheaply made paperbacks, held a special place of honor in the Hardy living room. But a collection devoted entirely to his own works was a dream the realization of which continued to elude Mr Hardy.

And then Mr Hardy received a letter from a publisher unfamiliar to him. Surely this was one he had never contacted, nor even read of in the trade journals to which he assiduously subscribed. The writer of the letter introduced himself as the proprietor of a new firm, Mantigore Press. He was seeking to publish the works of deserving but previously overlooked authors. He had been an admirer of Mr Hardy's atmospheric and effective prose for some years, and if Mr Hardy found himself in a position to place a collection of his stories with the new company, Mantigore Press was prepared to issue a contract immediately, and to offer a small but realistic advance payment against royalties to be earned.

The letter was signed, *Auric Mantigore*.

Regis Hardy was so excited that his wife had to spend the better part of an hour calming and soothing him. He then responded to Auric Mantigore's letter with a quick and enthusiastic reply in the affirmative.

Thus it was that, in due course, Mantigore Press announced the impending publication of *Return to Elmwood: the Collected Stories of Regis Hardy*.

Mantigore Press was headquartered in the city of Repentance, Maine, some 3,000 miles from Elmwood, California. At first Mr Hardy conducted his business with Mantigore by postal means, but when Auric Mantigore informed him that the distinguished artist and resident of Repentance, Simeon Dimsby, had been engaged to create a jacket painting and interior illustrations for *Return to Elmwood*, Mr Hardy could contain himself no longer.

Over a modest evening meal he broached his plan to his wife. 'We are both now retired, Helena. Our pensions are small but adequate to our needs, and we have some savings. I would like to travel to Repentance, Maine, to meet Auric Mantigore and the great Simeon Dimsby. I intend to write to Messrs. Mantigore and Dimsby and propose such a meeting. If they are amenable to my plan, I would be most pleased to have your company on the trip, and to arrange for your inclusion in our festive gathering.'

There were tears in Helena Hardy's eyes as she voiced her approval of her husband's notion.

Even before watching the evening news on that occasion, Regis Hardy penned letters to Auric Mantigore and Simeon Dimsby, broaching his plan. While similar in content, the two letters were not identical. That addressed to Simeon Dimsby included a paragraph in which Mr Hardy expressed his admiration for Dimsby's work. Many artists had attempted to capture the essence of Regis Hardy's stories, but none had fully succeeded, at least in his opinion. But he was confident of Dimsby's ability to do so, and hoped fervently to meet the great illustrator.

Not long after writing to Mantigore and Dimsby, Regis Hardy received responses from both. Mantigore explained that he was a busy man whose responsibilities occupied him for many hours each day. Further, he was obliged by commercial considerations to spend most of each month traveling. Consequently, he suggested that Hardy and Dimsby make such arrangements as they saw fit. If available, Mantigore would join them. If unable to do so, he would nonetheless offer his best wishes.

Regis Hardy was mildly disappointed by Auric Mantigore's letter, but he was positively elated when he read Simeon Dimsby's. The artist had developed a great fondness for Hardy's stories and was most enthusiastic about *Return to Elmwood*. He had already created preliminary sketches for his illustrations and worked out what he referred to as his 'concept' for the dust-jacket painting. He indicated a date by which he hoped to have the final versions of the drawings in hand, and suggested that Regis Hardy come to his, Dimsby's, home and workshop on that date.

Further correspondence confirmed that Mrs Hardy would also be welcomed at the Dimsby demesne, and that if it were convenient for the Hardys, the invitation would be so timed as to include dinner at the Dimsby home. Mrs Dimsby was an accomplished chef, Simeon Dimsby asserted, and would be pleased to prepare her finest dishes for the Hardys.

Regis Hardy could barely contain his joy. He dispatched an enthusiastic reply, jotted the date of the proposed dinner party in his desk planner, and made a note to phone a local travel agent and book a flight for himself and his wife to the airport nearest Repentance, Maine.

It was fortunate for Regis Hardy's peace of mind that Simeon Dimsby worked rapidly, for even so Mr Hardy found himself counting the days until his and Mrs Hardy's flight, like a child counting days until a birthday, or Christmas, or the end of the school year. Standing before the bathroom mirror in his pajamas, Mr Hardy took note of his lined visage, his largely naked scalp and the snowy whiteness of what little hair he retained.

He was an old man, but in his chest his heart leaped like that of an eager and joyous youth.

At last the long-awaited day arrived. The Hardys were driven to the airport by one Albert Tindle, a former colleague of Mr Hardy's at the Department of Social Services. They boarded the huge, sleek jetliner, Mr Hardy commenting almost involuntarily at the contrast between it and the far smaller, propeller-driven monoplanes of his youth.

Their journey was uneventful, and upon reaching Repentance, Maine, the Hardys checked into a motel. This was a locally owned affiliate of an international chain. It was well managed in accord with corporate guidelines. The Hardys' room was comfortably appointed in a standardized and impersonal style. Mrs Hardy remarked that they might as easily have been in Brazil, Syria, or Thailand, or even on the moon, had there been motels on the moon, for all the local character of their lodgings.

Mr Hardy telephoned the home of Simeon Dimsby. Mrs Dimsby took the call, reiterated the invitation to dine that evening, and even offered the services of her husband to pick up the Hardys at their motel. Mr Hardy expressed gratitude for the offer but indicated that he and his wife would take a cab to the Dimsbys' house.

Dusk was falling when the driver pulled to the curb at the address Regis Hardy had given him. The warm autumnal afternoon had yielded to a chill breeze with the disappearance of the sun, and an early moon was rising red and menacing above the eastern horizon. Mr and Mrs Hardy stood side by side, gazing at the tall frame structure. A brightness flickered in the front window as if electrification had somehow bypassed the Dimsby house and its occupants relied on old-fashioned oil lamps for illumination.

An unexpected chill caused Mr Hardy to shudder almost imperceptibly. He took his wife's hand and advanced, opening a protesting gate in the waist-high iron fence. The lawn surrounding the house had not been mowed in a very long time. The wooden stairs that led to the front porch creaked with each of Mr and Mrs Hardy's steps.

A search for a doorbell or knocker having failed, Mr Hardy rapped tentatively on the wooden panel with his knuckles.

At once the door swung back. A plump woman of below average height looked up at the Hardys. The roundness of her face was offset by the grey hair which she had pulled back into a bun. She wore a patterned housedress and cloth apron. A small birthmark above one eye evoked a mildly distasteful fantasy on Regis Hardy's part.

'You must be the Hardys. Come in. I'm Mrs Dimsby. Eustacia Whipple Dimsby. Please call me Eustacia.'

She took Mr Hardy's fedora and Mrs Hardy's wrap and escorted them to a parlor furnished as it must have been a century before. 'Mr Dimsby is in his workshop. Make yourselves comfortable while I fetch him.'

She disappeared down a hallway.

The Hardys exchanged glances.

A door slammed. The pendulum of a tall clock swung to and fro. There were footsteps. A figure appeared where Eustacia Dimsby had last been seen.

'I am Simeon Dimsby.'

Regis Hardy rose to his feet. Dimsby shook his hand, then bowed over Helena Hardy's as would have a Regency dandy. It took an effort for Regis Hardy to refrain from flinching away from Dimsby's icy fingers. The artist was cadaverously thin, his pale countenance set off by a high-collared white shirt and heavy black suit. Waves of cold seemed to waft from him.

'Forgive me,' he explained. 'My workshop is below the house and I keep it cool at all times, to preserve my compositions.'

'You work in oils?' Hardy asked. He knew little of artistic media.

Dimsby shook his head from side to side. 'No.' He offered no further explanation.

'But if you have to keep your work refrigerated, how do you deliver it to your publishers?' Dimsby did not answer at once, and

Hardy filled the silence. 'That is, your pictures are so fine, both your black-and-white illustrations and your paintings. Helena and I have admired them for a long time. I was thrilled when Mr Mantigore told me you were to illustrate my book, *Return to Elmwood*. But what do you use for ink? For paint? Wouldn't it spoil?'

'Such is the wonder of modern invention,' Dimsby explained. He had crossed the room and opened what appeared to be an eighteenth century cupboard. He turned with a graceful decanter in one hand and two round-bellied snifters in the other. 'The day has taken a chilly turn, has it not? Won't you each try some brandy to warm yourselves while Mrs Dimsby prepares our dinner.'

Each of the Hardys accepted a snifter of shimmering, copper-colored liquid. As Regis Hardy held it before his face the fumes of the liquor rose with a pleasant sharpness and warmth. It was delicious on his tongue. From the corner of his eye he observed his wife sampling the beverage.

'You were speaking of technology,' Hardy addressed his host.

'Yes.'

'And won't you have some brandy yourself?' Hardy asked.

'I do not,' Dimsby said. After a brief silence he resumed. 'My compositions would, ah, *de*-compose if exposed to heat,' he explained, laughing at his own play on words. 'Therefore I scan them into a computer and deliver them to my publishers in the form of electronic files.'

Hardy nodded. 'A shame. I was hoping – that is, I had thought, maybe – once *Return to Elmwood* is completed, that you might be willing to part with one of your originals. It would have a place of honor in our house, wouldn't it, dear? Especially if we might purchase – if Mr Dimsby would consider parting with – the jacket painting.'

His wife agreed that, yes, a Dimsby original would be treasured in the Hardy home.

'Alas, I fear that would be impossible,' Simeon Dimsby commiserated, 'but perhaps after dinner you would enjoy a tour of my workshop. You may have some comments on the renderings I have done for *Return to Elmwood*.' Before he could say more his wife returned from the kitchen and summoned them to the dinner table.

The Dimsby dining room, like the parlor, could have served as the set for a period motion picture, but there was no sense of artificiality or unreality to the room. Rather, upon entering its confines one had the impression of having stepped backward in time.

Mrs Dimsby bustled into the kitchen and returned bearing a large platter. It was covered with a green, shimmering mass of interwoven strips that reminded Mr Hardy of marine vegetation that he had seen on past visits to the Pacific Ocean near his home. Mrs Dimsby set the platter in the center of the gleaming linen cloth that covered the table.

Mr Dimsby asked if the Hardys would object to the old-fashioned practice of saying grace prior to dining. They did not. Mr Dimsby then folded his grey, bony hands in a manner unfamiliar to the guests. He lowered his head and closed his eyes, murmuring what Regis Hardy took to be his devotion. Mr Hardy had no notion of Simeon Dimsby's ethnic heritage or his religious affiliation. The prayer was in a language unfamiliar to Hardy, a disquieting mixture of sibilants and gutturals. As the prayer ended the room seemed to shudder. Accustomed as he was to occasional small earthquakes in California, Regis Hardy was unalarmed by the minor temblor, despite never having heard of earthquakes in Maine.

The green substance proved to be a pre-prandial salad. Its flavor was mildly unpleasant, the dressing of an odd gelatinous consistency and its odor peculiarly marine, but Mr Hardy managed to down a small portion of it, as did his wife.

Mrs Dimsby removed the platter and salad plates.

Mr Dimsby said, 'The main course is Mrs Dimsby's specialty, an old family recipe handed down ever since Colonial times here in Repentance. In fact, local legend has it that the dish was a favorite of the aboriginal inhabitants. Unlike other native peoples they neither died out nor moved away, but were assimilated by the settlers. Or, perhaps more accurately, one might say that the settlers were assimilated by the local inhabitants.'

Mr Hardy was about to ask if his host's prayer had been spoken in the natives' language, but before he could do so, Mrs Dimsby returned from the kitchen bearing a massive iron pot. Mr Hardy was amazed that the short woman could handle its weight, but she hefted it onto a blackened trivet. The contents of the iron pot bubbled and hissed, emitting visible columns of steam.

'I hope no one is allergic to shellfish,' she announced. Receiving no objections she nodded to her husband, who lifted a long-handled implement and dipped it into the pot. Beside him stood a stack of deep bowls. He ladled a portion into one for Helena Hardy, then for Regis Hardy, then for his wife, Eustacia, and finally for himself.

Regis Hardy gazed at the contents of his bowl. Taking his clue from Mrs Dimsby's comment, he assumed that the meal consisted of a shellfish stew or bouillabaisse. Not only bits of marine carapace but tiny tentacles, claws, and even eyestalks were clearly visible, floating in a viscid red broth. The meal must have been brought to the table while still a-boil, for bubbles rose to the surface, tentacles waved and minuscule claws seemed to snap at Mr Hardy's spoon. He shot a glance at his wife, sharing with her his distress.

He managed to secure a spoonful of the broth and convey it to his mouth, all the while staring at a small marine crustacean that seemed to stare back at him from his bowl. The broth was hot in both main senses of that word, and as it reached the back of Mr Hardy's tongue he could have sworn that a tiny, serrated claw nipped at his uvula, sending a wave of pain and nausea through him.

The Hardys managed to down a bare polite minimum of their meal while the Dimsbys emptied their bowls and refilled them repeatedly, smacking their lips and exclaiming in pleasure at the textures and flavors of the repast. Conversation was desultory, and it was with relief that Mr Hardy pushed his old ladder-back chair away from the table at the end of the meal, helping his wife to follow suit.

Eustacia Dimsby excused herself in order to clear the table and attend to her duties in the kitchen. Helena Hardy volunteered her assistance. Simeon Dimsby renewed his offer to Regis Hardy, to tour the subterranean workshop. Hardy attempted to beg off, pleading fatigue after the day's transcontinental travel, but yielded to Dimsby's persuasive words and the astonishingly powerful, even painful, grip on his elbow.

Dimsby insisted that Hardy precede him down a lengthy narrow stairway. The first flight was of creaking, wooden risers and treads. Thereafter the flight plunged more steeply into what seemed bedrock, the stairs carved out of ancient New England granite.

Illumination was provided by concealed fixtures.

Mr Hardy's breath rose coldly in visible clouds.

After an exhausting trek which left Mr Hardy wondering how he would ever be able to climb back to the surface, the staircase ended. He found himself in a small antechamber. A single iron door met his gaze.

Simeon Dimsby stepped past Mr Hardy. He drew an oversized, old-fashioned key from his suit pocket and inserted it in a massive, time-blackened lock. Turning the key, he snapped the lock open and pulled the door toward himself.

Inside the chamber the temperature seemed to plunge still farther. Mr Hardy stood, surrounded by magnificent yet macabre images. At a sound he turned and observed Simeon Dimsby, who had pulled the heavy door shut behind the pair of them with a jarring, metallic impact.

'Let me show you my sketches for *Return to Elmwood*,' Dimsby grated. 'We won't be disturbed. Only Auric Mantigore and I have keys to this door. Not even my wife, dear as she is, can enter unless we permit it.'

He opened a drawer in a rough wooden table and removed a huge envelope. He undid the hasp on the envelope and withdrew one of a sheaf of renderings on stiff illustration board. He turned toward Hardy. 'I hope you will be pleased.'

The top drawing was Dimsby's illustration for Mr Hardy's story 'Narcotics from Neptune'. The illustration for this tale in *Interstellar Stories*, by one Barton Gorgon, had been a literal representation of the climactic scene of the narrative, in which Hardy's beleaguered space voyagers, imprisoned by amoeboid creatures from the frigid outer planet, injected with a deadly, addictive drug and forced to work in the noxious mines of Neptune's rocky moons, confronted their captors in an apocalyptic rebellion.

Gorgon had focused on the haggard, bearded faces of the enslaved earthlings. Regis Hardy had always felt that Gorgon's drawing, while not ineffective, had lacked considerably in impact.

Not so Simeon Dimsby's version.

Dimsby had dealt directly with the aliens. His rendition of them was horrifying. Dimsby had transcended Regis Hardy's own description of the aliens' physical appearance and had managed in some undefinable way to capture their overwhelming sense of monstrous power.

Hardy gasped. 'How did you do this?'

A thin smile curled Dimsby's lips. 'Do you like it? The medium is a substance that I manufacture myself. The primary ingredient is the ink of deep-water Atlantic kraken. And there are other ingredients as well.'

Dimsby retrieved the drawing from Regis Hardy's grasp, replaced it carefully in the envelope and removed another. He looked at the drawing himself, smiled once more, again faintly, and extended the illustration toward Hardy's outstretched hand.

This time the drawing was clearly based on 'Vampire Town'. The tale had been Regis Hardy's first sale. Not his best work, he felt, but one for which he held a great affection because of its landmark importance in his career. The art director of *Mayhem Monthly* had assigned the story to Walter Wallace, a longtime hack illustrator who hadn't done a good drawing in thirty years, but who managed to eke out an existence on the basis of name recognition and long-standing connections if nothing more.

In contrast to Wallace's crudely gory imagery, Simeon Dimsby's night scene of the village – torch-wielding undead pursuing the last surviving day-dweller to his inevitable doom – was enough to send a shuddering *frisson* down Regis Hardy's spine.

Dimsby's images for Hardy's other stories were all powerful and frightening, but more than this they were strangely *disquieting*. As Regis Hardy looked at each drawing he felt as if Simeon Dimsby had seen past the prose of his story and penetrated into the nethermost and most fear-haunted recesses of his soul.

At last Simeon Dimsby's grey hand retrieved the last of the drawings from Regis Hardy's unsteady grasp. He returned the leaves to their envelope and the envelope to its drawer. He tilted his head on its abnormally long and flexible neck, twisted his thin lips into a suggestion of a smile, and asked, 'Had you any thoughts, Mr Hardy, regarding the jacket illustration for *Return to Elmwood*?'

'I thought you and Mr Mantigore had already made a choice,' Hardy replied.

'We have held several meetings and exchanged a number of notions, but Mr Mantigore felt that you deserved to be consulted before a final decision was made.' He paused. 'As the author, you see. Mr Mantigore has the greatest respect for us – what he calls, "creative geniuses." I believe that he uses the term in an ironic sense, but perhaps I am mistaken.'

He placed a bony, grey hand on Hardy's wrist. His grip was amazingly strong and his hand was frighteningly cold.

'Did you – have a medium in mind?' Hardy asked. 'I mean, I'm pretty ignorant where art is concerned, but I've heard of oils, watercolors, something called gouache.'

'You're not as uninformed as you pretend, Mr Hardy.' The artist still had hold of the author's wrist. He leaned closer, peering into Hardy's face. In Dimsby's eyes Hardy saw distant flames dancing, yet the eyes seemed oddly ice-like, almost crystalline, and the flames emitted chill instead of warmth.

'I don't – I don't really know,' Hardy managed to stammer.

Dimsby said, 'Well then, let me show you some of the materials I have left from my last painting.' He released Hardy's wrist and Hardy shrank back, breathing a sigh of relief. Dimsby knelt in front of a safe-like storage cabinet. He twirled the lock that held it shut, then pulled the heavy door toward himself. 'A pity that Mr Mantigore has been unable to join us,' he commented.

As if on cue there sounded a grating noise from the heavy lock on the iron door to Simeon Dimsby's workshop.

The great iron door swung back.

Regis Hardy had never met Auric Mantigore, never seen a photograph of the publisher, yet even so there was no doubt in his mind as to the identity of the newcomer.

Auric Mantigore was almost abnormally short, little more than four feet tall, yet he was built as massively as the iron safe that Simeon Dimsby had just opened. He might have been a blood relative of Dimsby's wife. 'Mr Hardy,' he said, 'I'd know you anywhere.'

He strode into the room. 'Your spouse was upstairs with Mrs Dimsby. Just moments ago I had the pleasure of making her acquaintance.' In the brighter illumination of Dimsby's studio, a small but disturbing birthmark was visible on Mantigore's forehead.

'Auric,' Hardy heard Dimsby saying, 'have you dined?'

Mantigore grinned broadly. He drew an oversized bandanna from his pocket and wiped a speck of red from the corner of his mouth. 'Yes,' he said.

'Well then, I was about to show Mr Hardy the kind of materials I use for my color work.'

'Were you, indeed?' Mantigore responded. 'Then my timing is apt, is it not?'

He slipped his suit coat from his shoulders and laid it carefully aside, drawing a large, glistening blade from an inside pocket.

Dimsby lifted a huge iron pot from the safe. It resembled the one Eustacia Dimsby had used in her kitchen, but was larger.

Far larger.

Dimsby placed it carefully on a work table very near to Regis Hardy. The author knew even before he peered into it what he would see, but he could not keep from looking.

His impulse to retch was forgotten in the terror and pain that he felt as Simeon Dimsby seized him by the elbows, his grip like ice-cold iron.

Auric Mantigore said, 'I'm so happy that I got to meet you this once, Mr Hardy. I do so admire your work. You can rest assured that Mantigore Press will do its very best with *Return to Elmwood*. I give you my word, we're going to make your book a success. We're going to cook up something really spicy to help put it over.'

He nodded as if in pleased agreement with himself. 'And yet, you may rest assured, it will be in the best of taste.'

THOMAS LIGOTTI

Our Temporary Supervisor

IN 1997, THOMAS LIGOTTI RECEIVED the Horror Writers Association's Bram Stoker Award for superior achievement for his novella 'The Red Tower' and both the Bram Stoker and British Fantasy Awards for his short-story collection, *The Nightmare Factory*.

His other books include *Songs of a Dead Dreamer, Grimscribe: His Lives and Works, Noctuary, The Agonizing Resurrection of Victor Frankenstein and Other Gothic Tales, In a Foreign Land In a Foreign Town* and *I Have a Special Plan for This World*.

The author describes 'Our Temporary Supervisor' as 'an extrapolation of the nightmare of the contemporary working world.' It is included in his latest collection from Durtro, *Teatro Grottesco*, which also features the companion tale to this piece, 'My Case for Retributive Action'. Also recently published is *My Work is Not Yet Done: Three Tales of Corporate Horror*, which includes a previously unpublished short novel. *Crampton: A Screenplay*, is a further title from Durtro, co-written with Brandon Trenz.

I HAVE SENT THIS MANUSCRIPT to your publication across the border, assuming that it ever arrives there, because I believe that the matters described in this personal anecdote have implications that should concern even those outside my homeland and beyond the influence, as far as I know, of the Quine

Organization. These two entities, one of which may be designated as a political entity and the other being a purely commercial entity, are very likely known to someone in your position of journalistic inquiry as all but synonymous. Therefore, on this side of the border one might as well call himself a *citizen* of the Quine Organization, or a Q. Org national, although I think that even someone like yourself cannot appreciate the full extent of this identity, which in my own lifetime has passed the point of identification between two separate entities and approached total assimilation of one by the other. Such a claim may seem alarmist or whimsical to those on your side of the border, where your closest neighbors – I know this – are often considered as a somewhat backward folk who inhabit small, decaying towns spread out across a low-lying landscape blanketed almost year-round by dense greyish fogs. This is how the Quine Organization, which is to say in the same breath my homeland, would deceptively present itself to the world, and this is precisely why I am anxious (for reasons that are not always explicit or punctiliously detailed) to relate my personal anecdote.

To begin with, I work in a factory situated just outside one of those small, decaying towns layered over with fogs for most of the year. The building is a nondescript, one-storey structure constructed of cinder blocks and cement. Inside is a working area that consists of a single room of floor space and a small corner office with windows of heavily frosted glass. Within the confines of this office are a few filing cabinets and a desk where the factory supervisor sits while the workers outside stand at one of several square 'assembly blocks.' Four workers are positioned on each side of the square blocks, their only task being the assembly, by hand, of pieces of metal that are delivered to us from another factory. No one whom I have ever asked has the least notion of the larger machinery, if in fact it is some type of machinery, for which these pieces are destined.

When I first took this job at the factory it was not my intention to work there very long, for I once possessed higher hopes for my life, although the exact nature of these hopes remained rather vague in my youthful mind. While the work was not arduous, and my fellow workers were congenial enough, I did not imagine myself standing forever at my designated assembly block, fitting pieces of metal into other pieces of metal, with a few interruptions throughout the day for breaks that were supposed to refresh our minds from the tedium of our work or for meal breaks to allow us to nourish our bodies. Somehow it never occurred to me that the nearby town where I and the others at the factory lived, traveling to and from our jobs along the same fog-strewn road, held no higher opportunities for me or anyone else, which no doubt accounts for the vagueness, the wispy insubstantiality, of my youthful hopes.

As it happened, I had been employed at the factory only a few months when there occurred the only change that had ever disturbed its daily routine of piece-assembly, the only deviation from a ritual that had been going on for nobody knew how many years. The meaning of this digression in our working lives did not at first present any great cause for apprehension or anxiety, nothing that would require any of the factory's employees to reconsider the type or dosage of the medication to which they were prescribed, since almost everyone on this side of the border, including myself, takes some kind of medication, a fact that is perhaps due in some part to an arrangement in my country whereby all doctors and pharmacists are on the payroll of the Quine Organization, a company which maintains a large pharmaceutical division.

In any case, the change of routine to which I have alluded was announced to us one day when the factory supervisor stepped out of his office and made one of his rare appearances on the floor where the rest of us stood positioned, in rather close quarters, around our designated assembly blocks. For the first time since I had taken this job, our work was called to a halt *between* those moments of pause when we took breaks for either mental refreshment or to nourish our bodies. Our supervisor, a Mr Frowley, was a massive individual, though not menacingly so, who moved and spoke with a lethargy that perhaps was merely a consequence of his bodily bulk, although his sluggishness might also have been caused by his medication, either as a side effect or possibly as the primary effect. Mr Frowley laboriously made his way to the central area of the factory floor and addressed us in his slow-mannered way.

'I'm being called away on company business,' he informed us. 'In my absence a new supervisor will be sent to take over my duties on a temporary basis. This situation will be in place tomorrow when you come to work. I can't say how long it will last.'

He then asked if any of us had questions for him regarding what was quite a momentous occasion, even though at the time I hadn't been working at the factory long enough to comprehend its truly anomalous nature. No one had any questions for Mr Frowley, or none that they voiced, and the factory supervisor then proceeded back to his small corner office with its windows of heavily frosted glass.

Immediately following Mr Frowley's announcement that he was being called away on company business and that in the interim the factory would be managed by a temporary supervisor, there were of course a few murmurings among my fellow workers about what all of this might mean. Nothing of this sort had ever happened at the factory, according to the employees who had worked there for any substantial length of time, including a few who were approaching an age when, I presumed, they would be able to leave their jobs behind them and enter a period of well-earned retirement after spending their entire adult lives standing at the same assembly blocks and fitting together pieces of metal. By the end of the day, however, these murmurings had long died out as we filed out of the factory and began making our way along the foggy road back to our homes in town.

That night, for no reason I could name, I was unable to fall asleep, something which previously I had had no trouble doing after being on my feet all day assembling pieces of metal together in the same configuration one after the other. This activity of assemblage now burdened my mind, as I tossed about in my bed, with the full weight of its repetitiousness, its endlessness, and its disconnection from any purpose I could imagine. For the first time I wondered how those metal pieces that we assembled had come to be created, my thoughts futilely attempting to pursue them to their origins in the crudest form of substance which, I assumed, had been removed from the ground and undergone some process of refinement, then had taken shape in some factory, or series of factories, before they arrived at the one where I was presently employed. With an even greater sense of futility I tried to imagine where these metal pieces were delivered once we had fitted them together as we had been trained to do, my mind racing in the darkness of my room to conceive of their ultimate destination and purpose. Until that night I had never been disturbed by questions of this kind. There was no point in occupying myself with such things, since I had always possessed higher hopes for my life beyond the time I needed to serve at the factory in order to support myself. Finally I got out of bed and took an extra dose of medication. This allowed me at least a few hours of sleep before I was required to be at my job.

When we entered the factory each morning, it was normal procedure for the first man who passed through the door to switch on the cone-shaped lamps that hung down on long rods from the ceiling. Another set of lights was located inside the supervisor's office, and Mr Frowley would switch those on himself when he came in to work around the same time as the rest of us. However, that morning the lights within the supervisor's office were not yet on. Since this was the first day that a new supervisor was scheduled to assume Mr Frowley's duties, if only on a temporary basis, we naturally assumed that, for some reason, this person was not yet present in the factory. But when daylight shone through the fog beyond the narrow rectangular windows of the factory, which included the windows of the supervisor's office, we now began to suspect that the new supervisor – that is, our temporary supervisor – had been inside his office all along. I use the word 'suspect' because it was simply not possible to tell – in the absence of the office lights being switched on, with only natural daylight shining into the windows through the fog – whether or not there was someone on the other side of the heavily frosted glass that enclosed the supervisor's office. If the new supervisor that the Quine Organization had sent to fill in temporarily for Mr Frowley had in fact taken up residence in the office situated in a corner of the factory, he was not moving about in any way that would allow us to distinguish his form among the blur of shapes that could be detected through the heavily frosted glass of that room.

Even if no one said anything that specifically referred either to the new supervisor's presence or absence within the factory, I saw that nearly everyone standing around their assembly blocks had cast a glance at some point during the early hours of the day in the direction of Mr Frowley's office. The assembly block at which I was located was closer than most to the supervisor's office, and we who were positioned there would seem to have been able to discern if someone was in fact inside. But those of us standing around our assembly block, as well as others at blocks even closer to the supervisor's office, only exchanged furtive looks among ourselves, as if we were asking one another, 'What do you think?' But no one could say anything with certainty, or nothing that we could express in sensible terms.

Nevertheless, all of us behaved as if that corner office was indeed occupied and conducted ourselves in the manner of employees whose actions were subject to profound scrutiny and the closest supervision. As the hours passed it became more and more apparent that the supervisor's office was being inhabited, although the nature of its new resident had become a matter for question. During the first break of the day there were words spoken among some of us to the effect that the figure behind the heavily frosted glass could not be seen to have a definite shape or to possess any kind of stable or solid form. Several of my fellow workers mentioned a dark ripple they had spied several times moving behind or within the uneven surface of the glass that enclosed the supervisor's office. But whenever their eyes came to focus on this rippling movement, they said, it would suddenly come to a stop or simply disperse like a patch of fog. By the time we took our meal break there were more observations shared, many of them in agreement about sighting a slowly shifting outline, some darkish and globulant form like a thunderhead churning in a darkened sky. To some it appeared to have no more substance than a shadow, and perhaps that was all it was, they argued, although they had to concede that this shadow was unlike any other they had seen, for at times it moved in a seemingly purposeful way, tracing the same path over and over behind the frosted glass, as if it were a type of creature pacing about in a cage. Others swore they could discern a bodily configuration, however elusive and aberrant. They spoke only in terms of its 'head part' or 'arm-protrusions,' although even these more conventional descriptions were qualified by admissions that such quasi-anatomical components did not manifest themselves in any normal aspect inside the office. 'It doesn't seem to be sitting behind the desk,' one man asserted, 'but looks more like it's sticking up from the top, sort of sideways too.' This was something that I also had noted as I stood at my assembly block, as had the men who worked to the left and right of me. But the employee who stood directly across the block from where I was positioned, whose name was Blecher and who was younger than most of the others at the factory and perhaps no more than a few years older than I was, never spoke a single word about anything he might have seen in the supervisor's office. Moreover, he worked throughout that day with his eyes fixed upon his task of fitting together pieces of metal, his gaze locked at a downward angle, even when he moved away from the assembly block for breaks or to use the lavatory. Not once did I catch him glancing in the direction of that corner of the factory that the rest of us, as the hours dragged by, could barely keep our eyes from. Then, toward the end of the work day, when the atmosphere around the factory had been made weighty by our spoken words and unspoken thoughts, when the sense of an unknown mode of supervision hung ominously about us, as well as within us (such that I felt some inner shackles had been applied that kept both my body and my mind from straying far from the position I occupied at that assembly block), Blecher finally broke down.

'No more,' he said as if speaking only to himself. Then he repeated these words in a louder voice and with a vehemence that suggested something of what he had been holding within himself throughout the day. 'No more!' he shouted as he moved away from the assembly block and turned to look straight at the door of the supervisor's office, which, like the office windows, was a frame of heavily frosted glass.

Blecher moved swiftly to the door of the office. Without pausing for a moment, not even to knock or in any way announce his entrance, he stormed inside the cube-shaped room and slammed the door behind him. All eyes in the factory were now fixed on the office in the corner. While we had suffered so many confusions and conflicts over the physical definition of the temporary supervisor, we had no trouble at all seeing the dark outline of Blecher behind the heavily frosted glass and could easily follow his movements. Afterward, everything happened very rapidly, and the rest of us stood as if stricken with the kind of paralysis one sometimes experiences in a dream.

At first Blecher stood rigid before the desk inside the office, but this posture lasted only for a moment. Soon he was rushing about the room as if in flight from some pursuing agency, crashing into the filing cabinets and finally falling to the floor. When he stood up again he appeared to be fending off a swarm of insects, waving his arms wildly to forestall the onslaught of a cloudy and shifting mass that hovered about him like a trembling aura. Then his body slammed hard against the frosted glass of the door, and I thought he was going to break through. But he scrambled full about and came stumbling out of the office, pausing a second to stare at the rest of us, who were staring back at him. There was a look of derangement and incomprehension in his eyes, while his hands were shaking.

The door behind Blecher was left half open after his furious exit, but no one attempted to look inside the office. He seemed unable to move away from the place where he stood with the half-open office door only a few feet behind him. Then the door finally began to close slowly behind him, although no visible force appeared to be causing it to do so, however deliberately it moved on its hinges. A little click sounded when the door pushed back into its frame. But it was the sound of the lock being turned on the other side of the door that stirred Blecher from his frozen stance, and he went running out of the factory. Only seconds later the bell signaling the close of the work day rang with all the shrillness of an alarm, even though it was not quite time for us to leave our assembly blocks behind us.

Startled back into a fully wakened state, we exited the factory as a consolidated group, proceeding with a measured pace, unspeaking, until we had all filed out of the building. Outside there was no sign of Blecher, although I don't think that anyone expected to see him. In any case, the greyish fog was especially dense along the road leading back to town, and we could hardly see one another as we made our way home, none of us saying a word about what had happened, as if we were bound by a pact of silence. Any mention of the Blecher incident would have made it impossible, at least to my mind, to go back to the factory. And there was no other place we could turn to for our living.

That evening I went to bed early, taking a substantial dose of medication to ensure that I would drop right off to sleep and not spend hour upon hour with my mind racing, as it had been the previous night, with thoughts about the origins (somewhere in the ground) and subsequent destination (at some other factory or series of factories) of the metal pieces I spent my days assembling. I awoke earlier than usual, but rather than lingering about my room, where I was likely to start thinking about events of the day before, I went to a small diner in town that I knew would be open for breakfast at that time of the morning.

When I stepped inside the diner I saw that it was unusually crowded, the tables and booths and stools at the counter occupied for the most part by my fellow workers from the factory. For once I was glad to see these men whom I had previously considered 'lifers' in a job at which I never intended to work for very long, considering that I still possessed higher hopes of a vague sort for my future. I greeted a number of the others as I walked toward an unoccupied stool at the counter, but no one returned more than a nod to me nor were they much engaged in talking with one another.

After taking a seat at the counter and ordering breakfast, I recognized the man on my right as someone who worked at the assembly block beside the one where I was positioned day after day. I was fairly sure that his name was Nohls, although I didn't use his name and simply said 'good morning' to him in the quietest voice I could manage. For a moment Nohls didn't reply but simply continued to stare into the plate in front of him from which he was slowly and mechanically picking up small pieces of food with his fork and placing them into his mouth. Without turning to face me, Nohls said, in a voice even quieter than my own had been, 'Did you hear about Blecher?'

'No,' I whispered. 'What about him?'

'Dead,' said Nohls.

'Dead?' I responded in a voice that was loud enough to cause everyone else in the diner to turn and look my way. Resuming our converation in extremely quiet tones, I asked Nohls what had happened to Blecher.

'That rooming house where he lives. The woman who runs the place said that he was acting strange after . . . after he came back from work yesterday.'

Later on, Nohls informed me, Blecher didn't show up for dinner. The woman who operated the boarding house took it upon herself to check up on Blecher, who didn't answer when she knocked on his door. Concerned, she asked one of her other male residents to look in on Mr Blecher. He was found lying face down on his bed, and on the nightstand were several open containers of the various medications to which he was prescribed. He hadn't consumed the entire contents of these containers but nevertheless had died of an overdose of medication. Perhaps he simply wanted to put the events of the day out of his mind and get a decent night's sleep. I had done this myself, I told Nohls.

'Could be that's what happened,' Nohls replied. 'I don't suppose that anyone will ever know for sure.'

After finishing my breakfast, I kept drinking refill after refill of coffee, as I noticed others in the diner, including Nohls, were doing. We still had time before we needed to be at our jobs. Eventually, however, other patrons began to arrive and, as a group, we left for work.

When we arrived at the factory in the darkness and fog some hours before dawn, there were several other employees standing outside the door. None of them, it seemed, wanted to be the first to enter the building and switch on the lights. Only after the rest of us approached the factory did anyone go inside. It was then that we found someone had preceded us into work that morning, and had switched on the lights. His was a face new to us. He was standing in Blecher's old position, directly opposite mine at the same assembly block, and he had already done a considerable amount of work, his hands moving furiously as he fitted those small metal pieces together.

As the rest of us walked onto the floor of the factory to take up position at our respective assembly blocks, almost everyone cast a suspicious eye upon the new man who was standing where Blecher used to stand and who, as I remarked, was working at a furious pace. But in fact it was only his hands that were working in a furious manner, manipulating those small pieces of metal like two large spiders spinning the same web. Otherwise he stood quite calmly and was very much a stock figure of the type of person that worked at the factory. He was attired in regulation grey work clothes that were well worn and was neither conspicuously older nor conspicuously younger than the other employees. The only quality that singled him out was the furiousness he displayed in his work, to which he gave his full attention. Even when the factory began to fill with other men in grey work clothes, almost all of whom cast a suspicious eye on the new man, he never looked up from the assembly block where he was manipulating those pieces of metal with such intentness, such

THOMAS LIGOTTI

complete absorption, that he didn't seem to notice anyone else around him.

If the new man seemed an unsettling presence, appearing as he did the morning after Blecher had taken an overdose of medication and standing in Blecher's position directly across from me at the same assembly block, at least he served to distract us from the darkened office that was inhabited by our temporary supervisor. Whereas the day before we had been wholly preoccupied with this supervisory figure, our attention was now primarily drawn to the new employee among us. And even though he filled our minds with various speculations and suspicions, the new man did not contribute to the atmosphere of nightmarish thoughts and perceptions that had caused Blecher to become entirely deranged and led him to take action in the way he did.

Of course we could forbear for just so long before someone addressed the new man about his appearance at the factory that day. Since my fellow workers who stood to the right and left of me at the assembly block were doing their best to ignore the situation, the task of probing for some answers, I felt, had fallen upon me.

'Where are you from?' I asked the man who stood directly across from me where Blecher once stood on his side of the assembly block.

'The company sent me,' the man responded in a surprisingly forthcoming and casual tone, although he didn't for a second look up from his work.

I then introduced myself and the other two men at the assembly block, who nodded and mumbled their greetings to the stranger. That was when I discovered the limitations of the new man's willingness to reveal himself.

'No offense,' he said. 'But there's a lot of work that needs to be done around here.'

During our brief exchange the new man had continued to manipulate without interruption those pieces of metal before him. However, even though he kept his head angled downwards, as Blecher had for most of the previous day, I saw that he did allow his gaze to flick very quickly in the direction of the supervisor's office. Seeing that, I did not bother him any further, thinking that perhaps he would be more talkative during the upcoming break. In the meantime I let him continue his furious pace of work, which was far beyond the measure of productivity anyone else at the factory had ever attained.

Soon I observed that the men standing to the left and right of me at the assembly block were attempting to emulate the new man's style of so deftly fitting together those small metal pieces and even compete with the incredibly productive pace at which he worked. I myself followed suit. At first our efforts were an embarrassment, our own hands fumbling to imitate the movements of his, which were so swift that our eyes could not follow them, nor could our minds puzzle out a technique of working quite different from the one we had always practiced. Nevertheless, in some way unknown to us, we began to approach, if somewhat remotely, the speed and style of the new man's method of fitting together his pieces of metal. Our efforts and altered manner of working did not go unnoticed by the employees at the assembly blocks nearby. The new technique was gradually taken up and passed on to others around the factory. By the time we stopped for our first break of the day, everyone was employing the new man's methodology.

But we didn't stop working for very long. After it became obvious that the new man did not pause for a second to join us in our scheduled break period, we all returned to our assembly blocks and continued working as furiously as we could. We surprised ourselves in the performance of what had once seemed a dull and simple task, eventually rising to the level of virtuosity displayed by a man whose name we did not even know. I now looked forward to speaking to him about the change he had brought about in the factory, expecting to do so when the time came for our meal break. Yet when that time finally arrived the rest of us at the factory never anticipated the spectacle that awaited us.

For, rather than leaving his position at the assembly block during the meal break that the company had always sanctioned, the new man continued to work, consuming his meal with one hand while still assembling those metal pieces, although at a somewhat slower pace, with the other. This performance introduced the rest of us at the factory to a hitherto unknown level of virtuosity in the service of productivity. At first there was some resistance to attempting these new heights where the new man, without any ostentation, was leading us. But his purpose soon enough became evident. And it was simple enough: those employees who ceased working entirely during the meal break found themselves once again preoccupied, even tormented, by the troubling atmosphere that pervaded the factory, the source of which was attributed to the temporary supervisor who inhabited the office with heavily frosted windows. On the other hand, those employees who continued working at their assembly blocks seemed relatively unbothered by the images and influences that, although there was no consensus as to their exact nature, had plagued everyone the day before. Thus, it wasn't long before all of us learned to consume our meals with one hand while continuing to work with the other. It goes without saying that when the time came for our last break of the day, no one budged an inch from his assembly block.

It was only when the bell rang to signal the end of the work day – sounding several hours later than we were accustomed to hearing it – that I had a chance to speak with the new employee. Once we were outside the factory, and everyone was proceeding in a state of silent exhaustion back to town, I made a point of catching up to him as he strode at a quick pace through the dense, greyish fog. I didn't mince words. 'What's going on?' I demanded to know.

Unexpectedly he stopped dead in his tracks and faced me, although we could barely see each other through the fog. Then I saw his head turn slightly in the direction of the factory we had left some distance behind us. 'Listen, my friend,' he said, his voice filled with a grave sincerity. 'I'm not looking for trouble. I hope you're not either.'

'Wasn't I working right along with you?' I said. 'Wasn't everyone?'

'Yes. You all made a good start.'

'So I take it you're working with the new supervisor.'

'No,' he said emphatically. 'I don't know anything about that. I couldn't tell you anything about that.'

'But you've worked under similar conditions before, isn't that true?'

'I work for the company, just like you. The company sent me here.'

'But something must have changed at the company,' I said. 'Something new is happening.'

'Not really,' he replied. 'The Quine Organization is always making adjustments and refinements in the way it does business. It just took some time for it to reach you out here. You're a long way from company headquarters, or even the closest regional center.'

'There's more of this coming, isn't there?'

'Possibly. But there really isn't any point in discussing such things. Not if you want to continue working for the company. Not if you want to stay out of trouble.'

'What trouble?'

'I have to go. Please don't try to discuss this matter with me again.'

'Are you saying that you're going to report me?'

'No,' he said, his eyes looking back at the factory. 'That's not necessary these days.'

Then he turned and walked off at a quick pace into the fog.

The next morning I returned to the factory along with everyone else. We worked at an even faster rate and were even more productive. Part of this was due to the fact that the bell that signaled the end of the work day rang later than it had the day before. This lengthening of the time we spent at the factory, along with the increasingly faster rate at which we worked, became an established pattern. It wasn't long before we were allowed only a few hours away from the factory, only a few hours that belonged to us, although the only possible way we could use this time was to gain the rest we needed in order to return to the exhausting labors that the company now demanded of us.

But I had always possessed higher hopes for my life, hopes that were becoming more and more vague with each passing day. *I have to resign my position at the factory* – these were the words that raced through my mind as I tried to gain a few hours of rest before returning to my job. I had no idea what such a step might mean, since I had no other prospects for earning a living, and I had no money saved that would enable me to keep my room in the apartment building where I lived. In addition, the medications I required, that almost everyone on this side of the border requires to make their existence at all tolerable, were prescribed by doctors who were all employed by the Quine Organization and filled by pharmacists who also operated only at the sufferance of this company. All of that notwithstanding, I still felt that I had no choice but to resign my position at the factory.

At the end of the hallway outside my apartment there was a tiny niche in which was located a telephone for public use by the building's tenants. I would have to make my resignation using this telephone, since I couldn't imagine doing so in person. I couldn't possibly enter the office of the temporary supervisor, as Blecher had done. I couldn't go into that room enclosed by heavily frosted glass behind which I and my fellow workers had observed something that appeared in various forms and manifestations, from an indistinct shape that seemed to shift and churn like a dark cloud to something more defined that appeared to have a 'head part' and 'arm-protrusions'. Given this situation, I would use the telephone to call the closest regional centre and make my resignation to the appropriate person in charge of such matters.

The telephone niche at the end of the hallway outside my apartment was so narrow that I had to enter it sideways. In the confines of that space there was barely enough room to make the necessary movements of placing coins in the telephone that hung on the wall and barely enough light to see what number one was dialing. I remember how concerned I was not to dial a wrong number and thereby lose a portion of what little money I had. After taking every possible precaution to ensure that I would successfully complete my phone call, a process that seemed to take hours, I reached someone at the closest regional centre operated by the company.

The phone rang so many times that I feared no one would ever answer. Finally the ringing stopped and, after a pause, I heard a barely audible voice. It sounded thin and distant.

'Quine Organization, Northwest Regional Centre.'

'Yes,' I began, 'I would like to resign my position at the company,' I said.

'I'm sorry, did you say that you wanted to resign from the company? You sound so far away,' said the voice.

'Yes, I want to resign,' I shouted into the mouthpiece of the telephone. 'I want to resign. Can you hear me?'

'Yes, I can hear you. But the company is not accepting resignations at this time. I'm going to transfer you to our temporary supervisor.'

'Wait,' I said, but the transfer had been made and once again the phone began ringing so many times that I feared no one would answer.

Then the ringing stopped, although no voice came on the line. 'Hello,' I said. But all I could hear was an indistinct, though highly reverberant, noise – a low roaring sound that alternately faded and swelled as if it were echoing through vast spaces deep within the caverns of the earth or across a clouded sky. This noise, this low and bestial roaring, affected me with a dread I could not name. I held the telephone receiver away from my ear, but the roaring noise continued to sound within my head. Then I felt the telephone quivering in my hand, pulsing like something that was alive. And when I slammed the telephone receiver back into its cradle, this quivering and pulsing sensation continued to move up my arm, passing through my body and finally reaching my brain where it became synchronized with the low roaring noise that was now growing louder and louder, confusing my thoughts into an echoing insanity and paralyzing my movements so that I could not even scream for help.

I was never sure that I actually had made that telephone call to resign my position at the company. And if in fact I did make such a call, I could never be certain that what I experienced – what I heard and felt in that telephone niche at the end of the hallway outside my apartment – in any way resembled the dreams that recurred every night once I stopped showing up for work at the factory. No amount of medication I took could prevent the nightly onset of these dreams, and no amount of medication could efface their memory from my mind. Soon enough I had taken so much medication that I didn't have a sufficient amount left to overdose my system, as Blecher had done. And since I was no longer employed, I could not afford to get my prescription refilled and thereby acquire the medication I needed to tolerate my existence. Of course I might have done away with myself in some other manner, should I have been so inclined. But somehow I still retained higher hopes for my life. Accordingly, I returned to see if I could get my job back at the factory. After all, hadn't the person I spoke with at the regional centre told me that the Quine Organization was not accepting resignations at this time?

Of course I couldn't be sure what I had been told over the telephone, or even if I had made such a call to resign my position with the company. It wasn't until I actually walked onto the floor of the factory that realized I still had a job there if I wanted one, for the place where I had stood for such long hours at my assembly block was unoccupied. Already attired in my grey work clothes, I walked over to the assembly block and began fitting together, at a furious pace, those small metal pieces. Without pausing in my task I looked across the assembly block at the person I had once thought of as the 'new man'.

'Welcome back,' he said in a casual voice.

'Thank you,' I replied.

'I told Mr Frowley that you would return any day now.'

For a moment I was overjoyed at the implicit news that the temporary supervisor was gone and Mr Frowley was back managing the factory. But when I looked over at his office in the corner I noticed that behind the heavily frosted glass there were no lights on, although the large-bodied outline of Mr Frowley could be distinguished sitting behind his desk. Nevertheless, he was a changed man, as I discovered soon after returning to work. No one and nothing at the factory would ever again be as it once was. We were working practically around the clock now. Some of us began to stay the night at the factory, sleeping for an hour or so in a corner before going back to work at our assembly blocks.

After returning to work I no longer suffered from the nightmares that had caused me to go running back to the factory in the first place. And yet I continued to feel, if somewhat faintly, the atmosphere of those nightmares, which was so like the atmosphere our temporary supervisor had brought to the factory. I believe that this feeling of the overseeing presence of the temporary supervisor was a calculated measure on the part of the Quine Organization, which is always making adjustments and refinements in the way it does business.

The company retained its policy of not accepting resignations. It even extended this policy at some point and would not allow retirements. We were all prescribed new medications, although I can't say exactly how many years ago that happened. No one at the factory can remember how long we've worked here, or how old we are, yet our pace and productivity continues to increase. It seems as if neither the company nor our temporary supervisor will ever be done with us. Yet we are only human beings, or at least physical beings, and one day we must die. This is the only retirement we can expect, even though none of us is looking forward to that time. For we can't keep from wondering what might come afterward – what the company could have planned for us, and the part our temporary supervisor might play in that plan. Working at a furious pace, fitting together those small pieces of metal, helps keep our minds off such things.

CHARLES L. GRANT

Whose Ghosts These Are

CHARLES L. GRANT WAS NAMED GRAND MASTER at the 2002 World Horror Convention in Chicago. It was a well-deserved accolade for a writer and editor with more than 100 books to his credit and a mantelpiece filled with awards, including the World Fantasy, British Fantasy and Nebula. His pseudonyms include 'Geoffrey Marsh' (pulp adventure), 'Lionel Fenn' (funny fantasy), 'Simon Lake' (Young Adult horror) and 'Felicia Andrews' and 'Deborah Lewis' (both romantic fantasies).

His 1986 novel *The Pet* has been optioned by the movies, the story 'Crowd of Shadows' was optioned by NBC as a TV film, while 'Temperature Days on Hawthorne Street' was adapted for the syndicated series *Tales from the Darkside*. His short fiction has been collected in *Tales from the Nightside*, *A Glow of Candles*, *Nightmare Seasons*, *The Orchard*, *Dialing the Wind*, *The Black Carousel* and *A Quiet Way to Scream*, and recent books include *When the Cold Wind Blows*, the fifth volume in the *Black Oak* series, and *Redmoor: Strange Fruit*, a major historical horror novel from Tor, which takes place between 1786 and the 1890s.

'When I was asked to contribute to another themed anthology, I decided to try another serial-killer piece,' explains Grant, 'except this time I made him a cop. The editor made a big deal about using the museum, so I did; as it turned out, though, hardly anyone else did. Go figure.'

T HE STREET DOES NOT CHANGE, morning to night. Shops open, shops close; pedestrians walk the crooked sidewalks, with or without burden, peering in the store windows, wishing, coveting, moving on; vans and trucks make their deliveries and leave, while automobiles avoid it because it curves so sharply, so often. To walk from one end to the other is like following the dry bed of a long-dead stream that snakes from no place to nowhere.

None of the buildings here are more than four storeys high, though they seem much taller because the street itself is so narrow. They are old, these buildings, but they are not frail. They are well-kept, mostly, almost equally divided between brick and granite facades with occasional wood trim of various colors. Nothing special about them; nothing to draw a camera lens or a sketch pad, a commemorative plaque, a footnote in a tourist guide. Stores, a few offices, at ground level on both ends, apartments and offices above; in the middle, apartment buildings with stone stairs and stoops, aged white medallions of mythical creatures over each lintel. Gateless iron-spear fences, small plots of grass, flower boxes, trees at the curb.

Nothing changes, and Hank Cabot liked it that way.

He walked this tree-lined block and the surrounding neighborhood for close to fifteen years, his uniform so familiar that in his civilian clothes people he saw every day sometimes had to look at him twice just to be sure he was who they thought he was. An almost comical look as well, as if he had shaved off a mustache and they weren't quite able to make out what was different about him.

It was a partial anonymity and he had never been able to decide whether it was good or bad.

Retirement, on the other hand, was, in the beginning, good.

He had loved his blue tunic and the brass buttons and the polished belt with its gleaming attachments, refusing promotions once he had reached sergeant because he'd wanted nothing to do with the politics of being an officer, nothing to do with other parts of the city, nothing to do with anything but his job as he had eventually defined and refined it.

He was a beat cop, nothing more, nothing less.

He wrote parking tickets and scolded kids who taunted other kids and old folks; he investigated minor break-ins and petty theft; he had heart-to-hearts with shoplifters and angry spouses;

he broke up fights and arrested drunks and gossiped and swapped jokes and had once spent an hour on a damp stoop with a little girl, trying to reattach the head of her doll.

He was a beat cop.

And now, at long last in his mid-fifties, he was something else, and he wasn't sure yet what that was.

That was the bad part.

In a way, it was kind of funny, that first day away from the Job. He had slept in, a sinful luxury whose guilt he had cheerfully grinned away; he had made a slow breakfast and read the paper and done a little cleaning of his second-floor apartment; and when at last habit grabbed him by the scruff, he had taken out a new denim jacket and had gone for a walk. The street first, of course, then several others north and south. Not too far afield, but far enough. Restraining himself from checking closed shop doors, the timing on parking meters, the alleys between buildings, the empty lots.

It had been an effort.

It had nearly worn him out.

It hadn't been until that evening, while he ate a sandwich in front of his living-room window and watched the street put itself to bed, that he'd realized no one had greeted him with anything more than a polite nod, complained to him, whined at him about the injustices the city had settled upon their shoulders and why the hell couldn't he do something about it.

The good part was, he didn't have to answer them anymore, didn't have to lie or be a confessor or a teacher or a parent who happened to have a gun on his hip.

The bad part was . . . nights when he couldn't sleep because he was supposed to be on shift, nights when he slept and didn't dream and woke up feeling as if he'd walked a hundred miles with a hundred-pound pack on his back, nights when nightmares of horribly distorted and twisted faces pressing close to his face made him sit up and scream – except the scream was only a hoarse croaking, and the nightmare itself eventually began to lose some of its terror when he figured they were the faces of the angry victims he couldn't help and the angry culprits he had apprehended over the course of thirty years.

Over a year later, he and the nightmares had become old friends. But his friends on the street still looked at him oddly.

'It'll take some getting used to, you know,' said Lana Hynes for at least the hundredth time, dropping into the chair opposite him at the Caulberg Luncheonette. She fanned an order pad at her neck as if it were muggy July instead of the cool middle of October. 'For them too, I mean. All this time, they don't know what you look like.'

'Oh, yeah, sure. I've lived here forever, right? I didn't have the uniform on all the time.'

But he thought he knew what she meant. He was, in or out of the Blue, nothing special. Not tall, a slight paunch, a face faintly ruddy, red hair fading much too swiftly to grey. An ordinary voice. Cops hated people like him – no one ever knew what they really looked like.

She grinned then, more like a smirk, and he felt a blush work its way toward his cheeks. This time he knew exactly what she meant. They had been lovers once, before he jilted her for the Job, and now, for better or worse, they were friends. So much so, it seemed, that lately she had taken to ignoring him when he came in, just to tick him off so she could tease him about it later.

'Knock it off,' he muttered at that grin, grabbing his burger quickly, taking a bite.

'Why, Mr Cabot, I am sure I do not know what you mean.' A laugh soft in her throat, and she leaned forward, crinkling the front of her red-and-white uniform blouse, the one that matched the checkered floor, the tablecloths, the pattern around the edge of the menu. It drove her crazy, and frankly, he was getting a little tired of hearing about it.

'The bill,' was all he said.

She scowled. 'Screw you, Cabot.'

His turn to grin: 'Been there, done that.'

A close thing, then: would she slap him or laugh?

It startled him to realize that he had, at some imprecise moment on some non-momentous day, stopped caring very much. Startled him, then saddened him, then angered him that she didn't realize it herself. Maybe it was time to start eating somewhere else.

All this in the space of a second, maybe two.

Damn, he thought; *what the hell's the matter with you, pal?*

She neither slapped nor laughed. She tapped a pencil against her pad and said, 'So, you been to that museum yet?'

Curtly: 'No.'

'Well, why not?' Her own red hair fell in carefully arranged curls over one eye. 'I'd've thought you'd like something like that. All those bad-guy exhibits. You know, like that Ghost guy.'

'That Ghost guy,' he said, knowing he sounded stuffy, 'is a killer, Lana. Nothing interesting about him, not at all. And I had enough of that on the Job, thank you.'

A hand reached out and slapped his arm lightly. 'Oh, please, give me a break, okay? No offense, but it's not like you were a detective. You didn't work with dead bodies every day, you know?'

'Yeah, maybe, but still . . .'

An impatient call from the counter brought Lana to her feet. She dropped his bill on the table, leaned over to kiss his cheek. And whispered in his ear: 'It's been over a year, Hank. Do something different for a change, before you turn into an old woman.'

He nodded automatically, gave her an automatic 'Yes, dear,' and laughed silently when she slapped him across the back of his head. Not so lightly. Another laugh, and he looked out at the street while he finished his lunch. The trees had turned, and sweaters and lined jackets had been rescued from storage. A puff of autumn cold surged against his ankles each time the door opened. A pleasant shiver, a comfortable reminder of how miserable the previous summer had been and how far away the next one was.

He spent the afternoon at a high-school football game. He didn't know the teams, didn't know the schools, just enjoyed the hot dogs and the soda and the cheerleaders who made him feel exceedingly old. A fair-to-middling dinner at a small Italian restaurant took him past nightfall, and he decided to walk off all the wine he had drunk.

With his collar snapped up and his hands deep in his pockets, he moved through the fleeting clouds of his breath, instinctively watching the dark that hid behind all the lights. The shadows he made as he passed under street lamps swung around him, fascinated him for a while. He wondered if, like fingerprints, everyone's shadow was different. When the angle was right, the light just so, his shadow took to a low brick wall and paced him a few strides, and he decided they weren't like fingerprints at all.

They were like ghosts who gave you an idea what it would be like to be dead.

Damn, he thought, and cast his attention out to the city instead. Where he glowered at a young couple arguing under the canopy of a luxury apartment building, whistled softly at a cat watching him narrow-eyed from a garbage-can lid. A taxi nearly ran him down when it took a corner too tightly; his footsteps sounded too sharp, and for half a block he tried to walk on his toes.

Halloween decorations everywhere, here and there mixed in with cardboard turkeys and cartoon-like Pilgrims. One damn store even had its Christmas lights up.

He felt his temper, so long with him that it was like an old comfortable coat, begin, like that coat, to wear thin at the edges. A shift of his shoulders, a brief massage to the back of his neck, and he quickened his pace, anxious to get to the three rooms that were his. The secondhand furniture, the old-fashioned kitchen, the rust-ring around the tub's drain that had been there when he'd moved in. It wasn't the warmth or the comfort; he just wanted to be away from the streets, the people, the traffic . . . the city.

Breathing hard. Watching his shadow. Following his shadow until he blinked and found himself at the living-room window, staring down at the trees that smothered most of the night's artificial light, leaving specks of it on the pavement, shimmering as an autumn wind rose while the moon set unseen.

A deep breath, a sigh for all the wine that had stolen some of his time, and he slept most of the day away. It felt good. It made him smile. Another habit broken, and he treated himself to dinner and a movie, and walked home again. He liked it so much he did it again a few nights later, and again the night after that, and a few nights after that, taking a child-like pleasure in once in a while losing track of the hour. No schedules, no meetings; just him and the street that never changes, morning to night.

A week after Halloween he finally returned to Caulberg's for an early supper. His usual table was already occupied, so he took a stool at the counter, waiting patiently for Lana to acknowledge him. When at last she did, with a look he knew well – *It's about time, you son of a bitch* – he felt a momentary crush of guilt for ignoring her for so long. She was a good friend, after all; probably . . . no, *absolutely* his only friend. But his temper came instantly to attention when she slapped a cup and saucer in front of him, poured coffee and said, 'Well, look who's here. The Lone Stranger.'

'Sorry,' he said flatly. 'Been busy.'

'Too busy to stick your head in, say hi or something?'

He shrugged a weak apology. 'Been busy,' he repeated.

'Yeah, right.'

He tried a smile. 'Hey, I'm retired, remember? Things to do, places to see. I'm going to the Riviera next weekend.'

Her expression suggested his eyes had changed to a none-too-subtle brown, and she moved away to place his order, take care of the only other customer at the counter, slip into the kitchen without looking his way again. She didn't return until his hamburger was ready, and she delivered it as if she were slapping his face with a glove.

He leaned back and gave her a look; she stepped back and folded her arms across her chest and gave *him* a look.

They stared at each other for several seconds before her lips twitched, and he pulled his lips in between his teeth.

'Laugh and you die, Cabot,' she said.

He nodded; the tension vanished.

She stepped back to the counter and leaned over it, forearms braced on the surface, her face only a few inches from his. 'The thing is, Cabot,' she said, keeping her voice down, checking to be sure no one could eavesdrop, 'we don't like it when you disappear, okay? I know what you think, but we depend on having you here all the time, just in case.'

'But I'm not a cop any—'

She shook her head. 'It doesn't make any difference.'

'And they barely—'

'It doesn't make any difference.'

'But—'

She grabbed his chin and held it tightly. 'Listen to me, you old creep, and none of your false modesty or any of that other crap, okay? We're worried about you.' She nodded sharply, once. 'You are, whether you know it or not, kind of important to us. God knows why, but you are. When you go off like that without telling anybody, it makes us nervous. I mean, that damn Ghost freak did it again last week. What, the fifth? The sixth time? Since July? They still don't know who the body belongs to.' Her hand slipped away as she straightened, lay flat against her stomach. 'We thought it was you, you son of a bitch. We thought he'd gotten you.'

He almost said, *We, or you?* but for a change he kept silent. Instead, he looked at his meal, tilted his head to one side in a brief shrug of not knowing what to say. All his complaining, and he had had no idea. None at all.

She pointed at his plate. 'Eat,' she ordered. 'Then get a goddam hobby.'

'Oh, right, like Dutch?'

Dutch Heinrich owned the butcher shop around the corner. This week, on top of his window display case, was a three-foot-tall cathedral fashioned entirely out of toothpicks, none of which were immediately visible because of the way the man had painted the model. It looked carved from stone.

Finally she smiled. 'You could do worse. He sells those stupid things for a fortune.' A wink, then; an eyebrow cocked; a gentle smile. 'Just do it, Hank. Stop lying to yourself, you're bored as hell. Make us all happy, just do it.'

A promise to think about it, a command from her that just thinking about it wasn't an option, and she left him alone to eat. As he did, he wondered; when he left, he headed for the small park a few blocks up, and it wasn't until he realized he had spent a full hour watching two very nearsighted old men playing a truly bad game of chess that he finally understood his year-long vacation was over. Fifty-something, with probably another thirty to go.

Good God, he thought; *I'll probably shoot myself next Christmas, and won't Lana be pissed.*

He laughed aloud, and the old men glared without really seeing him. He gave them a jaunty salute, and whistled himself back home, and to a vow that tomorrow he would either find himself a part-time job, or a time-gobbling hobby.

Which might be, he thought when he saw the next morning's newspaper, filing the necessary applications for an investigator's license. Job or hobby, it would give him an official-sounding excuse to be nosy. To poke around, uncover the true identity of the man they called the Ghost.

He had killed again.

The sixth time since the end of July, the second time in a week.

There wasn't much in the article, aside from recycled quotes from
psychologists and criminal experts about the mind of such a man,
but the police vowed they were on it with promising leads in an
intense investigation. He snorted. He had heard that story before
– it meant the victims had no common ground, no links; the cops
hadn't a clue and weren't about to get one. The worst kind of
killer – completely random. He also knew there had to be more;
something had been held back from the public so the nuts and
habitual confessers could be weeded out. He leaned back in his
chair, stared blindly at the kitchen ceiling. He could call in a favor
or two, find out what the missing information was, and take it
from there.

'Sure,' he said to the ceiling light. 'Take it where?'

He had a better question: 'Why?'

Because it was interesting? Fascinating? A puzzle that wanted
solving? A chance for a little action? An opportunity to do
something valuable with his time? A way to get himself involved
with the public again?

A way to justify the block's belief in him? Concern for him?

He made a derisive noise deep in his throat, folded the paper to
put the sports section on top – to read whenever he returned from
wherever he would go to pass the daylight hours – and pushed his
chair back. Flattened his palms on the small table and pushed
himself to his feet.

Why?

Because Lana was right. He was goddammed bored out of his
goddam mind, that was why.

Which wasn't the real reason, and he knew it, but it would do
for now. It would have to.

He walked.

He window-shopped.

He spent some time in a showroom, pretending he was thinking
about buying a car.

He had lunch in a place he had never been to before; he spent a
couple of hours on a tourist bus, seeing things he had never seen
before; he watched the sunset from a bench in a park he had never
been to, and when the sun's reflection slid out of the windows and
let in the dark, he flipped up his collar and made his way to a bus
stop, where a trio of kids cut in front of him so they could get on

first. When he said, 'Hey, dammit,' only one looked back, gave him a *sorry didn't see you* shrug; the others played push-and-shove until they found their seats.

Hank didn't get on.

He let the bus go, turned away from the exhaust wash, let his temper subside to a more manageable level. It wasn't easy. His jaw was so taut it trembled, and heat behind his eyes made him slightly dizzy until he closed them, tightly. It wasn't easy. If he had had the uniform, they wouldn't have done it. Maybe they would have been just as smart-ass, just as rude, but they wouldn't have done it.

Uniform or no, they never did it to him on the block.

A step back from the curb, head lowered, throat working to swallow, he stared at the tips of his shoes until the night's chill and the traffic's clamor forced him to move.

He found the museum a few minutes later.

There was nothing special about it that he could see – a single door in a narrow building that could have used renovation a decade or two ago. Lana hadn't been here herself; it was one of those heard-about-it-from-a-friend things, but she figured he would be interested, being a cop and all.

He hadn't been, and had been avoiding actively searching for it since she had first brought it up.

He was a beat cop, for God's sake. Didn't she understand that? An ordinary beat cop. He saw bodies, he saw blood, he saw the instruments that had drawn one from the other, but he wasn't the one who hunted the killers down. No, he was the one who found what was left of their prey.

On the other hand, he thought as he glanced up and down the avenue, feeling vaguely uneasy, as if he were about to walk into a porn shop or something, maybe this was a sign. *What the hell.* At the very least, it would keep her off his back for a while.

He grunted, shook his head quickly, scolded himself for being unfair. She meant well. She cared.

The museum door opened, and he looked down in surprise at the hand, his hand, that had turned the dull brass knob.

Okay, it was a sign.

A half-smile took him over the threshold and out of the cold. A brief unsettling sensation of déjà vu before he noticed a tiny wood table on his left that held an untidy stack of pamphlets – *The*

Museum of Horror Presents. He took one, opened it, and realized
the light was so dim that he practically had to put his nose
through the thin paper in order to read it. A simple diagram of the
interior, a few words, not much else. The main premise seemed to
be that he had to discover for himself the details of the exhibits.
Which were sealed upright cases ranged along narrow aisles, glass
cases touched with dust and annoying flared reflections of small
caged bulbs hanging from the ceiling, cases whose contents
startled him when he walked past, only glancing in until he
finally understood what he had seen.

'You're kidding me,' he said quietly.

The preserved bodies, or damn fine replicas, purportedly those
of murderers of the first rank, criminals of the mind, villains of the
body. Supposed personal items tucked around their feet and on
small glass shelves. He recognized none of the names, none of the
crimes, but it didn't make any difference; it was bad enough
looking at the corpses, real or not; it was worse reading what they
were supposed to have done.

Soft voices and whispers from other parts of the large room.

Soft footsteps and whispering soles.

The impulse to giggle in such a solemn place became an urge,
and he rubbed a hard hand across his lips. A second time, harder,
for a shot of pain to kill the laugh. Sniffing, grabbing a handkerchief to blow his nose and wincing at the explosive sound of it;
wandering the aisles, reading the legends now, thinking the
curator or whatever he was called had one hell of an imagination.
In spite of himself, stopping now and then to examine a body, the
clothes, flicking dust away to peer more closely at a face.

Soft voice.

Soft footsteps.

A check over his shoulder now and then, but he saw no one
else. Only heard them, felt them, had almost convinced himself he
was in here with ghosts when, rounding a corner, he nearly
collided with a woman, a teenager really, whose eyes widened as
large as her mouth when it opened to scream.

'Jesus, where the hell did you come from?'

He grinned. 'I'm haunting the place.'

Too much makeup, hair cropped unevenly, she sneered thick
lips at him and huffed away. 'Stupid creep,' she muttered.

He scowled at her back, half tempted to call after her and

demand . . . what? What the hell was he getting so pissed about? They had startled each other, they were mad because they'd been scared, what's the big deal, Hank?

He scratched the back of his neck, pulled at his nose, and looked at the case immediately to his left.

It was empty; a little hazy because of the light dust, but still, it was empty.

Yet there was a card, just like all the others, and this one claimed that what he saw, or didn't see, was the mortal remains of the recent serial killer known as the Ghost. It took him a few seconds of frowning before he caught the joke and smiled. Nodded his appreciation. Looked around, wishing there were someone nearby with whom he could share the curator's bizarre sense of humor.

No one.

He was alone.

And being alone, he checked again to be sure he was right, then reached out a finger and drew it gently along the case's seams, stretching to reach to the top, bending over to reach the bottom. The glass felt warm, but comfortably so, and there was a faint vibration – the traffic outside, footsteps in here. It would be cozy inside, he figured, and almost laughed again. Cozy. Snug. The Ghost making faces at those whose peered in, trying to make sense of what they weren't seeing.

This time he couldn't stop the laugh, and didn't want to.

'Boo!' he said to his reflection in the glass, and feigned stark terror, clamping a hand to his heart, staggering backward, nearly colliding with the exhibit behind him.

'Boo!' he said through a deep rippling laugh, and wiped a tear from one eye, pressed a hand to his side where a stitch had stabbed him.

He was coming apart, he knew it, and he didn't give a damn.

'Boo!' one last time, and he made his way to the exit, giggling, shaking his head and chuckling, on the street laughing so loudly he embarrassed himself even though he was alone.

He felt . . . great.

In front of Dutch's closed butcher shop he applauded when he saw that the cathedral was gone. Another sale. Bravo. Bravo.

He patroled the neighborhood, just like the old days, and like the old days saved his street for last. He didn't mind the damp

November cold that seeped up his sleeves and down his collar, the way the few remaining leaves hustled after him on the wind, the way his footsteps sounded flat, not October sharp.

He didn't mind at all.

He patroled until near sunrise, then slept the sun to bed. No nightmares, no croaking screams.

Just before Thanksgiving, Lana commented on his attitude as she served him his steak-and-potatoes dinner. 'Jesus, Cabot,' she said, 'it's like you're almost cheerful for a change.'

And he repaid her by leaning over the counter, taking hold of her arm, and planting a big one on her lips. 'Why, thank you, my dear,' he said as he sat back on his stool, picked up his knife and fork, and gave his meal a smile.

Lana, startled into silence, could only swallow, and touch her lips with a finger as if to test them. A dreamy smile, a scowl at her reaction, and when he finished she said, 'Hank, you all right? You're not . . . I mean, like, drugs or something?' A finger pointed. 'And don't you dare say you're just high on life.'

'My hobby,' he told her, dropping the price of his dinner on the counter.

'You're joking, right?'

'Nope.' He struck a pose. 'You want to hear one?'

'One what?'

'Poem.'

Her mouth opened, closed, and he said, 'Whose ghosts these are I think I know/Their graves are in my dreams, you know.'

She waited.

He watched her.

She said, 'Is that it?'

He shrugged as he zipped up his jacket. 'I'm still working on it.'

'It . . . kind of sounds familiar.'

'Maybe,' he said as he walked toward the door, a wave over his shoulder. 'Maybe not.'

Maybe, he thought as he caught the next bus uptown; *maybe not*.

He returned to the museum and gave himself five minutes before he made his way to the Ghost case, touched the seams and found them cold. His eyes closed briefly. His stomach lurched. He held one arm away from his body, for balance. He made his way carefully to the sidewalk where he looked up at a sky that the city's lights robbed of stars and moon. He didn't move until a gust of wind nudged him; he didn't choose a direction until he reached a corner and turned it; he told himself he didn't know what he was doing until he recognized his home, and saw a man in a topcoat and felt hat urinating against one of the iron-spear fences.

'Hey,' he said, his voice quiet but mildly angry. 'Kids play there, you know.'

The man zippered himself and buttoned his coat. 'You a cop?'

'Nope.'

'Then screw you, pal,' and he walked away.

Hank watched him go, looked at the windows above him, across the street, saw shades glow and dark curtains, and imagined he could hear the sounds of sleep and making love and television shows and stereos and children dreaming and old folks dying.

I'm a beat cop, for God's sake.

Stop lying to yourself, Lana had told him.

So he did.

He followed the man in the expensive topcoat for several blocks, out of the neighborhood and into a street where there was more night than night-lights. He moved swiftly then without seeming to, and when the man turned around, glaring at the intrusion, Hank took him by the throat with one hand and held him, knowing now, aware now, what the published reports did not say — that the bodies were somehow thinner. Older. Maybe drained, but not of blood or bone or muscle.

Hank held the topcoat man until he crumpled into the gutter, his hat rolling into the center of the street, stopping upside down. A sigh, but no regrets, and he took a bus uptown for the second time that night, did not marvel that the museum was still open. He went straight to the Ghost's case and ran his fingertips along the seams, feeling the cold eventually, slowly, become warm, watching the haze inside thicken . . . just a little. Placed a palm against the front and felt that faint vibration — not traffic or footsteps: it was the reverberation of faint screams.

If he looked closely enough, hard enough, he might even see his nightmare, not a nightmare any longer.

A quick smile, a ghost of a smile, and he left for home and slept the sun to bed.

Comforted in knowing that outside the street never changes from morning to night.

Comforted too in knowing that at night the street is haunted.

MURIEL GRAY

Shite Hawks

MURIEL GRAY IS A WRITER, BROADCASTER AND JOURNALIST, as well as being the joint managing director of one of Britain's biggest and most successful independent film and television companies, Ideal World Productions, responsible for such popular series as *Location Location Location*, *Driven*, *Vids*, *Equinox*, *Deals on Wheels* and the feature film *Late Night Shopping*.

As a presenter, she has hosted such TV shows as *The Tube*, *The Media Show*, *Frocks on The Box*, *Walkie Talkie* and *The Booker Prize*, amongst many others. She broadcast for hundreds of hours on BBC Radio One during the 1980s and 1990s and currently presents Radio Scotland's book review programme.

Along with a non-fiction book about mountaineering, *The First Fifty*, she has published three acclaimed horror novels: *The Trickster*, *Furnace* and *The Ancient*.

'I first became interested in the desert landscapes of huge landfill sites,' recalls Gray, 'when my television company shot a film that featured one in Glasgow, and met the real man with hawks employed to keep away seagulls. (Not remotely like the seedy figure in my fiction, I hasten to add.) A few weeks later I saw a rubbish-collection truck sporting a figure sitting up front in the cab that had been made out of refuse by the bin men who crewed it. It was horrific. It was meant to be funny, but the effect of its piecemeal construction was chilling. That was the start of not only "Shite Hawks", but also my novel *The Ancient*, which played with the same themes.

'I'm interested in how society is childishly desperate to conceal

and mask everything we break, use and discard and think of as
ugly, and there is a subtext in "Shite Hawks" that suggests how
that also applies to people.'

I HATE THE WAY SPANNER watches me when I eat. It's fucking
unnatural. It's not like he's looking at me. It's like he follows
the food from the moment it leaves the plastic bag, and keeps
his eyes on it as it travels the last few inches into my mouth. And
all the time, he's holding his own sandwich like it isn't really food
at all, but some synthetic approximation of the real thing, the
thing that I have and he doesn't. It bugs the fucking tits right off
me.

Especially today.

'What the fuck are you lookin' at, you retard?'

Spanner moves his eyes from the motion of the concealed food
in my cheeks to my eyes, and affects the look of a scolded child.
'Aw, hey, there's no call for that now. No call for that at all.'

Belcher looks up from behind his tabloid and shoots me a look.
'Mind your language, ye wee cunt.'

He sees no humour in that, and the idle line of latent violence in
his eyes tells me that even if I do, now is not the time to display it. I
glare back at Spanner whose stare is fixed back on my hand, the
one with the remains of the cheese sandwich in it, and I turn in
disgust to look out the window of the Portakabin. I have to wipe
an arc in the condensation to see out. It drips all day from the
bloody Calor gas fire Belcher keeps on, summer or winter, but
through the smear I can make out a figure.

It's not like the hawk guy to be late for his lunch break. That fat
moron's as lazy as a fucking woman. But here he comes, ten
minutes into the break and only just appearing over the last
mound of steaming rubbish, his scabby hooded bird swaying on
his wrist, trying blindly to compensate its balance for the bobbing
and stumbling gait of its master.

'Door,' is the only greeting he gets from Belcher as he enters,
and he shuts it behind him obediently.

I watch as he fetches out the stupid wee folding perch he keeps
in the pocket of his donkey jacket, erects it on the table, and
transfers the bird from his leather glove onto the four-inch piece

of dowelling. It obliges him by dropping a viscous brown and white marbled shit on the table.

'Aw, Jesus wept, man. We're eatin' here.' Spanner has taken his eyes off my moving jaw long enough to regard the slug-shaped dropping only inches from his Tupperware box of sandwiches.

'It's nature. What d'ye want him do? Go to the fuckin' bog an' wash his hands?'

Belcher looks up again. The motion promotes an instant and respectful silence. 'See anyone?'

The hawk guy looks at each of us turn. 'Naw.'

I look out the steamy window again, this time aware that my heart is increasing its pace.

'Naebody,' qualifies the hawk guy, as though we misunderstood him the first time.

The Portakabin is right in the middle of the vast toxic plain of the landfill, and today, as most days, the grey Scottish sky can barely distinguish a horizon against the near-colourless piles of waste. I suppose in reality, if you look closely, there's plenty of colour in the piles. Mostly primary colours. But it's funny how when you put them all together like that it just becomes the hue of mud. Sickly, diseased, reeking mud. Only the hooked dinosaur arm of Spanner's JCB breaks the monotony of these man-made rolling hills, abandoned as it is in a frozen predatory pose to the call of lunch. I stare at it for the visual relief it provides, and when Belcher speaks I can barely force myself to turn back towards the room. Of course I do. It wouldn't be smart not to.

'Kids?'

The hawk guy shakes his head. 'They sealed up the gap in the fence. Wee cunts cannae get through any mair.'

Belcher looks to Spanner. Tension beats in the air like a pulse.

For a minute we all think Belcher is going to let it pass. He sits back and folds the paper in front of him, examining the walls of the cabin like he's just noticed it. Instinctively I do the same. I let my eyes wander over his gallery. A ceramic plate with transfer pictures of Corfu around the circumference supports clock hands that have long since ceased to turn. Next to it a life-size plastic vacuum-moulded head of a Vegas Elvis grins down at all four of us like we were stage-side-table guests, and beneath, the Sellotape holding up a silk pennant from Oban is losing the battle to gravity as the red tassels droop and fold back, obscuring the 'n'.

But of course he's not looking at all that stuff. He's looking at that fucking doll, Blutacked to the wall, its feet resting on a little souvenir Swiss wooden shelf specially mounted there for the purpose. I glance at Spanner, who's also looking at it, and I lower my eyes.

'I telt ye to open it up, Spanner.' Belcher looks back lazily at the transfixed man. 'I believe I telt ye last week.'

Spanner opens his mouth, then closes it again. One long wisp of oily grey hair that he combs across and that adheres to his bald pate shifts from its base and falls across his shiny face. He pushes it back with familiar attention. 'Ah did.'

He's lying so nakedly, even the hawk guy looks away.

'Someone from the estate must've fixed it again since.'

We all know it's a lie. Especially me. I look steadily at Spanner to try and hide that.

There hasn't been a stranger on the landfill for over three weeks. Not a kid looking for interesting discarded treasure, not a junky or wino, not even the illegal dumpers who case the joint after the gates close. No one. Mind, there's nothing strange about that. There's no seagulls either. And that's no thanks to the fucking hawk guy who's getting paid a fortune to keep these non-existent gulls off the site with his scabby budgie. I sneaked a look at his invoice on Belcher's desk one day. 'East Glasgow Hawks' it said at the top of the paper.

And then EGH claimed to be owed nearly two hundred fucking pounds a week, just to keep that lazy bastard's mangy pet flying around all day pretending to keep off imaginary flying vermin. Spanner says the guy's got a contract at the airport too. Must be coining it in, the fat shite. And the worst of it is, the gulls wouldn't come here any more even if you were pumping fish out your arse. They wouldn't be so daft.

The rats went months ago. That leaves us. Only us.

I force myself to look back up at the doll again. Belcher's had it up there now for three days. That means The Rising is almost here. Like, really really almost here. He wouldn't dare have it out so long in case one of the Council suits dropped by and happened to ask what the fuck it was. So it must be almost now. Shit. Almost time, and no strangers. I can't help wondering what the mad cunt's plan is. You can't tell by looking at Belcher. You can't tell anything very much. So I look at the doll.

This is only the third time I've seen it, since I'm last in. Only been on the site sixteen months. Been to college, blew out, landed here, and it took me at least three months to murder my bloody vocabulary so they'd even talk to me, the under-educated thick bastards. So now I can talk in words of one syllable, or if it's Spanner I'm talking to, less. But I fit in now. I fit in fine. Only seen two Risings, and I can't get the last one out my head when I stare at that thing.

At least the doll can't stare back, on account of having no eyes. The head is a bleached rat's skull, delicate, nearly beautiful. It sits on top of a leather body, attached to it by a separate strip of leather that goes over the top of the skull almost like a World War Two flying helmet.

And then that obscene fucking body dangles below it. I can't even bring myself to think about who might have made the thing, what pair of hands held it and stitched it into that shape, but the thought of the maker is worse than the finished work. I used to wonder if Belcher had done it, but one look at his massive chapped hands would reassure you that those fingers would never be capable of any kind of craftsmanship. He can barely make a roll-up, and his fingers are so fat it's all he can do to force his forefinger up a nostril to pick the snotter out that ugly nose. Somehow that brings me comfort. No matter how repulsive it is, the doll is a work of art, but the thought that its maker could be in this room would give me the dry boke.

Its upper body has two thin arms dangling from it, the hands – or claws, I can't work out which – represented by tiny razor-sharp shards of tin cut meticulously from old cans. On the torso are two half-filled pendulous breasts, the nipples made from the ends of condoms, filled with God knows what, that give them a pink fleshy appearance. Hanging below is its distended belly. Maybe it's supposed to be pregnant, maybe not. But there's a slit up it leaving an empty oval chamber, about an inch in diameter, that's blackened and hardened inside like the interior of a bad walnut shell.

Just below is a two-inch-long thick, wrinkled cock.

The legs that try and straddle the massive swollen organ are stick-thin again, and end with the same metal claws; and because they bandy out like an old guy with rickets, those tin claws make the doll's bottom half look reptilian.

Belcher is looking at me now. I felt his gaze shift to my face as tangibly as if he'd stroked me. I look at the doll for a few beats more, resume chewing my sandwich, then try to look away casually.

He'll have a plan. We all trust that he knows what he's doing. The hawk guy makes a wee kind of chucking noise to his bird and strokes its tiny head with a finger, in a kind of affirmation that everything's going to be okay.

But I don't know. It feels different this time. I know I've done wrong but Belcher can't possibly know that. I'm just going to sit it out. The cheese in my mouth tastes like wax. I swallow.

'What about you?'

I blink, then swallow again. 'What?'

He waits. Not honouring my reply with one of his own. Spanner has moved his eyes to my face. The hawk guy is still fingering his fucking bird. I take the back of my hand over my mouth. 'Same, Mr Belcher. Not a soul.'

This time, Belcher gives a slight nod. He picks up his paper again, turns two pages, then folds it in half, in half again, and starts to read the fat origamied rectangle of newsprint as though he had never spoken.

No one breaks the silence. Not even the hawk, and that wee bastard can suddenly give an ear-piercing shriek when you least expect it. Even it senses Belcher's displeasure. We know him too well to think it's finished.

'Sun sets at six-fourteen. Meet at the beds at six.' He smoothes the paper, still squinting at the type. 'An' when ah say six, ah mean six, you dozy cunts.'

I've been driving the dumper all week. I like it fine. Although it's Spanner who fills me up with his digger, I don't have to see or talk to the stupid bastard. We're safe in our respective cabs, the only communication a wave of a hand from a window or a flash of headlights. And this afternoon all I have to do is think about The Rising.

I'm not thinking about what Belcher has in mind. I'm thinking what we all might get this time. I never thought it would work the first go. And I still don't know if it did, but it felt like it did. And I suppose I need to believe that it did. Yes, I really do.

I wanted that trail bike and I got that trail bike. Maybe it wasn't quite the way I thought, but I still got it. It was in the auction, the one I saw, sitting up high on its pink shocks the way an Arab racehorse stands on tiptoe before a gallop. I wanted it so badly, and even more badly when it didn't reach the reserve price and it got wheeled away. And then the one I got, just exactly like the one in the auction, was on the site, a few days after The Rising. Just left there, paint as good as new, even sporting two day-glo mudguards I hadn't bargained for. Well, okay, maybe it wasn't the exact same one. And so the fuck what that it had no back tyre and the carburettor was shot? It only took me sixty quid to fix, and that was several hundred notes short of what I'd have needed to buy the thing proper.

See, we all want things. Spanner wanted that woman from his estate. Christ knows why. What a dog. Dyed hair, three kids by three different guys, and her tits nearly down at her ankles. And even though she made Mother Teresa look like a supermodel she wouldn't spit on Spanner if he was on fire. But he wanted her. And one week after The Rising, he told me as we shovelled, that he was getting pissed with her and shagging her from behind in that pit of a flat she has above the shops. You see, that can't be coincidence, can it? I don't know what the hawk guy wants and I don't care. He gets enough for fucking nothing just by chucking that bird around.

But we all know what Belcher wants, and it worries me that it's too big. He's not going to get it. The worst of it is, the thing that really eats me up if I'm being honest, is that I think he'll keep on going, pulling any stunt he can, because he believes that one day his undoable thing will be done.

I saw his face one afternoon and that told me a lot. A lot I didn't want to know. He brought her in the car to the Portakabin on one of his days off, because he was on his way somewhere else. He must have forgotten something important – normally he'd never have done it.

The engine was still running and Belcher was inside the cabin, but I stopped and looked in the back of the car as I passed. I knew better than to come in because then he'd have known I'd seen her and I know he hates that. It's an old Ford Mondeo, and it's shite. There's rust bleeding all along the underside of the driver's door that you just know creeps right into the chassis where you can't see it, and you can hear that the engine's fucked even when it's idling. You see, that's what he should be asking for. A new car. I just think he'd get it. That The Rising could get him it. But like I said, it's not enough.

She's about fourteen, his daughter. She was strapped into what looked like a giant child-seat in the back, except it had kind of a headrest thing on either side of her temples with metal arms to position them like an anglepoise lamp. Her face was turned, looking out the window, although it was obvious she couldn't look at anything, the way her eyes were pointing in different directions and darting around like she was following two different shoals of fast fish. A long thread of foamy spittle hung from her bottom lip and stuck to her chest like a suspension bridge, and on that barrelled chest two thin arms rested, terminating in the clawed spastic hands that seemed frozen in a desire to tear at her own scrawny throat.

Then I glanced up at the Portakabin window and I saw him looking at me.

His face was a mixture of shame and anger, and much worse, a longing that was almost primeval in intensity. I backed away and he never mentioned I'd even been there. But I couldn't get his face out of my head.

What does he think? Does he think that after fourteen years she'll just get up out of that padded contraption and walk? That she'll open her slack twisted mouth and suddenly say 'Daddy'? That she'll untangle her misshapen wasted body and join the other teenagers on the street in choosing clothes, in laughing and drinking and living and shagging boys, and one day even make him a grandfather? It's too much. Way too much.

It's why I closed up that fence. His face. That empty longing. The knowledge that he'd do anything.

I didn't see the first guy. At the first Rising, I mean. I knew who he was, though. A good choice. They're all scum, that family of builders that always try and dump when we're on night shift. They used to drop him off by car at the gate. Didn't park, you see, so the nightwatchman or the cops who pass regularly couldn't get a licence plate. And then he'd come in and scout about, choose the site, then scarper with the details for the truck to follow in the days after. You see, we change the main pit every few days. Move it around. You have to know where we're burying. Fly bastards. Don't know where they picked him up again, but no car meant we could never spot him.

So they never knew where he went, you see. And when the cops came round, we'd never seen him. Like I say, that was the truth for me anyhow. I genuinely never saw him. Just where he was taken, and of course the bit of him that Belcher has to put in the doll's slit belly. Looked like the tip of a finger. Maybe not. I could be wrong. It was the tip of something, though.

But I saw the second guy. And all I can say is that fucking junkie was better off wherever he is now than walking the earth with decent people. Junkies make me boke. I can barely look at their sallow sunken faces in the pub where I drink without wanting to walk up and punch their fucking lights out.

So I watched, and I nearly saw it Rise before I had to look away, but I wasn't shamed that it took the bastard and that I'd helped this time. Those scumbags rob old ladies just to feed their veins. True. I was more shamed I didn't see what came for him. Because I was afraid. Anyway, that was when I got my bike.

But kids. I don't know. I just don't think so. I've watched them, the dirty underfed neglected little shits, pissing around on the heaps of rubbish by the fence in their shiny chain-store sports wear, and I could see what Belcher meant. But then you'd chase them, and behind those pinched wee masks of adult defiance that called you things you didn't know were in the English language, there were still glimpses of something like children. So I closed up the fence.

I took care, of course, to climb over and do it from the other side, so it'd look like one of those hacket hard faced 'mothers' from the estate had done it, the ones with necks so fat their thin-gold-chained crucifixes look as though they're choking them to death, instead of protecting their immortal souls. Belcher'll never know it was me.

Course, that's left us without a stranger for this time, but he knows what he's doing. He's the one that really wants something. He'll find a way.

I let myself think about what I want this time and there's no contest. In fact I don't want it, I need it.

Spanner interrupts my dreaming by missing the back of the truck by ten miles, and piles of shit spill over the edge and spew around my cab.

'You blind, you fucking maniac?'

He can't hear me. But I shout anyway, and drive off half full just to bug him. On my way to where this pile of crap needs to be I pass the beds, the mechanically smoothed runways on top of the deepest piles of rubbish that Belcher named, where we'll be meeting in half an hour, and I think about it again.

It's a Cosworth. Sex and power. Four doors, black, with a spoiler and alloy wheels. Gerry Kelly, the smooth fucker who works at the bookie's, is selling it for near on seven grand, and never in a million years can I get my hands on that kind of cash. But I want it. And you see, a thing like that can't just turn up on the site. Cars don't get dumped on the site. So it'll be interesting to see how I manage to get it. That is, if The Rising really does work. Maybe I want to know for sure that it works more than I actually want the car. Maybe.

I think about it some more as I dump the quarter-load that the shit-for-brains Spanner has tossed into the back and then I drive back slowly, imagining who I could shag in the back seat of that car and where we could go and how fast.

And before I know what time it is I see the hawk guy and Belcher making their way to the beds, and I pull up the dumper beside Spanner's digger, parked at an angle that'll force him to do a difficult reverse, and go and get ready to join them.

Of course there's no sunset. This is Glasgow. The grey sky just turns a darker grey, then the street lights of the city come on and stain it a sickly orange. That's how it works. But if Belcher says it's six-fourteen when the invisible sun pegs out and heads west, then it must be right. The air is thick with methane, so much tonight you can hardly breathe. That happens when the air is still, and even after sixteen months I sometimes think I won't be able to take it. But you do. You get used to anything.

Belcher is holding the doll casually, letting its legs hang from his square fist the way a toddler would take a teddy to bed, and he stops walking at some unspecified spot and waits. Spanner and the hawk guy stand on either side of him but a step behind, and so when I reach them, I choose the hawk guy's side and do the same. It's nearly dark now, but the halogens that ring the perimeter fence are picking us out and lighting up the beds like a football pitch. The shadows are so harsh that the ragged skin of the rubbish almost looks comforting in comparison.

Although it's been compacted – inexpertly, by Spanner, obviously – you can still make out the variety of human debris that makes up this unnatural surface. Cartons and plastic containers, broken bread crates, bits of abandoned machines, handles, telephone handsets, rotting vegetables, dried coffee grounds, ripped mattresses. It doesn't ever do to look too closely. It's best to treat it all like it was one thing. The one big thing that humanity has decided it doesn't want any more. The thing that's been eaten and shat on and torn up and soiled, and needs to be buried and covered by people like us, kept well out of sight.

I think I can feel something already under my feet, although to tell the truth it might just be my excitement. I never could wait for things.

The hawk guy hasn't got his hawk. I notice this and it's strange. It's also strange there isn't a stranger. But I don't make the rules, and I don't even know the rules. Maybe it's not always necessary. I don't know if I'm relieved or disappointed. I just know that whatever happens I'm going to watch all the way this time. Not chicken out. Keep looking until it comes and goes.

We wait in silence, hands held in front like we were at church, and then Belcher rubs his face with the hand not holding the doll. 'Ah fuckin' hate it when you wee cunts mess me about.'

He says this so quietly and wearily I wonder if he's talking to himself, or even to the doll. But he stops mashing his face and turns to look directly at me. My head feels hot, and I can start to hear my pulse beating in my ears, the way you can sometimes when you're pissed and your pillow's too hard. I stay silent. There might be a mistake. I might be misreading him. The other two are looking at their feet. I wonder if I should also lower my eyes, but Belcher's gaze is too intense.

'Ah mean, whit the fuck was a' that aboot? Ye think anybody would miss wan o' the wee bastards? Eh?'

I know, and he knows I know that he's referring to the fence. I try and hold his gaze.

'Well, do ye?'

He's nearly shouting. That's not like him. I have to answer. I start with a shrug. 'Just thought there'd be a fuss, Mr Belcher. You know, kids an' that. The cops. You know. The mothers.'

He steps right up to me and I can feel his breath on my face. His voice drops again. 'Those fat whores dinnae even know how many fuckin' kids they've got. Even if ye could drag them oot the pub long enough tae line them up and show them, there's no tellin' they'd recognize them.'

He closes his mouth and his back teeth grind together and make his jaw move. He speaks next in a near-whisper.

'Don't know the meanin' o' the fuckin' word "parent".'

When he says this his voice breaks on the word 'parent' and I use my embarrassment as a decent excuse to lower my gaze. This disgusting personal display somewhere between sentimentality and rage is making me more nervous than when he's just plain mad. I'm praying he'll stop it and go back to being a one-word fucker. Maybe the prayer works. He's calming down, the hardness back in his voice when he speaks again. All trace of the break healed. 'Ah watched ye close up the fence. You stupid wee arsewipe.'

I think about lying and then he's saying something chilling. 'Ye were last in.'

As I look quickly back up again three things happen.

Belcher closes his eyes and nods, like he's fallen asleep. Spanner and the hawk guy grab me by each arm, Spanner surprisingly strong for such a crap wee guy.

Then Belcher takes out his knife and slices the top of my left ear off.

I don't even cry out with the pain. I just open my mouth as wide as my jaw will allow and nothing comes out. Just a kind of gasp. Because I can feel it coming. The ground is moving.

I can't watch as Belcher puts the bit of ear in that oval slit and tosses the doll in front him. I can't watch because I'm looking at the undulating hump in the beds that's growing and changing and coming nearer.

The smell of methane is so strong now that a spark would ignite the whole site, and I gag and cough, trying to get my breath and my voice back.

I know stuff now. Here's what I know.

It makes itself. It just fucking makes itself out of whatever it can find. There's two dead dogs' heads melted together to make a thing with three eyes and what looks like all jaws and rotted teeth. The body's a mess of butcher's bones, bottle glass, bits of cat, newspaper and broken tiles. But the arms. Oh God, the arms. So much metal. And all ending in blades of tin and steel and rusted pointed broken industrial shrapnel, so that when the first pain comes it's mixed with a sharp almost fruity tang of oxidizing metal. It works fast but clumsily, like a newborn animal, and I know that we're helping make it even as it gets bigger.

And all I can think of, as I sink to my knees and drool on the ground in the pool of my own hot piss, is his daughter drooling the same way in her bed, and how this isn't going to make it better.

If I could ever talk again, if the ragged hole in my throat would close and stop pumping blood on the milk cartons and broken paperbacks, I would tell the stupid cunt again and again.

Shout it. Scream it.

It isn't going to make it better.

MICHAEL CHISLETT

Off the Map

MICHAEL CHISLETT HAS BEEN INFLUENCED by such writers as
Robert Aickman, M.R. James, Arthur Machen and Fritz Leiber.
His fiction has appeared in such magazines as *Ghosts & Scholars*,
All Hallows and *Supernatural Tales*, and in the anthologies *The
Young Oxford Book of Supernatural Stories*, *The Young Oxford
Book of Nightmares*, *Midnight Never Comes* and *Shadows and
Silence*.

He takes a perverse pleasure in inventing plausible 'fakelore' in
his stories, many of which are set in South London, where he was
born and has lived all his life (and that he feels he knows a bit too
well). He is currently working on a novel, *Jane Dark's Garden*,
which is set in the same area as 'Off the Map' and which one day
may even be finished.

About the following story, Chislett reveals: 'Machen is the
obvious influence behind the tale. He was adept at seeing the odd
and the hidden in the dullness of suburban London. The mysteries
behind closed curtains in Victorian villas and such. The mysteries
are still there and it is up to us, if we are so minded, to discover
them.

'The park and the streets leading up to it do exist. Not quite
so steep a climb, perhaps, and with not so many turnings, but
it is there. The view is not very good, though; one might well
be able to see London from it, but for the houses in between,
and there are no reports of any phenomena such as are
described in the story. If those of a curious turn of mind do
choose to seek the place out, then they should be very careful

of the maps that they consult first. There is, of course, no
station named "Mabb's End" in London, nor Mabb's Hill. If
they are on your map, then I would certainly like to see it. But
as for going there . . . well, it is best to be sensible about these
things, is all I can say.'

F LETCHER WAS, IN HIS PERVERSE WAY about such things,
    proud of still using his old *A to Z* when finding his way
around London. The street atlas had been published in the mid-
sixties and in the years since many places in the city had altered
out of all recognition. Streets had vanished, new ones been added,
and whole districts erased more effectively than by the Blitz. So
Fletcher thought of the book of maps as an indicator, albeit a not
very reliable one, of likely ways to go. But he was sure that, even if
the chart he steered by was no longer trustworthy, his instincts
would set him right. For he knew that London could never be
reduced to lines on paper, its nature was to change, and when
travelling in the metropolis it was often best to go as an explorer
entering unknown country.

'I am,' Fletcher would declare, 'one of those born with a natural
sense of direction.'

'Are you claiming never to have been lost at all?' asked his
friend Mathews.

'I have often been confused,' Fletcher admitted, 'but never
lost.'

They were standing in Greenwich Park atop the hill and
Mathews pointed at Canary Wharf.

'It is easy to get lost round there,' he said, 'even with a good
map. Imagine if you had lived in the area as a child and
returned after thirty or forty years, not knowing how things
had changed. It would be as if you had gone with the fairies
for what seemed but a night, to return to a world no longer
yours.'

'As one taken under the hill,' mused Fletcher. 'Not many places
like that on the Isle of Dogs.'

They stared at the glass and concrete buildings that dominated
the riverside. The setting sun was reflected by a thousand windows. When it was full dark, Fletcher would look at the lights on
Canary Wharf and think of the Last Redoubt in Hodgson's *The
Night Land*.

'If one had been taken away,' Fletcher said, 'or lost part of one's memory, so that you could only remember things as they had been years before, that would be . . . difficult.'

They walked in silence to the observatory, where they stopped once more to view the reach of the Thames. With silent contempt they turned their backs on the Dome to look upriver toward the setting sun.

'It has ruined it,' said Mathews, indicating the tower that dominated the north shore. 'Just think of how many painters have put on canvas the view of London from this spot. And now . . .'

He waved a hand expressively and shuddered.

'It is not a building that I could ever like,' said Fletcher, 'but it has a certain something.'

'I know that things must change,' Mathews allowed reluctantly, 'for London cannot be still. That's the best thing about a great city. But that building, well . . . it's everywhere.'

Fletcher could not disagree.

They walked out of the park and across the heath to Point Hill, where they stood looking down on the roofs below.

'Now this is an area that has hardly changed, except for the view, of course, since I was a child,' observed Mathews.

'One of the great high places of London, the Maidenstone,' said Fletcher. 'If it were not for the haze over the city we might see "Appy" Ampstead.'

'The air is cleaner now than for a couple of hundred years,' returned Mathews. 'The "London Particular" is a thing of the past.'

'Because there is no industry left,' said Fletcher who looked sadly upon the bow of the Thames as it rounded Deptford. It was empty now; but he recalled a river full with ships, its banks lined by busy warehouses and thriving factories. It had not been so long ago, but all trace of the working Thames was now gone.

The sun sank slowly, its brightness lingering in the air above the city as the shadows of evening seemed to rise up from the soil beneath their feet. The trees that bordered the high, flat place seemed to be oddly misshapen as, one by one, the street lamps came on down the hill. If there were others about on the Maidenstone the two friends were oblivious to them, for in the thickening twilight it was difficult to see things, even if they were close by; even if they were closer than one might wish.

'This is one of the last unspoilt places, one of the few left alone,' sighed Mathews.

'Amazing that it has never been built upon,' said Fletcher, adding: 'I suppose if anyone tried they would have been stopped.'

They walked down the steps from the hill, their route taking them between two rows of cottages. There was the unspoken promise of a pint or three ahead of them.

'I know of a similar place,' said Mathews, 'on a hill, still unspoilt, with steps leading between the houses as a short cut between the streets. Not the usual thing that you find in this part of London, and not really all that far from here.'

'Do you mean One Tree Hill at Honor Oak?' asked Fletcher, who prided himself on knowing all the high places of the city. 'The steps up the hill to the church there are very steep. They say that sometimes the ghost of a girl can be seen dancing on the steps.'

'No, not there, but close to it,' said Mathews. 'Mabb's Hill – it rises above the station.'

'Mabb's End,' said Fletcher with interest, 'a station where the trains rarely stop. I didn't know that there was anything there, despite the name.'

They had walked down Royal Hill and stood, undecided, before two adjoining pubs.

'Young's, I think,' said Fletcher.

'Pint of special will do nicely,' Mathews agreed.

They were soon sitting in the beer garden with their drinks. The summer night had grown humid and the lights strung from the trees and on the fence between the pubs glowed like fireflies. Fletcher had taken out his *A to Z* and studied the volume, with its tape-repaired spine, in the dim, uncertain light.

'Now just where is this place?' he asked. 'I have the station here.'

Mathews peered at the open book. Above the garden the air was dark, for the light seemed to enclose the place in a glowing box. The uncertain illumination made the lines of the streets in the outdated atlas shift in odd patterns, as if the geography of the city was mutating before his eyes.

'I can't remember the name of the road, but one walks up the hill from the station and into a twisting street of Victorian houses. It is quite a climb, for the road turns sharply several times as if it were built on a zigzag pattern. Easier to use the stairs between the houses? Yes, but I think it best to be quite sure where one comes out. It is a place that might be easy to get lost in – even for someone with such a phenomenal sense of direction as yourself, Fletcher. Ah! I think that this is it.'

Fletcher looked down, trying to make out the tiny lettering at the tip of his friend's finger.

'Overhill Road – very apposite. And I see that behind the station, below the hill presumably, is Underhill Road. Have you ever noticed how these names always seem to go together? But I see no park or open space marked there. There *is* a park, farther across, opposite the station, but that cannot be the vantage point you mean . . .'

'It is a very small place,' Mathews agreed, 'hardly more than the size of a couple of suburban gardens, but the view is splendid.'

Quite unaccountably, Fletcher felt suddenly unsure that his friend meant the view over London. He looked up at the night sky where no moon or stars showed as yet, for overhead all was a canopy of dark blue which turned to indigo and then black as his gaze swept from horizon to zenith. Moths danced beneath the hanging lights, flitting about the coloured glass.

'But is it splendid enough?' Fletcher asked. 'I mean, is it worth going out of one's way for?'

'If one is near there, yes,' said Mathews.

'But is it worth making a trip for?' persisted Fletcher.

Mathews appeared lost in thought for a moment.

'If you are disappointed then you will blame me for wasting your time,' he said at last, 'but it is an odd spot. I came across it completely by chance.'

He took a long pull at his beer, and Fletcher sensed that an anecdote was on its way. An anecdote or perhaps something more substantial.

'It was quite a long time ago,' began Mathews, 'when I was looking for a flat. I had been given the address but had got myself a bit lost.'

'I never get lost,' Fletcher could not resist boasting. Pointing to his *A to Z*, he added, 'It never lets me down.'

'Something to depend on in a turning world,' said Mathews dryly. 'Do you want another pint?'

As Fletcher awaited his friend's return he idly studied the atlas. He wondered if he might be due for new glasses for the lines on the page seemed to be all a-tumble, as if they were forming a new chart of the city, one that he could make no sense of.

Mathews returned with the ale and they sat silently for a few minutes, drinking contentedly.

'It was quite a while since I was there and the place may have changed a good deal,' Mathews said at last.

'In the darker reaches of history, then,' joked Fletcher. 'Well, I can't find any open space marked there at all.'

'It is a very small area,' said Mathews thoughtfully, 'like the place had been overlooked when the district was first built up. Not really a park at all.'

'Probably not worth going to,' said Fletcher, who was mildly annoyed at not being able to find the place in his book of maps. 'I really don't know why you bothered to tell me of it.'

'Oh, but it is worth going to, if one is near and can find it. For the view.' Mathews looked at Fletcher for a moment and raised his glass, but before drinking could not resist adding, 'Perhaps you do not know London quite as well as you think.'

Fletcher, as was his way, began to regale his friend with rather tall tales of his adventures in the odder and more neglected corners of the city. Soon the conversation turned to other, perhaps more interesting things, the Matter of London, the terrible decline in the standard of real ale and its rising price. The hill above Mabb's End and its wonderful view were forgotten, for the time being.

The conversation with Mathews had almost slipped Fletcher's mind until a few months later, when he unexpectedly found that business would take him near Mabb's End.

'I shall have the time,' he mused, 'so I might as well seek out Mathews's wonderful view.'

Later that day he stood outside the station consulting his battered street atlas. Fletcher saw that Overhill Road was almost directly opposite, and rose quite steeply, just as Mathews had described. On each side of the road, which curved sharply to the left, Victorian houses of three and four storeys rose sheer as cliffs. Fletcher set off and turned the bend in the road, only to find that another faced him but a few dozen yards away.

'Turn and turn again,' he muttered when, on navigating this second corner, he was confronted by yet another bend, only a house length ahead. Certain that the map had not shown all these sharp turns he opened the book and a slip of paper, one that marked the relevant page, fell out and, caught by a vagrant breeze, fluttered before his face. Fletcher, who had written an important address on the paper, snatched at it, but the scrap easily evaded him and floated just out of reach to land on the pavement by the steps of the house.

It was then that Fletcher noticed the old man who stood by the door watching with interest his contortions as he tried to catch the paper.

'It's there,' said the old fellow, pointing to the note, which lay before the steps at his feet.

As he retrieved the slip Fletcher suppressed the urge to retort that he was not blind, and instead thought it prudent to enquire if he was on the right road.

'Excuse me,' he asked, 'but is there a piece of open ground near here? A sort of park at the top of this road?'

Scratching his head thoughtfully, the old man looked up the hill, which rose ever more steeply above them.

'Don't know,' he said, adding by way of explanation, 'I've never been up there.'

'Oh! Don't you live here then?' asked Fletcher.

'Yes,' answered the old chap, 'right here.' He pointed, rather unnecessarily, to the house. 'I've never needed to go up there.'

Fletcher was at a loss to understand how someone could not take the trouble to walk to the end of their street. Was the man entirely rational? Then another explanation presented itself.

'Have you just moved in?'

The man gave him an odd look and replied, 'I've been here nearly forty years.'

'So in forty years you have never been to the end of your street?' Fletcher exclaimed.

'No point,' said the old fellow with a hint of pride. 'Nothing there.'

Fletcher felt a flicker of excitement. A place with nothing there. Of course, it was silly to put such a literal construction on the phrase. There was always something, even if it was not a very interesting something. With a nod to the old man he resumed his climb.

'Its a steep way up,' came a call from behind him.

'How do you know if you've never been up there?' Fletcher demanded, turning round.

A confused, anxious look passed across the man's face, as if the question was profoundly upsetting. 'My wife did once,' he said abruptly, and disappeared inside, slamming the door behind him.

How peculiar, thought Fletcher, with a shake of his head. He knew that some Londoners took a perverse pride in not knowing their city, but never having gone to the end of one's own street was taking parochialism a bit far. He shrugged – if he followed Overhill Road he must surely get to somewhere.

Resolutely, Fletcher set off again, noticing as he turned yet another bend that the higher he went, the taller the houses became. There were extra storeys topped off with sharply sloping roofs, and attics with steep gables that overlooked the street. He felt quite dizzy from staring up at them. Pausing for a moment to draw breath, he had the vague suspicion that he was on an Escher-like world, one where up and down, high and low did not quite mean what was normally accepted.

Then he noticed that, between two of the houses, a stepped alley ran. Recalling Mathews's description, he made for this, thinking to save time that would be wasted negotiating another bend. As he climbed the steps a young woman pushing a pram appeared at the top, and waited for him to ascend.

'Let me give you a hand,' he offered, pleased to be able to indulge in a little minor gallantry. The girl, who like so many mothers these days seemed to be distressingly young, smiled assent. Fletcher grasped the bar of the old-fashioned baby carriage, which despite its size felt quite light, and lifted it down with the girl holding on to the handle. On reaching the bottom of the steps he set the pram down and looked inside, ready to make an appropriate remark. But it was quite empty and he was at a loss for words.

'Keep on going,' said the girl, cheerfully. 'You'll get there before you know it.'

Fletcher smiled at her. He had begun to puff and pant rather and he thought he must be somewhat red in the face.

'The road does seem to go on for ever,' he said ruefully.

'It can do, if you let it,' said the girl, turning to head downhill.

'It's all right for you,' Fletcher laughed, 'with an empty pram.'

She turned her head and grinned back at him.

'It'll be full on the way back.'

So saying, she disappeared around the abrupt bend. Fletcher thought her smile, while by no means unwelcome, was rather too knowing. She was certainly right about his stamina. The climb was proving much more difficult than he could have anticipated. Mathews really had not properly described how absurdly steep the hill was. Fletcher was beginning to feel worn out and testy.

'There had better be something at the end of this,' he muttered darkly, and took out the *A to Z* again. As he opened the dog-eared paperback a page came loose. He looked at it in bewilderment. Despite its age the street atlas was in good condition, and this was the first time that it had shown signs of disintegration. Fletcher looked at the errant page, trying to see what part of the city had come adrift. He could not recognize it at all. Hood Lane, Hobb Street. None of the names were familiar. Ah! Here was a station – Pook End. He had never heard of it.

Then, as he stood shaking his head, Fletcher noticed something even stranger. The road seemed to have changed, for the slope had somehow levelled. For a moment he had the feeling that he might not have walked up the street but had gone down, and that he now stood in a dip or valley between two rises. Closing his eyes in bewilderment, he began to wonder if he had over-exerted himself. Could he be having a mild stroke? After a few seconds he opened his eyes and was relieved to find that the street had returned to normal – if such a punishing gradient could be described as normal.

Fletcher still held the loose page in his hand, but refused to look at it; instead, he placed the sheet between the cover and first page, resolving to study the map later. He saw with dismay that other sheets were coming loose too, and it struck him that the London he knew so well was now falling apart.

'That's it,' he said aloud. 'I'm going back down.'

'You've come too far now. You have to carry on.'

It was the girl with the pram, or at least it looked like her. But she was coming downhill towards him, moving rapidly, almost at a run, as if by her speed she could take off and all the faster reach the bottom, or wherever she might be going.

'Straight up?' Fletcher asked as she sped past. He could not now be sure if it was the same girl, for he saw that this pram had an occupant. But it sped past so fast that he had no time to make out who or what it was. As he spoke Fletcher pointed uphill to where the road made yet another sharp bend.

'It's hardly straight and it's not up,' she replied without looking back and vanished into the stepped alley, leaving only the sound of wheels clacking on stone. Fletcher decided that it must be a different girl. Perhaps there was a nursery nearby. This might explain why the first girl's pram was empty. She had deposited her baby somewhere. He took a deep breath and considered the girl's words. Well, he had come too far now to stop. It would not do to tell Mathews that he had given up on the hill.

Just as Fletcher set off again the sun burst through the cloud, and its warm light gave an odd sense of exuberance to the red-brown Victorian stonework around him.

'I've never seen anything quite like this!' he exclaimed in wonder. But even as he paused and spoke the moment of epiphany began to fade.

'Like what?'

A man stood on the pavement, washing a car. The sun gleamed on the bonnet and dazzled Fletcher's eyes, so that he had to shut them for a second before he replied.

'Oh, the way the sun shone on the houses – it made the street seem all aglow.'

The car washer looked doubtfully along the road at the houses with their darkening windows. As suddenly as it had emerged the sun retreated behind the clouds, leaving the road all grey and mundane once more.

'Dunno about that,' said the man, flicking water from his wash-leather before attacking the car's gleaming bonnet again.

'An interesting street, this,' said Fletcher, and immediately felt like an idiot. He knew from experience that any show of enthusiasm was viewed by most people with the deepest suspicion.

' 'S all right, I suppose,' the man acknowledged, 'compared to some.'

'I'm thinking of moving in, somewhere around here,' lied Fletcher, to prolong the conversation. 'Near the top of the hill.'

'Nothing much up there,' said the man dully.

'Always something,' replied Fletcher. 'Houses, views, prospects.'

'There *is* a bit of a view,' allowed the man, after pondering for a moment.

'A view over London?'

'Just down the hill.' The man frowned as if recalling something unpleasant. 'Been there and didn't like it.'

'You didn't like the view?' Fletcher probed.

'View?' the man seemed confused. 'No, not that. No, London – didn't think much of it.'

'Good Lord!' Fletcher exclaimed, amazed at the idea of anyone not liking London.

'Overrated. Couldn't see the point.'

The man turned back to the bonnet and resumed his polishing, and Fletcher found his gaze drawn to the metal. The sun's brief appearance had dazzled him, and in consequence there was a peculiar blackness at the edge of his vision. He saw his reflection in the car bonnet. How strange his face looked. Like he was trapped in a distorting mirror.

'You'd best hurry up,' said the man, 'before it turns to rain.'

Fletcher saw that the cloud had grown heavier and the sky now loured, black and brooding. It would not be pleasant to be caught out in it, if the rain did come.

'I should have brought my brolly,' he said, half to himself.

'Always brings it on,' the man muttered gloomily.

'Umbrellas?'

'Nah! When I wash me car,' the man said resignedly.

'Sympathetic magic,' said Fletcher, as he walked away. 'There's a lot of it about.'

Fletcher began to walk as fast as he could, for it seemed likely that he would be caught out in the open by the rain before he reached the crest. When he saw another of the peculiar stepped alleys he walked up it rather than tramp the length of the road – the road which, he now saw, had abandoned its habit of twisting and turning, and stretched well into the distance, the end of it quite out of sight.

Having climbed the last step he found himself standing by a small green space, in the centre of which stood a large and flourishing oak. He went to it, and from beneath its boughs surveyed his surroundings as the rain began to fall.

The open space covered little more than an acre. Beside the large oak a few smaller trees lined the edge of the grassy area. Some bushes and uncut grass suggested a spot left largely to its own devices; one rarely touched by hand – or, for that matter, foot – of man.

'Well, has it been worth all that walk?' he demanded aloud.

Receiving no answer, he defied the rain and crossed to where a low wooden fence stood at the edge of the untamed acre. He looked out and down over a valley, on the other side of which another hill rose steeply. He tried to orientate himself by looking toward London for landmarks – even Canary Wharf – but just the valley and hill could be seen, with the grey roofs of the tall houses darkening in the rain that he noticed was growing steadily heavier.

'It's not always like this.'

Fletcher turned on hearing the voice but at first he could see no one. From behind the oak a young girl of about twelve appeared, holding a bunch of wild flowers. She arranged the blooms carefully against the tree, and Fletcher saw that the shrivelled remains of other flowers surrounded the oak. After the girl had finished she came to stand beside Fletcher, and looked down the valley. He followed her gaze.

'You see different things at different times,' she said. 'Sometimes the houses are not there.'

Fletcher imagined that at the height of summer the trees would obscure the buildings to make the view appear deceptively rural.

'It must be a very nice view, then?' he asked politely.

The girl looked down with an intent frown, as though (Fletcher thought) she were trying to will the landscape to change. Or perhaps she willed it not to alter?

'Oh no,' she said firmly. 'Sometimes it is really horrible, worse than this.'

She spoke with such vehemence that Fletcher looked at her with surprise, then turned back to the view. It was nothing special. In fact he felt rather let down, and the rain was getting heavier. Why had Mathews bothered to mention the place? It really was a waste of time, and he would be soaked when he got home.

'The rain spoils the view, I suppose. It can make everything look horrible.'

'No,' she said. 'It's worse when the sun comes out, you can see more.'

Even as he looked Fletcher thought that the prospect was subtly changing. It must be the rain obscuring the landscape. For a moment he imagined that all was underwater in a drowned world, as if a second Flood had inundated the valley.

'You're lucky that you can't see it all – it's being covered.'

The girl's voice was oddly intense for one so young.

'You don't have to see it all the time. I do.'

The child was becoming distressed, almost about to cry. Embarrassed, Fletcher looked for what might have upset her, but could see nothing in the view that might be to blame. Indeed, as the air grew thick with ropes of rain the prospect had become almost totally obscured.

'It's like we're all underwater,' he said, and noticed for the first time that the girl was not dressed for the weather, either. Her shift, or whatever it was, seemed quite soaked.

Unfortunately this remark seemed to upset her all the more, and her lower lip quivered as she pointed out into the rain.

'Yes,' she said. 'They can swim at you through it, and when it's dry they creep up, slithering like snakes, or sneaking and crawling like spiders.'

Her words seemed to conjure the mysterious 'they', as Fletcher thought to see in the teeming rain a movement in the air, sinuous and slick. Shapes did move there, though what they were he could not quite decide. Rain dragons? Didn't the Chinese have them? He looked again, and the rain was like smoke, and things crawled in its obscurity. He could not help but recall an obscure passage from Blake about vast spiders crawling after their prey, making smoky tracks in the firmament. Powers of the Air indeed – and it was said by some that Hell was full of spiders.

'Wriggling and creeping,' she said, 'and hot like fires gone dead but that can still burn you.'

Fletcher wondered if this was what Mathews had seen, or something like it. No! He would surely have warned him.

'What do they do?' he whispered, fearful now for himself and the child.

'They show me things,' she answered, 'and tell me things too. It's not fair! That's why I'm here all of the time, for listening to them. I do wish that I hadn't!'

And she began to cry bitterly.

The landscape wavered in the subaqueous dimness. It was changing again, more rapidly. The houses had disappeared entirely, to be replaced by what at first Fletcher thought to be human-like figures of monstrous size. He took a fearful step backward, about to flee; but the girl stood still, now wearing a rapt, half-frightened expression. He stayed and looked out again, to see that the menacing forms had changed into – or might they have been so all of the time? – giant standing stones like those of Stonehenge or Carnac. There were many of them, but they formed no apparent pattern.

'They move,' she said, 'if you don't watch them, and sometimes they move anyway.'

'But how? Why?' Fletcher exclaimed. 'What are they?'

'Dolls, that's what the others told me.'

'But they are nothing like dolls . . . do you mean dolmen?'

Then Fletcher recalled that he had heard of *dhols* before, somewhere.

'Who are these others?'

His mind raced with wild conjecture as the floating nebulous shapes shifted and changed, looming above the alley. The shapes seemed well able to reach out a casual paw and swat at them, and Fletcher felt a sudden urge to protect the girl. But then she looked up at him, and he wondered how he could ever have mistaken her for a child.

'They showed me the ceremonies,' she said. 'The white one, the green one, but the best of all . . .'

Fletcher walked rapidly away, almost running, out from what now seemed a dark wood to where the road should have been – should have been but was not. Although he clapped his hands over his ears the voice of the false child still sounded in them as he fled.

'The scarlet ceremony, that is the best!'

The street he had walked up was gone, replaced by a landscape of such buildings as he had never imagined, temples and palaces, perhaps. Part of a new, or very, very old, London.

Flowers that rarely bloomed in our world spoke to him in insinuating whispers.

'I am not going mad,' Fletcher said aloud, 'I am not seeing or hearing this.'

'Oh, but you are.'

He did not look to see who – or what – had spoken. But the gloating voice pursued him through the landscape of bloody henges and monstrous standing stones. Why had he not seen it when he had walked up? Why had he not listened to those who had – in their own fashion – tried to warn him?

There were others now who followed him, all childlike in stature, adding their tones to the chorus.

'There is so much to see, and we have not even started the ceremonies.'

Fletcher raced through the avenue of stones that shifted about him, as if seen through a mist or in the depths of a smoky mirror, until they changed without warning into an ordinary suburban street. He stopped to stare, amazed and wondering at the new transformation. He looked back to the grassy space where trees shivered in the rain – just a few trees. What he had thought a great oak was a stunted relic that marked the centre of a dull plot, not worth the effort of visiting.

Some instinct made Fletcher reach for his *A to Z*. The pages were all loose now, so carefully he tried to find the street on which he stood. He could not, for not only were the leaves all out of order, but he saw whole districts that were unfamiliar to him and he could not help but think that he did not know the city quite as well as he had thought. The strange pages would have to be shown to Mathews. What would his friend make of it all?

Fletcher fumbled with the loose sheets, trying to get them back between the covers. Some fell from his hand, and he bent to retrieve them before they were soaked by the rain. But even as he gathered them up the print began to run before his eyes, the ink smudging and smearing his fingers.

'What could it be?' he exclaimed. 'Where have I been?'

As he spoke the girl pushing the pram appeared from around the corner of the stepped alley.

'It's easier going down than going up,' she told him and pointed to the alley. 'You'd best be quick, it might all change again.'

Thanking her, Fletcher was about to ask the girl if she knew where he had been; but, looking down at what the pram contained, he thought better of it. A broom lay there, an old-fashioned one with a head of what looked like birch twigs. A coverlet had been laid over it, reaching to just below where the twigs were tied to the stick.

'Isn't he lovely?' the girl said and smiled. 'He's my little poppet.'

She reached out and took the remains of the *A to Z* from him. Fletcher did not resist. She threw the book up into the air, and the pages came adrift and floated in the rain, hovering like birds. A vortex began to shape the loose, swirling pages into an almost recognizable form.

Not waiting to see what his once-familiar street atlas had become he walked down the steps, his pace increasing to a trot down the hill, not looking back until he reached the road by the station. Then he turned to see an ordinary street rising up a hill to end in a piece of waste ground of no interest, except for its offering a view over London.

'Not at all what I saw there,' said Mathews, who had listened without interrupting until his friend had finished. 'Just a rather nice view of the city. I took the trouble of going there this morning, I thought that I had better after getting that very odd phone call from you, and it was just as I remembered. Victorian streets rising up a rather steep hill, with steps connecting them. There were some sharp bends in the road, but not as many as you recall. The whole walk up from the station took barely ten minutes. There was nothing too unusual.'

'What do you mean, too unusual?' Fletcher demanded.

'When I reached the top I sat down on a bench beneath a stunted oak. I rather thought that it might have been lightning-blasted. There were some flowers around its base. Well, as I sat there a girl pushing a pram came along and sat down beside me, and we exchanged a few pleasantries – as one does – and I looked into the pram to admire the baby.'

'It was not a baby,' Fletcher stated firmly.

'Oh, it was a child all right. It would have been interesting to have seen the father, I fancy. Anyway, as I looked she made a suggestion that I chose not to take up. If I were a younger man, or a bit more adventurous . . . But you see, I think that would have entailed me being there for some time, in that place. Also I did not like the look of those other girls who were hovering about there.'

'What was the suggestion?' Fletcher demanded. 'Come on, Mathews, do tell.'

They were in a pub, as usual. Mathews took a long drink from his pint before saying: 'I'd rather not tell but I think that we both had a lucky escape.'

Fletcher thought his friend had a rather smug grin on his face, as if he were pleased about being so mysterious. But he knew that no amount of badgering would get him to reveal what – if anything – the girl had said. Fletcher had his own ideas.

'I suppose,' said Mathews, 'that we are lucky to have been the ones to have discovered them; privileged that the mystery was revealed to us. Part of the mystery, anyway. I think that others have had the same experience, but not recognized it for what it was.'

'At the end the mystery remains,' said Fletcher. 'It's those girls I feel sorry for. Do you think they are there for ever?'

'For a very long time, anyway, and I am afraid that there is nothing that we can do to help them.'

Mathews took another sup of his beer, then mused:

'Shame about your *A to Z*. Will you be getting a new one? I did see some pages lying in the gutter when I was there but they were quite sodden and unreadable. Do you think that you might have been mistaken about those streets? Hobb Lane, Hood Street, Pook End?'

'Hardly,' Fletcher snorted. 'I bought a new one this morning. They come in handy.'

He took the book from out of his pocket and laid it on the table. 'Surprising how different it all looks in this one.'

He opened the book at random.

'This could be a form of bibliomancy. One opens the book, puts a finger on the map and travels to the spot.'

'One could end up in Wealdstone,' said Mathews and leant over the table to where the atlas had been opened. 'Travel broadens the mind, they say, and the most mundane of places can be full of curiosities.'

'The best journeys take place in our minds,' said Fletcher, 'and are purely imaginary. Did I ever tell you of the time I was in North London and found a rather interesting park?'

'Was it anywhere near Stoke Newington?' asked Mathews.

'A shrewd guess.' Fletcher grinned. 'It was another case of so near and yet so far.'

And he began to recount to Mathews his most extraordinary adventure in North London.

KELLY LINK

Most of My Friends Are Two-Thirds Water

KELLY LINK'S STORY 'Louise's Ghost', from her 2001 collection *Stranger Things Happen* (published by Small Beer Press), won the Nebula Award. Her story 'Travels with the Snow Queen' won the James Tiptree Jr. Award in 1997 and her ghost story 'The Specialist's Hat' (reprinted in the tenth volume of *The Mammoth Book of Best New Horror*) won the World Fantasy Award in 1999.

She lives in Brooklyn with her husband, Gavin J. Grant, with whom she co-edits the occasional fanzine *Lady Churchill's Rosebud Wristlet*.

'My friend, a guy named Jak Cheng, called me up one day and said he had a great first line for a science fiction story,' Link reveals. 'I took his first line, and I also borrowed some of his life, and then, to be fair, I put some of my life in there as well. I'm not the narrator, not exactly, and my friend Jak isn't Jak, not exactly, but there are some family resemblances.

'So some parts of this story are true, and some parts are made up, and when I reread it, it's the made-up bits that I like best. They're less confusing. If I could, I'd e-mail Jak so I could tell you what bits he likes best – but he's off on an archaeological dig.'

'*Okay, Joe. As I was saying, our Martian women are gonna be blonde, because, see, just because.*'
— Ray Bradbury, 'The Concrete Mixer'

A FEW YEARS AGO, Jack dropped the c from his name and became Jak. He called me up at breakfast one morning to tell me this. He said he was frying bacon for breakfast and that all his roommates were away. He said that he was walking around stark naked. He could have been telling the truth, I don't know. I could hear something spitting and hissing in the background that could have been bacon, or maybe it was just static on the line.

Jak keeps a journal in which he records the dreams he has about making love to his ex-girlfriend Nikki, who looks like Sandy Duncan. Nikki is now married to someone else. In the most recent dream, Jak says, Nikki had a wooden leg. Sandy Duncan has a glass eye in real life. Jak calls me up to tell me this dream.

He calls to say that he is in love with the woman who does the Braun coffee-maker commercial, the one with the short blonde hair, like Nikki, and eyes that are dreamy and a little too far apart. He can't tell from the commercial if she has a wooden leg, but he watches TV every night, in the hopes of seeing her again.

If I were blonde, I could fall in love with Jak.

Jak calls me with the first line of a story. Most of my friends are two-thirds water, he says, and I say that this doesn't surprise me. He says, no, that this is the first line. There's a Philip K. Dick novel, I tell him, that has a first line like that, but not exactly and I can't remember the name of the novel. I am listening to him while I clean out my father's refrigerator. The name of the Philip K. Dick novel is *Confessions of a Crap Artist*, I tell Jak. What novel? he says.

He says that he followed a woman home from the subway, accidentally. He says that he was sitting across from her on the Number 1 uptown and he smiled at her. This is a bad thing to do in New York when there isn't anyone else in the subway car, travelling uptown past 116th Street, when it's one o'clock in the morning, even when you're Asian and not much taller than she is, even when she made eye contact first, which is what Jak says she

did. Anyway he smiled and she looked away. She got off at the
next stop, 125th, and so did he. 125th is his stop. She looked back
and when she saw him, her face changed and she began to walk
faster.

Was she blonde? I ask, casually. I don't remember, Jak says.
They came up onto Broadway, Jak just a little behind her, and
then she looked back at him and crossed over to the east side.
He stayed on the west side so she wouldn't think he was
following her. She walked fast. He dawdled. She was about a
block ahead when he saw her cross at La Salle, towards him,
towards Claremont and Riverside, where Jak lives on the fifth
floor of a run-down brownstone. I used to live in this building
before I left school. Now I live in my father's garage. The
woman on Broadway looked back and saw that Jak was still
following her. She walked faster. He says he walked even more
slowly.

By the time he came to the corner market on Riverside, the one
that stays open all night long, he couldn't see her. So he bought a
pint of ice cream and some toilet paper. She was in front of him at
the counter, paying for a carton of skim milk and a box of dish
detergent. When she saw him, he thought she was going to say
something to the cashier but instead she picked up her change and
hurried out of the store.

Jak says that the lights on Claremont are always a little dim and
fizzy, and sounds are muffled, as if the street is under water. In the
summer, the air is heavier and darker at night, like water on your
skin. I say that I remember that. He says that up ahead of him, the
woman was flickering under the street light like a light bulb.
What do you mean, like a light bulb? I ask. I can hear him shrug
over the phone. She flickered, he says. I mean like a light bulb. He
says that she would turn back to look at him, and then look away
again. Her face was pale. It flickered.

By this point, he says, he wasn't embarrassed. He wasn't
worried any more. He felt almost as if they knew each other.
It might have been a game they were playing. He says that he
wasn't surprised when she stopped in front of his building
and let herself in. She slammed the security door behind her
and stood for a moment, glaring at him through the glass.
She looked exactly the way Nikki looked, he says, when
Nikki was still going out with him, when she was angry

at him for being late or for misunderstanding something. The woman behind the glass pressed her lips together and glared at Jak.

He says when he took his key out of his pocket, she turned and ran up the stairs. She went up the first flight of stairs and then he couldn't see her any more. He went inside and took the elevator up to the fifth floor. On the fifth floor, when he was getting out, he says that the woman who looked like Nikki was slamming shut the door of the apartment directly across from his apartment. He heard the chain slide across the latch.

She lives across from you, I say. He says that he thinks she just moved in. Nothing like meeting new neighbours, I say. In the back of the refrigerator, behind wrinkled carrots and jars of pickled onions and horseradish, I find a bottle of butterscotch sauce. I didn't buy this, I tell Jak over the phone. Who bought this? My father's diabetic. I know your father's diabetic, he says.

I've known Jak for seven years. Nikki has been married for three months now. He was in Ankara on an archaeological dig when they broke up, only he didn't know they'd broken up until he got back to New York. She called and told him that she was engaged. She invited him to the wedding and then disinvited him a few weeks later. I was invited to the wedding, too, but instead I went to New York and spent the weekend with Jak. We didn't sleep together.

Saturday night, which was when Nikki was supposed to be getting married, we watched an episode of *Baywatch* in which the actor David Hasselhoff almost marries the beautiful blonde lifeguard, but in the end doesn't, because he has to go save some tourists whose fishing boat has caught fire. Then we watched *The Princess Bride*. We drank a lot of Scotch and I threw up in Jak's sink while he stood outside the bathroom door and sang a song he had written about Nikki getting married. When I wouldn't come out of the bathroom, he said good night through the door.

I cleaned up the sink and brushed my teeth and went to sleep on a lumpy foldout futon. I dreamed that I was in Nikki's bridal party. Everyone was blonde in my dream, the bridegroom, the best man, the mother of the bride, the flower girl, everyone looked like Sandy Duncan except for me. In the morning I got up and drove my father's car back to Virginia, and my father's garage, and Jak went to work at VideoArt, where he has a part-time job which involves technical videos about beauty school, and the Gulf War, and things like that. He mostly edits, but I once saw his hands on a late night commercial, dialling the number for a video calendar featuring exotic beauties. Women, not flowers. I almost ordered the calendar.

I haven't spoken to Nikki since before Jak went to Turkey and she got engaged.

When I first moved into my father's garage, I got a job at the textile mill where my father has worked for the last twenty years. I answered phones. I listened to men tell jokes about blondes. I took home free packages of men's underwear. My father and I pretended we didn't know each other. After a while, I had all the men's underwear that I needed. I knew all the jokes by heart. I told my father that I was going to take a sabbatical from my sabbatical, just for a while. I was going to write a book. I think that he was relieved.

Jak calls me up to ask me how my father is doing. My father loves Jak. They write letters to each other a couple of times a year, in which my father tells Jak how I am doing, and whom I am dating. These tend to be very short letters. Jak sends articles back to my father about religion, insects, foreign countries where he has been digging things up.

My father and Jak aren't very much alike, at least I don't think so, but they *like* each other. Jak is the son that my father never had, the son-in-law he will never have.

I ask Jak if he has run into his new neighbour, the blonde one, again, and there is a brief silence. He says, yeah, he has. She knocked on his door a few days later, to borrow a cup of sugar. That's original, I say. He says that she didn't seem to recognize him and so he didn't bring it up. He says that he has noticed that there seem to be an unusually high percentage of blonde women in his apartment building.

Let's run away to Las Vegas, I say, on impulse. He asks why Las Vegas. We could get married, I say, and the next day we could get divorced. I've always wanted an ex-husband, I tell him. It would make my father very happy. He makes a counterproposal: we could go to New Orleans and not get married. I point out that we've already done that. I say that maybe we should try something new, but in the end we decide that he should come to Charlottesville in May. I am going to give a reading.

My father would like Jak to marry me, but not necessarily in Las Vegas.

The time that we went to New Orleans, we stayed awake all night in the lobby of a hostel, playing Hearts with a girl from Finland. Every time that Jak took a heart, no matter what was in his hand, no matter whether or not someone else had already taken a point, he'd try to shoot the moon. We could have done it, I think, we could have fallen in love in New Orleans, but not in front of the girl from Finland, who was blonde.

A year later, Jak found an ad for tickets to Paris, ninety-nine dollars round trip. This was while we were still in school. We went for Valentine's Day because that was one of the conditions of the promotional fare. Nikki was spending a semester in Scotland. She was studying mad-cow disease. They were sort of not seeing each other while she was away and in any case she was away and so I went with Jak to Paris for Valentine's Day. Isn't it romantic, I said, we're going to be in Paris on Valentine's Day. Maybe we'll meet someone, Jak said.

I lied. We didn't go to Paris for Valentine's Day, although Jak really did find the ad in the paper, and the tickets really were only ninety-nine dollars round trip. We didn't go and he never asked me, and anyway Nikki came home later that month and they got back together again. We did go to New Orleans, though. I don't think I've made that up.

I realize there is a problem with Las Vegas, which is that there are a lot of blonde women there.

You are probably wondering why I am living in my father's garage. My father is probably wondering why I am living in his garage. It worries his neighbours.

Jak calls to tell me that he is quitting his job at VideoArt. He has gotten some grant money, which will not only cover the rest of the school year, but will also allow him to spend another summer in Turkey, digging things up. I tell him that I'm happy for him. He says that a weird thing happened when he went to pick up his last paycheck. He got into an elevator with seven blonde women who all looked like Sandy Duncan. They stopped talking when he got on and the elevator was so quiet he could hear them all breathing. He says that they were all breathing in perfect unison. He says that all of their bosoms were rising and falling in unison like they had been running, like some sort of synchronized Olympic breast event. He says that they smelled wonderful – that the whole elevator smelled wonderful – like a box of Lemon Fresh Joy soap detergent. He got off on the thirtieth floor and they all stayed on the elevator, although he was telepathically communicating with them that they should all get off with him, that all seven of them should spend the day with him, they could all go to the Central Park Zoo, it would be wonderful.

But not a single one got off, although he thought they looked wistful when he did. He stood in the hall and the elevator door closed and he watched the numbers and the elevator finally stopped on the forty-fifth floor, the top floor. After he picked up his paycheck, he went up to the forty-fifth floor and this is the strange thing, he says.

He says that when the elevator doors opened and he got out, the forty-fifth floor was completely deserted. There was plastic up everywhere and drills and cans of paint and bits of moulding lying on the floor, like the whole top floor was being renovated. A piece of the ceiling had been removed and he could see the girders and the sky through the girders. All the office doors were open and so he walked around, but he says he didn't see anyone, anyone at all. So where did the women go? he says. Maybe they were construction workers, I say. They didn't smell like construction workers, he says.

If I say that some of my friends are two-thirds water, then you will realize that some of my friends aren't, that some of them are probably more and some are probably less than two-thirds, that maybe some of them are two-thirds something besides water, maybe some of them are two-thirds Lemon Fresh Joy. When I say that some women are blondes, you will realize that I am probably not. I am probably not in love with Jak.

I have been living in my father's garage for a year and a half. My bed is surrounded by boxes of Christmas tree ornaments (his) and boxes of college textbooks (mine). We are pretending that I am writing a novel. I don't pay rent. The novel will be dedicated to him. So far, I've finished the dedication page and the first three chapters. Really, what I do is sleep late, until he goes to work, and then I walk three miles downtown to the dollar movie theater that used to be a porn theater, the used bookstore where I stand and read trashy romance novels in the aisle. Sometimes I go to the coffeehouse where, in a few months, I am supposed to give a reading. The owner is a friend of my father and gives me coffee. I sit in the window and write letters. I go home, I fix dinner for my father, and then sometimes I write. Sometimes I watch TV. Sometimes I go out again. I go to bars and play pool with men that I couldn't possibly bring home to my father. Sometimes I bring them back to his garage instead. I lure them home with promises of free underwear.

Jak calls me at three in the morning. He says that he has a terrific idea for a sci-fi story. I say that I don't want to hear a sci-fi idea at three in the morning. Then he says that it isn't really a story idea, that it's true. It happened to him and he has to tell someone about it, so I say okay, tell me about it.

I lie in bed listening to Jak. There is a man lying beside me in bed that I met in a bar a few hours ago. He has a stud in his penis. This is kind of a disappointment, not that he has a stud in his penis, but the stud itself. It's very small. It's not like an earring. I had pictured something more baroque – a great big gaudy clip-on like the ones that grandmothers wear – when he told me about it in the bar. I made the man in my bed take the stud out when we had sex, but he put it in again afterwards because otherwise the hole will close up. It was just three weeks ago when he got his penis pierced and having sex at all was probably not a good idea for either of us, although I don't even have pierced ears. I noticed him in the bar immediately. He was sitting gingerly, his legs far apart. When he got up to buy me a beer, he walked as if walking was something that he had just learned.

I can't remember his name. He is sleeping with his mouth open, his hands curled around his penis, protecting it. The sheets are twisted down around his ankles. I can't remember his name but I think it started with a C.

Hold on a minute, I say to Jak. I untangle the phone cord as far as I can, until I am on the driveway outside my father's garage, closing the door gently behind me. My father never wakes up when the phone rings in the middle of the night. He says he never wakes up. The man in my bed, whose name probably begins with a C, is either still asleep or pretending to be. Outside the asphalt is rough and damp under me. I'm naked, I tell Jak, it's too hot to wear anything to sleep in. No, you're not, Jak says. I'm wearing blue and white striped pyjama bottoms but I lie again and tell him that I am truly, actually not wearing clothes. Prove it, he says. I ask how I'm supposed to prove over the phone that I'm naked. Take my word for it, I just am. Then so am I, he says.

So what's your great idea for a sci-fi story? I ask. Blonde women are actually aliens, he says. All of them? I ask. Most of them, Jak says. He says that all the ones that look like Sandy Duncan are definitely aliens. I tell him that I'm not sure that this is such a great story idea. He says that it's not a story idea, that it's true. He has proof. He tells me about the woman who lives in the apartment across from him, the woman who looks like Nikki, who looks like Sandy Duncan. The woman that he accidentally followed home from the subway.

According to Jak, this woman invited him to come over for a drink because a while ago he had lent her a cup of sugar. I say that I remember the cup of sugar. According to Jak they sat on her couch, which was deep and plush and smelled like Lemon Fresh Joy, and they drank most of a bottle of Scotch. They talked about graduate school – he says she said she was a second-year student at the business school, she had a little bit of an accent, he says. She said she was from Luxembourg – and then she kissed him. So he kissed her back for a while and then he stuck his hand down under the elastic of her skirt. He says the first thing he noticed was that she wasn't wearing any underwear. He says the second thing he noticed was that she was smooth down there like a Barbie doll. She didn't have a vagina.

I interrupt at this point and ask him what exactly he means

when he says this. Jak says he means exactly what he said, which is that she didn't have a vagina. He says that her skin was unusually warm, hot actually. She reached down and gently pushed his hand away. He says that at this point he was a little bit drunk and a little bit confused, but still not quite ready to give up hope. He says that it had been so long since the last time he slept with a woman, he thought maybe he'd forgotten exactly what was where.

He says that the blonde woman, whose name is either Cordelia or Annamarie (he's forgotten which), then unzipped his pants, pushed down his boxers, and took his penis in her mouth. I tell him that I'm happy for him, but I'm more interested in the thing he said about how she didn't have a vagina.

He says that he's pretty sure that they reproduce by parthenogenesis. Who reproduce by parthenogenesis? I ask. Aliens, he says, blonde women. That's why there are so many of them. That's why they all look alike. Don't they go to the bathroom? I ask. He says he hasn't figured out that part yet. He says that he's pretty sure that Nikki is now an alien, although she used to be a human, back when they were going out. Are you sure? I say. She had a vagina, he says.

I ask him why Nikki got married then, if she's an alien. Camouflage, he says. I say that I hope her fiancé, her husband, I mean, doesn't mind. Jak says that New York is full of blonde women who resemble Sandy Duncan and most of them are undoubtedly aliens, that this is some sort of invasion. After he came in Chloe or Annamarie's mouth – probably neither name is her real name, he says – he says that she said she hoped they could see each other again and let him out of her apartment. So what do the aliens want with you? I ask. I don't know, Jak says and hangs up.

I try to call him back but he's left the phone off the hook. So I go back inside and wake up the man in my bed and ask him if he's ever made love to a blonde and if so did he notice anything unusual about her vagina. He asks me if this is one of those jokes and I say that I don't know. We try to have sex, but it isn't working, so instead I open up a box of my father's Christmas tree decorations. I take out tinsel and strings of lights and ornamental glass fruit. I hang the fruit off his fingers and toes and tell him not to move. I drape the tinsel and lights around his arms and legs and plug him in. He complains some but I tell him to be quiet or my father will wake up. I tell him how beautiful he looks, all lit up like a Christmas tree or a flying saucer. I put his penis in my mouth and pretend that I am Courtney (or Annamarie, or whatever her name is), that I am blonde, that I am an alien. The man whose name begins with a C doesn't seem to notice.

I am falling asleep when the man says to me, I think I love you. What time is it? I say. I think you better leave, before my father wakes up. He says, but it's not even five o'clock yet. My father wakes up early, I tell him.

He takes off the tinsel and the Christmas lights and the ornamental fruit. He gets dressed and we shake hands and I let him out through the side door of the garage.

Some jokes about blondes. Why did the M&M factory fire the blonde? Because she kept throwing away the Ws. Why did the blonde stare at the bottle of orange juice? Because it said concentrate. A blonde and a brunette work in the same office, and one day the brunette gets a bouquet of roses. Oh great, she says, I guess this means I'm going to spend the weekend flat on my back, with my legs up in the air. Why, says the blonde, don't you have a vase?

I never find out the name of the man in my bed, the one with the stud in his penis. Probably this is for the best. My reading is coming up and I have to concentrate on that. All week I leave messages on Jak's machine but he doesn't call me back. On the day that I am supposed to go to the airport to pick him up, the day before I am supposed to give a reading, although I haven't written anything new for over a year, Jak finally calls me.

He says he's sorry but he's not going to be able to come to Virginia after all. I ask him why not. He said that he got the Carey bus at Grand Central, and that a blonde woman sat next to him. Let me guess, I say, she didn't have a vagina. He says he has no idea if she had a vagina or not, that she just sat next to him, reading a trashy romance by Catherine Cookson. I say that I've never read Catherine Cookson, but I'm lying. I read a novel by her once. It occurs to me that the act of reading Catherine Cookson might conclusively prove that the woman either had a vagina or that she didn't, that the blonde woman who sat beside Jak might have been an alien, or else incontrovertibly human, but I'm not sure which. Really, I could make a case either way.

Jak says that the real problem was when the bus pulled into the terminal at LaGuardia and he went to the check-in gate. The woman behind the counter was blonde, and so was every single woman behind him in line, he tells me, when he turned around. He says that he realized that what he had was a one-way ticket to Sandy Duncan Land, that if he didn't turn around and go straight back to Manhattan, that he was going to end up on some planet populated by blonde women with Barbie-smooth crotches. He says that Manhattan may be suffering from some sort of alien infestation, but he's coming to terms with that. He says he can live with an apartment full of rats, in a building full of women with no vaginas. He says that for the time being, it's safest.

He says that when he got home, the woman in the apartment on the fifth floor was looking through the keyhole. How do you know? I say. He says that he could smell her standing next to the door. The whole hallway was warm with the way she was staring, that the whole hallway smelled like Lemon Fresh Joy. He says that he's sorry that he can't come to Virginia for my reading, but that's the way it is. He says that when he goes to Ankara this summer, he might not be coming back. There aren't so many blonde women out there, he says.

When I give the reading, my father is there, and the owner of the coffeehouse, and so are about three other people. I read a story I wrote a few years ago about a boy who learns how to fly. It doesn't make him happy. Afterwards my father tells me that I sure have a strange imagination. This is what he always says. His friend tells me that I have a nice clear reading voice, that I enunciate very well. I tell her that I've been working on my enunciation. She says that she likes my hair this colour.

I think about calling Jak and telling him that I am thinking of dyeing my hair. I think about telling him that this might not even be necessary, that when I wake up in the mornings, I am finding blonde hairs on my pillow. If I called him and told him this, I might be making it up; I might be telling the truth. Before I call him, I am waiting to see what happens next. I am sitting here on my father's living-room couch, which smells like Lemon Fresh Joy, watching a commercial in which someone's hands are dialling the number for a video calendar of exotic beauties. I am eating butterscotch out of the jar. I am waiting for the phone to ring.

CONRAD WILLIAMS

City in Aspic

CONRAD WILLIAMS IS THE AUTHOR OF *Head Injuries* (The Do-Not Press) and the International Horror Guild Award-nominated *Nearly People* (PS Publishing). His short fiction has most recently appeared in *Cemetery Dance*, *The Spook*, *Dark Terrors 6*, *Phantoms of Venice* and *The Museum of Horrors*. He is a past winner of the British Fantasy Award.

'City in Aspic' was written by an author who has never set foot in Venice. 'But,' argues Williams, 'it's one of those cities that worms its way into your consciousness, especially if you've seen *Don't Look Now*, which is simply one of the best, if not *the* best, horror films ever made. You can't help but feel you know that city, and working with a *Time Out Venice Guide* did me a few favours . . .'

It was the author's fondness for the Nicolas Roeg film that inspired him to write the tale. 'It is my tribute to the film,' continues Williams. 'The names of the characters in my story correspond to the names of the actors who appear in *Don't Look Now*, and the Europa is the hotel where John and Laura Baxter actually stayed.

'I'm hoping to go to Venice some day to find out how authentic this story managed to be in terms of its sense of place. Probably in the winter. No doubt I'll see a few mateless gloves flapping about. If you go out looking for them, they're everywhere.'

I T WAS A PLACE THAT needed people in order for it to come alive. In winter, the streets whispered with uncollected litter and nervous pigeons. The air grew so thick with cold that it became hard to walk anywhere. When night came, the water that was slowly drowning the city turned the darkness into an uncertain quantity. There was astonishing beauty here too, though, even where there oughtn't to be any. The crumbling structures, the occasional bodies dragged from the waterways, the bleach of winter that pocketed the city's colour for months on end: all of it had a poetry, a comeliness. Massimo understood this skewed charm. Where others saw moles, he saw beauty spots.

Many times Massimo had wished he could simply drift away like the tourists at the tail end of the season, or the leaves that blew from the trees. It would be nice to spend the coldest months of the year farther south, perhaps with his cousins in Palermo. But now that was not possible. He and Venice were stuck with each other until March.

He stood on the balcony of the honeymoon suite, smoking his last cigarette and enjoying the garlicky smells of *chicheti* that wafted up from the *osterie* on the Riva degli Schiavoni. One of Venice's interminable mists had risen from the Canale di San Marco and clung to the façades like great sheets hung out to dry. Behind him, from deep within the hotel, the sound of the vacuum cleaners on the stairs competed for a short while with the toots of the *vaporetto* and the bell of San Nicoló dei Mendicoli. The last of the guests had checked out that morning and in a little while Maria, the cleaner, would be finished and he could lock the great doors of the Hotel Europa until next year.

He could have his dinner here, on this balcony, every evening if he so wished. The corridors would be his alone to patrol. A different bed to sleep in whenever he liked, though such a choice disturbed him perhaps more than it ought. Deaths had occurred in some of the Europa's rooms; children and divorces had their origins on a number of those mattresses.

He flicked his cigarette end in the direction of the canal and returned to the room where he smoothed the bedspread before taking the stairs down to the ground floor. His father, Leopoldo, had told him this was a job of great responsibility; if he went about it with professionalism, then he would be considered for the post of reception clerk. He was under no illusions. He was a security guard, no more. In the seventies, his father had run the Europa with a touch of élan and much warmth. Tourists who stayed at the Europa came back the next year and the year after that. And then the hotel had been taken over by men in suits with large bellies and eyes that gleamed when they assessed his father's profits. They paid a hefty sum to take over the hotel. Massimo's father was tired. A stroke had robbed him of his personable nature. Though the hotel was Massimo's birthright, Massimo agreed that they should take the money in order that it should fund his father's senescence. But his father, though crippled by the stroke, clung to life and the money was running out.

Maria, who had been a cleaner here for as long as Massimo could remember, patted his arm before she left and told him that spring would be here before he was aware. 'Take advantage of the rest,' she advised him. 'You'll be busy again too soon.' Perhaps seeing the bitterness in his eyes, she smiled at him. 'Your father would be proud of you.'

And now, alone. The magazines had been read and the puzzle books completed. The evening stretched before him like the interminable carpets on the five floors above. He took a cursory stroll of the ground floor, checking the window catches in each room and the locks on the doors. The furniture was shrouded with dust sheets that reduced everything to the same lumpen shape.

He was about to return to the lobby and rewatch an old football video when he saw the single glove draped across the newel post. The stairwell reached up into darkness, those risers beyond the sixth step lost to a night that had fallen on the city as stealthily as snow. It was a lady's glove for the left hand, made from black leather and scuffed with age. The inside smelled of perfume. Maria must have come across it while she was preparing the rooms for the winter. He pocketed it and drew the curtains across the front entrance but not before noticing that the street was empty. He didn't like the way that Venice was abandoned each year. It was as if sunshine and long days were the only things of interest to visitors. Newly married couples ran the gamut of clichés before returning to their homes; the way the tourists clung to St Mark's Square or were punted around in boats suggested that Venice had nothing else to offer.

Irritated by this train of thought, Massimo turned off the

television and went out into his city, a place where he could still get lost in the dark, a place that thrilled and comforted him like no other. The somnolent lap of the water against the gondolas was the beat of a mother's heart. It was not merely a comfort. It justified him. It fastened him like a bolt to the earth and gave him substance.

He stopped for coffee and *grappa* at the *trattoria al canastrello* and watched from the window the black water as it ribboned beneath the Ponte di Rialto. One of his favourite occupations was observing people, but at this time of the year the only people around were the old and infirm. They drifted through the streets as if the weight of their experience was shoring Venice up, as much a support for the ancient city as the countless larch poles that cradled it beneath the waves. Venice, during the winter, seemed to run down like an old clock. Its streets and façades could still play a backdrop for anybody from any time over the last fifteen hundred years without them seeming anachronistic. He would not have been surprised to see Marco Polo himself hurrying along the Fondamenta del Vin. The people fastened Venice to the here and now. But when there were no people, it was as if the city were immune to history. Venice had the quality of an eternal ghost.

A woman with one hand paused at the apex of the bridge to look into the water, but then he saw how the light was absorbed by the dark glove on the limb that he thought had been missing, which made it seem invisible. She was moving away from the bridge, in the direction of the San Polo district, when Massimo remembered the glove in his pocket. He cast a handful of lire on to the table and burst out of the trattoria into the cold. The air was damp and settled heavily in his lungs.

By the time he was under the grand arch at the top of the bridge the woman was nowhere to be seen; she could have taken any one of the half-dozen exits away from the canal. Frustration bled through him. He glanced back to the warmth of the trattoria and saw that somebody had already taken his place at the window, was hunched over a newspaper. Angry, he stalked in the direction she had taken, rubbing at the glove in his pocket. It was an old thing. Tomorrow, no doubt, she would buy herself a new pair, thus rendering pointless this little chase of his.

Massimo walked for twenty minutes, until the fog had drawn

an ugly, persistent cough from his chest. He tugged at the collars of his coat but the damp was in him and around him now, settling on the thick black twill like dew. He heard a brief snatch of music from one of the *pensiones* but it was stolen away before he had the chance to place it. The absence of people disarmed him. During the day, this area was a hive of activity filled with *erberia* and *pescheria*, along with jewellers' shops and clothes stalls. Now it was lonely and its voice was any number of echoes. The lack of physicality, of motion, had taken away his confidence. The street names were made indistinct by the quickening mist. He had grown up in this city, and understood that part of its charm was its complication of alleyways, but never before had he felt so lost. His home had turned its back on him.

Shutters closed noisily on the night. Venice was sealing itself against the hour.

He stumbled gratefully upon the Campo San Polo where he was able to reorient himself. Eager to return to the hotel, he lingered as he heard the skitter of heels clatter through the arches toward him. She was still nearby, or somebody else was. He bit down on his compulsion to find her and hurried back to the Europa. Once there, he locked the glass doors and threw on the lobby lights.

He placed the glove behind the reception desk and checked the phone messages. There was just one, from his father, who felt well enough to take lunch with his son the following day, if the weather was fair.

In bed, Massimo allowed the creaks and sighs of the old hotel to lull him. At least here, among these well-known and much-loved sounds, he could feel at home, even if his city had shown him its inaccessible side tonight. He slept and dreamt of hands reaching out from the sacrament black waters. They would not rest until they touched him. And where they touched him, a little part of his happiness, his warmth inside, was switched off for ever.

Massimo wakened feeling hollow and feverish. He knew it was his blood-sugar levels in need of a boost, but could not resist blaming the dream on his skittishness. He wished, as was so often the case with other dreams, that he had been unable to remember it.

He took breakfast in another of the suites, white dust sheets covering the furniture and brightening the room, while also making it cold through its lack of definition. The mist had disappeared. Feeble sunlight splashed across the roofs and turned the surface of the canal into the colour of watered-down milk. Feeling better, he set the timer on the central heating to ensure that each room would be warmed for a few hours, and switched on the television.

In the night, a murder had been committed in Venice, at the *campanile* near the church of San Polo. According to the reporter, who was standing by the Palazzo Soranzo in the square, his nose red from the cold, the woman had been found just after midnight by a man walking his dog. The camera switched angles to show the crime scene, which was dominated by a white tent erected by the *carabinieri*, a number of whom were standing around with sub-machine guns hanging loose over their arms. Bystanders watched as a stretcher was shunted into an ambulance, a crimson blanket covering the body.

Shaken, Massimo switched off the bulletin and showered. He had picked up a sniffle after last night's adventure and he felt too ropy to go out. He considered calling his father to cancel lunch, but the old man did not take the air much these days; he would be looking forward to spending a little time in the sunshine with his boy.

Massimo toured the hotel, desultorily checking windows and locks. He flapped ineffectually at the pigeons that had settled on the terraces and made a mental note to buy some disinfectant and talk to Franco, the handyman, about getting some netting to drape from the roof, to prevent them nesting. With a heavy heart, he locked the hotel doors behind him. It was not so much the emptiness of the old building that got to him, but its silences. Coming back to a quiet place, that over the years had known so much bluster and happiness, was saddening in the extreme. It was a different hotel from the one his father had run. It was as if, at the time of Leopoldo's departing, its spirit had left too, perhaps clogged up with the cogs of the old-fashioned fob watch he wore in his waistcoat, or bunched in a pocket like one of his maroon silk handkerchiefs.

Massimo spotted his father easily. His beard was a white strap for his chin and he wore the only tie he owned, a dark blue knot against a badly ironed white shirt.

'Hi, pop,' he said, bending slightly to kiss the top of the old man's head. The beard was not clipped as neatly as it once had been; his hair was haphazardly oiled. He smelled of burnt toast.

'*Buon giorno*,' Leopoldo said, formally. '*Come sta?*'

Massimo ordered another glass of Prosecco for his father, despite his protestations, and a *grappa* for himself.

'You heard of the killing?' Leopoldo said, through the slewed mess of his mouth. He dabbed at the corner of it with a handkerchief every ten seconds or so. The left side of his face seemed to be sliding away from his head. It gave him a dismissive air that, Massimo suspected, pleased his father no end. He seemed distressed by the news, though.

'This morning, yes,' he replied. He could not help feeling guilty. His father's stare still had the capacity to find some speck of fault in him, even when there was none.

'A woman, they say.'

Massimo grunted.

'They say her left hand was skinned, like a rabbit.'

'I didn't know that.' Reaching for the glove in his pocket that, of course, was not there, Massimo betrayed more of his nervousness than even he expected of himself.

Leopoldo had noticed also. 'Are you all right, son?' He tried to reach out the withered nonsense of his own left hand but he could do no more than waggle it in Massimo's direction.

'I'm fine. It's the hotel. Strange to be there with nobody else around.'

'It is a good hotel. She will protect you.'

'I know, pop, I know.'

They were halfway through lunch when Massimo thought of something.

'How did you know about the hand?' he asked. 'You said it was skinned.'

'So they say.'

'Who are "they"?'

Leopoldo wiped his lips. His plate was littered with splinters of chicken bone. Much of the sauce patterned his shirt; he was having a good lunch.

'I have my friends,' he said. 'Friends all over Venice. They stay in my hotel sometimes. Maybe when they need a little help.

Polizia. I have friends there too. You don't think your papa has his contacts?'

Sadly, Massimo understood that, like his father, the only friends he could lay claim to were friends of the hotel first. They were friends by extension.

'It's nice to see you again, pop.'

'You too. We should do this more often. You should come visit me.'

'I will. I will.'

Massimo walked his father to the *vaporetto* and waved him off before deciding to investigate the murder site for himself. The crowd had dispersed since the body had been taken away, but the white tent remained, as did the *carabinieri*. Police tape sealed off the area. By day, the *campo* did not seem capable of possessing the menace it had exuded the previous night. All of its shadows had been washed clean by the sunlight.

He wanted to ask one of the policemen, or perhaps one of the louche reporters leaning against the wall smoking cigarettes, if they knew anything more about the death and whether or not Leopoldo's nugget of gossip bore any truth. Instead, he walked away. To say anything might be to incriminate himself. He could not help feeling in some small way responsible for the woman's death. If he had caught up with her, he might have been able to give her her glove; his presence alone might have been enough to dissuade her pursuer from attacking.

On the Ponte di Rialto he saw a dark cat withdrawn into the shade. His father had loved cats and had kept many at the Europa over the years. Massimo beckoned it to him but it did not come. It was only as he drew nearer that he realized it was not a cat at all. It was another glove.

Massimo did not go out that evening. He ate his dinner in the hotel kitchen and played patience in the lobby while the television murmured. He paid it no attention, but its burble was of some comfort. He thought about calling some of his old friends, people he had not seen for many years, and asking them round for drinks but he did not possess the courage. It would be too much to find that they had moved away from Venice or worse, that they had remained but did not remember him. The hotel had nailed him to this city. He might be taking care of it at the moment, but he saw now how it had more than taken care of him. He stopped dealing cards and looked up at the paintings on the walls, the worn carpet leading from the door to the reception area, the sofas under their dust sheets, the ashtrays on the fake marble tables. He suddenly despised the hotel, and the way his father had shackled him to it. He envied the old man's freedom. All of Massimo's formative years had been poured into the hotel and while it had remained robust, fashionable even, he had found himself at the doorway to his forties, his promise, his potential dwindling like the hair at his temples. Venice was like an ill-matched spouse that one gets used to, that one learns to if not love, then abide. Its waters lapped slowly at one's resolve; Massimo had been worn down by it. He had capitulated.

Evening had lost its ripe colours to the night. Faint drifts of cloud were scrapes at the bottom of a bowl of dark chocolate. A cold wind, a taste of winter, was coming in from the north, inspiring shapes among the twists of litter. Massimo sat back in his chair and reached for the bottle beneath the desk. His hand brushed against the gloves. He took two quick shots of *grappa* and picked up the telephone. His fingers remembered the number before he had fully mustered it in his thoughts. He was surprised by the readiness of this memory. *She can't still live there,* he thought, as the line burred with the ringing tone. The lights in the hotel dimmed and then grew very bright. He was about to hang up, embarrassed by this asinine plot, but he was startled into saying something when a voice leapt down the receiver at him: 'Pronto!'

Adelina Gaggio remembered him. How could she not, she had argued? Though it had been thirty years since they had last spoken at length, when they had both been at school, their conversation had been spiced and easy, as if they had never lost touch. Her voice had been a soft hand enclosing his, bringing him in from the cold.

Yes, she had eaten, but she was at a loose end tonight and would be thrilled to come and see him. She too lived in the Sestiere Castello, in Calle Dietro te Deum, and would be with him within the hour.

Massimo hurried around the lobby, stripping back the sheets to try to rouse some colour and warmth from the old building. He changed into clothes that were not so tired-looking and relieved the wine cellar of a few bottles of Bardolino. It was as he was wiping them clean and trying to remember which bunch contained the key for the dining room, where the glasses were stored, that he heard two very loud thumps above his head, as if somebody struggling to remove his shoes had managed to kick them across the room.

The spit vanished from his mouth. He had nothing in the way of a weapon, other than a broken snooker cue from the games room that had been waiting months for a repair that would never happen. He took the lower half of it, tight in his fist, and padded along the corridor to the stairs. Throwing the switches to illuminate the upper floors might scare the intruder off but the coward in Massimo could not bear to ascend in darkness. He was halfway up the second flight, the suite of rooms where the sound had come from in view, when the lights went out again, staggered, as though a finger was deliberately flicking off each set. Massimo's hand would not settle on the butt of the cue. He paused, his breath coming harder than this simple exertion ought to inspire, while his eyes accustomed themselves to the fresh dark.

A pair of pigeons had flown into a window, confused by the reflections in the glass. The electrics, old and unreliable in such a building, had fused. Hadn't they suggested their unpredictability to him downstairs just now? He clung to the possibilities like a child at the tit. But if the circuits had fused, shouldn't the lights go out as one?

There were different sets of switches. The ones he had thrown at the foot of the stairs and separate consoles for each floor. If there had been an intruder up here, then he was still up here. Where was the sense in breaking in, dashing downstairs and then killing the lights after the caretaker had gone to investigate? Massimo removed his attention from the inked-out column behind him and forced his focus to fix on the shadows ahead. Nothing moved up there that he could see, but now he could hear the slam of a window in its frame as the wind increased.

He swept up the final flight and stood at the end of the corridor. The door to room 29 was ajar. Biting down on his fear, he approached the room. He would swing first and ask questions later. The thought of violence encouraged his heart to beat faster.

Six feet shy of the door a moan slipped out of him as the gap in the doorway shrank and the door snicked softly shut.

Downstairs, the entry buzzer rasped.

The torpor of fear fell away from him like a chrysalis. Refreshed by the promise of an ally, he hurried back down the stairs and unlocked the doors. Adelina was standing hunched against the wind, a smile fading. She had taken off one of her gloves to press the buzzer. Her eyes went from his own to the makeshift cosh he brandished.

'Come in,' he said, grabbing her arm roughly.

She stiffened under his fingers. He apologized quickly and told her what was wrong.

'Call the police,' she said, as if she were explaining something simple to a child.

'I can't. I'm not sure.'

She rolled her eyes, the first expression she had shown him that he remembered from their youth. Time had bracketed her face with a kind heaviness that nevertheless had fogged his recollections of her until now. She marched past him and took the stairs two at a time. He noticed that the lights had come back on.

'Wait,' he said, and hurried after her. Despite his anger at himself, he stopped in the same place as before and watched her open the door. He saw the shadows spring back as the light went on and then noticed the counterpane on the bed diminishing, the narrowing of the watercolour on the far wall as the door swung slowly shut. He waited for her to cry out. A minute passed that felt the length of a season. If he went downstairs now, the frost would be gone from the car roofs and spring would have lent its freshness to the canals.

Adelina emerged, wiping her hands off against each other. She looked bored, as a person waiting for a bus in the rain might.

'A window had come loose,' she said simply, and brushed past him. 'Do you have something to drink?'

Massimo's attention kept returning to those hands, even after the first bottle had been consumed, when his body had relaxed into itself and his earlier panic seemed distant and foolish. They were slimmer than the rest of her body, as if they had once belonged to another woman. She used them to help shape her words, which had loosened with the drink, and their movements were accompanied with frequent laughter. It bothered him slightly that she refused to take off the left glove, but the wine was numbing him to his insecurities. It didn't matter. It didn't matter at all.

It seemed absurd to Massimo that their paths had not crossed, even by accident, in the three decades since they had shared classes at school. Since then, she had stayed in Venice for all but one of the following years, and had worked as a saleswoman for the Murano Glass Company since the mid-1990s. She had never married, but she had a teenage son, Bruno, who was currently travelling in England. 'My life now, I want to devote to animals. And then find myself a good husband. Have some happiness before they put me in my pretty little plot on San Michele.'

Towards midnight, the two bottles drained, they suddenly became aware of the passage of time. The wind had become a constant howl but Adelina declined Massimo's offer to take one of the rooms, gratis. She left with his telephone number, and promises that they would keep in touch now; that they had no excuses not to. Her kiss on his cheek stayed with him, like a line of poetry, or a new song that feels like an old favourite by the time it ends. He fell asleep in the chair.

When he wakened, he thought it was morning, but the light was the artificial spill coming from the brackets on the walls. His mouth was sticky with wine. He saw from his watch that he had been asleep a matter of two hours. It was cold, the heating having turned itself off, but that was not what had roused him.

Somebody had screamed. The wind was dead, so he couldn't blame the sound on that. He rose from his seat and switched off the lights in order to see better when he pressed his face to the window. Two hours was more than enough time for Adelina to have arrived home safely; nevertheless, unease spread like indigestion through his chest.

On the ground six feet away from the doors, a suede glove the colour of the cement it rested on flapped at him, as if agitating for help. There were no blocks of light in any of the other buildings that he could see, which suggested that he had imagined it after all. But another scream, this one deeper and somehow more liquid, stitched by frantic gasps, cut through his doubt. He closed his eyes and pressed his forehead against the cold glass, as if its chill might numb the distressed part of his mind. What could he do to help? The scream had been severed and originated from the maze of streets off the main drag. He could spend half an hour looking for its author, enough time for a body to be dumped in the canal and a killer to become a ghost. He might have opened the doors anyway, and tried his best, if it hadn't been for the grate of heels on the pavement. He moved back from the window into the sanctity of shadow and watched as a shadow lengthened in the frame afforded by the Europa's entrance. Something in its deportment rattled him. The shadow seemed too stiff, too jerky, as if the joints of the owner's body had been fused together. It became, in the second or two when he realized the figure was going to pass into view, dreadfully important that he did not look at who it was, regardless of the fact that the other would not be able to see him in the gloom. He turned away, like a child from a bad dream, and sensed eyes burn into him, scorching him away layer by layer. He felt raped by their awful scrutiny.

An age later, he craned his neck and saw that the figure had gone. The glove, though, remained on the ground, fingers curled skyward, like a dead animal that had withdrawn and hardened. Was it the woman he had seen the day before? He could almost believe that her presence had given the glove that solidified, bereft appearance and was grateful that he had lost her on the bridge that night. Because for the first time, he suspected that *she* had been tracking *him*.

Signorina Sinistra. Massimo heard the name a dozen times the next morning in the market place as he shopped for vegetables and fruit. 'She takes the skin from the left hand', a voice at his shoulder said as he was testing the ripeness of an avocado. Another, queueing behind him while he took coffee in a bar, confided: 'They found another body this morning. Near the Arsenale. A man this time. His hand, oh my Lord, his hand!'

Another body. That made two. A little premature, he thought, to start giving the killer a moniker, providing a myth before its time. And how could they be certain it was a female murderer? But then he thought of the footsteps outside the hotel and he shuddered. He must hurry back and burn the gloves that he was keeping under the desk. God only knew why he had bothered to collect them in the first place. They had brought him nothing but trouble. He suspected that his complicity in the murders had begun with the recovery of the first one, as if that simple act had been some kind of secret signal, a green light of sorts.

A police car was parked outside the hotel when he returned. A sombre-faced man with doughy jowls standing by the passenger door tried to smile at him but the curve of his lips only served to turn his mouth into a flat line. Massimo's heart lurched when he saw that the entrance doors to the hotel were open. Two police-men were standing inside.

Massimo said, 'I'm sure I locked that this morning.'

The sombre-faced man, who introduced himself as Inspector Scarpa, shrugged. 'It was for the best that we should stay until you returned. You are Leopoldo's son, yes?'

Massimo nodded. Inspector Scarpa aped him. 'My first job,' he said, 'when I joined the police, was here, at the Europa.'

'Oh?' Massimo moved away from the other man, into the warmth of the lobby. The two policemen looked at him as if he were trespassing. He saw a third policeman now, standing behind the reception desk with his hands clasped behind his back, watching the television screen. A football match was playing.

'Yes,' said the inspector, following Massimo into the hotel. 'A most terrible case. Your father must remember it. Some people staying here. Two men. They tortured a woman – a young girl, in fact – in one of the rooms. But they escaped.'

'I don't believe you,' Massimo spat, horrified that his hotel could be guilty of such a secret. His father had never mentioned such a thing to him.

'You must have been no more than a boy. It was in all the newspapers. Twenty-eight years ago. A big, big story. The girl died, as I recall. A complication. She developed infections. Nasty business.' He shrugged again, as if it was a game.

The policeman had grown bored of the football match and was picking through the coffee cups and notepads on the desk.

'Do you have a search warrant?' Massimo barked, and then smiled awkwardly at the inspector, hoping he would take the outburst as a joke. Inspector Scarpa's eyebrows had raised.

Now the policeman had seen something; Massimo could tell from his expression what it was.

'Well, thank you for looking after my hotel. I'm grateful to you. I'll make sure I'm more careful in future.'

'Careful in what way?' Inspector Scarpa said as the officer lifted the gloves into view and all eyes turned on Massimo.

He asked for a glass of *grappa* and they brought him one. The inspector looked like an indulgent uncle who has caught his nephew watching a pornographic film. The face seemed born to police work. *Tell me all about it,* was its message. It was big enough and friendly enough to absorb lots of information. The inspector was a sponge.

Massimo told them everything, right up until the previous night when he had seen the woman in the street. The only details he changed concerned the checking of the second-floor room: he could not admit to Adelina searching it for him. The inspector had made a barely imperceptible gesture with his hand when he mentioned Adelina's name and thereafter his concentration was qualified with a slight frown, as if he couldn't quite understand Massimo's dialect.

When he was finished, Inspector Scarpa said, 'Can we see the room?'

Massimo swallowed the last drops of the *grappa*; his 'Sorry?' was strangled slightly by its fire.

'The room you checked. Where you heard the intruder.'

'There was no intruder. Just a window that wasn't locked properly.'

'Can we see it?'

'I don't see why this is so—'

Inspector Scarpa held up his hand. In a soporific voice, he said: '*Per favore,* Signore Poerio. Please. Indulge us. We shan't take up too much more of your precious time.'

The first sting of sarcasm. It hit home more acutely, coming from Inspector Scarpa's affable mouth. They suspected him of something. *Well, let them.*

'This way,' he said, brusquely, and set off for the stairs without waiting for them to gather. On the second floor he slipped the bunch of keys from his waistband and hunted for the relevant master. As he did so, the inspector ran his fingers along the slender knuckles of his opposing hand, eliciting cracks from the joints with little tweaks and twists. The sounds were unbearably loud in the corridor. Massimo dropped his keys. Nobody seemed to mind.

'Adelina, you say?' muttered the inspector, in a faraway voice. 'Adelina?'

'Yes. What of it?'

Another shrug. 'It's familiar. It's familiar to me.'

Massimo opened the door and stood back to let the other four men into the room. In the mirror, before he could enter, he saw them looking down at a body. The crimson rug that it lay on had once been white. He reacted more quickly than he believed he could have, closing the door and locking it before the police had a chance to stop him. Fists pounded the door, yet still there was no rage in Scarpa's voice. He sounded saddened. Perhaps he and his father had been closer than he let on. What was it pop had said? *You don't think your papa has his contacts?*

Massimo hurried downstairs and pulled on his coat. His mind would not stand still long enough for him to formulate a plan. He should pack a suitcase. He should contact Adelina. Perhaps he should steal the police car.

Instead, he locked the hotel doors behind him and scurried west along the canal. Once past the Piazza San Marco he paused on the Calle Vallaresso, listening for sirens. In Harry's Bar, he pushed past the lunchtime gathering and found a telephone. He dialled and let it ring for a full three minutes but his father did not answer. Then he tried Adelina's number. An Englishman answered.

'Adelina,' Massimo said. 'I need to speak to Adelina.'

'*Non capisco, amico.*' His Italian was frustratingly poor.

'Adelina Gaggio. She lives there. Can you get her for me?'

'Non. Nobody here by that name.'

Massimo had punched in the correct number. There was no doubt. 'Please. You have to—'

'Hey? You deaf? I said nobody here called Adelina. *Testa di cazzo.*'

Massimo slammed the receiver down. He could go there, to the street Adelina had mentioned, but without an address it could take hours to find her and even then she might not be in. She might be at work.

The glass company.

Excitedly, he dialled 12 and obtained the number from directory services. When he got through to the receptionist at Murano her contact list did not contain any reference to Adelina Gaggio.

'Has she been with us long?' the receptionist tried. 'She might not be on our list if she joined us recently.'

'Five years,' Massimo said. A white, abject face stared at him from behind the bar. He was about to order a bellini from it when he realised it was his own, reflected in a mirror. 'At least five years.'

'I'm sorry.'

'She must—'

'Very sorry, sir.'

What now? He struggled to keep himself from crying out. He had nobody to go to, other than the police, and they would not be patient with a man who had locked some of their colleagues in a room with a woman he had ostensibly murdered. But surely they would see that his panic was inspired by innocence. If he had killed somebody in his own hotel, would he not take pains to dispose of the body, rather than blithely stroll around Venice having left the main entrance unlocked?

How could Adelina have lied to him? The coolness of the woman as she came out of the room. How could it be that he had called her after twenty years only to find that he had invited a deranged killer onto the premises? The police would not believe him if he told them this, but it was all he had to offer.

He dialled 112 and was patched through. He tried to explain but every time he finished a sentence, the police operator would ask him to expand on every iota of information or ask him to spell the names he mentioned. Then the operator would fudge the spelling and get him to repeat it.

'Adelina,' the voice buzzed. 'What's that? A-D-A . . . ?'

It dawned on him then, and he replaced the receiver gently. He glanced out of the front windows but how could he chance it? Then again, they would have any rear exit covered too. They would not expect him to leave by the front door.

He saw a group of suits standing to return to the office and he hurried after them, catching up with them, and purposefully barging into a middle-aged woman. He put on a big smile and apologized profusely as they filtered on to the street. He put his hand on her arm. There was wine in her. She was happy and forgiving. She covered his hand with her own and said it was perfectly all right. He asked her what she had had for lunch. He asked her the name of the perfume she was wearing. In this manner he passed along the street with his new friends. He didn't look back until he was in sight of a safe alleyway he could move down. Only now were the police cars drawing up outside Harry's Bar. He ran.

This time his father did pick up the phone. But he heard a click, as soft as a pair of dentures nestling together, and he understood that what ought to have been the safest house of all was now the most dangerous.

'I'm okay, pop,' he said. 'I'm all right.'

'Massimo,' his father said. 'I'm sorry.'

Massimo killed the connection, hoping that even those few seconds had not been enough to expose him to the authorities a second time. He had been running for days, it seemed, but it could only have been a matter of hours. The sunlight was failing now. The light on the canals was turning the colour of overripe peaches. From the east, a wedge of flat, grey sky was closing upon Venice like the metal lid to a box of secrets. Freezing air ran before it, as though the weather too was trying to escape the city's confused sprawl.

His thoughts turned to the inspector, who had seemed so understanding, yet had contained an edge as hard as the coming cold snap. The policeman's past seemed as caught up in the Europa as his own. He wished he had had the time to ask his father about the incident that Scarpa had mentioned. He would have been a ten-year-old when the hotel had provided a torture chamber for some of its guests. He couldn't remember a thing about it, but then he would have been shielded from such an appalling event. He thought of the way his father had said sorry and did not like what his mind came up with.

With no better task to turn to, Massimo caught a *vaporetto* to San Tomà and hurried the two hundred metres or so to the Campo dei Frari. The woman at the reception desk of the Archivio di Stato looked as impenetrable as a bad clam but she was sympathetic to his needs, even if the five-hour window for requesting materials had lapsed.

It didn't take long. Once he had been shown how to access the microfiches and blow them up on the viewer, it was simply a matter of trawling through the front pages of *Il Gazzettino* from 1973. A photograph of the Europa's exterior halted him before any of the words did. The headline took up much of the page but this had no impact on him once he had noticed the small photograph at the foot of the page, the torture victim who had died. He didn't need to read the caption to know it was the woman he had entertained in his hotel the previous night.

It was there, in black and white, and his brain had sucked it in even though he had averted his eyes, fearful of an image decades old. Yet he wasn't happy. They could have got it wrong. They could have mixed up her picture. They *must* have got it wrong. The alternatives were too outlandish to swallow.

Everywhere he looked, there were gloves lying companionless. In the canal, sitting on windowsills, hunched on the ground near lamp-posts and benches. His panic mounted as he counted them. Nothing looked quite so dismal as a discarded glove. Did each one signify a terrible death in the city? Just because two bodies three bodies had been found didn't mean that more were lying in wait, stretching back to a time when the killer had set out on her spree.

Snow had begun to fall on the city. Already the narrow streets and uneven roofs were dusted with white while the canal absorbed the flakes and remained black. In some areas, where the light was poor, the canals escaped from view completely. They became plumbless moats that one could look into without hope of ever finding an end.

At Fondamente Nuove he persuaded a *vaporetto* pilot preparing to go home to take him to San Michele. The promise of ten thousand lire if he waited to bring him back was enough of a lure. On the short journey, Massimo watched the waters creaming at the bow while Venice fell away behind them. A series of lights came on around the Sacca della Miscricordia, as though people had opened their windows to watch his journey.

The island loomed out of the dark. More and more, his father had made references to this place, with its pretty cypress trees. It would be expensive to find him a plot here, but it seemed, even through Leopoldo's oblique language, that his heart was set upon it.

Even from here, in such unsociable weather, Massimo could smell the perfume of cut flowers on the graves. As the *vaporetto* drew up alongside, the white stone of the Convento di San Michele seemed lambent in the murk.

'You know the cemetery is closed, Signor?'

'Just wait for me,' Massimo ordered, and then: 'Do you have a torch?'

The pilot sat back and rummaged for cigarettes in his jacket pocket. 'Yes. And I might allow you to hire it, if you ask me nice.'

It was not such a difficult cemetery to break into. Beyond the entry archway, the cloisters marked the beginning of the grave-yard proper. But Massimo ignored it. Adelina might well have been buried here, but she was not here now. The island could not take bodies indefinitely. Having gorged on the dead for so long, it had reached bursting point. Now the bones of the resting were lifted every ten years or so for another final journey to an ossuary on the mainland, in order to make way for the next wave of cadavers. If Adelina's name was to be found here, it would be on a plaque, not a headstone. Massimo trained the feeble torchlight on the neatly arranged plinths, readying himself for a long night's hunt. At least they were easier to read than the weathered slabs.

The snow that had begun to fall on the heart of the city found its way out here after half an hour. Massimo blew on his hands to keep them warm and tried to ignore the impatient hoots from the *vaporetto* horn. The pilot was going nowhere; his pockets would remain empty if he did.

He covered the cemetery in a slow strafing movement, his hopes lifting with every plaque that did not bear her name. Perhaps, simply, he was going mad after all. When he did not find her here, he could return to the mainland and find it had returned to normal. All he needed was this restorative jaunt to pick clean the tired crevices of his mind.

But then, of course, of course: *Adelina Gaggio, 1963–1973.* The characters were chiselled in marble as cleanly as if they had been formed that very afternoon.

He found himself back at the water's edge with no recollection of climbing over the monastery wall. The pilot had turned his back on him and was eyeing the wink of lights across the Venice coastline. It was a pale comfort to Massimo, but the longer he stared at his home, the more he wanted to be back there. He would turn himself in and try to help the police as best he could, even if it meant being charged for obstruction, or worse.

'Start the engine, friend,' he said, as he clambered on board. The pilot did not move. A white glove lay on one of the seats. Massimo struggled to piece together a sudden scattering of jigsaw pieces in his thoughts, but none of the pieces would fit: they seemed to be from different puzzles and he knew they could not match the complete picture he was striving for.

'I don't—' he began, but his words were coated with too much breath, too much saliva to complete his sentence.

He touched the pilot and watched as he toppled back in his seat. Massimo recoiled as he saw the pilot grinning at him. But the grin was too low on his face, and too wide and wet.

The glove was nothing of the sort. Or rather, it could only have fitted the pilot's hand. It had been skinned with a surgeon's precision.

'It doesn't fit,' she said. 'None of them ever fit.'

She solidified at his side, as if structuring herself from the particles of dark that helped to make up what the night was. Almost immediately it was as if she had always been there.

'Don't worry, Mass,' she whispered. 'When you called me, why, it wasn't you calling me at all. It was the hotel. It was the Europa, bringing me home. Our true resting place is never the final resting place, is it? It's where we drop. That's what takes our essence. The rug in the room you were so afraid of. That has the flavour of my final breath in its weave. It's an *always* place. More real, I suppose, than our city, trapped in a yesterday none of us believe in any more. More real than I ever was.'

He was paralysed with fear and doubt.

He saw her hand come free of the glove, which she dropped over the side of the boat. What he thought at first to be tattoos of some kind, a weird graffiti that sprawled across her flesh, revealed itself to him as the veins and sinews of a severely damaged hand. The fingernails were warped with the aftershock of septicaemia. They looked as thick and twisted as ram's horn.

'They sliced my fingers as though they were bits of meat, Mass. They stuck splinters under my fingernails and set fire to my palm. They skinned me. For fun. For *fun*. And your father took money for it. Hush money. He pocketed his bundle of notes and at the centre of them was my pain, wrapped so very tightly.'

Massimo was weeping now. 'I didn't know,' he said. 'You were my friend. I didn't know.'

She gently rubbed his neck with her grotesque claw. 'You saw what was happening. But you forgot. I called to you. The men shouted at you to go away. And your father gave you money to forget. But you saw all right. Every cry for help since, haven't you chosen to ignore it? Haven't you always turned your back and thought, "Well, what can I do?" You're like this city, Mass. You close your eyes to ugliness. And the blood that runs through you is as cold as the water in those canals.'

He had slumped against her. So exhausted was he, and so enchanted by the Venetian lights, that he failed to notice what her hand was doing until it was withdrawing.

She said, 'Your hand, when you held mine, Mass – didn't they fit together so perfectly?'

His flailing mind saw that her hand, with its five gnarled horns, was sheathed by a new glove. A really quite beautiful glove that waxed and waned in his eyes like the beat of water in the canals. It was a deep, glistening red. He was going to ask her what material produced such a fine colour, but he was too tired to speak. The last thing he saw before he became indivisible from the night was the flash of a cleaver as she pulled back the deep corners of her cloak. And even that was beautiful.

TANITH LEE

Where All Things Perish

TANITH LEE BEGAN WRITING at the age of nine, and after various employment, she became a full-time writer in 1975, when DAW Books published her novel *The Birthgrave*. Since then she has written and published around sixty novels, nine collections and over 200 short stories. She has also scripted two episodes of the cult BBC-TV series *Blakes 7*, and has twice won the World Fantasy Award for short fiction and was awarded the British Fantasy Society's August Derleth Award in 1980 for her novel *Death's Master*.

In 1998 she was shortlisted for the Guardian Award for Children's Fiction for her novel *Law of the Wolf Tower*, the first volume in the 'Claidi Journal' series. More recently, Tor Books has published *White as Snow*, the author's retelling of the Snow White story, while Overlook Press has issued *A Bed of Earth* and *Venus Preserved*, the third and fourth volumes respectively in the 'Secret Books of Paradys' series. She is currently working on a sequel to her novel *The Silver Metal Lover* for Bantam Books.

'Late one night, my partner John Kaiine and I fell to talking about ghost stories and other sinister matters,' recalls the author. 'Outside the by-then-darkened room, leaves were appearing on the trees and seeming to form strange shapes and faces. The idea of looking from windows took hold of us. Then, as is his wont, John produced an idea so perfect for a story that the usual scramble was on to grab a notebook. The spine of the work supplied, the characters began to arrive on their own, as is *their* wont.

'The story was almost entirely there, even its title, which came to me at once. Then I had only to think of a remedy. I went to sleep with my head well-filled by the tale, and woke up with the solution to everything shining darkly there on some efficient desk in my brain.'

I

It was glimpsing Polleto again, between trains, at that hotel in Vymart, which made me remember. Which, in its way, is quite curious, for how could I ever have forgotten such a thing? So impossible and *terrible* a thing. And yet, the human mind is a strange mechanism, and the human heart far stranger. Sometimes the most trivial events haunt our waking hours, even our dreams, for years after they have happened. While episodes of incredible moment, perhaps only because they have been marked indelibly upon us, stand back in the shadows, mute and motionless, until some chance ray of mental light discovers them. And then they are there, burning bright, towering and undismissable once more. At such times one knows they are more than memories, more than the mere furniture of the brain. Rather, they have become part of it, a part of oneself.

'What is it, Frederick, that you are staring at?'

'That little man at the table over there.'

'What, that little clerkish chap in the dusty overcoat? He hardly looks worthy of your curiosity. Of anyone's, come to that.'

'No, he probably isn't. A very ordinary fellow, the sort you wouldn't recall, I suppose, in the normal way of things.'

'I should think not. But you do?'

'Well, as it happens, he was resident in a place where something very odd once happened to me. And not to myself alone.'

'He was involved in this odd thing? He looks blameless to the point of criminality.'

'I imagine that he is. No, he was simply living there at the time, had been there two or three years, if I remember correctly. I met him once, in the street, and my aunt introduced him as a Mr

Polleto. We exchanged civilities, that was all. He had the faintest trace of a foreign accent, but otherwise seemed a nonentity. My aunt confessed they had all been very disappointed in him because, learning his name before his arrival, they'd hoped for some sort of flamboyant Italian theatrical gentleman, or something of the sort.'

'He looks more like a grocer.'

'My aunt's words exactly. Those were the probable facts, too, I believe. He'd been a shopkeeper, but had come into some funds through a legacy. He bought a house in Steepleford, which was where I was visiting my aunt.'

'This is a remarkably dull story, Frederick.'

'Yes.' I hesitated then. I added, 'The *other* story isn't, I can assure you.'

'The story which you recollect only since you caught sight of your Mr Polleto? Well, are you going to blab? We have four long hours before the Wassenhaur train. Let's refresh our glasses, and then you can tell me your tale.'

'Perhaps not.'

'Oh, come, this is too flirtatious. What have you been doing all this while but trying to engage my attention in it?'

'I protest.'

But the brandy bottle intervened. And presently, sitting on that sunny terrace of the Hotel Alpius, I recounted to my friend and travelling companion the story which I will now relate. That was the first time I ever told it to anyone. And this, now, I trust, will be the last.

II

The modest town of Steepleford had some slight notoriety in the eighteenth century, when it was one of the centres of a cult known as the Lilyites. These people believed so absolutely in the teachings of Christ, and acted upon them so unswervingly, that they soon turned the entire Christian church against them. There were a few hangings and some riots, as is often the way in these cases, until at last the cult lost both dedication and adherents, and ebbed away. Even so, through the succeeding years (from about 1750 to 1783), now and then some murmur might be heard of the Lilyites. Being, however, still generally feared and loathed for their extreme habits, they were soon rooted out and disposed of, one way or another. The last hint of the cult seemed to surface, nevertheless, in sleepy Steepleford. During the July of 1783, one Josebaar Hawkins was harangued in Market Square for holding a secret meeting of seventeen persons, at which they had, allegedly, sworn to slough their worldly goods and to love all men as themselves, in the celebrated Lilyite manner.

At his impromptu trial, Hawkins either denied all this, or ably recanted. He was said to have laughed heartily at the notion of giving up his fine house, which was the product of successful dealings in the textile industry and which stood to the side of Salter's Lane in its own grounds. He asked, it seems, if the worthies now questioning him thought that he would also abandon his new and beautiful young wife, who went by the unusual name of Amber Maria, or drag her with him in the Lilyite fashion, shoeless and penniless, about the countryside.

Hawkins was presently acquitted of belonging to the sect. No others were even interviewed upon the matter. Thereafter no more is heard, in the annals of Steepleford, of the Lilyites, but there is one more mention of Hawkins and his wife. This record states that in 1788, Amber Maria, being then twenty years of age, (which must have made her fifteen or less at her wedding), was taken ill and died within a month. Hawkins, not wishing to part from her even dead, obtained sanction for her burial in the grounds of his house.

All this, though possibly of local interest in Steepleford, where as a rule a horse casting its shoe in the street might cause great excitement, is of small apparent value on the slate of the world. Yet I must myself now add that even in my own short and irregular visits to the town, I had been, perhaps inattentively, aware of a strangeness that somehow attached itself to the Hawkins house, which still stood to the side of Salter's Lane.

The Lane ran up from Market Gate Street. It was a long and winding track, with fields at first on both sides, leading in turn to thick woodland that in places was ancient – great green oaks and mighty chestnuts and beeches, some over two hundred years of age. I can confirm from walks I have taken that there exist, or existed, areas in these woods which seemed old nearly as civilization, and when an elderly country fellow once pointed out to me a group of trees that had, he said, stood as saplings in the reign of King John, I more than half believed him. But this, of course, may be attributable merely to an imaginative man's fancy.

Some two miles up its length, Salter's Lane takes a sharp turn toward the London Road. At this juncture stands the house of Josebaar Hawkins.

It was built in the flat-faced style of those times, with tall, comfit-box-framed windows and a couple of impressive chimneys like towers, behind a high brick wall. Although lavish enough for a cloth merchant and his wife, the 'grounds' were not vast, more gardens, and by the time I first happened on the place these had become overgrown to a wilderness. Even so, one might make out sections of brickwork, and the chimney tops, above the trees.

Having found it, I asked my aunt about the house, idly enough I am sure. She replied, also idly, that it was some architectural monstrosity a century out of date, standing always shut up and empty, since no one would either buy it or pull it down. Perhaps I asked her even then why no one lived there. I know I did ask at some adjacent point, for I retain her answer. She replied, 'Oh, there's some story, dear boy, that a man bricked up his wife alive in a room there. She belonged to some wild sect or other, with which he lost patience. But she had, I think, an interesting name . . . now what can that have been?' My aunt then seemed to mislay the topic. However, a few hours, or it may have been days, later, she presented me, after dinner one night, with a musty thick volume from her library. 'I have marked the place.'

'The place of what, pray?' I inquired.

'The section that concerns the house of Josebaar Hawkins.'

I was baffled enough, not then knowing the name, to sit down at once in the smoking room and read the passage indicated. So it was that I learned of the Lilyites, of whom also I had never heard anything until then, and of Hawkins and his house off Salter's Lane. Included in the piece was the account from which I have excerpted my own note above on Hawkins's impromptu 'trial'. It also contained a portion quoted from Steepleford's parish register, with records of both the marriage and the death of Amber Maria Hawkins. This was followed by the notice of her burial in the grounds of the house, which had been overseen both by the priest and by certain officers of the town. Then my aunt's book, having set history fair and straight, proceeded, in the way of such tomes, to undermine it.

According to this treatise, Hawkins, at first an enraptured husband, had come suddenly and utterly to think his wife an evil witch. Growing afraid of her, he tricked her to an attic room of the house and here succeeded in locking her in. Thereafter he had both the door and the window bricked up by men who, being sworn in on the scheme with him, turned blind eyes and deaf ears to her screams and cries for pity. My aunt's book was in small doubt that the priest and the officers who later pretended to have certified Amber Maria's death and conducted her burial were accomplices in this hideous and extraordinary act. (I have to say that, perusing this, some memory did vaguely stir in me, but it was of so incoherent, slight and indeed uncheerful a nature, having to do, I thought, with a children's rhyme of the locale, that I did not search after it at all diligently.)

As I have already remarked, I seldom then visited Steepleford. On that visit I may have offered some comment on my reading, or my aunt may have done. I fail to recollect. Certainly the rest of my visit was soon over, nor, having gone away, did I return there for more than a year, and during my next dutiful brief holiday I remember nothing seen or said of the house in Salter's Lane.

But now I come to my next *relevant* visit, which occurred almost three years after those I have just described.

I had been in Greece for ten months and had come back full of the spirit of that place, thinking to find England dull and drab. But it was May, and a nice May, too, and by the time the train stopped at the Halt, I had decided to walk the rest of the way to the town through the woods and fields. So, inevitably, I found myself, just past midday, on the winding path of Salter's Lane. It was the most perfect of afternoons. The sky was that clear milky blue that certain poets compare (quite wrongly, to my mind) with the eyes of children. Among the oaks that clasped the track, green piled on green, wild flowers had set fire to the hedges and the grass, and sunlight festooned everything with shining jewels. Birds sang in a storm, and my heart lifted high. *What is Greece to this?* thought I, staring off between breaks in the trees at luminous glades, steeped in the most elder shadows. *Why, this might* be *Greece, in her morning.*

And then, between one step and another, there fell the strangest thing, which I could and can only describe as a sudden quietness; less silence than absence. I stopped and looked about, still smiling, thinking the world of nature had fallen prone, as is its wont, to some threat or fascination too small or obscure for human eye or mind to note. I waited patiently, too, for the lovely rain of birdsong to scatter down on me once more. It did not come.

Then, and how curious it sounded to me, as if I had never before heard such a thing, I picked up the song of a blackbird – but it seemed miles off up the Lane, the way I had come. And precisely at that moment, turning again, I saw something of a dull, dry red that thrust between the leaves. At once I knew it for a chimney of the Hawkins house.

I was taken aback. Imaginative as I freely admit I am, I would not say that I was especially superstitious. But something now disturbed me, and that very much. Not being able to divine what it was, beyond the presence of that wry old house, discomposed me further.

Accordingly, I stared at the house, right at it, and, crossing over the Lane, gazed up the outer wall over which the vines and ivies hung so thickly. What an ugly house it was, I thought, and no mistake. Even its windows of filthy glass, largely overgrown by creeper, were ugly. While that window there, above, was the ugliest of all, an absolute eyesore, stuck on at quite the wrong architectural moment.

While I was thinking this and standing there, staring so feverishly and insolently, the childish rhyme came back into my head with no warning, from out of some store cupboard of the brain. And with it a host of tiny bits and pieces that, over the years of my visits here, and all unconsidered, I had apparently garnered. I heard my aunt say again how a woman had been bricked up in 'that house', and I heard a friend of my aunt's, a titled lady I barely knew, saying once again, as she must have done years before: 'Oh, the peasantry won't go by the place after dark. No, it's a fact. They all go out of their way by Joiner's Crossing. And this, mark you, because of a tale more than a hundred years old.'

And the rhyme? I had doubtless heard children singing it in play, in the streets and yards of Steepleford, and maybe they still do so, although I wonder if they do. I will set it down, for having remembered it, I have never since forgotten.

> *She looks through water,*
> *She looks through air,*
> *She leaps at the moon*
> *And she looks in.*
>
> *Give her silver,*
> *Give her gold,*
> *And bind her eyes*
> *With a brick and a pin.*

'Aunt Alice,' I said to her that evening, when we were pursuing some sherry before the meal, 'I want to tell you about something I saw on my walk today, coming here to the town.'

Pleased to see me, she turned to me a willing, expectant face, but no sooner did I mention the house in Salter's Lane than she laughed.

'Dear boy, I shall have to think you obsessed by the place. Are you intending to buy it? I should certainly be delighted to have you live in the town, but not in such a miserable property.'

I replied, rather irritably, that nothing was further from my desires. Looking rather crushed, she sought to make amends. 'I'm sorry, Frederick. I am sure that London is more suited to your temperament than such a dreary backwater as Steepleford.' After which much of the evening was spent in my praising Steepleford and herself, for I felt ashamed of my bad temper. When I was a boy, this aunt had been very kind to me, and deserved far better of me than three-yearly visits laced with petty ill humour.

By ten o'clock we were friends again and playing cards, and so I reintroduced my topic. Although I admit I stuck strictly to the facts as I saw them, omitting all the other sensations I have outlined.

'The oddest thing, Aunt, is that I could swear the window that I saw had not been there previously. It was very high up, almost into the roof, rather small, yet somehow extremely noticeable. Although I have only once – to my recollection – looked at the house before, yet I thought I remembered it quite well, and I truly believe there never was a window in that position – however fantastic this may sound.'

As women will, my aunt then said something damningly practical. 'So many of the house windows there are closed up with ivy and creeper. Could some of this overgrowth simply have fallen away, and so revealed the casement you speak of?'

Such a banal solution had not occurred to me. I agreed that she was probably correct. To myself I said that I must put up with the necessary boredom of my visit, and not try preposterously to dress it up with invented supernatural flights.

The following morning, I penitently accompanied my aunt on her round of social calls. By midday, my face had set like cement in a polite smile, and thus, as we crossed Market Gate Street, I found myself beaming at a small, nondescript man in unostentatious dress who had touched his hat to us.

'Ah, Mr Polleto,' said my aunt, magnanimous to a fault. 'What fine weather we are having.'

Mr Polleto conceded that we were. He had a flat dusty voice, old even beyond his bent and well-aged appearance. In it my ears caught just the trace of some foreignness. Then I found myself introduced, and not standing on ceremony, as my aunt had not, I shook hands with him. What a hand he had! It was neither cold nor hot, not damp, but rather dry – it did not have much strength in it, certainly, yet nor was it a weak hand. But an uncomfortable hand it was. It did not seem to *fit* in mine, and I sensed it would not fit in anyone's.

'Mr Polleto has resided in the town for quite three years now, I believe,' said my aunt, when we had parted from him. She then told me of the general disappointment that he had not lived up to his name. 'He has the cottage by the old tiltyard.'

But I was not interested in Mr Polleto and his indescribable handshake. His face I had already mislaid, for he was one of those men who are eternally unmemorable, or seem so – for if ever seen again, somehow they are known at once, as I have already demonstrated, and later must demonstrate further.

However, now I wanted my lunch, and was dismayed to find my aunt was leading me to yet another doorstep. I rallied rather feebly. 'And which lady is this, Aunt Alice?'

'No lady, Frederick. This is the house of our local scholar. I have some purchases to make and will leave you here, with Mr Farbody, who has written and published pamphlets.'

'Indeed,' said I. But just then the maid let me in, and presently I was taking a glass of very drinkable Madeira in a sunlit library with Mr Farbody, who had at once addressed me thus: 'My good sir, I understand you are interested in the history of the Hawkins house.'

'Well, it is a curious tale,' Farbody continued, requiring little prompting from me. 'Did you know that the farmhands here-abouts, and workers and their families in the town, have kept up a tradition that the spot is cursed?'

'I remember someone saying that people refuse to go along Salter's Lane by night.'

'Well, that, of course, isn't always to be avoided, but they make a to-do about it. The thing is, it seems, not to *look* at the building. I've heard of girls, if they are due to be married, still binding their eyes with a scarf and having to be led, should they need to pass the house even in daylight.'

'And all this because Amber Maria Hawkins was thought a witch?'

'Ah, she *was* a witch, if the tales may be believed,' and here Farbody winked at me. 'She could see treasure in the ground, for one thing. No one knows her origins. Josebaar said he came across her one day in the woods. She was probably a gypsy girl, but all alone, bright-haired and straying with her arms full of wild flowers. He took a fancy for her, and perhaps she for him; it seems so – or else she liked the idea of his status in the town. He had already made some money and his family was an old one. And if she was a gypsy or itinerant, homeless and without kin, all that may have appealed to her, do you see. So there and then she is supposed to have said to him, "You may sport with me, and I will let you. Or you may marry me and I will make you rich." And he said, "How might that be, seeing you are in rags?' To which Amber Maria replied simply, "I will bring you silver and gold."'

At this, the rhyme came into my head again and I interrupted. 'I thought it was she who was to have the gold and silver?'

Farbody smiled, and lit his pipe. 'It does seem she could have been rich on her own account for sure, if she'd cared to be, for the next thing she did was point at the ground under a tree and say to Hawkins, "Dig there, and you will find a large store of coins." Even money likes money, so he dug in the ground, and – *hey presto!* – found a box of gold pieces, deep down and undisturbed for a century. When he asked her how she knew where to dig, she shrugged and said, "I saw them." Nor did Amber do this only once, but several times, apparently. And in the same way she could find items that had been lost. And once she is supposed to have seen a sheep that had fallen down a deep well, which animal was then got out alive. She could see, you understand, *through* things. Through the earth, through stone, and through certain other natural materials – though not, I think, through metal, which may account for the metals in the rhyme.'

'What does the rhyme mean?' I asked him.

'It's essentially to do with binding her, shutting her up where she couldn't do harm. You see, Hawkins was besotted with her some while, but then he began to be afraid of her. He's said to have told the priest, "She will sit quiet all day and only look at me." When the priest said that many a man would be thankful for such a placid, adoring wife, Hawkins replied she did not look *on* him, but *into* him. And he said that once he had told her hotly to leave off, for he was a sinner like all men, and if she would keep on staring in such a way, she would see his soul and mortal corruption. To which she gave this strange response: "Men say always they are wretched and tainted by flesh and sin, but in all men there is such goodness and beauty, as in the earth and all living things, that it is to me like my food and drink, and I can never be tired of having it."'

When Farbody told me this, there in that warm and pleasant room, the sunlight on the books and the domestic pipe-smoke mild in the air, the hair rose on my neck.

'In heaven's name,' I said.

The scholar smiled again, pleased with himself and with the peculiar tale he had memorized so well. 'Yes, something in that gives you a turn, doesn't it? She seems to be speaking so charmingly, innocently, and it makes the skin creep. I can tell you, sir, I read this story first when I was a boy of eleven, and I was awake nights after, until my mother scolded some reason into me and hid the volume I'd been reading. Which may explain,' he added amiably, 'my lifelong quest for such hidden trifles of knowledge.'

Farbody then went on with the narrative.

Josebaar turned quickly from love to shrinking horror at his young wife. At first he tried to arrange a separation between them, but she would have none of this; then he had thoughts of escaping her by going overseas. But she guessed his course, and is said to have assured him she loved him too well to let him go. If he must leave, she would find and follow him, and he did not doubt that she had the powers to do so.

In the end, Hawkins, pale and harried, went to his friends, among whom was the priest, and confessed he was in such fear that he should not 'soon remain alive, since the woman eats me up from the inside out'. By what grim stages the others came round to Hawkins's state of mind, Farbody said one might only conjecture, and similarly if any money was involved in it. 'But those were ignorant and superstitious times,' he reflected. 'Alas, they are still.' Whatever went on, whatever the span of its duration, a plan was presently devised to rid Josebaar Hawkins of the woman.

'He pretended to her that he had only been testing her with his talk of going off, to see how much she loved him. And finding her so faithful, he meant to reward her. He told her he had put by an especial gift for her, an heirloom of his family, kept in a wooden chest in the attics of the house. But it would amuse him if she would go up and look first *through the wood* of its lid, and so say what she saw, before he unlocked the chest and gave her the trophy. Well, it seems she could easily see through wood but not through her husband, and up she went. No sooner was she in the room with the empty chest than he slammed closed the door and secured it. And then at once came a gang of men and bricked the door up, and others came along the roof to seal and brick up the window.'

The bizarre quality of Farbody's recitation was added to, for me, by a sense of historical fact that seemed to underlie the whole. I found myself asking abruptly, 'Could she not have opened the window – or broken the pane, before the roof-gang reached her?'

'No, dear sir. Remember, the glass in those days was of much thicker and sturdier stuff than the flimsy crystal of our day. Besides, Hawkins had previously *pinned* the window shut. I mean, he had driven iron pins through the frame to the brickwork, and hammered in longer pins lengthwise all across.'

'Hence the horrible rhyme: a brick and a pin.'

'Just so. Besides, too, she was very high up, and the men anyway would have thrust her back — she was physically no match for them. They must have been a harsh crew. All the while they were doing it, blocking her in to die the slow death of starvation and thirst, Amber Maria was shrieking, imploring them. And after they had finished, she screamed and howled in her prison for uncountable days and nights, before she fell silent for ever. There are many reports of this.'

I shuddered. 'In God's name, you speak as if it really happened.'

He looked at me. 'My dear sir, it did. I can make no claims for her sorcery, but the facts of her death are undoubtedly true. Some years after, Josebaar Hawkins was hanged for her murder. For he confessed to it, having had not a quiet hour since.'

'And then? Did they unlock the room?'

'That they did not. The story concludes with that asseveration. No one would go near the house, let alone pull bricks away from any part of it. That they left, and leave, to the mercy of God.'

I sat some while in silence. Perhaps, very likely, I looked grim or rattled, for the scholar came and refilled my glass and moved the biscuit plate nearer my elbow.

'The children's rhyme,' said Farbody, 'as you're aware, has its own oddities. The brick and the pin relate to the window and door, the sealing of the room. I've come across one text which states that Amber Maria could see *only* through natural substances, and that therefore a brick, which is man-mixed, would defeat her gaze, just as would refined metal; obviously the very reason why she could detect coins in the ground, rather than see through these also. But do you recall that other line, *She leaps at the moon?*'

I said that I did.

'Salter's Lane,' said the scholar, 'has nothing to do with the salting trade. Indeed, one wouldn't expect it, so far as we are here from the sea. No, the word *salter* relates to the Latin *saltare*, *to leap*. In medieval times, that area of the woods was known to be a place where witches held their revels and danced the Wild Dance for their lord, Satan, "leaping high as the moon". Which moon, of course, is a calendar feature of the sabbat, whether full or horned for the Devil.'

Just then the doorbell jangled. My aunt had returned for me. I was astonished to see, glancing at Farbody's clock, that only half an hour had elapsed. But then, I suppose I was struggling back to my own time, across the centuries.

I thanked him and, going out with my aunt into the summer street, I resolved to shake myself free of the unnaturally strong emotion that had dropped upon me. And so we went to our luncheon.

Three or four days later I, reluctantly but evincing cheerfulness, accompanied my aunt to a church tea party, held in honour of the new bell which had recently been installed, and for which everyone had, the year before, been engaged in fund-raising. Here the social classes mingled with uneasy and ill-founded camaraderie, and I was revealed to a succession of people of all types, to whom it seemed my aunt wished to show off her nephew. Touched by her pride in me, I did my best to be jolly.

'And look,' said Aunt Alice, 'there is Daffodil Sempson. Or rather, Mrs King, as she is married to a hotel-keeper at St Leonards now, and has come for the first time to visit her sister. They are a somewhat estranged family. None of them is in service now, but in her youth, Daffodil was lady's maid to the Misses Condimer, and travelled all over Europe with them, before she was even seventeen. A great advantage for any girl.'

Struck, I admit, by the name Daffodil, I turned, and saw a very pleasing young woman, dressed most stylishly, a trick no doubt learnt during her travels with the minor aristocracy.

'By all means introduce me to her,' I told my aunt, with a more genuine enthusiasm.

But neither of us was able to catch the lady's eye. She seemed to be fixedly interested in something that was going on at the far end of the room, where several people were walking about, and the tables groaned beneath their loads of cakes and lemonade.

'I wonder what has engaged her attention so,' speculated my aunt.

Mrs King, née Sempson, was staring now almost unnaturally. Then I saw her turn her pretty head, seem to check, and then once more compulsively gaze back towards the tables.

Suddenly she quite changed colour. I have been witness to several instances of abrupt illness, slight or extreme. Mrs King seemed in the grip of the latter. Her face took on not a white but a thickly shining, greenish pallor. Without thinking I moved towards her. But in that moment she dropped to the ground.

At once she was surrounded by women, one of whom must have been her sister. Presently she was carried away.

From all sides came sympathetic murmurs concerning the heat.

To my sorrow, Mrs King did not return to enjoy the over-bountiful tea. My aunt made enquiries of her sister, who said that Daffodil was been obliged to be sent home in the pony cart. 'It is a great nuisance, as she intended returning to St Leonards tomorrow, and now she won't be well enough.'

'Is her indisposition more serious than we had hoped?' asked my aunt.

'Oh,' said the sister, blinking at me with eyes not half so fine as her sibling's, 'she makes a fuss about it. She has these delicate ways from her younger years. I may say, she'd never have dared go on so *then*. They would have dismissed her.'

'I thought,' said I sternly, 'that she seemed most unwell.'

'No, it isn't that she's ill,' declared the vulgar sister, whose hat might have been a lesson to us all in the virtues of regret. 'She says it's something that she saw in Austria, once.' My aunt and I evidenced incomprehension. The sister said, '*I* can say nothing of it. She refuses to explain. She says it's too dreadful, and it's taken her these six years to put it from her, and now she's been reminded and will need to stay in bed, with me expected to be flapping round her all day long, and neglecting my duties and Pa.'

We extricated ourselves from the uninspiring Miss Sempson and soon after left the tea party. As we were going out I remember that Aunt Alice said to me, 'There is disappointing Mr Polleto. I understand he contributed generously to the bell fund, which I find curious, since he's far from affluent, and never attends the church. Nor is he sociable. Did you happen to notice him this afternoon?'

I said that he might easily go unnoticed, but that I had not, I thought, seen him. Nor had I.

The day before my departure from Steepleford, I had planned a walk through the woods. Whether or not I would approach the stretch of the Lane that ran by Josebaar Hawkins's house I was myself unsure. In any event, a sudden thunderstorm erupted. Its violence and tenacity were such that I gave over any idea of walking, and spent all that last day with my aunt. The following morning we parted most affectionately, and I returned to London. A month later I went abroad and spent the rest of the year in Rome, in which ancient, imperial and legend-haunted city it may be supposed Steepleford and all its tales sank in my memory to a depth of fathoms.

Just after the New Year, I spent a day or so again at Steepleford. This time, there was snow down, but a flawless snow, thick and solid to tread upon, the weather chill and fine. Had I truly forgotten the house in Salter's Lane? I think that I had in everything but my heart. I took my way across the white fields, admiring the shapes of everything, each changed by its cover of pale fleece, then strayed off into the ancient woods, which were like a cathedral of purest ice.

And then somehow, in the way these things turn out, I took at random another of the silent avenues, and found myself ten minutes later at one of the several openings into the Lane. I had been walking by then for more than two hours, and it seemed foolish not to follow this path back to the town.

Soon I reckoned I had been wise to do so. The low afternoon sun was clouding over and a mauve cast hid the sky. So I strode briskly, thinking of a warm fire ahead and other cheer, and came level with the high wall of Josebaar Hawkins's ill-starred house.

At first I think I did not recognize it, for like everything else it was plastered with white. But then I got a great shock, and stopped dead in my tracks.

'What has happened here?' I asked, perhaps aloud. Until that time, the trees of the old estate had made a second wall behind the first, and the pile of the building had been visible only in portions, as I have previously described. Now, looking beyond one huge holly tree, I gained abruptly a view of the entire upper front aspect – all of it, its timber, stone and brickwork, the roof and chimneys, and every cold window, glaring as if it were eye to eye with me, like some person who has suddenly whipped from their face a mask.

Astonished, I attempted to reason how this should be. It was not that the trees were bare. No, it was that every tree, saving the holly, which in any case stood this side of the wall, had been brought down.

I confess that meeting the house like this, head-on, unnerved me. I made no secret of that to myself. But in a moment or so, I had a rational thought. Some vandals had been at work in the 'grounds'. They had chopped down the trees and carted them away, no doubt to provide firewood for needy winter hearths.

On the strength of this rationale, an unusual, perhaps a boy's desire took me, having seen so much, to scale the wall and peer over into the precincts of the house, now open to be studied. I have to say too that my peculiar eagerness to do this was prompted, I now think, more by an *aversion* to doing it, rather than a longing after secrets. It was like a dare one must not evade, for fear of being thought – worst of all by oneself – a coward.

I am quite strong and fit. The wall had inconsistencies and irregular stones in plenty. Despite the snow, I got up it in less than three minutes, and, perched there on the top, stared down into the gardens.

They were the most desolate sight. Patches of snow lay all about, but the ground had turned dark, and in places black, the snowfall having partly melted away as it already had on some of the higher trees in the woods. There was a good reason for this. Any sun that fell here must fall directly over everything since nothing now stood between it and the ground, only the house. Every tree and shrub that had grown, rampantly and untended, within the walls had been felled and, presumably, taken away. And I wondered who could have made so bold after all these hundred and more years.

Then something else caught my eye. There was, toward the side of the house, a sort of ornamental little building, perhaps a folly. It was ruinous and falling down, and its demise seemed to have been hastened by a young oak tree, which had toppled aslant upon its roof, and leaned there yet.

So why then, I wondered, had the wood-stealing vandals not carted off also this ready-felled tree? There it lay, as useful as any other timber, bare and exposed, its dislocated branches creaking in some unfelt wind, clear as complaining voices in the stillness.

There were no birds, of course. There was, as before, no sound – beyond, this time, the creaking of the fallen tree's branches. But this effect had been common through much of the woods, as the day advanced and the winter sun prepared to leave the earth. Until this point I had not noted it particularly.

Now I did. For here the absence of all sound, save that sinister creaking whine of broken branches, seemed heavy with presage. The air smelled sour, and faintly dirty, like one might expect in the centre of an industrial town, where smoke and cinders fall and make each breath lifeless, and potent with disease.

And then, even as I sat there gazing at it, the unlikeliest thing occurred. The leaning dead oak tree swayed, and out of it there burst a shower of dry pieces, splinters of wood ejected, and then one whole limb snapped off and dropped, disintegrating even as it went, so that by the instant it touched the ground, there was no more left of it than dust. What had caused such a thing? The action of some animal? No animal was in the vicinity, so much was plain. The simple process of a slow decay, then, electing to finish its work coincidentally with my scrutiny? I had the strangest notion that, simply by *staring* at the tree, I had hastened the branch's breaking off and dissolution.

And then, and then, I knew that it was not I. *I* had not caused it. Across my scalp my hair crawled as if filled by icy tricklings. Against my will, it seemed to me, yet no more resistible than as if at the pull of a chain of steel, my head turned and tilted back, and I looked up the unmasked face of that house, towards its highest casements.

There was not a creeper left upon any of them. Even the snow had been leached away. But oh, something white there was, which stood at the window, looking out, and out.

I can put down here only what I saw. I saw a woman's shape. Her gown I cannot detail, nor how her hair was dressed, though it seemed to me that both were disordered. Her features I could not see, and that had nothing to do with distance, and I believe nothing to do with light or shade. She *had* no features, none. That is, she had only one feature. She had two eyes. But her eyes were set in that featureless whiteness of a shape like two burned holes. They were not eyes at all – but . . . they *were* eyes, more eyes than are possible to any thing that lives.

I remember little of my descent of the wall. Perhaps I fell from it. Certainly I think some of it crumbled and broke away too, as I slipped down. And then I fled along the Lane, and this I do recall. I fled and I whimpered like a man pursued by the dogs of hell that are really fiends, and they will tear him, even his soul, if they catch him. But they did not catch me, and I reached the town. And then came maybe the most sinister and curious thing of all.

For running out into Market Gate Street in the wintry dusk, a carriage passed me, and in the carriage a friend of my aunt's who greeted me as she went by most graciously. And I raised my hat, and nodded, and then walked on to my aunt's door, like some man who has not just met the devil on the road.

'Aunt,' I said to her that evening, 'why not come up to London for a spell?'

'Oh, no, dear boy,' she said. 'I'm too comfortable here. Why should I wish to be in London?'

'Well, I am there. And half a dozen theatres and shops and museums that are the envy of the country.' But she would not be moved, saying it would put me against her, if she encroached upon my 'London World'.

And so, after another day, I went again away from Steepleford. And naturally, I had spoken to no one of what I had seen, and no one had asked me what I had seen. Nor did I hear a single mention of Hawkins's house, or its current state, about the town, let alone of anything else.

However, as I sat in the train, I took myself sternly to one side, and told myself that perhaps ghosts did exist, for there are nowadays even photographs of some of them. But of all things, the dead could not harm the living: their power was done.

III

Less than a month later, I was at a supper given by my then acquaintance, Lord D—. The food was of the best and the wines Olympian, which made up, somewhat, for the conversation. At midnight I well remember we had some music, amongst the rest an attractive rendition, given by a female singer of superb voice, of the words of Alexander Pope's *Pastorals*, the melody being, I think, Handel's. As it finished, one of the servants came discreetly in, and presently handed me a telegram.

To my dismay I read that my aunt had fallen seriously ill, and begged my attendance on her. My own man had taken alarm and brought the message directly on to me.

I hurried to my rooms and flung some things together, and was soon on the train for Steepleford Halt.

I have said that I had great affection for my aunt, and with good reason. My agitation was increased because she had never, until then, that I knew, been afflicted with any ailment not trifling and swiftly over. Other thoughts I believe I dismissed from my mind.

The morning was young when we arrived at the Halt, where her carriage had been sent in readiness. It was a dismal day in February, sleety and cold, with leaden skies. Everything looked horrible to me in the deadly light of it, and in the light of my anxiety, and all the station buildings, the gaunt trees, seemed covered by an air of desuetude and darkness. This impression only increased as we bumped through the wintry woods, and I cannot describe my abrupt unease when I thought we must turn along Salter's Lane. Then the carriage veered away, and went instead by the other route, to the Crossing. On asking the coachman, he told me that some trees had come down in the Lane, which made it impassable, and I dare say I was ridiculously relieved.

I barely noted the town. No sooner had we reached my aunt's than I sprang from the carriage and hastened indoors.

In the hall I met her doctor, a solid man, who reassured me somewhat. 'It is a kind of low fever we've been seeing in the town recently. Unfortunately, given your aunt's age, it has stayed with her longer than one might have hoped.'

Then he frowned, and I asked him why he did so.

He said, 'Ah, well, there have been rather a lot of such cases in the past month. But there. The old and the very young are always vulnerable. Your aunt, of course, is not yet sixty.'

I said, 'Have there been fatalities?'

'No, no, nothing like that.'

None of this prepared me for the sight of my aunt, who, lying propped on her pillows, looked white, and seemed, to me, near death. I took her hand, and she murmured at once, 'I called you here, my dear, because I was afraid I might not be able to remain much longer. But today I feel rather better.'

I told her she was a fraud, and that I was happy to find her so.

Despite my nervousness, my aunt rallied. She improved. But she did not entirely get well. Two weeks later, when pressing concerns of my own urged me to go back to London, she too implored me to leave. 'I was being very foolish,' she said. 'What nonsense. I shall see the New Century, I am determined on it.' And I realized I made her more uncertain by remaining so faithfully, as if hourly fearful of her collapse.

The doctor too grew confident. 'She is completely out of danger, or I'd never concur with your departure. And she has the best of care. I'd like to see more progress, but then her age has been against her a little. When the spring weather comes, then we should see a change for the better. Although,' he added, rather insensitively and ominously, 'I find that all those who have succumbed to this pernicious malady take a great while over mending. There's a young woman I have heard of, of only three-and-twenty, of the working families, you understand, but well nourished and fit, and the mother of healthy children, who has been sick with this same fever off and on for eight weeks. She was one of the first to contract it, and again and again she seems to throw it off, only to sink down once more.'

Receiving this news, I was now in two minds whether or not to go. However, in the end a telegram arriving the other way, from the metropolis, forced my hand, and I caught the train.

Truth to tell, it was a relief to escape the atmosphere of a convalescent house, not to mention all Steepleford, which had seemed unbearably dreary and run-down in the rain and mud of a newborn and unfriendly March. Indeed, I had never seen the place look so forlorn; it had depressed me. And when, having been returned to the city only a few days, a firmly written letter came from my aunt, assuring me she had now taken the upward path, and even given a tea party for some friends, I resolved to stay where I was. Soon after this, and in the light of a further optimistic bright epistle from Steepleford, I allowed myself to be lured to France with Nash and his brother, and then was persuaded on to Italy again.

In retrospect I gain a terrible impression of my short time there in the awakening summer, and of that previous more leisurely summer I had spent in Rome, happily wandering among the bronzes and the marbles of both inanimate and human subjects. Because concurrently there ran on and on, behind the veils of distance and inattention, that dreadful horror of which I could know nothing, and yet which I do believe I sensed. For had it not shown itself to me behind its own shadow, brushed me with its noiseless wing?

I shall not try to excuse myself. Perhaps I was afraid. I might have seen that there was good reason to be.

Certainly I did not ponder that chance vision I had had of a 'ghost' in the window of Josebaar Hawkins's house. I did not even offer the experience as a suitable Gothic tale, one hot Tuscan night among the soft blue hills when others were telling ghost stories. Did I even call it to mind? Perhaps – I cannot remember. But of course, too, what I had seen was not a ghost. Not that at all.

Needless to say, when I got back to England late in July, I was at once assailed by feelings of unquiet and guilt, and instantly wrote to Aunt Alice – there had been no letters from her waiting for me, but as a general rule she did not constantly put pen to paper. I asked how she did, and if I might come down and see her.

After a slight delay, I received her reply, which was brief and penned in a careful, rigid style. She said she was in her usual health, and would be glad if I would 'take time to call on her'. I thought the whole tone of her letter sulky, and was peeved that she had not mentioned some presents I had sent her on my travels – for which churlishness may I be forgiven.

For some reason, as I saw to the packing of my bag, I had upon my mind that fragment of Pope's *Pastorals*, which I had heard the very evening the telegram reached me informing me of my aunt's illness. The gracious verse was in every way unlike the rhyme that had accrued about Amber Hawkins and her murdering spouse, yet now it too lodged fast in my head, and repeated itself over and over. Never came warning in a stranger guise.

The words are well known, of course, but I shall put them down even so, such is their unconscionable significance to me now:

> *Where'er you walk, cool gales shall fan the glade,*
> *Trees, where you sit, shall crowd into a shade;*
> *Where'er you tread, the blushing flowers shall rise,*
> *And all things flourish where you turn your eyes.*

The train reached Steepleford Halt soon after three o'clock of a peerless summer afternoon. London had been somewhat stuffy and overheated, but as we entered the countryside beyond, a wonderful honeyed peace descended, balmy, lazy, and a-flicker with butterflies. Flowers blazed from every hedge and bank, the trees were laden with heavy green, the sky was as blue as the mysotis.

Descending from my carriage I was struck initially only by the sense of the huge sun, which was hammering the earth. But looking about me I perceived at once a quality in the light, both dry and harsh. Everything looked to me, in this glare, drained of colour, faded like a woman's lovely gown worn too often.

The veteran who oversaw the station was standing to one side, consulting his watch as the train pulled out again. It was my habit to exchange a few pleasantries with him when I met him, and I prepared to do so now, but he forestalled me. Looking up, his face was not as it had been, not so much older as used up. He nodded but did not smile.

'Good day. I regret the train was late.'

'No matter. It was a delightful journey today.'

'But a poor arrival, I dare to think,' he said. He sounded surly, which surprised me very much; he was not of this sort. Then he pointed straight by me. 'D'you see that tree?'

I turned, to humour him, and gazed towards an old copper beech that had guarded the ground above the railway for as long as I had been coming there, and no doubt for some regiments of years before that.

'The tree. Indeed I do.'

'See how it leans?'

'Why, yes – what can have happened?'

'The good Lord knows,' said he. 'The roots are out to one side. Dying, it is.'

'What a great pity. Can nothing be done?'

He made a noise. He was angry, not merely at my paltry concern, but at all things that had somehow conspired to ruin the beauty of the tree.

'It's got to be felled tomorrow,' he said. 'A danger to the trains if it falls, d'you see.'

I said again I was very sorry, as I was, and gave him something for his trouble, at which he looked as if the coins concerned were the Thirty Pieces of Silver themselves.

I was glad to get out of the station after that.

My intention had not been to walk; it was too sultry, and here for sure there was a dull storminess to the air that was already making my head ache. The station farther up the line lay five miles beyond the town, but in an outpost where a cab might be accosted. Here, however, I had been promised my aunt's carriage, which now, going out on to the path, I did not find. This I could have understood more readily if the train had been early, or on time.

I almost turned back to ask the stationmaster if a carriage might be procured from the local inn, but then thought better of it. The walk to the town would not take so long, providing I struck off at once for Salter's Lane, and followed that to Steepleford.

There I idled, on the gravel, under the impoverished shade of some spindly, desiccated sycamores, as if a decision had still to be made. I was reluctant to go on. But go on I must, and would.

Until this moment I had, I think, almost entirely suppressed or driven away my utter unease at the prospect of the Lane where witches once had leaped in their revels, and where lay the house of a murderer – and of his wife who, as I had seen and still believed, haunted its window. Now my fears rushed in like the sea tearing through one small crack in a dyke, carrying all before it.

I broke out into a sweat that even the leaden heat had not occasioned, for the moisture was cold, and my heart thudded in my breast.

Come, I thought, *in heaven's name, you are not a baby. What is there to be afraid of? If the wretched nook affects you so, do what the others do, and look away from it.*

What finally galvanized me was a dawning grasp of what the absence of the carriage might mean. In the past, when it had been promised, it had been reliable. If my aunt had forgotten to order it forth, or her coachman had not brought it, then something must have happened to interrupt the mission. And all at once I was vastly unsettled as to what.

Then I did set off, striding the path between the fields, towards the woodland that lay like a smoky cloud upon the nearest horizon.

I must have noticed as I went the state of those fields. They were bleached and barren-looking, the grain in parts fallen, and where it was still upright, then not normal in its colour. In other areas it seemed burnt. At the time I suspected a fire had taken place, or infestation of some sort. My mind was not truly on the fields, and did not want to be.

But then I reached the edge of the woods. And with the best will in the world, I could no longer delude myself.

Only after the most serious of gales would so many great trees have fallen. Looking in, at what had been the greenest of green shades, I now beheld bald, wide avenues, all railwayed with these broken pillars, which had tumbled in every direction, taking in every case more than one or two of their fellows with them. Besides these fallen giants, the standing wood was sickly. There could be no mistaking it. A yellowish tinge was on each leaf, or worse, a blackened scorching, as if some acid had been thrown over and among them all. The leaf canopy besides showed great holes.

I advanced like some soldier into enemy territory, where any lethal hazard or trap may be encountered. No sooner was I in, however, than I paused again. Upon the raddled ground, bare of anything but the most hardy weeds and brackens (and these burnt and brown), I had begun to see strange heaps and drifts of a dark dust. I knew at once what these were, but going over to one of the fallen trees, I tapped it, not very hard, with a strong-looking stick I had found on the outer path and picked up thoughtlessly, as one sometimes does on a walk. No sooner did the stick make contact than the bole of the prone trunk, for about five feet either side of the light blow, gave way in a shower of what appeared to be the finest black sugar. The sturdy-looking stick also snapped in half, brittle as charcoal. And the sugar-like substance sprayed out from it too. I dropped the stick then. As it hit the ground, it shattered into some twenty further fragments. The dust – the dust was all that remained of trees that, last summer, had seemed to touch the sky.

But I had to go on through this wreckage of a poisoned wood. I followed doggedly the carriage-ride, which normally at this time of year would have been rather overgrown. Surely I had seen it so myself – with sprinklings of woodland flowers everywhere the sun could penetrate, thick moss and large lacy ferns where it did not. There was no hint of that now. Not even the toadstools and other fungi that colonize any woodland, good or bad, had

ventured in. Nor was anything else to be come on. No beasts or
birds ran or fluttered or fluted through the trees, or played about
the tracks. Silence ruled the woods. Absence ruled them. And here
was I, forging on perforce, like the last man alive upon a dying
earth. And my feelings of horror and dejection increased with
every step I took.

By the time I got out into Salter's Lane, I may say I was
prepared for anything. Had I not been, the quantity of felled
trees that marked the exit point would have alerted me, and the
expanses of the deadly dust, which resembled here nothing so
much as the encroachment of a desert.

Even prepared, yet I halted where I stood. I looked down the
Lane, and knew it for an avenue accursed. It was – and I do not
exaggerate – like some landscape of the damned.

Nothing stood in it. Its length was paved by horizontal trees
and in between them the dust had formed mounds which had
partly solidified, in a friable, hopeless manner, perhaps from the
direct action of the weather. Where hedges had been, there were
sometimes left some bare black twigs and poles. I did not want to
enter the Lane. I did not want to travel over it.

But I had no choice – unless I turned back, retrod my path and
then went on to Joiner's Crossing, a detour which would now add
almost an hour to my urgent journey.

So I went on. I walked into the Lane and advanced, having,
every yard or so, to get over the fallen trees, most of which gave
way under my feet, meaning I must scramble and jump to save
myself from a fall. The mounds of dust were much the same; I
sank in them as in the dunes of some hellish beach, or else the
humps of powdery 'soil' they had formed crumbled, and I
slithered unsafely.

This was very exhausting, and additionally foul from the dust
that was constantly billowing up as if purposely to stifle me.

Above, the sky was no longer blue. It had a tarnished sheen to
it, like unpolished metal. True clouds were hung out on it, grimy-
looking and peculiar in shape, like torn banners, each a mile
across.

Of course, I knew that I must come to the house. I knew that I
must pass it. I had vowed I would not give it one glance. The perils
and obstacles of the Lane would assist me, surely, in that, since I
needed all my attention for the road.

However, I reached the house of Josebaar Hawkins, and did not keep to my vow.

The holly tree was gone. There was no trace of it – it had become one with the dust. The wall too had come down. It lay scattered all over the Lane, the bricks and bits of stonework disintegrating, like everything else. Behind the wall stretched a vast piece of ground that was like a bare, swept floor. It had nothing at all growing upon it, and even the dust had blown or otherwise vanished away. It was a nothingness, in colour greyish. And upon this table of death there rose – the house. Beside it was the little ornamental building that I had spied on my last excursion there. This I now saw, with an unnerving pang, had been a small mausoleum, no doubt the supposed resting place of Hawkins's wife. Now it comprised merely a part of a roof upon a couple of columns. Within, too, was nothing. Of the toppled oak that had leant there, no sign remained, naturally.

Of everything that had been there, of nature or contrivance, the house alone stood – but not intact. Its roof had come away in broad segments: one could see the gaping joists and beams, which were in turn collapsing. Both chimneys were down, crashed inwards. On the lower floors not one window had kept its antique glass or its boxed decorations. The creepers had slipped from the exterior walls and after them the bricks had tried and were still trying to come out. Yet the shell of the building, what there was of it, still jutted upright. And in that spot, this made it a thing of unbelievable terror. Ruined and distorted and every moment increasingly giving way, nevertheless *it* had so far *stayed*, where nothing else remained.

I perceived all this before I had raised my gaze beyond the lower floors. When I did raise it, I selected its targets with much care. But in the end, I knew I would have to do it, would have to look full-on at the upper window under the roof.

I had been in Rome, I had been in Siena and Venice. Among the hills and waters, among the bronzes, surely I had somehow understood that *she* still stood here, on and on, stood here looking out, eating with her eyes first the bricks and mortar, then the pins that sealed her up, patient as only a hopeless thing can be, taking a century over it; next eating out the glass, and next what lay beyond the glass – the trees, the air, the Lane, the countryside.

They must have known, the people of Steepleford town, in
1788, when they passed by on the Lane, hearing her weeping and
shrieking in agony and fear, all those endless days and nights.
They must have known what he had done to her. What then did
they do, but cross themselves, perhaps, or use some older, less
acceptable mark. But they knew, they knew.

She had loved too well, that was her sole crime. She had seen
too much in mankind that was beautiful and good, and for sure
too much in him, in Josebaar Hawkins, and for this they had
condemned her and killed her. How she must then have hated
them. How she must have *looked*, fixing despairingly her mad
eyes upon the impenetrable dark. And if she had not survived her
death, *something* that came of her, and of her hatred, and of those
eyes – and which learned too, new skills whereby to use those eyes
– that *did* survive, and lived still, and saw and looked – and fed.
And it was there, there in that window, drawing up the whole
world in its slow and bottomless net.

'Oh, God, Amber Maria, poor lost pitiable hideous residue—'

My gaze was fixed on her window, her death's window. My
gaze was stuck there and now could not pull away. I felt my heart
turn to water inside me and the occluded atmosphere blackened
over.

I did not quite lose my senses. Instead I found myself leaning on
my hands, kneeling in the desert of dust among the slaughter of
the trees.

To myself I said, *But what did I see this time?*

For I had not seen a single thing. The window – *her* window –
was empty of everything. Of creeper and of bricks, pins and glass.
Of light and shadow, and of any shape. As with the rest, nothing
was there. And yet . . . the nothing that was in that window was
not empty. No. *She* was there in it, there in the core of it, as things
hide in darkness. Or her eyes were there, those pits of seeing, her
looking was there, her *looking* looked out. It had looked even into
me, and through me, and away, to have all else.

Presently I got up. And, as before, I ran.

The town – I wondered afterwards why the stationmaster had not
warned me. I wondered too why the newspapers and journals in
London had not carried some mention of it, why no sensational
word seemed to have escaped from it. Perhaps there had been

some news which was not believed – or believed too well and suppressed. Besides, events had raced to their final act as swiftly as a wave.

I have read of times of siege and plague in medieval Germany, Italy, France. In certain of those occult little towns, crouched in the profundities of deep valleys, hung like baskets from the sides of cliffs, the dim and winding alleys make such images still all too credible. But Steepleford was a slow, flat, gentle settlement, prosperous and mild, where the horse, casting its shoe, caused a stir, and they had longed for a foreign theatrical gentleman to liven them up.

Getting near the outskirts, I saw a cloud hanging over the fields and town. It was a wreath of smoke. The dead gardens along the approach I had scarcely noticed, nor the untended houses, which seemed to have been afflicted too by a kind of partial hurricane, ripping the tiles from roofs and setting askew anything that had been in the slightest way vulnerable. There was a dearth of people going about their trades or gossip. Instead, there hung in the atmosphere a *presence* of incredible raw heat and turgid staleness. I have never smelled such air, even in the sinks of greater Europe.

I came into Market Gate Street before I properly knew it, and there, as in some canvas by Hieronymus Bosch, I saw what I took at once for plague fires burning in archways and at the corners of houses, reeking of sulphur and other purgatives.

The fumes by now were nearly as thick as a London fog, and in them, as I moved on, persons came and went anonymously, their heads down and swathed in scarves, none looking at another. They were creatures from the selfsame painting, at large between torments.

Then came the River Styx, for the street was awash with a black, stinking body of fluid. I had splashed into it before I could prevent myself, but in any case, there was no other way across.

Up toward my aunt's part of the town, a pony and trap leapt rattling by, the unhappy animal tossing its head and red-eyed as the horses of Pluto from the smoke. A man hailed me and pulled the horse in. Amazed to be recognized in the Inferno, I stopped. There was my aunt's doctor, peering down.

'Thank God you've arrived, young man. We sent off a wire this very morning.'

My heart clenched inside me. 'It must have missed me by an instant. Is she so bad, then?'

'I fear she is, now. It's the same all over the town. The deuce knows what the illness is. We have three specialists down from London, and one from the Low Countries, and they have drawn a blank on it. My own sister, who has never taken sick in her life – well. But besides all this business of burst pipes and subsiding walls across the entire town— But I won't trouble you with that, either.' The pony shook its head violently. The doctor raised his voice to curse. 'Be damned to these confounded fires! What do the fools think they're doing? Have they heard nothing of modern hygiene – our only reliable ally against disease – to fill up the air with such muck? Superstition, ignorance— Make haste to get on!' And with this baleful cry, whether to me or to the pony I was unsure, the doctor whipped the beast on, and like King Death himself flung off into the smother.

But I ran again, and so reached my aunt's house. And ten minutes later I was in her bedroom, by the side of her bed. But she, although living yet, did not see or hear me.

When I was a small boy, and my youthful mother died suddenly and without warning, this aunt of mine, then an elegant and pretty fashion plate of an Alice, herself not much above thirty-five, sheathed in softest clothes and scented by vanilla, took me in her arms and let me sob out my soul. And now again I stood beside her, and again I wept. But she never knew it, now. And oh, any pity I had felt for that other, for that thing once known as Amber Maria Hawkins, you can be sure I had given it up.

So now I must come to the strangest part of my abnormal tale. To a conclusion, indeed, that any writer of fiction would be ashamed to set before his audience, having brought them thus far, and by such a fearful road. Therefore, prior to the last scenes of the drama, I will say this: One piece evidently missing from my narrative has since been supplied, and only the discovery of that unique absentee has brought me, at this time, and so many years after these events took place, to write them down at all.

My aunt, where she lay on the bed, did not stir. Only the faintest movement indicated that she still breathed. I looked ardently for this proof, and once or twice it seemed to me that it faltered, and then I too held my breath. But always the slight rise and fall of her breast resumed. At least she was not in pain or distress. That was all, at this time, that I might be thankful for.

Near midnight the doctor called again. He was worn out, as I could see, by his conscientious tours up and down the stricken town, through the acrid fumes of the fires, the stenchful spilled waters, and the furnace heat, which even nightfall had not lessened. When he was done with his examination, a frighteningly swift one, I had them bring him some brandy, and he thanked me, then solemnly announced that he 'did not think it would be long'.

'Is there nothing that can be done?' I asked like a child.

The doctor shook his head. He was doubtless exhausted too by this question, which must have been asked of him everywhere that night, by tearful wives and white-faced husbands, by daughters, by fathers, by one-third of the folk of Steepleford. In that hour they had become the people of Egypt when the Angel of Death did not pass over them but took from them, across all the boundaries of age and condition, their first-born.

After the doctor had gone, I sat down again, and drank some of the wine that had been brought to me on an untouched dinner tray. Then I think I must have slipped into a doze.

I was woken, as were countless others, by the most fearsome noise I have ever heard.

Starting up, I gave a cry. As I did so, I heard below and above me in the house, and everywhere around, many other throats exercised in similar startled exclamation. I can only describe the sound as being like an exact representation of that well-known phrase: the Crack of Doom. It was as if a thunderbolt hurled from heaven had struck the town, cracking it open with one awful brazen clang.

Finding myself unharmed, and the house still entire about me, I turned in fear to the bed. But a glance at my aunt showed her to be still insensible. Going to the window then I stared out, but the street was thick with smoke and darkness, its few lamps half blind. Worse for being inevitably unseen, vague noises of fright and panic had risen all around, and I made out windows lighting up here and there like red eyes. Then a man came running by. I opened the casement and called down to him. 'What was that sound? Do you know?'

But he only raised to me a face peeled by terror, and flew on.

I truly believed some apocalyptic conclusion was about to rush upon us all. The most primal urge came on me, and going to my poor aunt I meant to lift her up in my arms, so that we might at least perish together. But as I reached the bedside, I stopped dead once more. For I saw her eyes were open and looking at me lucidly. And where the lamp shone on her face, her colour had come back, not feverish but soft, even attractive.

'How nice to see you, Frederick,' said my aunt. 'I have had the most refreshing sleep and feel so much better now.' Her voice was not weak, nor did she seem to be lying to console me. She added, nearly winsomely, 'I hate to trouble cook – I know the hour is late – but perhaps Sally might boil me an egg? An egg with a little toast. And oh, a cup of tea. I'm so thirsty.'

And then, before my astounded gaze, she was sitting herself up in the bed, and as I sprang to forestall and help her, she laughed. 'You're gallant, dear boy.'

When accordingly I went out into the passage, I found the maid, Sally, standing there and looking at me with great round eyes. Before I could speak of the wonder concerning my aunt, Sally announced, 'They say the new church bell has fallen right down the spire and landed in the chancel. The roof there is all damaged and come down, too. Did you hear the horrible noise, sir? We thought the End had come.'

Distractedly I asked, 'Was anyone hurt?'

'They say not.' (I learned later that 'they' was the carter's boy, who had bustled in with the news.) 'But the whole town has been woke up.'

This was, it turned out, true in more than one way, if the process of waking may be associated with revival. For my aunt was not alone in her abrupt and miraculous feat of recovery. It transpired, as over succeeding days I learned in more detail, that of all the six hundred-odd persons lying sick that night, or even, it was thought, at the point of death, not one but did not rouse up an instant or so after the appalling clangour of the bell. And not one thereafter but did not take quickly a swift and easy path to full recovery. (Even, or so I was assured, a cat that had been failing grew suddenly well, and a canary that had sunk to the floor of its cage flew up on its perch and began to sing.)

Shamelessly, it was spoken of as a miracle, this reversal of extreme illness to good health. And there were those who spoke religiously of the falling bell, some claiming that it had cast itself down in some curious form of sacrifice, which it achieved, having cracked and buckled itself beyond use. Others averred that it had been itself unlucky or impure in some sensational but mysterious way, and therefore fell like an evil angel, at God's will, after which the town was freed from its curse.

These notions, of course, were ludicrous, but everywhere for a while one heard them, and small suprise. For the saving of so many of the town's lives, both young and old, affluent and poor, and in so abrupt and unheralded a form, did indeed smack of divine intervention. While I did not for a moment credit this, yet I thanked God with everyone else there. And as the days went on, and Steepleford hoisted itself slowly but surely from its own ashes, the streets cleared of water and debris, the baleful fires vanished, and the summer sun took pity and shone with greater brightness and less heat. The smell of furnaces and dungeons melted away.

Ten days later, accompanying my aunt on her first walk up and down the thoroughfares, I saw fresh roses blooming in twenty gardens. Now and then, where a tree had come down or been axed, new growth could be seen rioting, shining green, from the stumps.

They had found by then that the bell rope had been eaten away. By rats, some said, as Steepleford moved, a rescued ship, back upon its even keel.

'Such a nuisance,' added my aunt, flighty as a girl. 'Now the rector will want another one.'

I said that this would mean more fund-raising bacchanals, and Aunt Alice remarked that the strange Mr Polleto at least would spare them all his disappointing presence. 'Lady Constance, when she called, told me that he had left the town only last Monday. Generally such a thing would never have caught her attention, but it seems the cottage is now for sale, and she wishes to buy it for a young painter she has found.'

But I had then no interest at all in Mr Polleto.

My aunt, meanwhile, had more than become herself again. She seemed to me younger and more active than she had been for years. The doctor too assured me that he now thought her 'good for three decades'. And when she said to me one evening, 'Do you know, dear boy, I think being ill has done me good,' I could only agree. And so, it must be confessed, once more at liberty to do so, I began to hanker after my own life.

Of course, I was bemused too. I wanted time to myself to think over events. One instant I felt I had been the involuntary party to a delusion. At another, the unreal seemed actual. But we seldom trust ourselves upon such matters, I mean upon matters that may involve the supernatural. There is always some other explanation that surely must be the proper one.

I am not unduly superstitious, and now, in the glow of returning normality, I began to prefer to think of myself as having been in the grasp of a wild obsession. In this state I had imagined some things and brooded upon others, until I could make them fit my vivid scenario.

When finally I commenced my preparations to leave Steepleford, I was told, in passing, by a neighbour that no carriage could now be driven along Salter's Lane.

'Are the fallen trees still uncleared?'

'No, no. It's the new growth shooting out there. It's become one great coppice, with trees bursting, they say, from the stumps. Those that have seen it say they've never known a sight like it. But there's a deal going on with trees and other plants, after that drought we had.' Here he gave me a long list of things, which I will not reproduce. Then, as I was tiring, he said this: 'Perhaps you may have noticed the old beech at the station? A fine old tree, but it was twisting and due for the axe. But now it's been spared, and they say the roots have dug down again, if such a thing is to be believed, and the trunk is straight again too. And the leaves are coming out on it as if it were May, not August. A strange business and no mistake. Did you ever get a peep at that house in the Lane? The Witch House, some call it.'

Sombrely I replied that I had.

'Well, that's all come down, like a house of cards. Not a wall of it standing, nor one stone on another. A great heap of rubble.'

I had a dream, not while I remained in the town but a month later, when Nash had persuaded me back to France, in the south, in a little village among the chestnut woods. I dreamed I was on the roof of Steepleford church, and pale, glassy arrows flew by through the air. They were the looks of a woman who stood at a window in Salter's Lane. These arrows severed the rope of the bell in the church spire. And when it fell there was no sound, only a great nothingness. But in the nothingness, I knew that woman was no more.

'What's up?' said Nash, finding me out in the village street, smoking, at four in the morning, the dawn just lifting its silver lids beyond the trees.

'Do you suppose,' I said, 'that something thought fully virtuous, if attacked, might rebound on the attacker, might destroy them?'

'History and experience relate otherwise,' said Nash.

And so they do.

IV

That, then, was my story of Steepleford, all I had of it at the time, but which I gave to my companion, Jeffers, on the terrace of the Hotel Alpius as we waited for the Wassenhaur train.

I was nevertheless moved to express to him my regret for the unsatisfactory lack of explanation concerning the final outcome of events.

'I haven't been back to the place for years now,' I finished, 'and so can add nothing. My aunt, you see, grew sprightly – she still is – and moved to London, where she has a fine town house.'

'Hmm,' said my companion. He drew upon his cigar, and looked covertly again at the instigator of my tale, that same quaint little shopkeeper Polleto, who still sat at his adjacent table.

Precisely at that moment the untoward took place. Or perhaps I should say the apt, as it had happened before, and neither of us could now miss its significance.

A party of three gentlemen and two ladies had just now been coming across the terrace, and had taken their seats to my right. So it was that I heard, from behind my right ear, a stifled little cry, and next the splintering crash of a water glass dropped on the paving.

Jeffers and I both turned sharply, in time to see that the second young lady of the party, ashen in colour, was being supported by her friends. As they fussed and produced a smelling-bottle, and called loudly for spirits, Polleto darted to his feet and went gliding quickly from the terrace.

'Now I fancy,' said Jeffers, 'you've witnessed something of this sort before. And I too, in a way, since you told me of it.'

'You mean Daffodil King, who fainted at the church tea?'

'Just so.'

'You imagine that she, and the lady over there, swooned for a similar reason – that they had seen Mr Polleto?'

'Don't you imagine it?' asked Jeffers laconically.

I thought, and answered honestly, 'Yes. But why?'

'I wonder,' said Jeffers, infuriatingly. Then he added, 'No, I'm not being fair to you. You see, I've read of the case, and viewed a rather poor photograph once, in a police museum, in circumstances I shan't bore you with. When you first pointed him out, I had a half-suspicion. But in the light of both ladies fainting at the sight of the man . . . Recollect, Austria is only over the border here. I believe you told me that the charming Daffodil had been in Austria once, and said she had seen something there so awful that it had taken her six years to recover from it?'

'Yes, or so her sister informed me.'

'What she saw then was that same man, Polleto, in the street probably, on the day that the people of a well-known Austrian spa almost lynched him. I have no doubts the other lady, to our right, saw him in a similar style. Unless she had the singular misfortune to have met him.'

'Then he's notorious?'

'No. Of course, his real name *isn't* Polleto. I was never told what his real name was. The documents referred to him only as the Criminal. And the crime too was hushed up in the end, and rich acquaintances got him away to avoid a most resounding scandal, which would, I believe, have brought down the Austrian government of the hour.'

'In God's name – what had he done?'

Jeffers shrugged. 'That's the thing, Frederick, what *had* he done? No one would say. Not even the file on him, which I was shown, would say anything as to the *nature* of his crime. Not even the policemen I spoke with. It was something so vile, so disgusting, so inhuman, that no scrap of it has ever been revealed by anyone who knows. They won't – can't – speak of it. They try to push it from their minds. And if they see him, like that lady across the terrace, some part of them withers. There now, she's looking a little better. All the better, no doubt, since what made her ill has left the vicinity.'

I sat staring at him.

Presently I said, 'Are you then saying to me what I suppose you must be?'

Jeffers stretched himself in his chair, and smiled at me. 'Even you,' said he, 'asked yourself whether or not something of great perceived virtue, like a church bell, could halt Amber Maria, should she set her sights on it. But it wasn't virtue she avoided, was it? She loved the earth and all the people in it. I, too, Frederick, have heard of the Lilyite sect, and of course she must have been a member of it. No doubt Josebaar Hawkins let her have her meetings in his house, and protected her afterwards by lying. But maybe, in later years, he feared that in her too, that she was one of the Lilyites and put the teachings of Jesus before all other things. What did she do but love others and want to help them with her precious gift of seeing, from which she herself had never tried to profit? She saw good and beauty in all men and all things, and loved them like – loved them *better than* – herself. And where have you heard such philosophy before, save from the lips of Christ?'

I was shocked a little, to have missed this clue. Humbly I waited for him to go on. He did so.

'Amber Maria looked with her eating eyes through her window, and after the blocked-up bricks and pins, she had the glass, and then, as you said, the trees, the air and the Lane. And next she ate up Steepleford with her eyes. And it would have gone on like this, like rings spreading from a pebble thrown into a pool, and God knows where it could have ended. But ended it must have done, at last. For in this world, along with all those who, despite their colossal failings, carry in them the seeds of goodness and beauty, there are a few, only a few, I trust, who have nothing like that inside them. Who are composed only of the grossest and most foul of atoms, who are, though human, like things of the Pit. In them there is not, I dare say, one hint of light. Perhaps there is no soul. And meeting one of these persons, Amber Maria, who fed on goodness and beauty and drained it to dust, fed instead upon the worst poison, that which would scald away the psychic core of any such vampire. It was Polleto, you see, Polleto, that little ghastly human demon, whose crime is so unspeakable that it is never spoken of, Polleto who had come to live in the town, placating it by helping it buy a bell, Polleto that at last her devouring eyes reached. Like everything else then, she tried to eat him up. And then she must have tried to spew him out. But it was too late. She had touched and tasted in a manner only vampires know. She who had once loved God and once loved others as herself, until they let her die in that atrocious manner. And after that she who hated and would have eaten the world, save in due course she came to Polleto and ate at Polleto. *Polleto*! And it killed her, Frederick, in each and every way. It killed her, sending her to a death more deep than any grave, more cold than any stone.'

GLEN HIRSHBERG

Struwwelpeter

THE FOLLOWING STORY ORIGINALLY APPEARED on SciFi.Com, and has been selected for *The Year's Best Fantasy and Horror: Fifteenth Annual Collection* as well as this volume of *The Mammoth Books of Best New Horror*.

Glen Hirshberg's novelette, 'Mr Dark's Carnival', which received its first printing in the Ash-Tree Press anthology *Shadows and Silence* and later appeared in *The Year's Best Fantasy and Horror: Fourteenth Annual Collection*, was nominated for both the International Horror Guild Award and the World Fantasy Award. He also has stories in *Dark Terrors* 6 and *The Dark*. His first novel, *The Snowman's Children*, is published in the United States by Carroll & Graf. Currently, he is putting the final touches on a collection of ghost stories and working on a new novel. He lives in Los Angeles with his wife and son.

About 'Struwwelpeter' the author notes: 'Ballard is an actual section of Seattle, but the neighborhood portrayed here bares little resemblance to it except for the rain and the duplexes and the lutefisk smell. This story is dedicated to Phil Bednarz, wherever he is, for taking me bell-ringing.'

> 'The dead are not altogether powerless.'
> – Chief Seattle

T HIS WAS BEFORE WE KNEW about Peter, or at least before we understood what we knew, and my mother says it's impossible to know a thing like that anyway. She's wrong, though, and she doesn't need me to tell her she is, either.

Back then, we still gathered, afterschool afternoons, at the Andersz house, because it was close to the locks. If it wasn't raining, we'd drop our books and grab ho-hos out of the tin Mr Andersz always left on the table for us and head immediately toward the water. Gulls spun in the sunlight overhead, their cries urgent, taunting, telling us, *you're missing it, you're missing it.* We'd sprint between the rows of low stone duplexes, the sad little gardens with their flowers battered by the rain until the petals looked bent and forgotten like discarded training wheels, the splintery, sagging blue walls of the Black Anchor restaurant where Mr Paars used to hunker alone and murmuring over his plates of reeking lutefisk when he wasn't stalking 15th Street, knocking pigeons and homeless people out of the way with his dog-head cane. Finally, we'd burst into the park, pour down the avenue of fir trees like a mudslide, scattering people, bugs, and birds before us until we hit the water.

For hours, we'd prowl the green hillsides, watching the sailors yell at the invading seals from the top of the locks while the seals ignored them, skimming for fish and sometimes rolling on their backs and flipping their fins. We watched the rich-people sailboats with their masts rusting, the big grey fishing boats from Alaska and Japan and Russia with the fishermen bored on deck, smoking, throwing butts at the seals and leaning on the rails while the gulls shrieked overhead. As long as the rain held off, we stayed and threw stones to see how high up the opposite bank we could get them, and Peter would wait for ships to drift in front of us and then throw low over their bows. The sailors would scream curses in other languages or sometimes ours, and Peter would throw bigger stones at the boat-hulls. When they hit with a thunk, we'd flop on our backs on the wet grass and flip our feet in the air like the seals. It was the rudest gesture we knew.

Of course, most days it was raining, and we stayed in the Anderszes' basement until Mr Andersz and the Serbians came home. Down there, in the damp – Mr Andersz claimed his was one of three basements in all of Ballard – you could hear the wetness rising in the grass outside like lock-water. The first thing Peter did when we got downstairs was flick on the gas fireplace (not for heat, it didn't throw any), and we'd toss in stuff: pencils, a tinfoil ball, a plastic cup, and once a broken old 45 which formed blisters on its surface and then spit black goo into the air like a fleeing octopus dumping ink before it slid into a notch in the logs to melt. Once, Peter went upstairs and came back with one of Mr Andersz's red spiral photo albums and tossed it into the flames, and when one of the Mack sisters asked him what was in it, he told her, 'No idea. Didn't look.'

The burning never lasted long, five minutes, maybe. Then we'd eat ho-hos and play the Atari Mr Andersz had bought Peter years before at a yard sale, and it wasn't like you think, not always. Mostly, Peter flopped in his orange bean-bag chair with his long legs stretched in front of him and his too-long black bangs splayed across his forehead like the talons of some horrible, giant bird gripping him to lift him away. He let me and the Mack sisters take turns on the machine, and Kenny London and Steve Rourke, too, back in the days when they would come. I was the best at the basic games, Asteroids and Pong, but Jenny Mack could stay on Dig Dug forever and not get grabbed by the floating grabby-things in the ground. Even when we asked Peter to take his turn, he wouldn't. He'd say, 'Go ahead,' or 'Too tired,' or 'Fuck off,' and once I even turned around in the middle of losing to Jenny and found him watching us, sort of, the rainy window and us, not the tv screen at all. He reminded me a little of my grandfather before he died, all folded up in his chair and not wanting to go anywhere and kind of happy to have us there. Always, Peter seemed happy to have us there.

When Mr Andersz got home, he'd fish a ho-ho out of the tin for himself if we'd left him one — we tried to, most days — and then come downstairs, and when he peered out of the stairwell, his black wool hat still stuck to his head like melted wax, he already looked different than when we saw him at school. At school, even with his hands covered in yellow chalk and his transparencies full of fractions and decimals scattered all over his desk and the pears he carried with him and never seemed to eat, he was just Mr Andersz, fifth-grade math teacher, funny accent, funny to get angry. At school, it never occurred to any of us to feel sorry for him.

'Well, hello, all of you,' he'd say, as if talking to a litter of puppies he'd found, and we'd pause our game and hold our breath and wait for Peter. Sometimes – most times – Peter said, 'Hey' back, or even, 'Hey, Dad.' Then we'd all chime in like a clock tolling the hour, 'Hey, Mr Andersz,' 'Thanks for the ho-hos,' 'Your hat's all wet again,' and he'd smile and nod and go upstairs.

There were the other days, too. A few, that's all. On most of those, Peter just didn't answer, wouldn't look at his father. It was only the one time that he said, 'Hello, Dipshit-Dad,' and Jenny froze at the Atari and one of the floating grabby things swallowed her digger, and the rest of us stared, but not at Peter, and not at Mr Andersz, either. Anywhere but there.

For a few seconds, Mr Andersz seemed to be deciding, and rain-rivers wriggled down the walls and windows like transparent snakes, and we held our breath. But all he said, in the end, was, 'We'll talk later, Struwwelpeter,' which was only a little different from what he usually said when Peter got this way. Usually, he said, 'Oh. It's you, then. Hello, Struwwelpeter.' I never liked the way he said that, as though he was greeting someone else entirely, not his son. Eventually, Jenny or her sister Kelly would say, 'Hi, Mr Andersz,' and he'd glance around at us as though he'd forgotten we were there, and then he'd go upstairs and invite the Serbians in, and we wouldn't see him again until we left.

The Serbians made Steve Rourke nervous, which is almost funny, in retrospect. They were big and dark, both of them, two brothers who looked at their hands whenever they saw children. One was a car mechanic, the other worked at the locks, and they sat all afternoon, most afternoons, in Mr Andersz's study, sipping tea and speaking Serbian in low whispers. The words made their whispers harsh, full of z's and ground-up s's, as though they'd swallowed glass. 'They could be planning things in there,' Steve used to say. 'My dad says both those guys were badass soldiers.' Mostly, as far as I could tell, they looked at Mr Andersz's giant library of photo albums and listened to records. Judy Collins, Joan Baez. Almost funny, like I said.

Of course, by this last Halloween – my last night at the Andersz house – both Serbians were dead, run down by a drunken driver while walking across Fremont Bridge, and Kenny London had moved away, and Steve Rourke didn't come anymore. He said his parents wouldn't let him, and I bet they wouldn't, but that wasn't why he stopped coming. I knew it, and I think Peter knew it, too, and that worried me, a little, in ways I couldn't explain.

I almost didn't get to go, either. I was out the door, blinking in the surprising sunlight and the wind rolling off the Sound through the streets, when my mother yelled, '*Andrew*!' and stopped me. I turned to find her in the open screen door of our duplex, arms folded over the long, grey coat she wore inside and out from October to May, sunlight or no, brown-grey curls bunched on top of her scalp as though trying to crawl over her head out of the wind. She seemed to be wiggling in mid-air, like a salmon trying to hold itself still against a current. Rarely did she take what she called her 'frustrations' out on me, but she'd been crabby all day, and now she looked furious, despite the fact that I'd stayed in my room, out of her way, from the second I got home from school, because I knew she didn't really want me out tonight. Not with Peter. Not after last year.

'That's a costume?' She gestured with her chin at my jeans, my everyday black sweater, too-small brown mac she'd promised to replace this year.

I shrugged.

'You're not going trick-or-treating?'

The truth was, no one went trick-or-treating much in our section of Ballard, not like in Bellingham where we'd lived when we lived with my dad. Too wet and dismal, most days, and there were too many drunks lurking around places like the Black Anchor and sometimes stumbling down the duplexes, shouting curses at the dripping trees.

'Trick-or-treating's for babies,' I said.

'Hmm, I wonder which of your friends taught you that,' my mother said, and then a look flashed across her face, different than the one she usually got at times like this. She still looked sad, but not about me. She looked sad *for* me.

I took a step toward her, and her image wavered in my glasses. 'I won't sleep there. I'll be home by eleven,' I said.

'You'll be home by ten, or you won't be going anywhere again anytime soon. Got it? How old do you think you are, anyway?'

'Twelve,' I said, with as much conviction as I could muster, and my mother flashed the sad look again.

'If Peter tells you to jump off a bridge . . .'

'Push him off.'

My mother nodded. 'If I didn't feel so bad for *him* . . .' she said, and I thought she meant Peter, and then I wasn't sure. But she didn't say anything else, and after a few seconds, I couldn't stand there anymore, not with the wind crawling down the neck of my jacket and my mother still looking like that. I left her in the doorway.

Even in bright sunlight, mine was a dreary neighborhood. The gusts of wind herded paper scraps and street-grit down the overflowing gutters and yanked the last leaves off the trees like a gleeful gang on a vandalism rampage. I saw a few parents – new to the area, obviously – hunched into rain-slickers, leading little kids from house to house. The kids wore drugstore clown costumes, Darth Vader masks, sailor caps. They all looked edgy, miserable. At most of the houses, no one answered the doorbell.

Outside the Andersz place, I stopped for just a minute, watching the leaves leaping from their branches like lemmings and tumbling down the wind, trying to figure out what was different, what felt wrong. Then I had it: the Mountain was out. The endless Fall rain had rolled in early that year, and it had been weeks, maybe months, since I'd last seen Mount Rainier. Seeing it now gave me the same unsettled sensation as always. 'It's because you're looking south, not west,' people always say, as if that explains how the mountain gets to that spot on the horizon, on the wrong side of the city, not where it actually is but out to sea, seemingly bobbing on the waves, not the land.

How many times, I wondered abruptly, had some adult in my life asked why I liked Peter? I wasn't cruel, and despite my size, I wasn't easily cowed, and I did okay in school – not as well as Peter, but okay – and I had 'a gentleness, most days', as Mrs Corbett (WhoreButt, to Peter) had written on my report card last year. 'If he learns to exercise judgment – and perhaps gives some thought to his choice of companions – he could go far.'

I wanted to go far from Ballard, anyway, and the locks, and the smell of lutefisk, and the rain. I liked doorbell ditching, but I didn't get much charge out of throwing stones through windows. And if people were home when we did it, came out and shook their fists or worse, just stood there, looking at us the way you would at a wind or an earthquake, nothing you could slow or stop, I'd freeze, feeling bad, until Peter screamed at me or yanked me so hard that I had no choice but to follow.

I could say I liked how smart Peter was, and I did. He could sit dead still for 27 minutes of a 30-minute comprehension test, then scan the reading and answer every question right before the teacher, furious, hovering over him and watching the clock, could snatch the paper away without the rest of us screaming foul. He could recite the periodic table of elements backwards, complete with atomic weights. He could build skyscrapers five feet high out of chalk and rubber-cement jars and toothpicks and crayons that always stayed standing until anyone who wasn't him tried to touch them.

I could say I liked the way he treated everyone the same, which he did, in a way. He'd been the first in my grade – the only one, for a year or so – to hang out with the Mack sisters, who were still, at that point, the only African Americans in our school. But he wasn't all that nice to the Macks, really. Just no nastier than he was to the rest of us.

No. I liked Peter for exactly the reason my mother and my teachers feared I did: because he was fearless, because he was cruel – although mostly to people who deserved it when it wasn't Halloween – and most of all, because he really did seem capable of anything. So many of the people I knew seemed capable of nothing, for whatever reason. Capable of nothing.

Out on the whitecap-riddled Sound, the sun sank, and the Mountain turned red. It was like looking inside it, seeing it living. Shivering slightly in the wind, I hopped the Anderszes' three stone steps and rang the bell.

'Just come in, fuck!' I heard Peter yell from the basement, and I started to open the door, and Mr Andersz opened it for me. He had his grey cardigan straight on his waist for once and his black hat was gone and his black-grey hair was wet and combed on his forehead, and I had the horrible, hilarious idea that he was going on a date.

'Andrew, come in,' he said, sounding funny, too formal, the way he did at school. He didn't step back right away, either, and when he did, he put his hand against the mirror on the hallway wall, as though the house was rocking underneath him.

'Hey, Mr Andersz,' I said, wiping my feet on the shredded green mat that said something in Serbian. Downstairs, I could hear the burbling of the Dig Dug game, and I knew the Mack sisters had arrived. I flung my coat over Peter's green slicker on the coatrack, took a couple steps toward the basement door, turned around, stopped.

Mr Andersz had not moved, hadn't even taken his hand off the mirror, and now he was staring at it as though it was a spider frozen there.

'Are you all right, Mr Andersz?' I asked, and he didn't respond. Then he made a sound, a sort of hiss, like a radiator when you switch it off.

'How many?' he muttered. I could barely hear him. 'How many chances? As a teacher, you know there won't be many. You get two, maybe three moments in an entire year . . . Something's happened, there's been a fight or someone's sick or the soccer team won or something, and you're looking at a student . . .' His voice trailed off, leaving me with the way he said 'student'. He pronounced it 'stu-*dent*'. It was one of the things we all made fun of, not mean fun, just fun. 'You're looking at them,' he said, 'and suddenly, there they are. And it's them, and it's thrilling, terrifying, because you know you might have a chance . . . an opportunity. You can say something.'

On the mirror, Mr Andersz's hand twitched, and I noticed the sweat beading under the hair on his forehead. It reminded me of my dad, and I wondered if Mr Andersz was drunk. Then I wondered if my dad was drunk, wherever he was. Downstairs, Jenny Mack yelled, 'Get off' in her fighting voice, happy-loud, and Kelly Mack said, 'Good, come on, this is *boring*.'

'And as parent . . .' Mr Andersz muttered. 'How many? And what happens . . . the moment comes . . . but you're missing your wife. Just right then, just for a while. Or your friends. Maybe you're tired. It's just that day. It's rainy, you have meals to make, you're tired . . . There'll be another moment. Surely. You have years. Right? You have years . . .'

So fast and so silent was Peter's arrival in the basement doorway that I mistook him for a shadow from outside, didn't even realize he was there until he pushed me in the chest. 'What's your deal?' he said.

I started to gesture at Mr Andersz, thought better of it,

shrugged. Footsteps clattered on the basement stairs, and then the Macks were in the room. Kelly had her tightly braided hair stuffed under a black, backward baseball cap. Her bare arms were covered in paste-on snake tattoos, and her face was dusted in white powder. Jenny wore a red sweater, black jeans. Her hair hung straight and shiny and dark, hovering just off her head and neck like a bird's crest, and I understood, for the first time, that she was pretty. Her eyes were bright green, wet and watchful.

'What are you supposed to be?' I said to Kelly, because suddenly I was uncomfortable looking at Jenny.

Kelly flung her arm out to point and did a quick, ridiculous shoulder-wriggle. It was nothing like her typical movements; I'd seen her dance. 'Vanilla Ice,' she said, and spun around.

'Let's go,' Peter said, stepping past me and his father and tossing my mac on the floor so he could get to his slicker.

'You want candy, Andy?' Jenny teased, her voice sing-songy.

'Ho-ho?' I asked. I was talking, I suppose, to Mr Andersz, who was still staring at his hand on the mirror. I didn't want him to be in the way. It made me nervous for him.

The word 'ho-ho' seemed to rouse him, though. He shoved himself free of the wall, shook his head as if awakening, and said, 'Just a minute,' very quietly.

Peter opened the front door, letting in the wind, and Mr Andersz pushed it closed, not hard. But he leaned against it, and the Mack sisters stopped with their coats half on. Peter just stood beside him, his black hair sharp and pointy on his forehead like the tips of a spiked fence. But he looked more curious than angry.

Mr Andersz lifted a hand to his eyes, squeezed them shut, opened them. Then he said, 'Turn out your pockets.'

Still, Peter's face registered nothing. He didn't respond to his father or glance at us. Neither Kelly nor I moved, either. Beside me, Jenny took a long, slow breath, as though she was clipping a wire on a bomb, and then she said, 'Here, Mr A,' and she pulled the pockets of her grey coat inside out, revealing two sticks of Dentyne, two cigarettes, a ring of keys with a Seahawks whistle dangling amongst them, and a ticket stub. I couldn't see what from.

'Thank you, Jenny,' Mr Andersz said, but he didn't take the cigarettes, hardly even looked at her. He watched his son.

Very slowly, after a long time, Peter smiled. 'Look at you,' he
said. 'Being daddy.' He pulled out the liner of his coat pockets.
There was nothing in them at all.

'Pants,' said Mr Andersz.

'What do you think you're looking for, Big Bàd Daddy?' Peter
asked. 'What do you think you're going to find?'

'Pants,' Mr Andersz said.

'And what will you do, do you think, if you find it?' But he
turned out his pants pockets. There was nothing in those, either,
not even keys or money.

For the first time since Peter had come upstairs, Mr Andersz
looked at the rest of us, and I shuddered. His face looked the same
way my mother's had when I'd left the house: a little scared, but
mostly sad. Permanently, stupidly sad.

'I want to tell you something,' he said. If he spoke like this in
the classroom, I thought, no one would wedge unbent paper-
clips in his chalkboard erasers anymore. 'I won't have it. There
will be no windows broken. There will be no little children
terrorized—'

'That wasn't our fault,' said Jenny, and she was right, in a way.
We hadn't known anyone was hiding in those bushes when we
toilet-papered them, and Peter had meant to light his cigarette,
not the roll of toilet paper.

'Nothing lit on fire. No one bullied or hurt. I won't have it,
because it's beneath you, do you understand? You're the smartest
children I know.' Abruptly, Mr Andersz's hands flashed out and
grabbed his son's shoulders. 'Do you hear me? You're the
smartest child I've ever seen.'

For a second, they just stood there, Mr Andersz clutching
Peter's shoulders as though trying to steer a runaway truck, Peter
completely blank.

Then, very slowly, Peter smiled. 'Thanks, Dad,' he said.

'Please,' Mr Andersz said, and Peter opened his mouth, and we
all cringed.

But what he said was, 'Okay,' and he slipped past his father and
out the door. I looked at the Mack sisters. Together, we watched
Mr Andersz in the doorway with his head tilted forward on his
neck and his hands tight at his sides, like a diver at the Olympics
getting ready for a backflip. He never moved, though, and
eventually, we followed Peter out. I was last, and I thought I

felt Mr Andersz's hand on my back as I went by, but I wasn't sure, and when I glanced around, he was still just standing there, and the door swung shut.

I'd been inside the Andersz's house fifteen minutes, maybe less, but the wind had whipped the late afternoon light over the horizon, and the Mountain had faded from red to grey-black, motionless now on the surface of the water like an oil tanker, one of those massive, passing ships on which no people were visible, ever. I never liked my neighborhood, but I hated it after sundown, the city gone, the Sound indistinguishable from the black, starless sky, no one walking. It was like we were some-one's toy set that had been closed up in its box and snapped shut for the night.

'Where are we going?' Kelly Mack said, her voice sharp, fed up. She'd been sick of us, lately. Sick of Peter.

'Yeah,' I said, rousing myself. I didn't want to soap car windows or throw rocks at street signs or put on rubber masks and scare trick-or-treaters, exactly, but those were the things we did. And we had no supplies.

Peter closed his eyes, leaned his head back, took a deep breath of the rushing air and held it. He looked almost peaceful. I couldn't remember seeing him that way. It was startling. Then he stuck one trembling arm out in front of him, pointed at me, and his eyes sprung open.

'Do you know . . .' he said, his voice deep, accented, a perfect imitation, 'what that bell does?'

I clapped my hands. 'That bell . . .' I said, in the closest I could get to the same voice, and the Mack sisters stared at us, baffled, which made me grin even harder, 'raises the dead.'

'What are you babbling about?' said Kelly to Peter, but Jenny was looking at me, seawater eyes curious and strange.

'You know Mr Paars?' I asked her.

But of course she didn't. The Macks had moved here less than a year and a half ago, and I hadn't seen Mr Paars, I realized, in considerably longer. Not since the night of the bell, in fact. I looked at Peter. His grin was as wide as mine felt. He nodded at me. We'd been friends a long time, I realized. Almost half my life.

Of course, I didn't say that. 'A long time ago,' I told the Macks, feeling like a longshoreman, a lighthouse keeper, someone with stories who lived by the sea, 'there was this man. An old, white-haired-man. He ate lutefisk – it's fish, it smells awful, I don't really know what it is – and stalked around the neighborhood, scaring everybody.'

'He had this cane,' Peter said, and I waited for him to go on, join me in the telling, but he didn't.

'All black,' I said. 'Kind of scaly. Ribbed, or something. It didn't look like a cane. And it had this silver dog's head on it, with fangs. A doberman—'

'Anyway . . .' said Kelly Mack, though Jenny seemed to be enjoying listening.

'He used to bop people with it. Kids. Homeless people. Whoever got in his way. He stomped around 15th Street, terrorizing everyone. Two years ago, on the first Halloween we were allowed out alone, right about this time of night, Peter and I spotted him coming out of the hardware store. It's not there anymore, it's that empty space next to the place where the movie theater used to be. Anyway, we saw him there, and we followed him home.'

Peter waved us out of his yard, toward the locks. Again, I waited, but when he glanced at me, the grin was gone. His face was normal, neutral, maybe, and he didn't say anything.

'He lives down there,' I said, gesturing to the south, toward the Sound. 'Way past all the other houses. Past the end of the street. Practically in the water.'

Despite what Peter had said, we didn't head that way. Not then. We wandered toward the locks, into the park. The avenue between the pine trees was empty except for a scatter of solitary bums on benches, wrapping themselves in shredded jackets and newspapers as the night nailed itself down and the dark billowed around us in the wind-gusts like the sides of a tent. In the roiling trees, black birds perched on the branches, silent as gargoyles.

'There aren't any other houses that close to Mr Paars's,' I said. 'The street turns to dirt, and it's always wet because it's down by the water. There are these long, empty lots full of weeds, and a couple of sheds, I don't know what's in them or who would own them. Anyway, right where the pavement ends, Peter and I dropped back and just kind of hung out near the last house until Mr Paars made it to his yard. God, Peter, you remember his yard?'

Instead of answering, Peter led us between the low stone

buildings to the canal, where we watched the water swallow the last streaks of daylight like some monstrous whale gulping plankton. The only boats in the slips were two sailboats, sails furled, rocking as the waves slapped against them. The only person I saw on either stood at the stern of the boat closest to us, head hooded in a green oil-slicker, face aimed out to sea.

'Think I could hit him from here?' said Peter, and I flinched, looked at his fists expecting to see stones, but he was just asking. 'Tell them the rest,' he said.

I glanced at the Macks, was startled to see them holding hands, leaning against the rail over the canal, though they were watching us, not the water. 'Come on, already,' Kelly said, but Jenny just raised her eyebrows at me. Behind her, seagulls dipped and tumbled on the wind like shreds of cloud that had been ripped loose.

'We waited, I don't know, a while. It was cold. Remember how cold it was? We were wearing winter coats and mittens. It wasn't windy like this, but it was freezing. At least that made the dirt less muddy when we finally went down there. We passed the sheds and the trees, and there was no one, I mean no one, around. Too cold for any trick-or-treating anywhere around here, even if anyone was going to. And there wasn't anywhere to go on that street, regardless.

'Anyway. It's weird. Everything's all flat down there, and then right as you get near the Paars place, this little forest springs up, all these thick firs. We couldn't really see anything.'

'Except that it was light,' Peter murmured.

'Yeah. Bright light. Mr Paars had his yard floodlit, for intruders, we figured. We thought he was probably paranoid. So we snuck off the road when we got close and went into the trees. In there, it was wet. Muddy, too. My mom was so mad when I got home. Pine needles sticking to me everywhere. She said I looked like I'd been tarred and feathered. We hid in this little grove, looked into the lawn, and we saw the bell.'

Now Peter turned around, his hands flung wide to either side. 'Biggest fucking bell you've ever seen in your life,' he said.

'What are you talking about?' said Kelly.

'It was in this . . . pavilion,' I started, not sure how to describe it. 'Gazebo, I guess. All white and round, like a carousel, except the only thing inside was this giant white bell, like a church bell, hanging from the ceiling on a chain. And all the lights in the yard were aimed at it.'

'Weird,' said Jenny, leaning against her sister.

'Yeah. And that house. It's real dark, and real old. Black wood or something, all sort of falling apart. Two storeys, kind of big. It looked like four or five of the sheds we passed sort of stacked on top of each other and squashed together. But the lawn was beautiful. Green, mowed perfectly, like a baseball stadium.'

'Kind of,' Peter whispered. He turned from the canal and wandered away again, back between buildings down the tree-lined lane.

A shiver swept up the skin on my back as I realized, finally, why we were going back to the Paars house. I'd forgotten, until that moment, how scared we'd been. How scared Peter had been. Probably, Peter had been thinking about this for two years.

'It was all so strange,' I said to the Macks, all of us watching the bums in their rattling paper blankets and the birds clinging by their talons to the branches and eyeing us as we passed. 'All that outside light, the house falling apart and no lights on in there, no car in the driveway, that huge bell. So we just looked for a long time. Then Peter said – I remember this, exactly – "He just leaves something shaped like that hanging there. And he expects us not to ring it."

'Then, finally, we realized what was in the grass.'

By now, we were out of the park, back among the duplexes, and the wind had turned colder, though it wasn't freezing, exactly. In a way, it felt good, fresh, like a hard slap in the face.

'I want a shrimp-and-chips,' Kelly said, gesturing over her shoulder toward 15th Street, where the little fry-stand still stayed open next to the Dairy Queen, although the Dairy Queen had been abandoned.

'I want to go see this Paars house,' said Jenny. 'Stop your whining.' She sounded cheerful, fierce, the way she did when she played Dig Dug or threw her hand in the air at school. She was smart, too, not Peter-smart, but as smart as me, at least. And I think she'd seen the trace of fear in Peter, barely there but visible in his skin like a fossil, something long dead and never before seen, and it fascinated her. That's what I was thinking when she reached out casually and grabbed my hand. Then I stopped thinking at all. 'Tell me about the grass,' she said.

'It was like a circle,' I said, my fingers still, my palm flat against hers. Even when she squeezed, I held still. I didn't know what to do, and I didn't want Peter to turn around. If Kelly had noticed, she didn't say anything. 'Cut right in the grass. A pattern. A circle, with this upside-down triangle inside it, and—'

'How do you know it was upside down?' Jenny asked.

'What?'

'How do you know you were even looking at it the right way?'

'Shut up,' said Peter, quick and hard, not turning around, leading us onto the street that dropped down to the Sound, to the Paars house. Then he did turn around, and he saw our hands. But he didn't say anything. When he was facing forward again, Jenny squeezed once more, and I gave a feeble squeeze back,

We walked half a block in silence, but that just made me more nervous. I could feel Jenny's thumb sliding along the outside of mine, and it made me tingly, terrified. I said, 'Upside down. Right side up. Whatever. It was a symbol, a weird one. It looked like an eye.'

'Old dude must have had a hell of a lawnmower,' Kelly muttered, glanced at Peter's back, and stopped talking, just in time, I thought. Mr Andersz was right. She was smart, too.

'It kind of made you not want to put your foot in the grass,' I continued. 'I don't know why. It just looked wrong. Like it really could see you. I can't explain.'

'Didn't make *me* want not to put my foot in the grass,' Peter said.

I felt Jenny look at me. Her mouth was six inches or so from my hair, my ear. It was too much. My hand twitched and I let go. Blushing, I glanced at her. She looked surprised, and she drifted away toward her sister.

'That's true,' I said, wishing I could call Jenny back. 'Peter stepped right out.'

On our left, the last of the duplexes slid away, and we came to the end of the pavement. In front of us, the dirt road rolled down the hill, red-brown and wet and bumpy, like some stretched, cut-out tongue on the ground. I remembered the way Peter's duck-boots had seemed to float on the surface of Mr Paars's floodlit green lawn, as though he was walking on water.

'Hey,' I said, though Peter had already stepped onto the dirt and was strolling, fast and purposeful, down the hill. 'Peter,' I called after him, though I followed, of course. The Macks were beside but no longer near me. 'When's the last time you saw him? Mr Paars?'

He turned around, and he was smiling now, the smile that scared me. 'Same time you did, Bubba,' he said. 'Two years ago tonight.'

I blinked, stood still, and the wind lashed me like the end of a twisted-up towel. 'How do you know when I last saw him?' I said.

Peter shrugged. 'Am I wrong?'

I didn't answer. I watched Peter's face, the dark swirling around and over it, shaping it, like rushing water over stone.

'He hasn't been anywhere. Not on 15th Street. Not at the Black Anchor. Nowhere. I've been watching.'

'Maybe he doesn't live there anymore,' Jenny said carefully. She was watching Peter, too.

'There's a car,' Peter said. 'A Lincoln. Long and black. Practically a limo.'

'I've seen that car,' I said. 'I've seen it drive by my house, right at dinner time.'

'It goes down there,' said Peter, gesturing toward the trees, the water, the Paars house. 'Like I said, I've been watching.'

And of course, he had been, I thought. If his father had let him, he'd probably have camped right here, or in the gazebo under the bell. In fact, it seemed impossible to me, given everything I knew about Peter, that he'd let two years go by.

'Exactly what happened to you two down there?' Kelly asked.

'Tell them now,' said Peter. 'There isn't going to be any talking once we get down there. Not until we're all finished.' Dropping into a crouch, he picked at the cold, wet dirt with his fingers, watched the ferries drifting out of downtown toward Bainbridge Island, Vashon. You couldn't really make out the boats from there, just the clusters of lights on the water like clouds of lost, doomed fireflies.

'Even the grass was weird,' I said, remembering the weight of my sopping pants against my legs. 'It was so wet. I mean, everywhere was wet, as usual, but this was like wading in a pond. You put your foot down and the whole lawn rippled. It made the eye look like it was winking. At first we were kind of hunched over, sort of hiding, which was ridiculous in all that light. I didn't want to walk in the circle, but Peter just strolled right through it. He called me a baby because I went the long way around.'

'I called you a baby because you were being one,' Peter said, but not meanly, really.

'We kept expecting lights to fly on in the house. Or dogs to come out. It just seemed like there would be dogs. But there weren't. We got up to the gazebo, which was the only place in the whole yard with shadows, because it was surrounded by all these trees. Weird trees. They were kind of stunted. Not pines, either, they're like birch trees, I guess. But short. And their bark is black.'

'Felt weird, too,' Peter muttered, straightening up, wiping his hands down his coat. 'It just crumbled when you rubbed it in your hands, like one of those soft block-erasers, you know what I mean?'

'We must have stood there ten minutes. More. It was so quiet. You could hear the Sound, a little, although there aren't any waves there or anything. You could hear the pine trees dripping, or maybe it was the lawn. But there weren't any birds. And there wasn't anything moving in that house. Finally, Peter started toward the bell. He took exactly one step into the gazebo, and one of those dwarf trees walked right off its roots into his path, and both of us started screaming.'

'What?' said Jenny.

'I didn't scream,' said Peter. 'And he hit me.'

'He didn't hit you,' I said.

'Yes, he did.'

'Could you shut up and let Andrew finish?' said Kelly, and Peter lunged, grabbing her slicker in his fists and shoving her hard and then yanking her forward so that her head snapped back on its stalk like a decapitated flower and then snapped into place again.

It had happened so fast that neither Jenny nor I had moved, but Jenny hurtled forward now, raking her nails down Peter's face, and he said, 'Ow!' and fell back, and she threw her arms around Kelly's shoulders. For a few seconds, they stood like that, and then Kelly put her own arms up and eased Jenny away. To my astonishment, I saw that she was laughing.

'I don't think I'd do that again, if I were you,' she said to Peter, her laughter quick and hard, as though she was spitting teeth.

Peter put a hand to his cheek, gazing at the blood that came away on his fingers. 'Ow,' he said again.

'Let's go home,' Jenny said to her sister.

No one answered right away. Then Peter said, 'Don't.' After a few seconds, when no one reacted, he said, 'You've got to see the house.' He was going to say more, I think, but what else was there to say? I felt bad, without knowing why. He was like a planet we visited, cold and rocky and probably lifeless, and we kept coming because it was all so strange, so different than what we knew. He looked at me, and what I was thinking must have flashed in my face, because he blinked in surprise, turned away, and started down the road without looking back. We all followed. Planet, dark star, whatever he was, he created orbits.

'So the tree hit Peter,' Jenny Mack said quietly when we were halfway down the hill, almost to the sheds.

'It wasn't a tree. It just seemed like a tree. I don't know how we didn't see him there. He had to have been watching us the whole time. Maybe he knew we'd followed him. He just stepped out of the shadows and kind of whacked Peter across the chest with his cane. That black dog-head cane. He did kind of look like a tree. His skin was all gnarly, kind of dark. If you rubbed him between your fingers, he'd probably have crumbled, too. And his hair was so white. A tree that was way too old.

'And his voice. It was like a bullfrog, even deeper. He spoke real slow. He said, "Boy. Do you know what that bell does?" And then he did the most amazing thing of all. The scariest thing. He looked at both of us, real slow. Then he dropped his cane. Just dropped it to his side. And he smiled, like he was daring us to go ahead. "That bell raises the dead. Right up out of the ground" '

'Look at these,' Kelly Mack murmured as we walked between the sheds.

'Raises the dead,' I said.

'Yeah, I heard you. These are amazing.'

And they were. I'd forgotten. The most startling thing, really, was that they were still standing. They'd all sunk into the swampy grass on at least one side, and none of them had roofs, not whole roofs, anyway, and the window slots gaped, and the wind made a rattle as it rolled through them, like waves over seashells, empty things that hadn't been empty always. They were too small to have been boat sheds, I thought, had to have been for tools and things. But tools to do what?

In a matter of steps, they were behind us, between us and the homes we knew, the streets we walked. We reached the ring of pines around the Paars house, and it was different, worse. I didn't realize how, but Peter did.

'No lights,' he said.

For a while, we just stood in the blackness while saltwater and pine-resin smells glided over us like a mist. There wasn't any moon, but the water beyond the house reflected what light there was, so we could see the long, black Lincoln in the dirt driveway, the house and the gazebo beyond it. After a minute or so, we could make out the bell, too, hanging like some bloated, white bat from the gazebo ceiling.

'It *is* creepy,' Jenny said.

'Ya think?' I said, but I didn't mean to, it was just what I imagined Peter would have said if he were saying anything. 'Peter, I think Mr Paars is gone. Moved, or something.'

'Good,' he said. 'Then he won't mind.' He stepped out onto the lawn and said, 'Fuck.'

'What?' I asked, shoulders hunching, but Peter just shook his head.

'Grass. It's a lot longer. And it's wet as hell.'

'What happened after "That bell raises the dead"?' Jenny asked.

I didn't answer right away. I wasn't sure what Peter wanted me to say. But he just squinted at the house, didn't even seem to be listening. I almost took Jenny's hand. I wanted to. 'We ran.'

'Both of you? Hey, Kell—'

But Kelly was already out on the grass next to Peter, smirking as her feet sank. Peter glanced at her – cautiously, I thought. Uncertain. 'You would have, too,' he said.

'I might have,' said Kelly.

Then we were all on the grass, holding still, listening. The wind rushed through the trees as though filling a vacuum. I thought I could hear the Sound, not waves, just the dead, heavy wet. But there were no gulls, no bugs.

Once more, Peter strolled straight for that embedded circle in the grass, still visible despite the depth of the lawn, like a manta ray half-buried in seaweed. When Peter's feet crossed the corners of the upside-down triangle – the tear-ducts of the eye – I winced, then felt silly. For all I knew, it was a corporate logo; it looked about that menacing. I started forward, too. The Macks came with me. I walked in the circle, though I skirted the edge of the triangle. Step on a crack and all. I didn't look behind to see what the Macks did, I was too busy watching Peter as his pace picked up. He was practically running, straight for the gazebo, and then he stopped.

'Hey,' he said.

I'd seen it, too, I thought, feeling my knees lock as my nervousness intensified. In the lone upstairs window, there'd been a flicker. Maybe. Just one, for a single second, and then it was gone again. 'I saw it,' I called, but Peter wasn't listening to me. He was moving straight toward the front door. And anyway, I realized, he hadn't been looking upstairs.

'What the hell's he doing?' Kelly said as she strolled past me, but she didn't stop for an answer. Jenny did, though.

'Andrew, what's going on?' she said, and I looked at her eyes, green and shadowy as the grass, but that just made me edgier still.

I shook my head. For a moment, Jenny stood beside me. Finally, she shrugged and followed her sister. None of them looked back, which meant, I thought, that there really hadn't been rustling behind us just now, back in the pines. When I whipped my head around, I saw nothing but trees and twitching shadows.

'Here, puss-puss-puss,' Peter called softly. If the grass had been less wet and I'd been less unsettled, I'd have flopped on my back and flipped my feet in the air at him, the seal's send-off. Instead, I came forward.

The house, like the sheds, seemed to have sunk sideways into the ground. With its filthy windows and rotting planks, it looked like the abandoned hull of a beached ship. Around it, the leafless branches of the dwarf trees danced like the limbs of paper skeletons.

'Now, class,' said Peter, still very quietly. 'What's wrong with this picture?'

'I assume you mean other than giant bells, weird eyeballs in the grass, empty sheds, and these whammy-ass trees,' Kelly said, but Peter ignored her.

'He means the front door,' said Jenny, and of course she was right.

I don't even know how Peter noticed. It was under an over-hang, so that the only light that reached it reflected off the ground. But there was no doubt. The door was open. Six inches, tops. The scratched brass of the knob glinted dully, like an eye.

'Okay,' I said. 'So the door didn't catch when he went in, and he didn't notice.'

'When who went in?' said Peter, mocking. 'Thought you said he moved.'

The wind kicked up, and the door glided back another few inches, then sucked itself shut with a click.

'Guess that settles that,' I said, knowing it didn't even before the curtains came streaming out the single front window, grey and gauzy as cigarette smoke as they floated on the breeze. They hung there a few seconds, then glided to rest against the side of the house when the wind expired.

'Guess it does,' said Peter softly, and he marched straight up the steps, pushed open the door, and disappeared into the Paars house.

None of the rest of us moved or spoke. Around us, tree-branches tapped against each other, the side of the house. For the second time I sensed someone behind me and spun around. Night-dew sparkled in the lawn like broken glass, and one of the shadows of the towering pines seemed to shiver back, as though the trees had inhaled it. Otherwise, there was nothing. I thought about Mr Paars, that dog-head cane with its silver fangs.

'What's he trying to prove?' Kelly asked, a silly question where Peter was concerned, really. It wasn't about proving. We all knew that.

Jenny said, 'He's been in there a long time,' and Peter stuck his head out the window, the curtain floating away from him.

'Come see this,' he said, and ducked back inside.

Hesitating, I knew, was pointless. We all knew it. We went up the stairs together, and the door drifted open before we even touched it. 'Wow,' said Kelly staring straight ahead, and Jenny took my hand again, and then we were all inside. 'Wow,' Kelly said again.

Except for a long, wooden table folded and propped against the staircase like a lifeboat, all the furniture we could see had been draped in white sheets. The sheets rose and rearranged themselves in the breeze, which was constant and everywhere, because all the windows had been flung wide open. Leaves chased each other across the dirt-crusted hardwood floor, and scraps of paper flapped in mid-air like giant moths before settling on the staircase or the backs of chairs or blowing out the windows.

Peter appeared in a doorway across the foyer from us, his black hair bright against the deeper blackness of the rooms behind him. 'Don't miss the den,' he said. 'I'm going to go look at the kitchen.' Then he was gone again.

Kelly had started away now, too, wandering into the living room to our right, running her fingers over the tops of a covered couch as she passed it. One of the paintings on the wall, I noticed, had been covered rather than removed, and I wondered what it was. Kelly drew up the cover, peered beneath it, then dropped it and stepped deeper into the house. I started to follow, but Jenny pulled me the other way, and we went left into what must have been Mr Paars's den.

'Whoa,' Jenny said, and her fingers slid between mine and tightened.

In the dead center of the room, amidst discarded file folders that lay where they'd been tossed and empty envelopes with plastic address windows that flapped and chattered when the wind filled them, sat an enormous oak rolltop desk. The top was gone, broken away, and it lay against the room's lone window like the cracked shell of a dinosaur egg. On the surface of the desk, in black felt frames, a set of six photographs had been arranged in a semicircle.

'It's like the top of a tombstone,' Jenny murmured. 'You know what I mean? Like a . . . what do you call it?'

'Family vault,' I said. 'Mausoleum.'

'One of those.'

Somehow, the fact that two of the frames turned out to be empty made the array even more unsettling. The other four held individual pictures of what had to be brothers and one sister – they all had flying white hair, razor-blue eyes – standing, each in turn, on the top step of the gazebo outside, with the great bell looming behind them, bright white and all out of proportion, like the Mountain on a too-clear day.

'Andrew,' Jenny said, her voice nearly a whisper, and in spite of the faces in the photographs and the room we were in, I felt it all over me. 'Why Struwwelpeter?'

'What?' I said, mostly just to make her speak again.

'Struwwelpeter. Why does Mr Andersz call him that?'

'Oh. It's from some kids' book. My mom actually had it when she was little. She said it was about some boy who got in trouble because he wouldn't cut his hair or cut his nails.'

Jenny narrowed her eyes. 'What does that have to do with anything?'

'I don't know. Except my mom said the pictures in the book were really scary. She said Struwwelpeter looked like Freddy Krueger with a 'fro.'

Jenny burst out laughing, but she stopped fast. Neither of us, I think, liked the way laughter sounded in that room, in that house, with those black-bordered faces staring at us. 'Struwwelpeter,' she said, rolling the name carefully on her tongue, like a little kid daring to lick a frozen flagpole.

'It's what my mom called me when I was little,' said Peter from the doorway, and Jenny's fingers clenched hard and then fell free of mine. Peter didn't move toward us. He just stood there while we watched, paralyzed. After a few long seconds, he added, 'When I kicked the shit out of barbers, because I hated having my hair cut. Then when I was just being bad. She'd say that instead of screaming at me. It made me cry.' From across the foyer, in the living room, maybe, we heard a single, soft bump, as though something had fallen over.

With a shrug, Peter released us and stepped past us back into the foyer. We followed, not touching now, not even looking at each other. I felt guilty, amazed, strange. When we passed the windows the curtains billowed up and brushed across us.

'Hey, Kelly,' Peter whispered loudly into the living room. He whispered it again, then abruptly turned our way and said, 'You think he's dead?'

'Looks like it,' I answered, glancing down the hallway toward the kitchen, into the shadows in the living room, which seemed to have shifted, somehow, the sheet some way different as it lay across the couch. I couldn't place the feeling, it was like watching an actor playing a corpse, knowing he was alive, trying to catch him breathing.

'But the car's here,' Peter said. 'The Lincoln. Hey, *Kelly*!' His

448   GLEN HIRSHBERG

shout made me wince, and Jenny cringed back toward the front
door, but she shouted, too.

'Kell? *Kell*?'

'Oh, what is *that*?' I murmured, my whole spine twitching like
a severed electrical wire, and when Jenny and Peter looked at me,
I pointed upstairs.

'Wh—' Jenny started, and then it happened again, and both of
them saw it. From under the half-closed door at the top of the
staircase – the only door we could see from where we were – came
a sudden slash of light which disappeared instantly, like a snake's
tongue flashing in and out.

We stood there at least a minute, maybe more. Even Peter
looked uncertain, not scared, quite, but something had happened
to his face. I couldn't place it right then. It made me nervous,
though. And it made me like him more than I had in a long, long
time.

Then, without warning, Peter was halfway up the stairs, his feet
stomping dust out of each step as he slammed them down, saying,
'Fucking hilarious, Kelly. Here I come. Ready or not.' He stopped
halfway up and turned to glare at us. Mostly at me. 'Come on.'

'Let's go,' I said to Jenny, reached out on my own for the first
time and touched her elbow, but to my surprise she jerked it away
from me. 'Jenny, she's up there.'

'I don't think so,' she whispered.

'Come *on*,' Peter hissed.

'Andrew, something's wrong. Stay here.'

I looked into her face, smart, steely Jenny Mack, first girl ever
to look at me like that, first girl I'd ever wanted to, and right then,
for the only time in my life, I felt – within me – the horrible thrill
of Peter's power, knew the secret of it. It wasn't bravery and it
wasn't smarts, although he had both those things in spades. It was
simply the willingness to trade. At any given moment, Peter
Andersz would trade anyone for anything, or at least could
convince people that he would. Knowing you could do that, I
thought, would be like holding a grenade, tossing it back and
forth in the terrified face of the world.

I looked at Jenny's eyes, filling with tears, and I wanted to kiss
her, though I couldn't even imagine how to initiate something like
that. What I said, in my best Peter-voice, was, 'I'm going upstairs.
Coming or staying?'

I can't explain. I didn't mean anything. It felt like playacting, no more real than holding her hand had been. We were just throwing on costumes, dancing around each other, scaring each other. Trick or treat.

'*Kelly?*' Jenny called past me, blinking, crying openly, now, and I started to reach for her again, and she shoved me, hard, toward the stairs.

'Hurry up,' said Peter, with none of the triumph I might have expected in his voice.

I went up, and we clumped, side by side, to the top of the stairs. When we reached the landing, I looked back at Jenny. She was propped in the front door, one hand on the doorknob and the other wiping at her eyes as she jerked her head from side to side, looking for her sister.

At our feet, light licked under the door again. Peter held up a hand, and we stood together and listened. We heard wind, low and hungry, and now I was sure I could hear the Sound lapping against the edge of the continent, crawling over the lip of it.

'OnetwothreeBoo!' Peter screamed and flung open the door, which banged against a wall inside and bounced back. Peter kicked it open again, and we lunged through into what must have been a bedroom, once, and was now just a room, a blank space, with nothing in it at all.

Even before the light swept over us again, from outside, from the window, I realized what it was. 'Lighthouse,' I said, breathless. 'Greenpoint Light.'

Peter grinned. 'Oh, yeah. Halloween.'

Every year, the suburbs north of us set Greenpoint Light running again on Halloween, just for fun. One year, they'd even rented ferries and decked them out with seaweed and parents in pirate costumes and floated them just offshore, ghost-ships for the kiddies. We'd seen them skirting our suburb on their way up the coast.

'Do you think—' I started, and Peter grabbed me hard by the elbow. 'Ow,' I said.

'Listen,' snapped Peter.

I heard the house groan as it shifted. I heard paper flapping somewhere downstairs, the front door tapping against its frame or the inside wall as it swung on the wind.

'*Listen,*' Peter whispered, and this time I heard it. Very low.

Very faint, like a finger rubbed along the lip of a glass, but unmistakable once you realized what it was. Outside, in the yard, someone had just lifted the tongue of the bell and tapped it, oh so gently, against the side.

I stared at Peter, and he stared back. Then he leaped to the window, peering down. I thought he was going to punch the glass loose from the way his shoulders jerked.

'Well?' I said.

'All I can see is the roof.' He shoved the window even further open than it already was. '*Clever girls!*' he screamed, and waited, for laughter, maybe, a full-on bong of the bell, something. Abruptly, he turned to me, and the light rolled across him, waist-high, and when it receded, he looked different, damp with it. 'Clever girls,' he said.

I whirled, stepped into the hall, looked down. The front door was open, and Jenny was gone. 'Peter?' I whispered, and I heard him swear as he emerged onto the landing beside me. 'You think they're outside?'

Peter didn't answer right away. He had his hands jammed in his pockets, his gaze cast down at the floor. He shuffled in place. 'The thing is, Andrew,' he said, 'there's nothing to do.'

'What are you talking about?'

'There's nothing to do.'

'Find the girls?'

He shrugged.

'Ring the bell?'

'They rang it.'

'You're the one who brought us out here. What were you expecting?'

He glanced back at the bedroom's bare walls, the rectangular, dustless space in the floor where, until very recently, a bed or rug must have been, the empty light fixture overhead. Struwwelpeter. My friend. 'Opposition,' he said, and shuffled off down the hall.

'Where are you going?' I called after him.

He turned, and the look on his face stunned me, it had been years since I'd seen it. The last time was in second grade, right after he punched Robert Case, who was twice his size, in the face and ground one of Robert's eyeglass lenses into his eye. The last time anyone who knew him had dared to fight him. He looked . . . sorry.

'Coming?' he said.

I almost followed him. But I felt bad about leaving Jenny. And I wanted to see her and Kelly out on the lawn, pointing through the window at us and laughing. And I didn't want to be in that house anymore. And it was exhausting being with Peter, trying to read him, dancing clear of him.

'I'll be outside,' I said.

He shrugged and disappeared through the last unopened door at the end of the hall. I listened for a few seconds, heard nothing, turned, and started downstairs. 'Hey, Jenny?' I called, got no answer. I was three steps from the bottom before I realized what was wrong.

In the middle of the foyer floor, amidst a swirl of leaves and paper, Kelly Mack's black baseball cap lay upside down like an empty tortoise shell. 'Um,' I said to no one, to myself, took one more uncertain step down, and the front door swung back on its hinges.

I just stared, at first. I couldn't even breathe, let alone scream, it was like I had an apple core lodged in my throat. I just stared into the white spray-paint on the front door, the triangle-within-a-circle. A wet, wide-open eye. My legs wobbled, and I grabbed for the banister, slipped down to the bottom step, held myself still. *I should scream*, I thought. *I should get Peter down here, and both of us should run*. I didn't even see the hand until it clamped hard around my mouth.

For a second, I couldn't do anything at all, and that was way too long, because before I could lunge away or bite down, a second hand snaked around my waist, and I was yanked off my feet into the blackness to my left and slammed against the living-room wall.

I wasn't sure when I'd closed my eyes, but now I couldn't make them open. My head rang, and my skin felt tingly, tickly, as though it was dissolving into the atoms that made it up, all of them racing in a billion different directions, and soon there'd be nothing left of me, just a scatter of energy and a spot on Mr Paars's dusty, decaying floor.

'Did I hurt you?' whispered a voice I knew, close to my ears. It still took me a long time to open my eyes. 'Just nod or shake your head.'

Slowly, forcing my eyes open, I nodded.

'Good. Now sssh,' said Mr Andersz, and released me.

Behind him, both Mack sisters stood grinning.

'You like the cap?' Kelly said. 'The cap's a good touch, no?'

'Sssh,' Mr Andersz said. 'Please. I beg you.'

'You should see you,' Jenny whispered, sliding up close. 'You look so damn scared.'

'What's—'

'He followed us to see if we were doing anything horrible. He saw us come in here, and he had this idea to get back at Peter.'

I gaped at Jenny, then at Mr Andersz, who was peering, very carefully, around the corner, up the stairs.

'Not to get back,' he said, so serious. It was the same voice he'd used in his own front hallway earlier that evening. He'd never looked more like his son than he did right then. 'To reach out. Reach him. Someone's got to do something. He's a good boy. He could be. Now, please. Don't spoil this.'

Everything about Mr Andersz at that moment astounded me. But watching him revealed nothing further. He stood at the edge of the living room, shoulders hunched, hair tucked tight under his dockworker's cap, waiting. Slowly, my gaze swung back to Jenny, who continued to grin in my direction, but not at me, certainly not with me. And I knew I'd lost her.

'This was about Peter,' I said. 'You could have just stuck your head out and waved me down.'

'Yep,' said Jenny, and watched Mr Andersz, not me.

Upstairs, a door creaked, and Peter's voice rang out. 'Hey, Andrew.'

To Jenny's surprise and Mr Andersz's horror, I almost answered. I stepped forward, opened my mouth. I'm sure Jenny thought I was getting back at her, turning the tables again, but mostly I didn't like what Mr Andersz was doing. I think I sensed the danger in it. I might have been the only one.

But I was twelve. And Peter certainly deserved it. And Mr Andersz was my teacher, and my friend's father. I closed my mouth, sank back into the shadows, and did not move again until it was over.

'*Andrew, I know you can hear me!*' Peter shouted, stepping onto the landing. He came, clomp clomp clomp, toward the stairs. '*Annn-drew!*' Then, abruptly, we heard him laugh. Down he came, his shoes clattering over the steps. I thought he might charge past us, but he stopped, right where I did.

Beside the couch, under the draped painting, Kelly Mack pointed at her own hatless head and mouthed, 'Oh, yeah.'

But it was the eye on the door, I thought, not the cap. Only the eye would have stopped him, because like me – and faster than me – Peter would have realized that neither Mack sister, smart as they were, would have thought of it. Even if they'd had spray paint. Mr Andersz had brought spray paint? Clearly, he'd been planning this – or something like this – for quite some time. If he was the one who'd done it, that is.

'What the fuck,' Peter muttered. He came down a step. Another. His feet touched flat floor, and still Mr Andersz held his post.

Then, very quietly, he said, 'Boo.'

It was as if he'd punched an ejector-seat button. Peter flew through the front door, hands flung up to ward off the eye as he sailed past it. He was fifteen feet from the house, still flying, when he realized what he'd heard. We all saw it hit him. He jerked in mid-air like a hooked marlin reaching the end of a harpoon rope.

For a few seconds, he just stood in the wet grass with his back to us, quivering. Kelly had sauntered past Mr Andersz onto the front porch, laughing. Mr Andersz, I noticed, was smiling, too, weakly. Even Jenny was laughing quietly beside me.

But I was watching Peter's back, his whole body vibrating like an imploded building after the charge has gone off, right at the moment of collapse. 'No,' I said.

When Peter finally turned around, though, his face was his regular face, inscrutable, a little pale. The spikes in his hair looked almost silly in the shadows, and made him look younger. A naughty little boy. Calvin with no Hobbes.

'So he *is* dead,' Peter said.

Mr Andersz stepped outside. Kelly was slapping her leg, but no one paid her any attention.

'Son,' said Mr Andersz, and he stretched one hand out, as though to call Peter to him. 'I'm sorry. It was . . . I thought you might laugh.'

'He's dead, right?'

The smile was gone from Mr Andersz's face now, and from

Jenny's, I noted when I glanced her way. 'Kelly, shut up,' I heard her say to her sister, and Kelly stopped giggling.

'Did you know he used to teach at the school?' Mr Andersz asked, startling me.

'Mr Paars?'

'Sixth-grade science. Biology, especially. Years ago. Kids didn't like him. Yes, Peter, he died a week or so ago. He'd been very sick. We got a notice about it at school.'

'Then he won't mind,' said Peter, too quietly, 'if I go ahead and ring that bell. Right?'

Mr Andersz didn't know about the bell, I realized. He didn't understand. I watched him look at his son, watched the weight he always seemed to be carrying settle back around his shoulders, lock into place like a yoke. He bent forward, a little.

'My son,' he said. Uselessly.

So I shoved past him. I didn't mean to push him, I just needed him out of the way, and anyway, he gave no resistance, bent back like a plant.

'Peter, don't do it,' I said.

The eyes, black and mesmerizing, swung down on me. 'Oh. Andrew. Forgot you were here.'

It was, of course, the cruelest thing he could have said, the source of his power over me and the reason I was with him – other than the fact that I liked him, I mean. It was the thing I feared most, in general, no matter where I was.

'That bell . . .' I said, thinking of the dog's head-cane, that deep and frozen voice, but thinking more, somehow, about my friend, rocketing away from us now at incomprehensible speed. Because that's what he seemed to be doing, to me.

'Wouldn't it be great?' said Peter. And then, unexpectedly, he grinned at me. He would never forget I was there, I realized. Couldn't. I was all he had.

He turned and walked straight across the grass. The Mack sisters and Mr Andersz followed, all of them seeming to float in the long, wet green like seabirds skimming the surface of the ocean. I did not go with them. I had the feel of Jenny's fingers in mine, and the sounds of flapping paper and whirling leaves in my ears, and Peter's last, surprising smile floating in front of my eyes, and it was enough, too much, an astonishing Halloween.

'This thing's freezing,' I heard Peter say, while his father and the Macks fanned out around him, facing the house and me. He was facing away, toward the trees. 'Feel this.' He held the tongue of the bell toward Kelly Mack, but she'd gone silent, now, watching him, and she shook her head.

'Ready or not,' he said. Then he reared back and rammed the bell-tongue home.

Instinctively, I flung my hands up to my ears, but the effect was disappointing, particularly to Peter. It sounded like a dinner bell, high, a little tinny, something that might call kids or a dog out of the water or the woods at bedtime. Peter slammed the tongue against the side of the bell one more time, dropped it, and the peal floated away over the Sound, dissipating into the salt air like seagull-cry.

For a few breaths, barely any time at all, we all stood where we were. Then Jenny Mack said, 'Oh.' I saw her hand snake out, grab her sister's, and her sister looked up, right at me, I thought. The two Macks stared at each other. Then they were gone, hurtling across the yard, straight across that wide-open white eye, flying toward the forest.

Peter whirled, looked at me, and his mouth opened, a little. I couldn't hear him, but I saw him murmur, 'Wow,' and a new smile exploded, one I couldn't even fathom, and he was gone, too, sprinting for the trees, passing the Macks as they all vanished into the shadows.

'Uh,' said Mr Andersz, backing, backing, and his expression confused me most of all. He was almost laughing. 'I'm so sorry,' he said. 'We didn't realize . . .' He turned and chased after his son. And still, somehow, I thought they'd all been looking at me, until I heard the single, sharp thud from the porch behind me. Wood hitting wood. Cane-into-wood.

I didn't turn around. Not then. What for? I knew what was behind me. Even so, I couldn't get my legs to move, quite, not until I heard a second thud, closer this time, as though the thing on the porch had stepped fully out of the house, making its slow, steady way toward me. Stumbling, I kicked myself forward, put a hand down in the wet grass and the mud closed over it like a mouth. When I jerked it free, it made a disappointed, sucking sort of sound, and I heard a sort of sigh behind me, another thud, and I ran, all the way to the woods.

Hours later, we were still huddled together in the Andersz

kitchen, wolfing down ho-hos and hot chocolate. Jenny and Kelly and Peter kept laughing, erupting into cloudbursts of excited conversation, laughing some more. Mr Andersz laughed, too, as he boiled more water and spooned marshmallows into our mugs and told us.

The man the bell had called forth, he said, was Mr Paars's brother. He'd been coming for years, taking care of Mr Paars after he got too sick to look after himself, because he refused to move into a rest home or even his brother's home.

'The Lincoln,' Peter said, and Mr Andersz nodded.

'God, poor man. He must have been inside when you all got there. He must have thought you were coming to rob the place, or vandalize it, and he went out back.'

'We must have scared the living shit out of him,' Peter said happily.

'Almost as much as we did you,' said Kelly, and everyone was shouting, pointing, laughing again.

'Mr Paars had been dead for days when they found him,' Mr Andersz told us. 'The brother had to go away, and he left a nurse in charge, but the nurse got sick, I guess, or Mr Paars wouldn't let her in, or something. Anyway, it was pretty awful when the brother came back. That's why the windows were all open. It'll take weeks, I bet, to air that place out.'

I sat, and I sipped my cocoa, and I watched my friends chatter and eat and laugh and wave their arms around, and it dawned on me, slowly, that none of them had seen. None of them had heard. Not really. I almost said something five different times, but I never quite did, I think because of the way we all were, just for that hour, that last, magic night: triumphant, and windswept, and defiant, and together. Like real friends. Almost.

That was the last time, of course. The next summer, the Macks moved to Vancouver, although they'd slowly slipped away from Peter and me anyway by then. Mr Andersz lost his job – there was an incident, apparently, he just stopped teaching and sat down on the floor in the front of his classroom and swallowed an entire box of chalk, stick by stick – and wound up working in the little caged-in accounting office at the used-car lot in the wasteland down by the Ballard Bridge. And slowly, over a long period of time, it became more exciting, even for me, to talk about Peter than it was to be with him.

Soon, I think, my mother is going to get sick of staring at the images repeating over and over on our tv screen, the live reports from the rubble of my school and the yearbook photo of Peter and the video of him being stuffed into a police car and the names streaming across the bottom of the screen like a tornado warning, except too late. For the fifteenth time, at least, I see Steve Rourke's name go by. I should have told him, I thought, should have warned him. But he should have known. I wonder why my name isn't up there, why Peter didn't come after me. The answer, though, is obvious. He forgot I was there. Or he wants me to think he did.

It doesn't matter. Any minute, my mother's going to get up and go to bed, and she's going to tell me I should, too, and that we'll leave here, we'll get away and never come back.

'Yes,' I'll say. 'Soon.'

'All those children,' she'll say. Again. 'Sweet Jesus, I can't believe it. Andrew.' She'll drop her head on my shoulder and throw her arms around me and cry.

But by then, I won't be thinking about the streaming names, the people I knew who are people no longer, or what Peter might have been thinking tonight. I'll be thinking, just as I am now, about Peter in the grass outside the Paars house, at the moment he realized what we'd done to him. The way he stood there, vibrating. We didn't make him what he was. Not the Macks, not his dad, not me – none of us. But it's like he said: God puts something shaped like that in the world, and then He expects us not to ring it.

And now there's only one thing left to do. As soon as my mom finally lets go, stops sobbing, and stumbles off to sleep, I'm going to sneak outside, and I'm going to go straight down the hill to the Paars house. I haven't been there since that night. I have no idea if the sheds or the house or the bell even exist anymore.

But if they do, and if that eye in the grass, or any of its power, is still there . . . well, then. I'll give a little ring. And then we'll know, once and for all, whether I really did see two old men, with matching canes, on the porch of the Paars house when I glanced back right as I fled into the woods. Whether I really did hear rustling from all those sideways sheds as I flew past, as though, in each, something was sliding out of the ground. I wonder if the bell works only on the Paars family, or if it affects any recently deceased in the vicinity. Maybe the dead really can be called back, for a while, like kids from recess. And if they do come back – and if they're angry, and they go looking for Peter, and they find him – well. Let the poor, brilliant, fucked-up bastard get what he deserves.

ELIZABETH HAND

Cleopatra Brimstone

ELIZABETH HAND GREW UP IN New York and lived in Washington, D.C., for a number of years before moving to the coast of Maine, where she now lives. She is the author of six novels, including *Black Light*, *Glimmering* and *Waking the Moon*, as well as a short-story collection, *Last Summer at Mars Hill*. Her work has received the Nebula, World Fantasy, Tiptree and Mythopeic Society awards, and 'Cleopatra Brimstone' won the International Horror Guild Award in 2002. She recently completed a novel called *Mortal Love*.

'This story was written when I had to cancel a long-planned (and much-anticipated) research trip to London and the West Country in October 2000,' recalls the author. 'To ease my disappointment, I picked up on an old story idea I'd abandoned, changed the setting to London's Camden Town (where I've spent a good deal of time in the last six years), and for two weeks devoted myself to recreating the place where I should have been.

'I have a lifelong fascination with insects, butterflies and moths in particular, but I must admit that I've never found my amateur's knowledge of lepidoptery terribly useful as a dating tool.'

For Mike Harrison

Her earliest memory was of wings. Luminous red and blue, yellow and green and orange; a black so rich it appeared liquid, edible. They moved above her and the sunlight made them glow as though they were themselves made of light, fragments of another, brighter world falling to earth about her crib. Her tiny hands stretched upward to grasp them but could not: they were too elusive, too radiant, too much of the air.

Could they ever have been real?

For years she thought she must have dreamed them. But one afternoon when she was ten she went into the attic, searching for old clothes to wear to a Halloween party. In a corner beneath a cobwebbed window she found a box of her baby things. Yellow-stained bibs and tiny fuzzy jumpers blued from bleaching, a much-nibbled stuffed dog that she had no memory of whatsoever.

And at the very bottom of the carton, something else. Wings flattened and twisted out of shape, wires bent and strings frayed: a mobile. Six plastic butterflies, colors faded and their wings giving off a musty smell, no longer eidolons of Eden but crude representations of monarch, zebra swallowtail, red admiral, sulfur, an unnaturally elongated hairskipper and *Agrias narcissus*. Except for the *narcissus*, all were common New World species that any child might see in a suburban garden. They hung limply from their wires, antennae long since broken off; when she touched one wing it felt cold and stiff as metal.

The afternoon had been overcast, tending to rain. But as she held the mobile to the window, a shaft of sunlight broke through the darkness to ignite the plastic wings, blood-red, ivy-green, the pure burning yellow of an August field. In that instant it was as though her entire being was burned away, skin hair lips fingers all ash; and nothing remained but the butterflies and her awareness of them, orange and black fluid filling her mouth, the edges of her eyes scored by wings.

As a girl she had always worn glasses. A mild childhood astigmatism worsened when she was thirteen: she started bumping into things, and found it increasingly difficult to concentrate on the entomological textbooks and journals that she read voraciously. Growing pains, her mother thought; but after two months, Janie's clumsiness and concomitant headaches became so severe that her mother admitted that this was perhaps something more serious, and took her to the family physician.

'Janie's fine,' Dr Gordon announced after peering into her ears

and eyes. 'She needs to see the ophthalmologist, that's all. Sometimes our eyes change when we hit puberty.' He gave her mother
the name of an eye doctor nearby.

Her mother was relieved, and so was Jane – she had overheard
her parents talking the night before her appointment, and the
words CAT *scan* and *brain tumour* figured in their hushed
conversation. Actually, Jane had been more concerned about
another odd physical manifestation, one which no one but herself
seemed to have noticed. She had started menstruating several
months earlier: nothing unusual in that. Everything she had read
about it mentioned the usual things – mood swings, growth
spurts, acne, pubic hair.

But nothing was said about eyebrows. Janie first noticed
something strange about hers when she got her period for the
second time. She had retreated to the bathtub, where she spent a
good half-hour reading an article in *Nature* about Oriental
Ladybug swarms. When she finished the article, she got out of
the tub, dressed and brushed her teeth, then spent a minute
frowning at the mirror.

Something was different about her face. She turned sideways,
squinting. Had her chin broken out? No; but something had
changed. Her hair color? Her teeth? She leaned over the sink until
she was almost nose-to-nose with her reflection.

That was when she saw that her eyebrows had undergone a
growth spurt of their own. At the inner edge of each eyebrow,
above the bridge of her nose, three hairs had grown remarkably
long. They furled back towards her temple, entwined in a sort of
loose braid. She had not noticed them sooner because she seldom
looked in a mirror, and also because the odd hairs did not arch
above the eyebrows, but instead blended in with them, the way a
bittersweet vine twines around a branch.

Still, they seemed bizarre enough that she wanted no one, not
even her parents, to notice. She found her mother's eyebrow
tweezers, neatly plucked the six hairs and flushed them down the
toilet. They did not grow back.

At the optometrist's, Jane opted for heavy tortoiseshell frames
rather than contacts. The optometrist, and her mother, thought
she was crazy, but it was a very deliberate choice. Janie was not
one of those homely B-movie adolescent girls, driven to Science as
a last resort. She had always been a tomboy, skinny as a rail, with

long, slanted violet-blue eyes; a small rosy mouth; long, straight
black hair that ran like oil between her fingers; skin so pale it had
the periwinkle shimmer of skim milk.

When she hit puberty, all of these conspired to beauty. And
Jane hated it. Hated the attention, hated being looked at, hated
that other girls hated her. She was quiet, not shy but impatient to
focus on her schoolwork, and this was mistaken for arrogance by
her peers. All through high school she had few friends. She
learned early the perils of befriending boys, even earnest boys
who professed an interest in genetic mutations and intricate
computer simulations of hive activity. Jane could trust them
not to touch her, but she couldn't trust them not to fall in love.
As a result of having none of the usual distractions of high school
– sex, social life, mindless employment – she received an Intel/
Westinghouse Science Scholarship for a computer-generated
schematic of possible mutations in a small population of viceroy
butterflies exposed to genetically engineered crops. She graduated
in her junior year, took her scholarship money, and ran.

She had been accepted at Stanford and MIT, but chose to
attend a small, highly prestigious women's college in a big city
several hundred miles away. Her parents were apprehensive
about her being on her own at the tender age of seventeen,
but the college, with its elegant, cloister-like buildings and lushly
wooded grounds, put them at ease. That and the dean's assur-
ances that the neighborhood was completely safe, as long as
students were sensible about not walking alone at night. Thus
mollified, and at Janie's urging – she was desperate to move away
from home – her father signed a very large check for the first
semester's tuition. That September she started school.

She studied entomology, spending her first year examining the
genitalia of male and female Scarce Wormwood Shark Moths, a
species found on the Siberian steppes. Her hours in the zoology
lab were rapturous, hunched over a microscope with a pair of
tweezers so minute they were themselves like some delicate
portion of her specimen's physiognomy. She would remove the
butterflies' genitalia, tiny and geometrically precise as diatoms,
and dip them first into glycerine, which acted as a preservative,
and next into a mixture of water and alcohol. Then she observed
them under the microscope. Her glasses interfered with this work
– they bumped into the microscope's viewing lens – and so she

switched to wearing contact lenses. In retrospect, she thought that this was probably a mistake.

At Argus College she still had no close friends, but neither was she the solitary creature she had been at home. She respected her fellow students, and grew to appreciate the company of women. She could go for days at a time seeing no men besides her professors or the commuters driving past the school's wrought-iron gates.

And she was not the school's only beauty. Argus College specialized in young women like Jane: elegant, diffident girls who studied the burial customs of Mongol women or the mating habits of rare antipodean birds; girls who composed concertos for violin and gamelan orchestra, or wrote computer programs that charted the progress of potentially dangerous celestial objects through the Oort cloud. Within this educational greenhouse, Janie was not so much orchid as sturdy milkweed blossom. She thrived.

Her first three years at Argus passed in a bright-winged blur with her butterflies. Summers were given to museum internships, where she spent months cleaning and mounting specimens in solitary delight. In her senior year Janie received permission to design her own thesis project, involving her beloved Shark Moths. She was given a corner in a dusty anteroom off the Zoology Lab, and there she set up her microscope and laptop. There was no window in her corner, indeed there was no window in the anteroom at all, though the adjoining Lab was pleasantly old-fashioned, with high arched windows set between Victorian cabinetry displaying *Lepidoptera*, neon-carapaced beetles, unusual tree fungi and (she found these slightly tragic) numerous exotic finches, their brilliant plumage dimmed to dusty hues. Since she often worked late into the night, she requested and received her own set of keys. Most evenings she could be found beneath the glare of the small halogen lamp, entering data into her computer, scanning images of genetic mutations involving female Shark Moths exposed to dioxane, corresponding with other researchers in Melbourne and Kyoto, Siberia and London.

The rape occurred around ten o'clock one Friday night in early March. She had locked the door to her office, leaving her laptop behind, and started to walk to the subway station a few blocks away. It was a cold clear night, the yellow glow of the crime lights giving dead grass and leafless trees an eerie autumn glow. She hurried across the campus, seeing no one, then hesitated at Seventh Street. It was a longer walk, but safer, if she went down Seventh Street and then over to Michigan Avenue. The shortcut was much quicker, but Argus authorities and the local police discouraged students from taking it after dark. Jane stood for a moment, staring across the road to where the desolate park lay; then, staring resolutely straight ahead and walking briskly, she crossed Seventh and took the shortcut.

A crumbling sidewalk passed through a weedy expanse of vacant lot, strewn with broken bottles and the spindly forms of half a dozen dusty-limbed oak trees. Where the grass ended, a narrow road skirted a block of abandoned row houses, intermittently lit by crime lights. Most of the lights had been vandalized, and one had been knocked down in a car accident – the car's fender was still there, twisted around the lamppost. Jane picked her way carefully among shards of shattered glass, reached the sidewalk in front of the boarded-up houses and began to walk more quickly, toward the brightly-lit Michigan Avenue intersection where the subway waited.

She never saw him. He was *there*, she knew that; knew he had a face, and clothing; but afterwards she could recall none of it. Not the feel of him, not his smell; only the knife he held – awkwardly, she realized later, she probably could have wrested it from him – and the few words he spoke to her. He said nothing at first, just grabbed her and pulled her into an alley between the row houses, his fingers covering her mouth, the heel of his hand pressing against her windpipe so that she gagged. He pushed her onto the dead leaves and wads of matted windblown newspaper, yanked her pants down, ripped open her jacket and then tore her shirt open. She heard one of the buttons strike brick and roll away. She thought desperately of what she had read once, in a Rape Awareness brochure: not to struggle, not to fight, not to do anything that might cause her attacker to kill her.

Janie did not fight. Instead, she divided into three parts. One part knelt nearby and prayed the way she had done as a child, not intently but automatically, trying to get through the strings of words as quickly as possible. The second part submitted blindly and silently to the man in the alley. And the third hovered above the other two, her hands wafting slowly up and down to keep her aloft as she watched.

'Try to get away,' the man whispered. She could not see him or feel him though his hands were there. 'Try to get away.'

She remembered that she ought not to struggle, but from the noises he made and the way he tugged at her she realized that was what aroused him. She did not want to anger him; she made a small sound deep in her throat and tried to push him from her chest. Almost immediately he groaned, and seconds later rolled off her. Only his hand lingered for a moment upon her cheek. Then he stumbled to his feet – she could hear him fumbling with his zipper – and fled.

The praying girl and the girl in the air also disappeared then. Only Janie was left, yanking her ruined clothes around her as she lurched from the alley and began to run, screaming and staggering back and forth across the road, toward the subway.

The police came, an ambulance. She was taken first to the police station and then to the City General Hospital, a hellish place, starkly lit, with endless underground corridors that led into darkened rooms where solitary figures lay on narrow beds like gurneys. Her pubic hair was combed and stray hairs placed into sterile envelopes; semen samples were taken, and she was advised to be tested for HIV and other diseases. She spent the entire night in the hospital, waiting and undergoing various examinations. She refused to give the police or hospital staff her parents' phone number, or anyone else's. Just before dawn they finally released her, with an envelope full of brochures from the local Rape Crisis Centre, New Hope for Women, Planned Parenthood, and a business card from the police detective who was overseeing her case. The detective drove her to her apartment in his squad car; when he stopped in front of her building, she was suddenly terrified that he would know where she lived, that he would come back, that he had been her assailant.

But of course he had not been. He walked her to the door and waited for her to go inside. 'Call your parents,' he said right before he left.

'I will.'

She pulled aside the bamboo window shade, watching until the squad car pulled away. Then she threw out the brochures she'd received, flung off her clothes and stuffed them into the trash. She showered and changed, packed a bag full of clothes and another of books. Then she called a cab. When it arrived, she directed it to the Argus campus, where she retrieved her laptop and her research on Tiger Moths, then had the cab bring her to Union Station.

She bought a train ticket home. Only after she arrived and told her parents what had happened did she finally start to cry. Even then, she could not remember what the man had looked like.

She lived at home for three months. Her parents insisted that she get psychiatric counseling and join a therapy group for rape survivors. She did so, reluctantly, but stopped attending after three weeks. The rape was something that had happened to her, but it was over.

'It was fifteen minutes out of my life,' she said once at group. 'That's all. It's not the rest of my life.'

This didn't go over very well. Other women thought she was in denial; the therapist thought Jane would suffer later if she did not confront her fears now.

'But I'm not afraid,' said Jane.

'Why not?' demanded a woman whose eyebrows had fallen out.

Because lightning doesn't strike twice, Jane thought grimly, but she said nothing. That was the last time she attended group.

That night her father had a phone call. He took the phone and sat at the dining table, listening; after a moment he stood and walked into his study, giving a quick backward glance at his daughter before closing the door behind him. Jane felt as though her chest had suddenly frozen: but after some minutes she heard her father's laugh: he was not, after all, talking to the police detective. When after half an hour he returned, he gave Janie another quick look, more thoughtful this time.

'That was Andrew.' Andrew was a doctor friend of his, an Englishman. 'He and Fred are going to Provence for three months. They were wondering if you might want to house-sit for them.'

'In *London*?' Jane's mother shook her head. 'I don't think—'

'I said we'd think about it.'

'*I'll* think about it,' Jane corrected him. She stared at both her parents, absently ran a finger along one eyebrow. 'Just let me think about it.'

And she went to bed.

She went to London. She already had a passport, from visiting Andrew with her parents when she was in high school. Before she left there were countless arguments with her mother and father, and phone calls back and forth to Andrew. He assured them that the flat was secure, there was a very nice reliable older woman who lived upstairs, that it would be a good idea for Janie to get out on her own again.

'So you don't get gun-shy,' he said to her one night on the phone. He was a doctor, after all: a homeopath not an allopath, which Janie found reassuring. 'It's important for you to get on with your life. You won't be able to get a real job here as a visitor, but I'll see what I can do.'

It was on the plane to Heathrow that she made a discovery. She had splashed water onto her face, and was beginning to comb her hair when she blinked and stared into the mirror.

Above her eyebrows, the long hairs had grown back. They followed the contours of her brow, sweeping back towards her temples; still entwined, still difficult to make out unless she drew her face close to her reflection and tilted her head just so. Tentatively she touched one braided strand. It was stiff yet oddly pliant; but as she ran her finger along its length a sudden *surge* flowed through her. Not an electrical shock: more like the thrill of pain when a dentist's drill touches a nerve, or an elbow rams against a stone. She gasped; but immediately the pain was gone. Instead there was a thrumming behind her forehead, a spreading warmth that trickled into her throat like sweet syrup. She opened her mouth, her gasp turning into an uncontrollable yawn, the yawn into a spike of such profound physical ecstasy that she grabbed the edge of the sink and thrust forward, striking her head against the mirror. She was dimly aware of someone knocking at the lavatory door as she clutched the sink and, shuddering, climaxed.

'Hello?' someone called softly. 'Hello, is this occupied?'

'Right out,' Janie gasped. She caught her breath, still trembling; ran a hand across her face, her fingers halting before they could touch the hairs above her eyebrows. There was the faintest

tingling, a temblor of sensation that faded as she grabbed her
cosmetic bag, pulled the door open and stumbled back into the
cabin.

Andrew and Fred lived in an old Georgian row house just west of
Camden Town, overlooking the Regent's Canal. Their flat occupied the first floor and basement; there was a hexagonal solarium
out back, with glass walls and heated stone floor, and beyond
that a stepped terrace leading down to the canal. The bedroom
had an old wooden four-poster piled high with duvets and down
pillows, and French doors that also opened onto the terrace.
Andrew showed her how to operate the elaborate sliding security
doors that unfolded from the walls, and gave her the keys to the
barred window guards.

'You're completely safe here,' he said, smiling. 'Tomorrow
we'll introduce you to Kendra upstairs, and show you how to
get around. Camden Market's just down that way, and *that*
way—'

He stepped out onto the terrace, pointing to where the canal
coiled and disappeared beneath an arched stone bridge. '—that
way's the Regent's Park Zoo. I've given you a membership—'

'Oh! Thank you!' Janie looked around, delighted. 'This is
wonderful.'

'It is.' Andrew put an arm around her and drew her close.
'You're going to have a wonderful time, Janie. I thought you'd
like the zoo – there's a new exhibit there, "The World Within" or
words to that effect – it's about insects. I thought perhaps you
might want to volunteer there – they have an active docent
programme, and you're so knowledgeable about that sort of
thing.'

'Sure. It sounds great – really great.' She grinned and smoothed
her hair back from her face, the wind sending up the rank scent of
stagnant water from the canal, the sweetly poisonous smell of
hawthorn blossom. As she stood gazing down past the potted
geraniums and Fred's rosemary trees, the hairs upon her brow
trembled, and she laughed out loud, giddily, with anticipation.

Fred and Andrew left two days later. It was enough time for Janie
to get over her jet lag, and begin to get barely acclimated to the
city, and to its smell. London had an acrid scent: damp ashes, the

softer underlying fetor of rot that oozed from ancient bricks and stone buildings, the thick vegetative smell of the canal, sharpened with urine and spilled beer. So many thousands of people descended on Camden Town on the weekend that the Tube station was restricted to incoming passengers, and the canal path became almost impassable. Even late on a week night she could hear voices from the other side of the canal, harsh London voices echoing beneath the bridges or shouting to be heard above the din of the trains passing overhead.

Those first days Janie did not venture far from the flat. She unpacked her clothes, which did not take much time, and then unpacked her collecting box, which did. The sturdy wooden case had come through the overseas flight and Customs seemingly unscathed, but Janie found herself holding her breath as she undid the metal hinges, afraid of what she'd find inside.

'Oh!' she exclaimed. Relief, not chagrin: nothing had been damaged. The small glass vials of ethyl alcohol and gel shellac were intact, and the pillboxes where she kept the tiny #2 pins she used for mounting. Fighting her own eagerness, she carefully removed packets of stiff archival paper, a block of Styrofoam covered with pinholes; two bottles of clear Maybelline nail polish and a small container of Elmer's Glue-All; more pillboxes, empty, and empty gelatine capsules for very small specimens; and last of all a small glass-fronted display box, framed in mahogany and holding her most precious specimen: a hybrid *Celerio harmuthi kordesch*, the male crossbreed of the Spurge and Elephant Hawkmoths. As long as the first joint of her thumb, it had the hawkmoth's typically streamlined wings but exquisitely delicate coloring, fuchsia bands shading to a soft rich brown, its thorax thick and seemingly feathered. Only a handful of these hybrid moths had ever existed, bred by the Prague entomologist Jan Pokorny in 1961; a few years afterward, both the Spurge Hawkmoth and the Elephant Hawkmoth had become extinct.

Janie had found this one for sale on the Internet three months ago. It was a former museum specimen and cost a fortune; she had a few bad nights, worrying whether it had actually been a legal purchase. Now she held the display box in her cupped palms and gazed at it raptly. Behind her eyes she felt a prickle, like sleep or unshed tears; then a slow thrumming warmth crept from her brows, spreading to her temples, down her neck and through her breasts, spreading like a stain. She swallowed, leaned back against the sofa and let the display box rest back within the larger case; slid first one hand then the other beneath her sweater and began to stroke her nipples. When some time later she came it was with stabbing force and a thunderous sensation above her eyes, as though she had struck her forehead against the floor.

She had not: gasping, she pushed the hair from her face, zipped her jeans and reflexively leaned forward, to make certain the hawkmoth in its glass box was safe.

Over the following days she made a few brief forays to the newsagent and greengrocer, trying to eke out the supplies Fred and Andrew had left in the kitchen. She sat in the solarium, her bare feet warm against the heated stone floor, and drank camomile tea or claret, staring down to where the ceaseless stream of people passed along the canal path, and watching the narrowboats as they plied their way slowly between Camden Lock and Little Venice, two miles to the west in Paddington. By the following Wednesday she felt brave enough, and bored enough, to leave her refuge and visit the zoo.

It was a short walk along the canal, dodging bicyclists who jingled their bells impatiently when she forgot to stay on the proper side of the path. She passed beneath several arching bridges, their undersides pleated with slime and moss. Drunks sprawled against the stones and stared at her blearily or challengingly by turns; well-dressed couples walked dogs, and there were excited knots of children, tugging their parents on to the zoo.

Fred had walked here with Janie, to show her the way. But it all looked unfamiliar now. She kept a few strides behind a family, her head down, trying not to look as though she was following them; and felt a pulse of relief when they reached a twisting stair with an arrowed sign at its top.

REGENT'S PARK ZOO

There was an old church across the street, its yellow stone walls overgrown with ivy; and down and around the corner a long stretch of hedges with high iron walls fronting them, and at last a huge set of gates, crammed with children and vendors selling balloons and banners and London guidebooks. Janie lifted her head and walked quickly past the family that had led her here, showed her membership card at the entrance, and went inside.

She wasted no time on the seals or tigers or monkeys, but went straight to the newly renovated structure where a multicolored banner flapped in the late-morning breeze.

AN ALTERNATE UNIVERSE: SECRETS OF THE INSECT WORLD

Inside, crowds of schoolchildren and harassed-looking adults formed a ragged queue that trailed through a brightly lit corridor, its walls covered with huge glossy colour photos and computer-enhanced images of hissing cockroaches, helgrammites, morpho butterflies, death-watch beetles, polyphemous moths. Janie dutifully joined the queue, but when the corridor opened into a vast sun-lit atrium she strode off on her own, leaving the children and teachers to gape at monarchs in butterfly cages and an interactive display of honeybees dancing. Instead she found a relatively quiet display at the far end of the exhibition space, a floor-to-ceiling cylinder of transparent net, perhaps six feet in diameter. In it, buckthorn bushes and blooming hawthorn vied for sunlight with a slender beech sapling, and dozens of butterflies flitted upwards through the new yellow leaves, or sat with wings outstretched upon the beech tree. They were a type of *Pieridae*, the butterflies known as Whites; though these were not white at all. The females had creamy yellow-green wings, very pale, their wingspans perhaps an inch and a half. The males were the same size; when they were at rest their flattened wings were a dull, rather sulfurous color. But when the males lit into the air their wings revealed vivid, spectral yellow undersides. Janie caught her breath in delight, her neck prickling with that same atavistic joy she'd felt as a child in the attic.

'Wow,' she breathed, and pressed up against the netting. It felt like wings against her face, soft, webbed; but as she stared at the insects inside her brow began to ache as with migraine. She shoved her glasses onto her nose, closed her eyes and drew a long breath; then took a step away from the cage. After a minute she opened her eyes. The headache had diminished to a dull throb; when she hesitantly touched one eyebrow, she could feel the entwined hairs there, stiff as wire. They were vibrating, but at her touch the vibrations, like the headache, dulled. She stared at the floor, the tiles sticky with contraband juice and gum; then looked up once again at the cage. There was a display sign off to one side; she walked over to it, slowly, and read.

CLEOPATRA BRIMSTONE
Gonepteryx rhamni cleopatra

This popular and subtly coloured species has a range which extends throughout the Northern Hemisphere, with the exception of Arctic regions and several remote islands. In Europe, the Brimstone is a harbinger of spring, often emerging from its winter hibernation under dead leaves to revel in the countryside while there is still snow upon the ground.

'I must ask you to please not touch the cages.'

Janie turned to see a man, perhaps fifty, standing a few feet away. A net was jammed under his arm; in his hand he held a clear plastic jar with several butterflies at the bottom, apparently dead.

'Oh. Sorry,' said Jane. The man edged past her. He set his jar on the floor, opened a small door at the base of the cylindrical cage, and deftly angled the net inside. Butterflies lifted in a yellow-green blur from leaves and branches; the man swept the net carefully across the bottom of the cage, then withdrew it. Three dead butterflies, like scraps of colored paper, drifted from the net into the open jar.

'Housecleaning,' he said, and once more thrust his arm into the cage. He was slender and wiry, not much taller than she was, his face hawkish and burnt brown from the sun, his thick straight hair iron-streaked and pulled back into a long braid. He wore black jeans and a dark-blue hooded jersey, with an ID badge clipped to the collar.

'You work here,' said Janie. The man glanced at her, his arm still in the cage; she could see him sizing her up. After a moment he glanced away again. A few minutes later he emptied the net for the last time, closed the cage and the jar, and stepped over to a waste bin, pulling bits of dead leaves from the net and dropping them into the container.

'I'm one of the curatorial staff. You American?'

Janie nodded. 'Yeah. Actually, I – I wanted to see about volunteering here.'

'Lifewatch desk at the main entrance.' The man cocked his head toward the door. 'They can get you signed up and registered, see what's available.'

'No – I mean, I want to volunteer here. With the insects—'

'Butterfly collector, are you?' The man smiled, his tone mocking. He had hazel eyes, deepset; his thin mouth made the smile seem perhaps more cruel than intended. 'We get a lot of those.'

Janie flushed. 'No. I am not a *collector*,' she said coldly, adjusting her glasses. 'I'm doing a thesis on dioxane genital mutation in *Cucullia artemisae*.' She didn't add that it was an undergraduate thesis. 'I've been doing independent research for seven years now.' She hesitated, thinking of her Intel scholarship, and added, 'I've received several grants for my work.'

The man regarded her appraisingly. 'Are you studying here, then?'

'Yes,' she lied again. 'At Oxford. I'm on sabbatical right now. But I live near here, and so I thought I might—'

She shrugged, opening her hands; looked over at him and smiled tentatively. 'Make myself useful?'

The man waited a moment, nodded. 'Well. Do you have a few minutes now? I've got to do something with these, but if you want you can come with me and wait, and then we can see what we can do. Maybe circumvent some paperwork.'

He turned and started across the room. He had a graceful, bouncing gait, like a gymnast or circus acrobat: impatient with the ground beneath him. 'Shouldn't take long,' he called over his shoulder as Janie hurried to catch up.

She followed him through a door marked AUTHORISED PERSONS ONLY, into the exhibit laboratory, a reassuringly familiar place with its display cases and smells of shellac and camphor, acetone and ethyl alcohol. There were more cages here, but smaller ones, sheltering live specimens – pupating butterflies and moths, stick insects, leaf insects, dung beetles. The man dropped his net onto a desk, took the jar to a long table against one wall, blindingly lit by long fluorescent tubes. There were scores of bottles here, some empty, others filled with paper and tiny inert figures.

'Have a seat,' said the man, gesturing at two folding chairs. He settled into one, grabbed an empty jar and a roll of absorbent paper. 'I'm David Bierce. So where're you staying? Camden Town?'

'Janie Kendall. Yes—'

'The High Street?'

Janie sat in the other chair, pulling it a few inches away from him. The questions made her uneasy, but she only nodded, lying again, and said, 'Closer, actually. Off Gloucester Road. With friends.'

'Mmm.' Bierce tore off a piece of absorbent paper, leaned across to a stainless steel sink and dampened the paper. Then he dropped it into the empty jar. He paused, turned to her and gestured at the table, smiling.

'Care to join in?'

Janie shrugged. 'Sure—'

She pulled her chair closer, found another empty jar and did as Bierce had, dampening a piece of paper towel and dropping it inside. Then she took the jar containing the dead brimstones and carefully shook one onto the counter. It was a female, its coloring more muted than the males'; she scooped it up very gently, careful not to disturb the scales like dull green glitter upon its wings, dropped it into the jar and replaced the top.

'Very nice.' Bierce nodded, raising his eyebrows. 'You seem to know what you're doing. Work with other insects? Soft-bodied ones?'

'Sometimes. Mostly moths, though. And butterflies.'

'Right.' He inclined his head to a recessed shelf. 'How would you label that, then? Go ahead.'

On the shelf she found a notepad and a case of Rapidograph pens. She began to write, conscious of Bierce staring at her. 'We usually just put all this into the computer, of course, and print it out', he said. 'I just want to see the benefits of an American education in the sciences.'

Janie fought the urge to look at him. Instead she wrote out the information, making her printing as tiny as possible.

Gonepteryx rhamni cleopatra
UNITED KINGDOM: LONDON
Regent's Park Zoo
Lat/Long unknown

21.IV.2001
D. Bierce
Net/caged specimen

She handed it to Bierce. 'I don't know the proper coordinates for London.' Bierce scrutinized the paper. 'It's actually the Royal Zoological Society,' he said. He looked at her, then smiled. 'But you'll do.'

'Great!' She grinned, the first time she'd really felt happy since arriving here. 'When do you want me to start?'

'How about Monday?'

Janie hesitated: this was only Friday. 'I could come in tomorrow—'

'I don't work on the weekend, and you'll need to be trained. Also, they have to process the paperwork. Right—'

He stood and went to a desk, pulling open drawers until he found a clipboard holding sheaves of triplicate forms. 'Here. Fill all this out, leave it with me and I'll pass it on to Carolyn — she's the head volunteer coordinator. They usually want to interview you, but I'll tell them we've done all that already.'

'What time should I come in Monday?'

'Come at nine. Everything opens at ten, that way you'll avoid the crowds. Use the staff entrance, someone there will have an ID waiting for you to pick up when you sign in—'

She nodded and began filling out the forms.

'All right, then.' David Bierce leaned against the desk and again fixed her with that sly, almost taunting gaze. 'Know how to find your way home?'

Janie lifted her chin defiantly. 'Yes.'

'Enjoying London? Going to go out tonight and do Camden Town with all the yobs?'

'Maybe. I haven't been out much yet.'

'Mmm. Beautiful American girl, they'll eat you alive. Just kidding.' He straightened, started across the room towards the door. 'I'll you see Monday then.'

He held the door for her. 'You really should check out the clubs. You're too young not to see the city by night.' He smiled, the fluorescent light slanting sideways into his hazel eyes and making them suddenly glow icy blue. 'Bye, then.'

'Bye,' said Janie, and hurried quickly from the lab towards home.

That night, for the first time, she went out. She told herself she would have gone anyway, no matter what Bierce had said. She had no idea where the clubs were; Andrew had pointed out the Electric Ballroom to her, right up from the Tube station, but he'd also warned her that was where the tourists flocked on weekends.

'They do a Disco thing on Saturday nights – Saturday Night Fever, everyone gets all done up in vintage clothes. Quite a fashion show,' he'd said, smiling and shaking his head.

Janie had no interest in that. She ate a quick supper, vindaloo from the take-away down the street from the flat; then dressed. She hadn't brought a huge number of clothes – at home she'd never bothered much with clothes at all, making do with thrift-shop finds and whatever her mother gave her for Christmas. But now she found herself sitting on the edge of the four-poster, staring with pursed lips at the sparse contents of two bureau drawers. Finally she pulled out a pair of black corduroy jeans and a black turtleneck and pulled on her sneakers. She removed her glasses, for the first time in weeks inserted her contact lenses. Then she shrugged into her old navy peacoat and left.

It was after ten o'clock. On the canal path, throngs of people stood, drinking from pints of canned lager. She made her way through them, ignoring catcalls and whispered invitations, step-ping to avoid where kids lay making out against the brick wall that ran alongside the path, or pissing in the bushes. The bridge over the canal at Camden Lock was clogged with several dozen kids in mohawks or varicolored hair, shouting at each other above the din of a boombox and swigging from bottles of Spanish champagne.

A boy with a champagne bottle leered, lunging at her.

' 'Ere, sweetheart, 'ep youseff—'

Janie ducked, and he careered against the ledge, his arm striking brick and the bottle shattering in a starburst of black and gold.

'Fucking cunt!' he shrieked after her. 'Fucking bloody *cunt*!'

People glanced at her but Janie kept her head down, making a quick turn into the vast cobbled courtyard of Camden Market. The place had a desolate air: the vendors would not arrive until early next morning, and now only stray cats and bits of wind-blown trash moved in the shadows. In the surrounding buildings people spilled out onto balconies, drinking and calling back and forth, their voices hollow and their long shadows twisting across the ill-lit central courtyard. Janie hurried to the far end, but there found only brick walls, closed-up shop doors and a young woman huddled within the folds of a filthy sleeping bag.

'*Couldya – couldya—*' the woman murmured.

Janie turned and followed the wall until she found a door leading into a short passage. She entered it, hoping she was going in the direction of Camden High Street. She felt like Alice trying to find her way through the garden in Wonderland: arched door-ways led not into the street but to headshops and blindingly lit piercing parlors, open for business; other doors opened onto enclosed courtyards, dark, smelling of piss and marijuana. Finally from the corner of her eye she glimpsed what looked like the end of the passage, headlights piercing through the gloom like landing lights. Doggedly she made her way towards them.

'Ay watchowt watchowt,' someone yelled as she emerged from the passage onto the sidewalk, and ran the last few steps to the curb.

She was on the High Street; rather, in that block or two of curving no-man's-land where it turned into Chalk Farm Road. The sidewalks were still crowded, but everyone was heading towards Camden Lock and not away from it. Janie waited for the light to change and raced across the street, to where a cobblestoned alley snaked off between a shop selling leather underwear and another advertising 'Fine French Country Furni-ture'.

For several minutes she stood there. She watched the crowds heading towards Camden Town, the steady stream of minicabs and taxis and buses heading up Chalk Farm Road towards Hampstead. Overhead, dull orange clouds moved across a night sky the color of charred wood; there was the steady low thunder of jets circling after takeoff at Heathrow. At last she tugged her collar up around her neck, letting her hair fall in loose waves down her back, shoved her hands into her coat pockets and turned to walk purposefully down the alley.

Before her the cobblestone path turned sharply to the right. She couldn't see what was beyond, but she could hear voices: a girl laughing, a man's sibilant retort. A moment later the alley spilled out onto a cul-de-sac. A couple stood a few yards away, before a doorway with a small copper awning above it. The young woman glanced sideways at Janie, quickly looked away again. A silhouette filled the doorway; the young man pulled out a wallet. His hand disappeared within the silhouette, re-emerged; and the couple walked inside. Janie waited until the shadowy figure withdrew. She looked over her shoulder, then approached the building.

There was a heavy metal door, black, with graffiti scratched into it and pale blurred spots where painted graffiti had been effaced. The door was set back several feet into a brick recess; at the top there was a metal slot with a grille and a flat steel strip inside that could be slid back, so that one could peer out into the courtyard. To the right of the door, on the brick wall within the recess, was a small brass plaque with a single word on it.

HIVE

There was no doorbell or any other way to signal that you wanted to enter. Janie stood, wondering what was inside; feeling a small tingling unease that was less fear than the knowledge that even if she were to confront the figure who'd let that other couple inside, she herself would certainly be turned away.

With a *skreek* of metal on stone the door suddenly shot open. Janie looked up, into the sharp, raggedly handsome face of a tall, still youngish man with very short blond hair, a line of gleaming gold beads like drops of sweat piercing the edge of his left jaw.

'Good evening,' he said, glancing past her to the alley. He wore a black sleeveless T-shirt with a small golden bee embroidered upon the breast. His bare arms were muscular, striated with long sweeping scars: black, red, white. 'Are you waiting for Hannah?'

'No.' Quickly Janie pulled out a handful of five-pound notes. 'Just me tonight.'

'That'll be twenty, then.' The man held his hand out, still gazing at the alley; when Janie slipped the notes to him he looked down and flashed her a vulpine smile. 'Enjoy yourself.' She darted past him into the building.

Abruptly it was as though some darker night had fallen. Thunderously so, since the enfolding blackness was slashed with music so loud it was itself like light: Janie hesitated, closing her eyes, and white flashes streaked across her eyelids like sleet, pulsing in time to the music. She opened her eyes, giving them a chance to adjust to the darkness, and tried to get a sense of where she was. A few feet away a blurry greyish lozenge sharpened into the window of a coat-check room. Janie walked past it, towards the source of the music. Immediately the floor slanted steeply beneath her feet. She steadied herself with one hand against the wall, following the incline until it opened onto a cavernous dance floor.

She gazed inside, disappointed. It looked like any other club, crowded, strobe-lit, turquoise smoke and silver glitter coiling between hundreds of whirling bodies clad in candy pink, sky blue, neon red, rainslicker yellow. Baby colors, Janie thought. There was a boy who was almost naked, except for shorts, a transparent water bottle strapped to his chest and long tubes snaking into his mouth. Another boy had hair the color of lime jello, his face corrugated with glitter and sweat; he swayed near the edge of the dance floor, turned to stare at Janie and then beamed, beckoning her join him.

Janie gave him a quick smile, shaking her head; when the boy opened his arms to her in mock pleading she shouted 'No!'

But she continued to smile, though she felt as though her head would crack like an egg from the throbbing music. Shoving her hands into her pockets she skirted the dance floor, pushed her way to the bar and bought a drink, something pink with no ice in a plastic cup. It smelled like Gatorade and lighter fluid. She gulped it down, then carried the cup held before her like a torch as she continued on her circuit of the room. There was nothing else of interest; just long queues for the lavatories and another bar, numerous doors and stairwells where kids clustered, drinking and smoking. Now and then beeps and whistles like birdsong or insect cries came through the stuttering electronic din, whoops and trilling laughter from the dancers. But mostly they moved in near-silence, eyes rolled ceiling-ward, bodies exploding into Catherine wheels of flesh and plastic and nylon, but all without a word.

It gave Janie a headache – a *real* headache, the back of her skull bruised, tender to the touch. She dropped her plastic cup and started looking for a way out. She could see past the dance floor to where she had entered, but it seemed as though another hundred people had arrived in the few minutes since then: kids were standing six-deep at both bars, and the action on the floor had spread, amoeba-like, towards the corridors angling back up toward the street.

'Sorry—'

A fat woman in an Arsenal jersey jostled her as she hurried by, leaving a smear of oily sweat on Janie's wrist. Janie grimaced and wiped her hand on the bottom of her coat. She gave one last look at the dance floor, but nothing had changed within the intricate lattice of dancers and smoke, braids of glow-lights and spotlit faces surging up and down, up and down, while more dancers fought their way to the centre.

'Shit.' She turned and strode off, heading to where the huge room curved off into relative emptiness. Here, scores of tables were scattered, some overturned, others stacked against the wall. A few people sat, talking; a girl lay curled on the floor, her head pillowed on a Barbie knapsack. Janie crossed to the wall, and found first a door that led to a bare brick wall, then a second door that revealed a broom closet. The next was dark-red, metal, official-looking: the kind of door that Janie associated with school fire drills.

A fire door. It would lead outside, or into a hall that would lead there. Without hesitating she pushed it open and entered. A short corridor lit by EXIT signs stretched ahead of her, with another door at the end. She hurried towards it, already reaching reflexively for the keys to the flat, pushed the door-bar and stepped inside.

For an instant she thought she had somehow stumbled into a hospital emergency room. There was the glitter of halogen light on steel, distorted reflections thrown back at her from curved glass surfaces; the abrasive odor of isopropyl alcohol and the fainter tinny scent of blood, like metal in the mouth.

And bodies: everywhere, bodies, splayed on gurneys or suspended from gleaming metal hooks, laced with black electrical cord and pinned upright onto smooth rubber mats. She stared open-mouthed, neither appalled nor frightened but fascinated by the conundrum before her: how did *that* hand fit *there*, and whose leg was *that*? She inched backward, pressing herself against the door and trying to stay in the shadows – just inches ahead of her ribbons of luminous bluish light streamed from lamps hung high overhead. The chiaroscuro of pallid bodies and black furniture, shiny with sweat and here and there red-streaked, or brown; the mere sight of so many bodies, real bodies – flesh spilling over the edge of tabletops, too much hair or none at all, eyes squeezed shut in ecstasy or terror and mouths open to reveal stained teeth, pale gums – the sheer *fluidity* of it all enthralled her. She felt as she had, once, pulling aside a rotted log to disclose the ants' nest beneath, masses of minute fleeing bodies, soldiers carrying eggs and larvae in their jaws, tunnels spiraling into the center of another world. Her brow tingled, warmth flushed her from brow to breast . . .

Another world, that's what she had found then; and discovered again now.

'*Out.*'

Janie sucked her breath in sharply. Fingers dug into her shoulder, yanked her back through the metal door so roughly that she cut her wrist against it.

'No lurkers, what the fuck—'

A man flung her against the wall. She gasped, turned to run but he grabbed her shoulder again. 'Christ, a fucking girl.'

He sounded angry but relieved. She looked up: a huge man, more fat than muscle. He wore very tight leather briefs and the same black sleeveless shirt with a golden bee embroidered upon it. 'How the hell'd you get in like *that*?' he demanded, cocking a thumb at her.

She shook her head, then realized he meant her clothes. 'I was just trying to find my way out.'

'Well, you found your way in. In like fucking Flynn.' He laughed: he had gold-capped teeth, and gold wires threading the tip of his tongue. 'You want to join the party, you know the rules. No exceptions.'

Before she could reply he turned and was gone, the door thudding shut softly behind him. She waited, heart pounding, then reached and pushed the bar on the door.

Locked. She was out, not in; she was nowhere at all. For a long time she stood there, trying to hear anything from the other side of the door, waiting to see if anyone would come back looking for her. At last she turned, and began to find her way home.

Next morning she woke early, to the sound of delivery trucks in the street and children on the canal path, laughing and squabbling on their way to the zoo. She sat up with a pang, remembering David Bierce and her volunteer job; then recalled this was Saturday, not Monday.

'Wow,' she said aloud. The extra days seemed like a gift.

For a few minutes she lay in Fred and Andrew's great four-poster, staring abstractedly at where she had rested her mounted specimens atop the wainscoting – the hybrid hawkmoth; a beautiful Honduran owl butterfly, *Caligo atreus*; a mourning cloak she had caught and mounted herself years ago. She thought of the club last night, mentally retracing her steps to the hidden back room; thought of the man who had thrown her out, the interplay of light and shadow upon the bodies pinned to mats and tables. She had slept in her clothes; now she rolled out of bed and pulled her sneakers on, forgoing breakfast but stuffing her pocket with ten- and twenty-pound notes before she left.

It was a clear cool morning, with a high, pale blue sky and the young leaves of nettles and hawthorn still glistening with dew. Someone had thrown a shopping cart from the nearby Sainsbury's into the canal; it edged sideways up out of the shallow water, like a frozen shipwreck. A boy stood a few yards down from it, fishing, an absent, placid expression on his face.

She crossed over the bridge to the canal path and headed for the High Street. With every step she took the day grew older, noisier, trains rattling on the bridge behind her and voices harsh as gulls rising from the other side of the brick wall that separated the canal path from the street.

At Camden Lock she had to fight her way through the market. There were tens of thousands of tourists, swarming from the maze of shops to pick their way between scores of vendors selling old and new clothes, bootleg CDs, cheap silver jewelry, kilims, feather boas, handcuffs, cell phones, mass-produced furniture and puppets from Indonesia, Morocco, Guyana, Wales. The fug of burning incense and cheap candles choked her; she hurried to where a young woman was turning samosas in a vat of sputtering oil and dug into her pocket for a handful of change, standing so that the smells of hot grease and scorched chickpea batter canceled out patchouli and Caribbean Nights.

'Two, please,' Janie shouted.

She ate and almost immediately felt better; then walked a few steps to where a spike-haired girl sat behind a table covered with cheap clothes made of ripstock fabric in Jell-O shades.

'Everything five pounds,' the girl announced. She stood, smiling helpfully as Janie began to sort through pairs of hugely baggy pants. They were cross-seamed with Velcro and deep zippered pockets. Janie held up a pair, frowning as the legs billowed, lavender and green, in the wind.

'It's so you can make them into shorts,' the girl explained. She stepped around the table and took the pants from Janie, deftly tugging at the legs so that they detached. 'See? Or a skirt.' The girl replaced the pants, picked up another pair, screaming orange with black trim, and a matching windbreaker. 'This color would look nice on you.'

'Okay.' Janie paid for them, waited for the girl to put the clothes in a plastic bag. 'Thanks.'

'Bye now.'

She went out into Camden High Street. Shopkeepers stood guard over the tables spilling out from their storefronts, heaped with leather clothes and souvenir T-shirts: MIND THE GAP, LONDON UNDERGROUND, shirts emblazoned with the Cat in the Hat toking on a cheroot. THE CAT IN THE HAT SMOKES BLACK. Every three or four feet someone had set up a boombox, deafening sound-bites of salsa, techno, 'The Hustle', Bob Marley, 'Anarchy in the UK', Radiohead. On the corner of Inverness Street and the High Street a few punks squatted in a doorway, looking over the postcards they'd bought. A sign in a smoked-glass window said ALL HAIRCUTS £10, MEN WOMEN CHILDREN.

'Sorry,' one of the punks said, as Janie stepped over them and into the shop.

The barber was sitting in an old-fashioned chair, his back to her, reading *The Sun*. At the sound of her footsteps he turned, smiling automatically. 'Can I help you?'

'Yes, please. I'd like my hair cut. All of it.'

He nodded, gesturing to the chair. 'Please.'

Janie had thought she might have to convince him that she was serious. She had beautiful hair, well below her shoulders; the kind of hair people would kill for, she'd been hearing that her whole life. But the barber just hummed and chopped it off, the *snick*

snick of his shears interspersed with kindly questions about whether she was enjoying her visit and his account of a vacation to Disney World ten years earlier.

'Dear, do we want it shaved or buzz-cut?'

In the mirror a huge-eyed creature gazed at Janie, like a tarsier or one of the owlish caligo moths. She stared at it, entranced, then nodded. 'Shaved. Please.'

When he was finished she got out of the chair, dazed, and ran her hand across her scalp. It was smooth and cool as an apple. There were a few tiny nicks that stung beneath her fingers. She paid the barber, tipping him two pounds. He smiled and held the door open for her.

'Now when you want a touch-up you come see us, dear. Only five pounds for a touch-up.'

She went next to find new shoes. There were more shoe shops in Camden Town than she had ever seen anywhere in her life; she checked out four of them on one block before deciding on a discounted pair of twenty-hole black Doc Martens. They were no longer fashionable, but they had blunted steel caps on the toes. She bought them, giving the salesgirl her old sneakers to toss into the waste bin. When she went back onto the street it was like walking in wet cement – the shoes were so heavy, the leather so stiff that she ducked back into the shoe shop and bought a pair of heavy wool socks and put them on. She returned outside, hesitating on the front step before crossing the street and heading back in the direction of Chalk Farm Road. There was a shop here that Fred had shown her before he left.

'Now, that's where you get your fetish gear, Janie,' he'd said, pointing to a shop window painted matte black. THE PLACE, it said in red letters, with two linked circles beneath. Fred had grinned and rapped his knuckles against the glass as they walked by. 'I've never been in, you'll have to tell me what it's like.' They'd both laughed at the thought.

Now Janie walked slowly, the wind chill against her bare skull. When she could make out the shop, sun glinting off the crimson letters and a sad-eyed dog tied to a post out front, she began to hurry, her new boots making a hollow thump as she pushed through the door.

There was a security gate inside, a thin, sallow young man with dreadlocks nodding at her silently as she approached.

'You'll have to check that. ' He pointed at the bag with her new clothes in it. She handed it to him, reading the warning posted behind the counter.

SHOPLIFTERS WILL BE BEATEN,
FLAYED, SPANKED, BIRCHED, BLED
AND THEN PROSECUTED
TO THE FULL EXTENT OF THE LAW

The shop was well-lit. It smelled strongly of new leather and coconut oil and pine-scented disinfectant. She seemed to be the only customer this early in the day, although she counted seven employees, manning cash registers, unpacking cartons, watching to make sure she didn't try to nick anything. A CD of dance music played, and the phone rang constantly.

She spent a good half-hour just walking through the place, impressed by the range of merchandise. Electrified wands to deliver shocks; things like meat cleavers made of stainless steel with rubber tips. Velcro dog collars, Velcro hoods, black rubber balls and balls in neon shades; a mat embedded with three-inch spikes that could be conveniently rolled up and came with its own lightweight carrying case. As she wandered about more customers arrived, some of them greeting the clerks by name, others furtive, making a quick circuit of the shelves before darting outside again. At last Janie knew what she wanted. A set of wristcuffs and one of anklecuffs, both of very heavy black leather with stainless steel hardware; four adjustable nylon leashes, also black, with clips on either end that could be fastened to cuffs or looped around a post; a few spare S-clips.

'That it?'

Janie nodded, and the register clerk began scanning her purchases. She felt almost guilty, buying so few things, not taking advantage of the vast Meccano glory of all those shelves full of gleaming, sombre contrivances.

'There you go.' He handed her the receipt, then inclined his head at her. 'Nice touch, that—'

He pointed at her eyebrows. Janie drew her hand up, felt the long pliant hairs uncoiling like baby ferns. 'Thanks,' she murmured. She retrieved her bag and went home to wait for evening.

It was nearly midnight when she left the flat. She had slept for most of the afternoon, a deep but restless sleep, with anxious dreams of flight, falling, her hands encased in metal gloves, a shadowy figure crouching above her. She woke in the dark, heart pounding, terrified for a moment that she had slept all the way through till Sunday night.

But of course she had not. She showered, then dressed in a tight, low-cut black shirt and pulled on her new nylon pants and heavy boots. She seldom wore makeup, but tonight after putting in her contacts she carefully outlined her eyes with black, then chose a very pale lavender lipstick. She surveyed herself in the mirror critically. With her white skin, huge violet eyes and hairless skull, she resembled one of the Balinese puppets for sale in the market – beautiful but vacant, faintly ominous. She grabbed her keys and money, pulled on her windbreaker, and headed out.

When she reached the alley that led to the club, she entered it, walked about halfway, and stopped. After glancing back and forth to make sure no one was coming, she detached the legs from her nylon pants, stuffing them into a pocket, then adjusted the Velcro tabs so that the pants became a very short orange-and-black skirt. Her long legs were sheathed in black tights. She bent to tighten the laces on her metal-toed boots and hurried to the club entrance.

Tonight there was a line of people waiting to get in. Janie took her place, fastidiously avoiding looking at any of the others. They waited for thirty minutes, Janie shivering in her thin nylon windbreaker, before the door opened and the same gaunt blond man appeared to take their money. Janie felt her heart beat faster when it was her turn, wondering if he would recognize her. But he only scanned the courtyard, and, when the last of them darted inside, closed the door with a booming *clang*.

Inside all was as it had been, only far more crowded. Janie bought a drink – orange squash, no alcohol. It was horribly sweet, with a bitter, curdled aftertaste. Still, it had cost two pounds: she drank it all. She had just started on her way down to the dance floor when someone came up from behind to tap her shoulder, shouting into her ear.

'Wanna?'

It was a tall, broad-shouldered boy a few years older than she was, perhaps twenty-four, with a lean ruddy face, loose shoulder-length blond hair streaked green, and deep-set, very dark blue eyes. He swayed dreamily, gazing at the dance floor and hardly looking at her at all.

'Sure,' Janie shouted back. He looped an arm around her shoulder, pulling her with him; his striped V-necked shirt smelled of talc and sweat. They danced for a long time, Janie moving with calculated abandon, the boy heaving and leaping as though a dog was biting at his shins.

'You're beautiful,' he shouted. There was an almost imperceptible instant of silence as the DJ changed tracks. 'What's your name?'

'Cleopatra Brimstone.'

The shattering music grew deafening once more. The boy grinned. 'Well, Cleopatra. Want something to drink?'

Janie nodded in time with the beat, so fast that her head spun. He took her hand and she raced to keep up with him, threading their way towards the bar.

'Actually,' she yelled, pausing so that he stopped short and bumped up against her. 'I think I'd rather go outside. Want to come?'

He stared at her, half-smiling, and shrugged. 'Aw right. Let me get a drink first—'

They went outside. In the alley the wind sent eddies of dead leaves and newspaper flying up into their faces. Janie laughed, and pressed herself against the boy's side. He grinned down at her, finished his drink and tossed the can aside; then put his arm around her. 'Do you want to go get a drink, then?' he asked.

They stumbled out onto the sidewalk, turned and began walking. People filled the High Street, lines snaking out from the entrances of pubs and restaurants. A blue glow surrounded the streetlights, and clouds of small white moths beat themselves against the globes; vapour and banners of grey smoke hung above the punks blocking the sidewalk by Camden Lock. Janie and the boy dipped down into the street. He pointed to a pub occupying the corner a few blocks down, a large old green-painted building with baskets of flowers hanging beneath its windows and a large sign swinging back and forth in the wind: THE END OF THE WORLD. 'In there, then?'

Janie shook her head. 'I live right here, by the canal. We could go to my place if you want. We could have a few drinks there.'

The boy glanced down at her. 'Aw right,' he said – very quickly, so she wouldn't change her mind. 'That'd be aw right.'

It was quieter on the back street leading to the flat. An old drunk huddled in a doorway, cadging change; Janie looked away from him and got out her keys, while the boy stood restlessly, giving the drunk a belligerent look.

'Here we are,' she announced, pushing the door open. 'Home again home again.'

'Nice place.' The boy followed her, gazing around admiringly. 'You live here alone?'

'Yup.' After she spoke Janie had a flash of unease, admitting that. But the boy only ambled into the kitchen, running a hand along the antique French farmhouse cupboard and nodding.

'You're American, right? Studying here?'

'Uh-huh. What would you like to drink? Brandy?'

He made a face, then laughed. 'Aw right! You got expensive taste. Goes with the name, I'd guess.' Janie looked puzzled, and he went on, 'Cleopatra – fancy name for a girl.'

'Fancier for a boy,' Janie retorted, and he laughed again.

She got the brandy, stood in the living room unlacing her boots. 'Why don't we go in there?' she said, gesturing towards the bedroom. 'It's kind of cold out here.'

The boy ran a hand across his head, his blond hair streaming through his fingers. 'Yeah, aw right.' He looked around. 'Um, that the toilet there?' Janie nodded. 'Right back, then . . .'

She went into the bedroom, set the brandy and two glasses on a night table and took off her windbreaker. On another table, several tall candles, creamy white and thick as her wrist, were set into ornate brass holders. She lit these – the room filled with the sweet scent of beeswax – and sat on the floor, leaning against the bed. A few minutes later the toilet flushed and the boy reappeared. His hands and face were damp, redder than they had been. He smiled and sank onto the floor beside her. Janie handed him a glass of brandy.

'Cheers,' he said, and drank it all in one gulp.

'Cheers,' said Janie. She took a sip from hers, then refilled his glass. He drank again, more slowly this time. The candles threw a soft yellow haze over the four-poster bed with its green velvet duvet, the mounds of pillows, forest green, crimson, saffron yellow. They sat without speaking for several minutes. Then the boy set his glass on the floor. He turned to face Janie, extending one arm around her shoulder and drawing his face near hers.

'Well then,' he said.

His mouth tasted acrid, nicotine and cheap gin beneath the blunter taste of brandy. His hand sliding under her shirt was cold; Janie felt goose pimples rising across her breast, her nipple shrinking beneath his touch. He pressed against her, his cock already hard, and reached down to unzip his jeans.

'Wait,' Janie murmured. 'Let's get on the bed . . .'

She slid from his grasp and onto the bed, crawling to the heaps of pillows and feeling beneath one until she found what she had placed there earlier. 'Let's have a little fun first.'

'*This* is fun,' the boy said, a bit plaintively. But he slung himself onto the bed beside her, pulling off his shoes and letting them fall to the floor with a thud. 'What you got there?'

Smiling, Janie turned and held up the wristcuffs. The boy looked at them, then at her, grinning. 'Oh, ho. Been in the back room, then—'

Janie arched her shoulders and unbuttoned her shirt. He reached for one of the cuffs, but she shook her head. 'No. Not me, yet.'

'Ladies first.'

'Gentleman's pleasure.'

The boy's grin widened. 'Won't argue with that.'

She took his hand and pulled him, gently, to the middle of the bed. 'Lie on your back,' she whispered.

He did, watching as she removed first his shirt and then his jeans and underwear. His cock lay nudged against his thigh, not quite hard anymore; when she brushed her fingers against it he moaned softly, took her hand and tried to press it against him.

'No,' she whispered. 'Not yet. Give me your hand.'

She placed the cuffs around each wrist, and his ankles; fastened the nylon leash to each one and then began tying the bonds around each bedpost. It took longer than she had expected; it was difficult to get the bonds taut enough that the boy could not move. He lay there watchfully, his eyes glimmering in the candle-light as he craned his head to stare at her, his breath shallow, quickening.

'There.' She sat back upon her haunches, staring at him. His

cock was hard again now, the hair on his chest and groin tawny in
the half-light. He gazed back at her, his tongue pale as he licked
his lips. 'Try to get away,' she whispered.

He moved slightly, his arms and legs a white X against a deep
green field. 'Can't,' he said hoarsely.

She pulled her shirt off, then her nylon skirt. She had nothing
on beneath. She leaned forward, letting her fingers trail from the
cleft in his throat to his chest, cupping her palm atop his nipple
and then sliding her hand down to his thigh. The flesh was
warm, the little hairs soft and moist. Her own breath quickened;
sudden heat flooded her, a honeyed liquid in her mouth. Above
her brow the long hairs stiffened and furled straight out to either
side: when she lifted her head to the candlelight she could see
them from the corner of her eyes, twin barbs black and glistening like wire.

'You're so sexy.' The boy's voice was hoarse. 'God, you're—'

She placed her hand over his mouth. 'Try to get away,' she said,
commandingly this time. *'Try to get away.'*

His torso writhed, the duvet bunching up around him in dark
folds. She raked her fingernails down his chest and he cried out,
moaning 'Fuck me, God, fuck me . . .'

'Try to get away.'

She stroked his cock, her fingers barely grazing its swollen
head. With a moan he came, struggling helplessly to thrust his
groin towards her. At the same moment Janie gasped, a fiery rush
arrowing down from her brow to her breasts, her cunt. She
rocked forward, crying out, her head brushing against the boy's
side as she sprawled back across the bed. For a minute she lay
there, the room around her seeming to pulse and swirl into
myriad crystalline shapes, each bearing within it the same line
of candles, the long curve of the boy's thigh swelling up into the
hollow of his hip. She drew breath shakily, the flush of heat
fading from her brow; then pushed herself up until she was sitting
beside him. His eyes were shut. A thread of saliva traced the
furrow between mouth and chin. Without thinking she drew her
face down to his, and kissed his cheek.

Immediately he began to grow smaller. Janie reared back,
smacking into one of the bedposts and stared at the figure in
front of her, shaking her head.

'No,' she whispered. 'No, no.'

He was shrinking: so fast it was like watching water dissolve into dry sand. Man-size, child-size, large dog, small. His eyes flew open and for a fraction of a second stared horrified into her own. His hands and feet slipped like mercury from his bonds, wriggling until they met his torso and were absorbed into it. Janie's fingers kneaded the duvet; six inches away the boy was no larger than her hand, then smaller, smaller still. She blinked, for a heart-shredding instant thought he had disappeared completely.

Then she saw something crawling between folds of velvet. The length of her middle finger, its thorax black, yellow-striped, its lower wings elongated into frilled arabesques like those of a festoon, deep yellow, charcoal black, with indigo eye spots, its upper wings a chiaroscuro of black and white stripes.

Bhutanitis lidderdalii. A native of the eastern Himalayas, rarely glimpsed: it lived among the crowns of trees in mountain valleys, its caterpillars feeding on lianas. Janie held her breath, watching as its wings beat feebly. Without warning it lifted into the air. Janie cried out, falling onto her knees as she sprawled across the bed, cupping it quickly but carefully between her hands.

'Beautiful, beautiful,' she crooned. She stepped from the bed, not daring to pause and examine it, and hurried into the kitchen. In the cupboard she found an empty jar, set it down and gingerly angled the lid from it, holding one hand with the butterfly against her breast. She swore, feeling its wings fluttering against her fingers, then quickly brought her hand to the jar's mouth, dropped the butterfly inside and screwed the lid back in place. It fluttered helplessly inside; she could see where the scales had already been scraped from its wing. Still swearing, she ran back into the bedroom, putting the lights on and dragging her collection box from under the bed. She grabbed a vial of ethyl alcohol, went back into the kitchen and tore a bit of paper towel from the rack. She opened the vial, poured a few drops of ethyl alcohol onto the paper; opened the jar and gently tilted it onto its side. She slipped the paper inside, very slowly tipping the jar upright once more, until the paper had settled on the bottom, the butterfly on top of it. Its wings beat frantically for a few moments, then stopped. Its proboscis uncoiled, finer than a hair. Slowly Janie drew her own hand to her brow and ran it along the length of the antenna there. She sat there staring at it until the sun leaked

through the wooden shutters in the kitchen window. The butterfly did not move again.

The next day passed in a metallic grey haze, the only color the
saturated blues and yellows of the *lidderdalii*'s wings, burned
upon Janie's eyes as though she had looked into the sun. When
she finally roused herself, she felt a spasm of panic at sight of the
boy's clothes on the bedroom floor.

'Shit.' She ran her hand across her head, was momentarily
startled to recall she had no hair. 'Now what?'

She stood there for a few minutes, thinking; then gathered the
clothes – striped V-neck sweater, jeans, socks, jockey shorts,
Timberland knockoff shoes – and dumped them into a plastic
Sainsbury's bag. There was a wallet in the jeans pocket. She
opened it, gazed impassively at a driver's license – KENNETH
REED, WOLVERHAMPTON – and a few five-pound notes. She
pocketed the money, took the license into the bathroom and
burned it, letting the ashes drop into the toilet. Then she went
outside.

It was early Sunday morning, no one about except for a young
mother pushing a baby in a stroller. In the neighboring doorway
the same drunk old man sprawled surrounded by empty bottles
and rubbish. He stared blearily up at Janie as she approached.

'Here,' she said. She bent and dropped the five-pound notes
into his scabby hand.

'God bless you, darlin'.' He coughed, his eyes focusing on
neither Janie nor the notes. 'God bless you.'

She turned and walked briskly back towards the canal path.
There were few waste bins in Camden Town, and so each day
trash accumulated in rank heaps along the path, beneath streetlights, in vacant alleys. Street cleaners and sweeping machines
then daily cleared it all away again: like elves, Janie thought. As
she walked along the canal path she dropped the shoes in one pile
of rubbish; tossed the sweater alongside a single high-heeled shoe
in the market; stuffed the underwear and socks into a collapsing
cardboard box filled with rotting lettuce; and left the jeans beside
a stack of papers outside an unopened newsagent's shop. The
wallet she tied into the Sainsbury's bag and dropped into an
overflowing trash bag outside of Boots. Then she retraced her
steps, stopping in front of a shop window filled with tatty

polyester lingerie in large sizes and boldly artificial-looking wigs: pink afros, platinum blonde falls, black-and-white Cruella DeVil tresses.

The door was propped open; Schubert lieder played softly on 3 2. Janie stuck her head in and looked around, saw a beefy man behind the register, cashing out. He had orange lipstick smeared around his mouth and delicate silver fish hanging from his ears.

'We're not open yet. Eleven on Sunday,' he said without looking up.

'I'm just looking.' Janie sidled over to a glass shelf where four wigs sat on Styrofoam heads. One had very glossy black hair in a chin-length flapper bob. Janie tried it on, eyeing herself in a grimy mirror. 'How much is this one?'

'Fifteen. But we're not—'

'Here. Thanks!' Janie stuck a twenty-pound note on the counter and ran from the shop. When she reached the corner she slowed, pirouetted to catch her reflection in a shop window. She stared at herself, grinning, then walked the rest of the way home, exhilarated and faintly dizzy.

Monday morning she went to the zoo to begin her volunteer work. She had mounted the *Bhutanitis lidderdalii*, on a piece of Styrofoam with a piece of paper on it, to keep the butterfly's legs from becoming embedded in the Styrofoam. She'd softened it first, putting it into a jar with damp paper, removed it and placed it on the mounting platform, neatly spearing its thorax – a little to the right – with a #2 pin. She propped it carefully on the wainscoting beside the hawkmoth, and left.

She arrived and found her ID badge waiting for her at the staff entrance. It was a clear morning, warmer than it had been for a week; the long hairs on her brow vibrated as though they were wires that had been plucked. Beneath the wig her shaved head felt hot and moist, the first new hairs starting to prickle across her scalp. Her nose itched where her glasses pressed against it. Janie walked, smiling, past the gibbons howling in their habitat and the pygmy hippos floating calmly in their pool, their eyes shut, green bubbles breaking around them like little fish. In front of the Insect Zoo a uniformed woman was unloading sacks of meal from a golf cart.

'Morning,' Janie called cheerfully, and went inside.

She found David Bierce standing in front of a temperature gauge beside a glass cage holding the hissing cockroaches.

'Something happened last night, the damn things got too cold.' He glanced over, handed her a clipboard and began to remove the top of the gauge. 'I called Operations but they're at their fucking morning meeting. Fucking computers—'

He stuck his hand inside the control box and flicked angrily at the gauge. 'You know anything about computers?'

'Not this kind.' Janie brought her face up to the cage's glass front. Inside were half a dozen glossy roaches, five inches long and the color of pale maple syrup. They lay, unmoving, near a glass petri dish filled with what looked like damp brown sugar. 'Are they dead?'

'Those things? They're fucking immortal. You could stamp on one and it wouldn't die. Believe me, I've done it.' He continued to fiddle with the gauge, finally sighed and replaced the lid. 'Well, let's let the boys over in Ops handle it. Come on, I'll get you started.'

He gave her a brief tour of the lab, opening drawers full of dissecting instruments, mounting platforms, pins; showing her where the food for the various insects was kept in a series of small refrigerators. Sugar syrup, cornstarch, plastic containers full of smaller insects, grubs and mealworms, tiny grey beetles. 'Mostly we just keep on top of replacing the ones that die,' David explained. 'That, and making sure the plants don't develop the wrong kind of fungus. Nature takes her course and we just goose her along when she needs it. School groups are here constantly, but the docents handle that. You're more than welcome to talk to them, if that's the sort of thing you want to do.'

He turned from where he'd been washing empty jars at a small sink, dried his hands and walked over to sit on top of a desk. 'It's not terribly glamorous work here.' He reached down for a Styrofoam cup of coffee and sipped from it, gazing at her coolly. 'We're none of us working on our PhDs anymore.'

Janie shrugged. 'That's all right.'

'It's not even all that interesting. I mean, it can be very repetitive. Tedious.'

'I don't mind.' A sudden pang of anxiety made Janie's voice break. She could feel her face growing hot, and quickly looked away. 'Really,' she said sullenly.

'Suit yourself. Coffee's over there – you'll probably have to clean yourself a cup, though.' He cocked his head, staring at her curiously, then said, 'Did you do something different with your hair?'

She nodded once, brushing the edge of her bangs with a finger. 'Yeah.'

'Nice. Very Louise Brooks.' He hopped from the desk and crossed to a computer set up in the corner. 'You can use my computer if you need to, I'll give you the password later.'

Janie nodded, her flush fading into relief. 'How many people work here?'

'Actually, we're short-staffed here right now – no money for hiring and our grant's run out. It's pretty much just me, and whoever Carolyn sends over from the docents. Sweet little blue-hairs mostly, they don't much like bugs. So it's providential you turned up, *Jane*.'

He said her name mockingly, gave her a crooked grin. 'You said you have experience mounting? Well, I try to save as many of the dead specimens as I can, and when there's any slow days, which there never are, I mount them and use them for the workshops I do with the schools that come in. What would be nice would be if we had enough specimens that I could give some to the teachers, to take back to their classrooms. We have a nice website and we might be able to work up some interactive programs. No schools are scheduled today, Monday's usually slow here. So if you could work on some of *those*—' he gestured to where several dozen cardboard boxes and glass jars were strewn across a countertop. '—that would be really brilliant,' he ended, and turned to his computer screen.

She spent the morning mounting insects. Few were interesting or unusual: a number of brown hairstreaks, some Camberwell Beauties, three hissing cockroaches, several Brimstones. But there was a single *Acherontia atropos*, the Death's-head Hawkmoth, the pattern of grey and brown and pale yellow scales on the back of its thorax forming the image of a human skull. Its proboscis was unfurled, the twin points sharp enough to pierce a finger: Janie touched it gingerly, wincing delightedly as a pinprick of blood appeared on her fingertip.

'You bring a lunch?'

She looked away from the bright magnifying light she'd been using and blinked in surprise. 'Lunch?'

David Bierce laughed. 'Enjoying yourself? Well, that's good, makes the day go faster. Yes, lunch!' He rubbed his hands together, the harsh light making him look gnomelike, his sharp features malevolent and leering. 'They have some decent fish and chips at the stall over by the cats. Come on, I'll treat you. Your first day.'

They sat at a picnic table beside the food booth and ate. David pulled a bottle of ale from his knapsack and shared it with Janie. Overhead scattered clouds like smoke moved swiftly southwards. An Indian woman with three small boys sat at another table, the boys tossing fries at seagulls that swept down, shrieking, and made the smallest boy wail.

'Rain later,' David said, staring at the sky. 'Too bad.' He sprinkled vinegar on his fried haddock and looked at Janie. 'So did you go out over the weekend?'

She stared at the table and smiled. 'Yeah, I did. It was fun.'

'Where'd you go? The Electric Ballroom?'

'God, no. This other place.' She glanced at his hand resting on the table beside her. He had long fingers, the knuckles slightly enlarged; but the back of his hand was smooth, the same soft brown as the *Acherontia*'s wingtips. Her brows prickled, warmth trickling from them like water. When she lifted her head she could smell him, some kind of musky soap, salt; the bittersweet ale on his breath.

'Yeah? Where? I haven't been out in months, I'd be lost in Camden Town these days.'

'I dunno. The Hive?'

She couldn't imagine he would have heard of it – far too old. But he swiveled on the bench, his eyebrows arching with feigned shock. 'You went to *Hive*? And they let you in?'

'Yes,' Janie stammered. 'I mean, I didn't know – it was just a dance club. I just – danced.'

'Did you.' David Bierce's gaze sharpened, his hazel eyes catching the sun and sending back an icy emerald glitter. 'Did you.'

She picked up the bottle of ale and began to peel the label from it. 'Yes.'

'Have a boyfriend, then?'

She shook her head, rolled a fragment of label into a tiny pill. 'No.'

'Stop that.' His hand closed over hers. He drew it away from the bottle, letting it rest against the table edge. She swallowed: he kept his hand on top of hers, pressing it against the metal edge until she felt her scored palm began to ache. Her eyes closed: she could feel herself floating, and see a dozen feet beneath her own form, slender, the wig beetle-black upon her skull, her wrist like a bent stalk. Abruptly his hand slid away and beneath the table, brushing her leg as he stooped to retrieve his knapsack.

'Time to get back to work,' he said lightly, sliding from the bench and slinging his bag over his shoulder. The breeze lifted his long greying hair as he turned away. 'I'll see you back there.'

Overhead the gulls screamed and flapped, dropping bits of fried fish on the sidewalk. She stared at the table in front of her, the cardboard trays that held the remnants of lunch, and watched as a yellow jacket landed on a fleck of grease, its golden thorax swollen with moisture as it began to feed.

She did not return to Hive that night. Instead she wore a patch-work dress over her jeans and Doc Martens, stuffed the wig inside a drawer and headed to a small bar on Inverness Street. The fair day had turned to rain, black puddles like molten metal capturing the amber glow of traffic signals and streetlights.

There were only a handful of tables at Bar Ganza. Most of the customers stood on the sidewalk outside, drinking and shouting to be heard above the sound of wailing Spanish love songs. Janie fought her way inside, got a glass of red wine and miraculously found an empty stool alongside the wall. She climbed onto it, wrapped her long legs around the pedestal and sipped her wine.

'Hey. Nice hair.' A man in his early thirties, his own head shaven, sidled up to Janie's stool. He held a cigarette, smoking it with quick, nervous gestures as he stared at her. He thrust his cigarette towards the ceiling, indicating a booming speaker. 'You like the music?'

'Not particularly.'

'Hey, you're American? Me too. Chicago. Good bud of mine, works for Citibank, he told me about this place. Food's not bad. Tapas. Baby octopus. You like octopus?'

Janie's eyes narrowed. The man wore expensive-looking corduroy trousers, a rumpled jacket of nubby charcoal-colored linen. 'No,' she said, but didn't turn away.

'Me neither. Like eating great big slimy bugs. Geoff Lanning—'

He stuck his hand out. She touched it, lightly, and smiled. 'Nice to meet you, Geoff.'

For the next half-hour or so she pretended to listen to him, nodding and smiling brilliantly whenever he looked up at her. The bar grew louder and more crowded, and people began eyeing Janie's stool covetously.

'I think I'd better hand over this seat,' she announced, hopping down and elbowing her way to the door. 'Before they eat me.'

Geoff Lanning hurried after her. 'Hey, you want to get dinner? The Camden Brasserie's just up here—'

'No, thanks.' She hesitated on the curb, gazing demurely at her Doc Martens. 'But would you like to come in for a drink?'

He was very impressed by her apartment. 'Man, this place'd probably go for a half-mil, easy! That's three-quarters of a million American.' He opened and closed cupboards, ran a hand lovingly across the slate sink. 'Nice hardwood floors, high-speed access – you never told me what you do.'

Janie laughed. 'As little as possible. Here—'

She handed him a brandy snifter, let her finger trace the back of his wrist. 'You look like kind of an adventurous sort of guy.'

'Hey, big adventure, that's me.' He lifted his glass to her. 'What exactly did you have in mind? Big game hunting?'

'Mmm. Maybe.'

It was more of a struggle this time, not for Geoff Lanning but for Janie. He lay complacently in his bonds, his stocky torso wriggling obediently when Janie commanded. Her head ached from the cheap wine at Bar Ganza; the long hairs above her eyes lay sleek against her skull, and did not move at all until she closed her eyes, and, unbidden, the image of David Bierce's hand covering hers appeared.

'Try to get away,' she whispered.

'Whoa Nellie,' Geoff Lanning gasped.

'Try to get away,' she repeated, her voice hoarser.

'Oh.' The man whimpered softly. 'Jesus Christ, what – oh my God, *what*—'

Quickly she bent and kissed his fingertips, saw where the leather cuff had bitten into his pudgy wrist. This time she was prepared when with a keening sound he began to twist upon the bed, his arms and legs shriveling and then coiling in upon themselves, his shaved head withdrawing into his tiny torso like a snail within its shell.

But she was not prepared for the creature that remained, its feathery antennae a trembling echo of her own, its extraordinarily elongated hind spurs nearly four inches long.

'*Oh*,' she gasped.

She didn't dare touch it until it took to the air: the slender spurs fragile as icicles, scarlet, their saffron tips curling like Christmas ribbon, its large delicate wings saffron with slate-blue and scarlet eye-spots, and spanning nearly six inches. A Madagascan Moon Moth, one of the loveliest and rarest silk moths, and almost impossible to find as an intact specimen.

'What do I do with you, what do I do?' she crooned as it spread its wings and lifted from the bed. It flew in short sweeping arcs; she scrambled to blow out the candles before it could get near them. She pulled on a bathrobe and left the lights off, closed the bedroom door and hurried into the kitchen, looking for a flash-light. She found nothing, but recalled Andrew telling her there was a large torch in the basement.

She hadn't been down there since her initial tour of the flat. It was brightly lit, with long neat cabinets against both walls, a floor-to-ceiling wine rack filled with bottles of claret and vintage burgundy, compact washer and dryer, small refrigerator, buckets and brooms waiting for the cleaning lady's weekly visit. She found the flashlight sitting on top of the refrigerator, a container of extra batteries beside it. She switched it on and off a few times, then glanced down at the refrigerator and absently opened it.

Seeing all that wine had made her think the little refrigerator might be filled with beer. Instead it held only a long plastic box, with a red lid and a red *Biohazard* sticker on the side. Janie put the flashlight down and stooped, carefully removing the box and setting it on the floor. A label with Andrew's neat architectural handwriting was on the top.

DR. ANDREW FILDERMAN
ST. MARTIN'S HOSPICE

'Huh,' she said, and opened it.

Inside there was a small red biohazard-waste container, and scores of plastic bags filled with disposable hypodermics, am-

pules, and suppositories. All contained morphine at varying
dosages. Janie stared, marveling, then opened one of the bags.
She shook half a dozen morphine ampules into her palm, carefully re-closed the bag, put it back into the box and returned the
box to the refrigerator. Then she grabbed the flashlight and ran
upstairs.

It took her a while to capture the Moon Moth. First she had to
find a killing jar large enough, and then she had to very carefully
lure it inside, so that its frail wing spurs wouldn't be damaged.
She did this by positioning the jar on its side and placing a
gooseneck lamp directly behind it, so that the bare bulb shone
through the glass. After about fifteen minutes, the moth landed on
top of the jar, its tiny legs slipping as it struggled on the smooth
curved surface. Another few minutes and it had crawled inside,
nestled on the wad of tissues Janie had set there, moist with ethyl
alcohol. She screwed the lid on tightly, left the jar on its side, and
waited for it to die.

Over the next week she acquired three more specimens. *Papilio
demetrius*, a Japanese swallowtail with elegant orange eyespots
on a velvety black ground; a Scarce Copper, not scarce at all,
really, but with lovely pumpkin-colored wings; and *Graphium
agamemnon*, a Malaysian species with vivid green spots and
chrome-yellow strips on its somber brown wings. She'd ventured
away from Camden Town, capturing the swallowtail in a
private room in an SM club in Islington and the *Graphium
agamemnon* in a parked car behind a noisy pub in Crouch End.
The Scarce Copper came from a vacant lot near the Tube station
at Tottenham Court Road very late one night, where the
wreckage of a chain-link fence stood in for her bedposts. She
found the morphine to be useful, although she had to wait until
immediately after the man ejaculated before pressing the ampule
against his throat, aiming for the carotid artery. This way the
butterflies emerged already sedated, and in minutes died with no
damage to their wings. Leftover clothing was easily disposed of,
but she had to be more careful with wallets, stuffing them deep
within rubbish bins, when she could, or burying them in her
own trash bags and then watching as the waste trucks came by
on their rounds.

In South Kensington she discovered an entomological supply

store. There she bought more mounting supples, and inquired casually as to whether the owner might be interested in purchasing some specimens.

He shrugged. 'Depends. What you got?'

'Well, right now I have only one *Argema mittrei*.' Janie adjusted her glasses and glanced around the shop. A lot of morphos, an Atlas moth: nothing too unusual. 'But I might be getting another, in which case . . .'

'Moon Moth, eh? How'd you come by that, I wonder?' The man raised his eyebrows, and Janie flushed. 'Don't worry, I'm not going to turn you in. Christ, I'd go out of business. Well, obviously I can't display those in the shop, but if you want to part with one, let me know. I'm always scouting for my customers.'

She began volunteering three days a week at the Insect Zoo. One Wednesday, the night after she'd gotten a gorgeous *Urania leilus*, its wings sadly damaged by rain, she arrived to see David Bierce reading that morning's *Camden New Journal*. He peered over the newspaper and frowned.

'You still going out alone at night?'

She froze, her mouth dry; turned and hurried over to the coffee maker. 'Why?' she said, fighting to keep her tone even.

'Because there's an article about some of the clubs around here. Apparently a few people have gone missing.'

'Really?' Janie got her coffee, wiping up a spill with the side of her hand. 'What happened?'

'Nobody knows. Two blokes reported gone, family frantic, sort of thing. Probably just runaways. Camden Town eats them alive, kids.' He handed the paper to Janie. 'Although one of them was last seen near Highbury Fields, some sex club there.'

She scanned the article. There was no mention of any suspects. And no bodies had been found, although foul play was suspected. (*'Ken would never have gone away without notifying us or his employer . . .'*)

Anyone with any information was urged to contact the police.

'I don't go to sex clubs,' Janie said flatly. 'Plus those are both guys.'

'Mmm.' David leaned back in his chair, regarding her coolly. 'You're the one hitting Hive your first weekend in London.'

'It's a *dance* club!' Janie retorted. She laughed, rolled the newspaper into a tube and batted him gently on the shoulder. 'Don't worry. I'll be careful.'

David continued to stare at her, hazel eyes glittering. 'Who says it's you I'm worried about?'

She smiled, her mouth tight as she turned and began cleaning bottles in the sink.

It was a raw day, more late November than mid-May. Only two school groups were scheduled; otherwise the usual stream of visitors was reduced to a handful of elderly women who shook their heads over the cockroaches and gave barely a glance to the butterflies before shuffling on to another building. David Bierce paced restlessly through the lab on his way to clean the cages and make more complaints to the Operations Division. Janie cleaned and mounted two stag beetles, their spiny legs pricking her fingertips as she tried to force the pins through their glossy chestnut-colored shells. Afterwards she busied herself with straightening the clutter of cabinets and drawers stuffed with requisition forms and microscopes, computer parts and dissection kits.

It was well past two when David reappeared, his anorak slick with rain, his hair tucked beneath the hood. 'Come on,' he announced, standing impatiently by the open door. 'Let's go to lunch.'

Janie looked up from the computer where she'd been updating a specimen list. 'I'm really not very hungry,' she said, giving him an apologetic smile. 'You go ahead.'

'Oh, for Christ's sake.' David let the door slam shut as he crossed to her, his sneakers leaving wet smears on the tiled floor. 'That can wait till tomorrow. Come on, there's not a fucking thing here that needs doing.'

'But—' She gazed up at him. The hood slid from his head; his grey-streaked hair hung loose to his shoulders, and the sheen of rain on his sharp cheekbones made him look carved from oiled wood. 'What if somebody comes?'

'A very nice docent named Mrs Eleanor Feltwell is out there, *even as we speak*, in the unlikely event that we have a single visitor.'

He stooped so that his head was beside hers, scowling as he stared at the computer screen. A lock of his hair fell to brush against her neck. Beneath the wig her scalp burned, as though stung by tiny ants; she breathed in the warm acrid smell of his sweat and something else, a sharper scent, like crushed oak-mast or fresh-sawn wood. Above her brows the antennae suddenly quivered. Sweetness coated her tongue like burnt syrup. With a rush of panic she turned her head so he wouldn't see her face.

'I – I should finish this—'

'Oh, just *fuck* it, Jane! It's not like we're *paying* you. Come on, now, there's a good girl—'

He took her hand and pulled her to her feet, Janie still looking away. The bangs of her cheap wig scraped her forehead and she batted at them feebly. 'Get your things. What, don't you ever take days off in the States?'

'All right, all right.' She turned and gathered her black vinyl raincoat and knapsack, pulled on the coat and waited for him by the door. 'Jeez, you must be hungry,' she said crossly.

'No. Just fucking bored out of my skull. Have you been to Ruby in the Dust? No? I'll take you then, let's go—'

The restaurant was down the High Street, a small, cheerfully claptrap place, dim in the grey afternoon, its small wooden tables scattered with abandoned newspapers and overflowing ashtrays. David Bierce ordered a steak and a pint. Janie had a small salad, nasturtium blossoms strewn across pale green lettuce, and a glass of red wine. She lacked an appetite lately, living on vitamin-enhanced, fruity bottled drinks from the health food store and baklava from a Greek bakery near the Tube station.

'So.' David Bierce stabbed a piece of steak, peering at her sideways. 'Don't tell me you really haven't been here before.'

'I haven't!' Despite her unease at being with him, she laughed, and caught her reflection in the wall-length mirror. A thin plain young woman in shapeless Peruvian sweater and jeans, bad haircut and ugly glasses. Gazing at herself she felt suddenly stronger, invisible. She tilted her head and smiled at Bierce. 'The food's good.'

'So you don't have someone taking you out to dinner every night? Cooking for you? I thought you American girls all had adoring men at your feet. Adoring slaves,' he added dryly. 'Or slave girls, I suppose. If that's your thing.'

'No.' She stared at her salad, shook her head demurely and took a sip of wine. It made her feel even more invulnerable. 'No, I—'

'Boyfriend back home, right?' He finished his pint, flagged the waiter to order another and turned back to Janie. 'Well, that's nice. That's very nice – for him,' he added, and gave a short harsh laugh.

The waiter brought another pint, and more wine for Janie. 'Oh really, I better—'

'Just drink it, Jane.' Under the table, she felt a sharp pressure on her foot. She wasn't wearing her Doc Martens today but a pair of red plastic jellies. David Bierce had planted his heel firmly atop her toes; she sucked in her breath in shock and pain, the bones of her foot crackling as she tried to pull it from beneath him. Her antenna rippled, then stiffened, and heat burst like a seed inside her.

'Go ahead,' he said softly, pushing the wineglass towards her. 'Just a sip, that's right—'

She grabbed the glass, spilling wine on her sweater as she gulped at it. The vicious pressure on her foot subsided, but as the wine ran down her throat she could feel the heat thrusting her into the air, currents rushing beneath her as the girl at the table below set down her wineglass with trembling fingers.

'There.' David Bierce smiled, leaning forward to gently cup her hand between his. 'Now this is better than working. Right, Jane?'

He walked her home along the canal path. Janie tried to dissuade him, but he'd had a third pint by then; it didn't seem to make him drunk but coldly obdurate, and she finally gave in. The rain had turned to a fine drizzle, the canal's usually murky water silvered and softly gleaming in the twilight. They passed few other people, and Janie found herself wishing someone else would appear, so that she'd have an excuse to move closer to David Bierce. He kept close to the canal itself, several feet from Janie; when the breeze lifted she could catch his oaky scent again, rising above the dank reek of stagnant water and decaying hawthorn blossom.

They crossed over the bridge to approach her flat by the street. At the front sidewalk Janie stopped, smiled shyly and said, 'Thanks. That was nice.'

David nodded. 'Glad I finally got you out of your cage.' He lifted his head to gaze appraisingly at the row house. 'Christ, this where you're staying? You split the rent with someone?'

'No.' She hesitated: she couldn't remember what she had told him about her living arrangements. But before she could blurt something out he stepped past her to the front door, peeking into the window and bobbing impatiently up and down.

'Mind if I have a look? Professional entomologists don't often get the chance to see how the quality live.'

Janie hesitated, her stomach clenching; decided it would be safer to have him in rather than continue to put him off.

'All right,' she said reluctantly, and opened the door.

'Mmmm. Nice, nice, very nice.' He swept around the living room, spinning on his heel and making a show of admiring the elaborate molding, the tribal rugs, the fireplace mantel with its thick ecclesiastical candles and ormolu mirror. 'Goodness, all this for a wee thing like you? You're a clever cat, landing on your feet here, Lady Jane.'

She blushed. He bounded past her on his way into the bedroom, touching her shoulder; she had to close her eyes as a fiery wave surged through her and her antennae trembled.

'*Wow*,' he exclaimed.

Slowly she followed him into the bedroom. He stood in front of the wall where her specimens were balanced in a neat line across the wainscoting. His eyes were wide, his mouth open in genuine astonishment.

'Are these *yours*?' he marveled, his gaze fixed on the butterflies. 'You didn't actually catch them—?'

She shrugged.

'These are incredible!' He picked up the *Graphium agamemnon* and tilted it to the pewter-colored light falling through the French doors. 'Did you mount them, too?'

She nodded, crossing to stand beside him. 'Yeah. You can tell, with that one—' She pointed at the *Urania leilus* in its oak-framed box. 'It got rained on.'

David Bierce replaced the *Graphium agamemnon* and began to read the labels on the others.

Papilio demetrius
UNITED KINGDOM: LONDON
Highbury Fields, Islington
7.V.2001
J. Kendall

Isopa katinka
UNITED KINGDOM: LONDON
Finsbury Park
09.V.2001
J. Kendall

Argema mittrei
UNITED KINGDOM: LONDON
Camden Town
13.IV.2001
J. Kendall

He shook his head. 'You screwed up, though – you wrote "London" for all of them.' He turned to her, grinning wryly. 'Can't think of the last time I saw a Moon Moth in Camden Town.'

She forced a laugh. 'Oh – right.'

'And, I mean, you can't have actually *caught* them— '

He held up the *Isopa katinka*, a butter-yellow Emperor moth, its peacock's-eyes russet and jet-black. 'I haven't seen any of these around lately. Not even in Finsbury Park.'

Janie made a little grimace of apology. 'Yeah. I meant, that's where I found them – where I bought them.'

'Mmmm.' He set the moth back on its ledge. 'You'll have to share your sources with me. I can never find things like these in North London.'

He turned and headed out of the bedroom. Janie hurriedly straightened the specimens, her hands shaking now as well, and followed him.

'Well, Lady Jane.' For the first time he looked at her without his usual mocking arrogance, his green-flecked eyes bemused, almost regretful. 'I think we managed to salvage something from the day.'

He turned, gazing one last time at the flat's glazed walls and highly waxed floors, the imported cabinetry and jewel-toned carpets. 'I was going to say, when I walked you home, that you needed someone to take care of you. But it looks like you've managed that on your own.'

Janie stared at her feet. He took a step toward her, the fragrance of oak-mast and honey filling her nostrils, crushed acorns, new fern. She grew dizzy, her hand lifting to find him; but he only reached to graze her cheek with his finger.

'Night then, Janie,' he said softly, and walked back out into the misty evening.

When he was gone she raced to the windows and pulled all the velvet curtains, then tore the wig from her head and threw it onto the couch along with her glasses. Her heart was pounding, her face slick with sweat – from fear or rage or disappointment, she didn't know. She yanked off her sweater and jeans, left them on the living-room floor and stomped into the bathroom. She stood in the shower for twenty minutes, head upturned as the water sluiced the smells of bracken and leaf-mold from her skin.

Finally she got out. She dried herself, let the towel drop and went into the kitchen. Abruptly she was famished. She tore open cupboards and drawers until she found a half-full jar of lavender honey from Provence. She opened it, the top spinning off into the sink, and frantically spooned honey into her mouth with her fingers. When she was finished she grabbed a jar of lemon curd and ate most of that, until she felt as though she might be sick. She stuck her head into the sink, letting water run from the faucet into her mouth, and at last walked, surfeited, into the bedroom.

She dressed, feeling warm and drowsy, almost dreamlike; pulling on red-and-yellow striped stockings, her nylon skirt, a tight red T-shirt. No bra, no panties. She put in her contacts, then examined herself in the mirror. Her hair had begun to grow back, a scant velvety stubble, bluish in the dim light. She drew a sweeping black line across each eyelid, on a whim took the liner and extended the curve of each antennae until they touched her temples. She painted her lips black as well and went to find her black vinyl raincoat.

It was early when she went out, far too early for any of the clubs to be open. The rain had stopped, but a thick greasy fog hung over everything, coating windshields and shop windows, making Janic's face feel as though it were encased in a clammy shell. For hours she wandered Camden Town, huge violet eyes turning to stare back at the men who watched her, dismissing each of them. Once she thought she saw David Bierce, coming out of Ruby in the Dust; but when she stopped to watch him cross the street saw it was not David at all but someone else. Much younger, his long dark hair in a thick braid, his feet clad in knee-high boots. He crossed the High Street, heading towards the Tube station. Janie hesitated, then darted after him.

He went to the Electric Ballroom. Fifteen or so people stood out front, talking quietly. The man she'd followed joined the line, standing by himself. Janie waited across the street, until the door opened and the little crowd began to shuffle inside. After the long-haired young man had entered she counted to one hundred, crossed the street, paid her cover and went inside.

The club had three levels; she finally tracked him down on the uppermost one. Even on a rainy Wednesday night it was crowded, the sound system blaring Idris Mohammed and Jimmie Cliff. He was standing alone near the bar, drinking bottled water.

'Hi!' she shouted, swaying up to him with her best First Day of School smile. 'Want to dance?'

He was older than she'd thought – thirtyish, still not as old as Bierce. He stared at her, puzzled, then shrugged. 'Sure.'

They danced, passing the water bottle between them. 'What's your name?' he shouted.

'Cleopatra Brimstone.'

'You're kidding!' he yelled back. The song ended in a bleat of feedback, and they walked, panting, back to the bar.

'What, you know another Cleopatra?' Janie asked teasingly.

'No. It's just a crazy name, that's all.' He smiled. He was handsomer than David Bierce, his features softer, more rounded, his eyes dark brown, his manner a bit reticent. 'I'm Thomas Raybourne. Tom.'

He bought another bottle of Pellegrino and one for Janie. She drank it quickly, trying to get his measure. When she finished she set the empty bottle on the floor and fanned herself with her hand.

'It's hot in here.' Her throat hurt from shouting over the music. 'I think I'm going to take a walk. Feel like coming?'

He hesitated, glancing around the club. 'I was supposed to meet a friend here . . .' he began, frowning. 'But—'

'Oh.' Disappointment filled her, spiking into desperation. 'Well, that's okay. I guess.'

'Oh, what the hell.' He smiled: he had nice eyes, a more stolid, reassuring gaze than Bierce. 'I can always come back.'

Outside she turned right, in the direction of the canal. 'I live pretty close by. Feel like coming in for a drink?'

He shrugged again. 'I don't drink, actually.'

'Something to eat then? It's not far – just along the canal path, a few blocks past Camden Lock—'

'Yeah, sure.'

They made desultory conversation. 'You should be careful,' he said as they crossed the bridge. 'Did you read about those people who've gone missing in Camden Town?'

Janie nodded but said nothing. She felt anxious and clumsy – as though she'd drunk too much, although she'd had nothing since the two glasses of wine with David Bierce. Her companion also seemed ill at ease; he kept glancing back, as though looking for someone on the canal path behind them.

'I should have tried to call,' he explained ruefully. 'But I forgot to recharge my mobile.'

'You could call from my place.'

'No, that's all right.'

She could tell from his tone that he was figuring how he could leave, gracefully, as soon as possible.

Inside the flat he settled on the couch, picked up a copy of *Time Out* and flipped through it, pretending to read. Janie went immediately into the kitchen and poured herself a glass of brandy. She downed it, poured a second one, and joined him on the couch.

'So.' She kicked off her Doc Martens, drew her stockinged foot slowly up his leg, from calf to thigh. 'Where you from?'

He was passive, so passive she wondered if he would get aroused at all. But after a while they were lying on the couch, both their shirts on the floor, his pants unzipped and his cock stiff, pressing against her bare belly.

'Let's go in there,' Janie whispered hoarsely. She took his hand and led him into the bedroom.

She only bothered lighting a single candle, before lying beside him on the bed. His eyes were half-closed, his breathing shallow. When she ran a fingernail around one nipple he made a small surprised sound, then quickly turned and pinned her to the bed.

'Wait! Slow down,' Janie said, and wriggled from beneath him. For the last week she'd left the bonds attached to the bedposts, hiding them beneath the covers when not in use. Now she grabbed one of the wristcuffs and pulled it free. Before he could see what she was doing it was around his wrist.

'Hey!'

She dived for the foot of the bed, his leg narrowly missing her as it thrashed against the covers. It was more difficult to get this in place, but she made a great show of giggling and stroking his thigh, which seemed to calm him. The other leg was next, and finally she leapt from the bed and darted to the headboard, slipping from his grasp when he tried to grab her shoulder.

'This is not consensual,' he said. She couldn't tell if he was serious or not.

'What about this, then?' she murmured, sliding down between his legs and cupping his erect penis between her hands. 'This seems to be enjoying itself.'

He groaned softly, shutting his eyes. 'Try to get away,' she said. 'Try to get away.'

He tried to lunge upward, his body arching so violently that she drew back in alarm. The bonds held; he arched again, and again, but now she remained beside him, her hands on his cock, his breath coming faster and faster and her own breath keeping pace with it, her heart pounding and the tingling above her eyes almost unbearable.

'Try to get away,' she gasped. 'Try to get away—'

When he came he cried out, his voice harsh, as though in pain, and Janie cried out as well, squeezing her eyes shut as spasms shook her from head to groin. Quickly her head dipped to kiss his chest; then she shuddered and drew back, watching.

His voice rose again, ended suddenly in a shrill wail, as his limbs knotted and shriveled like burning rope. She had a final glimpse of him, a homunculus sprouting too many legs. Then on the bed before her a perfectly formed *Papilio krischna* swallowtail crawled across the rumpled duvet, its wings twitching to display glittering green scales amidst spectral washes of violet and crimson and gold.

'Oh, you're beautiful, beautiful,' she whispered.

From across the room echoed a sound: soft, the rustle of her kimono falling from its hook as the door swung open. She snatched her hand from the butterfly and stared, through the door to the living room.

In her haste to get Thomas Raybourne inside she had forgotten to latch the front door. She scrambled to her feet, naked, staring wildly at the shadow looming in front of her, its features taking shape as it approached the candle, brown and black, light glinting across his face.

It was David Bierce. The scent of oak and bracken swelled, suffocating, fragrant, cut by the bitter odor of ethyl alcohol. He forced her gently onto the bed, heat piercing her breast and thighs, her antenna bursting out like quills from her brow and wings exploding everywhere around her as she struggled fruitlessly.

'Now. Try to get away,' he said.

CHICO KIDD

Cats and Architecture

CHICO KIDD'S DAY JOB IS IN ADVERTISING, for which she has won several awards, all, oddly enough, in the field of publishing.

Her first novel, *The Printer's Devil*, appeared in 1995 from Baen Books (under the name of Chico Kidd rather than A.F.), while almost all her short stories were finally collected together in one volume by Ash-Tree Press in *Summoning Knells and Other Inventions* (2000). She also writes stories in collaboration with Rick Kennett in Australia featuring William Hope Hodgson's character, Carnacki the Ghost-Finder. The Ghost Story Society published a collection of four stories in 1992, and this has been substantially expanded for the recent Ash-Tree collection, *Number 472 Cheyne Walk*.

'You could call "Cats and Architecture" a transitional tale between the old (and rather old-fashioned) "A.F." stories and the present series,' Kidd reveals. 'You could also call it an epiphany. Or a revelation. I suffered from writer's block for more than five years. It is a terrible affliction. This story started out as a typically Jamesian piece, and I'd been struggling with it for a long time. And then Captain Da Silva appeared, with a past and a personality and a lot of baggage I wasn't conscious of inventing. And since then I've been writing as if a dam has burst.

'One odd thing: the "proverb" quoted at the start of part two apparently isn't, at least my Portuguese friend has never heard it. Yet I must have found it somewhere as it was in my commonplace book (no source quoted). It wasn't until I was halfway through the third novel, earlier this year, that I discovered it was a saying of the Captain's mother.'

I

It was not carnival time in Venice, yet strangely enough a kind of charivari spirit seemed still to move along the city's narrow byways. Round the corner ahead you might hear the ghost of a laugh or a whisper of music, only to have it dissipate as you approached, or mutate into the soft plash of canal waters.

That the city is given to shades, and cannot escape its aura of being a place where time seems thin and stretched, is not a reason for the existence of such phantasms, any more than the human body is the cause or creator of its own internal organs—

Jo Da Silva put down her pen, her mind stuck in the groove of the movie *Don't Look Now*, and walked over to the window.

Out of season, Venice had indeed slipped back into the past that it inhabited after the majority of the tourists had departed, and had become a village again. The stinks of high summer were gone as well, and a kind of comfortable melancholy imbued its misty vistas.

The apartment looked out on a small, terracotta-coloured piazza (or campo, if you wanted to be pedantic about it). Its usual tenants were visiting relatives in Australia, and Jo was not one to turn down the offer of a month's free accommodation in La Serenissima; although she had done precious little in the way of the writing she had intended to knuckle down to in the week she had spent there. Its only drawback was her suspicion that the building harboured rats in its nether regions.

At the moment the campo appeared totally uninhabited, as if Jo were in a city on the moon, or perhaps in a de Chirico painting. It was almost completely filled up with shadows, and most of the windows in the other buildings that surrounded it were shuttered, like closed eyes. Potted plants made splashes of colour here and there.

Despite the direction of her last thoughts, she was not really expecting to see sinister little red-coated figures. The campo was so sleepy, in fact, that she was not expecting to see anything at all, which was why a movement in her eye's corner made her jump.

Diagonally across the square, one shuttered window stood slightly ajar. The shutter, half open, folded in on itself, as it were, gave a glimpse of darkness behind; and something whitish fluttered there. Not a curtain, for it had solidity. Not a person, either – but why had she thought that?

Ow, I seen it wive at me out the winder.

More ghost stories in her mind! That was *Oh Whistle and I'll Come to You.* On second thoughts, she rather wished that particular tale hadn't come to the surface.

. . . And I didn't like it.

Jo ran a hand though her short hair and decided it was definitely time to go and drink a cup of espresso, and possibly a glass of grappa as well. Or, even better, have a caffè corretto and combine the two – she liked the idea that coffee could be 'corrected' by the addition of alcohol. Besides, she had to go past the building with the window to get to the bar, and could take, therefore, a closer look.

Out in the red-shadowed, deserted campo, her steps echoed hollowly. The shadows had put a chill into the square, although above her the sky was still a hazed blue, only just beginning to fade towards evening.

A dog came sniffing out of an alley, busy on its own affairs, and Jo smiled; she liked dogs, but wished this one would do something to earn its keep, firstly by going after the rats and then, probably, doing something to deter the supercilious white cat that she had seen slinking around the vicinity most nights, like a pathfinder from the Countess of Groan's entourage. In Jo's opinion it was white cats that should be witches' familiars, leaving their black counterparts to bring, like chimney sweepers, luck where they would; silent and sneaky as all felines, to Jo the ghostlike pallor of the whites was far more suited to a supernatural role. *Darkness creeps on cat feet*, she thought, deliberately misquoting, and smiled to herself.

Now she was in the building's shadow, she looked up. It was older – and grander – than she'd thought at first: almost a demi-palazzo, it could have dated from the eighteenth century, but Jo's knowledge of architectural styles was sketchy at best. The window, on the top storey, was tall and possessed of a tiny balcony too small to sit on, but just wide enough for plant pots: indeed, others round the square were cluttered with flowers – the ubiquitous geraniums and petunias, whose hot pinks and reds clashed with the suntan-colours of the terracotta pots, and here and there a trail of magenta bougainvillea, like a Christmas paper chain.

Beside the front door, where now she stood, she saw a single bell-push – apparently the building had escaped being converted into apartments. After a moment's hesitation, she pressed it, hearing its dim buzz deep inside, like a trapped insect, but there was no reply.

She was conscious, then, of being on a cusp, presented with a clear choice between two routes. Either she could forget a thing, or a nothing, seen out of the edge of her eye in a building kitty-corner to her life; or, like the egregious Franz Westen, go in pursuit of it.

It brought a wry grin to her face. She may have been suffering from writer's block, but no one had ever accused her of lacking imagination, and nobody would ever say she was devoid of curiosity. And tending still towards feline metaphors, the significance of *that* was not lost on her.

Between the campo and the bar she had claimed as her own she passed a shop that sold masks, fantastical things of pasteboard and feathers and sequins and enamel, like an Ensor dream. Its window was always brightly illuminated, so that the colours of the masks gleamed in the hard bright light like phantasmagorical beetle-cases.

The Phantom of the Opera is here, inside your mind.

Jo shook her head to rid it of the irritating tune, but all she could think of as a substitute on the spur of the moment was poor mad Lucia, fluting '*Il fantasmo!*'; and the famous shot of Joan Sutherland, wild-haired in her bloodstained nightie, floated behind her eyes.

Reaching her destination, thoughts of corrected coffee drove out her introspection. Although the name *Il Bar Roberto* was written on the window in fading paint, the establishment was presided over by a tall thin unsmiling woman with an intimidating moustache; she was generally known as La Strega – although no cats, black, white or otherwise, were allowed past her door.

Under her aegis a number of young women who were too much
like her in appearance (although mostly lacking the facial hair)
not to be her daughters bustled about, serving customers, min-
istering to the espresso machine, and gossiping at the tops of their
voices. In one corner a television with the sound turned down
always seemed to be showing a football match, and usually a
number of men were clustered round it roaring encouragement,
or otherwise.

'Does anyone live in the house on the corner?' Jo asked one of
the daughters, who shrugged her shoulders and shook her head at
the same time. An older sister, passing with a tray of dirty cups
and glasses, was more knowledgeable.

'It belonged to an old boy called Della Quercia,' she told Jo.
'He didn't leave a will when he died; the children's lawyers have
been arguing over the house for years. So someone's getting fat
out of it. Why do you ask?'

'Just curious,' said Jo dismissively.

But when moonlight lay white on the campo that night, and
sleep eluded her, she got up, padded to the window and looked
out to see whether any pallid thing was waving to her. The corner
house was deep in shadow, and somehow that was more unsettling than seeing something. Even when she finally drifted off
to sleep, her dreams were populated with floating masks and pale
shrouds on the shores of stagnant waters.

Mist, which really came on cat feet, transformed the city the
next morning into a place of ghosts and shadows indeed, and
smelling strongly of the sea. Jo skulked in bed, fatigued from her
broken night, grumpy with lack of sleep; and then the phone
rang.

'Pronto,' she yawned into the mouthpiece. For a long time there
was nothing but the rush and clatter of the phone line, and then,
as she was about to hang up, very faint and faraway, a voice said,
'Are you coming?'

'What?'

Another long pause, and then, 'If you don't come to me, I'll
come to you.'

The line went dead, and left Jo staring at the receiver and
thinking about M. R. James.

And then she jerked awake with the compulsive indrawn
whoop of holding her breath too long, and stared round the

suddenly unfamiliar room without comprehension for nearly a minute.

She got out of bed, the old linoleum cold beneath her feet, and walked through to the main room, where she trod on something sharp that made her hop and curse. Investigating, she found it was a necklace: a rather pretty antique thing of opals and jade with a vaguely oriental look. Jo picked it up and put it on the table by the telephone, catching sight of her sleep-rumpled face in the mirror above. Not a jewellery person at the best of times – her idea of dressing up was a clean pair of jeans – she was hardly tempted to slip the necklace over her head to see how it would look. Even the fact that she could entertain such a thought made her smile, and she crossed to the window.

Opening the shutter nearly dislodged the white cat, which yowled angrily and took its leave in the feline equivalent of a huff. Outside, the weather truly *was* misty, so much so that the corner house was invisible and the sounds of people bestirring themselves were muffled, as if they had all put on boots of felt and decided, inexplicably, to speak in whispers. But then she heard the sharp bark of a dog, cutting through the dull cloud.

Not without suspicious glances at the telephone, Jo picked through the cards in the big dish beside it, until she found the one she was looking for.

'La Casa della Scala,' said Maurizio Giordano, whom Jo had been told knew everything there was to know about Venice. 'The House with the Stair.' Expecting, for no logical reason, a kindly gnome of a professor, she had been surprised to find a lumbering great young man who, had he been a dog, would have been a St Bernard, possibly crossed with an Irish wolfhound. He was the proprietor of an establishment called The Arcane Library – though even a brief glimpse at the shelves made Jo think 'eclectic' would be a better word.

'The House with the Stair?' she repeated, giving the words the same capitalization.

'That's right, it's quite famous. All the guides take the tourists to look at it. If you go through the archway on the right of the house you'll find a spiral staircase leading up the back, with a thing like a dovecote on top. It was built by a guy called Umberto Scimone, who most people think was as mad as a hatter. Because, you see, the staircase doesn't connect to the house at all, unless you want to jump two metres across and up or a metre down to get in through a window.'

'So what's the story?'

'Well, he built the staircase for cats, apparently. He was potty about cats. You know M. C. Escher?' Giordano asked, with apparent irrelevance.

'Yes?'

'Have you seen that print of all the curly-up critters going up and down one of his stair-mazes?' Jo nodded. 'That was the sort of thing Scimone had in mind. He even did a sketch of hundreds of cats doing much the same thing, up and down an endless stair. Though I don't think he was quite so fascinated by impossible geometry as Escher, being an architect, you see.'

Behind the professor, the open window gave onto a properly functional balcony on which stood a wicker chair, a small table, and a bay tree with a spiral trunk in a Chinese pot. From not too far away came the sounds of vaporetti plying the canals, but their clamour was currently being contested by some enthusiastic Verdi from somewhere nearby. Early, she thought; *Ernani*, perhaps. The air felt damp, although the mist was mostly gone, risen into the sky to dull the late-autumn sun and mock the eyes with air.

'And who was Signor Della Quercia?'

'As a matter of fact, he was my grandfather. On the wrong side of the blanket, though, as they say. But we're not yet done with Signor Scimone. Would you like a glass of wine?' Jo assented, and was shortly presented with a nicely chilled Vernaccia. That done, the professor continued, 'I assume you know what ley lines are?'

'Sort of,' she replied. 'Lines of . . . force, aren't they? *The Old Straight Track*,' she added, the title popping up unbidden, although she had never actually read the book.

'*Positive* force, to be exact,' said Giordano, and waited for Jo to nod her head. Sipping his wine, he continued, 'So it won't have occurred to you that they might have a negative equivalent?'

'Not really,' Jo said. 'I hadn't given it much thought.'

'Well, Signor Scimone did. And he came to the conclusion that Venice was riddled with the things. Lines of bad luck, if you like. Interestingly enough, it seems La Fenice was built on one.' Jo, who still grieved at the loss of the opera house, nodded. 'Scimone had quite a lot of . . . shall we say, individual ideas. Apart from the negative ley lines, he used all sorts of arcane formulae to influence his work.'

'What, sort of eighteenth-century Italian feng shui?'

Giordano laughed, a curiously high sound from such a huge frame. 'You could say that.' He got to his feet and hunted amongst his bookshelves, leaving Jo staring at a collection of what appeared to be grimoires. Finally he extracted a slim volume, the cover of which he showed to Jo: it featured the cat drawing he had mentioned earlier. It was called *Le Gatti e L'Architettura*; she missed the author's name.

Opening it delicately, he flicked through pages until he found what he was looking for. 'Here it is: *"Scimone's fascination with cats is well known, but perhaps the full extent of it is less common knowledge. In a letter to Fiorenza Tevere, he proposed the somewhat Brunoesque view that he saw them as merely the earthly manifestations of huge and benign beings which had their existence in another sphere entirely. As such, he believed their benevolence was a positive force for good, and planned every building to take advantage of this, especially those which had to be constructed on or near negative ley-lines."'*

'A cat-flap in every palazzo?' suggested Jo, not without sarcasm.

'Actually it was Galileo who invented the cat flap,' said Giordano, straight-faced, and Jo didn't know whether to believe him or not.

Closing the book, he refilled their glasses, and looked at her expectantly.

'And I suppose the house is on one of these negative ley lines?' she said.

'Exactly. Now listen, the plot thickens. Scimone built the house, properly the Palazzo Della Quercia, for one of my ancestors, carefully explaining to him the significance of the stairs, which were, in essence, a very grand cat flap, allowing them to come and go via an upper floor.'

'But didn't you say—'

'Yes, indeed. But originally the stairway *was* attached to the palazzo, by a sort of mini-Bridge of Sighs. Which, at some time in the late nineteenth or early twentieth century, simply disappeared. No one knows how. Or when. Or why. But I think I can hazard a guess at the why.' He paused.

'To *exclude* the cats?' hazarded Jo, feeling a little like the straight man in a vaudeville act.

'Yes, yes. But if we accept Scimone's use of cats as a kind of guardian against malign forces, removing the bridge very effectively cut off their protection.'

'But why would anyone want to do that?'

'Someone who wanted to contact the malign forces might. The Della Quercia family have enjoyed a . . . mixed reputation over the years. At one stage they were supposed to have owned some kind of powerful amulet brought back by Marco Polo, but nobody knows what became of that.'

Jo took a mouthful of wine and savoured the slightly metallic taste. 'Are we talking of a Della Quercia warlock?'

'Not a warlock,' the professor corrected her. 'A necromancer.'

There was a sudden silence, vaporetti and Verdi alike both mute for a long instant as a chill travelled down Jo's back.

'Someone who talks to the dead . . .'

'Oh, more than *talked*, I think. And not to the dead, exactly,' said Giordano softly, and suddenly he didn't seem a kindly figure at all.

Walking back from this meeting, Jo again felt surrounded by phantoms, but this time they had been conjured by speech and conjecture rather than atmosphere and legend ancient and modern. Things seemed to want to unravel, as if the knowledge of Scimone's negative ley lines had opened a third eye that was capable of seeing or at least sensing them all around her, an almost palpable cat's cradle in the air.

Her footsteps rang and echoed in the deserted campo, in the hollow of her head. She found herself, once more, standing outside the house with the stair, but instead of looking up at the windows (and whatever might be waving out of them) she followed Giordano's remembered instructions and headed through the archway he had described, unsurprised to disturb the white cat, which had been basking in an errant patch of sunlight. It shot her a very human look of annoyance at having its rest interrupted.

The tower struck her as a beautiful thing; somehow, in her speculations and imaginings, she had not been prepared for beauty. There was something so patently perfect about it that it took her breath away. Yet its *absolute* perfection was marred.

Lacking its bridge, it was incomplete, like an unfinished song. Jo sighed, looking up at the blank brick back of the palazzo, all shutters fastened, all secrets hidden away.

But she could climb the tower, she thought. Perhaps from the top she would see something enlightening. Almost automatically she walked towards it, and set her foot on the first marble step. Dizziness enclosed her briefly, and a phrase of Giordano's came to her.

Impossible geometry.

Jo shook her head to clear it, and began to ascend. An almost overwhelming sensation of déjà vu possessed her, instantly recognizable, unlike most such. Many years earlier, before the authorities closed it to the public, she had climbed the bell tower at Pisa, had lurched like a spacewalker up steps that threw her balance from one side to another: up had not been consistently up, was sometimes almost down; just so would a climber of one of Escher's edifices experience their endless turning, twisting stairs.

She tried to concentrate on the steps. They were not worn by the soft insubstantial tread of cats, with their feet as light as mist; nor was the marble furred with dust, for it shone whiter than the airy translucence of the Taj Mahal that looks, from a distance, like lace painted on the dawn. There was no handrail, so she trailed her left hand around the central column as she climbed – widdershins, of course.

With a suddenness that was startling, she reached the top, a circular chamber on whose floor the sunlight lay bright and striped by the shadows of the columns that surrounded it. Breathing a little heavily, she put her hands on her protesting thighs and bent slightly to recover.

It was strangely peaceful at the top of the cat tower. Across from Jo the blind façade of the palazzo loomed, uncompromising, shutters still covering its windows, one – she did a double-take and looked back at an area her gaze had already passed over – slightly ajar. She walked to the edge and looked out over the void, drawn by the darkness behind the shutter. What wealth of secrets was hidden within? And what guardian might be set over them?

Vertigo tugged at her and she steadied herself on a marble column, gravity – and the human fear of it – reasserting itself as the sudden squeal of an angry cat captured her attention. Feeling a trifle embarrassed (she was, after all, trespassing), Jo descended the stair and crept back out into the quiet campo and home again.

Why did she still feel such a compulsion to get into Della Quercia's house?

If you don't come to me, I'll come to you.

Jo paced the room, nervily. Night had stolen up on her – night, and too much caffeine. She knew she wouldn't sleep in this state, and that irritated her further.

'Damn and blast it,' she muttered, finding herself at the open window again, and staring out across the campo at the Casa della Scala.

All at once, she was convinced that there was someone standing behind her. No noise disturbed the silent apartment, no breath shared her air, but someone was in the room with her, and her back went icy cold. For no apparent reason, she thought of rats – rats in the walls.

She gripped the windowsill in unreasoning terror, and her blood thundered in her ears. Unwillingly, her gaze moved side-ways, to look at the room's slanted reflection in the open window.

Nothing, nothing, nothing, went her thoughts like a mantra. The lamp on the table, the one with the shade of Murano glass, shed a pool of soft light; everything else was in shadow. She could see no one reflected in the flat shiny glass. Yet she could not, physically could not, turn round, for fear of what stood in the room with her, watching.

Smiling. *Now why do I think that?* Jo shut her eyes, squeezed them tight, and the sense of being no longer alone vanished abruptly. Drawing a few deep breaths, she turned to face the room before opening her eyes again, and then scurried for the light switch to turn on all the illumination she could.

As she came back to the table, strewn with her papers and notes, she saw a key lying beside her pen.

Her scalp prickled. She eyed the key suspiciously. It was a large key for a deadlock, much like the one that opened the main door downstairs. There was no doubt in her mind what door this one would open.

So she stretched out her hand to pick it up, only to jump back, startled into alarm by the sudden squalling shriek of an angry cat.

Her heart tried to high-jump out of her chest, and she let out her breath in a sharp curse.

Up to her windowsill, ghost-pale like a spectre, leapt the white cat, its ears back, hissing defiance at something outside. Jo threw a ball of paper at it, which the cat ignored, and jumped down into the room, miaowing loudly at her. She tried to take evasive action, but it bumped her legs, twined itself round, its voice raucous in the silence.

'What do you want, Signor Gatto?' she asked, catching its tail, which it carried aloft like a banner. It continued to weave around her legs, and Jo sighed. 'I haven't got any food,' she told it. 'Unless you like uncooked pasta.'

The cat head-butted her in the shin. She sat down to stroke it, despite not considering herself a cat person, and it surprised her by jumping onto her lap and sitting there with none of the usual kneading.

'Oh, all right, if you insist,' she said, and picked up the newspaper.

Morning light flooded in, chill and white, without a hint of fog. It brought with it an air so icy that it might have come straight from the peaks of the Dolomites. Jo woke cold and cramped, but with a warm place in her lap that evoked a very recently departed cat. Surprised, she stretched herself, got up carefully in case of cricked necks or other joints, and closed the window – not without a faintly suspicious glance out onto the campo. Which was deserted: she looked at her watch and found the hour ungodly.

Some time later, washed, brushed and flossed, she headed towards Roberto's with an extra key in her jeans pocket. She had also, for some reason, picked up the antique necklace.

There was still a marked chill in the air, heralding that summer's tenacious rearguard might finally be admitting defeat. The bright sky was already clouded over, grey above the wind. Jo tucked her hands deep in the pockets of her duffel-coat, and walked faster.

In the steamy espresso-scented warmth, La Strega's daughter said to her, 'I hear that house has been sold at last, the one you were asking about,' and put a small cup on the table. Jo drank her coffee thoughtfully, and forgot to leave a tip.

At the front door, Jo paused to check whether she was

observed; seeing no one, she quickly inserted the key and turned it
before she could change her mind. The door swung inward, its
hinges creaking only very faintly, and she stepped inside as soon
as the gap was wide enough. Behind her, it shut quietly, leaving
her in a shadow-hung hall that smelled of mildew and the sea,
musty and salty, damp and sharp. And under that, another,
ranker odour, like something left to rot: a drainy, sewery stench.

Her feet crunched on the floor as she took a tentative step, and
she looked down to see fallen plaster shards. They had flaked off
the walls, leaving them with the look of diseased flesh. Further
down the passage lay decorators' detritus: a pair of scabrous
buckets, a grubby dust sheet piled in a heap, a paint-stained
stepladder. As she started up the wide staircase she heard rain
start to rattle outside. Vague ideas of accessing the cat tower
flitted through her thoughts, but the pull of the open window was
too strong.

Part of her mind noted in passing that the upward leprousness
of the walls ceased halfway up the first flight of stairs, and
presumed that the house had fallen victim, during its disuse, to
the curse of *acqua alta* – no respecter of persons or places, palazzi
included. What she was noticing much more insistently, however,
as she ascended further, was the smell. Now the sweetish stink of
decay had gained the upper hand, making her try to breathe
shallowly. But her heart was pounding with anticipation and her
lungs wanted extra oxygen, not less; so she resorted to pulling a
hanky from her pocket and hiding her nose in that. It had,
unfortunately, very little effect.

Something's dead up here. The conclusion was inescapable.
Jo started to sweat, felt it crawling through her hair. Suddenly
she didn't want to enter the room, but her volition carried her
to the door and put her fingers round the handle; even as she
turned it, pushing the door open, her mind was telling her not
to go in.

But the room was empty. Not even a curtain at the window that
might have explained what she had seen from across the square.
Jo came out, puzzled, and started to check the other rooms,
feeling that strange reluctance to enter any of them. All she found
were crusted paint pots, dirty rags and a glass jar containing a
dried-out paintbrush that smelled faintly of white spirit. Outside,
thunder rumbled and muttered.

On the topmost floor, at the back of the house, a long room ran the whole width of the building: the door to this stood slightly ajar. She pushed it, anticipating nothing again, but it swung in lightly and much further than she had expected. Something fell to the floor with a noise like the end of the world, making her swear explosively and get a full ripe breath of the foul stench, which set her coughing.

When her heart had stopped racing, she ventured cautiously into the room, and the mystery of what had fallen was solved: more decorators' debris in the form of a plank and two stepladders, which the door had caught glancingly and sent tumbling. But she forgot it as she saw what was on the floor in the centre of the room, clearly visible in the light that stole round the sides of the ill-fitting shutters at the windows.

There a figure had been drawn, a circle enclosing some other shape which was too scuffed for her to recognize, and in the centre of that, something flayed. Jo gulped, clasped her handkerchief more firmly over her nose and mouth, and advanced towards it.

The animal was unrecognizable, rags of decaying flesh and gobs of dried blood. It had been spreadeagled, pegged out by its four limbs, and eviscerated. Disgusted, she turned away, only to see a small pale pile of fur that had been flung to one side. She approached it, and almost stooped to look, but realized in time what it was and turned away, gagging.

It was the pelt of a white cat.

'Oh, shit,' she whispered 'God, oh, that's disgusting.' Why would someone do that? It was evidently a ritual of some kind. Divination by entrails? Summoning demons? What sort of demon would be impressed by the sacrifice of a cat? Unless, as Scimone had apparently believed, cats really were more than they seemed.

Don't be so damned stupid, she admonished herself. *The man believed in ley lines. You'll be looking for aliens next.*

Although, in a house built by Scimone, the sacrifice might take on a deeper significance.

A necromancer . . . Giordano's words came back to her. She swallowed, suddenly apprehensive, and the back of her neck prickled; she felt sweat slide down her ribs. The stench of the murdered cat filled her nostrils, coated her tongue, making her want to spit. Moving her head from side to side, she moved towards the door, and as she did so some trick of the shadows made the walls of the room appear to bulge inwards for a second.

Her heart gave another unpleasant startled little lurch, and she paused her hand on its journey to the doorknob.

Whatever you do, don't open the door. The thought popped into her mind with such utter certainty that she stood stock-still, convinced beyond all reason that something inimical was outside. She knew it without needing to see it, just as she knew where everything stood in her own home, how to persuade the sticky back door to open in wet weather, and which stairs creaked.

> *From the hag and hungry goblin*
> *That into rags would rend you . . .*

Jo shook her head to clear it. Quickly, she crossed to one of the windows and peered out around the shutter. Rain teemed down outside, and she turned away in despair, believing herself trapped completely.

Her gaze flicked around the room, skittering away from seeing the cat's remains, but they were centre stage and not to be pushed aside. Perhaps, she thought, she could remove it, even – assuming she could get out of the building – give it a decent burial. The difficulty of doing this in Venice did not enter her mind.

To this end, she inspected the tumbled decorating apparatus by the door and found a paint-scraper and a tray encrusted with solidified emulsion. Armed with this, she advanced upon the pathetic little corpse.

But the moment her foot passed the smudged circle, the floor seemed to fade beneath her, and she fell, gasping with alarm, clutching at nothing – but it was not, she realized a second later, the dizzying headlong fall from a top floor to shatter on a pavement, but, incomprehensibly, more as she imagined free fall to be: buoyed on the air itself, floating on something completely insubstantial. Around her, a wind from nowhere began to blow, forming a spiral around her so that she drifted in the centre of a vortex.

And still she fell.

II
Death in Venice

Por dinheiro bailo o perro.
The dog dances for money.
Portuguese proverb

A multitude of candles sputtered and smoked, so many of them that it might have been the inside of a church. The heat they gave off filled the room, and the ceiling above them was blackened; apart from the candles, the room was bare. It was a long room, stuffy and airless; heavy curtains covered its five tall windows, and the curtains, like the ceiling, were stained with soot. Despite all the candles, shadows lurked in its corners.

Leaning against the wall, Captain Da Silva watched, a frown on his face, as Della Quercia inscribed an elaborate figure on the floor with chalk. Da Silva was an unremarkable man, not tall, his only memorable feature a pair of blue eyes – legacy of an English grandmother – but he had a competent, reliable look. Right now he was a little nervous, a little sceptical, a little annoyed; and more than a little sickened, knowing what his employer intended to do with the white cat which stared out with golden-green eyes between the bars of the cage. And he badly needed a smoke.

Most of all, though, he wished very heartily that he had never got involved in this at all, but that would have been impossible anyway. He shook his head irritably, annoyed at wasting time on pointless speculation: Della Quercia owned him, more or less. Owned the *Isabella,* his ship, anyway, even if she was mortgaged to the gunwales – like everything else the Venetian had left of his forefathers' empire. This house included.

Da Silva had spent most of his life at sea, and had thought that he had seen and endured enough to be pretty much hardened to anything life could throw at him. Until Arturo Della Quercia had commandeered the *Isabella* and flung him into a world far removed from the mundane dangers of Cape Horn and the Roaring Forties; though he would have preferred a hundred-foot sea or a screaming hurricane any day, given the choice. Which, of course, he wasn't.

Like Venice herself, the Della Quercia fortunes and influence had declined over the centuries, and a once-proud shipping empire had dwindled to a single vessel and a decaying palazzo whose ground floor was unusable thanks to the combined effects of *acqua alta* and neglect. Even here, on the top floor, a damp and stagnant odour lingered.

Now Della Quercia, like many a desperate man before him, intended to wager everything upon one last throw: to take a final gamble for all or nothing. Yet the stake the Venetian was playing with was a higher one than Da Silva would ever hazard. He was wagering his soul.

Months before, he had taken passage on the *Isabella* to Macau – not, in itself, a particularly unusual thing for an owner to do. But he had also had a task to demand of her captain.

It had been in this house, Da Silva remembered, that the nightmare had begun. In the room directly below this one. And he hadn't even known it for a nightmare at the time.

'I need your help, Da Silva,' Della Quercia said, twirling his glass in the lamplight so that the wine, quickened by the flame, turned a deep, translucent ruby. 'Have you ever heard of Marco Polo's amulet?'

The Portuguese captain shook his head, and sipped at his own wine, an unexpected and uncharacteristic courtesy from his employer. 'No, Signore. Is it valuable?'

A deep laugh shook the older man. 'Yes, Captain – you might call it valuable. But suffice it to say that it was once in the possession of my family, and now it is not. I am told, however—' he looked at Da Silva as if summing him up '—that it is, at present, in Macau.' He drained his glass, and refilled it at once from the decanter.

'Was this thing stolen from your family, then?' Da Silva asked.

Again, Della Quercia laughed, but there was no mirth in it. 'Inasmuch as the person in whose possession it is now paid no money for it, yes.'

Da Silva sighed, but soundlessly. Della Quercia liked this sort of game, got pleasure out of needling him. But he had learned long ago that you did not show impatience, or for that matter any kind of expression or emotion, in the Venetian's presence. Not if you wanted to keep your freedom as well as your job. And Da Silva had no wish to sample the hospitality of an Italian jail, far less the hempen embrace of a noose. 'Then I assume you wish to acquire it back from this person? In Macau?'

'Yes, Captain, I do. But I shall need you to do the "acquiring". Since the person is a Portuguese person and speaks no civilized language.'

He did not mention at this stage that the Portuguese person was, in fact, a dead Portuguese person, nor that she had been dead for more than a hundred years. Not, Da Silva thought ruefully, that it would have made any difference. When Della Quercia said 'Jump!' all he could say, all he could ever have said, was 'How high?'

The place they came to eventually, after many false meanderings, was deep in the maze of buildings around the docks, hidden in the twists and turns of alleys between the godowns. Unfamiliar stinks assailed their nostrils; and the place, though it seemed – but for the ubiquitous rats – deserted, was noisy in odd ways – bursts of confused shouting, snatches of song, strange brassy instruments being struck, even a roaring that sounded like some kind of engine. Da Silva did not know, and did not really want to know, how his employer had come by the knowledge that had brought them here. His revolver was in his hand, but privately he was more glad of the long knife he wore concealed down his back.

It was also darker than it had any right to be, darker than the inside of a coal-sack, and Della Quercia's lantern made everything around its cold beam even blacker by contrast.

But they had arrived at last, and the captain knocked at the door in a rhythm that had been described to him. Presently a wizened, ancient Chinese woman, her face a mass of wrinkles, opened it a crack and peered out at them suspiciously.

'We came from the White Unicorn,' he said, in Mandarin, as he had been told, and passed her an ivory token.

Unsmiling, the woman nodded, and let them in, tottering on bound feet, although she wore the black pyjamas of a lower-class Chinese. 'Wait here,' she said. The door banged shut behind them, and Da Silva put his revolver back in his pocket.

They could see very little, although Da Silva identified the place as a dispensary. The scent of desiccated herbs was very faint, but Della Quercia's lantern showed him labels on drawers: ginseng, phoenix heart, dragon's claw. Presently the old woman returned and beckoned to them, her own hand like a claw.

So far, so mysterious; but Da Silva had moved easily through this world thus far, since it was a milieu with which he was familiar, and one he knew how to manipulate. At some point as they descended the steep wooden stair, however, he suddenly felt as though he had crossed a barrier: moved sideways, as it were, into some place that was not so familiar. His neck prickled, and he wondered whether his employer had felt the same thing; although he doubted it, Della Quercia being, he thought to himself, an insensitive son of a whore. But what manner of person would inhabit the cellar of a Chinese pharmacist's shop in an alleyway that was almost impossible to find? The answer came back at once: someone with something to hide.

He was entirely unprepared, however, for the sight that met him in the cellar. For though the floor was of hard-trodden dirt, a magnificent table sat in the centre of the room, and on it was a coffin. No, the word was sarcophagus: the great, ornate, glass-sided casket reminded him of nothing so much as the tomb of St Francis Xavier – which held the saint's uncorrupted mortal remains – in the city of Old Goa.

Da Silva was not a particularly religious man, nor even as superstitious as most sailors, but he crossed himself before thought caught up with instinct, and muttered 'Mary, Mother of God,' under his breath without even realizing he had done so.

Beside him, Della Quercia breathed out in triumph. 'María Alvares,' he whispered.

God gave the Portuguese a tiny country as their cradle, but all the world as their grave, thought Da Silva sourly. The words were António Vieira's but the sentiment was pretty accurate.

'So, with whom do I have to haggle for your charm, Signore?' he asked with as much asperity as he ever dared to use with Della Quercia.

'With her,' the other replied, gesturing at the coffin. Da Silva felt his jaw drop. 'With María Alvares, the necromancer, who stole it from my great-grandfather.'

'I—', began Da Silva, rendered momentarily speechless. 'How?'

'Open it,' Della Quercia said. 'Open the casket.'

The captain looked round, but the Chinese woman had vanished; so he found the catches that secured the carved lid in place and snapped them open, then heaved at the lid. It was so heavy that he was half afraid its weight would drag out of his grasp and smash the glass side. But it opened smoothly enough, and rested solidly back on its hinges when he lowered it carefully down.

Instead of the foul miasma he had expected, the breath from the coffin smelled faintly of roses. He let out the lungful of air he hadn't realized he was hanging on to, and looked down at the woman in the casket. A trickle of sweat ran down his face: he wiped it absently with his hand.

'The amulet keeps her uncorrupted,' said Della Quercia quietly; but *uncorrupted* did not mean *unchanged*, for the corpse thus revealed was exactly that: a corpse. María Alvares, whoever she had been, had mummified in her coffin: the flesh had shrunk off her bones, her skin had dried and tanned to leather that had moulded itself to the shape of her skull, the contours of the skeleton. Her hair still lay black as the night before moonrise, glossy and thick, but her eyeballs were desiccated in their sockets and her lips were drawn back from her teeth.

She wore her funeral finery, a dress of black silk, and around her hollow throat was the amulet: a necklace of pale jade and opals with fiery depths that took Da Silva's breath away.

'It's beautiful,' he said softly.

'Take it,' said Della Quercia. The captain hesitated. What was the catch? 'Do it, Da Silva.'

Grimacing, the captain reached behind the mummy's neck to unclasp the jewel, forcing out of his mind the memory of living women around whose necks he had fastened trinkets of far less value. But the contact was too intimate and too similar to forget entirely.

Then the shrivelled eyes rolled round in their sockets, and a wizened hand gripped his wrist before he had time to react, the nails digging into his flesh like talons. The skull snapped upward, leaving the mass of shining hair behind like a pillow, and the dead jaw moved.

'And who, pray tell, are you?' rasped the corpse.

For a long moment the captain was quite incapable of speech. Then, shaking with horror, he managed to croak, 'Luís Da Silva.'

He tried to pull away from her iron grip, but without success; then she sat up and seized the back of his neck with her other hand. The bones, in their glove of skin, clutched him like a vice and drew his face close to hers.

'Of what city, Luís Da Silva?' Her voice put him in mind of stones clashing together.

'Lisbon,' he whispered.

'At last,' replied María Alvares, and he fancied he saw a topaz glint in her shrivelled eyes. Then, knowing it had to be done but dreading it with all his soul, he asked the question Della Quercia had brought him here to put to her.

'What price do you want for this necklace?'

María Alvares seemed to exhale a breath of roses; she seemed to smile. 'A kiss,' she said, and pulled his head down.

Da Silva's mind wanted to go away somewhere, the way the body fights the agony of dreadful wounds by shutting down. But, quite to the contrary, everything was terribly clear: her dried lips, her leathern tongue, her coated teeth, and worst of all, his own desire that rose treacherously despite the fact that he was being kissed by a corpse and that he could feel blood trickling down the back of his neck from the sharp grip of her claws. With his free hand he fumbled for the clasp of the necklace, and managed to unfasten it; the amulet came away and María Alvares fell back into her coffin in sudden decay, the scent of roses turning mephitic in an instant.

He sank to the floor, his legs unable to support him, the opal-and-jade necklace clutched in his hand.

Della Quercia had never seen naked horror so clear on anyone's face before, but the matter was only of academic interest to him: the Portuguese had retrieved the amulet from his long-dead countrywoman, and now it could return to its rightful place – and its rightful use.

Bending to retrieve it, he saw that Da Silva's eyes were still open, though the captain was surely unconscious; he shook him roughly by the shoulder. At length Da Silva drew a shuddering breath, and sat up.

The edges of the jade circles had drawn blood from his hand, but the several little cuts from María Alvares's fingernails hurt more. There were five blue crescents on his wrist and a further selection on his neck where they had dug into him. But that was not, would never be, the worst of it; for physical wounds always heal.

Da Silva had, without realizing it, closed his eyes at the recollection; now he opened them to find that Della Quercia had finished his floorboard calligraphy. He ran his fingers over the faint scars on his wrist, and sighed, shifting his weight. A loose board rocked under his foot.

'Bring the cat here,' his employer instructed him, and Da Silva walked over to the cage and picked it up, his jaw rigid with distaste. Like most sailors, he liked cats: they killed rats, which were such a vile pest on every ship that ever put to sea. But that, Della Quercia had told him, was precisely why a cat had to be sacrificed here; and why he had done away with the little bridge that had connected the house to that curious tower behind it, although Da Silva was still not entirely sure he comprehended the reason for that. He did not know why it had been called the cat tower, nor of the architect Scimone's philosophies.

However, he understood that it was some kind of rat demon that Della Quercia needed the cat's death to summon, because that, apparently, was the purpose of the amulet. The necklace was its lodestone and blood its magnet; and, according to Della Quercia, demons could be compelled to reveal the whereabouts of hidden treasure.

Nineteen years before, Da Silva had killed a man whom he had caught in the act of rape – killed him with his long knife; yet the thought of cold-bloodedly slaughtering a cat made him squeamish. He did not regret his earlier action, since he was still married to the woman he had helped that day; indeed he knew he would do the same thing again. Unfortunately, though, the man he had killed had been named Aldo Della Quercia, and his elder brother had witnessed the entire incident. His revenge had been nothing so subtle as the Bible recommended: Da Silva's sentence had been life, not death.

So he did not watch what the Venetian did to the cat. The poor beast's yowls were bad enough, and the iron stench of its blood.

At last the animal's sounds of pain ceased, and Da Silva looked up, alerted by some sixth sense. His eyes narrowed, and he stared suspiciously past the blazing banks of candles. Della Quercia was still muttering in some kind of bastard Latin, but the quality of the

darkness in the room's corners seemed to have changed. The
shadows were thick and clotted, like congealing blood; the candle
flames themselves looked blurred, as if they had slowed. A
peculiar deadness crept into the air, a heaviness that was the
opposite of languor, for it bred a reflex of fear, a desire to flee. Da
Silva wiped sweat from his face, and found his hand was shaking
slightly. His mouth felt dry.

Della Quercia finished his incantation, and held his hands up.
His arms were streaked to the elbows with scarlet. For a bare
instant, everything seemed to hold its breath, and then Da Silva
smelled, rich and corrupt, the feral stink of rats.

In the centre of the figure Della Quercia had drawn, where the
bloody rags of flesh that were all that was left of the cat lay
crucified, a form began to take shape. It coalesced, as far as Da
Silva could see, out of the very air itself; and yet, as it grew, it
seemed more substantial, more solidly real, than the increasingly
shadowy image of the Venetian.

Da Silva had been leaning against the wall; now he tried to
burrow into it. What he saw was not, as he had expected, a
monstrous rat: it was worse than that. Though it had character-
istics of rathood – something in its stance, a hint of fang, of
disease in its yellow eye – it was manlike in form, down to its
dangling genitals. The captain shuddered, and growled like a dog,
yet he found himself unable to look away.

The creature dipped its horrid head to the butchered cat, and
Da Silva heard an appalling sucking noise. He unsheathed his
long knife, but gave serious thought to taking out his revolver too.
Not for the rat-demon: he knew it would have no effect. For
himself. It looked up then, and eyed him knowingly, drawing its
lips back from long yellow teeth. There was far too much
intelligence in that gaze, too much cunning.

From a long distance, he heard Della Quercia's voice, imperative in command although he could make out no words – he
knew that tone well enough – and knew with terrible certainty
that it would not work, that his employer could not compel this
thing.

And then he realized what was wrong. For all that Della
Quercia was the one with arcane knowledge, despite his having
told Da Silva what the amulet's purpose was, he had not put it
within his diagrams of protection.

He was wearing it around his own throat.

Though the traitorous thought went through Da Silva's mind that letting this rat-thing kill Della Quercia would solve all his problems, he let it slide by without considering it. As, within the barrier that he knew was useless, the creature flexed its corded muscles and prepared to pounce, Da Silva crossed the room in two strides and knocked the Venetian to the floor, reaching once again for the clasp of the amulet.

But he was too late, for the rat-demon was faster than any man could be. It flung him aside, a clawed hand slashing casually across his face, and he crashed into the wall six feet behind with an impact that turned the world black for a second.

When he came round, an instant later, his left eye was too full of blood to see out of, and the pain took his breath away; but with his other eye he saw the summoned thing, grown huge now, bend and suck at Della Quercia as moments ago it had fed off the cat's corpse. Which had, he noticed, vanished completely; though he did not think the rat-demon had, precisely, eaten it.

It drank and guzzled for only a short time before looking up and meeting Da Silva's gaze again with that dreadful knowing expression. Then it licked its bloody lips with a pointed tongue that reminded him too much of María Alvares's and slid, in a way he could neither comprehend nor describe, into the body of Arturo Della Quercia.

Da Silva cursed weakly, tasting his own blood in his mouth. The offhanded way the rat-thing had thrown him against the wall made him doubt his capacity to fight it. But appalled, he knew he had to try.

He retrieved his knife and staggered to his feet, gasping at the pain in his face and his left eye. Perhaps the creature was still disoriented; perhaps it could not immediately coordinate the body it had seized.

And perhaps, again, Da Silva thought wearily as Della Quercia lurched to his feet, this was just a novel way of committing suicide.

'Threaten me, little man?' It was Della Quercia's voice, but somehow distorted: the timbre hollower, louder, like a shout but with blurred edges.

'Oh yes,' Da Silva said, and lunged with his knife, opening

Della Quercia's arm from elbow to shoulder. Blood followed the
slash, but sluggishly. Da Silva would bleed to death quicker from
his head wound. He ducked under a flailing blow and hit out
again, catching Della Quercia glancingly in the neck – on the
amulet itself, he realized at the sudden spark, and tried to follow it
up, to hook the point under the chain. But the other grabbed the
blade of the knife and twisted the stroke aside with terrible
strength.

Wincing at the very thought of grasping the knife – he knew
how sharp it was – Da Silva fought just to keep hold of it.
Sweat ran into his good eye, and he knuckled it away. He was
close enough to the possessed man to attempt a knee in the
crotch, but Della Quercia caught the blow on his thigh and
backhanded Da Silva across the face again. His fingers had to
be nearly severed by now, but he seemed to feel no pain –
unlike Da Silva, who was almost blinded by the anguish of the
last blow.

They were so close now that he could smell rat-stink on Della
Quercia's breath, and see the yellow that had crept into his eyes.
He had only one chance now, and so he let go of the knife's
handle and used both hands to reach round the back of the
Venetian's neck and unfasten the amulet once more.

It slipped from his sweaty fingers, and both he and Della
Quercia went for it. But the moment it lost contact with the
possessed man's flesh, the Venetian collapsed to the ground like a
puppet whose strings had been cut. Da Silva kicked the necklace
across the room, out of reach, then doubled over, breathing
heavily, his hand over his face, trying to relieve the pain flaring
through his head.

Looking down, he saw brown suddenly bleed into the prone
man's eyes again, and Della Quercia looked out of them for a
final time, his mouth opening and closing, but no sound coming
out.

Kneeling, Da Silva picked up his knife, drew back the man's
head by its hair, and cut his employer's throat. The blade slid
through the Venetian's flesh as though it was cutting butter, but
the blood trickled out so slowly that it reinforced the captain's
thought that Della Quercia had been dead for at least a quarter of
an hour. Neither was Da Silva surprised when the corpse
crumbled into dust much as had that of María Alvares; although

he was relieved that no body was left to be discovered on the top floor of the palazzo.

He still had to dispose of the amulet, though, tired to the bone and in pain as he was; and covered in his own blood as he was, he had no intention of touching the item. Getting to his feet made him dizzy and he staggered, a floorboard creaking as he trod on it. By the door, he recalled, there was a loose board: he had felt it move earlier. It came up easily with the point of his knife.

Some months later, the one-eyed captain, Luís Da Silva, left Venice for good, taking his wife and children to Lisbon aboard his ship, the *Isabella*.

In the walls of the Casa Della Scala, the rat-demon waited.

III

Jo was in a place of Escher architecture, a place of more than four dimensions. Whether that was the reality, or she was seeing by metaphor, she had no idea.

But real or imagined, her feet were on the ground again, such as it was, and it made her feel better. Her mind did not understand how she had got here, wherever 'here' was, so she put that on the back burner and set about looking for a way out.

Instead of the stairs and interiors that she associated with Escher, this was a place of bridges, interconnecting roads and paths, and cats scampering across them, pursuing rats hither and thither, up and down, upside down. White cats, black cats, piebald cats, grey cats; ginger, calico, tabby; tiger-striped and leopard-spotted.

It didn't take a genius to figure that one out, Jo thought, laughing.

So it was a dream, she concluded; and as if to reassure her that that *was* all it was, the scene changed. A pulse boomed in her head, centred on her brow, drilled through like a migraine, and a red mist suffused her vision. She blinked, and flinched back as a huge rat's face swelled at her and receded. It was hideous, but she was only dreaming—

—And she was back in the room at the palazzo and it was *still there*.

Jo backed away until she hit the wall, then realized that the giant rat was confined by the figure in the centre of the floor, which now looked fresher and sharper, newly drawn. Not only that, but the beast was fairly insubstantial: she seemed to be able to see through its edges, as though it were an image projected into the room.

But it was still pretty frightful, and an almost palpable stink of menace radiated from it like heat from a stove. It was because it was so *big*, she realized: almost any small thing blown up huge offends one's sense of what is right; as if it no longer fitted into the small rat-shaped hole in her map of the world, and that made her hackles rise.

Belatedly, she noticed that the flayed cat was no longer pegged out in the centre of the chalked diagram. Had it ever been really there? Or was she still dreaming? She still felt a presence with her, but could not determine whether it was *in* the house or *of* the house.

'Della Quercia,' she said, and her voice cast strange echoes in the empty room, off the pallid faded walls, the stained ceiling. 'Della Quercia, what do you want?'

Her mind answered: he wants *you*. And that seemed to clarify everything. It cut through her panic and left her head clear, as if she had woken healed after a long illness.

Keeping her eyes on the monstrous rat, she sidled to the tall central window and fumbled at its latches, finding bolts top and bottom in addition to the central fastening. A sense of urgency pressed her, but she pressed it back firmly. The window open, she sought for catches on the shutter, and found those too after a moment. It banged back in the wind, and chilly rain blew in; the cold light illuminated the gigantic thing crouched scratching in the middle of the room, trying to dig through the barrier of air that surrounded it. It hissed at her as she looked in its direction and caught its malevolent yellow eye: the thought of its getting free, and the sight of it, insubstantial as it was, impelled her to make haste.

Skirting the circle, she crossed the room again. As she passed the imprisoned rat, it started to fling itself against invisible walls in a frenzy, clawing at the barrier it could not pass through, biting at it. The sight of its great curved fangs was the stuff of nightmare.

Trying to ignore it, and the horror it engendered, Jo examined the plank her entry had dislodged. It was about eight feet in length: she hoped it would be long enough. It was also heavy, and awkward to carry. In the end, she simply dragged it to the window and pushed the end out, balancing it with her own weight, towards the cat tower.

Slowly, infinitely slowly, and taking infinite care, she inched the plank across the gap. It was so heavy that she had to struggle to keep control of it; the rain lashed at her, sweat ran down her sides, her arms shook with the effort, but inch by inch it moved across the gap. The opening she was aiming for was somewhat lower than the window, a fact for which she was extremely grateful, even though it made her worry that her bridge might slip when she tried to cross it.

As the end neared the cat tower, the plank grew more and more difficult to control. But at last it thumped onto the sill of the opening she'd been aiming for, and she breathed a great sigh of relief. At the same time, she felt rather than heard a sound like a chord of music, so loud it could have been the plucking of the constellation of the Lyre, and the back of her neck prickled. It gathered momentum, swelled; became, suddenly, perfection: too much to bear, because she was only human. Tears sprang into her eyes at the sheer beauty of it.

And in that melodious instant, the bridge grew whole again, despite its being only a plank of wood. Stones grew around it, coalesced out of the air that was nothing, and nowhere, and endless, into the semblance of a real bridge; and as she watched, the white cat jumped up onto the far end and sauntered across, flirting its tail.

Following their white pathfinder came a feline army, more than in her dream, dozens of cats, a myriad of them, moving purposefully and in silence across a road closed to them for more than a hundred years, coming to confront their old enemy.

Jo stood to one side to let the white cat spring lightly down to the floor, and as it did she felt a burning sensation in her back pocket, as if something in there had suddenly gone red-hot. She yelped and hauled it out: it was the antique necklace she'd forgotten picking up, and it burned her hand as she flung it away.

In mid-air it exploded, a flash of actinic light splashed with sparks like phosphorus and a number of lesser cracks that shot tiny burning shards of shrapnel across the room. At the same time the cats launched themselves like furry missiles at the giant rat, straight through the barrier that confined it. It cowered back, squealing, as the cats tore it to pieces, Jo fled from their fury.

She stepped up onto her bridge, and though she knew that it was just a narrow plank and there was far too much air below her, she also knew that harmony was restored and the Casa della Scala was complete again, after too long in limbo.

Rain lashed through the open sides of the bridge as she crossed it, but she took no notice. At the other end she stepped through into the cat tower with a gasp of relief, then sank to the floor, her legs gone suddenly wobbly. She sat and hugged her knees, closing her eyes thankfully for an instant.

An insistent miaow brought her back to the present, and she looked up to see a pair of bright yellow-green eyes in a white-furred face. Jo stroked the cat, but it wanted to be away, so she got to her feet and followed it down the stair.

From below, it still looked like a plank, but if she half-closed her eyes and tried not to look directly at it, she could see a kind of ghost of what the bridge should be.

'Yes, I've got it,' said Giordano. 'How remarkable. I wonder if my cousin Pasquale can see it.'

'Now it's your turn,' Jo told him.

'I think you credit me with too much knowledge, if that's not an oxymoron. I don't know the contents of all the books in the library.'

'Maybe not,' she acknowledged as they walked along the calle that led to Roberto's. 'But I expect you have some family history you can delve into.'

'Well, I don't know a huge amount about my wicked ancestor, except that he was said to dabble in black magic. Summoning demons, or trying to.'

Jo stopped, as she always did, to look in the mask shop. 'He managed to summon one, anyway,' she said, watching her own reflection, a palimpsest on the display. 'With that necklace, I think.'

The other nodded. 'Yes, an artefact like that could well be used for summoning a demon.'

'He wanted me to put it on,' Jo said thoughtfully, starting to walk again.

'It's a good thing you didn't.'

'Yes. That rat-thing could have . . . possessed me?' The modern part of her mind expressed incredulity at the concept.

'Oh, I think so,' said Giordano. 'Don't you?'

She did not reply, and they walked in silence until they reached the bar. At the door she turned and asked him, 'How did your "wicked ancestor" die?'

'Arturo Della Quercia? Nobody knows. He disappeared. No one ever found his body.' Giordano followed her in, saying, 'Ciao, Signora Renata' in passing to the mustachioed proprietress.

When they had found seats, at a minute table by the window, Jo took the key out of her pocket. 'I should give you this while I think of it.'

Giordano eyed it with suspicion. 'If I were you, I'd throw it in the canal.'

'Okay,' she said.

Their espressos arrived, and Giordano spent some time sugaring his and stirring it. After a while he looked up and said, 'Do you mind telling me where your family comes from?'

Taken aback by the sudden change of subject, she replied, 'Well, Portugal, as you might guess from the name. Lisbon. But there was some kind of family feud and the parents came to England before I was born. Why?'

'Because you have blue eyes.'

'What?'

Her companion looked embarrassed. 'It's just that the captain of one of Arturo Della Quercia's ships was called Da Silva.'

'It's a pretty common name,' said Jo, picking up her cup.

'Maybe,' Giordano agreed. 'But they called this chap *"occhio azzurro"*.' He shrugged, and picked up his own coffee. 'Perhaps it's a coincidence.'

'But you think there's a connection. Why? Why would Arturo Della Quercia want that—' she lowered her voice '—demon to do me harm, if I'm a descendant of someone he employed?'

Putting his cup down, Giordano eyed her levelly. ' "Harm" is rather too mild a term, you know. When you think that "possession" is another word for "owning". Owning you, in life and

death, body and soul. For ever. Whatever he had against the Da
Silva family, you were lucky to get out.'

'Well,' said Jo, looking out of the window at a white cat that
had wandered into view, 'you could say I had help.'

STEPHEN JONES & KIM NEWMAN

Necrology: 2001

ARTHUR C. CLARKE'S ICONIC DATE saw the passing of many writers, artists, performers and technicians who, during their lifetimes, made significant contributions to the horror, science fiction and fantasy genres (or left their mark on popular culture in other, often fascinating, ways) . . .

AUTHORS/ARTISTS

Children's author **Catherine Storr**, whose classic 1958 novel *Marianne Dreams* was filmed in 1988 as *Paperhouse*, died on January 6th, aged 87. A former editor at Penguin Books, eleven of her supernatural stories were collected in *Cold Marble and Other Ghost Stories*, while her collection of stories for young children, *Clever Polly and the Stupid Wolf*, was published in 1955 and remains on the curriculum of many British primary schools.

Wartime cryptographer and screenwriter **Leo Marks** died on January 15th, aged 80. He scripted Michael Powell's cult classic *Peeping Tom* and *Twisted Nerve*.

Gordon B. Love, who produced the fanzine *Rocket's Blast/ Comicollector* in the 1960s, died on January 17th following an automobile accident. He was 62.

Comics artist **Frederic E. Ray, Jr.**, who illustrated *Superman* and *Tomahawk* for DC Comics during the 1940s and 1950s, died on January 23rd.

Fantasy and military SF writer **Rick Shelley** died of complications from a massive heart attack on January 27th, aged 54. His books include the 'Varayan Memoir' trilogy, the 'Lucky 13th' series, plus *The Wizard at Meq* and *The Wizard at Home*.

Canadian-born fantasy and SF writer **Gordon R.** (Rupert) **Dickson** died of complications from asthma on January 31st, aged 77. Best known for the 'Childe Cycle', 'Dorsai' sequence and 'Hoka' stories (written with Poul Anderson), the Hugo and Nebula Award-winning author published his first story in 1951 and wrote more than eighty books and around 200 short stories. His 1976 novel *The Dragon and the George* won the British Fantasy Society's August Derleth Award.

British horror author **Gerald Suster** died of an apparent heart attack on February 4th, aged 49. A former teacher before becoming a full-time writer in the late 1970s, his many occult thrillers include such titles as *The Devil's Maze*, *The God Game* and *The Labyrinth of Satan*, which formed a loosely linked trilogy. His other novels include *The Elect*, *The Scar*, *The Offering*, *The Block*, *The Force* and *The Handyman*. A devotee of Arthur Machen, whose writing was a major influence on his own work, Suster also wrote a number of non-fiction volumes based on his personal interest in the occult, including *Hitler and the Age of Horus*, *The Truth About the Tarot*, *The Hellfire Friars* and a biography of Aleister Crowley. He also contributed a regular column to the esoteric magazine *The Talking Stick*.

Slovakian-born **John L. Nanovic**, who worked as an editor under the name 'Henry Lysing' for Street & Smith on such pulp magazines as *Doc Savage* and *The Shadow*, died on February 9th, aged 94.

Peggy (Margaret) **Cave**, the wife of pulp author Hugh B. Cave, died of cancer complications on February 12th after two weeks in hospital. She was 86.

Popular horror author **Richard** [Carl] **Laymon** died of a massive heart attack on February 14th, aged 54. The current President of the Horror Writers Association, his many novels include the 'Beast House' series (*The Cellar*, *The Beast House* and *The Midnight Tour*), along with *The Woods Are Dark*, *Out Are the Lights*, *Beware!*, *All-Hallows Eve*, *Resurrection Dreams*, *The Stake*, *Quake*, *Bite*, *Cuts*, *Once Upon a Halloween*, *The Travelling Vampire Show* and *Night in the Lonesome October*. As well as writing two novels under the pseudonyms 'Carl Laymon' and 'Richard Kelly', his short fiction was collected in *A Good Secret Place* and *Dreadful Tales*, while the autobiographical study *A Writer's Life* appeared from Deadline Press. He was set to be guest of honour at the 2001 World Horror Convention in May.

Italian composer **Pierro Umiliani** died the same day, aged 75. He composed the scores for more than 100 films, including *The Amazing Doctor G.*, *Five Dolls for an August Moon*, *Witchcraft '70*, *Night of the Devils* and *Baba Yaga*.

Eccentric Irish Ufologist and author **Desmond** [Arthur Peter] **Leslie** died in France on February 22nd, aged 79. He collaborated with George Adamski on the controversial 1953 bestseller *Flying Saucers Have Landed*.

Film and TV composer **Richard Stone** died after a long battle with pancreatic cancer on March 9th, aged 47. Besides writing the music for such movies as *Sundown The Vampire in Retreat* and *Pumpkinhead*, he also won seven Emmys for his work on *Animaniacs* and such other cartoon TV series as *Freakazoid*, *Histeria!*, *Pinky and the Brain* and *Tazmania*.

25-year-old **Jenna A.** (Anne) **Felice**, an editor at Tor Books, died on March 10th of complications from a severe allergic reaction and asthmatic attack after spending nearly a week in a coma. She also worked with her life partner Rob Killheffer on the small-press magazine *Century*.

73-year-old bestselling thriller writer **Robert Ludlum** died of a massive heart attack at his Florida home on March 12th, after recently undergoing heart surgery. A former television and stage actor and theatre director, his first book *The Scarlatti Inheritance* was written in 1971 'as a lark', since when he sold more than 220 million copies in forty countries. His many titles include *The Holcroft Covenant* (made into a film starring Michael Caine), *The Bourne Identity* (made into a TV mini-series with Richard Chamberlain and a theatrical film with Matt Damon), *The Matarese Circle*, *The Scorpio Illusion*, *The Apocalypse Watch* and *The Prometheus Deception*, which appeared on the bestseller lists of the *New York Times*, *Los Angeles Times* and *Publishers Weekly*.

Veteran pulp author **J.** (John) **Harvey Haggard** died on March 15th, aged 87. A distant relative of H. Rider Haggard, from 1930 until 1960 his stories appeared in such titles as *Amazing*

Stories, Planet Stories, Thrilling Wonder Stories, Future Fiction, Fantastic Universe and Ray Bradbury's 1939 fanzine *Futuria Fantasia*. He had two stories reprinted in the 1997 volume *Ackermanthology*.

Dr Donald A. (Anthony) **Reed**, founder and president of The Academy of Science Fiction, Fantasy and Horror Films, died of heart failure and complications from diabetes on March 18th in Los Angeles, aged 65. Reed, who founded the Academy in 1972, was instrumental in the promotion of the Saturn Awards and also founded and served as president of the Count Dracula Society since 1962.

'Papa' **John** [Edmund] **Phillips**, who founded the 1960s California pop group the Mammas and the Papas, died of heart failure the same day, aged 65. After years of drug and alcohol abuse, he had had a liver transplant several years earlier. Phillips wrote such classic 'flower power' songs as "Monday Monday", 'California Dreamin', 'Creeque Alley' and 'San Francisco (Be Sure to Wear Some Flowers in Your Hair)'. He also scored the movies *Brewster McCloud, Myra Breckinridge* and *The Man Who Fell to Earth*.

British supernatural fiction writer **R.** (Ronald) [Henry Glynn] **Chetwynd-Hayes**, described by one of his publishers as 'Britain's Prince of Chill', died of bronchial pneumonia in a London nursing home on March 20th, aged 81. His first book was *The Man from the Bomb*, a science fiction novel published in 1959 by Badger Books, since when he published a further twelve novels, twenty-three collections, and edited such anthologies as *Cornish Tales of Terror, Scottish Tales of Terror* (as 'Angus Campbell'), *Welsh Tales of Terror, Tales of Terror from Outer Space, Gaslight Tales of Terror, Doomed to the Night*, twelve volumes of *The Fontana Book of Great Ghost Stories* and six volumes of *The Armada Monster Book* for children. In 1976 he ghost-edited and wrote almost all of the one-shot magazine *Ghoul*, and his own short stories were adapted for the screen in the anthology movies *From Beyond the Grave* and *The Monster Club* (the author was portrayed in the latter by John Carradine). In 1989 R. Chetwynd-Hayes was presented with Life Achievement Awards by both The Horror Writers of America and The British Fantasy Society for his services to the genre.

Daniel Counihan, British journalist, radio reporter and author of the children's fantasy *Unicorn Magic* (1953), died on March 25th, aged 83.

82-year-old Italian comic-strip artist **Luciana Giussani** died in Milan after a long illness on March 31st. With her sister Angela (who died in 1987) she created the popular crime comic *Diabolik* in 1962 (filmed by Mario Bava in 1967 as *Danger: Diabolik*) and together they founded the Astorina publishing house.

Novelist and TV scriptwriter **Gene Thompson**, a teenage protégé of Groucho Marx, died of cancer on April 14th, aged 76. He wrote the occult novel *Lupe* and scripts for such shows as *Gilligan's Island*, *My Favorite Martian*, *Love American Style* and *Columbo*.

Judy (Judith) **Watson**, the 61-year-old wife of science fiction/fantasy writer Ian Watson, died on April 14th of heart failure brought on by emphysema, from which she suffered progressively for the past few years. Her artwork appeared in *New Worlds* and *Oz*, and she bequeathed her body to the Department of Human Anatomy of the University of Oxford.

New York singer/songwriter and drummer **Joey Ramone** (Jeffrey Hyman) died after a long battle with lymphatic cancer on April 15th, aged 49. He formed his punk band The Ramones in March 1974. Following a fist fight in 1983, Ramone underwent emergency brain surgery. The band released twenty-one albums until they disbanded in 1996 and they appeared in the cult 1979 movie *Rock 'n' Roll High School* and recorded the theme for *Pet Sematary*.

Film and TV scriptwriter **George F. Slavin**, whose credits include *Mystery Submarine*, *The Rocket Man* and the *Star Trek* episode 'The Mark of Gideon', died on April 19th, aged 85.

Noted anthropologist and former SF writer **Dr Morton Klass** died on April 28th of a heart attack, aged 73. The brother of Philip Klass (aka author William Tenn), his short fiction appeared in the 1950s and 1960s in *Astounding*, *The Magazine of Fantasy & Science Fiction* and *Worlds of If*.

39-year-old Chicago model, singer, artist and writer **Lynne Gauger** (Lynne Sinclaire), best known as a companion to late horror authors Karl Edward Wagner and R. Chetwynd-Hayes, died on May 2nd after a long illness. She had been taking a variety of painkillers and other medication ever since being injured in a

STEPHEN JONES & KIM NEWMAN

car crash several years earlier, and had apparently lost the will to live. Her collaborative story with Rex Miller, 'Vampires of London', appeared in the anthology *The Hot Blood Series: Kiss and Kill*.

British songwriter **Michael Hazlewood**, whose best-known hits were probably '(All I Need is) The Air That I Breathe' and 'It Never Rains in Southern California', died of a heart attack on May 6th while on vacation in Florence, Italy. He was 59, and his other hits included the Pipkins' irritating 'Gimme Dat Ding' and the equally awful 'Little Arrows' by Leapy Lee.

American songwriter **James E. Myers** died on May 9th from leukaemia, age 81. With more than 300 songs to his credit, Myers co-wrote 'Rock Around the Clock' in 1953 (as 'Jimmy De-Knight') and changed the world. The two-minute, eight-second song was recorded by Bill Haley & His Comets the following year and quickly went to No.1 in the charts. It has since been recorded by more than 500 other artists, and used in more than forty movies, earning Myers a reported $10 million in royalties.

49-year-old British author **Douglas** [Noël] **Adams** died of a massive heart attack on May 11th while exercising in Santa Barbara, California. His writing career began with the BBC, working as a script editor and writer for *Doctor Who* from 1978 to 1980. At the same time, he wrote a humorous SF radio series entitled *The Hitch-hiker's Guide to the Galaxy*. The original six episodes were so popular that they led to a novelization that would eventually sell more than fourteen million copies worldwide, a television series and a stage show. Various sequels followed, including *The Restaurant at the End of the Universe*, *Life the Universe and Everything*, *So Long and Thanks for All the Fish* and *Mostly Harmless*, along with *Dirk Gently's Holistic Detective Agency* and its sequel *The Long Dark Tea-Time of the Soul*; the comedy dictionary *The Meaning of Liff* (with John Lloyd); a non-fiction book on conservation, *Last Chance to See*; and the computer game *Starship Titanic*. Eleven chapters from his unfinished 1996 novel, *The Salmon of Doubt*, were included in a collection of the same title published exactly a year after the author's death.

Controversial and hedonistic author and television scriptwriter **Simon** [Arthur Noël] **Raven** died of a stroke on May 12th, aged 73. His 1961 vampire novel *Doctors Wear Scarlet* was filmed as

Incense for the Damned (aka *Bloodsuckers*), while his other books with genre elements include *The Sabre Squadron*, *The Roses of Picardie* and its sequel *September Castle*, *The Islands of Sorrow* and the collection *Remember Your Grammar and Other Haunted Stories*. He edited the 1960 collection *The Best of Gerald Kersh*, and his script work includes such projects as the James Bond film *On Her Majesty's Secret Service*, *Unman Wittering and Zigo* and TV's *Sexton Blake and The Demon God*. Suffering with Krohn's disease since the early 1990s, he had lived as a pensioner in Sutton's Hospital, Charterhouse, an alms house for impoverished gentlemen in London.

Hank (Henry King) **Ketcham**, who created the comic strip character *Dennis the Menace* in 1951, died of heart disease and cancer on June 1st, aged 81. Although the strip appears in 1,000 newspapers around the world, he stopped drawing the character himself in 1994. Ketcham got his first job as an animator for Woody Woodpecker creator Walter Lantz, and he went on to work on such Disney classics as *Pinocchio*, *Bambi* and *Fantasia*. The artist suffered from post-traumatic stress disorder after active service in the armed forces and was estranged from his son, Dennis.

British fan writer and publisher **Alan Dodd** died on June 5th. During the 1950s and 1960s he contributed to a number of fanzines and produced his own title, *Camber*.

Legendary blues guitarist and singer **John Lee Hooker** died in San Francisco on June 21st, aged 83.

81-year-old E.C. comics artist **George Evans** died on June 22nd of terminal leukaemia following a heart attack. He began his career working for the aviation pulps, such as *Dare-Devil Aces*, before moving into comics after World War II. Starting out as a staff artist with Fiction House, he also worked at Fawcett (where he illustrated adaptations of *When Worlds Collide* and *Captain Video*), E.C., Classics Illustrated, Dell, Gold Key (*The Twilight Zone*), DC Comics and Marvel. Evans also produced the daily newspaper strips *Terry and the Pirates* and *Secret Agent Corrigan*. For Karl Edward Wagner's Carcosa imprint he illustrated *Far Lands Other Days* by E. Hoffman Price (1975) and *Lonely Vigils* by Manly Wade Wellman (1981).

Finnish author and illustrator **Tove** [Marika] **Jansson**, best known for her *Moomin* children's fantasies, died on June 27th, aged 86.

Emmy Award-winning scriptwriter **Harold 'Hal' Goldman** died of lung cancer in Los Angeles on the same day, aged 81. A member of Jack Benny's writing staff for more than two decades, he collaborated with George Burns from 1978 until the comedian's death in 1996. During that time he co-scripted the movie *Oh, God! Book II* starring Burns.

Guitarist and record producer **Chet** (Chester) [Burton] **Atkins** died of cancer on June 30th, aged 77. From the mid-1950s until the 1990s he released more than 100 albums and won fourteen Grammy Awards. As a session guitarist he played on Elvis Presley's 'Heartbreak Hotel', Hank Williams's 'Jambalaya' and the Everly Brothers' 'Wake Up Little Susie' and 'Bye Bye Love'.

Film and TV scriptwriter **Arnold Peyser** died of cancer on July 1st, aged 80. His credits include Elvis's *The Trouble With Girls* and such series as *Mission: Impossible*, *My Favorite Martian* and *Gilligan's Island*.

Canadian novelist and screenwriter **Mordecai Richler**, whose books include the children's fantasies *Jacob Two-Two Meets the Hooded Fang* and *Jacob Two-Two and the Dinosaur*, died of cancer on July 3rd, aged 70. He is best known for *The Apprenticeship of Duddy Kravitz* (filmed in 1974).

British composer/arranger **Delia Derbyshire**, best remembered for arranging composer Ron Grainer's electronic theme for *Doctor Who*, died of kidney failure the same day, aged 64. She also worked on *The Legend of Hell House*.

Indian-born British composer **James Bernard** died in London on July 12th, aged 75. Educated at Wellington College, where his fellow pupils included Christopher Lee, Bernard was encouraged by the great British composer Benjamin Britten, whom he first met when he was seventeen. After serving in the RAF for three years, and a short stint with BBC Radio, he wrote his first score for Hammer Films, *The Quatermass Experiment*, in 1955 for £100. His subsequent output of scores for the studio comprised *Quatermass 2*, *The Curse of Frankenstein*, *X The Unknown*, *Dracula* (one of the greatest and most influential horror film scores ever recorded), *The Hound of the Baskervilles*, *The Stranglers of Bombay*, *The Terror of the Tongs*, *The Kiss of the Vampire*, *The Gorgon*, *Dracula Prince of Darkness*, *The Plague of the Zombies*, *She*, *Frankenstein Created Woman*, *Dracula Has Risen from the Grave*, *The Devil Rides Out*, *Frankenstein Must*

Be Destroyed, Taste the Blood of Dracula, Scars of Dracula, The Legend of the 7 Golden Vampires and *Frankenstein and the Monster from Hell*. He also composed the score for *Torture Garden*, an anthology film from Hammer's rival Amicus, and in 1997 he wrote the score for Channel 4/Photoplay Production's restoration of F.W. Murnau's 1922 *Nosferatu*. His final work appeared the following year in Kevin Brownlow's documentary *Universal Horror* for Turner Classic Movies. As co-writer of the original story for the 1950 atomic thriller *Seven Days to Noon*, he was one of the few composers to win an Academy Award for something other than music.

American book-cover illustrator **Fred Marcellino** died of colon cancer the same day, aged 61. For over a decade he produced more than forty covers a year, including Charles L. Grant's *The Ravens of the Moon*, Clive Barker's *The Inhuman Condition* and *In the Flesh*, Ray Bradbury's *Death is a Lonely Business* and Peter Ackroyd's *First Light*. He later illustrated classic children's books.

British film poster illustrator **Tom** (Thomas) **'Chan'** [William] **Chantrell** died on July 15th, aged 84. From *The Amazing Dr Clitterhouse* in 1938 to *Star Wars* in the late 1970s, he produced around 7,000 poster designs, averaging three posters a week. Hammer Films' James Carreras would often commission his posters before the films were made, and Chantrell painted himself as the Count on *Dracula Has Risen from the Grave*, while his second wife Shirley appears as a radio operator on *The Bermuda Triangle* and as a cannibal victim on *Eaten Alive!*

43-year-old author **James H. Hatfield**, whose book *Fortunate Son: George W. Bush and the Making of an American President* was recalled and pulped by St. Martin's Press in 1999 after it was discovered that he had lied about his credentials, was found dead of a drug overdose on July 18th. His earlier books include a number of unauthorized trivia challenges, biographies and encyclopedias (many co-written with George Burt) based around such movies and TV shows as *Star Wars*, *Deep Space Nine*, *Lost in Space*, *The X Files* and *Star Trek The Next Generation*. Hatfield had been found guilty in 1988 of plotting to kill his bosses at a Dallas real-estate firm in a failed car bombing and in 1992 of forging a signature to cash $22,000 in Federal cheques.

Norman Hall Wright, the last surviving writer of Walt Disney's *Fantasia* ('The Nutcracker Suite' sequence), died on July 21st, aged 91. He also worked on various cartoon shorts and was a sequence director on *Bambi*.

Lynrd Sknyrd bassist **Leon Wilkeson** died on July 27th, aged 49. The cause of death was under investigation.

Children's author **Elizabeth Yates** died on July 29th, aged 95. In 1949 she ghost-edited the anthology *Spooks and Spirits and Shadowy Shapes* and included one of her own stories.

Science fiction and fantasy author **Poul [William] Anderson** died of prostate cancer around midnight on July 31st, aged 74. He had returned home that day after a month in hospital to await the end with his close family. After making his debut in *Astounding* in 1947, he wrote more than 100 books, including *Vault of the Ages* (1952), *Three Hearts and Three Lions*, *The High Crusade*, *A Midsummer Tempest*, *A Knight of Ghosts and Shadows*, *Tau Zero* and two collaborations with Gordon R. Dickson (who died in January), *Star Prince Charlie* and *Hokas Hokas Hokas*. A winner of three Nebula and seven Hugo awards, his penultimate novel, *Genesis*, won the 2000 John W. Campbell Memorial Award.

Robert H. (Henry) **Rimmer**, author of the 1966 free-love novel *The Harrad Experiment* (filmed in 1973) and several volumes of *The X-Rated Videotape Guide*, died on August 1st, aged 84. His other books include *The Zolotov Affair*, *Love Me Tomorrow* and *The Resurrection of Ann Hutchinson*.

68-year-old **Ron Townsend**, co-founder and one of the lead singers of 1960s group 5th Dimension, died of renal failure on August 2nd after a four-year battle with kidney disease. The Grammy-winning group's greatest hits include 'Up Up and Away' and 'Aquarius/Let the Sun Shine In'.

Author **Frederick A. Raborg, Jr.**, who was a regular contributor to Marvin Kaye's anthologies under the pseudonym 'Dick Baldwin', died on August 13th, aged 67. His stories appeared in *Brother Theodore's Chamber of Horrors*, *Ghosts*, *Masterpieces of Terror and the Supernatural* and *Devils & Demons*, amongst other titles.

HarperCollins editor **Robert S. Jones**, whose authors included Clive Barker, died of cancer in New York on the same day, aged 47.

American composer **Jack Elliott**, who wrote the music for

Starsky and Hutch, *Charlie's Angels*, *The Love Boat* and other 1970s TV shows, died of a brain tumour on August 18th, aged 74. His film credits include *Oh, God!*, and the series *The Fresh Prince of Bel-Air* was loosely based on Elliott's family.

Controversial British astrophysicist and SF author **Sir Fred Hoyle**, who coined the term 'Big Bang' to describe the creation of the Universe (a theory he always personally disputed), died on August 20th after suffering a severe stroke in July. He was 86. Founder of the Institute for Astronomy at Cambridge University and fellow of the Royal Society, Hoyle's novels include *The Black Cloud* and *Ossian's Ride*, and he co-wrote the BBC TV series *A for Andromeda* and its sequel, *Andromeda Breakthrough*, with John Elliott.

Comics artist **Chuck Cuidera**, who created *Blackhawk* at Quality Comics in 1941, died on August 25th, aged 86. He also created *Blue Beetle* and continued to ink *Blackhawk* after the title was sold to DC Comics until 1967. He worked on several other DC titles before leaving the field in 1970.

Philanthropist and publisher **Paul Hamlyn** (Paul Bertrand Hamburger), who became a multi-millionaire with his eponymous mass-market imprint, died on August 31st, aged 75. Among the books he published are *Supernatural Stories for Boys*, *The Best Ghost Stories*, *The Best Horror Stories* and *Spinechilling Tales for the Dead of Night*. He reissued Algernon Blackwood's *Tales of the Uncanny and the Supernatural* and *Tales of the Mysterious and Macabre* under his Spring Books imprint, and was also chairman of the Octopus Publishing Group from 1971 97.

Pauline Kael, the influential film critic of the *New Yorker* magazine, died of Parkinson's disease on September 2nd, aged 82. Her collected essays were published as *I Lost It at the Movies*, *Kiss Kiss Bang Bang*, *Going Steady*, *Deeper Into Movies* (winner of the National Book Award), *Reeling* and *For Keeps*.

54-year-old **Douglas J. Stone**, vice-president of Odyssey Press, which prints and mails *The New York Review of Science Fiction*, was aboard the doomed American Airlines Flight 11, which was crashed by terrorists into New York's World Trade Center on September 11th.

Long-time fan and former president and co-founder of the Southern Fandom Confederation, **Meade Frierson, III** died of cancer on September 24th, aged 61. With his wife Penny he edited the influential H.P. Lovecraft fanzine *HPL* in the early 1970s.

George Gately [Gallagher], creator of the *Heathcliff* newspaper comic strip, died of a heart attack on September 30th, aged 72. From 1973 until he retired in the late 1990s, he drew the eponymous cartoon cat, before which he created the *Hapless Harry* strip.

E.C. comics artist **Johnny Craig** also died in September, aged 75. After entering the industry in the late 1930s, he joined E.C. in 1950 where he contributed to *Tales from the Crypt*, *Vault of Horror*, *Haunt of Fear*, *Two-Fisted Tales* and other titles. His other credits include Warren Publishing's *Creepy* and *Eerie* and various titles for Marvel and DC.

69-year-old **Gregory** [Hancock] **Hemingway**, the youngest son of Ernest, died of hypertension and cardiovascular disease on October 1st while being held at a women's detention centre in Florida (he had apparently had a sex-change operation late in life and called himself 'Gloria'). Hemingway had been arrested five days earlier for being naked in public and was charged with indecent exposure and resisting arrest. His book about his father, *Papa: A Personal Memoir*, was published in 1976.

Scottish illustrator **Charles William Stewart** died on October 3rd, aged 85. As well as producing artwork for Beckford's *Vathek* and Le Fanu's *Uncle Silas*, he also edited *Ghost Stories and Other Horrid Tales* for the Folio Society, to which he contributed twenty watercolour plates.

Nuclear physicist, author and SF fan **Milton A. Rothman** died of heart failure on October 6th, aged 81. One of the hosts for the first SF convention in America, he chaired three Worldcons (including the one in 1953 that introduced the Hugo Award) and published fiction in *Astounding* under the pseudonym 'Lee Gregor'.

British-born composer and songwriter **Joel Lubin**, best known for such songs as 'Move Over, Darling' and 'Glass Bottom Boat' for Doris Day, died of heart failure on October 9th, aged 84. During the 1960s he developed a number of music artists, including Jan and Dean, and he co-wrote 'Tutti Frutti' with Little Richard.

Poet, editor and literary critic **Anne Ridler O.B.E.** (Anne

Barbara Bradby), who edited *Best Ghost Stories* for Faber & Faber in 1945, died in Oxford on October 15th, aged 89.

Oscar-winning American songwriter **Jay Livingston**, who with Ray Evans wrote such classics as 'Buttons and Bows', 'Mona Lisa' and 'Que Sera Sera', died of pneumonia on October 17th, aged 86. The duo's first big hit was 'G'bye Now' from Olsen and Johnson's 1941 revue *Hellzapoppin'*, which led to a ten-year contract with Paramount. Their TV themes include *Bonanza* and *Mister Ed* (which featured Livingston's voice). Livingston also worked on the scores for *When Worlds Collide* and *The Mole People*.

90-year-old TV writer **Norman Lessing**, whose credits include episodes of *Shirley Temple Storybook* (which he associate produced) and *Lost in Space*, died on October 22nd of congestive heart failure and complications from Parkinson's disease.

Best known for his depictions of Terry Pratchett's 'Discworld' on book covers, calendars and other media since 1984, British artist **Josh** (Ronald William) **Kirby** died unexpectedly in his sleep on October 23rd, aged 72. In a career that spanned fifty years, he produced more than 400 paintings, some of the best of which are collected in *The Josh Kirby Poster Book*, *In the Garden of Unearthly Delights*, *The Josh Kirby Discworld Portfolio* and *A Cosmic Cornucopia*. Beginning in 1956 with a paperback cover for Ian Fleming's *Moonraker*, he illustrated such authors as Ray Bradbury, Edgar Rice Burroughs and Alfred Hitchcock. Kirby won the British Fantasy Award for Best Artist in 1996, and amongst his other work he also produced film posters for *Starflight One*, *The Beastmaster*, *Krull*, *Morons from Outer Space*, *Return of the Jedi* and an unused design for *Monty Python's Life of Brian*.

Irish storyteller and stage actor **Éamon Kelly** died on October 24th, aged 87. His stories were collected by the Mercier Press.

American author **Richard Martin Stern**, whose novel *The Tower* helped inspire the 1974 movie *The Towering Inferno*, died on Halloween, aged 86.

British screenwriter and playwright **Anthony Shaffer** died of a heart attack in London on November 6th, aged 75. The twin brother of playwright Peter Shaffer, he is best known for his stage success *Sleuth* (filmed in 1971). His other screenplays include Hitchcock's *Frenzy*, *Absolution*, a trio of Agatha Christie adaptations (*Death on the Nile*, *Evil Under the Sun* and *Appointment with Death*) and the cult classic *The Wicker Man* (which he novelized in 1979).

Comics artist **Gray** (Dwight Graydon) **Morrow** died the same day, aged 67. He had been suffering from Parkinson's disease for several years and according to some reports took his own life. While illustrating various SF digest magazines and paperback book covers in the 1960s (including more than 100 covers for the *Perry Rhodan* series), he began contributing comic strips to Warren Publishing's *Creepy* and *Eerie*. In 1978 he adapted several stories for *The Illustrated Roger Zelazny*, and a retrospective volume entitled *Gray Morrow: Visionary* appeared in 2001. He also worked on a number of newspaper strips, including *Secret Agent X-9*, *Rip Kirby*, *Buck Rogers* and *Flash Gordon*, and was the longest-running artist on *Tarzan*, which he illustrated for eighteen years. He was reportedly despondent over his recent replacement on the strip by a new artist.

Ken (Kenneth) [Elton] **Kesey**, best known as the author of *One Flew Over the Cuckoo's Nest* (filmed in 1975) and the man who coined the term 'acid', died of complications from surgery for liver cancer on November 10th, aged 66. In 1966 Kesey fled to Mexico to avoid going to trial for marijuana possession and was eventually sentenced to six months in jail. He and his fellow 'Merry Pranksters' were the heroes of Tom Wolfe's influential 1968 book about psychedelia, *The Electric Kool-Aid Acid Test*.

60-year-old horror author and film-maker **Michael O'Rourke** died unexpectedly on November 14th, possibly as a result of toxic mould poisoning. Two years earlier O'Rourke and his wife were evacuated from their home and a lawsuit is ongoing. His books include *Darkling*, *The Bad Thing*, *The Undine* and *The Poison Tree* (under the byline 'F.M. O'Rourke'), and he scripted the films *Deadly Love* (which he also directed), *Hellgate* and *MoonStalker*.

TV writer **Peggy Chantler Dick**, whose credits include *Bewitched*, died of heart failure on November 20th, aged 78.

Author and illustrator **Seymour** [Victory] **Reit**, who created *Casper the Friendly Ghost* with animator Joe Oriolo, died on November 21st, aged 83. Reit and Oriolo sold all rights to the cartoon character to Famous Studios for just $200 in the mid-1940s, since when the franchise has generated millions through film shorts, TV series, movies and Harvey's on-going comic book series. Reit also worked on such cartoons as *Gulliver's Travels* (1939) and the *Popeye* and *Betty Boop* series, and he created the early 1940s comic strip characters Auro, Cosmo Corrigan and Super American, as well as drawing for *Archie, Little Lulu* and *Mad Magazine*.

Self-appointed busybody **Mary Whitehouse**, who formed the Viewers and Listeners Association in an attempt to censor films and television in Britain, died on November 23rd, aged 91. She won't be missed by many.

TV scriptwriter and producer **William Read Woodfield**, whose credits include *The Hypnotic Eye* and the TV movies *Earth II* and *Satan's Triangle*, died of a heart attack on November 24th, aged 73.

Former Beatles guitarist **George Harrison** died of cancer on November 29th, aged 58. His film appearances include *Help!*, *Yellow Submarine*, *A Magical Mystery Tour* and *Monty Python's Life of Brian*, and he produced the latter along with *The Time Bandits* and other movies under his production company Hand-Made Films, which he co-founded. At the time of his death the singer/songwriter was reportedly worth £120 million, and his 1970 single 'My Sweet Lord' briefly topped the UK charts again, replacing the late Aaliyah's 'More Than a Woman'. It was the first time that a posthumous No.1 hit was replaced by another.

75-year-old comic-strip artist **Dave Graue**, who took over the syndicated strip *Alley Oop* from its creator Vincent T. Hamlin in 1973, was killed in a car crash near his home in North Carolina on December 10th.

British TV writer **Alan Fennell** died of cancer on December 11th, aged 65. After teaming up with Gerry Anderson on the comic strip adaptations of the puppet series *Four Feather Falls* and *Supercar*, he began scripting many of Anderson's TV series, including *Fireball XL5*, *Stingray*, *Joe 90*, *Thunderbirds* and *U.F.O*. Fennell edited the children's magazine *Look-In* from 1971–74 and in 1991 he became editor of Fleetway's *Thunderbirds* comics.

Archie Comics artist **Dan DeCarlo**, who created *Sabrina the Teenage Witch*, died on December 18th, aged 82.

Writer and editor **Keith Allen Daniels** died of cancer the same day, aged 45. His SF and fantasy poetry appeared in *Analog*,

Asimov's, Weird Tales and other magazines, and he founded Anamnesis Press in 1990.

British ghost story author and former television scriptwriter and playwright **Sheila Hodgson** died of a stroke on Christmas Day, just three days after her 80th birthday. During the late 1970s she wrote a series of supernatural plays, three of which were based upon ideas suggested by M.R. James in his essay 'Stories I Have Tried to Write'. These were broadcast on BBC Radio 4 and subsequently published as stories in such periodicals as *Blackwood's Magazine* and *Ghosts & Scholars*, as well as being reprinted in Karl Edward Wagner's *The Year's Best Horror Stories XI* and *XVI*, and Ramsey Campbell's anthology *Meddling With Ghosts*. In 1998, Ash-Tree Press collected twelve of her tales featuring James as the central character in a volume entitled *The Fellow Travellers and Other Ghost Stories*.

Composer **Florian Fricke**, whose credits include Herzog's *Nosferatu*, died of a stroke on December 29th, aged 57.

British author **Victor [Joseph] Hanson** died of complications from a stroke in mid-December, aged 81. Best known for his hard-boiled crime and Western novels, in the early 1960s he published *The Twisters*, *Creatures of the Mist*, *Claws of the Night* and *The Grip of Fear* under the pseudonym 'Vern Hansen'.

ACTORS/ACTRESSES

American character actor **Ray Walston**, best known as TV's *My Favorite Martian* (1963–66) and the Devil in *Damn Yankees* (on Broadway and in the 1958 film), died on January 1st, aged 86. His numerous other credits include *The Happy Hooker Goes to Washington*, *Popeye*, *The Fall of the House of Usher* (1980), *Galaxy of Terror*, *O'Hara's Wife*, *Blood Relations*, *Saturday the 14th Strikes Back*, *Blood Salvage*, *Popcorn*, *Addams Family Values*, the 1999 *My Favorite Martian* movie, the Stephen King mini-series *The Stand* and a recurring role in *Star Trek Voyager*. He also narrated the title sequence of Steven Spielberg's *Amazing Stories* TV series (1985–87).

Character actress **Nancy Parsons** died after a long illness on January 5th, aged 58. She appeared in *Motel Hell* and on TV's *Nightmare Classics: Eyes of the Panther*.

Film and TV character actor **Scott Marlowe** died of a heart attack on January 6th, aged 68. He appeared in *The Subterraneans* and the TV movie *Night Slaves* along with episodes of *The Outer Limits*, *Thriller*, *The Wild Wild West* and many other shows.

65-year-old British stage and television actor **Michael Williams**, the husband of Dame Judi Dench, died of cancer on January 11th after a seventeen-month battle against the disease. He appeared in the RSC's 1966 movie *Marat/Sade*, and between 1989 and 1998 he portrayed Dr Watson to Clive Merrison's Sherlock Holmes for the entire canon of Sir Arthur Conan's Doyle's fifty-six short stories and four novels broadcast on BBC Radio 4.

Canadian character actor **Al Waxman** died during heart surgery on January 17th, aged 65. His many credits include *When Michael Calls*, *I Still Dream of Jeannie*, *Heavy Metal*, *Spasms* (aka *Death Bite*), *Millennium* and *Bogus*.

Hollywood musical comedy star **Virginia [Lee] O'Brien** died on January 18th, aged 79. Related to Civil War General Robert E. Lee, she appeared in sixteen movies between 1940 and 1947 and in 1955 had a small role in *Francis in the Navy*. She was married to *Superman* star Kirk Alyn (who died in 1999) from 1942–55.

Veteran Shakespearean actor **Joseph O'Conor** died in London on January 21st, aged 84. His films include *Gorgo*, Hammer's *The Gorgon* and *Devil Ship Pirates*, and *Doomwatch*, and he appeared on TV in the 1973 adaptation of M.R. James's *A Ghost Story for Christmas: Lost Hearts* and the recent children's series *The Belfry Witches*.

American actress **Sally Mansfield**, who portrayed Vena Ray on the 1950s TV series *Rocky Jones, Space Ranger*, died of lung cancer on January 28th, aged 77.

French leading man **Jean-Pierre Aumont** (Jean-Pierre Salomons) died on January 29th, aged 92. His many films include *Siren of Atlantis*, *Cauldron of Blood* (with Boris Karloff), *Castle Keep*, *The Happy Hooker* and *Don't Look in the Attic*. One of his three wives was Maria Montez, whom he married in 1946 and with whom he had a daughter, actress Tina Aumont.

BBC television announcer and co-host (with Derek Bond) of the long-running weekly show *Picture Parade*, **Peter [Varley] Haigh** also died in January, aged 75. He married Rank starlet Jill Adams in 1957.

Actor **Titus Moede**, who appeared in Ray Dennis Steckler's *The Incredibly Strange Creatures Who Stopped Living and Became Mixed-Up Zombies!!?*, *Rat Pfink and Boo Boo* and *The Thrill Killers*, died of colon cancer on February 6th. As 'Titus Moody' he was a pioneer in adult films.

Dale Evans (Frances Octavia Lucille Wood Smith), former band singer and the widow of Hollywood cowboy Roy Rogers, died of congestive heart failure on February 7th, aged 88. She had suffered a stroke in 1996 and was confined to a wheelchair. Known as 'The Queen of the Cowgirls', she appeared in twenty-eight films with her husband (who died in 1998) and they worked together on TV in *The Roy Rogers Show* (1951–57) and *The Roy Rogers and Dale Evans Show* (1962). She was named California Mother of the Year in 1967 and Texan of the Year in 1970. The couple lost three of their children, two of them in tragic accidents.

British character actor **Reginald Marsh** died on February 9th, aged 74. His numerous credits include *It Happened Here*, *Berserk* and the TV movies *The Stone Tape* and *Hammer House of Mystery and Suspense: Mark of the Devil*.

Former European middleweight champion boxer and actor **Tiberio Mitri** was run over by a train on February 12th, aged 74. The Italian boxer, who famously survived fifteen rounds in the ring with Jake La Motta at Madison Square Garden, went on to appear in a number of films, including *Ben-Hur* (1959) and numerous spaghetti Westerns and *peplums*. Following the premature deaths of his son and daughter, he developed a drinking problem and was living among Rome's homeless population.

British leading man **Michael** [Anthony] **Johnson** died on February 24th, aged 62. Best known as a television actor (notably opposite Herbert Lom in *The Human Jungle* [1963–65]), his only starring role on screen was in Hammer's *Lust for a Vampire* (1971).

American character actress **Rosemary DeCamp**, who played James Cagney's mother in *Yankee Doodle Dandy* despite being thirteen years his junior, died of pneumonia on February 20th, aged 90. She also appeared in *Jungle Book* (1942), William Castle's *13 Ghosts*, *Saturday the 14th* and the TV movie *The Time Machine* (1978).

American actress **Peggy Converse**, who starred in *The Thing That Couldn't Die*, died on March 2nd, aged 95.

TV actor **Louis Edmonds**, who portrayed various members of the Collins family in the daytime soap opera *Dark Shadows* (1966–71) and the movie *House of Dark Shadows*, died of respiratory failure on March 3rd, aged 77.

Edward Winter, who starred as Captain Ben Ryan in the TV series *Project U.F.O.* (1978–79), died of Parkinson's disease on March 8th, aged 63.

Obnoxious talkshow host and chain-smoker [Sean] **Morton Downey, Jr.** died of lung cancer and other respiratory problems on March 12th, aged 68. After composing such hit surf-rock numbers as 'Pipeline' and 'Wipeout' in the early 1960s, his syndicated TV series *The Morton Downey Jr. Show* debuted in the New York City area in 1987. He also appeared in more than twenty movies and TV shows, including *Predator 2* and episodes of *Monsters* and *Tales from the Crypt*.

Calypso singer **Sir Lancelot** (Lancelot Victor Pinard), whose credits include Val Lewton's *I Walked With a Zombie, The Ghost Ship* and *Curse of the Cat People*, plus *Zombies on Broadway* and *The Unknown Terror*, died the same day, aged 97.

Hollywood actress and light comedienne **Ann Sothern** (Harriette Lake) died of heart failure on March 15th, aged 92. Her many films include *Super-Sleuth*, *Lady in a Cage*, *Golden Needles* and *The Manitou*, and she was the voice of the car in the TV fantasy sitcom *My Mother the Car* (1965–66). Sothern was nominated for an Academy Award for her role in *The Whales of August* (with Vincent Price). Her daughter, designer Tisha Sterling, was also an actress.

Voice actress **Norma MacMillan**, who was the voice of *Casper, The Friendly Ghost* in the 1950s Paramount cartoon series, died in Canada on March 16th, aged 79. She also voiced Gumby in the Claymation series *Pokey and Gumby* and Sweet Polly Purebread in *Underdog*.

British leading man of the 1950s **Anthony** [Maitland] **Steel** died on March 21st, his 81st birthday. His credits include *Helter Skelter* (1948) and *West of Zanzibar* (1954). Later in his career he appeared in *The Story of O* (1975) and portrayed film producer Lintom Busotsky (a role originally intended for Peter Cushing) in the 1980 R. Chetwynd-Hayes adaptation, *The Monster Club*. He was briefly married to Anita Ekberg.

American stage and screen actor **Anthony Dexter** (Walter

Fleischmann) died on March 27th, aged 82. After being cast as
Rudolph Valentino in the 1951 biopic, his career never recovered
and he found himself in such films as *Fire Maidens from Outer
Space*, *The Story of Mankind*, *12 to the Moon* and *Phantom
Planet*.

Alleged serial killer **Henry Lee Lucas**, who confessed to more
than 300 homicides and was the inspiration for *Henry: Portrait of
a Serial Killer*, also died in March. He was apparently the only
man whose death sentence was commuted by Governor George
W. Bush of Texas.

British stage, screen and television actress **Jean Anderson** died
on April 1st, aged 93. Her occasional film credits include Disney's
The Three Lives of Thomasina, *The Night Digger* and *Scream-
time*.

German-born stage and screen actor **Brother Theodore** (Theodore Gottlieb) died of pneumonia in New York City on April 5th,
aged 94. A survivor of Dachau concentration camp, his film
credits include Orson Welles's *The Stranger*, *Nocturna*, the 1976
porno spoof *Gums*, *The Invisible Kid* and Joe Dante's *The 'burbs*.
He also narrated Al Adamson's *Horror of the Blood Monsters*
and voiced Gollum in the animated TV movies *The Hobbit* and
The Return of the King. *Brother Theodore's Chamber of Horrors*
was a 1975 paperback anthology co-edited with Marvin Kaye.

Oscar-winning American actress **Beatrice Straight**, who played
the paranormal investigator in *Poltergeist*, died of pneumonia on
April 7th, aged 86. She also won a Tony Award as Best Supporting Actress in the 1953 Broadway production of Arthur Miller's
The Crucible and was nominated for an Emmy for her role in the
1978 mini-series *The Dain Curse*. She had a recurring role as the
Queen of the Amazons in the 1977 TV series *Wonder Woman*.

American TV and film actor **David Graf**, best known for his
recurring role in the *Police Academy* movies, died of a heart
attack on the same day, aged 50. His other credits include *Burnin'
Love* and *Skeleton*.

Jerome Barr, estranged from his daughter Roseanne after she
publicly accused him in 1991 of molesting her as a child, died of
a heart attack on April 9th, aged 71. Barr, who had always
denied the allegations, won a casino jackpot just days before his
death.

New Zealand-born actress **Nyree** (Ngaire) **Dawn Porter** died suddenly in London on April 10th, aged 61. In Britain since 1960, she made her name as Irene in the 1967 BBC serial *The Forsyte Saga* and as the co-star of *The Protectors* (1972–74), and appeared in such films as AIP's *Jane Eyre* (1970), the Amicus productions *The House That Dripped Blood* and *From Beyond the Grave*, and in the 1980 TV mini-series of Ray Bradbury's *The Martian Chronicles*.

Welsh-born comedian and singer **Sir Harry [Donald] Secombe** died of prostate cancer on April 11th, aged 79. From 1951–60 Secombe co-starred in the surreal BBC radio programme *The Goon Show* (as Neddie Seagoon) along with Michael Bentine, Spike Milligan and Peter Sellers. His film appearances include *Helter Skelter* (1948), *Down Among the Z Men*, *Svengali* (1954) and *The Bed Sitting Room*.

British stage and screen actor **Paul Daneman** died on April 28th, aged 75. His film credits include Richard Lester's surreal *How I Won the War* (1967).

Argentine actress **Mabel Karr** died in a Madrid hospital from complications from an infection on May 1st, aged 66. She starred in Jesus Franco's *The Diabolical Dr Z* and *The Killer Tongue*.

Actress and singer **Deborah Walley**, who starred in *Gidget Goes Hawaiian*, *Beach Blanket Bingo*, *Ski Party*, *Dr Goldfoot and the Bikini Machine*, *The Ghost in the Invisible Bikini*, *Sergeant Deadhead the Astronaut*, *It's a Bikini World*, the 3-D *The Bubble* and *The Severed Arm*, died of oesophageal cancer on May 10th, aged 57. She had been diagnosed in February and was given just six months to live. Her other film credits include *Spinout* (with Elvis Presley). She also wrote children's books and divorced actor John Ashley in 1966.

The same day, actress turned pot dealer **Jennifer Stahl**, who had a small role in *Necropolis* and appeared as a dancer in *Dirty Dancing*, was one of three people found shot to death in a drug deal that went wrong in a sixth-floor apartment above Manhattan's Carnegie Deli.

87-year-old Italian-American crooner and former barber **Perry Como** (Pierino Roland Como, aka Nick Perido) died at his home in Florida on May 12th after suffering from Alzheimer's disease for two years. He appeared in a small number of films during the 1940s, and by the late 1950s was America's highest-paid TV performer. With record sales of more than 100 million, his laid-back hits include 'Catch a Falling Star', 'Magic Moments' and 'It's Impossible'.

American actor and playwright **Jason Miller**, who won a Pulitzer Prize and a Tony Award for his 1973 play *That Championship Season* and was nominated for an Oscar for his portrayal of Father Damien Karras in *The Exorcist*, died of heart failure in Pennsylvania on May 13th, aged 62. His other credits include *The Ninth Configuration*, *The Exorcist III* and such TV movies as *The Dain Curse*, *Vampire* (1979) and *The Henderson Monster*.

British leading man of the stage and screen, **Jack Watling**, died on May 22nd, aged 78. His credits include *Meet Mr Lucifer*, Hammer's *The Nanny*, *11 Harrowhouse* and TV's *Invisible Man* and *Doctor Who* (both opposite his daughter, Deborah).

Veteran TV character actor **Harry Townes** died in Alabama on May 23rd, aged 86. He played Dr Greenwood in the 1958 movie of Fredric Brown's *The Screaming Mimi* and appeared in episodes of *Inner Sanctum*, *Alfred Hitchcock Presents*, *Climax!*, *One Step Beyond*, *The Twilight Zone*, *Thriller*, *The Outer Limits*, *Star Trek*, *Night Gallery*, *The Sixth Sense* and numerous others. He semi-retired from acting thirty years ago to become an Episcopalian priest in his home town of Huntsville.

French actor **Jean Champion**, whose many credits include TV's *Belphegor*, died the same day, aged 87.

American actress and TV personality **Arlene Francis** (Arlene Kazanjian), best known as a panellist on the quiz show *What's My Line?*, died of cancer on May 31st, aged 93. Her occasional film appearances include *Murders in the Rue Morgue* opposite Bela Lugosi.

British film journalist and arts administrator **David Prothero** committed suicide in the summer. He contributed to *Shivers*, *The Dark Side*, *Scapegoat* and Kim Newman's *The BFI Companion to Horror* as well as publishing his own magazine, *Bloody Hell*.

Stuntman **Russell Saunders** died on June 1st, aged 86. His numerous credits include *The Thing* (1951), *Earthquake*, *The Poseidon Adventure* and *Logan's Run*.

Comedienne-actress **Imogene Coca** died on June 2nd, aged 92. Best known for her TV appearances, with guest spots on *Bewitched*, *Fantasy Island*, *Night Gallery* and *Monsters*, she also had roles in several films, including *Alice in Wonderland* (1985).

A former Broadway dancer, she was married to her second husband, actor King Donovan, from 1960 until his death in 1987.

Mexican-born Hollywood star and former boxer **Anthony Quinn** (Anthony Rudolph Oaxaca) died in a Boston hospital on June 3rd, aged 86. Best known for his 1964 film *Zorba the Greek*, he also appeared in *Bulldog Drummond in Africa*, *Television Spy*, *The Ghost Breakers*, *Road to Morocco*, *Sinbad the Sailor*, *Ulysses* (1955), *The Hunchback of Notre-Dame* (1956, as Quasimodo), *The Shoes of the Fisherman*, *The Magus*, *Ghosts Can't Do It* and *Last Action Hero*. On television he was in a 1951 episode of *Lights Out* and portrayed Zeus in five *Hercules The Legendary Journeys* TV movies in 1994. Married three times (once to Cecil B. DeMille's daughter Katherine), he had at least thirteen children by five different women.

76-year-old stage, film and TV actor **Carroll O'Connor**, best remembered for his Emmy Award-winning portrayal of Archie Bunker on the CBS-TV sitcom *All in the Family* (1971–79), died of a heart attack brought on by complications from diabetes on June 21st. He also appeared in the TV movie *Fear No Evil* (1969), and such series as *The Outer Limits*, *The Man from U.N.C.L.E.*, *Voyage to the Bottom of the Sea*, *Time Tunnel* and *The Wild Wild West*.

French-born actress **Corinne Calvet** (Corinne Dibos) died of a cerebral haemorrhage in Los Angeles on June 23rd, aged 75. Her film credits include *Bluebeard's Ten Honeymoons*, *Dr Heckle and Mr Hype*, *The Sword and the Sorcerer* and the TV movie *The Phantom of Hollywood*. Actor John Bromfield was one of her five husbands, and she once filed a $1 million slander suit against Zsa Zsa Gabor for alleging that she was not French.

Hollywood star **Jack Lemmon** (John Uhler Lemmon III) died of a cancer-related illness on June 27th, aged 76. The two-time Academy Award winner, best known for his long screen partnership with Walter Matthau (who died almost exactly a year earlier), appeared in such early TV series as *Suspense* and the movies *Bell Book and Candle*, *How to Murder Your Wife*, *Airport 77*, *The China Syndrome*, *JFK*, *Hamlet* (1996) and, uncredited, in *The Legend of Bagger Vance* (which he also narrated).

71-year-old British character actress **Joan Sims** died the same day after a long illness and years of heavy drinking and depression. Best known as the star of twenty-four *Carry On* comedies (including *Carry On Screaming*), she also appeared in *Colonel March Investigates* (with Boris Karloff), *Meet Mr Lucifer*, Disney's *One of Our Dinosaurs is Missing* and *The Canterville Ghost* (1996), and was a regular on TV's *Worzel Gummidge* (1979–81).

British actress **Patricia Hilliard**, who appeared in *The Ghost Goes West* (1936) and had a role in *Things to Come* (1936), died in mid-June, aged 85.

British character actor **Jack Gwillim** died on July 2nd, aged 91. Best known for his royal roles on stage, his films include *Circus of Horrors*, *Jason and the Argonauts* (1963, as King Aeetes), Hammer's *Curse of the Mummy's Tomb*, *Kiss the Girls and Make Them Die*, *Clash of the Titans* and as Van Helsing in *The Monster Squad*. On TV his career ranged from *A for Andromeda* to *Conan*.

British stage and screen actress **Eleanor Summerfield** died on July 13th, aged 80. Her film credits include *Scrooge* (1951) and Disney's *The Watcher in the Woods*.

Hollywood actress **Molly Lamont**, who appeared in *Scared to Death* (with Bela Lugosi), *Devil Bat's Daughter* and *Jungle Princess*, died on July 15th, aged 91.

'England's Premier Ventriloquist', **Arthur Worsley**, died on July 19th, aged 80. With his cheeky dummy Charlie Brown he worked with such acts as Laurel and Hardy, Elvis Presley and The Beatles.

Stage and TV actor **Steve Barton**, who played Raoul in both the original London and Broadway productions of Andrew Lloyd Webber's *The Phantom of the Opera*, died of heart failure in Germany on July 21st, aged 47. He also played the Beast in an Austrian production of Disney's *Beauty and the Beast*, appeared in the short-lived 1993 Broadway musical *The Red Shoes*, and originated the role of Count von Krolock in Jim Steinman's stage adaptation of *Dance of the Vampires* in Vienna in 1997.

American actor **Alex Nicol** died on July 28th, aged 85. He appeared in *The Clones*, *The Night God Screamed*, *A*P*E* and *The Screaming Skull*. He also directed the latter, along with *Point of Terror*.

British-born actor **Christopher Hewett** died of complications due to diabetes in Los Angeles on August 3rd, aged 80. Best known for the role of *Mr Belvedere* on TV from 1985–90, he also appeared in such films as *The Producers*, *Massarati and the Brain* and *Ratboy*. For the final season of *Fantasy Island* (1983–84) he played Mr Roarke's new sidekick Lawrence, after Hervé Villechaize left the show.

64-year-old TV scriptwriter, producer and cartoon voice **Lorenzo Music** (Gerald David Music), who played Carlton the Doorman in *Rhoda* (1974–78), which he co-created, and *Garfield the Cat* on the Saturday morning series, died of cancer on August 4th. He won an Emmy in 1969 as a writer on *The Smothers Brothers Comedy Hour*.

British actress **Dame Dorothy Tutin**, who played Peter Pan for two seasons (1971–72) on the London stage, died of leukaemia on August 6th, aged 71.

Hollywood leading lady **Dorothy McGuire** died of heart failure on August 13th, aged 85. She had broken her leg three weeks before. Her many films include *The Enchanted Cottage* (1945), *The Spiral Staircase* (1945, as the mute heroine), Disney's *The Swiss Family Robinson*, *The Greatest Story Ever Told* (as the Virgin Mary) and the TV movie *She Waits*.

Stage and occasional movie actress **Kim Stanley** (Patricia Beth Reid) died of uterine cancer the same day, aged 76. Her movies include *Seance on a Wet Afternoon* (for which she was nominated for an Oscar) and *The Right Stuff*.

Raymond Edward Johnson, who hosted the radio show *Inner Sanctum* (1941–52) as the macabre Raymond, died on August 15th, aged 90. He also played the lead in radio's *Mandrake the Magician* series.

Daytime soap opera star **Gerald Gordon**, who also appeared in the TV movie *It Happened at Lakewood Manor*, the original *Twilight Zone* series, *Highway to Heaven* and *Knight Rider*, died on August 17th after a long illness, aged 67.

Soul singer **Betty Everett**, who topped the US charts in 1964 with 'The Shoop Shoop Song (It's in His Kiss)', died on August 18th, aged 61.

American character actor **Walter Reed** (Walter Smith) died of kidney failure on August 20th, aged 85. Since making his debut in 1929 at the age of thirteen, he appeared in nearly 100 films and serials including *Flying Disc Man from Mars*, *Government Agent* *vs. Phantom Legion, Superman and the Mole Men, How to Make a Monster, Macumba Love* and *The Destructors*.

American character actress **Kathleen Freeman** died of lung cancer on August 23rd, aged 78. Best remembered as the fearsome Sister Stigmata (aka 'The Penguin') in both *Blues Brothers* movies, she made almost 100 films, including *Monkey Business, The Magnetic Monster, The Fly* (1958), *Psycho Sisters, Heartbeeps, Innerspace, Teen Wolf Too, Gremlins 2 The New Batch, Hocus Pocus, Nutty Professor II The Klumps, Shrek,* and ten with Jerry Lewis (including the original *The Nutty Professor*). She was also a regular on the 1953–55 *Topper* TV series and was appearing in the Broadway production of *The Full Monty* at the time of her death.

Howard Hughes discovery and Hollywood's leading *film noir* actress, **Jane Greer** (Bettejane Greer), died of complications from cancer on August 24th, two weeks short of her 77th birthday. Her films include *Out of the Past, Dick Tracy* (1945), *The Falcon's Alibi, Sinbad the Sailor* (1946), *Run for the Sun* and the Lon Chaney Sr. biopic *Man of a Thousand Faces*. She was briefly married to actor/crooner Rudy Vallee, and her family was descended from the poet John Donne.

22-year-old American R&B singer and actress **Aaliyah** (Dana Haughton) was one of nine people killed on August 25th, when a 'substantially overloaded' light airplane crashed shortly after take-off in the Bahamas, where she had been filming a music video. The niece of Gladys Knight, she was rumoured to have married singer/producer R. Kelly when she was only fifteen. After appearing in *Romeo Must Die*, she starred in the Anne Rice adaptation *Queen of the Damned* and had just completed pre-production on the two *Matrix* sequels. Her parents subsequently launched a legal action against Virgin Records and several video production companies alleging negligence led to the plane crash.

75-year-old Spanish actor **Francisco Rabal**, who suffered from bronchitis, died of emphysema on August 29th on a flight from Montreal, where he had received a lifetime achievement award. His nearly 200 films include *The Witches* (1967), Umberto Lenzi's *City of the Walking Dead* (aka *Nightmare City*), *Treasure of the Four Crowns* and *Dagon*.

American leading lady **Julie Bishop** (Jacqueline Brown, aka Jacqueline Wells) died on August 30th, her 87th birthday. After starting out as a child actress in silent films, she went on to appear in *Alice in Wonderland* (1933), *Tarzan the Fearless* (with Buster Crabbe), *The Black Cat* (with Karloff and Lugosi), *Torture Ship* and *The Hidden Hand*. Lionel Atwill was once her step father-in-law and her daughter is actress Pamela Shoop Sweeney.

Former American teen idol **Troy Donahue** (Merle Johnson, Jr.) died on September 2nd of a massive heart attack the 65-year-old had suffered while returning from a gym three days earlier. His film roles include *The Man With a Thousand Faces*, *Monolith Monsters*, *Monster on the Campus*, *My Blood Runs Cold*, *Rocket to the Moon* (aka *Those Fantastic Flying Fools*), *Sweet Saviour*, *Seizure*, *The Love-Thrill Murders*, *Cyclone*, *Deadly Prey*, *Dr Alien*, *Bad Blood*, *The Chilling*, *Omega Cop*, *Shock 'em Dead*, *Cockroach Hotel* and *The Godfather Part II*. Amongst four divorces, he was married to co-star Suzanne Pleshette for a year, and in the 1970s became addicted to drink and drugs, spending a summer homeless in New York's Central Park. In later years he gave acting lessons to passengers on a cruise line.

53-year-old American actress and photographer **Berry Berenson**, the widow of actor Anthony Perkins and younger sister of actress Marisa Berenson, was one of the ninety-two passengers and crew on American Airlines Flight 11, en route from Boston to Los Angeles, that terrorists crashed into the North Tower of New York's World Trade Center on September 11th. She appeared in such movies as *Cat People* (1982) and *Winter Kills*.

Former TV reporter, Beat poet, Second City founding member and belated character actor, **Victor [Keung] Wong** died in his sleep on September 12th, aged 74. His nearly thirty films include *Big Trouble in Little China*, *The Golden Child*, *Prince of Darkness* and *Tremors*. He retired in 1998 after suffering two strokes.

46-year-old **Lani O'Grady** (Lanita Rose Agrati), best known for playing the eldest daughter in the TV series *Eight is Enough* (1977–81), was found dead at her California home on September 25th. The actress, whose other credits include *Massacre at Central High* (aka *Blackboard Massacre*), *The Curious Case of the Campus Corpse* and the TV movie *The Kid With the Broken Halo*, had suffered from panic attacks, agoraphobia and alcohol and drug abuse.

Actress **Gloria Foster**, who appeared as The Oracle in *The*

Matrix, died of complications from diabetes in New York on September 29th, aged 64.

Early American TV sex symbol **Dagmar** (Virginia Ruth Egnor, aka Jennie Lewis) died on October 9th, aged 79. The buxom blonde appeared on Broadway with comedy duo Olsen and Johnson in the mid-1940s, and guested on TV alongside Jerry Lester, Morey Amsterdam and Milton Berle during the following decade. She retired in the 1970s.

American actor **Otis Young** died of a stroke on October 12th, aged 69. His films include *The Clones*, *The Capture of Bigfoot* and *Blood Beach*.

British actress **Linden Travers** (Florence Lindon-Travers), best remembered for her role as Mrs Todhunter in Hitchcock's *The Lady Vanishes*, died on October 23rd, aged 88. Her other films include *The Terror* (1939), *The Ghost Train* (1940), *The Bad Lord Byron* and *No Orchids For Miss Blandish*, which was banned in Britain for several years. Her younger brother was actor Bill Travers.

British character actress **Jenny Laird**, who appeared in *Village of the Damned* (1960) and the TV movies *A Place to Die* and *The Masks of Death* (as Mrs Hudson, opposite Peter Cushing's Sherlock Holmes), died on Halloween, aged 84. She also appeared in episodes of TV's *Doctor Who* and *Hammer House of Horror*.

Actor and Tony award-winning composer **Albert Hague**, who played the cantankerous Mr Shorofsky in *Fame* and the spin-off TV series, died of lung cancer on November 12th, aged 81. In 1966 he scored the animated short *Dr Seuss' How the Grinch Stole Christmas!* (narrated by Boris Karloff), and also appeared in *Nightmares*, *Space Jam* and TV's *Tales from the Darkside*.

American actor **Byron Sanders**, who appeared in *The Flesh Eaters* and also modelled for Salvador Dali's 'Crucifixion', died the same day, aged 76.

Veteran British comedienne and character actress **Peggy Mount** died on November 13th, aged 86.

33-year-old British actress **Charlotte Coleman**, best remembered as Hugh Grant's room-mate in *Four Weddings and a Funeral*, died of a severe asthma attack in London on November 14th. She also appeared in *The Young Poisoner's Handbook*,

Bearskin: An Urban Fairytale and TV's *Worzel Gummidge*, as
well as providing voices for the feature cartoon *Faeries*.

79-year-old Australian actor and screenwriter **Michael St. Clair**
died of a brain aneurysm while driving to an audition on
November 22nd. He appeared in *Skullduggery* and the TV movie
The Hound of the Baskervilles (1972), and scripted *Mission Mars*
and co-wrote *The Body Stealers* (aka *Thin Air*).

Actor and opera singer **Norman Lumsden**, best known as
author J.R. Hartley looking for a copy of his own book on fly-
fishing in the British *Yellow Pages* TV commercial, died on
November 28th, aged 95. His first job was as a commercial
artist for publisher Hodder & Stoughton, where he designed
book covers for Leslie Charteris's *The Saint* series and other
titles. Benjamin Britten wrote the part of Peter Quince in his
1960 opera of *A Midsummer Night's Dream* with Lumsden in
mind.

John Mitchum, the actor brother of Robert, died of a stroke on
November 29th, aged 82. He appeared in *Bigfoot*, *High Plains
Drifter*, *Telefon* and *Escapes*.

American character actress **Pauline Moore**, who played one of
the bridesmaids in the 1931 *Frankenstein*, died of complications
from Alzheimer's disease on December 7th, aged 87. Her other
credits include *Charlie Chan at the Olympics*, *Charlie Chan on
Treasure Island* and *Charlie Chan in Reno*.

Veteran Indian actor **Ashok Kumar** [Ganguli], who appeared
in more than 300 films during a career that spanned over sixty
years, died of a heart attack on December 10th, aged 90.

Singer **Rufus Thomas**, best known for his novelty hit 'Do the
Funky Chicken', died of apparent heart failure in Memphis,
Tennessee, on December 15th, aged 84. The Rolling Stones
covered his 'Walking the Dog' on their first album in 1964.

72-year-old British actor **Sir Nigel Hawthorne** died of a heart
attack on December 19th after a two-year battle against pancreatic cancer. He won a Tony Award for his stage performance
as C.S. Lewis in the 1991 Broadway production of *Shadowlands*
and was forced to pull out of playing Jack the Ripper in *From
Hell* (2001) when potentially lethal blood clots were discovered
on his lungs prior to filming. He also appeared in *DreamChild*,
Demolition Man, *Richard III*, *Memoirs of a Survivor*, *Firefox* and
the 1981 TV movie of *The Hunchback of Notre Dame*, and

contributed voice characterizations to *Watership Down*, *The Plague Dogs* and Disney's *The Black Cauldron* and *Tarzan*.

American character actor **Lance Fuller** died in a Los Angeles nursing home after a long illness on December 22nd, aged 73. He portrayed the Metaluna Mutant in the classic *This Island Earth*, and also appeared in *The She Creature* (1956), *Voodoo Woman*, *The Bride and the Beast*, *The Andromeda Strain* and episodes of TV's *Thriller* and *The Twilight Zone*.

American character actress [Anna] **Eileen Heckart** died after a three-year battle with cancer on December 31st, aged 82. Among her many roles, she appeared in both the Broadway and film productions of *The Bad Seed*, gaining an Academy Award nomination for Best Supporting Actress in the part ot Mrs Daigle. Her other movies include *No Way To Treat a Lady* and *Burnt Offerings*. She retired from acting in 2000.

Swiss-born leading man **Paul Hubschmid** (aka Paul Christian) died in Berlin of a pulmonary embolism the same day, aged 84. He appeared in *Bagdad*, *The Beast from 20,000 Fathoms*, Fritz Lang's *Tiger of Eschnapur* (aka *Journey to the Lost City*), *Funeral in Berlin*, *The Day the Sky Exploded* and *Skullduggery*.

FILM/TV TECHNICIANS

British cartoon film-maker **Alison de Vere** died on January 2nd, aged 73. In 1967 she helped create the backgrounds for The Beatles' *Yellow Submarine* and made a cameo appearance as one of the photographed figures in the 'Eleanor Rigby' sequence.

American independent film producer/director **James Hill** died of Alzheimer's disease on January 11th, aged 84. After working as a contract screenwriter at MGM, he joined actor Burt Lancaster and agent Harold Hecht in a production partnership. In 1958, he became Rita Hayworth's fifth and final husband. The marriage lasted two years.

Following years of poor health (his death was prematurely announced in 1996), Spanish writer/director **Amando De Ossorio** died on January 13th, aged 82. His many films include *Malenka The Niece of the Vampire*, *Tombs of the Blind Dead*, *Return of the Evil Dead*, *Night of the Sorcerers*, *Horror of the Zombies* (1974), *Night of the Seagulls* and *The Sea Serpent*.

Film exhibitor **Ted Mann**, who changed the name of Hollywood's famed Grauman's Chinese Theatre to his own in 1973, died of a stroke on January 15th, aged 84. He also produced the 1969 adaptation of Ray Bradbury's *The Illustrated Man* and *Krull*, and was married to actress Rhonda Fleming.

Sam Wiesenthal, who was production manager to Carl Laemmle, Jr's vice-president at Universal Pictures, died on February 11th at the Motion Picture & Television Hospital, aged 92. With Laemmle, he was responsible for *All Quiet on the Western Front* (1930) and the studio's *Frankenstein* and *Dracula* franchises. After Universal was sold in 1936, he moved on to other studios and later became an independent producer.

Screenwriter/director **Burt Kennedy**, best known for his comedy Westerns, died of cancer on February 15th, aged 78. He had undergone heart surgery the previous month, after which his kidneys had failed. Among his many credits are *The Killer Inside Me*, *Suburban Commando* and the TV movies *The Wild Wild West Revisited* and *More Wild Wild West*.

Former president of production at Paramount, producer **Howard W. Koch** reportedly died of Alzheimer's disease on February 16th, aged 84. His credits include *The Manchurian Candidate*, *The President's Analyst*, *On a Clear Day You Can See Forever*, *Heaven Can Wait* (1978), *Dragonslayer*, *The Keep* and *Ghost*. During the 1950s he was a partner with Aubrey Schenck in independent production company Bel-Air, which produced such low-budget chillers as *The Black Sleep*, *Pharaoh's Curse* and *Voodoo Island*, and he directed *Frankenstein 1970* starring Boris Karloff.

French film director **Robert Enrico**, whose early films include the Oscar-winning 1961 short *La Rivière Du Hibou* (*Incident at Owl Creek*), based on the story by Ambrose Bierce, died of cancer in Paris the same day, aged 69. In America, his short film was shown as part of *The Twilight Zone* TV series.

American producer/director **Stanley** [Earl] **Kramer**, whose classic films include *High Noon*, *The Caine Mutiny* and *Judgment at Nuremberg*, died of pneumonia on February 19th, aged 87. His other credits include *The 5,000 Fingers of Dr T*, *On the Beach* (1959), *Inherit the Wind* and *It's a Mad Mad Mad Mad World*. During the 1950s he kept Lon Chaney, Jr. in high-profile films, while both Karloff and Lugosi were scrabbling for work.

German-born American cinematographer **Ralf D. Bode**, whose credits include *Dressed to Kill*, died of lung cancer on February 27th, aged 59.

The same day saw the death of film and TV producer **Stan Margulies** from cancer at the age of 80. His credits include *Willy Wonka and the Chocolate Factory*.

Former actor, director and cinematographer **John A. Alonzo** died on March 13th, aged 66. After starring in *The Hand of Death* (1962), the Mexican-American cinematographer began as James Wong Howe's camera operator on *Seconds* (1966) before working with such directors as Martin Ritt, Roger Corman, Roman Polanski, John Frankenheimer and Brian De Palma. He photographed parts of Steven Spielberg's *Close Encounters of the Third Kind*, *Look What's Happened to Rosemary's Baby*, *Blue Thunder*, *Terror in the Aisles*, *The Guardian*, *Meteor Man*, *Star Trek Generations* and the live TV movie remake of *Fail Safe* (2000).

British film director **Ralph Thomas**, the older brother of the late *Carry On* director Gerald Thomas, died after a long illness on March 17th, aged 85. Best known for his series of *Doctor* comedies (1953–70), based on the novels by Richard Gordon, his other films include *Helter Skelter* (1948), *The 39 Steps* (1959), *Hot Enough for June*, *Deadlier Than the Male*, *Some Girls Do*, *Percy*, *Percy's Progress* and *Quest for Love* (based on a story by John Wyndham). His son is producer Jeremy Thomas.

Motion picture designer and conceptual artist **Mentor Huebner**, who designed Robby the Robot for MGM's *Forbidden Planet*, died on March 19th after several vascular bypass surgeries on his right leg. He was 83, and among his more than 250 other credits are many conceptual drawings for Alfred Hitchcock's films, *The Time Machine* (1960), *Planet of the Apes* (1967), *King Kong* (1976), *Flash Gordon* (1980), *Blade Runner*, *Dune* (1984), *Cat's Eye*, *The Addams Family*, *Honey I Shrunk the Kids*, *So I Married an Ax Murderer*, *Total Recall* and *Bram Stoker's Dracula*. Early in his career he had worked at Disney as an animator, drawing the 'Heigh-Ho' sequence for *Snow White and the Seven Dwarfs*.

Cartoon director and producer **William [Denby] Hanna**, who with partner Joseph Barbera founded Hanna-Barbera Productions in 1957, died on March 22nd, aged 90. He had been in declining health for several years. Among the many TV shows he helped to create were *The Flintstones*, *The Jetsons*, *Jonny Quest*, *Captain Caveman* and *Scooby-Doo*, winning eight Emmys for his work. The duo began their collaboration in 1937 at MGM, where they won seven Oscars for *Tom and Jerry* before the studio closed down its animation department in 1957. They also combined cartoon sequences with live action for such films as *Anchors Aweigh*, *Dangerous When Wet* and *Invitation to the Dance*.

Lawrence M. Lansburgh, who joined Walt Disney in the mid-1940s and directed eighteen features and episodes of TV's *The Wonderful World of Disney*, died on March 25th, aged 89.

Polish-born cinematographer **Piotr Sobocinski** was found dead in a Vancouver hotel room on March 26th, soon after completing the Stephen King adaptation *Hearts in Atlantis*.

67-year-old **Larry Tucker** who, with Paul Mazursky, co-developed, co-produced and scripted *The Monkees* TV series, died on April 1st of complications from multiple sclerosis and cancer. A former stand-up comedian, he appeared in Samuel Fuller's *Shock Corridor* and produced and scripted Mazursky's *Alex in Wonderland*.

French film director **Jean-Gabriel Albicocco**, whose credits include the 1966 international hit *Le Grand Meaulnes* (*The Wanderer*), died forgotten and destitute in Brazil on April 10th. He was 65.

French-born Canadian film and TV producer **Nicolas Clermont,** who as co-founder of Filmline International was responsible for the long-running *Highlander* series and *The Secret Adventures of Jules Verne*, died of cancer on April 11th, aged 59.

American visual effects artist **Sean Dever** died on April 13th, aged 32. His credits include such overblown blockbusters as *Red Planet*, *Thirteen Days*, *The Sixth Day*, *Waterworld*, *Angels in the Outfield*, *True Lies*, *The Fifth Element*, *Flubber*, *My Favorite Martian*, *Sphere* and *Batman and Robin*.

American film and television director **Michael Ritchie** died of complications from prostate cancer on April 16th, aged 62. His credits include *The Island*, *The Golden Child*, *A Simple Wish* and TV's *The Man from U.N.C.L.E.*

Italian director **Giacomo Gentilomo** died the same day in Rome, aged 92. His films include *Goliath and the Vampires* and *Hercules Against the Moon Men*.

Director, producer and writer **Jack Haley, Jr.,** the son of the Tin

Man in *The Wizard of Oz*, died on April 21st, aged 67. He created MGM's *That's Entertainment!* series and numerous award-winning TV specials and documentaries based around the Golden Age of Hollywood (*The Making of the Wizard of Oz*, etc.). He also directed the 1970, 1974 and 1979 Academy Award shows and was once married to Liza Minnelli.

British screenwriter and director **Ken Hughes** died of complications from Alzheimer's disease in a California nursing home on April 28th, aged 79. A former cinema projectionist, his film credits include *The Brain Machine*, *The Atomic Man* (aka *Timeslip*), *Joe Macbeth*, *Chitty Chitty Bang Bang* and *Casino Royale* (both based on books by Ian Fleming), *Sextette* with an 86-year-old Mae West and the slasher film *Night School* (aka *Terror Eyes*).

Veteran animator **Maurice J. Noble** died on May 18th, aged 91. Co-director of the Oscar-winning short *The Dot and the Line*, he worked on such Disney classics as *Snow White and the Seven Dwarfs*, *Bambi*, *Fantasia* and *Dumbo*, and more than sixty Warner Bros. cartoons (including *Duck Dodgers in the 24$\frac{1}{2}$ Century*). With business partner Chuck Jones he also produced many Dr Seuss (Ted Geisel) cartoons, including *The Cat in the Hat*, *Horton Hears a Who* and *How the Grinch Stole Christmas!*.

83-year-old **Herbert Wise Browar**, former vice-president of production at Filmways Television, died of a cerebral haemorrhage on May 19th. He served as an associate producer on such popular TV shows as *Mr Ed* (1961–65) and *The Addams Family* (1964 – 66).

Italian director **Alfonso Brescia** died on June 6th, aged 71. He directed more than fifty films (often credited to 'Al Bradley'), including *The Conqueror of Atlantis*, *The Super Stooges vs. the Wonder Women*, *War in Space*, *Battle of the Stars*, *Iron Warriors* and many more.

French cinematographer **Henri Alekan**, whose credits include Jean Cocteau's *Beauty and the Beast* and Wim Wenders's *Wings of Desire*, died on June 15th following a brief hospitalization for leukaemia. He was 92.

Michael Green, the chairman of leading independent British film distributor Entertainment, died on June 17th, aged 84. After co-founding Regal Films International in the late 1950s, he launched Entertainment Film Distributors in 1978, since when the company has released everything from *Hellraiser* to *Lord of the Rings* and produced the sci-fi flop *Slipstream*.

Entertainment attorney **Paul Schreibman**, who was responsible for making the deals with Toho to bring Godzilla, Mothra, Varan etc. to America, died on June 23rd, aged 92.

Oscar-winning special effects supervisor **A.D. Flowers** died from complications of emphysema and pneumonia on July 5th, aged 85. Chief of mechanical special effects at Twentieth Century-Fox for many years, his film credits include *The Poseidon Adventure*, Steven Spielberg's *1941* and *Apocalypse Now*.

Disney animator **Ted Berman** died on July 15th, aged 81. He worked on *Fantasia*, *Bambi*, *Alice in Wonderland*, *Peter Pan*, *Mary Poppins*, *Bedknobs and Broomsticks* and co-scripted and co-directed *The Black Cauldron*.

Producer **Jules Buck**, whose credits include *What's New Pussycat* and *The Ruling Class*, died on July 19th, aged 83.

Record producer and songwriter **Milton Gabler**, who founded the independent jazz label Commodore Records in 1937 and produced Bill Haley and the Comets' 'Rock Around the Clock' in one take, died on July 20th, aged 90.

Film and TV director **Alan Rafkin** died of complications during heart surgery in Los Angeles on August 6th, aged 73. A former nightclub comic, he began his career in 1958 with such TV series as *77 Sunset Strip*, directing more than eighty prime-time sitcoms along with a number of movies, including *Ski Party*, *Angel in My Pocket* and *The Ghost and Mr Chicken*.

Former film editor and TV producer **Art Seid** died on August 9th, aged 87. He edited *Lost Horizon* (1937) and *A Taste of Evil*.

Oscar and Emmy Award-nominated American sound designer and sound editor **Richard Jay Shorr** died of melanoma at his home in Paris on August 13th, aged 58. In 1979 he wrote and directed *Witches Brew*, a comic adaptation of Fritz Leiber's novel *Conjure Wife*, which was completed by Herbert L. Strock. Switching to sound production, Shorr also worked on *The Day After*, *Die Hard*, *Poltergeist III*, *Teenage Mutant Ninja Turtles* and *Highway to Hell*.

Music editor **Daniel Adrian Carlin** died of lung cancer and pulmonary fibrosis on August 14th, aged 73. His credits include *Ghost*, *Ghostbusters*, *Fatal Attraction* and *All That Jazz*.

Hollywood make-up artist **John Chambers**, best known for

creating Mr Spock's Vulcan ears on TV's *Star Trek* (1966 – 68) and the make-up for the original *Planet of the Apes* (1967) and its sequels, died of diabetes complications on August 25th, aged 78. His many other credits include *The Three Stooges in Orbit*, *The Human Duplicators*, *Slaughterhouse-Five*, *The Mephisto Waltz*, *Superbeast*, *Sssssss*, *Phantom of the Paradise*, *Embryo*, *The Island of Dr Moreau* (1977), *Halloween II* and TV's *Beauty and the Beast* (1976). Chambers won an honorary Oscar for his work on *Planet of the Apes*, and he was also rumoured to have created the famous Bigfoot creature filmed by Californian 're-searchers' in 1967.

Film editor and producer **Thomas Ralph Fries**, the son of producer Charles Fries, died of a protracted cardiopulmonary illness on September 10th, aged 47. His credits include *The Martian Chronicles*, *Starcrossed*, *Bridge Across Time* and *Flowers in the Attic*. In 1989 he produced *Phantom of the Mall: Eric's Revenge*.

54-year-old American television producer **David Angell** and his wife Lynn were among the sixty-five passengers and crew aboard United Airlines Flight 175, travelling from Boston to Los Angeles, that terrorists crashed into the South Tower of New York's World Trade Center on September 11th. The co-creator and executive producer of NBC-TV's *Frasier*, he also scripted episodes of the comedy shows *Wings* and *Cheers*, sharing six Emmy Awards for his television work.

Fred (Frederick) **De Cordova**, who directed *Bedtime for Bonzo* and *Bonzo Goes to College* starring Ronald Reagan and a chimpanzee, died on September 15th, aged 90. His fifty-year career included directing numerous TV shows (including episodes of *Bewitched*) a TV version of *Blithe Spirit* starring Noel Coward, Lauren Bacall and Claudette Colbert, and he was executive producer of Johnny Carson's *The Tonight Show* (1971–92).

Samuel Z. Arkoff, the cigar-chewing executive producer and co-founder (with James H. Nicholson, who died in 1972) of American International Pictures, died on September 16th, aged 83. His many films date from *The Beast With a Million Eyes* (1955) to *Hellhole* (1985), and include *I Was a Teenage Werewolf*, *I Was a Teenage Frankenstein*, *Blood of Dracula*, Roger Corman's Edgar Allan Poe series, *The Amityville Horror* (which grossed $65 million in America) and *Dressed to Kill*. His autobiography (with Richard Trubo), *Flying Through Hollywood by the Seat of My Pants*, was published in 1992. Arkoff's wife Hilda, who provided home-cooked meals for AIP wrap parties, died on July 26th.

Canadian-born film and TV director **Gerald Mayer**, the nephew of legendary MGM mogul Louis B. Mayer, died of complications from pneumonia on September 21st, aged 82. His credits include episodes of *Thriller*, *Voyage to the Bottom of the Sea*, *The Invaders*, *Tarzan*, *Six Million Dollar Man* and *Logan's Run*.

Computer special effects wizard **Robert Abel**, who created the slit-scan effect for the 'Star Gate' sequence in *2001: A Space Odyssey* and also worked on Disney's *Tron*, died on September 23rd, five weeks after suffering a heart attack. He was 64.

William ['Herbert'] **Coleman**, Alfred Hitchcock's associate producer and right-hand man for a decade, died on October 3rd, aged 93. He worked on such titles as *Rear Window*, *The Trouble With Harry* and *Vertigo*, and produced the TV series *Alfred Hitchcock Presents* and *The Alfred Hitchcock Hour*.

British TV special effects director **Jim Francis** died on October 5th, aged 47. His numerous credits include *Doctor Who*, *Red Dwarf*, *Blakes 7*, *The Hitch-hiker's Guide to the Galaxy*, *The Tenth Kingdom* and such films as *Hardware*, *Nostradamus* and *Grim*.

American director, dancer and choreographer **Herbert Ross**, who often collaborated with Neil Simon, died of heart failure on October 9th, aged 76. After staging the musical sequences for the Cliff Richard films *The Young Ones* and *Summer Holiday*, he worked on *Doctor Dolittle* before becoming a director with such films as *Play It Again Sam*, *The Last of Sheila*, *The Seven-Per-Cent Solution* and *Pennies from Heaven*. From 1988–2001 he was married to Jackie Kennedy's sister, Lee Bouvier Radziwell.

Italian opera designer, film director, writer and illustrator of children's books, **Beni Montresor** died on October 11th, aged 75. During the 1950s he worked at Rome's Cine Citta studios, where Ricardo Freda asked him to design *I Vampiri* (aka *The Devil's Commandment/Lust of the Vampire*) in 1956.

Music director and supervisor **Raoul Kraushaar**, who supplied music cues for such cartoons as *Huckleberry Hound* and *Yogi*

Bear, died on October 13th, aged 93. He was also involved in the music for *SOS Coast Guard, Prehistoric Women, Bride of the Gorilla, Untamed Women, Invaders from Mars* (1953), *Curucu Beast of the Amazon, The 30 Foot Bride of Candy Rock, Island of Lost Women, Jesse James Meets Frankenstein's Daughter, Billy the Kid vs. Dracula* and the Abbott and Costello TV show.

Known as the 'father of television syndication', **Frederic W. Ziv** died the same day, aged 96. Among the many shows his company created were *Science Fiction Theatre, Sea Hunt* and *The Cisco Kid.*

Sound supervisor **Robert Reed Rutledge,** who won an Oscar for his work on *Back to the Future,* died of a heart attack on October 15th, aged 53. His other credits include *Star Wars, The Beastmaster* and *The Witches of Eastwick.*

British film editor **Ray Lovejoy,** whose credits include Stanley Kubrick's *2001: A Space Odyssey* and *The Shining,* died on October 19th. His other films include *The Ruling Class, Aliens, Krull, Batman* and *Lost in Space.*

65-year-old Czechoslovakian director **Jaromil Jires,** whose best-known film is *Valerie and Her Week of Wonders,* died on October 24th after a long illness caused by head injuries sustained in a serious car accident.

John Roberts, who borrowed $1.8 million against his trust fund to co-produce *Woodstock* (1969), died of cancer on October 27th, aged 56.

American director **Adrian Weiss,** whose credits include Edward D. Wood, Jr.'s *The Bride and the Beast,* died on October 28th, aged 88.

British film director and producer **Roy Boulting,** best remembered for his affair with young star Hayley Mills, whom he later married, died after a long illness on November 5th, aged 88. With his twin brother John (who died in 1985) he became director of British Lion Films in the 1960s, and their films together include *Thunder Rock, Brighton Rock, Seven Days to Noon, Twisted Nerve* and *Endless Night.* Roy also directed *Run for the Sun,* another variation on 'The Most Dangerous Game'. His son with Hayley Mills, Crispian, became the lead singer of the pop group Kula Shaker.

American TV director **Paul Krasny** died in Las Vegas on November 12th, aged 66. His many credits include episodes of

Gemini Man, Logan's Run, The Powers of Matthew Starr and *Wizards and Warriors*.

Former actor turned director **Gunnar Hellstrom** died of a stroke on November 28th, aged 73. His credits include *The Name of the Game is Kill* and episodes of TV's *The Powers of Matthew Starr*.

British independent film distributor **Charles Cooper**, who founded Contemporary Films in the early 1950s as a supplier of high-quality foreign and artistic movies, died the same day, aged 91.

Former matador and maverick director **Oscar 'Budd' Boetticher, Jr.**, best known for his 'B' Westerns starring Randolph Scott and Audie Murphy, died of multiple organ failure from cancer on November 29th, aged 85. His first wife was actress Debra Paget, and his other film credits include *Escape in the Fog* and the Boston Blackie entry *One Mysterious Night*.

Oscar-winning Italian costume and set designer **Danilo Donati**, who worked with such directors as Luchino Visconti, Franco Zeffirelli, Pier Paolo Pasolini and Federico Fellini, died of heart failure on December 1st, aged 75. His other films include *Flash Gordon* (1980) and *Red Sonja*, and at the time of his death he was working on the sets for Robert Benigni's *Pinocchio*.

Animator **Faith Hubley** died of cancer on December 14th, aged 77. His films include *Moonbird*, *The Hole* and *Of Men and Demons*.

TV director **Alan Crosland, Jr.** died on December 18th, aged 83. His many credits include episodes of *Men into Space*, *Alfred Hitchcock Presents*, *Twilight Zone*, *The Outer Limits*, *Voyage to the Bottom of the Sea*, *The Sixth Sense*, *The Gemini Man*, *The Six Million Dollar Man*, *The Bionic Woman*, *Wonder Woman*, *Cliffhangers: The Secret Empire* and *Automan*.

American director and former editor **Paul Landres**, whose credits include *The Vampire*, *The Return of Dracula* (aka *The Fantastic Disappearing Man*), *The Flame Barrier* and TV's *The Veil: Destination Nightmare* (with Boris Karloff), died of complications from cancer on December 26th, aged 89.

Hollywood producer **Jack Grossberg** died on December 28th, aged 74. His credits include *The Producers*, *Sleeper*, *King Kong* (1976) and *Brainstorm*, after which he became a unit production manager on such films as *Back to the Future* and *Little Monsters*.

Animation director **Ray Patterson** died after a lengthy illness on December 30th, aged 90. After working at Disney on *Fantasia* and *Dumbo* he joined Hanna and Barbera at MGM in 1941, directing over sixty *Tom and Jerry* cartoons and the animated sequences for *Anchors Aweigh*. In 1967 he produced the animated TV series *Spider-Man* before moving to Hanna-Barbera, where he co-directed the cartoon feature *Charlotte's Web* and helmed *The Jetsons*, *Mr Magoo*, *Trollkins*, *The Flinstones Meet Rockula and Frankenstone*, *Scooby-Doo and Scrappy-Doo*, *The New Scooby-Doo Mysteries*, *The 13 Ghosts of Scooby-Doo*, *A Pup Named Scooby-Doo*, *The Addams Family* (1992–93) and numerous other shows.

Film and TV director **David Swift**, who began working at Disney as an assistant animator on such films as *Snow White and the Seven Dwarfs*, *Fantasia*, *Dumbo*, *Pinocchio* and *Peter Pan* and returned in the early 1960s as a live-action director, died on December 31st, aged 82. In the early 1950s he created the live TV series *Mr Peepers* starring Wally Cox.

Hollywood producer **Julia Phillips**, the first woman to win an Academy Award for Best Picture, died of cancer the same day, aged 57. Her many hits include *The Sting*, *Taxi Driver*, *The Big Bus* and *Close Encounters of the Third Kind*. When Steven Spielberg reportedly 'kicked her off' the latter, her career went into decline through drugs and alcohol. In 1990 she published her controversial autobiography *You'll Never Eat Lunch in This Town Again*.

USEFUL ADDRESSES

THE FOLLOWING LISTING OF ORGANIZATIONS, publications, dealers and individuals is designed to present readers with further avenues to explore. Although I can personally recommend all those listed on the following pages, neither myself nor the publisher can take any responsibility for the services they offer. Please also note that the information below is subject to change without notice.

ORGANIZATIONS

The British Fantasy Society <www.britishfantasysociety.org.uk> began in 1971 and publishes the quarterly newsletter *Prism*, produces other special booklets, and organizes the annual British FantasyCon and semi-regular meetings in London. Yearly membership is £25.00 (UK), £30.00 (Europe) and £35.00 (USA and the rest of the world) made payable in sterling to 'The British Fantasy Society' and sent to The BFS Secretary, c/o 201 Reddish Road, South Reddish, Stockport SK5 7HR, UK. E-mail: <syrinx.2112@btinternet.com>.

The Horror Writers Association <www.horror.org> is a worldwide organization of writers and publishing professionals dedicated to promoting the interests of writers of Horror and Dark Fantasy. It was formed in the early 1980s. Interested individuals may apply for Active, Affiliate or Associate membership. Active membership is limited to professional writers. HWA publishes a monthly *Newsletter* and organizes the annual Bram Stoker Awards ceremony. Standard membership is $55.00 (USA), £45.00/$65.00 (overseas); Corporate membership is $100.00 (USA), £74.00/$120.00 (overseas), and Family Membership is $75.00 (USA), £52.00/$85.00 (overseas). Apply online or send to HWA Membership, PO Box 50577, Palo Alto, CA 94303, USA. If paying by sterling cheque send to HWA, c/o Jo Fletcher, 24 Pearl Road, London E17 4QZ, UK.

World Fantasy Convention <www.worldfantasy.org/> is an annual convention held in a different (usually American) city each year, oriented particularly towards serious readers and genre professionals.

MAGAZINES

Cemetery Dance Magazine <www.cemeterydance.com> is edited by Richard Chizmar and Robert Morrish and includes fiction, interviews, articles and columns by many of the biggest names in horror. Cover price is $4.00 and a one-year subscription (six issues) is $22.00 payable by cheque or credit card to 'Cemetery Dance Publications', PO Box 943, Abingdon, MD 21009, USA. E-mail: <Cdancepub@aol.com>.

Now published by Celeste C. Clarke and edited by Dan Persons, **Cinefantastique** <www.cfq.com> is a bi-monthly SF/fantasy/horror movie magazine with a 'Sense of Wonder'. Cover price is $5.95/Cdn$9.50/£4.30 and a 12-issue subscription is $48.00 (USA) or $55.00 (Canada and overseas) to PO Box 270, Oak Park, IL 60303, USA. E-mail: <mail@cfq.com>.

Gothic.Net <www.gothic.net> is the weekly webzine of horror fiction, presenting fifty-two original short stories for an annual subscription of $15.00. Featured authors have included David J. Schow, Richard Matheson, Ramsey Campbell, Poppy Z. Brite, Caitlín R. Kiernan, Nancy Collins and many, many more. E-mail: <support@gothic.net>.

Interzone is Britain's leading magazine of science fiction and fantasy. Single copies are available for £3.50 (UK) or £4.00/$6.00 (overseas) or a 12-issue subscription is £34.00 (UK), $60.00 (USA) or £40.00 (overseas) payable by cheque or International Money Order. Payments can also be made by MasterCard, Visa or Eurocard to 'Interzone', 217 Preston Drove, Brighton, BN1 6FL, UK.

Locus <www.Locusmag.com> is the monthly newspaper of the SF/fantasy/horror field. $4.95 a copy, a 12-issue subscription is $46.00 (USA), $52.00 (Canada), $85.00 (International Air Mail) to 'Locus Publications', PO Box 13305, Oakland, CA 94661, USA. Dollar or Sterling cheques only can be sent to Fantast (Medway) Ltd, PO Box 23, Upwell Wisbech, Cambs PE14 9BU, UK. Subscription information with other rates and order form are available on the website. E-mail: <locus@locusmag.com>.

The Magazine of Fantasy & Science Fiction <www.fsfmag.com> has been publishing some of the best imaginative fiction for more than fifty years, now under the capable editorship of new owner Gordon Van Gelder. Single copies are $3.99 (USA) or $4.99 (Canada) and an annual subscription (which includes the double October/November anniversary issue) is $29.97 (USA) and $39.97 (rest of the world). US cheques or credit card information to 'Fantasy & Science Fiction', PO Box 3447, Hoboken, NJ 07030, USA, or subscribe online.

Rabbit Hole is published semi-regularly for members of The Harlan Ellison Recording Collection. Edited by Susan Ellison, each issue contains exclusive news and articles about Harlan Ellison, along with occasional fiction. There is also the opportunity to purchase signed Ellison books and audio recordings at special discount prices to HERC members. A four-issue subscription is just $10.00 (USA) or $14.00 (overseas) and includes a bonus audio tape, to: 'The Harlan Ellison Recording Collection', PO Box 55548, Sherman Oaks, CA 91413-0548, USA. Ellison is also currently fighting an important and costly legal battle against the electronic piracy of copyrighted work. For more information visit the web site: <harlanellison.com/kick>.

Rue Morgue <www.rue-morgue.com> bills itself as 'Canada's Premier Horror Magazine' and covers horror in culture and entertainment. Edited by Rod Gudino, the glossy bimonthly title costs $5.95 (USA) or $6.95 (Canada) and a six-issue subscription is $30.00 (USA) or $35.00 (Canada). Cheque or money order to 'Marrs Media, Inc.', 700 Queen Street East, Toronto, Ontario M4M IG9, Canada. E-mail: <info@rue-morgue.com>.

Science Fiction Chronicle <www.dnapublications.com/sfc> is

'SF, Fantasy & Horror's Monthly Trade Journal' featuring news, interviews, columns, markets, letters, calendar and extensive reviews. Single copies are $4.95 (USA) and $5.95 (Canada), and a one-year subscription is $45.00 (USA), $56.00 (Canada) and $75.00 (rest of the world, airmail). Make cheques payable to 'DNA Publications' and send to PO Box 2988, Radford, VA 24143–2988, USA. E-mail: <info@dnapublications.com>.

SF Site <www.sfsite.com> has been posted twice each month since 1997. Presently, it publishes around thirty to fifty reviews of SF, fantasy and horror from mass-market publishers and some small presses. They also maintain link pages for Author and Fan Tribute Sites and other facets including pages for Interviews, Fiction, Science Fact, Bookstores, Small Press, Publishers, E-Zines and Magazines, Artists, Audio, Art Galleries, Newsgroups and Writers' Resources. Periodically, they add features such as author and publisher reading lists. Past examples include Jonathan Carroll, Charles de Lint, Philip K. Dick, Paul J. McAuley, Ian McDonald, Kim Stanley Robinson, Dan Simmons and Michelle West.

The 3rd Alternative <www.ttapress.com> is a quarterly magazine of new horror fiction, interviews, artwork, articles and reviews. Cover price is £3.75/$6.00, and a six-issue subscription is £21.00 (UK), £24.00 (Europe), $33.00 (USA) or £27.00 (rest of the world) to 'TTA Press', 5 Martins Lane, Witcham, Ely, Cambs CB6 2LB, UK. US orders can be sent to 'TTA Press', PO Box 219, Olyphant, PA 18447, USA. You can also subscribe by credit card via the secure website. E-mail: <ttapress@aol.com>.

Video Watchdog <www.cinemaweb.com/videowd> is a monthly magazine described as 'the Perfectionist's Guide to Fantastic Video'. $6.50 a copy, an annual 12-issue subscription is $48.00 bulk/$70.00 first class (USA), $66.00 surface/$88.00 airmail (overseas). US funds only or VISA/MasterCard to 'Video Watchdog', PO Box 5283, Cincinnati, OH 45205-0283, USA. E-mail: <Videowd@aol.com>.

Weird Tales <www.dnapublications.com> is now in its 79th year of publication. This latest large-size incarnation of 'The Unique Magazine', edited by George H. Scithers and Darrell Scheweitzer, is published four times a year by DNA Publications, Inc. in association with Terminus Publishing Co., Inc. Single copies are $4.95 (USA),

$6.00 (Canada) and $9.00 (elsewhere) in US funds. A four-issue subscription is $16.00 (USA), $22.00 (Canada) and $35.00 (elsewhere) in US funds and should be sent to 'DNA Publications, Inc.', PO Box 2988, Radford, VA 24143–2988, USA. An e-mail version of the magazine's writers' guidelines (no electronic submissions) is available from <www.owlswick@netaxs.com>.

BOOK DEALERS

Cold Tonnage Books offers excellent mail order new and used SF/fantasy/horror, art, reference, limited editions etc. Write to Andy & Angela Richards, Cold Tonnage Books, 22 Kings Lane, Windlesham, Surrey GU20 6JQ, UK. Credit cards accepted. Tel: +44 (0)1276–475388. E-mail: <andy@coldtonnage.demon.co.uk>.

Ken Cowley offers mostly used SF/fantasy/horror/crime/ supernatural, collectables, pulps, videos etc. by mail order. Write to Trinity Cottage, 153 Old Church Road, Clevedon, North Somerset, BS21 7TU, UK. Tel: +44 (0)1275–872247. E-mail: <kencowley@excite.co.uk>.

Richard Dalby issues semi-regular mail order lists of used ghost and supernatural volumes at very reasonable prices. Write to 4 Westbourne Park, Scarborough, North Yorkshire YO12 4AT, UK. Tel: +44 (0)1723 377049.

Dark Delicacies <www.darkdel.com> is a friendly Burbank, California, store specializing in horror books, vampire merchandise and signings. They also do mail order and run money-saving book club and membership discount deals. 4213 West Burbank Blvd., Burbank, CA 91505, USA. Tel: (818) 556–6660. Credit cards accepted. E-mail: <darkdel@darkdel.com>.

DreamHaven Books & Comics <www.dreamhavenbooks. com> store and mail order offers new and used SF/fantasy/ horror/art and illustrated etc. with regular catalogues. Write to 912 West Lake Street, Minneapolis, MN 55408, USA. Credit cards accepted. Tel: (612) 823–6070. E-mail: <dream@dreamhavenbooks.com>.

Fantastic Literature <www.fantasticliterature.com> mail order offers new and used SF/fantasy/horror etc. with regular catalogues. Write to Simon and Laraine Gosden, Fantastic

Literature, 35 The Ramparts, Rayleigh, Essex SS6 8PY, UK.
Credit cards accepted. Tel/Fax: +44 (0)1268–747564. E-mail:
<sgosden@netcomuk.co.uk>.

Fantasy Centre <www.fantasycentre.biz> shop and mail order
has mostly used SF/fantasy/horror, art, reference, pulps etc.
at reasonable prices with regular bi-monthly catalogues.
Write to 157 Holloway Road, London N7 8LX, UK. Credit
cards accepted. Tel/Fax: +44 (0)20–7607 9433. E-mail:
<books@fantasycentre.biz>.

House of Monsters <www.visionvortex/houseofmonsters>
is a small treasure-trove of a store only open at weekends
from noon, that specializes in horror movie memorabilia,
toys, posters, videos, books and magazines. 1579 N.
Milwaukee Avenue, Gallery 218, Chicago, IL 60614, USA.
Credit cards accepted. Tel: (773) 292–0980. E-mail:
<Homonsters@aol.com>.

Mythos Books <www.abebooks.com/home/mythosbooks/>
mail order presents books and curiosities for the Lovecraftian
scholar and collectors of horror, weird and supernatural fiction
with regular e-mail updates. Write to 351 Lake Ridge Road,
Poplar Bluff, MO 63901–2160, USA. Credit cards accepted. Tel/
Fax: (573) 785–7710. E-mail: <dwynn@LDD.net>.

Porcupine Books offers extensive mail order lists of used fan-
tasy/horror/SF titles via e-mail <brian@porcupine.demon.co.uk>
or write to 37 Coventry Road, Ilford, Essex IG1 4QR, UK. Tel:
+44 (0)20 8554–3799.

Bob and Julie Wardzinski's **The Talking Dead** offers
reasonably priced paperbacks, pulps and hardcovers, with
catalogues issued regularly. They accept wants lists and are also
the exclusive supplier of back issues of *Interzone*. Credit cards
accepted. Contact them at 12 Rosamund Avenue, Merley,
Wimborne, Dorset BH21 1TE, UK. Tel: +44 (0)1202 849212.
E-mail: <talking.dead@tesco.net>.

Kirk Ruebotham <www.abebooks.com/home/kirk61/> sells
out-of-print and used horror/SF/fantasy/crime and related non-
fiction, with regular catalogues. Write to 16 Beaconsfield Road,
Runcorn, Cheshire WA7 4BX, UK. Tel: +44 (0)1928 560540
(10:00am–8:00pm). E-mail: <kirk@ruebotham.freeserve.co.uk>.

Weinberg Books at **The Stars Our Destination**
<www.sfbooks.com> is a monthly mail order service from

the friendly Chicago bookstore offering the latest horror, fantasy, science fiction and art books with regular catalogues featuring cover illustrations by Randy Broecker. Visit them at 705 Main Street, Evanston, IL 60202, USA. Credit cards accepted. Tel: (847) 570–5919. Fax: (847) 570–5927. E-mail: <stars@sfbooks.com> or <weinberg@sfbooks.com>.

MARKET INFORMATION AND NEWS

The Fix <www.ttapress.com> features in-depth reviews of all SF/fantasy/horror magazines publishing short fiction; interviews with editors, publishers and writers; stories; news and comment columns; artwork and much more. Six-issue subscriptions are £15.00 (UK), £18.00 (Europe), $28.00 (USA) and £21.00 (rest of the world). Payable to 'TTA Press', 5 Martins Lane, Witcham, Ely, Cambs CB6 2LB, UK. US orders can be sent to 'TTA Press', PO Box 219, Olyphant, PA 18447, USA. You can also subscribe by credit card via the secure website. E-mail: <ttapress@aol.com>. Try before you buy: to sign up for the free *e-Fix* send a blank e-mail to <e-Fix-subscribe@yahoogroups.com>.

The Gila Queen's Guide to Markets <www.gilaqueen.com> is a regular publication detailing markets for SF/fantasy/horror plus other genres, along with publishing news, contests, dead markets, anthologies, updates, etc. A sample copy is $6.00 and subscriptions are $45.00 (USA), $49.00 (Canada) and $60.00 (overseas). Back issues are also available. Cheques or money orders should be in US funds only and sent to 'The Gila Queen's Guide to Markets', PO Box 97, Newton, NJ 07860–0097, USA. E-mail: <GilaQueen@worldnet.att.net>.

Hellnotes <www.hellnotes.com> is described as 'Your Insider's Guide to the Horror Field'. This weekly Newsletter is available in an e-mail edition for $21.00 per year or hardcopy subscriptions are available for $50.00 per year. To subscribe by credit card, go to: <www.hellnotes.com/subscrib.htm>. To subscribe by mail, send US cheques or money order to: 'Hellnotes', 27780 Donkey Mine Road, Oak Run, CA 96069, USA. Tel/Fax: (916) 472–1050. E-mail: <dbsilva@hellnotes.com> or <pfolson@bresnanlink.net>.

Brian Keene and Kelly Laymon's **Jobs in Hell!** is a weekly Internet guide to horror markets for professional horror writers and artists, A one-year, 52-issue subscription costs $20.00. E-mail: <jobsinhell@hotmail.com> for a complimentary issue.